The Year of the Red Door

A Fantasy

by

William Timothy Murray

"Whosoever discovers the Name of the King,

so shall he become King."

The Year of the Red Door

Volume 5

To Touch a Dream

William Timothy Murray

"Whosoever shall discover the Name of the King,

so shall he become King."

To Touch a Dream
Volume 5 of The Year of the Red Door

Second Edition

ISBN: 978-1-944320-39-3

For permissions, review copies, or other inquiries, write to:
Penflight Books
P.O. Box 857
125 Avery Street
Winterville, Georgia 30683-9998
USA
infodesk@penflightbooks.com

Be sure to visit:

www.TheYearOfTheRedDoor.com

This work is dedicated to
the writers and authors,
artists, composers, musicians,
and movie makers,
storytellers all, ancient and new,
with names that are known,
and with names unknown,
who have nourished my spirit,
kindled my imagination,
enlightened my mind,
and opened my heart.

Table of Contents

Part I

Table of Contents
(continued)

ix

Preface

Welcome to *The Year of the Red Door.* For those of you who are curious, I invite you to visit the accompanying web site:

www.TheYearOfTheRedDoor.com

There you will find maps and other materials pertaining to the story and to the world in which the story takes place.

The road to publishing *The Year of the Red Door* has been an adventure, with the usual ups and downs and rough spots that any author may encounter. The bumps and jostles were considerably smoothed by the patient toil of my editors who were, I'm sure, often frustrated by a cantankerous and difficult client. Nonetheless, I have upon occasion made use of their advice, which was sometimes delivered via bold strokes, underlines, exclamation points, and a few rather cutting remarks handwritten across the pristine pages of my manuscripts. Therefore, any errors that you encounter are due entirely to my own negligence or else a puckish disregard of good advice.

For those of you who might be a bit put off by the scope and epic length of this story, I beg your indulgence and can only offer in my defense a paraphrase of Pascal (or Twain, depending on your preference):

I did not have time to write a short story,
so I wrote a long one instead.

The Author

X

Maps

A Note from the Cartographers

The geography and place names depicted on the following maps are generally accepted to be accurate as of the year of their preparation (869 Second Age). Distances are approximate, given the scales of the maps. However, these are only intended to give a general sense of the scale and relationship of the various regions and features. They are not intended for travel or navigation. Any mishap as a result from the use of these maps for such purposes of travel are the responsibility of the user, not the mapmakers.

For maps more suitable for travel within particular regions of the world, all interested parties are invited to inquire at our establishment.

Brannon & Gray Cartographers
No. 16, Miller's Pond Lane
Duinnor City

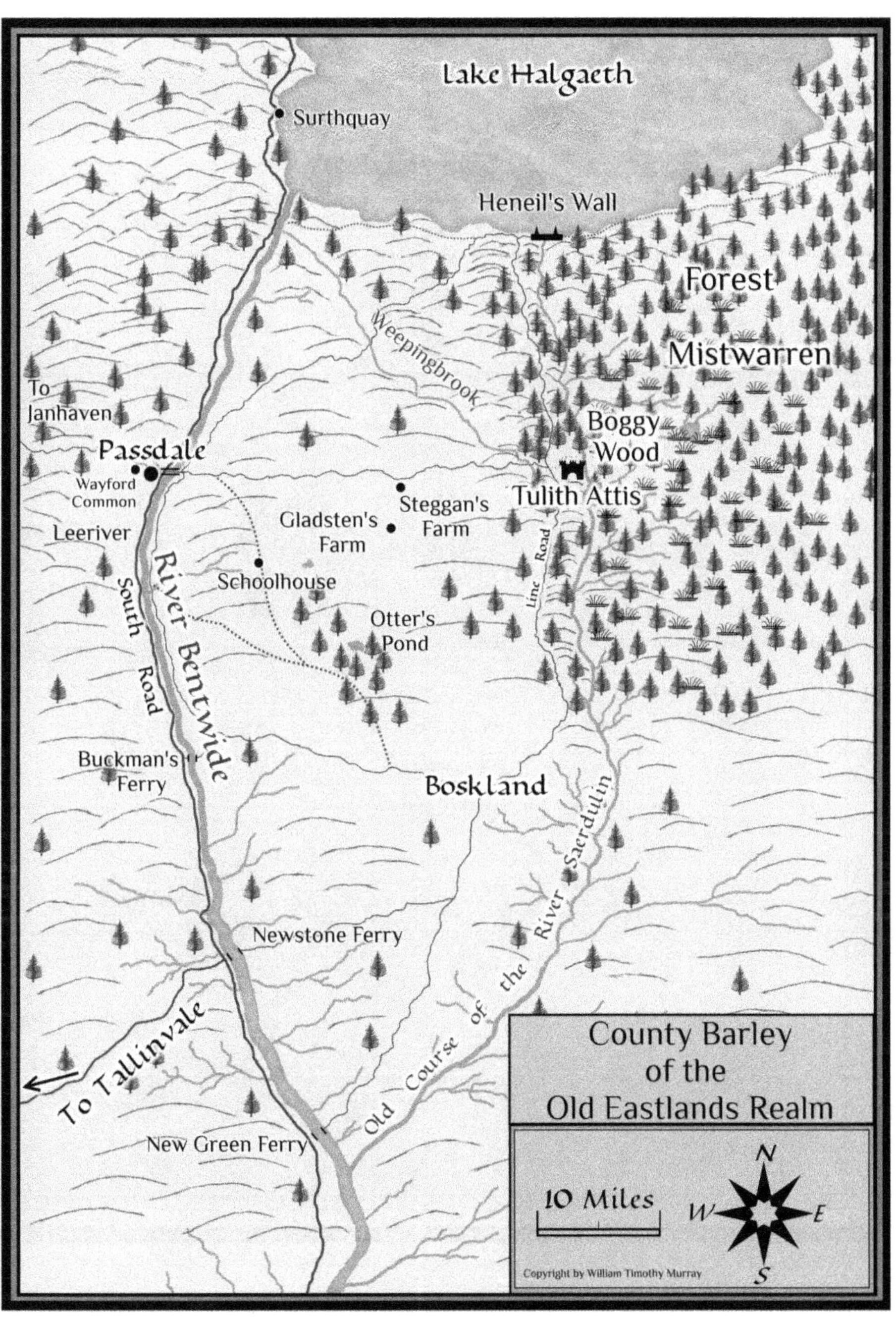

County Barley
Detailed maps can be found at:
www.TheYearOfTheRedDoor.com

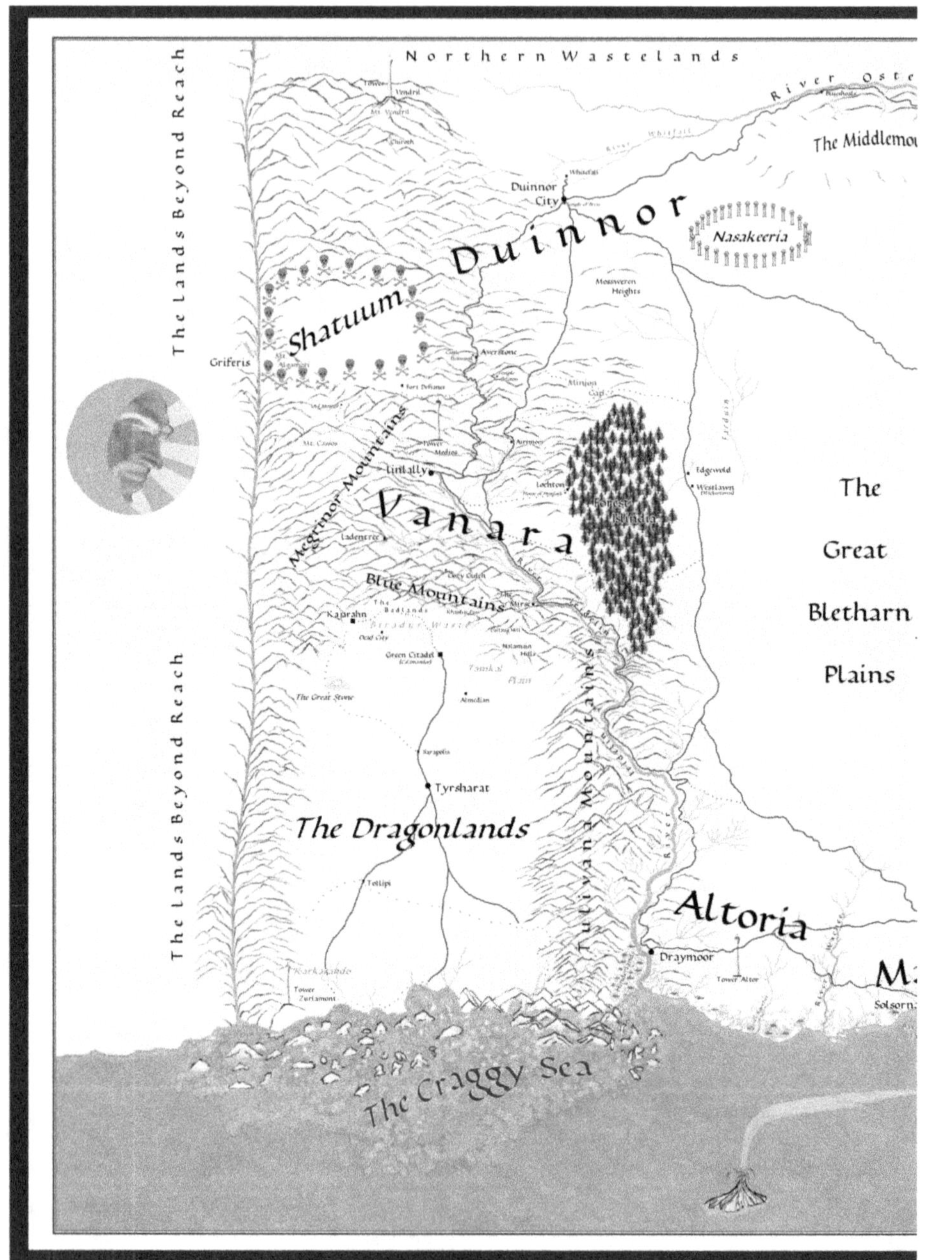

The Western World

Detailed maps can be found at:
www.TheYearOfTheRedDoor.com

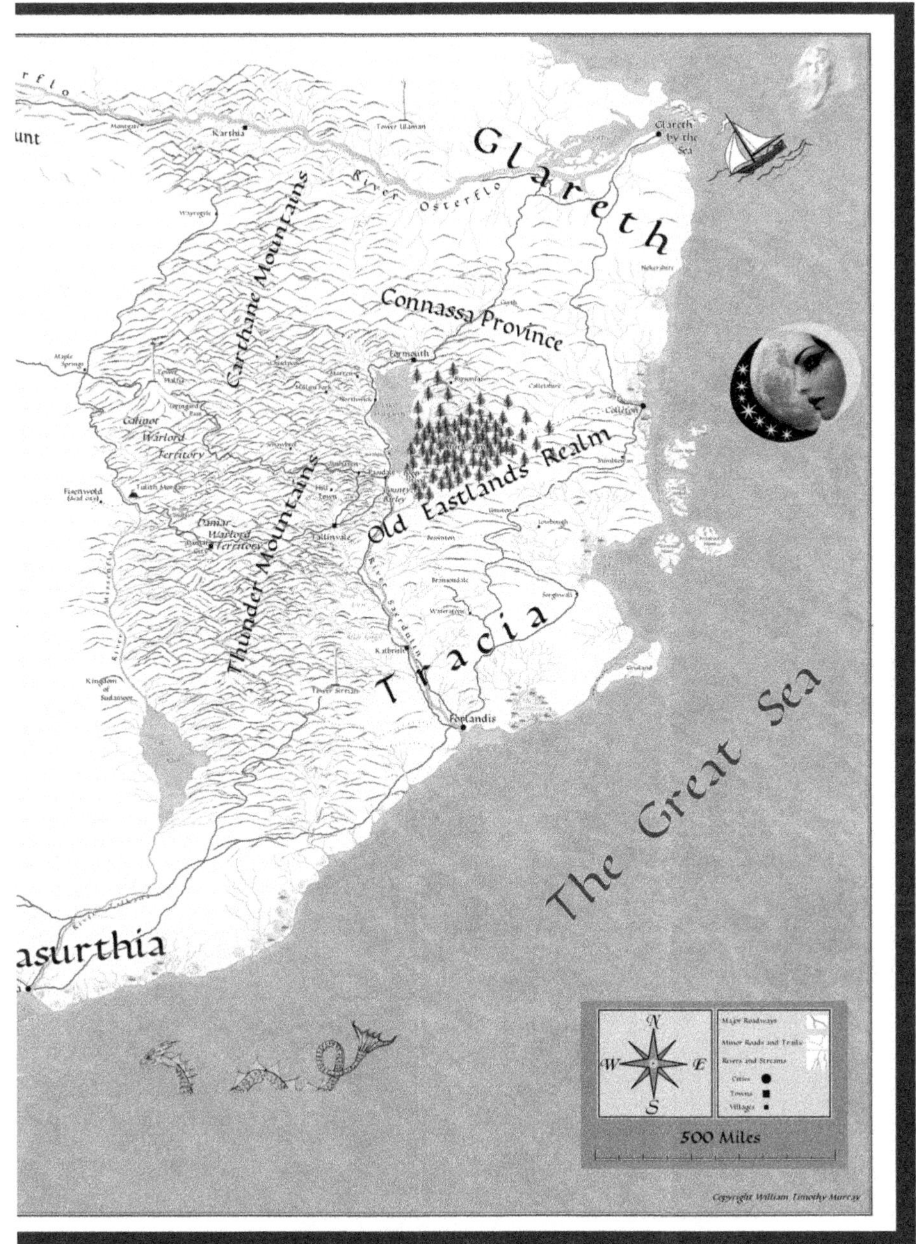

The Eastern World
Detailed maps can be found at:
www.TheYearOfTheRedDoor.com

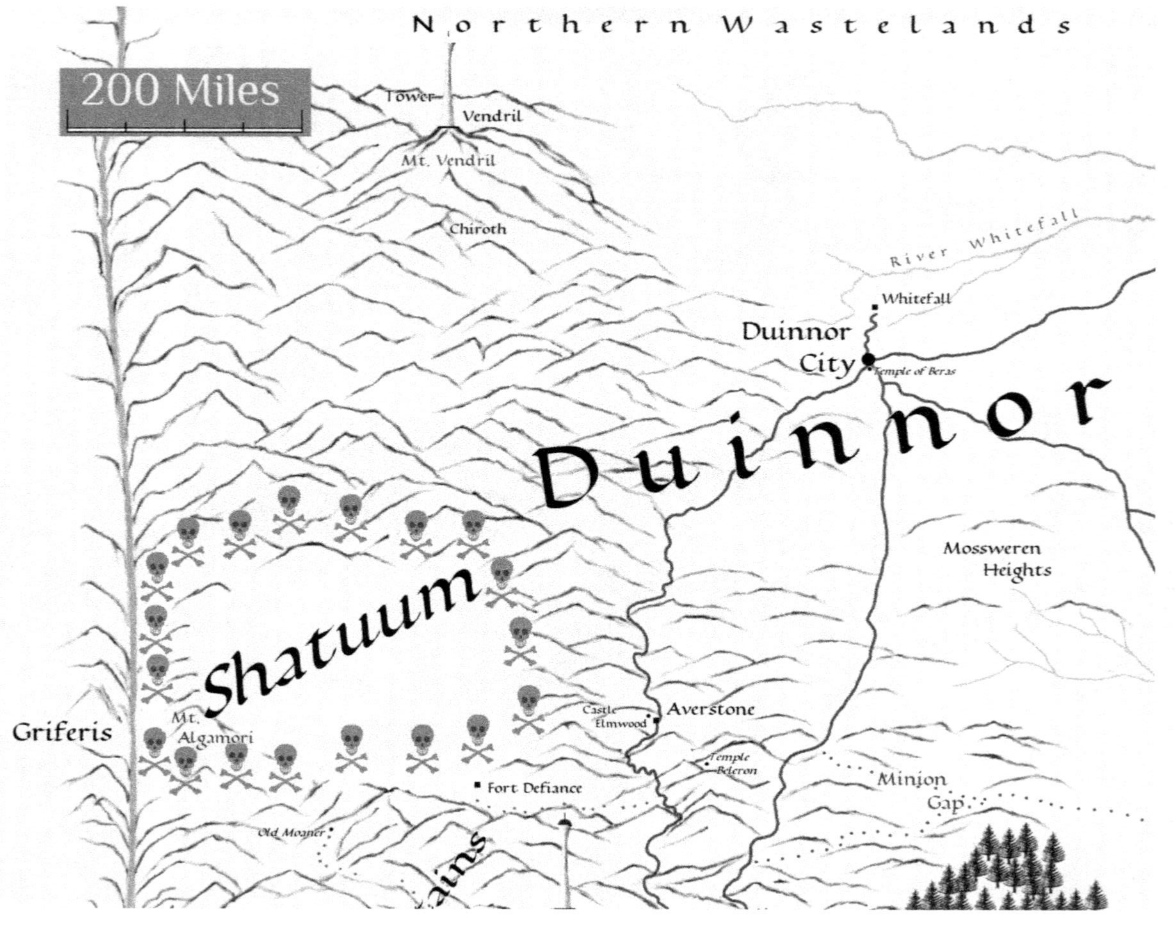

Duinnor & Shatuum
Detailed maps can be found at:
www.TheYearOfTheRedDoor.com

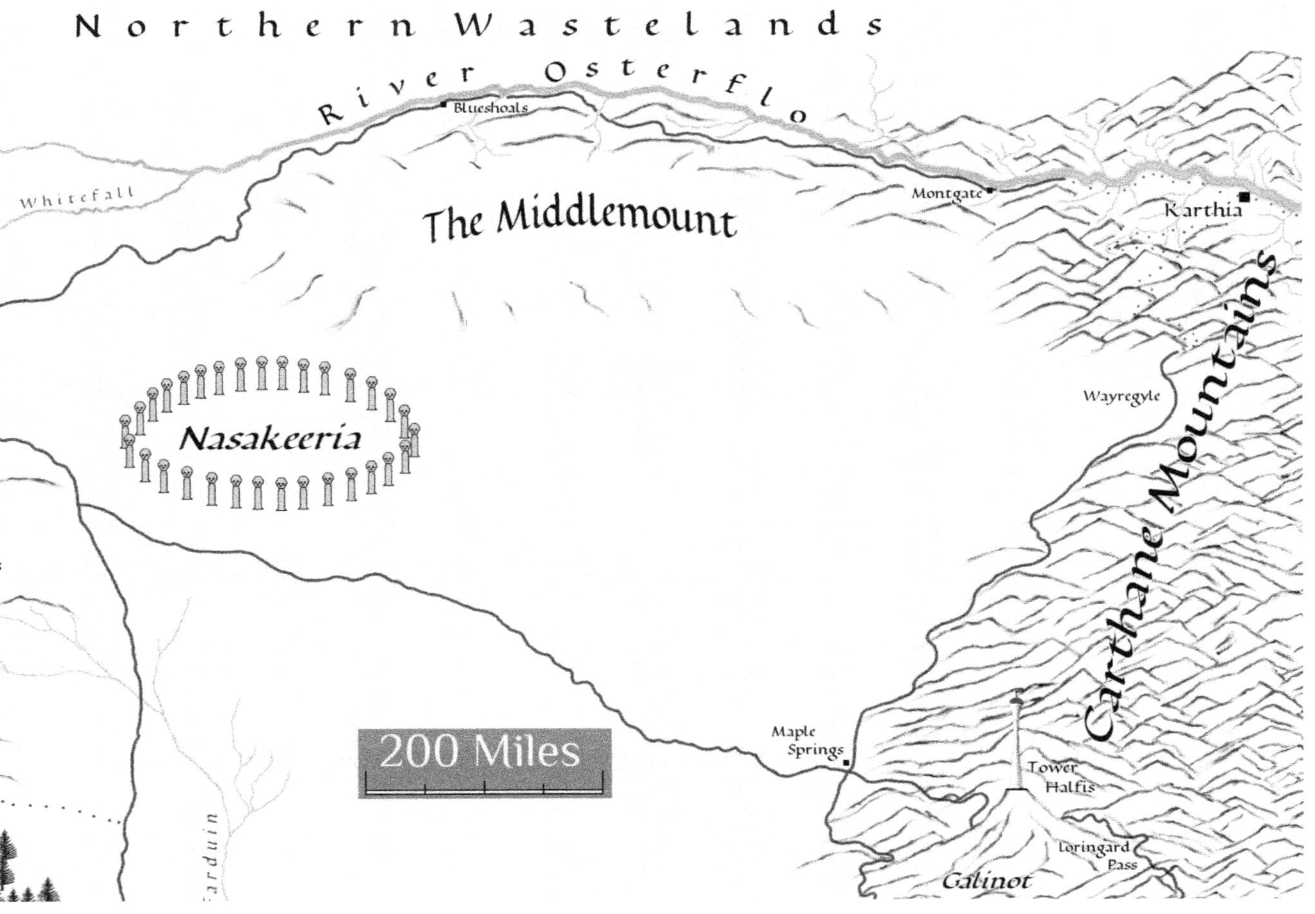

Middlemount & Nasakeeria
Detailed maps can be found at:
www.TheYearOfTheRedDoor.com

Glareth
Detailed maps can be found at:
www.TheYearOfTheRedDoor.com

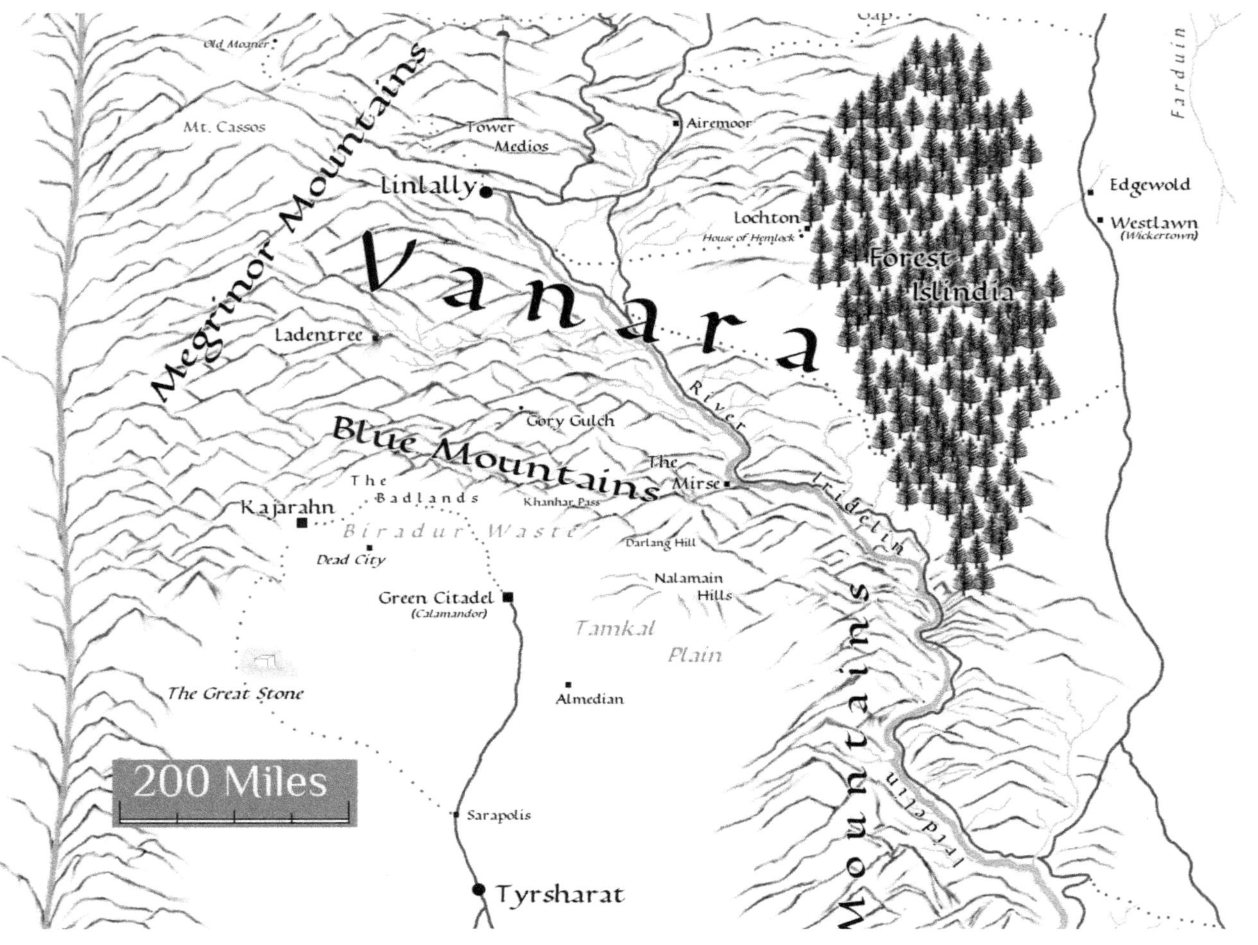

Vanara
Detailed maps can be found at:
www.TheYearOfTheRedDoor.com

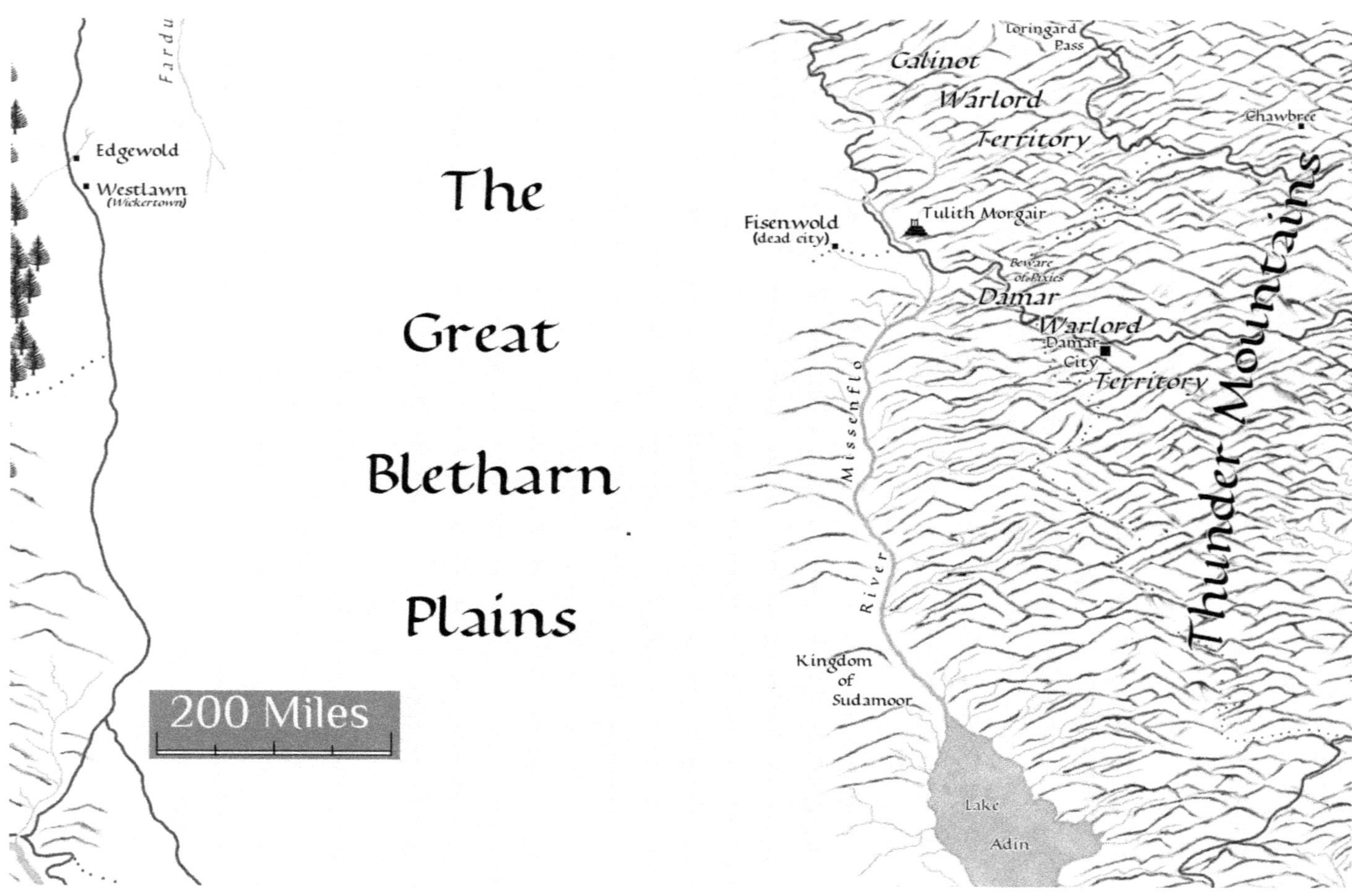

The Great Plains of Bletharn
Detailed maps can be found at:
www.TheYearOfTheRedDoor.com

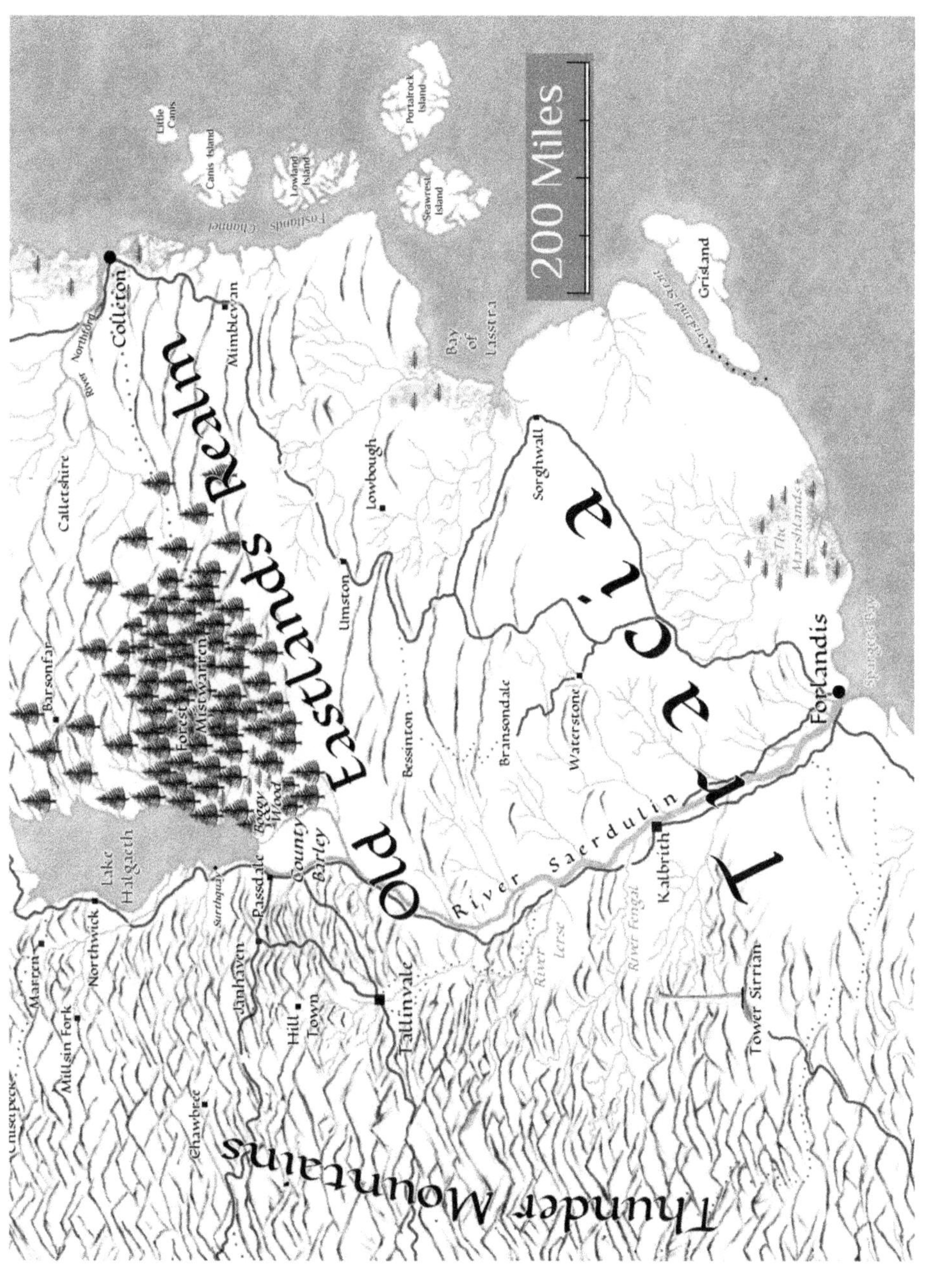

Tracia & the Old Eastlands Realm
Detailed maps can be found at:
www.TheYearOfTheRedDoor.com

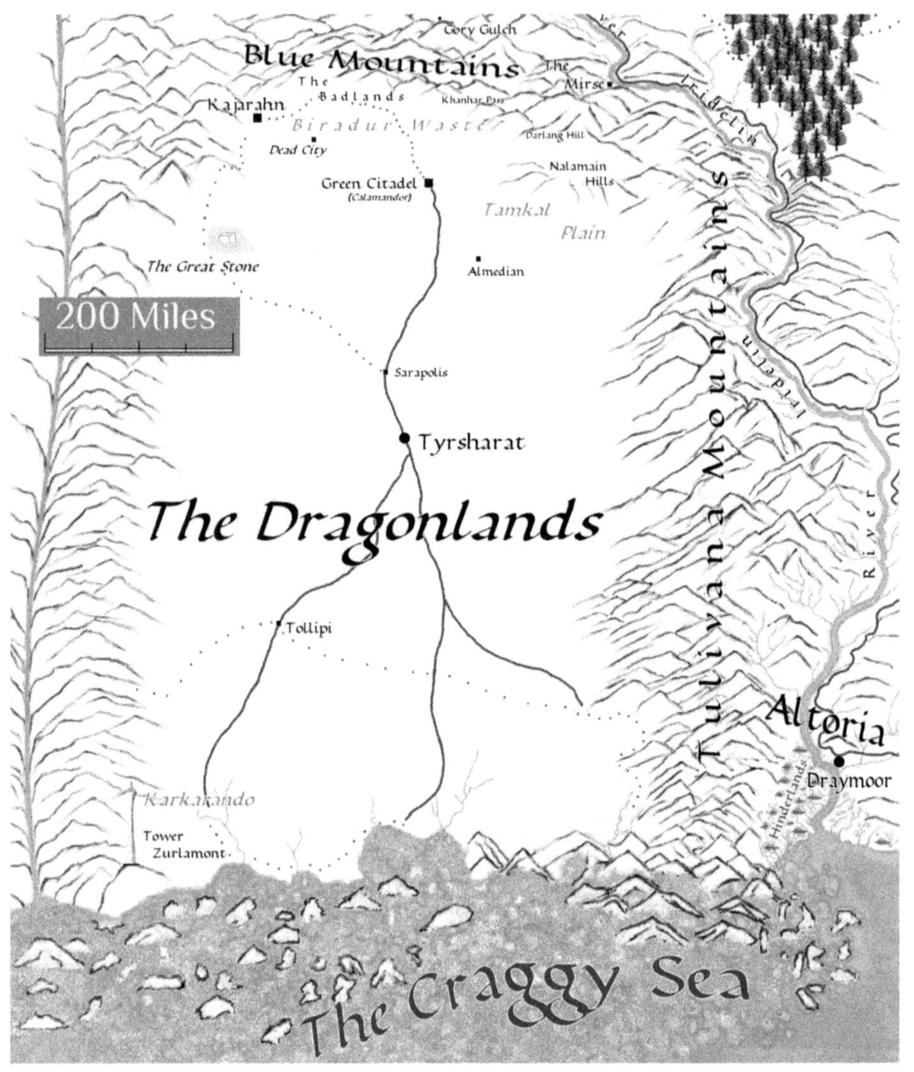

The Dragonlands
Detailed maps can be found at:
www.TheYearOfTheRedDoor.com

Altoria & Masurthia
Detailed maps can be found at:
www.TheYearOfTheRedDoor.com

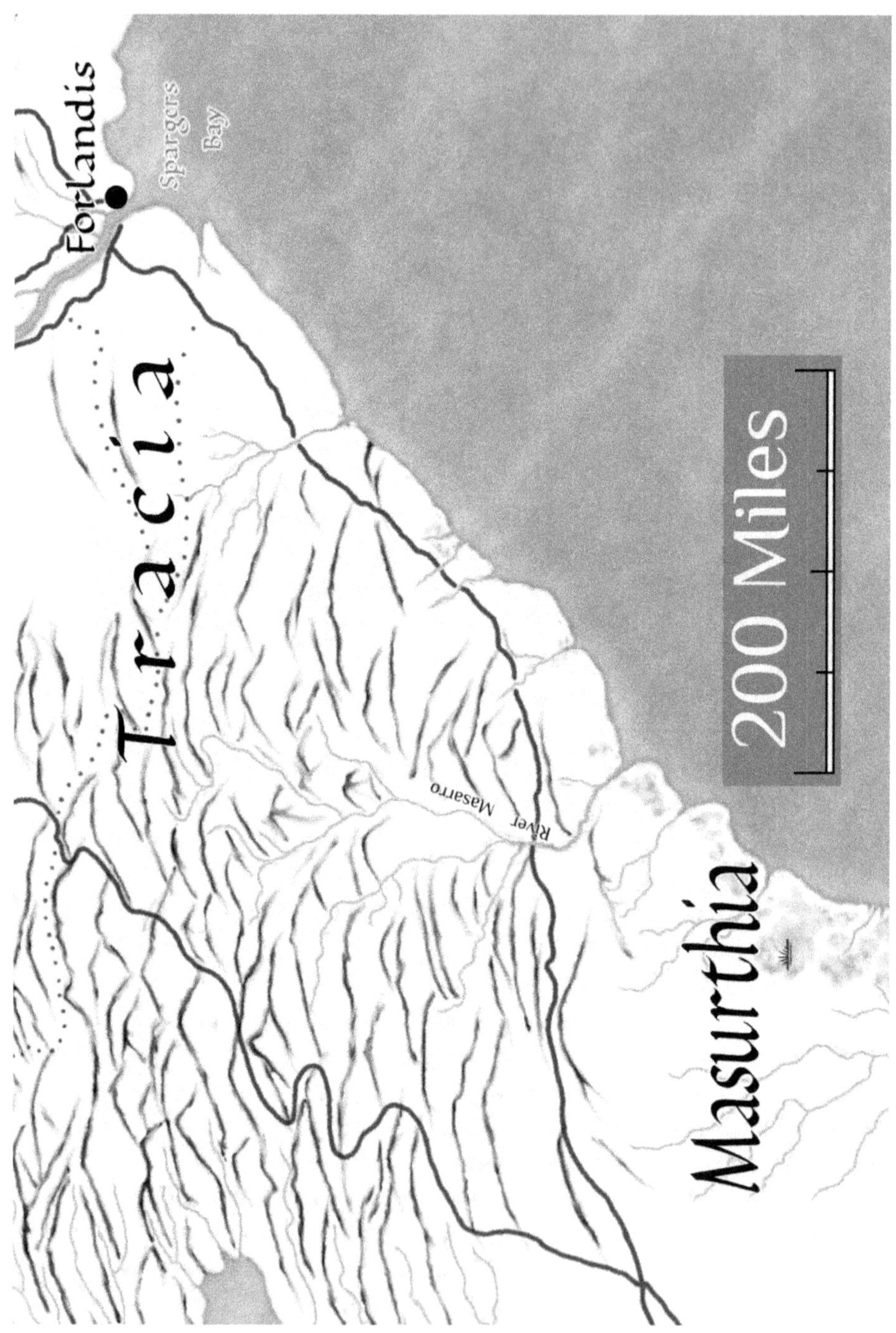

The Frontier between Tracia and Masurthia
Detailed maps can be found at:
www.TheYearOfTheRedDoor.com

To Touch a Dream

Prologue

Banis

The Fifth Unknown King of Duinnor kept his reign only ten years more after Tulith Attis fell to the Dragonkind. The fall of Tulith Attis was a severe blow to his secret plan. It was worrisome that the body of his agent, who was at the fortress when it was overrun, had not been found amongst the slain, nor was he with the few prisoners that Queen Serith Ellyn's army freed during the Battle of Saerdulin. The King felt betrayed, and assumed that his agent had failed utterly, and that Lyrium and Heneil managed to escape with the objects that he coveted. While others sought to find and recover the lost treasure of Tulith Attis, the King of Duinnor sent his Kingsmen and other less honorable men to scour all the Realms for Lyrium and Heneil. They were ruthless in their zeal, even reckless. Seventy rode brazenly into Nasakeeria. They never came out, though their bones did, raining down from the upward blast of fire that consumed all flesh, rattling onto the gruesome ring that surrounded that forbidden land. The King sent out more men who were just as determined in their search for Lyrium as they were in their hunt for those who were foretold might someday challenge the King, those whose names were unknown to any living person. His men rode down through the plains, into Sudamoor and Masurthia. Some went into Altoria, while others infiltrated the court of Glareth. More were sent to the war-ravaged Eastlands and Tracia, looking for survivors who, it was rumored, had escaped Tulith Attis before its gate was mysteriously opened to the besieging horde.

It was the Bloodcoins that he desired to possess, those jewel-centered gold disks that Aperion delivered into the world and gave to the Elifaen as a means of their escape from the strife of the world. The Forty-Nine, they were called, seven sets of seven dazzling and hypnotic objects, each no larger than could fit into the palm of one's hand, each made of heavy red gold cast with strange symbols. Seven embedded with diamond-white, seven of emerald-green, seven of amethyst-purple, of amber-gold, of ruby-red, of topaz-orange, and seven of sapphire-blue. As long as any Bloodcoins were free in the world, Men would not gain ascendancy over the descendants of the Faerekind, could not subjugate the Elifaen. The King already had two sets of seven, and he expected a third set would be delivered to him when an expedition returned from the frozen wastelands of the far north. And, besides those still held by Serith Ellyn, he now knew the location of two more sets, those that had belonged to Lucinda of Faircedar and those that had once belonged to Ormace of Fairbirch. He would have Serith Ellyn's soon enough, but all would be useless to him without Lyrium's.

He was determined to have them all.

While the Fifth Unknown King had his men scour the earth for the Bloodcoins, others who served him dealt with those who might take his throne. To that end, both in Glareth and in Masurthia, the King's ruthless assassins located and eliminated seven boys and three girls whom, it seemed, had no True Name. The agents of the King asked questions, such as, "Are there people in this region who hold with the old ways, who give their newborn to dying relatives for naming?" But such questions often raised suspicion, and many claimed, or feigned, ignorance of any such practice.

Some may have wondered at the men who came and went from the High Tower of Duinnor, summoned by the Avatar to have their thoughts sifted and scrutinized by the King only to be sent back out into the world.

Five years after the fall of Tulith Attis, they still searched for Lyrium and Heneil and the Seven precious objects that the House of Fairfir had safeguarded. Forty-two intrepid Kingsmen hacked their way into Forest Islindia, but like those who dared to cross Nasakeeria's border, none of these were heard from ever again, and not even their bones were found. The King even sent agents along secret and circuitous routes into the Dragonlands. These were laden with precious gems and gold, and their aim was to find any who may have fought at Tulith Attis and who also made it back to their own lands. They found very few, and with their gold they bribed them to tell their stories, and to tell if they knew of any survivors among the Elifaen defenders of Tulith Attis. But these agents failed to learn anything, either.

Seven years after the fall of Tulith Attis, the Fifth Unknown King recalled his men, and turned his mind to other matters. He had other grand plans and magnificent schemes to carry out, and with patience and determination, he would increase the power of Duinnor and assure its dominion over all other Realms.

Then came the unexpected challenger, one who had eluded his men. One who knew the secret Name and how to use it. The struggle was not quick, and it was not merciful. After a fearsome battle that lasted three days and nights, filling the sky over Duinnor with fiery bolts of lightning and thick smoke, the Fifth Unknown King was dead. It was spring's first day, and the first day of the Royal Year. The Golden Mantle, that robe which obscured the King's visage and befuddled the minds of those in its presence, passed from the Old King to the New King. Thus, as the Avatar changed its form from one thing to the next, the Year of the Quill ended, and it became the Year of the Golden Chalice.

At first, the Sixth Unknown King seemed satisfied with all of the officers of the court, the lords of the land, the generals of his armies, and his judges and magistrates. It was a great relief to the people of Duinnor that very little changed, and life went on pretty much as it had before. Perhaps the New King was content to follow the ways of the previous one, and maybe under his leadership the Dragonkind could be held within their own lands. And so the first years of the Sixth Unknown King of Duinnor passed without great change and with lessening anxiety of his people.

Then, in the ninth year of his reign, during the Year of the Golden Ring, there came pouring out from obscure and secret places demons and witches, bogles and wraiths, goblins and haints, filling the forests and the plains with their terror and dark magic as they had done in the time of Cupeldain. Flesh eaters, they were, and those who fell under their spells who were not consumed outright were taken away, never to be heard of again. The gates of the city were closed, but some of the foul creatures still made it within, killing and eating their human prey, making sickness and vile enchantments on the people of Duinnor as they did throughout the world. For years, the forces of Duinnor and all the other realms had little success against the awful marauders, for they were cunning and their appetites voracious. But then there appeared a Melnari known as Collandoth, and if it had not been for him and his brave band of eight Men and Elifaen, things would have been much different. They fearlessly hunted the creatures of darkness, giving them no quarter, and came to be called the Nine Banes of Duinnor for their work. They freed Duinnor of the creatures and drove them out from Vanara, too, and they traveled throughout all the Realms to track down the bloodsuckers and marauders, even going deep into the Dragonlands to pursue them.

Surely the King was pleased at this turn, though he did not do much, it seemed to his people, except take the opportunity that those fearsome times presented to make changes in Duinnor. For it was during those dark years that the Sixth Unknown King began replacing the old guard of Duinnor with a new faction of lords more suitable to his designs. Although most of those who now rose to power were Men, one was Lord Banis, a Firstborn Elifaen. It was the same Banis who for a time during the First Age had served King Parthais of Vanara. However, Lord Banis, like so many others, fell victim to the paranoia of Parthais and so lost his position and power and nearly his life. He fled Vanara, and he remained in hiding until Parthais was dead. When Queen Serith Ellyn came to Vanara's throne, and the Second Age began, Banis returned for a time to serve her as a High Judge of Vanara, just as he had done for her father before her. But Banis grew dissatisfied with that position and he resigned his judgeship. A few years later, he moved to Duinnor, joining the Ministry of Justice, and slowly rose in rank and power. During the time of the Fifth Unknown King, Banis watched, preparing his plots and his plans for advancement. When the

Sixth Unknown King came to power, Banis was ready. And so, whilst the Nine Banes of Duinnor fought and eradicated the evil beings that plagued the lands, Lord Banis quietly cultivated his following and increased his influence in Duinnor.

For nearly a century, Lord Banis served as Second Lord of the Exchequer and as an advisor to the Sixth Unknown King's First Lord of the High Chamber, Lord Harstaff. Harstaff's power was thereby increased, for Banis always seemed to know when conspiracy brewed, and he was able to bring malcontents to justice before their plots against the King were hatched. The King rewarded Banis, through First Lord Harstaff, and lavished wealth and honor upon him. But Lord Banis was not satisfied, and desired for himself the position of his superior, and the ear of the King. Knowing that he must make himself indispensable to the King, and also that he needed to hide his own secret affairs from the Throne, Banis put his long-brewed plan into action.

It was the 420th year of the Second Age, that is, the Year of the Winecork and the ninetieth year of the Sixth Unknown King, when Lord Banis, on the pretense of taking care of pressing matters at his old estate in northern Vanara, departed Duinnor and traveled south. Once he was beyond the sight of Duinnor's spyglasses, he turned to the southwest and traveled through the unsettled forests and mountains toward the lands of Shatuum. As he neared day by day, he saw numerous signs of Shatuum's sinister presence in those lands. He passed through swaths of forest covered with choking vines, and other places that smoldered, burned entirely away by pitch and fire. He saw bones, many bones, and the remains of hapless travelers who had ventured too close to that land, their impaled bodies picked by vultures. Holding his handkerchief to his nose, Lord Banis continued on determinedly.

At last, as evening vaguely descended on an overcast day, he came before the black wall of Shatuum and halted. No one stirred atop the battlement, and no flag or banner fluttered, for the air did not move, and all was heavy silence.

"I come to speak with Secundur!" he cried out loudly.

No one answered, not even an echo. Banis sat on his nervous buckmarl and waited. Every so often, he shouted his challenge again, again to be swallowed by the breathless air. Still he waited. Day fell, and a starless night blackened the land until Banis could see neither the looming wall in front of him nor even his hand before his face. Then, though the air was warm and heavy, his buckmarl shivered, and a chill crawled up his spine.

"What have you to do with me?" a soft voice spoke into his ear.

Startled, Banis twisted in his saddle, but he could see no one in the blackness.

"It is I, Secundur," spoke the voice. "I watched your approach, and I know from whence you came. I was curious, and so I kept back my subjects who strongly desire your flesh. So, tell me, why do you come, oh foolish Fallen One?"

"Lord Secundur," said Banis, "I know your history, for I was in the world when you served Morgasir and when you escaped his fate. I was in Vanara when, as it was recorded, Parthais gave to you the lands you now occupy. I know your hatred for my race and my people, and yet I also know how you sought the hand of Islindia and blighted her forest when she rebuffed you. Moreover, I have surmised what it is that you most desire, which is revenge upon those of my kind. Revenge and spite upon Aperion, and upon He who made the Faerekind. I come, therefore, with tidings that bear upon all those things, tidings that I think you would wish to know."

"I am listening," Secundur replied.

"I shall beg a boon from you in return for my news," he said. "And, if that goes well, I shall give you something else, too."

"Speak what it is that you wish from me."

"The ear of the Unknown King listens to the thoughts of all who stand before him, and he delves into the hearts of those within his presence as one might read a book. I seek a way of hiding a portion of my heart from him, so that he may not know all that is within my thoughts."

"That is easy enough to do, for the willing and for those strong enough to endure the spell. And I will see it done for you, if what you tell me is valuable. But first I must hear it."

"Then I will tell you: The present King, as the King before him, collects the Keys to the Nimbus Illuminas, and he presently has thirty-five of the Forty-Nine Bloodcoins. He is patient, he is subtle, and he is made immortal, as all Unknown Kings are made who wear the Golden Mantle. So, in the years to come, he will surely acquire those Seven of Vanara and locate the remaining Seven, too, those which Lyrium once held."

Banis felt a cold, sulfurous wind blow across his face, as Secundur breathed down upon him.

"So the King means to open the gate and release the Elifaen from earthly bondage. It is so that the earth will be the domain of Men alone."

"That is what I think, too, oh Lord of Shadow."

"You, who are Elifaen, do not wish that he do this?"

"I care not, for I do not intend to go, even if the King succeeds, and I will not be forced away."

"And why do you think that I would care one way or the other?"

"I think that you do, for you have ever sought to spite the will of Beras."

"Do not speak that name in my presence!"

Banis recoiled at the shriek, and his buckmarl snorted and shifted violently. Pulling the reins tight, Banis regained control of his mount as Secundur came back to him.

"Your news is valuable to me. What you wish to have, I shall grant. In two nights, return here to this very place. I shall send three witches to you, and they shall utter incantations over you, giving you a second heart within your heart, one that only you may see."

"Thank you, Lord Secundur. And I have yet another proposal, for our mutual benefit. Lend to me a few of your black eagles, and give unto me the means to see what they see and hear what they hear, and let me send them forth on the business of the King. In that way, we may both understand what the King plans to do by where he casts his eye."

"That is a greater thing than you know. And I doubt if you have anything of like worth to exchange for them."

"You may be the judge. I offer my daughter, Esildre, to be your concubine, to do with as you wish. It would spite Islindia, and be a pleasure for you, for my daughter is beautiful."

Secundur thought upon this for a long while. Then, in a fading voice, he said as he withdrew, "Be here two nights from hence. The witches shall bring my answer to you."

• • •

A week later, Banis was recovered from his ordeal with the witches, and he made his way back to Duinnor. He was weak, exhausted from the loss of blood that they required of him, and he was uncertain if Esildre would do as he instructed.

She did. Her eyes had seen too much at Tulith Attis and at Saerdulin, and her love of the world was gone from her.

"What better place than Shatuum to withdraw to?" Banis said to her. "I have been given to understand that Secundur is pleased by your beauty, and surely he will give you all that you may wish for."

Thus, by such words and many others, Esildre was easy to convince. She went to Shatuum, and Secundur took her unto his bed. He lavished his desires upon her, though she was cool toward him. And so it was that the black eagles, in return for Esildre, came for the first time to serve Duinnor. For some years, their roost was upon the high roof of Banis's house within Duinnor City. But when First Lord Harstaff suddenly and mysteriously died, and when Banis was made the new First Lord by the King, those birds found a new perch atop the highest tower of Duinnor.

Slowly, steadily, Lord Banis removed those who questioned his authority under the King, and those who opposed Duinnor's growing dominion over Vanara. And, discouraging the King from going forth into the city, Lord Banis came to speak for the Throne in many matters, seldom requiring that anyone but Banis go up to the High Chamber. With the gift from Secundur, Banis shielded a portion of his heart from the King, and he was able to guard his own activities from the scrutiny of others. Thus he garnered ever more power as the years passed. Using the black eagles, he kept watch on the happenings of the world, forewarning the King, when it suited him to do so, of events far and near, long before news came to Duinnor.

Yet Lord Banis did not have an easy time with his ambitions. Not only was he continually failed by incompetent associates, but there were vexing aspects to his pact with Secundur. For one, the eagles ever yearned to go to Shatuum, and it was often that Lord Banis wished he could keep the news that the eagles shared to himself, not wishing for even Secundur to know. And, for another, the spell that the witches of Shatuum had put on him, that enchantment which gave him a secret room within his heart into which the King could not see, affected him in a most peculiar and nagging way. As the years passed, he took to locking himself in his chambers late at night, falling into a trance of paranoia and desperation. During these bouts, he feverishly took quill and ink to paper and wrote down all those things that he had done that day, all those most secret plots he had planned and hatched, and all of their outcomes. Afterwards, gripped with panic, he hid those scribblings in secret places within his chambers. As the years passed, the writings were too many to keep in his apartments, but Banis could not bring himself to destroy them. So he took over the old prison at Northgate within the city in order that he could not only torture and intimidate his enemies away from the eyes of watchful Kingsmen, but also lock away his trunks of journals and diaries within the cells of that vile place.

Then, in the Year of the Loom, his own son, Navis, threatened to undo all by traveling to Shatuum to release Esildre. Banis could no longer do without the black eagles, and he pleaded with Navis to put such notions out of his head. But Navis was hotheaded and determined to free his beloved sister from Secundur, and his prowess at arms knew no equal. It was Navis, after all, who had slain Jatarak the Ogre, pursuing the creature into the Crevasse of Fire to do so, returning with the monster's head. It was Navis, too, who single-handedly slew a legion of Dragonkind at the Battle of Saerdulin. If any could enter Shatuum and bring Esildre out, it was he. Lord Banis therefore consented, but, since he had grown dispassionate of all but his own ambition, he enlisted the help of one called Bailorg to stop his son. Navis went on his expedition, and Bailorg went with him as a guide to the borders of Secundur's domain. Only Bailorg returned, saying, as he was instructed to do, that Navis had entered Shatuum. It was a lie. Navis was dead. Esildre remained in Shatuum, and the black eagles would remain at the beck and call of Lord Banis.

Many, many years later, when Esildre emerged from Shatuum by her own means, Banis once again thought that he was undone, and he fully expected Secundur to withdraw the black eagles. However, to his surprise, the eagles remained to do his bidding. Perhaps Secundur needed them too much, for once they delivered their messages to Lord Banis they always flew away to the southwest, presumably to say to Secundur what they had told Banis. Meanwhile, Banis grew confident that Esildre suspected nothing of the true fate of Navis, and he was smugly pleased that she debauched herself in her castle far off in the Vanaran frontier. Secundur had evidently left his mark on her, and Banis relied on that curse to keep her out of his way.

All was well. The years passed, and the power of Lord Banis steadily grew. He even came to hold the reins of the Duinnor Regulars who were ever keen to march into Vanara and on into the desert lands for King and glory, and for spoils. By the time of the Year of the Red Door, everything was ready for the last piece of his plan, one that would assure he would never be forced to leave the earth, in spite of the King's secret efforts. It was the year that Queen Serith Ellyn showed her Seven Bloodcoins to her people, as was her tradition to do every twenty-four years. Within a fortnight, she departed for Glareth, and, as very few knew, she took her Seven Bloodcoins with her. Banis knew, through his spies and his eagles, and he sent his agents to ambush the Queen's party. Soon he, and not the King, would have her Seven, and even if Lyrium's missing Seven were found, Banis would be certain they could never be used, for all Forty-Nine Bloodcoins were needed to open the Nimbus Illuminas.

Lord Banis waited patiently for the arrival of his agent with the fabled objects. Weeks passed into months, and he slowly grew worried. Then came the night when all the bells of Duinnor rang of their own accord and panic swept the lands. The great gates of the city were shut and barred, and all the Kingsmen and all of the Duinnor Regulars were called to the defense of the walls. Banis, as did all of Elifaen blood, was filled with a terrible urge to fly eastward, to take up arms and to fight all comers, though he could not say why he felt as he did. For nearly an entire day, he was so stricken with grief and worry that the King could hardly speak with him, so confused and incoherent were the feelings of Banis's dark heart. The King was sorely displeased at the uselessness of his highest official at such a time, and the sting of his harsh rebuke bit Banis so keenly that he feared he would be removed from his position of power.

The crisis passed without incident or attack, and Banis regained control over himself, having been humiliated before the King. Yet the merciful King retained Banis as First Lord. In the city, panic subsided, and the skittish population of Duinnor slowly returned to their usual ways and concerns. But Banis was restless and distracted, and he worried that the King was now mistrustful of him. He had too many secret irons in secret fires. Perhaps the strange event with all the bells somehow weakened Secundur's spell, and the King had glimpsed something amiss in Banis's heart. Doubts and mistrust nagged Banis, and they made him more dangerous than ever.

Then word came to him reporting the failure of his plot against the Queen of Vanara. Just as his agents, led by the zealous Captain Faradan, had closed in on Serith Ellyn's sleeping camp far out on the plains and were ready to attack and take the precious Seven, disaster struck. That was the night when all of the bells of Duinnor rang. As Lord Banis would later learn, it was the same night that the Bell of Tulith Attis tolled. The profound tolling of Heneil's bell served to raise the alarm in Serith Ellyn's camp, far away out on the plains, just as it had done in Duinnor, and Faradan was forced to withdraw without the Seven.

Banis was furious. His anger was tempered only by a new fear, one that now made him the King's strongest ally: the certain knowledge that the Bell of Tulith Attis had at last been rung could only mean that someone of great power had come into the world. Someone who might threaten King and First Lord alike.

When the black eagle that he sent to Bailorg, his old accomplice, finally returned, Banis learned much, and did not withhold it from the King. Bailorg was dead, killed by the Bellringer himself, who was a mere boy. The eagle witnessed the killing, and heard, too, the boy's confession. A second eagle arrived only a few weeks later, reporting that a party of travelers that included the boy was making its way west through the Thunder Mountains. And Collandoth of the Nine Banes was with him. They were on their way, the King was convinced, to take the throne. And the King wanted the boy captured before they reached Duinnor so that all conspirators could be identified and dealt with. Banis was not so certain. Why should they come directly to Duinnor? Would they not first seek aid from Vanara? The more Banis thought on it, the less convinced he was of the King's fears.

So while the King sent out his Arrest Summons to all Kingsmen along the plains and other routes the boy might take, Banis secretly sent word to his man in Vanara, Count Dialmor. If the boy showed up there, he was to be eliminated at all costs and without hesitation. This time, Captain Faradan must not fail.

But, as we know, he did.

Part I

14

Chapter 1

The Better Man

As Prince Carbane sent forth his many ships, a mighty fleet bound on a long voyage, his son, Prince Danoss, and Mr. Robigor Ribbon rode hard for ten days to catch up with the Glareth army already dispatched and quickly marching toward Formouth. Two weeks later, the Glarethians met with those mustered from the region around Formouth, swelling their forces to nearly four thousand strong, and they encamped in the woods and fields on the north shores of Lake Halgaeth. After two busy days of organizing, Mr. Ribbon, Prince Danoss, and five hundred soldiers of Connassa boarded onto eighty lake boats. While the bulk of the Prince's army set out on the road that ran around the western side of Halgaeth, the boats sailed swiftly southward. Owing to the skill of the Lakemen, to the nimbleness of their sturdy boats, and to Sir Wind's persistent encouragement, the boats made the trip in only a few days. By the morning of their fourth day, they could see the fiery braziers lit by an advance party of Lakemen, held aloft by the two ancient welcoming arms of the old landing of Surthquay. Taking turns, they landed their boats, maneuvering carefully to and from the dock throughout the day until all of the Lakemen under Prince Danoss and those of Glareth under his command had disembarked with their weapons and supplies and a fair number of horses that were glad, indeed, to be upon unshifting land once more. Waiting for them was a delegation from Passdale and County Barley, brought there by the party of Lakemen who had reconnoitered the region ahead of the expedition's arrival. They were Frizella Bosk, Mrs. Greardon, Mr. Clingdon, Mr. Furaman, Captain Makeig, and Mr. Winterford, all come to see a certain Barleyman whom they were assured would soon be arriving.

Mr. Ribbon was aboard one of the last boats to make its approach. He saw and recognized his old friends standing on the quay and moving back and forth to keep out of the way of the disembarking soldiers and those unloading the boats. As his own boat at last made its approach, Mr. Ribbon felt certain by the fact of their presence, if not by their somber bearing, and by the absence of his wife, that the news they had for him was dire. When he finally stepped from the boat that carried him, Frizella's cheeks were already running with tears as she came and threw her arms around him.

Prince Danoss watched from only a few feet away as Mr. Ribbon and Mrs. Bosk both sank to their knees, still embracing, and wept. Captain Makeig, his hat in his hand, solemnly and correctly greeted the Prince, and briefly told him of the death of Mr. Ribbon's wife. As Mr. Clingdon, Mr. Furaman, and Mrs. Greardon gathered around Frizella and Mr. Ribbon, offering their own condolences and support, Captain Makeig and Mr. Winterford held back, and the Prince waved away his captains, and put off his own duties so that he could remain nearby to Mr. Ribbon. He ordered his tents immediately set, and for them to be made available to these people without reservation, and for all their needs to be attended without question. But the Prince was needed by the urgencies of his army, and it was not until a few hours later, when all were encamped for the night and food was being prepared, that he was able to return to Mr. Ribbon. The Barleyman was sitting in the Prince's own chair, surrounded by his friends and by the Hill Town men, his head down, wiping his eyes continually with his handkerchief. So touched was Prince Danoss that he struggled to keep his own eyes clear.

Kneeling and putting his hand on Mr. Ribbon's shoulder, he said, "My dear friend. I offer my deepest sympathy. I cannot say how sorry I am to have held you so long from here only to be greeted by such terrible news. The Captain has related to me, though, that you could not have prevented your wife's death. The blame rests upon none but me alone for not rushing immediately with my personal guard, to come at once against the Redvests."

"I've told the Prince, Mr. Ribbon, that it would've only been a bloody massacre of the Prince's men," said Makeig softly. "To come in great force was the only prudent thing."

Mr. Ribbon nodded, and looked at the Prince, trying to smile.

"Ye do me great honor, Prince," he said. "But, had ye done as ye say, ye most likely would be dead, an' Glareth wouldn't have been warned. I thank ye for sayin' so, though."

Prince Danoss sighed, gave Mr. Ribbon a firm squeeze on the shoulder, and stood.

"Please let me know what you may need," he said to the sad group. "You should all eat, and there is plenty hot and ready. And there are tents with bedding reserved for you. We march tomorrow toward Tallinvale and shall go through Passdale on the way. I'll leave a small group there, and send another to Janhaven, to serve in what way you deem best. Please. Eat, and try to get some sleep."

• • •

They struck camp at dawn, formed their lines, and marched south toward Passdale on the road that traced its way alongside the old Bentwide. Mr. Ribbon, none too eager, after all, to go home, rode at the rear of the column with Frizella and Mr. Furaman and the others of Barley, while Martin Makeig and Winterford rode at the front with the

Prince, giving him as much news as they could. When the army came to the outskirts of Passdale, they were greeted by all of the people, relieved to see them at last, hoping that they might prevent another invasion. They were already quite busy trying to pick up the pieces of their lives and quite literally the pieces of their town. The Redvests had made the place a mess, having vandalized all of the homes and shops, making off with virtually everything that was not nailed down, and fouling the place with the litter of their occupation. But Captain Makeig's mission prevented the town from being burned, and for that everyone was grateful, and so he and the Prince were greeted by cheers as they rode in. The Passdale people watched, hugging each other, as the gallant Lakemen marched by, but after the army passed on through, and they saw Mr. Ribbon coming along, they became subdued and somber. They offered their salutes and bows, those who wore hats removed them as he passed by, and the womenfolk curtseyed. He hardly looked at the charred remains of the bridge, parts of its deck still hanging by stubborn cables and other timbers a-jumble in the shallow stream below. And he did not seem aware of the heartfelt gestures of those he rode past, for his eyes were as if made of stone, looking ahead toward his store and home. He saw the fine horse tethered to the hitching post, but had only a passing curiosity about it as he dismounted and tied his own mount beside it. Swallowing a thick lump in his throat, he looked at the shattered doors as he stepped onto the porch. Just then, a little girl ran up to him and gave him a posy of winter blossoms. He took them, giving the girl a little pat on the head, then took off his hat and walked into the gloomy store.

His home was very nearly empty. All of the goods were long stolen away, and most of the shelves and cabinets were gone, broken for kindling or other uses, while others were turned over and shattered. The floor was littered with broken glass, splintered wood, and, having been left open to the elements, his feet crunched on dry windblown leaves and glass shards. But what received his attention as soon as his eyes adjusted to the dark interior was not the wrecked condition of the store, but the figure of a man who sat hunched on the only remaining stool, facing somewhat away from the door with his head turned, gazing up the stairs. He was dressed in a plain brown coat, his travel cloak thrown across his knees, and Mr. Ribbon could see that he had only one arm. His hair was long and white, hanging loose and shaggy over his shoulders and down his back. Mr. Ribbon recognized him, and when he stepped closer, Lord Tallin stirred from his thoughts and turned his head to his son-in-law. They looked at each other for a long time.

"I would give all to not be sitting here, looking at the home where my daughter spent her happiest years," Tallin said at last. "I would give all. Even my memories of her."

Mr. Ribbon stepped closer and stood beside Tallin.

"I look at the place of her true happiness," Tallin went on, "and I have met those who were her friends. They were more of a family to her than I ever was. Yet, I always thought, that is, I always hoped..."

His words trailed off, then he stood.

"I must return to Tallinvale. I will not disturb you any longer," he said. "Only, I wish to say that if I hadn't been such a fool for so long, I think I should have enjoyed your company, and the company of your family. Please forgive me."

"Capt'n Makeig told me that ye tried to convince her to go to Tallinvale," said Mr. Ribbon. "But that she wouldn't do it."

"That is so. She was committed to her people. And, alas, Tallinvale was not such a safe place, after all."

Mr. Ribbon glanced at Tallin's empty sleeve. "I suppose not."

"What will you do?"

Mr. Ribbon shook his head. "I dunno. I imagine she'd a wanted me to keep on. But it hardly seems worthwhile."

Tallin nodded. The silence between them spoke more than words could, as silence sometimes does. So he went to the door, pulling on his cloak, and struggled for a moment to fasten it with his remaining hand.

"I dread goin' up thar," Mr. Ribbon said, looking up the staircase.

Tallin turned back to him, following Mr. Ribbon's eyes.

"I once thought that memories were a curse," he said. "They are painful. But they are also sweet. It's in the fighting of them, though, wherein evil lurks. I am the sorry example of that. If only I had listened to them, to guide my heart, instead of blaming them, perhaps I would have been a better father. A better man. You must indulge the memories, and endure them, if they are ever to stop hurting. It's unbearable, I know. But there's nothing else to do. I have a feeling they will fade soon enough. Too soon, perhaps. I never thought I'd say that."

"Yer an odd feller," Mr. Ribbon said.

"I know," Tallin nodded and was about to leave, then paused again, turning his head to speak over his shoulder. "Would you mind if I came to see you? From time to time. Just to talk."

"I reckon that'd be alright."

"Did Mrs. Bosk tell you that Robby came to Tallinvale on his way west?"

"She did."

Tallin nodded again.

"A fine man. One that any father would be proud of."

Tallin glanced at Mr. Ribbon, who was nodding, then strode off the porch to his horse.

• • •

After Lord Tallin rode away, Frizella and Furaman came to the door and saw Mr. Ribbon sitting at the bottom of the stairs. In his hand he held a small box that he had found there. He had almost stepped on it, but when he picked it up he instantly recognized it, even though it had been over twenty-one years since he had last seen it. Frizella tugged Furaman's sleeve, and the two decided to leave Mr. Ribbon alone a little longer. He had just opened the lid of the box and was looking at the many loose jewels it contained.

When Mr. Ribbon had last held this box, giving it back to Lord Tallin after a year of not even opening it, it contained only a speck of Lord Tallin's wealth. And Tallin would not have missed it one bit if Mr. Ribbon had thrown it into the Bentwide. Now it held all the wealth left to Lord Tallin after he had poured out his riches to his people. Throughout all those years since Mr. Ribbon handed it back to the stern lord, Tallin kept it just as it was. He never removed a single jewel, and every emerald, every diamond, every ruby and sapphire was still there. At first, they served only to goad and irk Lord Tallin. In those years, he almost hoped that Mirabella would come back home, having come to her senses concerning the ordinary life she had chosen to live. Then, slowly, the small box and its contents came to be a symbol of things more valuable than gold. And, later, in the last years of Mirabella's life, the small box sitting on Tallin's desk was a reminder of who was the better man, the great and powerful lord, or the not-so-simple Barleyman. It was sometime in those last years that Lord Tallin scrawled out a short note and put it within the box.

Mr. Ribbon puzzled over the box and the jewels, knowing nothing about the loss of Tallin's fortunes. As he fingered the stones within, he saw tucked behind them the slip of parchment placed there years before. Taking it out, he held it up in the dim light and squinted to read what was written upon it.

To Whomever It May Concern:

Be it known that this box and its entire contents
are the property of Mr. Robigor Ribbon
of Passdale and County Barley.

Danig Saheed Tallin

Chapter 2

That Other Place

Day 184
61 Days Remaining

Eldwin stood just inside the door of the same room that Robby had occupied when he visited Tallinvale. He watched and listened, and he remained silent, not wishing to intrude. Across the room, Esildre sat in a chair beside the bed, holding Tyrin's hand with her head down upon his arm. She had not left Tyrin's side since he had been brought here from the infirmary, waiting upon him day and night. At first, the physicians gave him little chance of survival, owing to the severity of his wounds and his great loss of blood. After two days, Tyrin briefly woke, and seeing Esildre beside him, he said weakly, "You must've dearly missed our conversations to have traveled so far to continue them." She laughed, nearly bursting into tears of joy as she stroked his brow.

"You do have the most beautiful eyes," he added. But it was all that he could manage, and after a short while of smiling, he lost consciousness once again. By the end of the third day, it was apparent that some poison had worked its way into him, for his body was racked by chills and fever.

Esildre did not sleep or eat, and she had neither the need nor any desire to do so. Several times each day for the next week, Eldwin looked in upon them, often sitting with Esildre to keep her company. But his words of encouragement gave her little comfort, and now as he stood by, he had none left to give. She knew, as Eldwin did, that Tyrin was dying. Though her head was down and he could not see her face, Eldwin heard her speaking to Tyrin.

"…and so we shall go to Glareth. We shall look upon the sea together, and walk along the shore, and you will recover your strength. Whenever it is a fine day, you will take me out upon the old canal in a punt, and we shall float along the oak-lined waterway amongst the lily-pads. If it is cold, our hearth will blaze, and we'll make jokes, and you will make me laugh most unlady-like. And should you ever think to take a wife, I hope it shall be me. I shall give you fine, joyous children. You will spoil them, I know, giving them whatever they want, playing every manner of game with them, climbing trees, and lying upon the hillside with them, pointing at the sky, studying the animal shapes in the clouds with a long stem of grass in your teeth. In the summer, when it is hot, we shall picnic upon the windy bluffs overlooking the bay and watch the dolphins dance. At night, we shall all gather around you to hear whatever story you may spin of your adventures, until the children are asleep on the floor at your feet and in your lap. We shall take them up to their beds and tuck them in, one by one, saying our blessings over them, and kissing their brows good-night. When the lamps are at last extinguished, and Lady Moon and her children light our bedroom window, we shall make love once again, and lie in each other's arms until dawn comes and our children fling themselves upon us to begin a new day. If I should scold them for being so rambunctious, you would scold me for being so severe. Then we'll dress and have our breakfast until they drag us away to another day filled with love."

Eldwin could hardly bear to listen, yet could not tear himself away. He thought of his own family and how he missed them so. His fellow Nowhereans had departed days ago, to return home and to ponder what they should do next. Esildre had sent her great-nephews back with them, to give Eldwin's people some modicum of protection. But Eldwin could not bring himself to leave Esildre. She had no one else, it seemed, besides Tyrin. She had not said much to Eldwin about Tyrin, but Eldwin knew that she was in love with him. It was this man, he had realized, that she had mentioned to him back in Nowhere, while sitting beside the Pool of Desire. How unfair it was, he thought, for her to find him in this manner, mortally wounded. Or was it? At least she was able to be with him. Eldwin fingered the locket that he still wore, remembering the soldier who had given it to him, dying alone with no one but a stranger to hear his last words, no one but a stranger to give him some small bit of comfort. At least Esildre gave Tyrin a last look at love's eyes. It could not be enough, could it? Enough to make up for the lost days of a future together?

He pondered the question, and she grieved. Time does not pass for the Elifaen as it does for mortals. A day may as well be an eyeblink, and a moment might seem a year. These past days, at Tyrin's side, were a terrible joy to her, stretching moment by moment as one bittersweet eternity into the next. Never could she have hoped that their paths would cross again since he left her at the Temple in Duinnor. If it was to be that he should die, as all mortals do, then the next best thing was for her to find him before he did, to stay with him as long as he had the breath of life in him, to utter words of love to him, to pet him, and to soothe him. What more had she to hope for? What more had she to give?

Finally, after her long sorry history, full of violence, madness, and regret, cursed and scorned, she finally understood. Somehow, she knew that he loved her. She did not need to understand why, nor did she need to understand how love had entered her heart somewhere along the road to Duinnor. She only understood that they did love each other, with the kind of love that few would ever know. The kind that she would never know again. It was more than she had ever hoped for. As he lay dying, he healed her. She could not loathe herself any longer if she was to be true to him. She did not deserve his love, but that was his gift to her. That is what she finally understood without even thinking about it. She did not think about the next moment, or the previous one. She remained by his side simply because she could not bear to be parted from him ever again.

"Oh, Tyrin, my love," she cried out suddenly, raising her head and looking at him. "Do not die yet! Not if you have the strength to live but a little while longer." Her voice softened, her tears rolled from her eyes, and she whispered, "But if you are too weary of life, sweet love, then go to sleep. Go to sleep, my dear, go to sleep. Find the peace and healing that abiding here with me cannot give. But, please, I beg you, do not go just yet!"

But he was gone.

Glassy-eyed, Esildre stared at Tyrin for a long while, her shoulders drooping and her head bobbing as if she was growing faint. Eldwin took a step forward. He watched her put her head down upon Tyrin's shoulder. She heaved a long final sigh. Her eyes remained open, but it was only a moment before Eldwin realized that she, too, was gone.

• • •

Eldwin picked a place on the north hills overlooking Tallinvale, a place that would not be disturbed for an age. He did not want them to rest within the barrows now being constructed for the dead of battle. Let the brave soldiers have that honored place.

He removed their linen-wrapped bodies from the wagon by himself, carried one and then the other on his small, strong shoulders, and he laid them gently down. The wagon driver offered to help, but Eldwin refused, thanking him and telling him that he would not need a ride back to the city. He dug the grave near an oak sapling that he thought might someday shade the place. He worked without rest, then carefully placed Tyrin and Esildre side by side, and he began the work of covering them over. When he was finished, he leaned against the spade for a long while, not yet ready to leave them. They were together, given back to the earth. Perhaps, he thought, they were now in that other place, too. He had seen too much, by now, to hope for anything other than simple peace when death came. If there was some other realm, some other place beyond hurt and pain, beyond hatred and strife, then his hope was that Esildre and Tyrin were there. Maybe, if he had been able to read, and if he had the right books to read from, he might be more certain about the hereafter from the writings of wiser men who were learned about such things. What pained him the most was that he did not understand how Esildre could be so hurt, so ruined by life to give it up so easily. Eldwin had seen death come in all its varied ways, from the fatigue of long illness to the terrible violence of war. But he had never seen life leave a body as Esildre's had done. Did the loss of

Tyrin pull at her heart with the sad weight of an unbearable millstone, a weight too much for even an immortal Elifaen to bear?

"Surely yer love for Tyrin must have been great," he said aloud, looking at the grave. "Why else may it have seemed unbearable to be without him? But how could it have come to this? What manner of pain was done upon ye so that ye could not carry forth Tyrin's memory, letting yer love of him speak through life to others? Who hurt ye so badly that death might seem preferable to becomin' love's widow, so to say? Ye once told me, back months ago, that ye cared about yer blind servants, an' that ye wished to return to them so that ye could take care of them as ye promised to do. What is to happen to them, now, dear lady?"

He turned to look over the battle-wrecked north fields, the strange trolls standing in the pits amongst the rubble and mire of the collapsed fields. They stood like a thousand moving columns, thick and tall, but with only their square heads and shoulders visible, turning to look this way and that as if bewildered. They bothered none of the workers who were already rebuilding the bridges and clearing away mangled bodies and equipment. It was an awful sight, but Eldwin, owing to his long life, could and did imagine that it was once a beautiful place, and he thought that it might be so again, someday. It would be a nice view, in future years, for any who might sit under the grown-up oak, looking across the valley in company with Tyrin and Esildre. He put his hat on, and turned back to the grave.

"I suppose if ye could have stayed," he said, "ye would have. So I reckon it is up to me, now, to carry on. An' I hope ye won't mind if I look into things for meself, to see what I might see. So, I bid ye goodbye, an' I wish ye both peace and rest."

He snapped his fingers and departed. His aim was to return to Nowhere to see Esildre's kin who were there. Then, if they could not answer him, he meant to go west and find Robby or Ullin Saheed, or maybe the wise Ashlord, or any one of his companions so they might tell him something of Esildre's story. This Eldwin was determined to do, for he had a powerful notion that some form of revenge was in order, and he meant to be the bringer of it.

Chapter 3

The Scathing

Ullin spent several days camping nearby to where Ayreltide had left him, and he spent much of that time fishing with good success. Being careful not to slip from the ice-covered banks into the frigid stream, he fashioned several lines from the thread and needles of his sewing kit, and made some fish traps out of sticks bound together with some of the cords from his pack. Between the lines and his traps, he caught a fair number of trout of reasonable size. After eating his fill on his second day in camp, his exhaustion truly caught up with him, and he slept all the rest of that day and through the night, rising only occasionally to stoke the fire. The next few days he rested and fished, and even managed the work of smoking some of the fish to carry with him. He also found walnuts not yet ruined by the winter or taken by chipmunks. Encouraged by Micerea to stay as long as he required to regain his strength and to treat his painful wound, he enjoyed the solitude, and, though wary, he was reasonably unafraid. This region, north of Shatuum but still far west of Duinnor, was bountiful, indeed, with water aplenty, good wood for fire and shelter, and fish and nuts to eat. So the quiet, snow-blanketed forest provided for him, and though it was cold, especially at night, he did not worry about freezing or starving. At first, he moved about only with great pain from the wound that Shatuum's captain had inflicted on him. But, with care and by treating it with the salve that Robby had obtained in Vanara, his wound began to heal and the pain subsided. As the days passed, he stayed busy, catching and smoking fish, gathering and roasting the nuts he found, and mending the tears in his shirt and vest, preparing himself to continue his journey. And, after several days, he began to feel his old self, again.

On his seventh night in camp, when Micerea took him to her palace rooms, he asked about Robby.

"What news is there from Griferis?" he asked. "Do you see Robby very often?"

"Not since he took me to Islindia," she answered. Ullin sat upon the windowsill looking out at Almedian, Micerea's home, its people fast asleep, the windows of their quiet houses dark under the bright stars. She stood beside him, put her arms around his neck, and kissed him tenderly on his temple. Sensing that he was preoccupied by something, she sat beside him on the other side of the broad window. "Robby has other worries, and he trusts me to aid you. So there is little need for Robby and me to see each other right away."

"I see. And are you beginning, as I am, to recover some of your rest?"

"Yes. We are not together very long, these nights, and I feel much better."

"And do you go elsewhere? Besides to see me?"

"Yes. I must look in upon those things happening in other parts. I travel, by dreamwalking, to the far southeastern reaches of my land. Most of the armies of my kind have been ordered there, and they gather in great numbers near the coast and along the mountains west of Altoria. A mountain is nearby, high up on the Altorian side of the range. It spews fire and ash, and puts out wide flowing streams of molten rock into the Hinderlands, and the ground shakes well into the desert lands. But the armies gathering beneath its clouds do not seem afraid of it. They are told it is their Dragon Father who puts forth his fire as prelude to their invasion. I fear they prepare to move very soon. They gather great stores of weapons and supplies, and they deplete all the lands of food and take many slaves to serve them. Yet I have not been able to delve how they intend to cross into Altoria, whether by sea or through the mountains."

"You have told me that the mountains are impenetrable, and that your kind have no ships worthy of the Craggy Sea on the southern coast of your land."

"That is so. Most of the trees suitable for shipbuilding have long since been cut. Small boats are used by our fishermen, but they do not venture far, owing to the poor wood they are made of and the deadly rocks and currents along our coast. As for the mountains, I have learned that several large parties of soldiers somehow did make it through them, but became lost in the marshy Hinderlands. I do not know how the generals think they can move their armies without great loss before they even encounter the Altorians."

"Well, they must have found a way and have a plan of some kind. I do hope that you are not exposing yourself to risk of discovery by your efforts."

"I am careful."

"And your father? You told me last night that this is his house. I am curious how much he knows about us."

Micerea nodded. "He knows. I share much with him. He knows how we feel about each other, and he does not disapprove. He is indebted to you for saving my life. And it was he, remember, who suspected that the new King of Duinnor might come from the House of Fairoak. He thought it might be you, and instructed me to keep an eye on you. That's how I found Robby."

"Yes, as you have told me. And what of your father's associates? Those who wish for better things than what your leaders are inclined toward?

Do they communicate with their counterparts in the north? Those for whom we once carried dispatches?"

"He tells me nothing about them. Not even when he meets with them or how he communicates with them. I have not been to the Free City for some time, and did not carry messages the last time I went. I think that whoever those people are, they must be highly placed, powerful people."

"I see."

"What worries you, my Ullin?"

"Everything. It would be nice to know if your father's league has any hope of making any change, should they get the chance."

"Hm, yes. I wish we could know. Sometimes I think that it is too much to hope for, since my people have lived in bondage for so long and are tied by tradition and blood to their ways. As long as the king and his priesthood control the darakal herb, and mete it out only as a way of retaining power, there is little that others can do. Sometimes I wish the herb would go away, except that suffering would be too great without it, and, anyway, I and many others are the beneficiaries of its properties."

Ullin shifted his posture, and looked at Micerea.

"I am thinking that I will ask Robby to release me from service, once I deliver these items that I carry to Duinnor."

"Oh?"

"Yes. And then making my way back to Kajarahn. Would you meet me there?"

"If you were there, how could I stay away, my love? But don't you need to go back to Tallinvale? And go to see the little ones in Nowhere, to accept the treasure that is there and release them from their curse? And what about going to Nasakeeria, as Robby wishes you to do?"

"I suppose I would need to do all that. But that would not keep me. I could do all that and be in the Free City within a year, or a year and a half at the most."

"We have talked before of such possibilities," Micerea reminded Ullin, "and of the dangers we might face in Kajarahn. I think it is too soon to say if that is the best thing. There is much we must do beforehand."

"Yes. I know."

• • •

The next morning, filled with restlessness, Ullin prepared his things, packed his supply of food, and broke camp. After a few hours of trudging through the varied terrain of the mountains, along frozen streams and up through deep drifts of snow between the slopes, he altered his course to go uphill seeking to gain the ridge above him. His course was eastward, and he did not wish to become boxed in or forced back the way he had come by snow too deep to go through. Hoping, too, that he could see the best way to proceed from the heights, he filled his water flask and began the arduous and slippery climb. Fortunately, trees for grasping hold of were plentiful, and it happened that the way he went became less steep after an hour or so. He reached the top of the ridge well before sundown, and was relieved to see that it ran more or less east before him. But it was unprotected from the icy wind and topped with crusty layers of snow that would make walking hazardous and slow.

"Oh, what would I not give for a warm bed!" he exclaimed, his words carried off by the wind. "I don't even know if Duinnor is straight east, or somewhat north or south. I must ask Micerea tonight if she can tell me."

Whichever way it was, Duinnor was still a very long way off, he knew, so he pulled out Swyncraff to use as a walking stick and, wasting no time, resumed his trek.

• • •

That day, when Micerea took her afternoon nap, she went to Griferis to see Robby, but was surprised when, before she could locate him, Finn stepped into her dream.

"May I help you?" he asked.

Somewhat taken aback, she hesitated, not knowing how to respond.

"You are Finn, are you not?" she asked. "I have seen you with Robby, and he told me that he was teaching you to dreamwalk."

"Yes, I am Finn. And I am Chamberlain of this place, by King Philawain's order. He has appointed me to see to any who may come here."

Micerea tried to move around Finn, looking for Robby, but Finn moved, too, and put himself before her.

"May I help you?" Finn repeated.

"I have come to see Robby."

"Please address him as King Philawain, or His Majesty. May I ask the nature of your visit?"

"Nature? I'm not sure I like being put off in this manner."

"If your business is pressing, I shall pass along your desire to see him. Then, if he wishes, I shall inform you when you may do so. Or, if he wishes to do so, he will come to you himself."

"I don't understand," Micerea said. "Robby, I mean, King Philawain has always seen me. We saw each other just over a week ago."

"I am as uncomfortable with this as any," Finn said, his expression remaining blank, "but I am determined to do as the King has instructed, if it is in my power. I know that you may go around me, as it were, and wait until I am no longer asleep or dreamwalking, when I cannot act as I do now. But I trust that you will honor my lord's wishes, too. Is your need to see him urgent? May I help you with anything?"

"No. I mean, it is not urgent that I see him right away."

"Please do not be upset, Lady Micerea," Finn said, "or else you will attract cindergnats, and possibly other creatures that enjoy anxious dreams. When I am free to do so, I should like nothing better than to tell you more as to why the King cannot see you just now. And it may be several days before I, or he, may do so."

No one had ever addressed her as Lady Micerea before now, and she thought at first that Finn was being sarcastic. But there was nothing in his tone or expression to support that notion, and she realized that Finn was actually being respectful of her.

"I do not have that title," she said. "Am I to understand that Rob, I mean King Philawain makes Griferis his sovereign domain?"

"He already has made it so. And I was instructed to address you as Lady Micerea."

"I see. But what of Duinnor? Has he given up his ambition for that throne?"

"That remains to be seen, but I would not assume that he has. The King of Duinnor is sometimes referred to as 'King of Kings' because he reigns over all the Seven Realms. I believe King Philawain has it within his power to take that title, should he desire it. Whether he does so, and whether he rules from here or from Duinnor, are matters for him to decide."

Micerea looked at Finn and glanced around him at the palace. She perceived a disturbance, a reddish-purple glow that indicated a dreamer surrounded by varying swarms of cindergnats as well as the more pleasant blue insects that feed and are fed by dreams. She had seen this before, and knew it to be evidence of a dream that wavered back and forth from nightmare to pleasant visions.

"Is the King ill?" she asked, and in response to her question Finn's expression changed. He sighed.

"I can see that it will be difficult to withhold from you the situation," he said. "I believe he is being Scathed. He has, for the past many days, been in the throes of a terrible malady. It is like nothing I have ever encountered. Come, then, and I shall show you."

Almost instantly, Finn guided her to Robby's bedchamber. He thrashed about in his bed, as in a delirious fever, and she was appalled to see that he was tied by his wrists to the bedposts.

"Why is he bound like that?"

"Because I have four times only narrowly prevented him from doing himself great harm," Finn answered.

Robby cried out, wailing in a most animal-like way. Around him exploded sudden violent dreams that almost immediately collapsed or transformed into other dreams in which he floated joyously over beautiful forests and mountains. In one moment, he participated in the most ghastly violence, swooping down on broad, feathered wings, plunging his sword into innocent Dragonkind, and pulling out their guts with his bloody hands as he flew off. In the next, he groaned with remorse as he ascended. Suddenly, his wings hardened and cracked like glass, shattering into millions of shimmering splinters as he plummeted from dizzying heights, screaming as he fell. Just before he struck the earth, he would awake, crying out in terror, then sinking into sobs until, as exhaustion overtook him, he would fall back into sleep, briefly dreaming of sweet freedom and joy until nightmares came once more.

During all this, red and blue cindergnats swarmed around Robby, as confused over the violent coming and going of his visions as Micerea was. She also noticed dark shapes on the edge of his dreamscapes, hunched on all fours like wolves, pacing back and forth, sometimes stepping closer when Robby's dreams were most violent, only to retreat, as if disappointed, when they turned pleasant.

"His body is feverish," Finn told Micerea, "and I must bring him water quite often, and force him to drink. Yesterday, he hardly slept at all, sitting peacefully in his bed staring at the window for hours without moving or speaking. Although he did not respond to me when I spoke to him, I thought he was recovering. But, today, the illness has returned, and it seems to have the upper hand."

"I must go to his mother," Micerea said. "She will know what to do for him, since she, too, went through it."

"You cannot. She is dead."

"What?"

"The King told me that his mother was killed by the invaders of his homeland. She was alone when it happened, sent by him on a mission to stop a Tracian man who threatened to uncover the secret plans of his mother's people."

"Oh, no! This is awful news!"

She immediately thought of Ullin, and her heart sank further at the prospect of telling him. They watched Robby in silence for a few moments as he was racked by a violent fit of anger, gnashing his teeth and pulling on his restraints.

"Isn't there someone we can go to for help?" Micerea asked.

"I do not know of anyone," Finn shrugged. "When I realized what was happening to him, I hurriedly consulted what books I could find to see if anything was written about the Scathing. But they do not say much, except to attend to the obvious needs of the person, with a mind to safety, primarily, since many take their lives during the change."

"What of his back? Have the scars formed? If so, he must be in great pain."

"Yes, they are forming. It was when I saw the blood running from his back that I realized what was happening to him. It is as if the flesh was torn away where some kind of long appendages were. Wings, I suppose. During the first day, he lost a great deal of blood. You can see how pale he is. But after a day, the bleeding stopped. I have applied salve and have changed the bedsheets repeatedly. Today, the scabs have begun to fall away. I see no sign of infection, but I continue applying the salve. I do not know what else to do."

"What about the girl who lives here? Does she know what is happening?"

"No. I have not told her, only to say that he is under the weather. I don't think she would understand. But I am certain she senses my anxiety."

"I think you should ask her to help you," Micerea said with sudden sympathy for Finn, for now she saw how truly exhausted he appeared.

"I have thought of it. But I am reluctant to allow her to see him this way."

"I don't think you have much choice. You cannot watch over him every moment."

"I know. It has been difficult. But you are right. I shall enlist Celia, if she is willing."

"Have you tried to visit him in his dreams?"

"Time and again. To try to calm him, to ease his anxiety. But, though we may see somewhat of his dreams, I have not been able to penetrate them."

Without asking, Micerea immediately tried. When she put her hand upon the bubble that was Robby's dream, it was as if it was made of glass, hard and cold. She pushed harder and as she did so, some of the cindergnats gathered around her hand, as if they desired to get their stingers into Robby.   It was no use.

"Is this the way it is with the Elifaen?" Finn asked.

"No. I have dreamwalked with one recently. Her dreams are no different, essentially, than anyone else's. Melancholy, she was, forlorn, and prone to dwelling upon the past."

"You must be speaking of Islindia. He told me that he took you to meet her."

"Yes, and her dreams were just as easy to enter as anyone's. This must be something peculiar to one while being Scathed."

"Hm. Perhaps the barrier to us will pass once he recovers somewhat. I hope so, anyway."

"You need to rest," Micerea said to Finn. "I will watch over him for a while."

"Very well," Finn agreed. "Please forgive my earlier reluctance to bring you before him. King Philawain instructed me, before all this began, to shield him from visitors. He has been quite busy, going hither and yon, and gathering himself to act. I think he wanted some privacy to think, without having to answer questions."

"I understand," Micerea said. "And I will honor that wish. I will watch over him until you feel ready to resume. Get some rest. When I see that you are up and about, I shall retreat. He knows how to find me. And, I suspect that you do, too."

"Thank you."

Chapter 4

Recoveries and Discoveries

Day 190
55 Days Remaining

Micerea avoided Ullin's dreams for two nights because she could not bear to tell him about his aunt's death, though she still watched over him as he made his way slowly eastward. In the meanwhile, she went to Passdale and looked in on Robby's father, finding him alone, sweeping the floors of his store and his house, and cleaning out the debris left over by the Redvests. She followed him when he left the store and walked around back to an old garden plot where there was a new grave. He sat on the stool that he had left there, and reported his day's activities.

"I've got some good news," he said. "Frizella's been reunited with her husband. It seems that when the roof fell in on his manor, Garend was already off it, along with some of his men, an' were makin' thar way through the cellar along the tunnel that went over to the spring house. They all got clean away, an' almost immediately set at work robbin' an' attackin' the Redvests along the road south of Buckman's Ferry. It's been a fine reunion, too! They both came by to see me this mornin'. Now if only Robby an' Billy'd come back, all might be on a fairly even keel again. But I imagine they've got their hands full, wherever they may be."

Mr. Ribbon sat for a very long while, saying nothing, his hands on his knees, and his head bowed.

"Well," he said suddenly, "I thought I'd just fill ye in a little. Seems like I'm needin' more rest, these days, than ever I needed afore. So I'd best get back to my sweepin' an' cleanin'. Ye know I miss ye most terribly. But I keep me tears down to a minimum, on account of that's how ye'd want it. I reckon I'm used to bein' lonely by now, so don't fret. We'll chat again tomorrow, if not sooner."

• • •

Micerea watched him go back inside, then she went to Griferis to look in on Finn and Robby. Robby was sitting up in bed, unbound, laughing hysterically, tears running down his face. Outside his door, Finn took a tea tray from Celia before entering Robby's room. Celia remained outside in the hall for a few minutes, then reached down and picked up her rabbit before walking away. It seemed to Micerea that Robby was beginning to recover, for the bouts of severe emotion, from insane joy to abject depression, seemed less frequent these past few days. So she went away to Ullin, and found him making his camp for the night. When he was asleep and began to dream, she knew she could put off no longer. She took him to her chambers to experience the illusion of a warm place, but he immediately sensed that something was wrong.

"I have terrible news," she said. Her heart was suddenly full of Mr. Ribbon's grief, and she burst into tears. "Your aunt Mirabella is dead."

Ullin stared at her, his eyes welling.

She reached out to touch Ullin, saying, "She died at the hands of the Redvests. I am so sorry, Ullin."

The dream they shared darkened with his sadness. Suddenly he woke up from her, and sobbed into his blanket beneath his improvised shelter of pine boughs.

"I should have remained in Janhaven!" he cried out. Micerea watched helplessly, her tears flowing freely across her face to soak the pillow where she slept.

When the shock of what she told him had somewhat passed, Ullin fell asleep once again, and again Micerea took him away.

"You should not blame yourself," she told him. "You may not have been able to prevent it, and your friends needed you with them."

Ullin shook his head, unconvinced.

"Your aunt's husband has recently returned to Passdale from Glareth," she said. "He has been back for a few days. Let me show you something."

She took Ullin to Passdale and showed him Mirabella's grave.

"This is where she was buried by her friends," she said. "Her husband sits on that stool every day and speaks to her, telling her about his day. I was here today, and I listened as he spoke. He said that Billy's father is not dead, but has spent these past months harrying the enemy along the south road with his band of Boskmen."

"Oh. Billy will be overjoyed to hear that," Ullin said, looking somberly at the stool. "I look forward to telling him the news when I see him in Duinnor."

"I have been to Tallinvale, too," she said to him. "Shall I take you there to see it?"

"I don't know if I have the heart," said Ullin. "Is it destroyed?"

"No. But there was a costly battle, and many died. Your grandfather was wounded, but survived. And he prevailed over the enemy."

"Then show me."

She took him, and they stood on the hill from which Eldwin had just recently departed. Indeed, they stood not ten feet from the grave of Tyrin and Esildre, though they did not notice it. By now, much of the water that covered the north fields was draining away so that the work of cleaning the battlefield could begin. Ullin was pained by the devastated forest, where only a few saplings still stood here and there, among a vast sea of stumps, the litter of the abandoned camps, and smoking brush. But the city's streetlamps were lit, and Ullin could see in the distance the lighted windows of Tallin Hall.

"What happened here?" Ullin gestured at the north fields. "It looks as though the ground sunk in all across there."

"I do not know what happened," Micerea answered. "I was not witness to the battle. The landscape has vastly changed from when I last viewed Tallinvale."

"Did the Nowhere people come?"

"I cannot say. I have not looked for them. But I did see many soldiers wearing the uniforms of Kingsmen."

"Kingsmen? Here?"

"Yes."

"Now that is something! Where did they come from?"

"I have not looked into it, and I cannot guess. I have been busy, Ullin."

"I'm sorry. Of course you have. Forgive me. But, Kingsmen!"

"There is something else you should know," Micerea said. "Your cousin undergoes the Scathing."

"He does? Oh, dear. How does he fare? Does he suffer much?"

"Yes, he does suffer. It was terrible to see him. I think he begins to recover, though. He has a friend named Finn who takes care of him. And there is a little girl that is in their charge, too, who helps somewhat, I think."

"I remember Robby telling me about Finn. Can you take me to see him?"

"I am not permitted to do so."

"Why not?"

"Because, Ullin, he is no longer Robby. He was no longer the Robby that we knew before the Scathing began, since he re-entered Griferis. You saw how he was changed. He is now Philawain, Lord and King of Griferis. He has taken Griferis from those before him to make it his own domain."

"Philawain, did you say? King? Is Philawain his true name?"

"It must be. It is what Finn said I was to call him. It seems our friend has become a king, only not the king that we thought he would."

"What about Duinnor's throne?"

"I asked Finn about that," Micerea said, "but he could not say. Or would not say. I am not sure which. Perhaps Finn does not know. But we should not go to Griferis without being invited. Robby, or Philawain, that is, will summon us when he is ready to, I am sure."

They looked at the dark valley and the lights of the city for a while longer as Ullin took in what Micerea had told him. Ullin had known all along that Robby would suffer the Scathing sooner or later. But how it might affect him was beyond Ullin's experience. And it was a worry that he had made himself lord of Griferis, calling himself king.

"I think he has outgrown us," Ullin said at last. "I doubt whether we should even try to guess his next move."

"I agree."

"What about my other friends, Ashlord, Sheila, Ibin, and Billy? Have you looked in on them?"

"No. Our King has asked me to leave Duinnor to him until the time came for me to do my part. That was over a week ago, before his present ordeal began."

"I see. Our King. Sounds strange to hear you say that."

"If I am to hope for a just king, then I must place my hope in Griferis. Should the King of Griferis become also King of Duinnor, then all the better."

Ullin looked at Micerea, nodding in agreement.

"I thank you for all that you have done for me," he said, "and for our King."

"I love you, Ullin Saheed. And I have come to love my King. Only in a different way, as is fitting for a subject to do. And, speaking of what is fitting, I should return you to your sleep. You need your rest."

• • •

The next morning, as Finn entered Robby's room, he was somewhat baffled by the smile on Robby's face. Robby followed Finn with his eyes as he put down the tray and poured a cup of tea.

"Finn," said Robby, "how goes the dreamwalking?"

Finn was surprised. It was the first intelligible sentence from Robby since the Scathing began.

"I am becoming quite good at it, my lord," Finn said tentatively, handing Robby a steaming cup. "How are you, today?"

"I am different," Robby said, taking the teacup. "Thank you."

"Different, sir?"

Robby sipped, closing his eyes. The flavor was new and intense, and he could almost see in his mind the leaves collected to make it, and taste the sun that shown upon the plants, and smell the soil from which they had grown.

"Yes. Different. I feel very long. Long in coming, long in going. But things fade. I remember everything, and I do mean everything, up until going for a walk along the parapets. Then, well, all is a muddle. I think if I did not have so much to do that I might be content just to sit here for months and try to remember it all. Everything seems very slow. It is as if an entire day has passed since you poured this cup. It is difficult to explain. But it is a terrible temptation to do nothing at all. To just enjoy the sun and moon, to enjoy this tea, to bask in every moment leading into the next."

"Hm. Perhaps it is just as well for you to rest, sire."

"No. In the first place, I don't need any rest. I've had enough. And, in the second place, I am no less determined than I was before to do what I set out to do. Perhaps even more so. Definitely more so. Now I know the terrible cost that the Elifaen pay each and every day. To anyone else, it could be overwhelming. I imagine it is, in fact. And that's why they are so prone to black moods and terribly dark dreams. But I am not anyone else. I have already died once, in a manner of speaking, and have had a glimpse across the void. And, besides, I have a chance to change things. I don't mean to squander that chance. How long has it been since I fell ill?"

"It has been about five days, my lord."

"Five days! Oh, my! An eternity, indeed! I must get up!"

"Then I take it you might wish for us to resume our work?"

"Absolutely. I do."

"And, if you need little rest, as the Elifaen seem to be constituted differently than the rest of us, will you still be able to sleep? And to dreamwalk?"

"I feel sure of it. I have never had much of a problem sleeping. And I feel that, should I wish to, I could close my eyes right now to a nice nap. That's another way I feel different. I feel I may be able to do things that I could not do before. It remains to be seen, though. Thank you for the tea, Finn."

"Celia made it for you, my lord."

"Oh?"

"Yes. I have taught her, of necessity, somewhat about certain chores."

"She helped you with me?"

"Yes, my lord. Only minor things. I would not permit her to enter your room. Frankly, sire, I was afraid to permit it."

"Hm. I can't say as I blame you. Well. I should get dressed, don't you think?"

"Yes, my lord. And, sir, perhaps we should first discuss the matter of the approaching party. Those prisoners who are being brought along the ledge from the south."

"Yes, a priority. How far along have they come during my absence?"

"I'm afraid they are rather close by. In another day or two at the most they will be at the low point in Shatuum's walls, the place where ladders are put down for them to climb."

"I see. Yes, we need to address that situation right away. Allow me to dress, then we'll plan their rescue and reception."

"Certainly, my lord."

"Finn?"

"Yes?"

"I have been taken care of so many times," Robby said, looking earnestly at Finn, "even by complete strangers. What I mean to say is thank you, Finn. Thank you."

• • •

When Sheila suddenly sat up in her bed, Ashlord put his book onto his lap and looked at her. She stared at the open window across the room, not seeming to notice his presence. Ashlord waited, hoping that the worst was over, but not trusting that it was. Certina nudged her way out from behind his collar and looked, too. Sheila suddenly flung her bedcovers off, leapt up, and raced straight at the window as fast as she could go, her arms out to dive through it. Halfway there, the tether around her ankle pulled taut, and she fell flat onto the floor with such a hard thud that Ashlord winced. He shook his head as she clawed her way closer to the window, dragging the bed to which she was tied. Sighing as he stood, he put his book down, went to her, and lifted her up. She did not fight him as she had after her previous attempts, which was something, but she looked at him with an expression of pleading confusion.

"I need to go," she said. "I must fly away with Cupeldain to fight the Dragonkind."

"That fight is over," Ashlord told her, as he had said to her before, and he coaxed her to her feet and back to the bed. She complied, nodding.

"Oh, yes. That's right. Then I should go with Aperion," she said, trying to turn back to the window. "He calls."

"He and his host have already departed. You will have to await your turn, my dear."

"Oh. I don't know if I can wait."

"Ah, but you must. I am sorry. Perhaps he will call again."

Ashlord sat Sheila down on the bed and examined the back of her nightgown, noting that there were hardly any bloodstains since changing her shredded clothes the night before.

"Lie back," he said, easing her down onto the mattress. He covered her over again with the cast off blankets, felt her brow, and went to the door. Outside in the hall, Farby stood up from his chair, as did Billy and Ibin when Ashlord put his head out.

"Billy, would you be so kind as to tell Miss Tarrier that we shall have yet another bout momentarily? But tell her that I think the worst has passed."

Billy nodded, put his book on his chair, and hurried downstairs. Before he had gotten down even the first flight, he heard Sheila's bloodcurdling wail. By the time he turned the last landing, Miss Tarrier appeared at the bottom of the stairs.

"Again?" she asked.

"Yep," said Billy.

"That's four times today."

"Don't I know it! But Ashlord says the worst of it's done with."

"Oh, I hope so! I dearly hope so for our neighbors' sakes!"

Billy turned to go back when suddenly Sheila's cries ceased. Freezing, he glanced back at Miss Tarrier, then took the stairs by twos all the way up. Panting as he came around the top landing, he saw Ibin and Farby on down the hall peering into Sheila's room. Ibin turned and put his finger on his lips as Billy hurried to them.

"Look!" Ibin said in a whisper.

Inside, Ashlord was bent over Sheila, one hand up to halt anyone from entering while the other rested on her brow. He breathed a sigh of relief, tossed off the covers around her ankle, and untied the tether. Coming to the door and into the hall, he closed the door softly behind him.

"She sleeps," he whispered. "Her fever is gone. And at last she truly sleeps!"

"Whew!" said Billy.

"That's, that'sgood, that'sgoodisn't it, Ashlord?" asked Ibin.

"Of course it is, old man!" grinned Farby, slapping Ibin on the back.

"Yes, it is," agreed Ashlord. "Mr. Farby, I thank you for your dedication to Lady Shevalia these past many days. Now that she begins her recovery, I'm sure that you may wish to resume your routine. And I happen to know that your parents wonder what has become of you."

"Yes. I suppose I should go. But only if you assure me that if anything changes for the worse, or if there is the slightest need, that you will send word by the quickest possible courier."

"You have my promise."

"Well, sir, I shall relinquish your room. I thank you for allowing me to stay. Please, should the opportunity arise, give Lady Shevalia my fondest regards."

"I shall do so. Oh, and would you be so kind as to tell Miss Tarrier that Lady Shevalia is now resting easy, but to send up a change of bedsheets when it is convenient."

As Farby departed homeward to his own bed, a bath, and a change of clothes, Miss Tarrier sent Reysa up with breakfast for the men. They ate in the parlor, as they had been doing so that they could be near Sheila at every moment, and their spirits were very much lifted. None had gotten much sleep, nor had Miss Tarrier or Reysa, owing to the fierce screaming and carrying on coming from Sheila's rooms at all hours for the past several days and nights. During that time, Miss Tarrier constantly went back and forth to the neighbors, pleading their indulgence and patience, explaining that the fever that gripped Lady Shevalia was sure to pass at any hour. After so many days and nights without rest, they all now felt the heaviness of their fatigue. It was not long after breakfast that everyone within the house except Ashlord was sound asleep. He needed no sleep, and he paced back and forth in the parlor, engaged in a fierce debate with himself.

"So she is Elifaen," he muttered as he paced. "And if Steggan brought her out of Tracia, as we were told, then those Bloodcoins that the Starharts had, that Steggan paid them with, must have come with her. But how did that come about? If her mother was Elifaen, which she most certainly was, then who was she?"

Certina watched from the mantel, following Ashlord's movements back and forth across the room. Ashlord stopped and turned to her.

"It actually would explain much," he said to Certina. "Much indeed. How easily she learned, her bearing, her yearnings and sensibilities, the speed of her healing, her resilience from suffering. Her sadness. It seems that I was right all along, old girl. I should have been more certain. I should have! Yes, yes. I know. A deeper mystery now surrounds her."

• • •

Banis pounded the table with such violence that his plate and utensils jumped and his wineglass was nearly upset. The soldier that stood at the far side of the dining table winced at the interruption of his report.

"Of course they are in the city by now," Banis said smoothly and calmly in counterpoint to his clenched fist.

"My lord," ventured the soldier, "we watch all of the men that you instructed us to watch. No one fitting Collandoth's description has been seen. No one but the tenants of Raynor's apartment house has been seen there, with the exception of those visiting them."

"What tenants? Who are they?"

"A lady called Shevalia. Two of her servants and her guardian, my lord."

"Shevalia?"

"Yes, my lord. A young lady."

"Of what House?"

"House of Pradkin, my lord."

"Pradkin? I have never heard of it. Where is their estate?"

"I do not know, my lord."

"Then you must find out, mustn't you? They have visitors, you said."

"Yes, my lord. The usual social greeters. One young man who seems to seek the attentions of the young lady. And Lady Highleaf, sir."

"Highleaf, eh? That busybody! It's not enough that her father was a thorn in my side for years. Now his meddling daughter blunders onto the scene. Be careful around her. She may seem foolish, but she is very powerful and influential. As for Lady Shevalia, find out who she is and what business she has in the city."

"Yes, my lord, but she has been ill, it seems. At least that is what the neighbors say. Some fever."

"And her guardian? What is his name?"

"Sootking, my lord."

Banis stared at the soldier with such a look of incredulity that the man winced again.

"Yes, my lord. An odd name, indeed, sir."

"Sootking. Soot. King. You stupid fool! Ash. Lord. Have you no intelligence whatsoever?"

"But, my lord, he is a red man. His hair, his skin, all red! The description we have is of a man with long black hair and beard."

"He disguises himself! That is Ashlord. It must be. Lady Shevalia must be the girl."

"But what of the others? There are only two men with them, not four, Lord Banis, and neither are a Kingsman."

"The other two must be nearby."

Banis rose suddenly and went to a nearby bureau and wrote a note in his careful hand. He put his seal on it and gave it to the soldier.

"Use your girl to put Ashlord out of the way," Banis commanded. "And use this writ for the rest of them."

Chapter 5

Thunderfoot

"Our King needs your help," Finn said to Micerea. She was surprised to see him so soon, and assumed that Finn came to fetch her to Griferis to see Robby, or King Philawain, as Finn insisted that he be called. But, at his statement, she suddenly worried that Robby had taken a turn for the worse.

"What has happened? I thought he was recovering," she said.

"Oh, he has fully recovered, but there is an urgent matter that he would like for us to take care of. And there isn't much time."

"What can I do for our King?" she asked.

Finn smiled, glad to hear her address Robby in that manner.

"He wishes us to work together to free some prisoners being brought to Shatuum."

Finn quickly told her about the approaching party that traveled along the precarious ledge that lined the Crack Between Worlds, and that some of the prisoners were Dragonkind. As he spoke, he took her to see them. They were a pitiful group, barely able to walk a few steps without being struck or whipped by the wraiths that drove them on. Finn also showed her on ahead to the place where they were to climb up ladders to a low rampart and thus enter Shatuum.

"It is King Philawain's wish that they be freed, then led on to Griferis. He will put out ropes for them to climb up from the ledge to the gate upon Algamori. From there, they will be permitted to cross the causeway into Griferis, which the King will put out for them."

"But they are chained. And they appear quite weak. How are they to overcome their guards and be free of them?"

"King Philawain says that he will see to their chains," Finn explained. "Once free, they should have little problem overpowering their guards, if they work together. But they must be forewarned so as to be ready. That is where we come in. We are to go to them and enter their dreams, Man and Dragonkind together, and tell them what to do. They are bound not to trust one another, but if we stand before them together, we should convince them to unite against their captors."

"I see. But are they permitted to sleep?"

"Yes. Their guards are as weak as they are, and must frequently rest. At each stop, the prisoners almost immediately fall asleep. So we must watch and be ready."

"Very well. I will do whatever I can to convince them," Micerea nodded. "And when they get to Griferis, what is to become of them?"

"They will be offered sanctuary, or, if they wish, they will be allowed to leave, but must then make their way on their own. I know. It doesn't seem like much of a choice, but our King wishes them to know that they will not be forced to stay within Griferis. Those who stay will be asked to serve Griferis for a time."

"How do you know that you can trust them?"

"We do not know. But King Philawain wishes to deny Shatuum anything, or anyone, that is within his power to keep from there. He is convinced that these prisoners will soon become like the guards who bring them, transformed by Secundur's dark arts to be his servants."

"Look, they stop."

Indeed, the staggering line had halted. The prisoners sat and leaned against the cliff. As soon as the first one dozed off, Micerea and Finn went to work. It was not easy. In the first place, it was difficult to convince the dreamers that they were not illusions of their fatigued state of imagination. And, just when they had delivered their message to the second one, the guards were rousing everyone back up onto their feet.

"Drat!" Micerea said.

"We must give them a sign to share with one another," said Finn, "so that they may know with only a few words that they have all received the same message."

"What sort of sign?"

"I don't know."

"I know! A word. An unusual word or name. Or something of the sort."

"Yes, we shall do that."

• • •

Robby also watched the group. At the pace they made, it would be less than a day before they reached the rendezvous place, where it would be too late to do anything. His plan depended on freeing them before they got that far. It would then be up to the prisoners to overpower their guards and rush as fast as they could beyond the ladders of Shatuum. Meanwhile, between dreamwalking naps, he searched frantically to find the items he needed to fashion some means by which they could climb up to the gate at the Landing and thus gain access to his causeway. He only hoped that this side of Mount Algamori still had some quality about it that kept Secundur from sending his forces to it, but he could not be sure. At least he knew from the memory of his forebears, memories given him when he learned his true name, what tools and devices to look for in Griferis. And, after searching a dozen large storage rooms, pushing a wheelbarrow from room to room, he found what he needed. He tossed several long coils of rope into the wheelbarrow, and also put in two large blocks, the kind used to hoist heavy weights. He hurried off, awkwardly pushing the unwieldy wheelbarrow as he went, stopping to carry the load, then the wheelbarrow up stairs.

"We truly need an apparatus like Lord Tallin has in his house!" he muttered as he dragged the wheelbarrow up yet another flight. "Or like in Linlally, powered by the waterfalls."

He sat down for a little nap, immediately fell asleep, and went to look in on Finn and Micerea. They were presently engaged in conversation with one of the Dragonkind women. Satisfied that they had things in hand, he woke himself and stood to continue his work. He knew Finn would come to him as soon as he and Micerea had accomplished their task.

"Now, to put out the causeway," Robby said to himself. Rushing up to the east tower, he climbed the stairs to the topmost floor and entered a circular room windowed all the way around. On the wall was a small glass case from which he removed a long glass key. He placed the key into another cylinder, also of glass, that jutted up from the floor of the room and gave it a turn. The cylinder began to glow with a pale blue light, and a low hum filled the room. Although he knew what to do, from studying the texts in the library, he did not know what to expect.

Next he went to the broad window. Below he could see the palace gate, a broad courtyard on this side of it and an abyss on the other side, and he looked out across the wide empty space to the far shelf where the gate stood upon Algamori. He placed each of his hands on top of copper posts that rose up from the floor to either side of him.

"I am Philawain," he said softly. "King of Griferis. Let those rightfully invited come to my domain."

A painful blare of trumpets hit his ears, and he flinched and closed his eyes as a jolt of lightning shot up the copper poles and through him. The bolt traveled out from the tower into the sky, and suddenly a mighty storm raged all around Griferis. Opening his eyes, he could see that a star-like light emanated from the distant gate at the mountain and the causeway now spanned across the abyss from there to Griferis. He pulled his hands away from the copper posts and the storm froze. Looking through the windows, he saw jagged lightning hanging in the billowing clouds, their blinding glare coloring the scene in an eerie blue-white light.

"Whew!" he said, hurrying to the stairs. "I wasn't sure that it would work, in spite of what the book said!"

It took him much longer than he expected, owing to the great distance that he had to haul the ropes and equipment. But within two hours, he had the blocks wound with rope, fixed to one of the uprights of the arched gate, and another knotted rope thrown over the side to the ledge below. Satisfied that all was ready, he jogged back across the mysterious bridge to his castle in the air.

• • •

"The two strongest must climb up first," said Micerea. "At the top you will find those things needed to hoist the others up."

"When all of your companions are up, immediately cross together over the causeway," instructed Finn. "You will be greeted at the gates of the King's Palace, wherein you will be safe."

"Once you are free of your chains, you cannot hesitate," added Micerea.

The Dragonkind man whom they addressed shook his head.

"I am baffled by this dream," he said, "although you have shown me that this is no ordinary dream."

"The King of Griferis is King of Dreams," said Micerea, "and it is he who sends us to you."

"Know by the words of your companions that this is no ordinary dream," said Finn. "Say aloud the word, 'Celia,' and your fellows will answer you with the word, 'Boxer.'"

"The word 'Celia' is always to be answered by 'Boxer,'" said Micerea. "Do this and you will know what kind of dream this is. Heed our words and be saved."

"Heed not, and become like those who take you to Secundur!"

This Dragonkind man was the last to receive their message, and when he awoke, kicked by a foul wraith wielding a serrated sword, he cried out, "Celia!"

Immediately, those around him muttered, "Boxer."

Then one of the women nearest to him said, as they got to their feet, "Celia."

"Boxer is the reply," he said in return.

"Quiet!" cried one of the wraiths, turning upon him with a grin. "Or I will fill my hungry belly with your guts."

They shuffled on, shivering in the cold, the chains around their ankles and wrists rattling dully. Soon they were all once again too miserable to have any glimmer of hope from a strange, fleeting dream.

"What's that odd light?" one wraith asked another, pointing far ahead to the bright glowing clouds.

"Must be that accursed castle," was the answer.

Then, just when the lead wraith pointed with his sword to the ladders a few yards away, the prisoners' shackles began to burst asunder, falling from their feet and hands.

"What's this?" said the wraith, staring at the chains that the man just behind him was now swinging. Before the creature could react, he was knocked off the ledge, joined almost immediately by two other guards as the remaining guards were knocked senseless.

"Let's go! As fast as we can!"

"Stay together!"

They could not go very fast simply because they had little strength left to them. But they were heartened somewhat by the mysterious light that drew them on, though it was several hours before they were close enough to see any details of it. Yet, as they neared, they were filled with increasing wonder and more than a little fear. It was as if a vast painting hung in the air, depicting a terrible storm surrounding a castle above them. But the wind did not blow, the lightning simply hung in the clouds like blinding jagged cracks, and the raindrops they now encountered did not fall to the ground.

"Surely this is a place of great power!" said one of the women.

"Or else a terrible trick."

When they came directly underneath the causeway, they found the ropes that were foretold. One of the men went up first, not without some difficulty, and after another hour, all of the others had been hauled up. At first, they were hesitant to go onto the causeway, for the storm still hung in the air, and, besides, there were no supports for the long span. Indeed, the causeway appeared spindly and insubstantial compared to the gulf that it crossed and the peaks surrounding. And the distant castle to which the causeway led was truly weird, hanging among the storm clouds, like the bridge, without any visible reason that it should not plummet into the abyss. Cold and hunger and the greater fear of pursuit coaxed them to give it a try. First one then another cautiously stepped across the threshold of the gate and onto the causeway, and soon all were hurrying along it, sometimes glancing over their shoulders to see if they were being pursued. After a while, they were far enough along the bridge to see a figure standing at the far end. As they neared, they saw he was dressed in a magnificent suit of green and gold velvet, a broad, dark blue sash over his shoulder, and a glittering hat, flecked with specks of gold and emeralds. He stood with one hand upon his hip and another hand upon a tall staff of spiral-banded gold. When they reached him, they all fell to their knees.

"King, we beseech thee to give us shelter in your strange and mysterious domain!" implored one of the women.

"The King of Griferis sends his welcome to you," said the figure. "But do you not recognize me? I am Finn, who was sent to you by my King to give you tidings and instruction through your dreams. I am the King's Chamberlain, and I come to bring you forth into Griferis, to have succor from my King, who rescues you from Secundur. I bid you enter!"

Finn gestured for them to come past him into the courtyard. They did so, wide-eyed and amazed, but the last one to pass turned to Finn.

"My lord," he said, "will we not be pursued into this place along yon bridge?"

"No. You are safe, for behold the power of King Philawain!"

Finn pointed through the gate at the causeway. Suddenly there was a deafening boom of thunder, and a powerful wind swept the scene with hard drops of rain. Then, just as suddenly, all noise ceased, the air cleared, and the causeway was gone with nothing but clear air beneath a blue sky between them and the edge of the chasm.

Finn led them into the palace and along a corridor to the north wing. There he took them to a dining room where a long table was set with food and drink.

"Eat," he said to them. "To each of you a room is provided. You will also have new clothes and the means to tend to your wounds. But first, eat. I, myself, will come again to see you after a little while."

"My lord," asked one of the young Dragonkind, who was no more than a girl, "can you tell us about your King? None of us have heard of him, or of this realm. Is he a conjurer-king?"

"You will learn of him in due time, when you are ready to present yourselves to him."

• • •

They ate as if they were famished, which, of course, they were. And they were so weak that they began to feel the heavy fatigues of their tortured journey almost as soon as a few morsels had been consumed. Finn, knowing this would be the case, returned in but a short while, and he took them to an adjoining foyer between two halls.

"I direct you ladies to go to the right," he said, "and the men to the left. You will each have your own room. Each room has a lock set into the door. The key is on the bedside table. You may lock your door or not, as you wish. Within each room you will find clothes that the King hopes will be suitable to your needs, at least for the time being. There is also wood and coal for the hearths, warm blankets, and, it is hoped, a comfortable bed. You are free to come and go as you wish within this wing, to the dining room to have an additional repast, or to visit with each other. However, I warn you: The King will not tolerate any ill-will amongst you, and he will not abide any rude behavior betwixt the men and the ladies. Is that understood? Good. One final warning: You may not attempt to leave this wing. You will succeed only in being cast out from this place. That said, I bid you good-night."

• • •

Later, when Finn locked the doors leading into and out from the north wing, he went to find Robby in the library, to have their usual meeting. Robby grinned as Finn entered, and rushed up to shake his hand.

"I congratulate you, my Chamberlain!" said Robby enthusiastically. "Well done! Splendid work! Almost as splendid as your outfit!"

"Thank you, sire. I fear my clothes are a bit overblown. They mistook me for you!"

"I know. I was looking on. No, I think they were suitably impressed," Robby said, guiding Finn to their table. "I only hope that I can do half as well when I greet them."

"I'm sure you will exceed my performance, sire."

"I wouldn't bet on it. By the way, I've been thinking. I should move out of my little bedroom and into the upstairs south wing. Don't get me wrong. I love my room. But I think I have a role to play, and I'll eventually need rooms befitting. So I may as well move tonight, if that is not too much trouble."

"No, sire. Whatever you wish. I agree that you deserve more suitable accommodations. It will be easier, in the long run, anyway. At least in the south wing you can be assured of your privacy and security. Besides, sire, it should also be much more comfortable."

"Then I'll do it. Now, let's talk about my upcoming meeting with our guests. You know what I have in mind to discuss with them. I do not wish to reveal too much too soon. And, whether they accept my offer or not, we still need to bring more people here. I have a notion as to how we may accomplish that, though it will only bring us a few at a time. First things first, though. Tell me again what you know of our guests, and add anything new that you and Micerea may have learned."

Once Robby and Finn completed their business together, and they were prepared for the morrow, Finn helped Robby gather all of his meager belongings from his bedchamber.

"I must say I'll miss the place," Robby said, closing the door behind them. "After all, it has been my cozy little home for the past twenty-eight years."

"Yes, sire," answered Finn, following along with some of Robby's books. "But I have a feeling that your new rooms will suit you better, once you are accustomed to them."

When they got to the upstairs south wing, Finn showed Robby to the rooms that he felt were suitable, and Robby liked what he saw. It had been a few weeks since he had explored this part of Griferis, and he remembered being somewhat taken aback at the opulence of the rooms. Indeed, even the hall leading to the suite that would be his was impressive, richly carpeted floors, wonderful drapes, and even a fountain located in the foyer where several hallways came together.

His personal rooms were no less lavish, but what impressed Robby the most was the spectacular view from the windows and balconies. The snowcapped peaks either side of the void receded southward, and the great chasm itself, filled with clouds, disappeared into the horizon. Standing with his arms still full of his things, he nodded.

"Yes. I think I could get used to waking up to this each morning!" he said. "Thank you, Finn. I know you are tired and need rest. Just as Micerea always reminded me, dreamwalking takes it out of you, doesn't it?"

"I must admit that I am quite done in," Finn answered, putting the books onto a desk. "Your bedrooms are just through that door, sire. The other door leads to a small library. I'll just turn down your bed for you."

"No, that is alright. Thank you, but I'll manage. I think that will be all. I have a few errands to run, if you know what I mean, so I bid you a good-night."

"Good-night, Your Majesty."

"You know, don't you, that I'll never get used to your way of addressing me? I wish you'd just call me Robby."

"If that is your command, I shall do so, sire."

"It isn't a command, Finn. Just a request."

"Then I shall endeavor to change my ways, sire."

Finn smiled, and Robby chuckled.

• • •

Almost as soon as Robby was alone, he flung himself into one of the comfortable chairs, went to sleep, and then raced eastward across the earth, diving down into the troll caves near Janhaven. They were still clogged with the reeking bodies of the Redvests killed in the intense battle that had taken place over two weeks earlier. Robby tried to ignore them as he found his way between a crack in the stones and continued down into the depths of the hidden chambers far below. There, Thunderfoot lay chained, and he was asleep. As soon as the King of the Trolls began to dream, Robby approached.

"It is time, King Thunderfoot," he said.

"Time?" bellowed Thunderfoot in a low gravelly voice. "Time does not impress me."

"Then let this! And remember our bargain!"

Robby swept his hand through the massive cuff that was forged around the troll's ankle. It rang so loudly that Thunderfoot instantly awoke, as if a great bell was struck, and he saw the iron burst asunder, scattering the heavy links of chain that passed through its ring.

Thunderfoot stared at the shards at his feet, picking up the heavy iron scraps in his massive hands. His blockish head turned and looked around his prison chamber in disbelief. He stood, free of his bonds, and raised his arms in a great stretch, yawning.

"I am impressed!" he cried, the rumbling of his statement bringing dust down from the high ceiling. "And I think I shall do as I said I would do!"

Thunderfoot tore into the walls, striking out the heavy blocks one by one until he came up to the place where the old hall was, the place where Bailorg had been killed. Thunderfoot stomped from the caves, squishing and crunching through the bodies that littered the place, and came out on the west side into the broad daylight. There, again, he stretched and yawned, then strode off southward, his footsteps giving back the name of the Thunder Mountains, his rock-crushing feet shaking the snow from the trees and making drifts slide down the slopes. With a stride as long between footfalls as an ordinary man was tall, he quickly made the south road to Tallinvale and pounded his way along it, scattering deer and foxes ahead of him. From time to time, he roared out his name, sounding like the word it was made of, and he took great joy in doing so.

Long before he reached Tallinvale, his people felt his approach, the bump of his footfalls coursing through the ground and coming up through their feet. Still standing where they had since they cast aside the lintels they had held aloft for so many years, they turned their neckless heads and looked northward at the hilly rim of the valley. Around the trolls, the workers who labored to repair the bridges and clean up the debris of war fled back to the city, as alarmed soldiers rushed to the north walls prepared for battle. Hearing that the blockheads, as the Tallinvalers had come to call the trolls, were at last stirring, General Teracue hurried to the north gate with Weylan and found Lord Tallin and Prince Danoss already there just as the booming was felt and heard from the distance, growing rapidly closer. As for the trolls, they did not move except to look toward the hill, or to scratch themselves. Thunderfoot appeared at the ridge, as tall as two men, and he halted to survey the scene.

"It is a great troll," said Teracue, peering through a spyglass. "He wears fine clothes and appears to have a square hat of gold."

"The hat is a crown, made to fit his head. It is Thunderfoot," said Tallin.

"Thunderfoot?" asked Weylan. "King of the Trolls?"

"Yes, the very same."

"Then he is not just legend," said Teracue, quickly looking up and down the wall to see that the soldiers were preparing for their next engagement.

"Our weapons will avail us nothing," said Tallin. "Should he decide to lead them against us, there is very little we may do to withstand them."

"I hope I didn't come all this way," said Danoss, "only to be pounded into mush by rock trolls."

"Then it was his people who built these walls," said Weylan. "My lord, what manner of bargain did you make with Thunderfoot?"

"I made no bargain with him," said Tallin. "And that's my worry."

At that moment, Thunderfoot rumbled out a long low growl merely by clearing his throat. The sound set the walls of Tallin City buzzing so that dust rose up from the entire scene, as sand might dance on the head of a kettledrum.

"Coooooooommmmmmeeee toooooo meeeeeeeeeee!" Thunderfoot then bellowed. All of those not of his kind threw their hands over their ears at the intense rumble. Several windows in the city shattered, horses bucked and neighed, and every bird within miles took to the air. Immediately, the thousands of trolls, who until recently had served Lord Tallin's purpose, began climbing from the pits in which they stood and made their way to stand before their king, the thunder of their shuffle like a great storm cracking and booming over the valley. This lasted a good while, but faded away as the trolls gathered before Thunderfoot, who stood above them on the hill with his hands on his hips. He was pleased by their obedience, and he nodded.

"Folloooooow meeeeeeeeee hoooooommmmme!" he said, and he turned and strode off westward, right through the wreck of the decimated forest. The trolls ordered themselves into a line and followed, every one of the thousands of them, and it was a mighty procession, making an earthquake by their tromping. Everyone was greatly relieved that the creatures were going away, but none more so than Lord Tallin, who breathed an audible sigh, as if he had been holding his breath.

"Well," he said, "I hope that is the end of a long-held worry!"

Chapter 6

The Forty-Nine

"Tell me again when you last saw Ullin?"

Lyrium adjusted her cane and stiffly turned to look at Ullin's mother. Both women looked frail, but Ullin's mother was truly so. Lyrium put her empty teacup and saucer on the sideboard. By now, she was accustomed to Lady Sharyn's lapses and did not mind at all repeating.

"I'm sorry, my lady," said the maid, who was hurrying back into the room after closing the shutters. "I should have taken care of that for you."

"It is no bother, thank you," said Lyrium.

Mortals grow old in different ways, Lyrium knew, and some more quickly than others. Truly, when Lady Sharyn's husband, Aram Tallin, died, she began to age rapidly. Unlike most mortals married to Elifaen, her youthfulness did not outlast her husband's death. Though she was barely sixty, something inside had been irrevocably broken when Aram died, setting off a sort of chain of upsets. First went her hair, once as brown as walnut and now entirely white. The rest of her body followed. Her eyesight rapidly diminished, and whereas she was once a strong, hefty woman, she was now as spindly as Lyrium's cane, hardly able to walk without assistance. And, finally, these past few years, her mind began to falter. Although Lyrium had only met Lady Sharyn soon after seeing Ullin and his friends at Tallin Hall, and was at first shocked by her condition, she quickly had the story of her decline from Sharyn's maid and from others.

Having taken a cottage nearby for the seclusion it offered, Lyrium was happy to learn that her nearest neighbor was Lady Sharyn. Since her arrival in Glareth, Lyrium had visited Lady Sharyn almost every day, walking the mile or so along the path that ran atop the bluffs to do so. With each visit, Sharyn's maid prepared tea for them and patiently waited upon the two old ladies while they chatted, Lyrium often reminding Sharyn of things she had already been told.

"It was this past autumn," she said, coming over to Sharyn's chair and bending over to kiss her on the top of her head. "I must go, now. I shall miss our visits."

"Oh, yes. You are going away, aren't you? I had forgotten. Will you be seeing my son again?"

"I hope to. And I hope to see you again, too."

"Aram will be sorry that he missed you," said Sharyn. "He's away in the deserts, you know."

"Yes, I know. I am sorry that I missed him, too. Please take care and mind your maid."

"Did I tell you that Ullin came to see me? When was it? Oh, yes. It was last summer, wasn't it, Jenny?"

"Yes, ma'am, it was," answered the maid.

"Yes, Sharyn, you told me. Goodbye."

Jenny saw her to the door, saying, "She will miss you, Lady Lyrium. Your visits have removed much tedium from her days."

"Thank you, Jenny. Please watch after her for me. And take good care of yourself, too."

Lyrium departed, and with her cane to help her, she hobbled along the bluff back to her own cottage. It was a blustery day, the sea foam blew thick along the beach far below, and there was a scattering of wind-driven snow. As she went, her back straightened, her cane thickened to a worthy walking stick, her wrinkles vanished, and, under the hood of her cloak, her hair thickened, becoming long and black as coal. When she came within sight of her cottage, she saw her daughters standing outside at the gate, their long cloaks pulled close against the wind.

"Welcome, our mother," said Belmira. "We have it all ready."

"The floor is swept clean," said Elmira, "and the fire burns steady."

"We hope that your vision will come to you soon."

"Though clouds are quite thick and will block Lady Moon."

"Indeed, it is a heavy blanket of clouds," nodded Lyrium, "but I thank you, my daughters. I will try one last time, with or without Lady Moon. Then we must go to the Queen. Is everything ready for our departure?"

"All is quite ready, and by your request…"

"…our coach comes at dawn to carry us west."

They went inside, and Lyrium saw that her daughters had cleared away the furniture, pushing it to the side of the great room. A fire blazed in the hearth, with ample wood to stoke it as night fell. Belmira took Lyrium's cloak as Elmira handed her a small rolled-up rug. Lyrium unrolled it onto the floor in the center of the room, revealing a small cloth sack within. She knelt on the rug, facing the fire, and began removing small stones and bones from the sack, arranging them carefully in groups before her. Her daughters retreated into the shadows to watch and to attend, if needed.

"Blood of my blood, bone of my bone," Lyrium said as she took a dagger from her belt and made a quick cut across her palm. Holding her hand like a fist, she squeezed the dripping blood out, making a circle of splattered dots on the floor before the wound healed. "Quicken mine eyes. Show me what you will, what I need to see."

She picked up a bone and a stone and dropped them into the circle.

"Quicken mine eyes."

She picked up another set, and dropped them into the circle.

"Show me what you will. What I need to see."

She went on for a while, scattering bones and stones, chanting her refrains as her daughters watched. They knew that with each passing year their touch with the world faded somewhat more than the year before. And with each year, Lyrium's Sight grew dimmer and more difficult to summon. It was many years, indeed, since she could enter the Place of Sight without preparation, having once been able to call upon the skill whenever she wished. Once, she could look at the stars and See, or at the flowing water of a sparkling stream. She once could See in her sleep, through dreams, or Sight might come to her suddenly, while turning over a leaf, or holding a seashell to her ear. Her skill was something from the old days, the Time Before Time, when all things spoke to the Faerekind of all other things. But, as that Time faded away from memory, so too did the ways of the world fade from the Fallen Ones. These late years, there were many nights when Lyrium chanted until dawn, trying to summon her waning skill without success.

This night, a long while after sunset, her daughters knew by the tone of her voice when she neared the Place of Sight. Now, her voice low and hoarse, she crouched over the circle, still on her knees, propped up with one hand while she picked up and dropped her charms, her long black hair draped downward on the floor, hiding her face. Then, as she reached to pick up a pair of stones, she froze, her hand inches away from them, and she ceased chanting.

To her eyes, the pattern of bones and stones formed a moving scene, their small shadows dancing in the flickering firelight. She abruptly straightened up, putting her hand before her eyes as she gazed at the fire, squinting, as if looking into the sun.

But it was not the sun, nor was it the firelight that made her squint so. It was the bright background of a clear blue day. The figure she saw was only a shadow against this background, standing on a high wall. As her eyes grew accustomed to the light, she saw that it was a man, probably in his late-forties, judging by his graying hair and beard. He looked out from the wall, his arms crossed. The flags that blew from masts around the wall attracted her gaze. They were dark blue, as the night sky, bordered in white. In the center of each flag was embroidered seven stars, each with seven points, all in a circle with the top star the largest, and in the center of the circle of stars was a winged key. When Lyrium's Sight turned back to the figure standing at the wall, he turned to face her, and she recognized the man as Robby Ribbon. Upon his head was a circlet of gold, set with seven glittering diamonds. Her vision blurred as the scene receded. Dizzied, she instinctively reached out for something to hold to, and her daughters, alarmed, took a step toward her. But Lyrium steadied herself before they could reach her, and now she stared at the flickering shadows dancing from the stones she had cast.

Suddenly she jumped up and dashed across the room for the pewter water pitcher. Going back to the circle, she swept away the bones and stones with her hand and poured water into the circle. Tossing aside the pitcher to bang and bounce across the floor, she knelt back down, and swirled the water-thinned blood as a child might do a finger-painting. After a moment, she recoiled, then bent closer to stare at it. The firelight shimmered through the pink puddle, and Lyrium felt herself being pulled into the cloudy water. She saw, standing before her, a woman attired in royal robes, a queen, bearing in one hand an arrow of gold and in the other a mirror, held so that Lyrium could see her own face, glowing with flickering firelight. The queen's hair was golden-brown, her eyes like honey in sunlight, and her face stern. Fear blew across Lyrium's skin like an icy breeze. Above the queen's head was a black canopy of stars held up by Serith Ellyn who was dressed as a servant might be, and upon the skirt of the canopy were set the Forty-Nine Keys to the Nimbus Illuminas, the Forty-Nine Bloodcoins. When Lyrium looked again into the mirror, she saw a fabulous fiery rainbow, bent across a dawn sky, going away from the earth and receding into the starry heavens. She felt drawn into the mirror. Halfway in, she reached out with her finger and touched the rainbow itself. Instantly, she was filled with a powerful longing to follow the rainbow upward, away and into the heavens, and she felt her spirit tugging, urging her to depart.

Lyrium gasped and inhaled violently and loudly, as if she had held her breath underwater for too long and had just now broken the surface. She staggered to her feet, gasping for air and backing away from the circle. Her daughters caught her as she fell unconscious.

• • •

"Thrice the same vision has come of her rite," said Belmira as they put their mother in her bed, "the first just the same as the last."

"And thrice has our mother recoiled from the Sight," answered Elmira, pulling the covers around Lyrium, "as never she did in the past."

"And, now as before, she cries and weeps."

"Her tears run the more, though she now sleeps."

Indeed, Lyrium's dreams were filled with that same powerful longing to depart from the earth, as so many of her kind had done with Aperion. And though she would not wake for hours, her tears would run and run until she did.

• • •

As Lyrium finally slept, so, too, did Serith Ellyn a few miles away in the city of Glareth by the Sea. Her dreams were nearly as sad and melancholy as Lyrium's. The Queen of Vanara was plagued, as she had been for many nights, by a recurring vision. It always began differently, depending on what she dreamed on a given night, but it always ended the same. This night, she dreamed she was flying upward into the sky, chasing after Aperion's Host that moved away from her. Realizing they would not wait, and that she could not catch up to them, she let herself fall, watching her wings shred away like dry leaves scattering before an autumn wind. She landed, of all places, before her fabulous throne in Linlally. It was quite the same as it ever was since its making by Cupeldain, but as she watched, the tips of the throne's ornate wings began to crack. She watched in horror as the entire chair snapped and popped as cracks traveled all through it, like thin ice breaking beneath one's footsteps. Soon the entire throne was riddled with these cracks, and just as she felt it would crumble to pieces before her, blood began oozing from each fissure, dripping down onto the floor and running across the tiles, just as her father's blood had done the night she slew him.

That is how this dream began. Backing away from the spreading pool, she entered the courtyard outside, staring at the encroaching red as it poured from the doorway.

"Psst!"

A shadow crossed her as she turned toward the sound and squinted into a nearly blinding sky. Standing on the wall that bordered the courtyard was the dark outline of a person.

"I need your Seven," he said.

"Who are you?"

"Will you give them over to me?"

"I most certainly will not! Who are you?"

"You know who I am."

But the dream then ended, as it always did, when she woke and sat up with a start. Infuriated, she threw her covers off to begin her day. The sun was not yet up, but as she glanced from her balcony window she saw that the clouds that rolled eastward to the rim of the sea were growing somewhat light. Gaiyelneth, who seemed always to sense when the Queen was up, soon came in to help her dress. Today, Serith Ellyn decided to dress for war, but she would leave off the armor until her visitors had departed. So she put on her loincloth, then her short battle toga and her wristbands. Gaiyelneth laid out her skirt of overlapping plate, her mail, and her breast and back plates. Finally, she took out from their cases Serith Ellyn's helmet, her sword, and her mace.

"I think the shield is a bit much for traveling, Gaiyelneth."

"If you ask me, my Queen, it is all a bit much."

"You are as impertinent as ever."

"Yes, ma'am. I try to stay sharp. I apologize."

"When I desire your apology, I shall ask for it," Serith Ellyn said. "Hand me my housecloak. I feel a chill in the air."

"Yes. It tries to snow, I think. I'll attend to the hearth directly."

"Leave it. I do not intend to stay long enough to enjoy what warmth it may yield. Even though winter here is not nearly as cold as in Vanara, I have felt the cold of Glareth worse than I can remember since arriving."

"They say it is the sea air in winter, ma'am. It gets into the bones, and brings a chill."

"Oh? Is that what they say?"

"Yes, ma'am."

A knock came. It was Gaiyelneth's brother, Captain Chanter.

"Pardon me, Queen," he said, bowing. "Thurdun sends me to say first that all is prepared for our departure. Secondly, that Lyrium's coach is now entering the Palace grounds."

"Very good, Captain. Thank you."

When he had departed, Serith Ellyn looked at Gaiyelneth and sighed.

"I think you do not look forward to seeing Lyrium, my lady," Gaiyelneth said.

"She came out of hiding suddenly, after so many centuries, having mysteriously survived Tulith Attis," Serith Ellyn said, tossing aside a decorative hairpin and handing another to Gaiyelneth. "Now, just when things seem to be coming to a head. And yet, except for one visit when she first arrived in Glareth, she has remained aloof of us. She has Sight, but she cannot control it anymore, it seems. She cannot look where she wishes to, and cannot see what may be useful. So I wonder why she came at all. Leave it! I have no need to look my best for her."

• • •

They went to the great parlor and were joined by Thurdun after a few moments. He and his sister then went out onto the balcony and watched as the last of Prince Carbane's ships hoisted their sails and made ready to move on the tide.

"It seems that Glareth will soon be empty, Thurdun."

"Yes. And, frankly, I feel we should have departed weeks ago, as soon as you obtained news about the attack on Linlally," said Thurdun.

"Perhaps," his sister said. "But Seafar has things in hand. I know, since your heart longs to go with Carbane, that you are anxious to take action. That time will come. It will be good to be home after so long."

"And we came all this way," Thurdun said, "only to carry back with us what we brought. You never even brought up the matter with Prince Carbane."

"No, I did not. You think it is too risky to carry them back?"

"I did not say that. I only wonder if your dream has anything to do with it. You had it again, did you not?"

Before she could answer, Gaiyelneth opened the door behind them.

"My Queen," she said. "Lyrium is here."

Serith Ellyn and Thurdun went in, and Gaiyelneth followed, closing the door against the cold air. Standing in the room before them was Lyrium and her two daughters.

"Queen," Lyrium bowed, as did her daughters. "Thank you for seeing me."

"It is my pleasure to do so," Serith Ellyn said stiffly. "Please be seated."

Lyrium waited for Serith Ellyn to seat herself and then chose a chair close by. Thurdun, Elmira, and Belmira remained standing as Gaiyelneth left the room.

"As you know, my lady," Lyrium said, "I came here to report about my visions concerning the Passdale lad. I foresaw that I would meet him, and that he would seek Griferis. And so I came out of hiding and went to Lord Tallin's estate."

"Yes, as you told me when you first arrived, when you did me the courtesy of sharing your impressions of him."

"Yes, ma'am. But, as I said to you then, my impressions were mixed. In the first place, the Ribbon boy was not at all as I had expected. He was not proud, and had no hunger for power."

"Yes," Serith Ellyn said, knowing that she must let Lyrium have her say in her own way. "You said that he rejected Ethliad, and he also rejected the Ring of Hearing and destroyed it."

"That is so, my lady. Having the gift of Seeing does not mean that I rightly interpret those things that I See. Indeed, my gift is natural to me, having come to me without Blessing or instruction. Many times I have misinterpreted what I have Seen. Just as at Tulith Attis, when I thought that I foresaw a Man leading wolves into the heart of the fortress, and when I warned my husband on that matter so that he was prompted to build the great dam upon the lake, to have the magic Bell forged and hung, and the stony guard likewise placed around the fortress. All these things that he did were based on a false interpretation of what I saw. I am still baffled by my mistake, yet it seems I was fated to make it, setting the stage for the fulfillment of my vision. For had I not been mistaken, the Bell would have never been made and the Ribbon boy would have never rung it. Had he not, it is likely the wolves would have killed him."

"Yes, it seems it was a fortuitous mistake, Lady Lyrium. But all this you have already told me. Have you had some new vision?"

"Yes, I have. Since last I saw you, I determined to be isolated from others of this court, taking a small cottage on the coast nearby. Now, as we prepare to return to our homes, I must tell you what I Saw, though it is worrisome. With the assistance of my daughters, I have thrice striven to See, casting my charms and entering the Place of Sight when it opened to me. Each time, I delved into my visions, straining to discern something that has greatly troubled me."

"Oh? And what may that be, other than the times that are upon us?"

"That is just it, dear Queen. What I have seen with my Sight, I cannot understand. Thrice I have seen the same thing, yet I do not know why. Though I cast my charms to see the outcome of Robby Ribbon's quest for the throne of Duinnor, I see instead the girl, his companion, Sheila Pradkin, Sheila being a diminutive of her right name, Shevalia. When I met her in Tallinvale, I knew instantly that she was someone very special, someone key to the success of Ribbon's quest. I hoped that I might rightly see if the boy would succeed, so that I could give you and others fair warning if he failed. For if he does not assume the throne of Duinnor, things will be dire indeed."

"That is so, as events are shaping up," Serith Ellyn said. "If the present King remains, there is no reason to expect him to act before all is in ruins."

"Just so. But I see the Ribbon boy wearing another crown, my lady, and standing under flags that I do not recognize. Not those of Duinnor. And I see him as an older man, as if many years have passed."

"Your Sight, if I understand it correctly, does not always look upon the present. Perhaps you see the future?"

"Yes, that may be so. But as soon as I see him, the Sight removes my vision from him to reveal to me a great and mighty lady, beautiful and terrible in aspect."

Lyrium went on to tell of the vision, describing all to the Queen of Vanara, even how she saw Serith Ellyn holding the canopy. At this, Serith Ellyn stiffened, but listened on to hear about the mirror. When Lyrium described the skyward rainbow, and how its lure was nearly irresistible, Serith Ellyn stood and went to the window and faced away. Lyrium immediately stood, hesitated, then completed the telling of her vision, and fell silent. All eyes were upon the Queen, but none said a word for many moments.

"Who was this woman that you saw?" Serith Ellyn asked, still looking away.

"It was Shevalia, who was introduced to me as Sheila, Robby Ribbon's companion and, as I learned, his lover. But in my vision she was much changed from when I met her. Her countenance, her bearing, everything."

"Shevalia."

"Yes, my lady."

"And what do you think your vision portends?"

"Upon the banner that I saw flying over Robby Ribbon's head were seven stars. Just as the next King of Duinnor would be the seventh and final King of that realm. Or so the legends have it. But the banner was not of Duinnor colors, and its emblem, a winged key, is unknown to me. Perhaps Ribbon will so greatly change Duinnor, that the old colors will be struck and put away. I do not know."

"And the girl. Shevalia? Does your Sight tell you that I will someday serve her?"

"Yes, Queen. I think it does."

"This is preposterous!" Serith Ellyn exclaimed, turning around to face Lyrium. "And does it also tell you that she holds the means to open the Nimbus Illuminas?"

"Yes, Queen."

"It is truly remarkable that you should have such a view. Indeed, your ability must fail you, or else your powers of interpretation. Or both! I have the only remaining Seven. I! The King in Duinnor, by every conceivable account, can only have five of the Sets. At most only five!"

Serith Ellyn paced back and forth in front of Lyrium as she spoke, giving her anger and indignation full vent.

"The Nimbus Illuminas can never be opened! The Forty-Nine are no more, for those at Tulith Attis were scattered and lost when the Dragonkind took them. Or have you forgotten, Lady Lyrium? You, who witnessed that massacre!"

"Queen Serith Ellyn," Lyrium said, "the Seven of Fairfir House were not lost to the Dragonkind. I sent them away before the end came."

Everyone, including Lyrium's daughters, stared aghast at the statement.

After a long smoldering glare, Serith Ellyn said, "Please explain yourself."

"I knew the end was coming. I had seen, in a dream, that we would not be victorious, and I knew that we were betrayed. I arranged for the Seven to be smuggled out with my maidservant and five trusted soldiers of my personal guard. Then, when the fortress was overrun, I and a few others fought our way through the hordes and made our escape. A few loyal Men stayed behind, to defend the treasury room as if it still held the Seven. This gave the Dragonkind some distraction from chasing my party. I knew it was the Seven they were after, for why else did they lay siege to Tulith Attis when they could have isolated us and moved against Glareth? And I knew that when they found them missing, the Dragonkind would not rest until they had me. Of course, I did not know that you with your armies would be coming. Meanwhile, I hoped that my maidservant, a fierce and cunning fighter, could make it through the enemy lines by boats down the river, and by night and by stealth to go south and away. It was our plan for them to go into hiding with the Seven until the Dragonkind had dispersed, then make their way to a place in Glareth Realm where I would leave a message for her so that she would know where to find me. But she never came."

"And did you not search for her?"

"I did, Queen. I eventually located one of my maidservant's party, who is called Tyrillick. He was being held prisoner by the Men of a Tracian clan who thought that he was a deserter from Tulith Attis since he was not with the armies that swept away the Dragonkind. When freed, Tyrillick told me that his party was scattered when their boats struck chains that the Dragonkind had stretched across the Saerdulin. The boats were all upset, and all were thrown overboard and carried downstream for many miles. Tyrillick and three others made it ashore but were soon taken by Men. Only Tyrillick survived captivity. He could not say what became of my maidservant. And I never found any sign of her."

Serith Ellyn sat back down heavily.

"So, whether taken and melted down by Dragonkind, or sunk to the bottom of the Saerdulin, the Seven are still lost. What of it?"

"Ma'am. My maidservant's name was Faeanna, and her mother was Shevalia, daughter of Desira who was sister of Tiryna of the House of Elmwood. Tiryna was wife of Lord Banis."

"I knew Desira, and I was with her when she died at Tamkal Plain. As for Shevalia, she died long before her mother, amongst those who were murdered with my grandfather, Cupeldain. Since then, many have undoubtedly had that name."

"No, ma'am, and to the contrary, it appears that Shevalia is a name rarely given. Glareth keeps copies of all census records of the Eastlands. When the Prince of Tracia was ousted, he had already sent his archives to Glareth. I have had the same vision three times, now. After the first time, I searched both the Glareth and the Tracian census records. I found no Shevalia listed in any of the records until I came to those census records of only a few years ago. Shevalia was the daughter of Lord Waterstone of Tracia. His wife's name was given as Faeanna, but I found no previous records of that name. She and her husband are now dead, but they had a daughter, named Shevalia, who died at three years of age. That was exactly the year before Sheila Pradkin's name was first entered into the annual census of County Barley, there recorded as being four years of age and niece to Steggan Pradkin. It was her I met with Robby Ribbon in Tallinvale. A most remarkable girl, her aura was dense with portent, but I could not see what that portent was. Not until I arrived here and had the first Seeing."

"So you think, somehow, she has the Seven? That they were somehow passed down to her by your maidservant, Faeanna?"

"Yes. I do."

Again, silence fell upon the group. Thurdun shifted his weight from foot to foot, looking down at his boots, his lips pursed in thought. Finally, he looked up, glancing at Lyrium first, then at Serith Ellyn.

"My sister," he said, "the Forty-Nine Keys to the Nimbus Illuminas are being gathered once more, for the first time since the days of Cupeldain. Lyrium's vision implies that the girl will obtain them all, wherever they are. And it seems that you have a role to play."

"I well know, brother, what role is implied by Lyrium's vision!" Serith Ellyn retorted, leaping to her feet once more, her face crimson. "A servant's role, indeed! I think not! Would you have me find the girl and hand our Seven over to her? To do so would end my rule over Vanara, and it would lead to calamity. Need I remind you of Shatuum's growing power? Does our Gray Guard watch that place in vain? It is not the Dragonkind that I fear most. Let their armies come! We shall defeat them as we always have. No, it is our father's pact with the Shadow Lord that I fear. For is not Griferis locked within Secundur's lands? It is the power of Griferis that I fear Secundur will someday master. A power that, as you know, I have seen for myself from within that place. And Duinnor?"

Serith Ellyn walked back and forth as she spoke, nearly spitting her words.

"Duinnor thinks too much of the faraway Dragonlands, and too little of nearby Shatuum! But it is all a-purpose! Why else do the black eagles find roost in Duinnor? Why else does Duinnor sap the strength of Vanara, year by year? Duinnor does Secundur's work for him!"

"Surely you do not think so, my Queen," said Thurdun.

"Do I not? Watch your tongue, Thurdun! Remember the fate of Cupeldain, our grandfather, who last sought to assemble the Forty-Nine. It cannot be done without peril! Collandoth and his conspirators! Bah! They have played into Secundur's hand, distracting us with the false hope of rebellion in the Dragonlands, the false hope of peace, while the Dragon King makes his alliances with Tracia. And now, with false hope of a new king in Duinnor! Now is not the time for the Forty-Nine! Now is not the time for our kind to depart! Now is the time for steel and for blood, I say! Yes, blood and steel! And woe be unto Duinnor if it thinks it has ever seen the true might of Vanara! This interview is at an end. Leave me, all of you. Go, I say!"

Thurdun escorted Lyrium and her daughters out and walked with them to the end of the hallway.

"I apologize for the Queen's temper," he said to Lyrium. "I have rarely seen her act so."

"Perhaps she is vexed by being so far from home for so long," said Lyrium graciously, "especially when so much has come to pass since she has been away."

"Surely that is so, Lady Lyrium. And, I think, she wearies of the world, as all of our kind do."

"Yes," Lyrium nodded. "Certainly, we languish all the more each day as time grows upon us, knowing not which way to turn or what to do but carry on. But I do not think she can stand in the way of the Nimbus Illuminas, one way or the other. I was appalled, momentarily, by her tone. But it served only to make it clear to me that the world is about to be remade, for good or ill, with or without her help."

"I hope that you are right," Thurdun said. "And I hope, too, that you are wrong."

• • •

Thurdun watched Lyrium depart in her uncanny coach, which seemed hardly to touch the ground and traveled out of sight faster than one would think possible. When he returned to his sister a short while later, he found her again out on the balcony, gripping the rail tightly with both hands. He put one hand upon one of hers and his arm around her lovingly.

"I made a fool of myself in there," she said.

"No. I don't think so."

"Oh, yes. I did. And, the thing of it is, Lyrium was right. I know in my heart she was. And so were you. And so has been Collandoth, all these years! Lyrium only served to confirm the foreboding of my insistent dreams. Oh, Thurdun! We have given up so much during our time. Neither of us has known what it is like to love a family, to raise children, or to be loved for our own sake. All these eons of our existence, forgetting where we came from, forgetting our language, and even forgetting, in spite of our scars, what it truly meant to have wings. And, in the long meantime, you and I have forgotten how to live life."

She pulled her hands away from the railing and looked at them, rubbing them together.

"I still have our father's blood upon my hands," she said. "And, I fear that I sink into the madness that took him."

"Never, little sister!" Thurdun said, squeezing her tighter.

"Do you think, my brother, that if Heaven's Rainbow was opened, that we would be forced to depart? Or do you think we would be made, once again, to choose whether to stay or to go?"

"I think the choice would be ours to make. But, I think also that, should we remain, we will again be changed, as we were before. I imagine, if we chose to stay, the new change would be just as hard for us as it was when we lost our wings, and just as unexpected."

"Just as hard? In what way?"

"My mind falters upon that point. I do not know in what way. It makes me hopeful, though, the prospect of change, just as it makes me shudder to think upon it."

Serith Ellyn nodded, then pulled away from Thurdun and looked at him earnestly.

"I will tell you, then, that I believe Lyrium saw in her vision the same person who speaks to me in my dreams."

"The Ribbon boy?"

"Yes. How the girl plays into it I cannot even guess. But I think it is Ribbon who wishes to have our Seven, not her. His emblem is the winged key, Lyrium says. And it is within a circle of seven stars with seven points."

"Ah," Thurdun nodded. "The Forty-Nine."

Chapter 7

A Fatal Hand is Dealt

Day 192
53 Days Remaining

"Mother, I have no interest whatsoever in attending one of her parties," Farby said as he put on his jacket and turned in the mirror to see if it still fit. His mother came into view behind him. Not pleased with the weight he had recently put on, he turned away from the mirror to face her. "I'm sure you and Father will have a splendid time without me."

"You know very well what your father would say to that," said Lady Elyna. "You have certain obligations to this family, and to yourself. You cannot just do as you please. Disappearing for nights on end, only to show up in the very same clothes that you departed in nearly a week ago. Your father is furious. The least you can do is attempt to live up to one or two of your social responsibilities. Besides, Lady Highleaf assures me that the finest youth of the town will be there."

"That will be a first!"

"Don't be rude!"

"I am sorry, Mother."

"Anyway, there will be many young ladies who would be glad to see you, I'm sure."

"I'm sure."

"Grantham!"

"Mother, I'd only embarrass you in front of your friends. And there are no young ladies in Duinnor who would be interested in me. And they are right not to be. I know as well as any the reputation I have."

"Nonsense. That is all in the past. And there may be some at the party who may not be so familiar with you and may be apt to give you a chance. Besides, I have never been embarrassed or ashamed of you. Put out, now and then, surely. But not embarrassed."

"You're sweet for saying so, Mother, even if I know better."

"Well, be that as it may, I am pretty sure there will be someone quite interesting at the party. A Lady Shevalia, who is by all accounts quite good-looking. And she is young, too, so they say."

"Lady Shevalia?"

"You have heard of her?"

"Only in passing."

"Well. I have been told that she was invited and is certain to be there. And so shall you! When our carriage leaves to drive to Starlight Hall, you, young man, will be inside of it!"

"Oh, good grief! Very well, Mother. But I'll only put in an appearance. Don't expect me to stay all night. Now, let me kiss you goodbye."

"Where are you off to? You come home only to pass out as if you have been on a drinking binge, except I know you better than that. You sleep all day, then all night, and now you leave once more? Your father will have something to say about this behavior when he comes home."

"I know already what he'll say, so I needn't be present when he says it. I go to call on an acquaintance who has been ill."

"Oh? Who?"

"Just someone I met recently," Farby replied, giving his mother a kiss. "I'll not be out late."

• • •

Anxious to get back to Shevalia after having been gone from her for an entire day and night, Farby rode quickly across the city, impatient with the traffic along the busy streets. When at last he came around the bend of Crescent Avenue, he saw a fancy carriage in front of Lady Shevalia's apartments and instantly recognized the livery of the footmen as being of the House of Highleaf.

"Oh! How very inconvenient! That woman is the theme of the day, it seems."

He rode on past, turned left down the next street, and came to a halt. Dismounting, he led his horse on and was just turning to go down an alley when from it emerged two ordinary looking men in dirty work clothes. He nodded to them as they passed, then turned to look back at them.

"Odd," he said to his horse, "their clothes are dirty, but their hands are clean. And they wear polished boots of soldiers."

Farby knew that the next street led back to the left toward the apartments and that, from a certain alley off from Crescent Avenue, he could watch for Lady Highleaf's departure. He would see her at the party that his mother wanted him to attend, which would be soon enough for him. It was not that he disliked Lady Highleaf—he was actually somewhat fond of her—it was just that going up to see Lady Shevalia while she was there would only invite too many awkward questions that he would prefer not to answer. Already, while he stayed in the apartments to be near Shevalia, he had narrowly missed Lady Highleaf, ducking into Mr. Sootking's room as she came up the stairs. It would be awkward enough for him to see Shevalia. That is, if she would receive him. But, since Farby would be satisfied with a word or two of assurance from Mr. Sootking as to Lady Shevalia's recovery, he did not see the point in pressing his luck. He determined to wait and watch, and, as soon as Lady Highleaf departed, he would make his arrival.

However, Farby's plan was dashed when he saw four men standing at the very spot where he wished to wait. They were loitering at the alley corner with their backs to Farby as he approached, and they were leaning around the corner to peer at Highleaf's carriage on down the way and across the street.

"Now why would they be doing that?" he muttered. "And, what's this? They wear polished boots, too, though they are dressed in working clothes."

With a casual smile, he continued past them, but he could feel them watching him. Suddenly, he stopped and turned back to face them.

"What? Have you never before seen a fine horse?" he demanded. "And why do you loiter here, rather than being at your workplaces, eh? Up to no good, I think. Waiting your chance to waylay some lady or gent, I'd wager. I shall pass this way again soon, and with the King's Constabulary, too, so I advise you to move along."

Before they could respond, Farby mounted and cantered away. But instead of going to fetch a Kingsman, it being they who routinely patrolled the city for the enforcement of law, he circled around once more, this time going the long way to come up on the far end of the alley from where the men were. Dismounting, he carefully looked around the corner and saw that they were now engaged in heated debate. Tying his reins to a gutter pipe, he crouched and entered the alley, ducking behind rubbish barrels and coal stalls, and trying not to slip on the ice that paved the alley as he neared the men.

"It won't be a good thing, that's certain, if Kingsmen get involved," one was saying.

"Let's just wait," said another, "an' see if Farby carries out his threat."

"It don't matter, none, anyhow," said a third. "We've got our writ from Banis, an' the Kingsmen'll back down as soon as they see it."

"Don't be a fool!" said the fourth. "The writ is only to be used, if needed, when we take them. After our little gal does her bit and fetches us. So we save the writ just in case there might be questions at that point. Until then, we can't afford meddling Kingsmen. After we carry out our orders, the writ will see to the rest. And it won't matter then, anyway. So let's be off for awhile, and come back in a few hours."

The men gave up their post and came toward Farby, who crouched behind a woodpile, wondering how they knew his name.

"Do you think your girl will do it? And keep her mouth shut?" said one as they passed his hiding place.

"I haven't spent the better part of a year training her for nothing," was the reply. "She's plenty capable. And she'll do it, too. She had better, if she wants her folks to come out from Northgate alive. And if she speaks, it'll be her neck in the noose, now won't it?"

Farby peered out and saw them reach the end of the alley. One of the men shot his hand out, pointing.

"What's this? Ain't that the brat's horse?"

"It certainly is!" said another, "which means he must be nearby."

"There he is! I bet he heard every word we said!"

By now, Farby was running the other way, the footfalls of his pursuers loud in the alley. He turned and ran away from the apartments, darting down another lane. He took several more turns, squeezing around narrow corners, and down another narrow alley. Halfway, he stopped as two of the men appeared at the far end, drawing their rapiers. Realizing that they had gone around the other way to cut him off, and that the other two would soon be coming up behind him, he quickly studied his surroundings, looking for a way out of the situation. The alley, almost narrow enough for him to touch each opposing wall, was eerily quiet given the danger that choked the space. Above him, the back windows of several houses were open, and he heard a child's voice singing in the distance. To one side was a door, but it was bolted from within. To the other side was another door, also bolted, and beside it was a wheelbarrow of coal that had not yet been shoveled into the home's coal chute. Farby picked up a lump and tossed it up and down a couple of times, judging its throwing potential. Two of the men were about twenty yards off, grinning as they came. Turning, Farby saw the other two men coming up behind him. He saw a short coal shovel leaning against the wall. He dropped the lump of coal, picked up the shovel, and charged at the two nearest men, yelling as he came at them. As Farby swung the shovel, his target ducked and slipped on a patch of ice, falling aside, causing the shovel to whack the other one in the elbow with a loud bang. The victim yelled and stumbled aside, dropping his rapier. Farby grabbed it up just as the first man got to his feet, joined by the other two. He gave the owner of the rapier another bang, this time on the head, then gripped the shovel just under the scoop. Using it as a buckler, he parried, quickly getting a feel for the inferior rapier. He caught one of the attackers on the back of his neck with a lucky swipe of the shovel, and the man was dead before he hit the ground. But the other two, wielding daggers as well as their rapiers, came at Farby even harder. It was a cramped space to fight within, and Farby was somewhat rusty from being too long without a sword. One of the attackers lunged, sending his rapier through Farby's pocket flap. He parried the following dagger swipe, and shot his own sword through the other man's heart. Before he could deal with the last one, the man backed his sword out from Farby's jacket and stood back a few feet. Farby glanced at his ruined jacket.

"Oh, I cannot let that pass!" he said, tossing the shovel down and facing his remaining opponent.

"You'll not find me so easy to prick as the others," said the man. "I'll have you know that I have been the top swordsman in my battalion for the past six years, with the winnings to show for it. And I shall momentarily demonstrate that fact upon you."

"Winnings, you say? Oh, a game, is it? Well, I call your swordsmanship, and I raise you a handkerchief," Farby retorted, "by which means you shall presently be dead."

"You what?"

Farby reached into his pocket and drew out a large silk handkerchief with a flourish.

"Oh, yes," he said, tossing away his rapier and waving the handkerchief about. "I only used the rapier because I had no choice, being pressed in the matter. And, since I am banned from carrying a sword in the city, I have been relegated to dueling with this," Farby waved the handkerchief again at the man, "and I have not yet lost a single combat."

"You little twit!" the man growled, lunging and swiping twice, missing both times as Farby leaned backwards, then twisted around. In a quick twirl, and by slight of hand, Farby had the handkerchief wrapped around the man's dagger wrist. The attacker instinctively tried to pull his weapon away but, before he realized what was happening, Farby gave a quick twist and released one end of his handkerchief and the man's arm suddenly shot back. Farby then stepped calmly away, folding his handkerchief as his opponent gaped down at his chest and the dagger put there to the hilt by his own hand, which still gripped it.

"I warned you," Farby said, wiping the coal grime from his hands. "But I suppose you would claim that I forced your hand."

The man fell over dead, Farby put away his handkerchief, and he searched the man's pockets, finding a folded parchment with the seal of Lord Banis. He broke the seal and read the writ as he walked back to the man with the shattered elbow and cracked skull, and who was just now getting to his feet and trying to stumble away, staggering drunkenly from one side of the alley to the other.

"Hm," Farby said, walking alongside the man, who now fairly hugged the wall in fear and pain. "I see here that Lord Banis gives the bearer of this writ the authority to arrest any person or persons, and to hold them at Northgate Keep for questioning. It also says that any person who is witness to events transpiring at or around the address of Number Three Crescent Avenue is to be compelled likewise to Northgate. Hm, now what sort of events might this refer to?"

Farby looked at the man questioningly. But the fellow only pressed himself against the wall all the harder, gripping with his fingernails the cracks between the bricks.

"No clue?" Farby asked him. With a shrug, turning his eyes back to the writ. "Oh, and this is interesting. It says here that the bearer of this writ may use any force whatsoever. Now, who might Banis desire to arrest this week? Come now, you must have some idea. I think I'll have it out of you, one way or the other. Now that I hold the writ, I think perhaps I should use it on you, and take you to Northgate Keep myself. I'm sure Lord Banis would be glad to see you there."

Shrinking away from Farby, the man cried out, "I'll not be Banis's guest!" He then produced a dagger and cut his own throat. Farby watched him die, then folded the writ and put it into his pocket next to his deadly handkerchief.

"Oh, fiddlesticks," Farby said, shaking his head at the dead man.

He shrugged, then walked to the end of the alley. There he stopped, hands on his hips, and looked to the right and then to the left.

"Now, where did I put my horse?"

Meanwhile, high above him, a little owl took off from the eaves overhanging the alley and shot away.

Chapter 8

Attacks Near and Far

"Are ye sure 'bout that, Ashlord?"

"Yes, Billy, I am quite sure. Certina showed it to me, though I do not know how she came to see it, or how she may have gone there."

Billy looked askance at Certina, who was perched on the mantel preening. A tiny downy feather floated away from her, rising with the heat from the fireplace to drift across the room. Billy sneezed. When he recovered, shaking his head as if to jangle the contents within back into place, he looked again at Ashlord.

"An' she showed ye, truly, that the Redvests are gone from Barley?"

"Yes, Billy. For the fourth time, yes. They are gone."

"An' Pop is alive an' well!"

Ashlord crumpled the paper he was reading into his lap and glared at Billy.

"But ye said ye saw him die."

"Billy," Ashlord said, "as far as I know, as of this morning, anyway, I have been mistaken about things three hundred and seven times thus far during my lifetime. And I am apt to be wrong once or twice again. Some of my mistakes were big ones. Others were stupendous. I saw your father on the roof of your house. Then I saw the roof collapse in a terrible conflagration of flame. I did not and still do not understand how anyone could have survived that event. I was mistaken not to figure that your father, being as clever as they come, had some way out while making the enemy suffer. Indeed, just before the collapse, I saw at least three dozen Redvests storm into the house. However your father managed his escape, I'm sure he did not share it with them. And your sister, Raenelle, is also safe."

Billy did not know whether to laugh or cry, and his eyes glistened with joyful, if not confused, emotions.

"An' so, as ye say, thar ain't no threat thar, no more."

"*Is* no threat. Not for the time being. That is why, when you relate your news, you must emphasize the threat farther south, where the Redvests mean to join with the Dragonkind."

"But won't they scoff at the idea of the Dragonkind gettin' out of the desert lands? I mean, they ain't never done it afore, has they?"

"*Have* they."

"I was askin' ye that."

"Yes, they have. Remember your lessons!"

"Oh, yeah. Lemme see. Once, back when they overran the Eastlands an' Haven Hill. An' another time, when they ran into Nasakeeria. So they mean to do it again."

"That's right. But, this time, they'll not make those mistakes. The eastern passes of the Hinderlands are heavily defended. And, to the north, Vanara stands in their way. No doubt the Dragon King has found a new way for his hordes to break out."

"So what about Tallinvale? I mean, if the Redvests are out of Barley, don't that mean they must've taken Tallinvale?"

"No. Tallinvale has prevailed."

"Certina told ye that, too?"

"Yes. She did."

"An' so all should make ready to defend against the south."

"Just so. You have it. Tell them just that. And there is one other even greater threat."

"Oh?"

"Shatuum."

"Oh? What about Shatuum?"

"Secundur will surely take advantage of the situation," said Ashlord. "We all know that he builds an army."

"I didn't know that."

"You do now, since I just told you. And you should have known before, if you had been paying any attention."

"Oh, yeah! The witch. An' the demon, too. That's the kind of army ye mean."

"Yes. And worse."

"An' worse?"

"On my word and honor!" Ashlord muttered, storming over to the desk to pick up his pipe. "I have never known such a dim-witted—"

Just then, Reysa knocked and entered.

"Hello, Reysa," Billy said, grinning and standing. "An' how might ye be this day?"

"Oh, I'm quite well, Mr. Bosk. Thank you, sir. And I hope that you and Mr. Sootking, are doing well today."

Ashlord grunted as he packed his bowl.

"Oh, mighty fine! Mighty fine!" Billy said. "Let me take that! Oh, that's much too much for a young lass as yerself to carry."

Billy took the bucket of wood from her and put it near the hearth.

"Thank you, Mr. Bosk. And Mr. Brinnin says to tell you that it's time for brunch downstairs, sir," she said. "If you'd care to join him, sir."

"Will ye be servin'?"

"Oh, no, sir. I must see to Lady Shevalia's room before she returns."

"Very good, then."

Reysa curtseyed to Billy, and he managed a rather elegant bow as she departed.

"Don't mind if I do join Ibin," he said to Ashlord. "All this news has given me a pow'rful appetite!"

Ashlord nodded and waved his pipe at Billy's exit, then he opened the window so that Certina could go find her brunch, too.

"All eating, and not an ounce of wit added!" he said, taking up the newspaper and sitting back down. After a moment, he gave up on reading the news and stared at the window. After a little while longer, his barely puffed pipe was cold, his eyes fixed upon the window in contemplation. It was quiet in the house, and he enjoyed the peace. Sheila was out with Lady Highleaf, and now that Billy was downstairs, Ashlord had only the pop and crackle from the hearth to disturb the silence.

And, today, Ashlord had much to meditate on. The mystery of how Certina could have seen what she saw in Passdale and in Tallinvale baffled him. He knew that she had not left Duinnor since their arrival, and probably had not even flown more than a mile from their apartments. But the visions she shared with him were clear. Mr. Bosk was speaking with Mr. Ribbon on the porch of the store in Passdale. Mr. Ribbon had a dustpan in his hand. Certina did not relate the words of their conversation, but she did show him that the town was wrecked, though not demolished. And there was not a Redvest in sight. And she showed him, too, General Teracue going about the walls of Tallin City with Lord Tallin, and Redvest prisoners building barrows under the direction of Kingsmen soldiers. The visions Certina had shared were clear, yet she could not express how she came to have them, only that she urgently needed Ashlord to see those things. And that was not all that Certina showed Ashlord. She had witnessed something that had happened nearby, only a few streets away.

Ashlord's hand absently went to his housecoat pocket, and there his fingers touched a note that had been delivered to him just a short time before his chat with Billy. The note, along with the visitor who had delivered it, confirmed what Certina had already revealed to Ashlord concerning the rather dangerous state of things within the neighborhood.

Then there was Sheila. She was much changed since her Scathing. That was to be expected, but whereas before she merely acted the part of a great and important lady, there was now something in her demeanor that was not an act, something solemn, something fierce.

Still pondering Sheila's transformation, Ashlord heard Reysa enter, probably to take away the tea tray. But she was ever respectful, never noisy, and never bothered his trance-like meditations. After a moment or two, realizing that he had no interest in the paper in his lap, he put down his pipe and folded the paper. Just as he leaned over to put the paper on the other side of the table, a long, narrow-bladed dagger swept down, barely missed Ashlord, and pinned the sleeve of his housecoat to the table. Instantly he shifted around, pulling at his sleeve, and saw Reysa poised with another dagger as she reached to pull the first from the table. Ashlord leaned backwards and the blade barely missed his throat.

"Reysa!" he cried, jumping up. He managed to kick his chair at her. Her face was white, her expression determined, and in the split second that the chair was flying at her, Ashlord realized his peril. She deftly kicked the chair away and got her dagger unpinned from the table. Ashlord stumbled backwards, and Reysa came at him with fighting daggers in both hands. In the next few moments, Reysa swung and jabbed, and Ashlord dodged and leaned. When he saw an opening, he snapped his fingers before her face, and a brilliant flash momentarily stunned Reysa. Blinking, she blindly lunged, but her daggers cut only air as Ashlord leapt to the side and reached for his walking stick leaning against the bureau. Reysa was already upon him. He got his stick with one hand, and, leaning far over, he delivered his foot against her chest so hard that she flew across the room and flipped backwards over the couch. She was back on her feet and came at Ashlord with unbelievable speed. All he could do was deflect with his sturdy walking stick, but he could get no counterstroke through her own parries. Then he saw his chance and swung at her head. She was too quick. She dropped to the floor, and his walking stick barely missed her head. Then she whirled around on one foot while her other leg stuck straight out, catching Ashlord behind the ankles. He went down backwards.

Billy opened the door and sauntered in just in time to see Reysa send one of her daggers flying down at Ashlord. Ashlord twisted aside, and the dagger embedded into the floor. Dumbstruck, Billy stared. Reysa briefly froze, and Ashlord rolled onto his feet, swinging his stick. Billy's hand went to his sword as Reysa dodged Ashlord's swing. Reysa kicked Billy against the doorframe violently and then kicked the door which struck him hard. Then she turned back to Ashlord. Now she was grunting, and her arms were a blur of deadly steel. Billy, shaking his head, recovered quickly enough to draw, and he came at her from one side while Ashlord engaged her on the other. Now between the two, she parried her opponents' thrusts and jabs, dodged their swings, and managed to deliver enough kicks to keep them at bay. But she bore on against Ashlord much harder than against Billy, driving the Melnari against the mantel so that he had little room to maneuver.

"Stay out of this, Billy!" she cried. Then she ducked and elbowed him in the jaw. Billy staggered backwards. She turned back to Ashlord in time to parry his next swing, doing so by dropping one of her daggers and catching Ashlord's stick in her hand. She surprised Ashlord by the move, and she wrenched it from him and flung it across the room. She raised her other dagger, and Ashlord threw a left hook, then a right cross, both of which she deflected with her forearm. Her dagger arm cocked just as her bodice split open and the long blade of Billy's rapier shot through her, its point coming precariously near Ashlord's throat. Her arms went limp as blood gurgled from her mouth, her eyes fixed upon Ashlord. Billy withdrew his blade. Reysa staggered and raised her dagger weakly at Ashlord. Then she fell dead to the floor.

"Reysa!" Billy cried, throwing his rapier away and kneeling beside her. "Reysa, Reysa!"

Her eyes were open, but Billy could see that life's fire was gone from them. He looked up at Ashlord with a painful expression of shock and bewilderment.

"Are ye alright, Ashlord?" he asked.

"Yes. Quite. And I owe that fact to you!"

"Dang, dang, dang! She truly had me goin'! All nicey-nice. All the while waitin', I bet, just to get at ye! But why?"

"We may never know," Ashlord said, crouching down to check her. "She's dead. Poor dear!"

"Poor dear? She nearly had us both done in!"

"Lower your voice. She was put up to it, I'm sure," answered Ashlord. "Close the door, Billy. I must think. Do we notify the authorities? Yes, I think we must. And what will Miss Tarrier do?"

"She's liable to kick us out, at the very least!"

"Is she in the house?"

"I reckon so. She was earlier. Oh, me! Oh, me! What've I done?"

"By the way, why did you come back upstairs?"

"I never went downstairs," Billy shrugged, shaking and stammering. "I went to me room to fetch one of them books to take down with me. Then I remembered that I left it in here, yonder on the card table."

"Lucky for me! Let's go down to see Miss Tarrier. And let me do all the talking."

Billy was staring aghast at Reysa, tears flowing from his eyes. Ashlord took him by the arm, and firmly pulled him away.

"Come along, Billy," Ashlord said. "Perhaps it would be best for you to go to your room and remain there until I call for you."

• • •

"How well do you know Reysa, Miss Tarrier?"

"I'm sure I don't know what you're asking me," she said, putting down the kettle. "She's me niece, ain't she?"

"Has she ever been in trouble of any kind?" Ashlord asked. "Tell me truthfully."

"Well, yes. I'm sorry to say she got caught up with a few of them Duinnor Regulars while she was with Lady Dassath, over in North Hill. Lord Banis keeps them to guard his street, and, well, she was caught being rather free with one of them. It was said that it went on for nearly two years before the two got caught down in Lord Dassath's cellar. I never asked Reysa about it, so I'm just repeating what got back to me. And from what I heard, the housekeeper quite nearly let her go on the spot, but instead took up the matter with Lady Dassath, who had a liking for Reysa.

Then, apparently the fellow Reysa was caught with had the ear of Lord Banis, and the great lord sent a note over to Lady Dassath asking her not to be so harsh but to give Reysa another chance."

"Lord Banis?"

"That's what I heard, Mr. Sootking. But there was never any more trouble afterwards that I heard of. And Lady Dassath did give Reysa a nice letter of reference when they departed Duinnor. Mind you, Reysa has been acting out of sorts, lately, but wouldn't say why when I put it to her. Until yesterday morning, that is, when I heard from an acquaintance that Reysa's parents, my half-brother and his wife, were taken to Northgate a week ago. I asked Reysa, and she told me it was all a terrible mistake. Something to do with a business partner of Reysa's father making free with borrowed money and laying the blame on Reysa's father."

"Northgate? The old prison?"

"That's right, Mr. Sootking. And nobody ever comes out of that place, so they say. So no wonder poor Reysa has been worried and fretful of late."

"Hm. I see. Well, Miss Tarrier, I think you should sit down, now. Ibin, would you go see if Mr. Yarman is available, and, if so, ask him to fetch the Constabulary. That's it, Miss Tarrier. Now, look at me. I have some very bad news to give you."

• • •

The Ladies Shevalia and Highleaf arrived to see a number of horses and a cart in front of the apartment, as well as a fair number of onlookers. Just as they stepped from their carriage, Reysa's body was brought out.

"What has happened?" cried Sheila, hurrying to the litter. "What happened to Reysa?"

"She was killed, ma'am," said one of the bearers as they lifted the litter onto the cart. "Done in by one of the men of this place. Or so I overheard."

"What? What happened?"

"Apparently, she tried to cut the throat of one of the gents stayin' here. Or somethin' of the sort, ma'am."

Lady Highleaf pulled Sheila away. "Let us go up and see Ashlord."

When the two ladies finally talked their way past the Kingsmen in the foyer who sought to bar the way, and they had made their way upstairs, they found Ashlord, Ibin, and Billy gathered in the third floor parlor along with several Kingsmen. One of the Kingsmen was speaking but stopped as they entered. A sheet had been thrown over the spot on the floor where Reysa had fallen, and a blot of dull red showed through it.

"I take it this is Lady Shevalia," said the Kingsman. Then he bowed slightly. "And Lady Highleaf, an honor to see you, present circumstance excepting, of course."

"Captain Thrubold. Do not let us interrupt."

"Very well. Mr. Ashlord, I do understand why you felt you must use an assumed name if, as you say, you felt some threat. And I appreciate the fact that you have told me about it, flat out, rather than keeping up pretenses. I know your reputation, sir. One of the Nine Banes. A Melnari, too. So I find it somewhat strange that a little girl could sneak up on you so easily."

"I had no reason to suspect her, Captain," said Ashlord. "Had it not been for my friend, Mr. Bosk, here, I might be the one being taken away on a litter."

"Right. Mr. Bosk, one more time, if you will. You saw her attempting to kill your friend, and you killed her in his defense."

"Like I said already," Billy nodded. "That's how it came about. They was in the middle of it, when I came in. Then she turned on me, too. It all happened too fast. I never saw the likes of it, the way she fought. Anyways, I ran her through. Ooh! Sorry. I'm still purty shook up."

"I'm sure," Thrubold said, squinting at Billy who was obviously very upset.

"Captain Thrubold," Lady Highleaf said, stepping forward, "I have known Ashlord for a very long time, and I can vouch for him as can a hundred others in Duinnor."

"No doubt, Lady Highleaf."

"Then why do you take the tone that you do? My understanding is that Mr. Bosk and Mr. Brinnin are here to protect Lady Shevalia and her guardian, Mr. Ashlord. It is apparent that the young man did his job. Now, what else are you looking for?"

"I look for a reason, ma'am. A reason why there has not been so much as an apple stolen in this district in the two years it has been under my watch. Then, within just a few hours, there are five killings."

"Pardon me?"

"Yes, five. I was just down the street, not a stone's throw away, looking at four bodies found an hour ago, when I was summoned here," Thrubold said. Turning back to Billy and Ashlord, he continued. "One had his neck broken, one was run through by a sword, and the other two seemed to have taken their own lives. And there were signs of a struggle. Perhaps a murder-suicide. You gentlemen wouldn't know anything about any of that, would you?"

"We have been within this house all day," said Ashlord.

Certina flew back to the window and landed on the sill. Captain Thrubold looked at her quizzically for a brief moment.

"Hm. Yes. Just as Miss Tarrier and Mr. Yarman have said. And, yet, there is an odd way in which the girl and those dead men are connected, I think."

"Oh?"

"I am fairly certain the dead men were all in the employ of Lord Banis," Thrubold said. "And one of them, as I recall, was involved about a year or so ago with the girl. A minor thing, but I happened to hear about it. Yes, and the man involved was found with his own dagger through his heart, his hand still upon it."

"Oh?"

"You do not seem surprised."

"Forgive me, Captain," Ashlord shrugged, "if I am not easily surprised by such things. She was a fair lass, and I suppose she may have had a number of men interested in her. Perhaps he was jilted by her and was overtaken with grief and madness."

"Hm. Perhaps. But I doubt it."

Captain Thrubold nodded, then looked at Ashlord, then at Billy, frowning at the both of them. Ashlord guessed that Thrubold was grappling with some decision, and that Thrubold must possess a copy of the summons that compelled the Kingsman to bring Ashlord and the others to Lord Banis. But Ashlord had already made his calculations, well before sending for the Kingsmen, and he now waited to see if his reckoning of things would bear out, or if they would all be arrested on the spot. There was a long silence in the room while Captain Thrubold made his own guesses and calculations. Then, abruptly, he turned to the other soldier who was sitting at the desk with a tablet of paper and a pen, copying everything said.

"Do you have everything, Waters?"

"Yes, sir. I believe so."

Thrubold nodded and turned back to Billy and Ashlord.

"Very well, sirs. That will be all for now," the Captain said. "I am reporting this as a case of defense, and I am giving your name as Sootking, since that is how you are known to this establishment. There may be a hearing. Until then, I see no reason to detain you, but please do not leave the city without my permission."

After the Captain departed, Sheila let go of Lady Highleaf's hand, which she had been clutching the whole while, to permit the lady to sit.

"So this is where the deed was done!" Lady Highleaf exclaimed. "Oh, come now, Ashlord. We both know that Banis has had it in for you. Captain Thrubold probably knows, too."

"What is this all about?" Sheila finally asked, hardly able to restrain her tears.

"I do not precisely know," said Ashlord. "A terrible thing, though. You heard enough to know about as much as we do. She tried to kill me, and Billy killed her before she could do it."

"What of them fellers the Capt'n mentioned?" Billy asked. "Do ye think Reysa knew 'em?"

"If they were who I think they were," Ashlord said, "then they have been watching this house since the day we arrived. Perhaps longer."

"But why would Reysa want to kill you?" asked Sheila, sitting on the divan beside Lady Highleaf.

"I do not know. I can only assume that she was made desperate enough to try by some despicable situation between her and Lord Banis or his men. Her relatives are in Northgate Prison, a notorious place from which few emerge once taken there. Perhaps she was being blackmailed. Billy and I just learned, after the attack but before Thrubold arrived, that Reysa was under some kind of protection of Lord Banis. So, whatever her reasons, he was surely behind it."

"Oh, poor Reysa!" Sheila uttered. Looking at Billy, she saw that he was as upset as any, and she stood and went to him, putting her arms around him. "I am sorry, Billy. I know you did what you had to do. And, what is worse, I know you liked her a great deal. We all did."

"I appreciate yer sayin' so. But it ain't right," he said, "just ain't right that she felt so cornered to try somethin' like that. I wish she'd have asked for our help with whatever was goin' on. I wish she'd been less sweet! Excuse me! Please, excuse me!"

Billy pushed Sheila aside, bowed to Lady Highleaf, and hurried from the room. Ibin went to the door to follow him, then hesitated, looking back at the others.

"Give him a few moments, Ibin. Then go to him," Ashlord said. "I don't think he will soon get over all this. I, for one, am sorry that I ever brought her into our employ."

"Don't be," Sheila said. "How could you have known things would turn out so?"

"And she was a poor lady's maid, anyway," declared Lady Highleaf. "Don't look at me so! I only say the obvious. Oh, she wasn't so bad as to deserve skewering, but one can never be too careful about such things."

"I am not sure that I appreciate your remarks," said Sheila.

"I am sure you do not, my dear," said Lady Highleaf. "And that is one reason why I like you. You are young and full of ideals and right-thinking. Perhaps from Ashlord's influence. Or perhaps you have always been so. But I am not Elifaen, as you now are, and so I come by my coldness slowly and naturally, rather than having it forced upon me. I think your old habits, and old heat, will go from you. You will likely be as cool and dispassionate as I in but a short while. And you will have all of eternity to warm up again, if you ever do. Much of my warmth, as all of my youth, is behind me, never to come again, I fear. So you must indulge an old lady her frankness."

Lady Highleaf smiled kindly as she spoke, as if begging for forgiveness without ever hinting at such a request.

"Now," Lady Highleaf addressed Ashlord, "what shall we do with you?"

"What do you mean?"

"Well! Once Banis hears about his men, he'll certainly redouble his efforts, whether or not you had anything to do with their demise. Especially if the girl was in his pocket. As I am sure you know, he is not to be trifled with."

"Oh, I doubt that he would attempt anything again very soon. Not now that the Kingsmen are involved and his men are out of the way."

"Kingsmen! It is the King who protects Banis! As he always has. If Banis thought you were a threat before, what do you suppose he will think, now?"

"Ashlord," Sheila interrupted, "when the Captain asked you if you knew anything about those men who were found dead, you never actually answered him."

"No. I suppose I did not."

"You do know something about it, don't you?"

"Yes, as it happens. I do. Certina saw the incident and reported it to me, in her way. Through her eyes, I also saw it. It took place just before you and Lady Highleaf departed the house this morning."

"Who is this Certina that you speak of?" asked Lady Highleaf. "Not this little bird that has followed you everywhere these past many years?"

"The same," said Ashlord. "She is a Familiar."

"My heavens! You mean to tell me that she talks?"

Ashlord and Sheila both nodded. Lady Highleaf then nodded, too, looking at Certina.

"Well, perhaps she could just share what she saw with all of us?"

"It doesn't work that way," said Sheila.

"Anyway, I would prefer not to tell all of what she told me," said Ashlord, "nor what happened after the incident. I will say that almost immediately upon learning from Certina what transpired in the back alleys down the way from here, I had a visitor. For now, his identity must be kept secret, for his own good, but he delivered to me this writ, which was taken from one of the dead men. The writ gives great authority to the bearer, and it is particular about giving the power to arrest anyone who might witness events that happen in this house. When I saw the writ, I thought that it must surely pertain to Lady Shevalia's late condition, for she made quite a stir in the neighborhood. But that was the first of two mistakes I made today. Three hundred and eight, and three hundred and nine."

"Surely they waited to be summoned by the girl once the deed was done," said Lady Highleaf.

"Yes. That seems apparent. They wanted me out of the way, perhaps thinking I exert some protection over the others. Or, perhaps Raynor has been so uncooperative that they felt it would be useless to apprehend another Melnari."

"I'll wager that the writ says that everyone else, that is, those who survived the girl's attack, were to be carted off to Northgate, never to be heard from again," Lady Highleaf concluded with some satisfaction. She stood abruptly. "Lady Shevalia, let us see to your things. You are to leave this house immediately and come with me to Starlight Hall."

"What?" Sheila asked, rising to her feet.

"In the first place," Lady Highleaf explained, "no lady would stay in this house after what has just transpired. It just wouldn't do! And, in the second, I don't trust Banis not to try all over again. That red-headed young man can't be everywhere, can he? Ashlord must look after himself for a while, I'm afraid."

"I can't just run off and leave!"

"Oh, but you can! And you must! Not another word. Let us see to your things. We've far too much to do to dawdle. The party is but a few days away, and I must keep my eye on the preparations. Come, child!"

Ashlord nodded to Sheila. "Go. You'll be safe at Starlight Hall, I'm sure."

"I'm not worried for myself!"

"Then, do," Ashlord said, guiding her to the door where Lady Highleaf waited. "It is important that you carry on with things. Just pack those few things that you'll need for tonight. I'll have Mr. Yarman bring over the rest of your belongings tomorrow."

* * *

Outside, Captain Thrubold sent away his men and walked with his assistant, Waters, back to the Constabulary quarters.

"Sir," Waters said. "Shall I amend the report?"

"No," answered Thrubold. "But we will delay things until I have had General Chadler's impression of it. Meanwhile, I'll not honor a summons with Banis's name upon it, if that is what you are wondering. At least not unless Chadler orders me to do so."

Waters nodded, and handed his tablet of notes to Thrubold.

"Things are coming to a head, then," commented Waters, as they crossed a busy street.

"So it seems."

* * *

While Lady Highleaf and the whimpering Miss Tarrier helped Lady Shevalia pack, Lord Banis, author of the events that prompted them to do so, was at the Palace, where he had been all morning. As events took their course on the east side of the city, Banis waited in the anteroom of the King's High Chamber. One of the black eagles had just returned from the Eastlands, and Banis was notified by a Kingsman before dawn. The eagles did not like the High Tower where the King lived, and only came there if Banis was present. Otherwise, they came to roost on the wall of the south courtyard where Banis had his Palace chambers, and that was where Banis would normally receive their messages. He knew that the King would have been informed, probably before he himself was, and was not surprised when, shortly after receiving the visions from the winged beast, four Kingsmen came to fetch him to the Tower.

When the doors to the High Chambers opened, and Banis entered, he found the King already waiting.

The King's voice came from the swirling light of his cocoon.

"I wish to speak with you aloud."

Banis knelt, grateful that, for now at least, the King's mind would not touch him. He glanced at the Red Door hovering to one side. In all his years serving the King, he had never grown accustomed to the Avatar, and he feared it almost as much as he feared the King.

"What news?"

"Tallinvale has prevailed, my King," Banis stated. "Aided by the Fourth Army under General Teracue, fifteen days ago."

"Teracue has always been impetuous," said the King smoothly. "Now we know why we have not heard from him for so long."

"Yes, Your Majesty."

"What else?"

"The eagle reports that the Tracian Redvests that besieged Tallinvale were utterly defeated, and that no remnant remained to rejoin those still massing in the south."

"And Glareth?"

"The eagle revealed nothing to me concerning Glareth, King."

"What good are your eagles, Banis, if all they report is what we may surmise? Does Serith Ellyn remain in Glareth? Does she have her Seven with her? This is what I wish to know. And, as for the Missing Seven, are they in the possession of the Triumvirate upstarts? Is that why they are so bold in their war-making plans?"

Banis knew better than to answer. He remained on his knees as the King floated to the window and, as Banis supposed, gazed out.

"What about the Melnari, Raynor? Has he given you the information that you sought?"

Banis suddenly felt trapped. He knew that the dungeon answered to the King, and that the King could learn easily enough what went on there.

"He has not been cooperative, Your Majesty. He has not revealed the names of the conspirators who are in league with him."

"Hm. And does this surprise you? Now I will tell you something. Last night, word reached Duinnor that Serith Ellyn's palace in Vanara was attacked. It seems that a band of Duinnor soldiers were behind the incident. A Captain Faradan led the assault. I'm sure that you know him, since he dined at your house several times over the past few years."

"Yes, I know him."

"It seems your agent there, Count Dialmor, disappeared at the time of the attack, and was seen riding south from Vanara."

"King, I left orders with Dialmor to stop Robby Ribbon from leaving Vanara, should he appear in that Realm."

"And was it also in your orders that the Queen's own home was to be attacked? Do not squirm! I know that you have sought to obtain the Queen's Seven. I know that you sent Faradan after the Queen, too, and that he failed in his attempt to assassinate her and take her Seven."

"My King! I knew that you desired to have them!"

"Do not presume to know our desires! We do not wish for war with Vanara!"

Now the King's mind touched Banis full and hard, and Banis instinctively put his hands over his ears and cringed as the thunder in his chest resonated.

"You would have Duinnor face the Dragonkind and Vanara, too!"

"No, King!"

"Secundur laughs at us! He knows we sap Vanara of her strength. A fine line we walk. Too weak, and Vanara cannot serve Duinnor. Too strong, and Duinnor will serve Vanara! Your task was simple: to prevent the youngster from reaching Griferis. Of a thousand ways you could have done it, you selected the least subtle, most provocative thing imaginable!"

"Yes, King. Forgive me, I beg you!"

"And what of Ashlord? Has he entered the city? Or was he in Vanara as well?"

"I believe he is here, my King. I should have confirmation this day or tomorrow."

"Then obtain it! And send forth your eagles! I must know where the boy is, whether he was murdered by Faradan, or if he escaped. Do not fail me in this, Banis! Now leave me!"

Chapter 9

The Ghouls of Shatuum

In the land of Shatuum, there were many keeps and towers. All were made of dark stone, unadorned except by the chains and braziers upon them. Many dated from those early days in Shatuum when Secundur's first warlords vied for his favor by gathering to themselves followers and fighting those others who did likewise. But it was Throgallus who rose up among them as overlord, putting down those of lesser cruelty and power, killing most and subjugating the rest. It pleased Secundur that it was so, for Throgallus was his own protégé, encouraged by Secundur's whispers and goading, and rewarded by Secundur's gifts. In his own castle, Throgallus enjoyed the company of the fairest witches and sorceresses of Shatuum, those whose duty it was to convert new prisoners into new wraiths. Many of these witches had come to Shatuum seeking refuge when Collandoth and the Nine Banes persecuted them all across the world. From the forests of Duinnor to the deserts of the south, they came, and from the salty coasts of the Eastlands to the very door of Shatuum itself. Those who had chased and harried the witches and sorcerers could not know that they only served Secundur's purpose, forcing those who escaped their stakes and mallets and their arrows of witchbane to take up their abode in Shatuum. Secundur was only too glad to give these vile immigrants a place to hide, and, as he did with Throgallus, he drew them into his shadows and nurtured their fears and their anger.

When the warring lords of Shatuum fought each other, the witches split their ranks amongst them, turning their spells and hexes on each other. But Throgallus and his forces triumphed over those who opposed him, and he spared not witch nor warlock, nor any who ever stood against him. Now, the victorious survivors of that purge gave themselves over to Throgallus, to please him with their favors, knowing that it would also please Secundur. They cast their charms around him, and they shared his bed just as they had once joined with the mighty demon, Valkose, and had spawned from that demon the Thirteen Captains of Shatuum. When Valkose was lured away and destroyed, and his spirit driven back to Shatuum by the hand of Aperion, the witches took the demon's waning ghost and tore it asunder with their spells, giving a portion of the elixir they made to each of the Captains. Of the voice of Valkose, they made the crack that would come from their whips, and of his breath they filled their whips with fire. And a portion of the potion they gave to Throgallus, to reign over the Captains, second only to Secundur.

Now the castle of Throgallus was the lair of those witches, needing no demon for their consummation, and his castle was also their brooding place, out of which the ranks of Shatuum were swelled with their hideous offspring. And, too, they converted many prisoners and beasts to serve Secundur. Men and Elifaen, they remade, and Dragonkind, too. But all prisoners were first brought to Throgallus to question, leaving it not to others to interrogate. And he always began with the same question to each one.

"Look upon my face," he would say, removing his helmet and stepping into the light of a fiery brazier. "Do you know my name?"

The answer was always the same, and none who were brought before him could ever name him.

"Do you know of the one called Lyrium?" he would then ask. And if the prisoner indicated that he knew that name, Throgallus would ask, "Where is she?"

None could say, or would say, no matter how much he threatened or tortured them, and no matter what reward he offered to them.

"What do you know of the Bloodcoins?" he would then demand of them. "How many are there, and where are they kept?"

No one he interrogated could account fully for the Forty-Nine, knowing not even how many were possessed by the King of Duinnor. Throgallus was always unsatisfied with these answers, ever doubtful of their words, and ever wary of the naggings of his own smoldering heart. More and more prisoners he demanded of his legions, particularly if they were Elifaen captured near Shatuum. But he also desired those captives, regardless of their race, that were purchased from the renegades of the far desert lands. His obsession over the fate of the Bloodcoins blackened his heart and made him sullen and mistrustful.

So when Throgallus was told that the latest group of prisoners had somehow broken free, just when they were near to Shatuum, he was enraged. With several of the Captains, he immediately went to the place where the chains were broken, and with his own hands he slew all of the surviving wraiths that had been in charge of the prisoners. He walked along the ledge northward, following the way the prisoners had taken, but when he came under the western shoulder of Algamori and neared the place where the Gate of Griferis stood, he stumbled and his head rang with a steady, painful note. Backing away, he cursed the mountain, and returned to his castle. There, his favorite enchantress came to him, seeking to apply her charms and her body as salve to his mood. He cast her aside so violently that her body flew across the room and cracked against the wall, leaving a great splatter of black blood. Then he drank an entire rundlet of heavy wine, which served to calm him somewhat, so that he uncharacteristically fell into a groggy stupor.

Of all the inhabitants of Shatuum, only Throgallus and Herzees the dreamwalker were permitted sleep. It was Secundur's law that none but those two could sleep, so fearful of dreamwalkers was Secundur, and of the subversive dreams they might bring. But Secundur knew that the dreams of Throgallus were a torment as nothing else could be, and Secundur needed Throgallus to be continually tormented. Furthermore, Secundur told Throgallus that if he ever fell asleep outside of his castle, he would be killed instantly by one of the Captains. In this way, Secundur guarded the sleep of Throgallus so that no dreamwalker could come to him without Herzees knowing.

This day, when Throgallus groaned in his drunken sleep, and when he dreamed, it was the same dream that always came to him. He dreamed of pleasant days and a faraway land, when he thought that his pact with the Fifth Unknown King would lapse unfulfilled. But, unless the King received those objects that were demanded of Throgallus, the King would unleash his assassins to hunt down and kill Throgallus's only son. Yet the King offered no help to Throgallus, no army, not even a company of Kingsmen. It did not matter. And the Dragonkind came, just as the King foresaw. And Throgallus suspected the reason they had come to Tulith Attis was because they also wanted the objects that the King desired. That also did not matter to Throgallus. At least, not at the time. For Throgallus thought that he was more powerful than those who assaulted Tulith Attis. He thought he was more cunning than the Dragonkind, and more cunning than Heneil and Lyrium, too. He did not need the King's help. Or so he thought. But the Dragonkind were too many, and too determined, and it was too late for anyone to help. All this was repeatedly reviewed in the mind of Throgallus as he dreamed, and it was so this night, too.

Then, as always, his dream descended into the chaos of war, into the bloody carnage of battle. In his slumber, he watched and fought again, unable to control what he saw or what he did, powerless to change the outcome. No one at the Battle of Tulith Attis fought as Throgallus fought, and yet it was useless. The Dragonkind came, and they came and came, like an endless tide, overwhelming his own brethren, slaughtering his kinsmen and allies, and pressing their attack upon his own person. When he had no more choice, Throgallus yielded, throwing aside his broken sword. The encircling Dragonkind did not kill him. They did not strike at him even when he taunted them to do so. And they backed away a little more when Bailorg appeared. Seeing Bailorg, he knew his fate. Throgallus put on that which Bailorg provided, the black armor with the red hourglass that he still wore to this very day. And, in that armor, he opened the gates of his own stronghold, and let the enemy in.

Again and again, Throgallus dreamed this dream of remembrance. Over and over for centuries he relived those moments. And a thousand times over, he stood in the Treasury Room with Bailorg, looking at the empty case where the Seven had been kept.

Except, this time, someone else was there, hovering in the shadows of the blood-mired place. When Throgallus turned upon him, the figure did not cower.

"I know your name," the figure said to Throgallus. "You were once called Pellen."

At hearing his name spoken for the first time in 548 years, a shiver went up his spine.

"The King of Duinnor trapped you, for he knew that you would not give over those objects he sent you to take, except to save yourself. That is why he sent Bailorg to you. But the King did not know that Bailorg also served Secundur and brought to you the armor that you wear. Lyrium foresaw your treason, and suspected you before the Dragonkind ever saw Tulith Attis. Because of her, the things that the King desired were taken from this room."

"Who are you? Reveal yourself to me!"

"I am your descendant, and also the descendant of those you betrayed."

Throgallus awoke with a start. He stumbled to his feet, knocking over a brazier and careening back and forth across the room until he gained a steady grip on the foot railing of his bed. There he crouched for hours, his skin crawling with fear beneath his armor as he tried to regain his sobriety and composure. He did so at last, and he threw on his helmet and marched away, determined to tell all to Secundur. But when he got to the gate of Secundur's tower, he paced back and forth for a long while in deep meditation as the Captains silently watched him. Then, leaving them behind, he strode on into the crooked place and up the many flights of dark stairs to the topmost floor, the darkest place of all, where never even the weakest light ever was, the place where Secundur always waited.

"What troubles you, my general?"

"It is time, my lord, for us to release our might against the world!"

"Why do you think so? Have we yet achieved our preparations? Do the armies of the Dragonkind march against Duinnor? Do the Redvests draw Glareth to its destruction? Is Vanara yet in revolt against the Sixth Unknown King?"

"No, my lord. None of those things have yet come to pass, as far as any may tell. There was an incident. Shatuum is no longer safe from the meddling of outsiders."

"Has another of our captains gone missing? Or perhaps more of our untrustworthy servants have left Shatuum. Do not worry, the captain that I sent out will find them before they may give us away."

"No, my lord. It is another matter. A number of prisoners escaped before they could be brought before me. By all accounts, their bonds were broken by invisible hammers, and fell away as if of their own accord."

"Ah."

Throgallus felt Secundur recede for a moment into the silence of the room that was as thick as the darkness within it. Secundur returned and drew near once more, and Throgallus heard his master's soft consoling voice in his ear.

"So, in spite of our efforts, your Bellringer has come at last. Invisible, you say? I think not. Surely he struck off their chains while your guards were not looking. Or perhaps they slept when they should not have."

"I do not think so, Lord Secundur."

Although Throgallus could not see him in the dark, he cast a glance in the direction where he imagined Secundur's dreamwalker lay sleeping.

"You think the Bellringer has the power to dreamwalk? That may be so. But no one may touch the material world while dreaming. And none may dreamwalk in my realm without being detected."

"I am not convinced, my lord."

"Do you think my dreamwalker would sacrifice his family with a lie to me?"

"No, my lord. Only perhaps he does not know all there is to know about the dream world that he is to watch for you. And perhaps he may not comprehend the power that some might bring into that realm. My lord, send me forth with our armies!"

"You grow impatient, and doubt feeds your longing for conquest. The loss of a few prisoners is not enough to merit ill-advised haste. If our forces go now, before the world is ripe for them, we will be defeated."

"And the missing Seven? What if they have been found?"

"Why do you mention them? Do you still fear that Lyrium may have them?"

"Yes, my lord."

"She does not. They are lost forever. The Fifth King failed to find them, and the Sixth King shall also fail. He may do whatever he wishes, and Serith Ellyn, too, with those they have. The ones they possess are useless without all others of the Forty-Nine, as you know. The Elifaen are trapped in the world, just as you are, just as we wish them to be. Go, now. Send new expeditions to the south, if you wish. I shall send my eagles to prepare the way so that more captives will be taken for you and your whores. Or, if that does not console you, put forth one of your raiding parties against the Gray Guard. Do not speak to me again of releasing our might until I order it done. Now leave me."

Throgallus departed. Secundur turned to another person who had waited unseen by Throgallus, listening to the exchange.

"My lord," said this person, "if the time does not come soon, I fear you will lose Throgallus. His will is strong, and he fills your Captains with a yearning to move upon the world."

"Is not your spell upon his armor still strong, Tythos?" Secundur asked, knowing the answer.

"It is, my lord. When you call for him, he comes without knowing why, just as he was drawn to you when he first donned that armor."

"Then I do not fear what he may do. As for the other matter. Have you yet divined a way to lift the spell upon the western slopes of this mountain?"

"No, my lord. I have not discovered a way to protect your Captains from that place."

"I see. Are you at least up to your other task?"

"It is being done as we speak. The skin of Valkose was given over to me by the witches, with the proper spells laid upon it, just as you said they would do. My work requires only a starless night. Then you shall have the conveyance that you desire. No light shall penetrate it, yet you shall see outside from within it. No one may touch it, lest they die, but you may reach from it to touch or speak to any within your sight. It shall weigh no more than a shadow, so that you may transport yourself by any means that you wish. Upon the wings of a fly, should you desire it."

"Very good. Once I am convinced of your words, and have that which you have promised, you shall be at my right-hand side. We will need Throgallus no longer, for together we shall lead our armies forth. The Kings of Duinnor may have their cloak, but I shall have mine."

"Yes, Lord Secundur."

• • •

As far as Robby was concerned, Tythos was far more dangerous than Throgallus with all his Captains. He had learned by watching that Tythos possessed the power to conjure the spirits from once-living things. It was Tythos who made the wraiths from the spawn of the witches, and he who had created the Thirteen Captains from the witches' spells. It was Tythos who had placed the incantations upon the armor that Bailorg carried to Tulith Attis. And Robby remembered from the Last Book of Nimwill that it was Tythos whom Parthais summoned to bring Secundur unto him. Throgallus knew nothing of Tythos, thinking that it was the witches alone who did all those things. But the power that Tythos wielded came from Secundur who infused his secret servant with his own hatred, his own malevolent venom, and who gave over to Tythos terrible secrets and awful recipes for perverting the forms of beasts. Robby only discovered these facts by standing within Secundur's chamber and listening to the whisperings of the Lord of Shatuum. For Secundur was ever restless and, when alone, was ever mumbling. Eventually, when visiting the dark lord's chamber between his other tasks, Robby saw Tythos come to Secundur, and he followed Tythos when he went away to his secret chambers far beneath the mountain. It was there that Robby saw him make the vile creatures that populated Shatuum, wraiths from the offspring of the witches. And from the prisoners held there, brought from all parts of the Seven Realms, Tythos stripped all that was their former selves, and he made of them goblins and ghouls, filled with a hunger for human meat and blood. Crowding every corner of Shatuum, these were the creatures that Secundur planned to unleash upon the world. It would be, as Ashlord had warned, worse than nightmare. Robby knew that no army on earth could contain them; only Throgallus and his Captains could hold them back.

As awful as it would be, far better for the world to face all the legions of Shatuum with Throgallus at their head, than for Secundur to lead them forth with Tythos at his side. And there was only one way to rob Tythos of the source of his power: Secundur must be destroyed, once and for all. Robby knew how it could be done, too. But he lacked the means to carry it out.

Chapter 10

New Servants for the King

On the afternoon following the night of their arrival, the guests of Griferis were rested, clean, and dressed in the new clothes provided to them. Finn led them through the halls of the palace and ushered them into the Great Circle Room to meet the King, closing the doors behind them. On the far side of the room stood Robby, dressed in a coat of splendid dark blue fabric, and simply cut white knee breeches buttoned around stockings over black silver-buckled shoes. His hair was neatly combed and tied in a short ponytail, and his beard was trimmed. He stood with his arms crossed and watched as Finn ordered the group into a semicircle so that all could face the King together.

"Wait just here, if you please," Finn instructed the group. He strode across the wide open space, and knelt before Robby. Finn spoke softly, but in the empty room his rehearsed words could be heard clearly by those who waited.

"Philawain, King of Griferis, I have brought those who were freed from Secundur to stand before you. What is your pleasure, sire?"

"Rise, good servant, and bring them forward to stand before me."

Finn rose and took a few steps back toward the group and beckoned to them. When they came close enough, he raised his hand for them to halt.

"Hail, Philawain, King!" Finn said loudly, striking the floor with his staff. At this, all of the guests bowed low. "Philawain, King, by whose power you were rescued from the cruel hand of Secundur, welcomes you to his domain! The King bids you be not afraid, for while within Griferis you need have no fear of Shatuum. King Philawain, who sees that which is hidden to others, bids you introduce yourselves to him."

Finn moved off to one side between the King and his guests. Robby remained where he was, his arms still crossed, and he said nothing for a few moments longer. Then he pointed at the Dragonkind man.

"You, sir. Come forward. What is your name, sir?"

"I am Radasa of Kajarahn, my lord," the man said, bowing.

"From the Free City? And to whom do you swear fealty?"

"I am a Freeman, sire. I have allegiances to my city only, and to my tribe and family, but am vassal to no lord."

"I see. And these others of the desert lands who are with you. Are they not members of your family?"

"Yes, my lord," the man answered uncomfortably, surprised that Robby could know that.

"Your wife and your three daughters?"

"Yes, my lord," the man said, glancing back at the others.

"Your wife and your daughters are very beautiful."

"Thank you, sire."

"You did not tell the other prisoners of your party," Robby stated. "Perhaps from fear that your family would be set one against the other, as I hear Secundur likes to do for sport."

"That is the legend, sire."

"I see. How came you and they to be captured?"

"Sire, as we traveled back to the Free City with a caravan, we were attacked and taken by renegades. It was they who sold us into captivity."

"Hm. A trader, I think. Surely your caravan was armed."

"Yes, King. But we were betrayed, for our guards abandoned us in the night just moments before our capture."

"I see. Very well. That is all for now."

The man bowed as he retreated back to his family, and his wife grasped his hand. Meanwhile, Robby pointed at the three Elifaen, "You, you, and you. Please come forward. Do the others here know that you are Elifaen?"

The three, two men and a woman, all appeared to be no more than teenagers but were actually older than anyone else present, except perhaps Finn. At the King's question, they looked at each other, then shook their heads.

"You are Hathrain, of the Masurthian House of Fairrose, and this is Unther of the Glareth House of Seafoam. Your name, my lady, is Winnefras of the House of Sandspur whose estate once graced the southern shores near Altoria. You three were captured by renegades, too, after you foolishly rode together from Vanara to look upon the Gory Gulch, where you hoped to retrieve the bones of your friend who died there many years ago. You did not know that those parts are now infested with bandits and deserters. Is it not so?"

"Yes, my lord," said Unther. "All that is true."

"Yes, King. It was foolish of us," said Hathrain.

"But, sire, if I may, we three fought together at the Gulch, and lost many friends," said Winnefras. "It was a dear comrade whose bones we sought to retrieve, for we heard that his father and his son grieve for him, and his wife wished to have his tomb nearby to her in her old age."

"I know," said Robby. "And I know whose bones it was that you sought. An admirable sentiment, one no doubt inspired by a powerful love for your friend. That is all."

Next, Robby directed his gaze at a man who stood, he felt, somewhat too proudly.

"I know you, too," Robby said to him. "Tell me, and speak truthfully, why were you in such a great hurry to travel from Vanara? Who was it that you traveled to meet?"

"Sire," the man said, "I traveled in haste in order to reach the Free City. There I was to meet one with whom I had a business interest."

"Hm. You are of Duinnor, are you not, of high station?"

"Yes, sire."

"And did you not have pressing matters in Vanara that needed your attention?"

"I had every reason to think they would hold until my return."

Finn slammed his staff onto the floor loudly. "Address yourself properly to the King!"

"My apologies, sire. I meant no disrespect to the King."

Robby glared at the man, dropping his arms and letting his fists hang. All present felt that he was offended by the man's familiar tone, but Robby was angry for another reason entirely, which he decided to keep to himself for the moment.

"One last question to you, sir," Robby said. "While you were in Vanara, did you ever meet a Kingsman named Ullin Saheed Tallin?"

The man visibly paled and hesitated. After a moment, Finn pounded his staff again.

"Answer the King!"

"Yes, sire. I met him."

"When did you meet him?"

"Not yet two months ago, sire. I attended a meeting in which he gave a report."

"And do you know what may have become of him?"

"No, King. That I do not know."

"I believe you. That is all for now, Count Dialmor."

The last man, the most nervous of all, waited to be called. Robby gestured for him to approach and looked at him for a long moment before speaking.

"Lafkin, son of Harrin, your companions owe their lives to you, sir," Robby said, "for it was you who slew the wraith that blocked the way. And it was you who climbed the ladder and all by yourself pulled up the first of your companions."

"Yes, sire. I did those things."

"You are a fighter of much experience, also of Duinnor. Before we speak of how you were captured, tell me: why were you never a Kingsman?"

"Sire," the man said, almost too nervous to speak, "I am not of a Named House. I attended the King's Academy when I was granted a commission by an honored patron. But I had the misfortune to bear witness against a fellow Kingsman in a case that was unjustly settled in his favor. As a result, I was forced to give up my commission and muster out of the ranks of the Kingsmen."

"And you found employment with the Duinnor Regulars."

"Yes, King. With the Eighth Army, Second Battalion, Second Company."

"Now, tell me, and do not fear to answer truthfully, how came you to become a renegade, throwing off your allegiance to Duinnor?"

The others in the group, hearing this, were filled with sudden anger that one of their captors was amongst them, and they looked at each other in surprise, muttering. Finn pounded the floor.

"Order! The King addresses not you but he!"

"Sire, I had little choice. I served with honor and dignity, I swear to you. I was assigned to go with a company of my fellows to capture a traitor and to bring him back to Duinnor for trial. But when my captain sought instead to ambush and kill him, I intervened to remind him of our orders, and I prevented both his death and his capture. I do not know why my captain did not kill me on the spot. He was a cruel man, and he tied me to a stake in the desert to fry in the heat. I was found by a party of renegades and offered a chance to fight against one of their band for my life, to become a member of their band if I was victorious. I won the contest. And, because I knew that I could not return home, I had no choice but to remain with those criminals. That, oh King, is the truth."

"Ah. And do you know the name of the man you were sent to capture? The traitor?"

"No, sire. It was never told to me, and I never learned his name. And I never came close enough to him to see his face. I can only say that he was wily and experienced, worthy of respect for that, at least, King."

"And were you told what act of treason the fellow committed?"

"Yes, sire. We were told that he carried dispatches to our enemies, the Dragonkind, from his accomplices in the north. But that is all we were told."

"I see. Now, how did it come to pass that you were sold into bondage with these others?"

"Again, sire, I intervened to prevent an injustice. The party of renegades that I was with mainly stole horses and goods from passing caravans, selling those in the Free City so that we could eat. But I slew one of my group who was about to murder an innocent traveler who had no goods to steal. The renegade that I slew had a brother who was a powerful criminal in the Free City. When next my band went there, I was taken and held to be traded to those who came there by night from Shatuum. It was only much later, sire, that others were put with me. First the three Elifaen, then the Dragonkind and his family, and lastly this man, Count Dialmor. That, my lord, is a truthful account."

"Yes. It is. Do you know the Count?"

"No, my lord. I had never met nor heard of him before he joined us as a prisoner."

"I see. Very well. That is all for now."

The man stepped back, remaining apart from the others as none of them wanted to stand close to him. Seeing this, Robby nodded, crossed his arms and turned his back to the group. He paced back and forth in thought, sometimes looking over his shoulder at Dialmor and sometimes at other members of the group. At last, he faced them again.

"I establish the first of my many kingdoms here in the place called Griferis," he said. "Perhaps some of you have heard of this place, in legend or tales. To some of you, or perhaps to all, I shall permit a choice: serve me for a time, or depart from here. Should you remain, you will be instructed in your duties. Should you decide to depart, the way will be made open for you to do so. But hear me! Once you leave this place, you will have no help from Griferis Kingdom."

Robby looked at Finn, then threw a glance at Lafkin. Finn tapped his staff and bowed low as Robby walked away through the doors behind him. The others also bowed. Finn took them all back to their wing. Before he departed from them, he gestured to Lafkin.

"Come with me, sir," Finn said. "The King wishes to speak further with you."

"Yes, my lord," the man said, somewhat relieved to be taken from the group who now seemed inclined to shun him.

Finn took Lafkin through a labyrinth of halls and passageways, up many flights of stairs, and finally outside to walk along one of the high walls that surrounded Griferis. There stood Robby, now in a long woolen overcoat, looking over the chasm at the far western peaks. Finn picked up a cloak fluttering in the wind on the parapet nearby and handed it to Lafkin.

"I shall leave you with the King," he said to Lafkin. "Put this on. It gets rather windy up here."

Lafkin put the cloak on and watched Finn retreat.

"Walk with me," said Robby.

"Yes, sire."

"I think you have already made up your mind," Robby said. "Is it because you have nowhere to go?"

"That is the gist of it, sire."

"Yet, of all in your party, you stand the best chance of returning home."

"My home, sire, is gone to me. When I lost my commission, then defied my captain, I erased any hope of returning to Duinnor, where I would be treated as a traitor."

"And serving me would be no worse than the deserts."

"To be blunt, sire. Yes."

"What if I turned out to be a despot? What if I demanded too much of you, or asked you to do that which your sense of right would deem improper?"

"I do not know, sire. But, if those things came to pass, I think I would fail you."

"I see. Well. In that case, I shall try not to be a despot, and I shall try not to compel you to do wrong things!"

Lafkin looked at Robby somewhat suspiciously.

"I need a fighting man," Robby went on. "Someone who can handle himself. I also need someone who can lead others. To train them in the use of arms, and, should the need arise, to see that they will faithfully use them in my service."

"Sire, although I have seen quite a few battles, I have never led men into one," Lafkin said. "I am afraid that I may not be the best person for the task. Surely there are others in your service already who are better qualified."

"I do not think so," said Robby. "Look."

Robby halted and waved his hand toward the palace.

"How many others in service to me do you see?"

Lafkin scanned the walls, gazed down at the courtyards, and then looked at Robby quizzically.

"You see none because there are none. My power grows. Until now, I have not needed the use of arms to accomplish my goals. However, I must prepare this kingdom for the day when arms might be needed. I offer you this opportunity to serve as my First General."

"King, I wonder, your general over what?"

"Your first duty will be to the safety of my person," Robby said, "then, to the safety of Griferis, defending my reign against all threats that may come. And, if the need arises, I shall ask you to carry out punishment on those who defy my will, or upon those that I direct you to punish. In that duty, you must be stern and ruthless, as the hand of my might. At first, you will be alone in these duties. But I shall amass the forces necessary to carry out your other duties. In return, I offer you a home and honorable work. Beyond that, there is not much else I may give until some time has passed. I cannot give you happiness. I cannot make your loneliness go away. I cannot change the injustice that has already befallen you. Still, though I cannot make it a promise, I might someday be able to restore your good name, and restore you to your home and family."

"Forgive me, sire. All of this seems somewhat improbable. I still do not understand what men would serve under me."

"You will have them. They will arrive in various ways. There is much for you to do before they come. Do you agree to my offer?" Robby held out his hand to Lafkin, who stared at it.

"How do you know that you can trust me, sire?"

"If you want my trust," Robby said, "you must earn it. Just as I must earn yours."

Lafkin put his hand into Robby's, and they shook.

"Good! Now, let us get straight to it!" Robby said, turning to continue their walk. "You will learn soon enough that I am no ordinary king. Someday, you may learn my story. You already know enough of my power to know that I can see into your dreams, when I wish to, or send others to look upon your dreams. And you saw for yourself something of my power when your chains fell away from you. These and other powers are but tools to me. I will use them as diligently as I shall expect you to use your skills. Foremost are your training and experience. The first thing that I desire of you is a complete plan for keeping order within Griferis. The number of guards needed, how they should be armed and trained, what their duties should be, and so forth. Second, I would like for you to prepare a list of all those arts, crafts, and skills needed to support a small army. Blacksmiths, armorers, and so forth. Do you follow? Assume you are to start from scratch, as it were."

"Yes, sire. I think I understand."

"Good. Finn will take you to your chambers. You will not be taken back to the group, but will have a separate place for a while. You will find writing tools and materials for making your lists. Oh, and Lafkin, if you know of any particular men or women, be they Men, Elifaen, or Dragonkind, that have the skills that you will require, and who may be willing to join our cause and serve honorably, please make a list of their names and where they might be found."

"Sire, what cause is it that you set about to accomplish?"

"I intend to extend my rule," Robby said. "In fact, I have already begun that work. You will learn more. Now, I must ask you to go with Lord Finn. Here he is. If you have any questions, put them to Finn."

"Yes, my King."

Robby watched Finn depart with Lafkin, and smiled.

"Well," he said to himself, "that was pretty simple. Now for the next ones!"

• • •

"Mr. Lafkin will not be rejoining you," Finn told the waiting group. "At least not for a few days. The King would now like to see our Elifaen guests."

The three Elifaen looked at each other and nodded to Finn. Finn took them to the Library where they saw Robby standing at the upstairs balcony with a book in his hand.

"I asked Finn to bring you here, for within this place are records of the histories of the world," said Robby, looking down at them. "They are, for the most part, accountings of one sorry conflict after another, not only between Men and their Elifaen allies against the Dragonkind, which is the sorriest, most egregious conflict of all, but also here is recorded many conflicts between and among Men and Elifaen. But what say you to the wars with the Dragonkind? Are they just?"

His guests looked at each other, none wishing to speak.

"I have asked you a question," Robby said. "Speak your answer!"

"Sire," said Hathrain, "who knows whether the wars have been just or not? We have fought because it has been our duty to do so."

"Duty?" Robby asked. "Tell me, are you loyal or disloyal to your people?"

"We are loyal, sire!"

"And therefore, if you felt the wars were not necessary to your people, you would not fight in them. Is that the way of it? Or do you have a love of bloodshed?"

Hathrain hesitated, but Unther stepped forward.

"Sire, we would fight, and have fought, because we were ordered to do so, not because we lust for blood."

"I see. Were you acting under orders when you went back to Gory Gulch to retrieve the bones of your slain comrade? Upon whose orders were you acting?"

"None, sire. We acted on our own."

"You acted without orders. I suppose your commanders simply did not care that you would go there to do what you set out to do? And so you were not disloyal to them?"

"You have us, King," Winnefras said. "Indeed, all of that land is forbidden for any soldier to enter without orders from the highest authority. But our friend was dear to us, and it grieved us to know that his kin ceaselessly mourn for him."

"I shall ask you again, and I beg that each of you search your heart and tell me: Are the wars with the Dragonkind just?"

"My heart tells me they are not," said Winnefras. "I speak only for myself, sire."

"I, too, have my doubts, sire," said Unther.

"Sire, I have seen too much to say if they are just," said Hathrain. "And I have blood on my hands. My mind hopes that what I have done, for Queen and for King, has been just. Yet, truthfully, my heart is troubled, and in my sleep I am haunted by my memories. It is a poor answer, sire, but the only one that I have to give."

Robby nodded, placed his book onto a nearby table, then walked down the stairs to stand before them.

"What would you give to change things?" he asked. "What would you give for peace between the Dragonkind and the Elifaen?"

"What wouldn't we give, King?"

"Would you give up your lives? Would you give yourselves for only the hope of peace, even if it was not assured? Would you lay your bodies down for it?"

"If there was hope, I would, sire," said Unther unhesitatingly. "I know why the wars began, for I have read and heard the tales of Cupeldain and of the goading of Secundur. I know of the Great Stone and the pride of Kalzar. I have seen with mine own eyes the way that the

Dragon people are treated by their masters. And I know, too, how Duinnor ever prods them to war with Vanara, keeping our homelands weak. All these things, sire, we three know, as do most of our kind. Yet we go on the way we have done for two thousand years, since we see little hope for change."

Robby nodded, looking at the other two who appeared by their expressions to be in full agreement with Unther.

"Then I tell you that there is hope," he said to them, "and I ask you two last questions. First, would you fight alongside Dragonkind to bring about peace?"

They looked at each other, as if surprised by the question, but Winnefras spoke first.

"Sire, it was a Dragonkind woman who came to us in our dreams, and because of her we are safe here before you," she said. "And, if in order to bring about peace I must fight against those who do not desire it, then I would fight beside any to accomplish it."

"I say so, too!" said Unther.

"And I!" proclaimed Hathrain. "If peace is to be had, King, surely it cannot be brought about by one side alone."

"Very well, then," said Robby. "My last question: Will you give to me one year of service, to do as I or my agent bids you to do, to serve me over all else, and to give every measure of your effort to my cause? For one year, renouncing all loyalties to any other queen or king, and forsaking your homes and your families?"

They nodded, looking at one another, and knelt before Robby.

"I am pleased by your answers," Robby said. "Arise, and hear me. I shall place you under the command of my High General. He will instruct you as to your duties, and you must obey him with zeal and determination. In a few days, you will meet him. Meanwhile, go with Lord Finn to your new quarters, and await my summons."

• • •

When Finn returned to the group, now consisting of the Dragonkind trader, his family, and Dialmor, he told them that the Elifaen would not be rejoining them, at least for the time being.

"Be not alarmed," he said. "They are safe and are being taken to quarters more suited to them. In the meantime, the King would like to see you, Radasa, and your family. Come with me, please."

"Lord Chamberlain," Dialmor interrupted, "what about me? Does not the King wish to interview me further?"

"Undoubtedly," Finn said. "However, you must await your turn, sir."

Finn led Radasa and his family to Robby's suite of rooms, and showed them into one of the rooms that seemed best for entertaining small groups. It was luxuriously appointed with carpets and draperies, fine glittering lamps, and many comfortable chairs and divans. Robby was standing beside the window facing them as they entered. Finn stood to one side as the man and his wife and children bowed. Robby returned the gesture and went to a chair and sat.

"How am I to address your wife, sir?" he asked Radasa.

"Her name is Kinsiri, sire. We do not use surnames as is common in the Northlands."

"Kinsiri. A lovely name. And your daughters? What are their names?"

"This is my eldest, Halyari. My middle child, Valcea. And my youngest, called Leena."

Each bowed when introduced.

"I am pleased to make your acquaintance, ladies. Please make yourselves comfortable on the divan, there. Sir, please sit, too, perhaps in this chair nearer to me, here."

"Thank you, sire."

"I hope that you have had a comfortable night and day thus far," Robby said to Kinsiri. "And that your needs have been met."

"Yes, King. We thank you. We have had a good night's sleep, and ample to eat, too."

"I am glad to hear it," Robby said. "Radasa, I will come straight to the point. I am in need of a good and experienced trader. One who can obtain for my kingdom all those things that I might need or desire. I wonder, then, would you be interested in a position within my domain, to serve by procuring for Griferis such things as you may?"

"Sire, I would gladly serve you in any capacity to repay the debt that I owe for saving my family."

"You owe me nothing, sir. Since you are of the Free City, I assume that you must be very experienced in bartering, trading, and negotiating with many who are less than reliable. I have been there, and I know that it is full of thieves and cheaters."

"Yes, sire. It is full of those kinds of people. But also many fair-minded traders and craftspeople, too. May I ask what sorts of things you might wish for that your representatives have not been able to obtain for you?"

"My representatives?" Robby chuckled, glancing at Finn. "I can honestly say that I will need virtually everything, sir. Fabric, raw iron, tools, wood of all kinds, ink, buttons, swords, armor, bows, glass, paint, leather goods, and practically anything and everything else one might imagine. And I shall also need craftsmen and women, and artisans of all kinds skilled in the making of things, too."

Baffled, Radasa held out his hands, gesturing all around.

"You seem to lack nothing, sire. Though I confess that I find it somewhat strange that we have seen few servants since we have arrived."

Robby nodded, then looked up at the ceiling for a moment, absently rubbing the scar on his wrist. Finn waited, wondering how much Robby would say.

"I shall tell you how it is," said Robby at last. "This is a new kingdom. I recently ascended to rule here, after a labor of many years. The previous occupants, seeking perhaps to thwart me, abandoned this place. There are now very few of us here. I mean to do great things, and it is my aim to make this but the first of many kingdoms that I shall rule. Imagine for yourself the kind of king that might exert his power over all of the Seven Realms of the North, and also over all of your own lands, too. It is also my aim to confront Shatuum, and destroy the power that is there. Such a king would be powerful, indeed, would he not?"

"Yes, sire. The mightiest ever."

"I am he. And this is the place of my beginning. I ask that you serve as my trader for one year. You shall be given safety and comfort, and your family, too. In return, you shall be made wealthier than you could have ever become in the Free City. If you refuse, I shall find another to serve me. But I think you have had a taste of my power, and I think you are too shrewd to pass on this offer."

"Sire, I never sought wealth, only to make a good living so as to provide for my family. I shall serve you. And I hope that you shall be satisfied with me. Only, I do have a worry."

"What is that?"

"Sire, we have been without the herb darakal for almost four months. While at the Free City, I could obtain that which my family needs, though it is expensive and dangerous to do so."

"How often do you normally take the elixir?"

"Every three months, if I have the gold."

"Tell me, Radasa," Robby asked, "how long has it been since you left the Dragonlands?"

"We were held for a month in the mountains west of Kajarahn, then another month and a half along the way, sire."

"And the wraiths that brought you along the Great Chasm fed you and gave you water?"

"Yes, sire. Such food that was revolting to eat, at first. And there was water aplenty falling from the heights above us."

"I know that you are all much fatigued and travel-weary, but do you feel the desert sickness at all?"

"No, sire," Radasa said, looking at his wife and daughters. "I do not think we have begun to suffer from the sickness that plagues our kind."

"And I do not think you shall," said Robby. "It is my belief that the sickness that wears down your people comes from the dust of the desert, and its waters are for the most part polluted with that dust. The darakal elixir is not a cure, as you know. It only makes the symptoms abate. However, here there is nothing to cause the sickness in the first place. I think that, once you have recuperated from your arduous journey, you will begin to feel stronger than you ever have before."

"I hope that what you say is true, sire."

"You must inform me should you or any of your family feel poorly, such as might be felt when the sickness comes," said Robby. "If that happens, I shall endeavor to obtain the herb for you."

"Thank you, sire. You do us great honor."

"Sire," Kinsiri spoke, "may I speak?"

"Certainly, my lady."

"I, too, am not without skill, and my daughters also have talents. I know fabrics and sewing, and the art of dyeing linen and other fabrics. My daughters have all three served in great houses of our city, each to a different lord who resides there, and may serve this House, if it pleases you for us to serve."

"That would please me very much, my lady. I am happy to hear you say so. Children—if I may address you so, for you are all three young women—what say you to your mother's suggestion?"

"We would honor our mother and father by serving the King in the best way that we may," said Halyari. "I am a good cook, accustomed to preparing fine meals for demanding lords and ladies, sire. My two sisters are both nearly as accomplished in the art of sewing as our mother. And, should it please the King, we all sing and dance quite well, too."

"Oh? Well, then! Radasa, you have no choice. I am compelled to command you and your family to stay and serve me!" Robby declared, grinning as he stood. He offered his hand for Radasa to shake. "Finn will now take you to your new rooms, where I think you'll be much more comfortable. He will also come to you when he has the time and present to you greater details of your new duties. I thank you all!"

"Thank you, Your Majesty!"

• • •

Several hours later, Finn returned to Robby and reported that Radasa's family were settling into their new rooms, Lafkin was already busy making his lists, and that the Elifaen, too, were in their new quarters.

"That leaves only Count Dialmor, sire," said Finn. "I sense that you have some concern over him. Do you know the man?"

"No, Finn," Robby said. "I do not. But I have watched his dreams, and there is something that keeps coming up. I'm afraid I don't know what to make of it, but it has to do with the time Ullin Saheed and I were in Vanara. In his dreams, I keep seeing Dialmor reading a sheet of paper with our names on it. Then, I see him speaking with a soldier of Duinnor, giving him the paper. Captain Faradan. That is the soldier's name. But there is something very disturbing about the mood of the dream. Very—I don't know—sneaky."

"Is there someone in Vanara that you might visit, dreamwalking, and ask?"

"Yes. I think so. But would you mind doing that for me? I was out late last night, and I'm quite worn out. And, yet, I still have a few errands that I must run, so to speak."

"I would be happy to do as you ask, my lord. I am quite rested."

"Good, thank you. Seafar is who you must find. Lord Seafar. He is Regent while Serith Ellyn is away, and he keeps chambers at the White Palace of Linlally. Ask him, if you can, about Dialmor and Faradan. And, while you are out, please look in on Micerea. I'd like to know how she is doing, and how Ullin gets along."

"Certainly, my lord."

"And one last thing," Robby said, walking Finn to the door. "Have you had a chance to prepare a list of staff for our service?"

"Why, yes, I have. It is an incomplete listing, based on my dreamwalking. I have looked far and wide and have discovered nearly three dozen candidates for your consideration. Shall I ask Micerea to do the same, sire?"

"Yes, do. Thank you."

• • •

Throughout the day, while Robby conducted his interviews, news of the attack in Vanara spread throughout Duinnor City and competed with stories about the strange murders that had taken place in broad daylight in an alley near Crescent Avenue. Then there was the story, too, that was going about concerning a young serving girl who had apparently been killed whilst attempting to carry out yet another murder. Printing presses were busy with these sensational stories, and by the afternoon so many versions of the events were written and read by the citizenry that some people passed the stories off as pure rumor. Others clamored to know what it meant if Vanara was truly attacked by Duinnor agents. What would Queen Serith Ellyn do? How should those Vanarans within Duinnor be treated? By nightfall, some even suggested that all Vanarans should be detained until further news arrived. The Vanaran Ambassador and all of the Vanaran Kingsmen advocated calm and assured their colleagues and counterparts that Lord Seafar and Queen Serith Ellyn would not react rashly.

Meanwhile, for those less interested in distant events, the case of the five deaths in the eastern part of the city was also cause for alarm. And while the printed stories at first mentioned Lady Shevalia in connection with the young girl's death, Lady Highleaf sent a note to every printer in the city assuring each that, should Shevalia's name continue to be bandied about so freely, she would withdraw her patronage and her financial support in favor of a competitor.

By the following morning, things were calmer. The broadsheets that circulated about the city mentioned Shevalia only in passing, and only to lament her bad luck to have employed such a conniving and ill-fated maid.

As the day progressed, little else was written about the deaths, except that it came out, in one late edition, that the men who were found dead were actually members of the Duinnor Regulars. It was an insinuating reference to Lord Banis, as most knew that the Regulars answered to him, but nothing more was written. It was enough to prompt some to look at each other with a wink and a nod, and with some amount of satisfaction that those employed by Banis were not immune to such a fate. While many reacted with guarded smugness, most were still too concerned with the attack upon the White Palace of Vanara, and could not but think that it must be interpreted by Vanara as an act of war.

The following day, Lady Highleaf was pleased to see that the stories she read were only retellings of what had already been written before. She was especially pleased to see several stories describing the upcoming party at Starlight Hall, reporting with some accuracy a few of the distinguished guests who would be in attendance. In the most flattering terms, Starlight Hall's splendid past was reviewed, favorably mentioning Lady Highleaf's late father who had built Starlight Hall, and recounting some of the previous sumptuous gatherings that had taken place there over the years. All this served to soothe her pride somewhat, and she spent the rest of the day selecting gowns for Lady Shevalia to choose from that would be most suitable to the occasion.

The morning after that, what she read filled her with disappointment and frustration. All of the printers had decided to embellish the tales coming out of Vanara with the most appalling accounts of bloodshed and violence, and not a single mention of her party was to be found in any of the broadsheets that covered her breakfast table. Matters only grew worse throughout the day. If the stories were to be believed, all of Duinnor was fretting away with worry as to what the attacks upon Linlally might portend. She spent the day making last-minute changes to party plans that were entirely unnecessary, much to the exasperation of her patient staff. And she dispatched new notes to the printers to remind them of the evening's ball.

To Lady Highleaf, the most important aspect of all this was that these stories served to distract everyone from the great event about to take place at her estate. It was a tremendous frustration that her party, planned for so long and which would normally be prominent upon the pages of the press as well as the lips of the city, now seemed somehow less consequential. This served to put her in a petulant temper, and she scurried about chastising cooks and chamberlains, secretaries and seamstresses, and footmen and serving maids. In short, anyone who came within her sight was apt to reap her ire about something trivial.

That is, anyone except Lady Shevalia. All of Lady Highleaf's bluster and blast simply fell to bits as soon as she came within Sheila's presence. This effect baffled Lady Highleaf as much as it did her servants, who could not fail to notice. And, it was also noticed that the change in Lady Highleaf lasted for some while afterwards. This quickly endeared the staff even more toward Lady Shevalia who treated them all with such simple courtesy that they contended with each other to wait upon her as she prepared for the evening.

Chapter 11

When All Moments May End

Day 195
50 Days Remaining

Wysteria Place was one of the oldest estates in all of Duinnor City, and one of the most beautiful, and its grounds covered nearly twenty acres of groves and gardens in the northwest district of the city. After the death of Lord Highleaf many years ago, it had been lovingly restored and was cared for by his eldest daughter, Lady Victoria Highleaf, and her vast fortune. In the middle of the estate, Starlight Hall rose up four stories, not counting the corner towers. This night, Starlight Hall's pale blue stones glowed, bathed by the light of the many lamps of its courtyards and by those that lined the long cobblestone drive leading up to the broad steps that ascended to its entrance. The Hall's roof, sheathed in glass and copper, had many crystalline domes, as did its towers, and these sparkled blue and white under the steady beams of the Five Stars of Duinnor that ardently glimmered overhead, lending the hall its name.

Though it was not even an hour after sunset, already carriages and coaches had long been arriving in a steady procession, delivering the proud and powerful, the important and interesting, as well as the eccentric and elegant people of the city. In short, a throng of varied individuals came that had in common amongst them a desire to attend one of the grandest parties of the season, and an invitation in hand to do so.

They entered within, passing through the grand foyer where winter coats and cloaks were dutifully taken by Starlight servants, as well as rapiers and swords (except those carried by Kingsmen, who were exempt from any such disarming). From there, the guests passed on to the landing at the top of a long wide staircase of white marble that flowed down into the expansive great hall. While music wafted lyrically from a balcony above, each guest was announced at the top of the stairs and then descended proudly to join those already enjoying the food, wine, and conversation that was shared in such abundant diversity. There were Kingsmen in their white breeches and green tunics trimmed with gold, and lords with shiny black shoes and colorful satin jackets, some handling fine walking sticks of rare wood and inlaid silver or gold. There were powerful and rich tradesmen, hardly distinguishable from the lords by their dress and attitude. And there were others, less fashionably dressed, perhaps, who were important citizens or who (by Lady Highleaf's judgment) were simply too interesting not to invite. And, certainly, there were ladies, titled and not titled, ever-so-many ladies in their long colorful gowns, their gloves to their elbows, and their jewels competing with their figures to attract the attention and envy of others. Old and young and every age between these ladies were, all wearing what they hoped was the most elegant, or the most fashionable, or the most provocative attire. Some bulged with layers of petticoats and lace, others sported dashing and colorful hats and caps, full of jewels and feathers, while others, particularly the Elifaen ladies who were impervious to cold (or those who wished to compete with them), wore so little that their attire bordered precariously close to scandalous.

The great hall was long and wide—somewhat like that of Tallin Hall, but much larger in every dimension—with many fireplaces roaring cordially and marvelous crystal-shimmering lamps atop marble posts. Hence, the place was nearly as warm and as bright as a spring day. But whereas Tallin Hall was lovely in its own way, Starlight Hall was glorious. The floor was paved in blue marble so polished that it appeared like the still, mirror-like pool of a mountain lake. One could look down and clearly see in the reflection the details of the ceiling above, painted with such skill and cunning that the clouds and Faerekind depicted seemed to move and change their shapes. And, not to be outdone by their backdrop, a dozen acrobats, suspended from thin, almost invisible threads, danced high above the guests, waving their gossamer wings while their mica-flecked bodies floated and rolled and spun around in dramatic bounds and graceful pirouettes with never a mishap nor a single awkward motion from one end of the hall to the other and back. And there, on the far side of the Hall, another staircase curved and flowed gently down to the floor like a frozen stream. Along this descent Lady Highleaf floated in her midnight blue gown, her hair up beneath a diamond-studded headband, and her bosom supporting a web of tiny silver-entwined diamonds so numerous that it appeared as if her skin was made of light. In one hand she held a folded fan while casually perched on her other hand was Certina, as proud, or more so, than any in attendance.

"Lady Highleaf!" the porter announced, thumping his staff.

She continued down the stairs gracefully, but not slowly, and was soon surrounded by bows and curtseys. One gentleman was in the fine garb of a Kingsman general with his broad red sash across his tunic. He was accompanied by a pale young girl in a simple but refined gown. He bowed low and kissed Lady Highleaf's hand.

"Lady Highleaf, a great honor to be in Starlight Hall once again!"

"It is my great pleasure to see you here, General Pelham. I hope your journey has not been too arduous."

"No, madam, thank you. It was without incident or strife. But it was a long trek, and I am glad to be back. May I present my daughter? Lady Highleaf, this is Trishka."

"Oh, at last," Highleaf declared, curtseying to the young lady. "I am so happy to meet you!"

"The pleasure is entirely my own, Lady Highleaf!" The girl curtseyed. "I have so looked forward to coming to Duinnor and seeing Starlight Hall."

"And what do you think of my little place?"

"It is fabulous!" Trishka declared, full of girlish thrill.

"I am glad you find it so," said Highleaf, smiling. "And I do hope you will enjoy yourself."

"I am sure that I shall, Lady Highleaf. Is that your pet? Is it a baby owl?"

"Hardly a baby, my child! And she is not my pet, but an honored guest. She is called Certina."

"Oh, how cute she is!" said Trishka. When Certina turned her full gaze upon the girl, she added quickly, "In a fierce sort of way!"

Certina, who was at first understandably put out by the girl's questions, was somewhat appeased by her last comment. Although the girl wanted to speak further, the press was so great around them that her father courteously and gently nudged her aside so that others could give their own greetings to Lady Highleaf and to Certina. Soon the two were cordially pulled this way and that, each enjoying the attention they received as Lady Highleaf leisurely moved through the crowd.

"Lord and Lady Garworth!" thumped the porter just as Lady Highleaf was about to speak to a rotund lady in a puffy green gown.

"Oh, my!" said the lady putting her hand on her bosom. "Must he thump like thunder?"

"Lady Bunsit," answered Lady Highleaf, leaning in close to her guest's ear, "the louder he thumps, the more important they are. Or so they may think!"

"Oh!" Lady Bunsit laughed, glancing at the elderly pair proudly descending the stairs. "I don't think those two would know any different since they are each as deaf as a doorknob!"

"That is yet another reason to thump so!"

By now, the hall was so filled with people that the music could hardly be heard over their talk and laughter, and the porter had to fairly shout, which he did admirably well.

"The Farbys of Duinnor!" he called out. Lady Highleaf smiled at the trio at the top of the stairs, and she breathed an inaudible sigh of relief that Lord and Lady Farby had actually talked their son into coming after all. She moved closer to the stairs to greet them, although it was several minutes before the well-wishers in attendance permitted her and the Farbys from reaching each other. When they did come together, she saw that Grantham Farby already appeared bored, even though he smiled courteously.

"Lady Highleaf," his father bowed. "An honor to be here."

"I am so glad to see you, Blain. My sister Elyna," said Lady Highleaf, kissing Grant's mother, "I'm so happy that you are all here."

"It took some doing!" Lady Elyna said, nodding at her son. "But here we are! Oh, I so love coming back to Starlight! You have outdone yourself!"

"Thank you."

"Lady Highleaf." Grant bowed and kissed Lady Highleaf's hand.

"Oh, come, Grantham. Don't be so put out!" Lady Highleaf grinned. "I know you'd rather be off on one of your adventures, but the town needs to have a new look at you."

"You and my mother are quite in agreement," he said, unable to keep himself from grinning at his exuberant aunt. "So here I am!"

Just as Lady Elyna was about to ask about the owl, Certina flew over to land on Grant's shoulder.

"Oh, my! You have already made a new friend, you see?" Lady Elyna said. "And what is its name?"

As Lady Highleaf repeated to her sister what she had already said so often this evening, Grant was tapped on his other shoulder. Turning, he saw an old schoolmate.

"Farby! You old rascal! So you are back in Duinnor!" declared the fellow, offering his hand.

"Good to see you, Reggie. Yes, I have been back for a few weeks, now."

"And not once have you come to see me. Inexcusable! Where have you been keeping yourself?"

"My apologies. I have been somewhat busy."

"Well, come have a glass with me."

"Oh, no, you don't!" commanded Lady Highleaf. "Reginald, you'll have to wait your turn, for our guest of honor must be properly presented. Or, if not properly, at least presented."

Lady Highleaf took her nephew by the elbow and led him back to the main stairs, gesturing to the porter. Certina flew off to perch on the banister of the balcony, apparently to distract the musicians from their notes with her penetrating glare, but the cadenced thumping of the porter's staff brought the music to an end before she could succeed.

"Lady Highleaf wishes to present the honorable Grantham Farby!"

All who did not already hold a glass in their hands quickly obtained one as Lady Highleaf and Grant made their way up a few steps of the stairs and turned to the gathering. A server came, and they each took a glass from his tray, then waited patiently for a moment or two as the guests became quiet and turned to look their way.

"I welcome you to Starlight Hall," Lady Highleaf said to them. "My dear nephew has recently completed his studies abroad, and this occasion is to celebrate his return to Duinnor. I hope that old acquaintances shall be remade and new ones begun. Some of you may be a little reluctant to do so, based on the extraordinary tales told about him. But I can only say that Grantham is superbly well-mannered, admirably conversant, and, if I say so, quite handsome. And, most importantly, as you can see, he is unarmed!"

There was some polite but nervous laughter at this remark, just as Lady Highleaf hoped.

"But I warn you!" she went on, grinning at Grant. "His wit, equal only to his charm, is as sharp as any blade in Duinnor!"

"Oh, Auntie!" Grant said over the giggles and laughter.

"I give you my nephew, Grantham Farby!" She raised her glass to Grant. As he bowed to her, the crowd roared back his name and raised their glasses. He bowed to them, then held up his hand.

"Lady Highleaf is most kind, even if she does exaggerate my qualities," he said. "But I cannot gainsay her enthusiasm, which is matched only by her beauty. To say the very least, I am honored by her gesture and by your attendance. I look forward to enjoying your company this evening. And so, without any further ado, I raise my glass to the finest and most beautiful aunt ever to be had. Lady Highleaf!"

"Lady Highleaf!" resounded the crowd, and those without glasses applauded loudly as Lady Highleaf curtseyed to Grant and to the crowd.

They descended back onto the floor as the music resumed, and Grant was soon surrounded by well-wishers and friends, schoolmates and family acquaintances, all introducing or re-introducing themselves. Many of them begged Grant to make the acquaintance of their particular niece or sister or cousin, just as many girls and ladies imposed upon him to put his name on their dance cards. Others followed at a demure distance, batting their eyes ridiculously whenever they thought he might glance toward them as he attempted to make his way back to his friend Reggie.

The gathering began to organize itself by slowly moving to the sides of the hall, clearing the floor in preparation for the dance. Additional chairs were brought out and arranged all around the room for the onlookers, and it was during this activity that the porter thumped very loudly.

"First Lord of the High Chamber of Duinnor, Lord Banis!"

A hush, pleasing to Lord Banis, passed over the room as he descended the stairs in his burgundy-trimmed cream jacket and his high, burgundy boots. He smugly nodded to those who bowed before him as he gained the floor, but it was only when he met with Lady Highleaf that he bowed, and most elegantly.

"Lady Highleaf."

"Lord Banis." She curtseyed very low.

"I am honored by your invitation."

"As I am by your attendance, my lord."

"It appears that all of Duinnor is in company tonight," Banis commented, casting his eye across the crowd, now resuming their chatter but keeping their distance, "as is appropriate and in keeping with the fine tradition of your little get-togethers."

"Thank you, my lord," answered Lady Highleaf. "Once again, the people of Duinnor honor Starlight Hall."

"Your popularity never wanes, but is as steady as the Stars of Duinnor."

"You are very kind."

"Not at all. I see that I am just in time for the dance. May I have the honor?"

"It would be mine to give, my lord, but the first is promised to the object of this celebration."

Lord Banis raised an eyebrow, just as Grant came up beside Lady Highleaf, who put her arm through his.

"Lord Banis." Grant bowed.

"Mr. Farby, I presume. It is a pleasure to meet you at last, sir."

"Thank you, my lord. If you'll excuse us," Grant said as he began to lead Lady Highleaf away. "And allow me to offer my deepest condolences on your recent loss."

"My loss? I do not know what you mean, sir."

Grant stopped and looked back at Banis quizzically. Lady Highleaf's smile froze.

"Your men, my lord. Those who were recently found deceased in some back alley somewhere. It was in all of the broadsheets."

Lord Banis's face reddened ever-so-slightly, and his smile was strained. Lady Highleaf visibly paled, and while she still smiled, she turned to look at Grant, her eyes shooting arrows of annoyance at him, for she knew all too well Grant's penchant for provocation.

"If you refer to those unfortunate gentlemen who were murdered nearby to Crescent Avenue," Banis said, "then I must tell you that I am in no way associated with them. I must wonder what makes you say so."

"Oh? Forgive me, my lord. I thought that I saw it writ somewhere. I was obviously in error. In that case, instead of my condolences, please accept my apology. Lady Highleaf? Shall we take our place?"

Lord Banis watched them go, fuming at the arrogance of Farby's insinuations, however accurate they were. He glanced around, realizing that many had overheard the exchange. It was bad enough that the men were found at all, and worse since the writ they had with his name on it was not found on them. If the Kingsmen had found the writ, the entire incident would have been passed over into Lord Banis's own investigators. But, as it was, the writ was apparently missing. Could Farby know? Banis then saw his least-favorite Kingsman general, and smiled as he made his way toward him, hoping to unnerve the man with some veiled and untrue insinuations of his own.

"That brat will repent his tone very soon," he muttered under his breath as he bowed to the general.

• • •

"Grantham, you are too rash!" said Lady Highleaf as the two took their positions. "You should bite your tongue before insulting Lord Banis."

"Did I insult him? Well, he is a blight upon the Throne!" answered Grant, bowing to Lady Highleaf as the music began. "A presumptive, arrogant, corrupt, criminal. An embarrassment and a slap in the face to every good Elifaen that I know, even if he is a Firstborn."

"Grantham, please! Dear me, boy!"

But he continued as they joined hands and danced.

"No wonder Vanara is ever suspicious of Duinnor!" Grant went on. "Everyone knows who controls the Regulars that vex Vanaran lands. Now that Linlally has been attacked, it will not go well for our Realm. And anyone with an ounce of sense must suspect Lord Banis of some role in that assault."

"Not another word, I beg you! Do not make this occasion one that I shall regret."

"I'm sorry, Auntie. Forgive me. I shall not ruin your night."

"It is not my night, sweetie, but yours. I know you hate crowds, and perhaps that has put you off your mood. I beg you put aside your fears and opinions, if you can, and enjoy yourself just this once."

"Yes, my lady. I am rightfully rebuked."

"Good! Now, what do you think of Lady Dayshall? Isn't she beautiful?"

"Oh, she's pretty, I suppose."

"Hm. I think you have very high standards, then. But I promise that you'll be smitten before the night is over."

"Oh? And how will you manage that, I wonder?"

• • •

Naturally, Lady Highleaf hoped that her other very special guest would impress Grant, as sure as she would impress everyone else. And she hoped that Grant, especially, would be so animated with desire for Lady Shevalia's attentions that he would give up his wanderlust for good and apply himself to winning her over. That he and Shevalia were already acquainted never entered her mind, much less that he was already stricken with heartache over her.

When the music stopped, and the dancers' applause of congratulation faded away, the porter at the far side thumped.

"Lady Shevalia!"

All eyes turned to the tall exotic beauty standing at the top of the far stairs. She stood for a moment, feeling not the least awkward, appearing proud and aloof, yet smiling serenely, and then she began her descent. She was likened unto a Faere queen of yore, her hair banded with glittering rubies that matched the dark red of her airy gown. As she floated down the stairs, the part in her gown flowed away from her legs, her figure a vision of womanhood at its most stunning, and many onlookers gaped while others instinctively bowed. Every woman was instantly filled with awe mixed with jealousy, and the heart of every man and boy brimmed with fear and desire. Yet no one was so shaken nor so flooded with terrible ardor as was Grantham Farby. From the opposite side of the room, he watched her descend like one might gaze at a meteor blazing slowly down from heaven itself, and, to him, the rubies in their diamond-crusted settings that glittered from her breast were mere embers to the sun.

"Oh, how beautiful she is," Lady Highleaf said absently, no less struck than anyone else.

"Quite," said Grant, overhearing her. He slowly shook himself from his thoughts, and he tried to swallow the lump that seemed caught in his breast. "Oh!," he said, "I think I see an old chum over there. Excuse me, if you will, Lady Highleaf."

Before she could protest, and just as Sheila entered the gathering, Grant hurried away toward one of the side doors, pulling a fellow along with him.

"Jonboy!" Farby said. "How wonderful it is to see you! Come, let's have a glass together."

The fellow obliged as he was fairly jerked away from the girl he had been speaking with, and the two young men disappeared.

"That annoying boy!" Lady Highleaf muttered. "Oh, good evening, Mr. Hanborn. I would love to dance, but I must greet Lady Shevalia."

Lady Highleaf made her way quickly across the room toward Sheila, who was only a few steps away from the stairs she had descended but was already surrounded by several ladies and many men. Lady Highleaf passed quickly by Lord Banis, who was staring at Shevalia with a look of complete and utter disbelief, for he had mistaken her for Esildre. So alike were Shevalia and Esildre in appearance and in bearing, so like shameless Esildre was Shevalia's attire, and still hot from Farby's insulting tone, Banis convinced himself immediately that this was some ploy, contrived by Lady Highleaf and Esildre, to shock and disconcert him. He picked up a glass of wine and quaffed it uncharacteristically, slamming it down onto the server's tray so hard that the stem broke, and then he made his way toward the two ladies.

Shevalia did not curtsey to her admirers, but dipped her head gracefully as they made their introductions.

"Lady Shevalia," one man said, offering his hand. "Allow me to introduce myself. Cargill Thornglass, at your service."

"I am pleased to make your acquaintance, sir," she answered. He bowed and kissed her hand, and she was not certain whether he gazed at her necklace or at her other nearby attributes, clearly visible between the folds of her gown. But she did not care. Why should she? She was Elifaen, and with that transformation there came to her a new way of being, one proud of who and what she now was, proud of her womanhood, her immortal body, and the power that she felt coursing across her very skin, down into her soul, and up into the sky. When she turned to greet another admirer, she displayed her exposed back to all. There, her new scars ran like lines of polished copper, following the curve of her waist to disappear into the low back of her gown.

Lord Banis stopped his advance, seeing her scars. Now he was convinced, for they were identical to Esildre's and could not be duplicated by any measure of paint or prowess. For the first time in many years, he suddenly did not know what he would say. Fortunately for him, Lady Highleaf was now at Shevalia's side, laughing and making proper introductions. Banis slowly continued to advance through the surrounding group, and those who recognized him bowed away while those who did not frowned at him as he squeezed through ahead of them.

"Ah, Lord Banis," Lady Highleaf said when she saw him. "Allow me to present Lady Shevalia."

"Lord Banis," Sheila said, giving him a lower dip of her head than she had to the others, and she offered her hand.

"Lady Shevalia," Banis said, bowing curtly and kissing her hand properly.

"I have heard of you," said Sheila. "You have a great deal of influence in Duinnor, or so I am told."

"That may be," answered Banis, somewhat squinting at her. There was something different about Esildre, some slight change in her complexion that baffled him, or a difference in how she smiled. "I have also heard of you, Lady Shevalia. Would you remind me of your House?"

"Pradkin, my lord. A virtually unknown and unnamed house of the Old Eastlands Realm, somewhat near to Tulith Attis, if you know the place."

Lord Banis nodded while, at the mention of the old fortress, a rare shiver ran up his neck.

"I do not know the house, but I know of the region. Who does not know of Tulith Attis? Yet, I think we have met."

"Have we? I would recall it, I am sure, for you are remarkably handsome, my lord. And you have the air of a Firstborn."

"That I am. Firstborn, that is to say."

"Lady Shevalia is new to town," interrupted Lady Highleaf, who was enjoying Banis's apparent awkwardness. "Perhaps you have read or heard of the unfortunate attack that took place against her guardian? Well, I insisted that she come to Starlight Hall and stay with me while all that was sorted out."

"Oh, yes. I did hear of it."

Lady Highleaf hesitated, wondering at his odd expression and his intense gaze at Sheila. It was Sheila who brazenly commented upon it.

"Why do you look at me so, my lord?" she asked calmly. "Have I already offended you in some way after such a short acquaintance? Or do you glare so at everyone that you meet?"

"My apologies. I was only somewhat shaken by how remarkable you are in appearance to someone else that I know."

"Oh? I have been told that before. Perhaps I have one of those faces, as they say, that looks like all others."

"No, certainly not."

"Who is it, may I ask, that you think I resemble?"

"Why, my daughter, no less. Esildre."

"Esildre? I have heard of her, too. Is she not Secundur's mistress?"

Banis instinctively stiffened, as did all else who listened in. As Sheila spoke the name, it seemed that the lamps in the place momentarily dimmed, the music struck a slightly discordant note, and many felt a sudden but brief chill. The moment passed, and Banis smiled.

"It is said that she was, for a time," Banis said smoothly.

"I would think that you would know if such was true," Sheila persisted, "being her father. And do you have any other children? I believe I heard that you do. Another daughter, in Vanara? And a son. Navis, I believe. Is that your son?"

"My other daughter was killed in battle. My son, too, is dead, my lady."

"Oh, I am sorry to hear that. How did he die, if you don't mind that I ask?"

Banis blinked. For the second time this evening, he felt accused, not by words but by the tone that he heard. Baffled by his daughter's innocent play-acting, he nonetheless could not bring himself to out her before the others. And before he could answer, Lady Highleaf once again intervened.

"Lady Shevalia, let us talk of happier things! Lord Banis, did you know that Lady Shevalia is an accomplished skater?"

"I beg your pardon, dear ladies," Banis said abruptly. "I just remembered that I must attend to some important business of the King before morning. If you would excuse me, I am afraid that I must take my leave of you. Lady Shevalia, it has been my pleasure. I hope to see you again. Lady Highleaf. Good evening to you both."

Banis bowed and walked quickly away. He went across the length of the hall toward the main stairs, marching right through the dancers in their ordered reel. He waved his arm at what he thought was a very large and insistent moth that suddenly fluttered past his nose, but was actually a small owl, the result of which was that he struck a dancer on the back of the head, requiring him to stop momentarily and offer a curt apology. He then quickly went up the stairs, ignoring those who bowed at his passing, and he walked almost at a trot to his carriage before the surprised footmen could even have it brought around for him.

"Take me home," he ordered his driver. "No! To the Palace!"

• • •

"Oh, my! I think he was upset by your brash questions," said Lady Highleaf. "And that's twice in one night that he has been flustered! I'm sure he'll try to spite us for it, too."

"I apologize, Lady Highleaf," said Sheila. "But I find it difficult not to say what I wish, these days."

"Well. In that case, let us make our way around the dancers to find a particular someone who shares that quality with you! This way, if you will. And, by the way, that is not the gown that I instructed to be laid out for you."

"No. But it suits my mood better."

"I see. I am sure we shall read all about it in tomorrow's broadsheets."

Before she could respond, Sheila heard the porter thump his staff and call out, "Misters Sootking, Brinnin, and Bosk!"

Looking up at the far stairs, Sheila saw the trio, and then she burst in to laughter. Ibin and Billy, in their fine velvet suits, were looking very smart, but it was Ashlord's appearance that made her nearly hysterical. He was dressed in a bright red longcoat, with red leather boots, red breeches, and a red, brimless hat. And, of course, he had the complexion to match.

"Oh, my word!" Lady Highleaf exclaimed, not the least bit amused at his outfit. "What has gotten into everyone? To make such a spectacle!"

"I can't say!" Sheila answered, trying to regain her composure.

"Well, I hope...oh, hello, Mr. Blithe."

"Lady Highleaf, how do you do?" A burly man in a black suit had suddenly appeared before the two ladies, and he bowed.

"Very well, thank you. Allow me to present Lady Shevalia."

"Ah, Lady Shevalia," said the man, bowing again to Sheila. "We have met before, and I do hope that you are fully recovered from the fall."

"Pardon me? The Fall?" Sheila asked, wincing at the sudden memory of her wings burning from her back as she plummeted.

"I was there," he explained. "At Miller's Pond. I, along with a few others, helped you into your carriage."

"Oh, sir! That! I'm sorry that I do not remember you. But I thank you for your kindness."

"It was nothing, my lady. I was glad to be of assistance."

"Thank you. And, yes, I am completely recovered."

"I am so glad to hear it. And to see you looking so radiant this evening!"

"Once more, I thank you, sir."

"Not at all, ma'am."

"Please do excuse us," said Lady Highleaf, impatiently craning her neck in an effort to see around Mr. Blithe. "We are just on our way to see someone."

Lady Highleaf only managed to escort Sheila a few more yards before their way was once again blocked by greeters, this time a group of ladies, all in even more revealing gowns than Sheila's, if that could be imagined.

"Lady Shevalia," said one of them even before being introduced. She was a woman of around forty with gray-streaked reddish hair and far too much rouge for her complexion. "I was just remarking on what a striking figure you have."

"Thank you—"

"And we were wondering if you might care to join us for a glass of wine? We were going to have some punch, but since Starlight cellars are next to none, we thought we'd sample the offering."

"Well, I—"

"This is Lady Truvilla," Lady Highleaf stiffly said to Sheila, "and Ladies Glanndire and Ballidora, all sisters, as you can see from their resemblance to one another."

"I'm pleased to meet you," Sheila said to them.

"Oh, and we are pleased to meet you at last," said Ballidora, a plumpish youngster of indeterminate age between fifteen and twenty-five. "We read all about the horrible attack upon the person of your guardian—"

"Bally!" said Glanndire, a blond young lady who casually fingered the emerald-studded chain around her neck as she tapped her younger sister on the shoulder with her fan. "I'm sure Shevalia has heard enough about that from everyone else." Then, smiling at Sheila, she went on, "I think we would be more interested in hearing about your home. Rumor has it that it is an ancient estate. Is that true?"

• • •

Having successfully avoided Lord Banis as he angrily charged through the foyer and out of Starlight Hall, and having made his grand entrance, Ashlord now led Billy and Ibin through the hall, giving their greetings and making their introductions. Since those already there could not all surround Lady Shevalia at once, and because many were passed by as Lady Highleaf attempted to lead Sheila through the place, many guests settled upon the next best thing which was, as many of them knew, the newly arrived trio of men who were Shevalia's close associates. Ashlord smiled and nodded amiably as he entered the crowd. Ibin grinned and bowed, dividing his attention equally between watching where he was going, gazing up at the acrobats floating overhead, and peering around in hope of taking another hors d'oeuvre from a passing tray. Billy trailed, tried to pay attention to everyone that was introduced to him, some by Ashlord, some by others, and he also tried his best to keep up with every word that Ashlord uttered. He was determined to take his cues from Ashlord, but it was difficult for him not to gawk at all of the beautiful ladies of the place, many of whom came straight up to him and introduced themselves with surprising enthusiasm. Billy knew that there was some method to Ashlord's advance through the crowd, skirting the dancers making their squares and runs, and that he would soon be called upon to give his story. He smiled nervously, nodded and bowed, and, much to his dismay, he had to break away from an especially pleasing and potentially fruitful conversation with a pretty young lady in order to hurry back to

Ashlord's side. All in all, Ashlord was pleased, Ibin was enthralled, and Billy was quite frustrated.

"Of all the places not to be on me own," he muttered, glancing at the fair lass he had just met and abandoned. Turning back, he nearly collided with a tall man in the green dress tunic of a Kingsman. Apologizing, he was about to move past the soldier when he looked again at the frowning face.

"Do I know ye?" Billy asked.

"If I am not mistaken, we met in the region of Edgewold," the man stated.

"Oh, right, I remember ye! Yer the silly basterd what took away our horses!" Billy blurted out.

"Ah, yes. I did my duty. And, some days later, I led a party to find you and your companions in order to offer them back."

"Ye did what?"

"When Teracue heard what I had done," the man said, "he was furious. Chewed me out with such a tongue lashing that I feared he would reduce me in rank on the spot!"

"An' well ye deserved it, I'd say."

"You speak your mind quite freely, sir," the Kingsman commented, appearing not the least disturbed by Billy's tone. "Just as my general eventually saw it, I had no choice. It was an unfortunate circumstance that his aides made the mistake of not rescinding our standing orders."

"Well," Billy squinted at the man, "I reckon yer a soldier an' must do as yer told 'til told otherwise."

"That is so. Still, I cannot fathom how on earth your company managed to elude us. We found your saddles and other belongings, and we tracked you from there all the way to Forest Islindia. When we found your tracks leading into that place, we all gave up hope that you would ever be seen again. And I was certain that I would lose my commission."

"Well, we made it through," Billy said. "An' I hope Teracue warn't too hard on ye."

"A strange thing," the Kingsman said. "As it turned out, Teracue seemed rather pleased that we did not find you. Said something about a summons unanswered being an answer unsummoned. Or some such. I was reassigned to Duinnor, and so I am here. My name is Blue, Tom Blue."

Billy shook the man's hand. "Billy Bosk."

"I would love to hear how you made it through Ibn Islindia."

"An' I'd love to tell ye," Billy said. "But I must stay with me companions, just yonder."

"I won't detain you, then."

"Ha! That's a good'un!" Billy laughed. The Kingsman chuckled, and offered his hand again.

"Perhaps we'll see each other later, then."

"Mebbe so!"

Billy pushed on through the crowd, taking a glass from a server as he went, and caught up with Ashlord and Ibin as Ashlord was finishing a brief chat with a little boy, bending down to speak to the child.

"...and that is why I am red all over, from head to toe!" he said to the lad.

"And did it hurt terribly?"

"Oh, no more than a passing pain, such as when you lick your fingers to snuff out a candleflame."

"Oh!"

"Now, where are your parents, young man? You should not be running about all by yourself. I am surprised that they do not watch you more carefully!"

"Oh, they watch me all the time, sir," the boy pointed upward, "and never let me out of their sight. And, when I get bigger, I'm going to join them up there!"

Billy felt a pang, knowing what it felt like to have a dead parent, even though he was just recently relieved of that sensation. That the child was already looking forward to rejoining his loved ones in the hereafter was quite upsetting to the Boskman.

"Ah, there you are!" Ashlord said to him. Seeing Billy's pained expression, Ashlord glanced at the little boy who was ambling off to accost someone else.

"Oh, no, you misunderstand. There they are!"

Billy followed Ashlord's upward gesture just as a pair of acrobats swept by, hand in hand in a graceful spin, the gauze of their wings spiraling around them.

"Oh! Right!"

"Now," Ashlord said so that only Ibin and Billy could hear, "I have made our presence known to those we need to speak with, so let us make our way easily toward those doors across the hall. Yes, Ibin, we shall first loiter at the side table."

• • •

The night went on. Certina tried her best to discombobulate or bedevil anyone she could, from the servers by landing on their trays, to the chamber ensemble at the balcony by variously darting past their noses or plucking with her beak the string of an idle cello. She tried her luck with innumerable ladies, spoiling their hair with her fluttering wings, or landing unceremoniously on the shoulder of a lord, only to be shooed away. She finally decided that she preferred the balcony, and she settled on the railing to lend her own piercing squawks to the music with such spirit and exuberance that Ashlord, hearing her from across the hall, burst into laughter as he picked up a fruit dainty.

"I ain't seen Lady Shevalia yet," said Billy.

"You *haven't* seen her."

"I know."

"Yes, you have."

"Huh?"

"You have looked straight at her exactly seventeen times so far this evening," Ashlord said, nodding as he chewed. "Mmmm. Very nice."

He gestured with his snack, and Billy looked to see Sheila not even ten yards away, facing away from them as she stood next to Lady Highleaf.

"Oh…my…GOSH!" he exclaimed, far too loudly. "Why, she's, that's, I mean, she's, ohmegosh!"

"Yes," Ashlord nodded, taking a glass of wine. "Quite stunning. And just the distraction that we need. Remember what I told you to say to Kecker when things get along. You'll see my signal."

"Yeah, yeah. I remember."

"So you may as well let our lady know that you are here, in keeping with our plan."

"Right away," Billy said as he emptied his glass and put it down. He tugged on his jacket, pulled on his frilly cuffs, and marched off.

"Hm!" Ashlord watched, taking a sip. "Can't say as I approve of her attire. But it does rather get the job done. Oh, well! She is who she is, now. Whoever that may be."

•　•　•

"Lady Shevalia, Lady Highleaf." Billy bowed low and elegantly. "I bid ye a good evenin', ladies!"

"Good evening, Mr. Bosk," said Lady Highleaf with an amused smile. "I hope you are enjoying yourself."

"Oh, I am, ma'am, I do say that I am!"

"How do you do tonight, Mr. Bosk?" Sheila asked. She smiled at her old friend, pleased and happy at how well he appeared in his fine velvet coat and breeches.

"Quite well, me lady," Billy bowed again, "I thank ye."

"I hope you will not feel compelled to keep a very close watch upon me tonight," Sheila said. "I think I am quite safe and in good company."

"Oh, no, Lady Shevalia. All is quite in hand, I want ye to know. I only wanted to make me greetin' an' let ye know that I am nearby."

"Thank you, Mr. Bosk. I am gratified by the gesture."

"Then I'll leave ye to yer many admirers."

Billy bowed again, and returned to Ashlord.

"Very good, Billy," Ashlord said. "Now, that door there. Ibin, keep an eye on Lady Shevalia, please. But do not disturb her unless absolutely required."

"Yes, sir. I'll, I'll, Iwill."

Ashlord led the way, and Billy followed him through a side door into a hallway. They passed a room wherein several older gentlemen were sitting in comfortable chairs drinking and smoking their pipes, past another room where some animated discussion was taking place among a group of young men, and then walked farther down to the next door. Ashlord glanced up and down the hall, then quickly opened the door and entered, closing it after Billy. Within was a small dimly-lit library with dark glass-doored cabinets, a few tables and chairs, and a fireplace that had been allowed to burn low. Four men were there, two standing up from their chairs when they entered, and the other two bent over some maps spread across the table.

"Ah, Ashlord," said one older man as he came over to shake Ashlord's hand. "It is good to have this chance to speak."

"Yes, at last. Allow me to introduce Mr. Bilaylin Bosk, of Bosk Manor, the Old Eastlands Realm. This is Lord Arata, one of seven Supreme Judges of Duinnor that oversee all lesser judges and their courts."

"Pleased to meet ye, Lord Arata."

"And you, sir. Ashlord knows all who are here with me, but let me introduce you to them. This is General Chadler of the Kingsman First Army. He is third in command over all Kingsmen in Duinnor, and has extensive experience here and abroad. He just completed a five-year tour of duty as head of the King's Palace Guard, until the term of his posting there ended. He now serves as commander of the City Kingsmen, those who act as law enforcement officers within the city. This is General Kecker, who is Kingsman liaison with the Foreign Ministry. And this is Ambassador Burgee, of Glareth. I'm afraid Ambassador Galdarin of Vanara could not attend, with all that is taking place."

Billy bowed and shook hands with all of the men, readying himself for the interview.

"Ashlord, I profoundly regret that Raynor is still under arrest," Lord Arata said. "He has not been charged. A writ of habeas corpus was submitted for Lord Banis to present to the King, but Banis refuses to inform us if or when it was presented. Moreover, he will not answer our inquiries as to Raynor's condition. I am sorry that there is not much more that I can do on my own. But I shall be attending a Conclave of Judges in ten days, and I hope to convince them to add their names to a new writ."

"I appreciate your efforts, Lord Arata. Raynor's fate is not in our hands, it seems. Our other work must move forward, regardless."

"We quite understand," Ambassador Burgee said. "Along those lines, perhaps we might now hear, in as much detail as possible, the news concerning the situation in the east. In two days, I am to send my regular dispatch down the Osterflo to Prince Carbane, and I would like to include any pertinent news."

"Certainly, Ambassador. But first allow me to ask General Kecker if there has been any news from the Triumvirate delegation here in Duinnor concerning the Eastlands?"

"No, I am afraid all is quiet. I have not made stringent inquiries, though, not wishing to tip our hand."

"I see," nodded Ashlord. "Ah, you have some maps out. May I take a look before we begin?"

"Certainly," said General Chadler, puzzled by Ashlord's request. As the general showed Ashlord the maps, Ashlord made a slight nod to Billy, who went to stand next to General Kecker.

"Genr'l Kecker," Billy said, "I heard tell ye like to fish."

"Oh, I have drowned a worm or two," replied the Kingsman, his brows raised. "Do you have an interest in such?"

"Why, no, not so much meself, sir. But me employer, Lady Shevalia, drops a line when she takes the notion. That is, when she ain't losin' arrows in the shrubbery."

"What do you mean? She enjoys archery, too? Why that is also a keen interest of mine."

"Ye don't say?"

• • •

While Ashlord and Billy began their meeting, Grant Farby, only a few doors down, listened distractedly as several of his former schoolmates debated the news.

"It means war," said one young man in Kingsman regalia. "I am certain of it. I mean, would we tolerate such an attack upon our King?"

"I agree," said another fellow. "Vanarans are fiercely loyal to their Queen."

"But she wasn't there."

"Doesn't matter. It was still an attack upon her realm."

"I don't know. Even if they were Duinnor Regulars who did it, who's to say they weren't some rogue band of overzealous men, like those Banis has in his pocket?"

"No matter. It was still an act of war."

"You've been awfully quiet, Farby. What do you say?"

Until now, Grant only leaned against the mantel, staring at the fire, thinking little of the conversation as it went back and forth.

"Vanara and Duinnor may go to war with each other over many things," he said, "but this is not one of them. Seafar is too wise to permit it. There are over six thousand Duinnor Regulars in Vanara, and four thousand Kingsmen. So Seafar will do nothing rash. My guess is that he will move to have the Regulars withdrawn. They are ever seeking spoils and making mischief. The Kingsmen are better respected, and better disciplined, so he probably won't push to have them removed."

Farby turned away from the fire to see that all were hanging on his words.

"But who can say? We have abused Vanara for centuries. And they burn with resentment against us. If there is to be war between Duinnor and Vanara, it will be due to longstanding rifts between us, rather than a result of this incident. My concern is not that Vanara will make war on us, but that we might make war upon them."

"Why ever would Duinnor attack Vanara?"

"To punish Vanara for executing that captain. Faradan, I believe his name was. Trying and executing him was in violation of our treaties. Some in Duinnor will view that as all the excuse we need to overthrow Serith Ellyn and to take from Vanara what we haven't already managed to steal."

"Farby, old man, your opinion borders upon treason."

"Call it what you will, Reggie. I never swore the Kingsman oath, remember. They didn't let me graduate. As a citizen, I am sworn to obey and defend Duinnor, not the King."

"The King *is* Duinnor!"

"I beg to differ. Duinnor was here before the Unknown Kings, and will be here after they are all gone."

• • •

"It was my desire for you to meet my nephew," said Lady Highleaf to Sheila in a rare moment of peace when no one needed to be introduced, addressed, or avoided. "His parents are dancing just there, so he must still be here, somewhere. I imagine he has ensconced himself in some side room, for crowds make him petulant and restless. But I do have another surprise for you that I know will not run away and hide. It has been in preparation for over a week, and I think you will like it."

"I am sure I will, whatever it is," Sheila said. "But I see someone approaching who seems to desire my attention."

"Oh?" Lady Highleaf turned and saw General Kecker approaching. "Oh. Him."

"Lady Highleaf, how do you do?"

"General Kecker. I am well, thank you. May I introduce Lady Shevalia?"

"I am quite honored." General Kecker bowed and kissed Sheila's hand. "And I was just speaking with one of your companions, a Mr. Bosk."

"Oh?"

"Why, yes. And he tells me that you are particularly fond of hunting and angling?"

"Angling, sir?"

"Fishing, my lady. With hook and line."

"Oh! Yes, I have done a bit of that."

"And, or so he tells me, you are quite the expert with bow and arrow, too."

"I have managed to place a few arrows where I intended."

"Well, then! We have much to talk about! I am something of an expert in both activities. Might I trouble you for this dance while we share our notions on those topics?"

"General Kecker," Lady Highleaf began, shaking her head to put off the Kingsman. Before she could prevent it, Sheila took the general's offered elbow.

"I would be delighted," Sheila said, winking at Lady Highleaf. "I hope you have thick boots on, for I tend to step on more toes than tile when dancing."

"Oh, I doubt that!"

Lady Highleaf watched them go to the dance floor, then she heaved a sigh of despair. It was all according to plan, she knew. Still, she thought, why couldn't Ashlord get rid of Kecker with one of his conjurer's tricks?

• • •

"An' thar ye have it, gentlemen," Billy concluded. "The Redvests made it all the way north to Barley, without the least bit o' trouble. An', word is, they cleaned out the place, movin' everythin' useful to supply armies down south."

Billy looked at Ashlord, who nodded, quite satisfied with the way Billy had handled himself, relating only the gist of events.

"Now, before I relate what I know about Tallinvale," Ashlord took up before questions could be asked, "let us skip ahead somewhat and hear what Mr. Bosk has to say about the Dragonkind seen on the Plains of Bletharn. And then he will tell us about events in and around Edgewold, to add to the reports you have already received about the Wickerman uprising."

"Right," nodded Billy. "So we were travelin' along from east to west, mindin' our own business, ye see."

Ashlord moved into the shadows once more, giving Billy ample space to gesticulate. While Billy told the gathering about the Dragonkind and the hidden well, Ashlord watched the reactions of those present. Already they wore solemn looks, but now their expressions became stern, jaws set, and General Chadler paced back and forth on the far side of the room as he listened to Billy. Billy did an admirable job of staying to the subject, and also of going right into the battle at Soltani Pass. When he described the monster that was encountered later on the day of the battle, the mood in the room was positively grim. When Billy completed this part of his tale, Ashlord stepped up again.

"Now, you must wonder why I encouraged General Kecker to leave our meeting," Ashlord said. "His ties to Tracia are close, and it is known that his sympathies are with the Triumvirate and their Redvests. You saw how smug he appeared, and was not concerned in the least to hear Mr. Bosk's report. It would have done no harm for him to remain for that part of our discussion, but what I am about to tell you he must not know, else I fear he will warn his Tracian friends who are in attendance here tonight. You have already had word from me concerning Lord Tallin's plan to draw in as much Redvest strength as he can and to engage them as long as possible. He has done so, and Tallinvale has been under siege these many weeks. I have recently learned more concerning the situation there. To cut a long tale short, after an epic march across the plains, General Teracue and the Fourth Army arrived in Tallinvale and joined in the fighting there, helping Tallinvale to utterly defeat the besieging Redvests. The siege of Tallinvale failed, and now there is a Kingsman army in the Eastlands. Precisely what the Triumvirate feared the most."

"You don't say!"

"That's incredible news! Wonderful!"

"That old Teracue! Only he and the Fourth could achieve such a feat!"

"Gentlemen," Ashlord interrupted their celebratory outbursts, "it is but a small victory for our side, in the great scope of things. No doubt you have had reports sent by General Teracue whilst he was still at Edgewold concerning those Dragonkind that Mr. Bosk and his party saw."

"Tonight is the first that I have heard of it," Ambassador Burgee stated, "and I find it most alarming!"

"It is being kept secret," said General Chadler. "High Command does not wish for word to leak out before we have had an opportunity to hear back from our own sorties sent forth from Duinnor to scour the plains."

"An understandable stance," said Ashlord. "However, it seems likely, almost a certainty, that the Redvest overlords and the Dragonkind have reached an accord. Certain people that I know in the south have sent replies to my inquiries that seem to confirm it. Their plan seems obvious. The Triumvirate will send their armies to take Masurthia, and the Dragonkind will take Altoria. The two armies will join and march north against Duinnor. That is why Tracia needs all of the supplies it can obtain, and why Dragonkind advance parties dig wells."

"Ashlord, the Dragonkind must know they cannot pass through The Mirse as they did during their Great Invasion," said Chadler. "It is too well fortified against them. That only leaves the mountains of Tulivana and the Hinderlands as an invasion route."

"But how will the Dragonkind cross the Hinderlands?" asked Lord Arata.

"My question, exactly," said Chadler.

"How matters little, my lord, since it is unlikely we could stop them at this late date," answered Ashlord. "Suffice to say they must have found a way through. I would send fast riders south, if I were you, General Chadler, to raise the alarm in Altoria and Masurthia. I am certain that Lord Seafar has had a report from Commander Tallin, and has already sent his messengers to Altoria and Masurthia. But it may be wise to add your concerns to his, so that they will take the warnings seriously. There is always a chance, if Altoria is vigilant, that they may discover the method by which the Dragon King plans to send his hordes through the Hinderlands. At the very least, perhaps our warnings will prevent Altoria from being taken by surprise, but they might also manage to mount an effective defense."

"Masurthia cannot hope to withstand the Redvests," said General Chadler. "It has virtually no standing army, and is in complete disarray, with internal squabbles between its regents and the Ruling Prince, who is not yet of age to govern. Even if Tallinvale turns its forces southward, Lord Tallin and Teracue cannot reduce the Redvests enough for Masurthia to defeat them."

"I know. Still, Masurthia and Altoria might slow our enemies by fighting rearguard actions as they retreat northward. That could give Duinnor time to arouse its might and join with Vanara."

"I do not wish to be premature," said Lord Arata, "but my contacts in the Dragonlands say that there is great unrest in the southern deserts and in the river valleys near the sea. Conscription of soldiers and laborers has increased over the past year, and darakal elixir is being more freely distributed to the army, presumably to build the strength of their soldiers. It might be time to act."

"Do we have the means to foster an uprising?" asked Chadler.

"Not a general uprising, no. But Gurasa is still alive. His people are loyal to him, and many others will rally to his banner. He seems willing to mount an insurgent campaign against Belsalza. But he needs assurances that we will provide supplies via the Free City and will keep our forces out of the desert."

"That is hardly an option," said General Chadler. "Only the King may order such support, otherwise it would be considered treason. And Serith Ellyn would have to agree to it, as well."

"An uprising in the desert lands would come too late, I think," said Ashlord. "At any rate, arms could not be prepared and shipped in time. What is of greater concern is that the invasion from the south is but one threat that looms. I fear that the moves by Tracia and the Dragonkind are but the opening gambits in a far worse attack being prepared."

"Oh?" Lord Arata said. "What do you mean?"

"I will tell you in a moment, but perhaps you could tell me what it would take to convene a Congress of the Seven Realms?"

"A Congress?"

"Only the King may call for that," said General Chadler. "It has not been done in, well, not since before I was born."

"Nor in my lifetime, either," said Ambassador Burgee.

"Nor mine," added Lord Arata. "It would take a general outcry over some situation, I imagine, before the King is moved to do so. Once or twice it has come up as a petition, but it was never done."

"Then perhaps it would be a good idea to let the city's printers know what is afoot abroad," suggested Ashlord. "There are at least three competing broadsheets each day, are there not?"

"Yes. And two weeklies."

"I do not suggest that we incite panic, only, shall we say, serious concern?" Ashlord said with a slight twinkle in his eye.

"I believe it would be a start. It would have to be done very carefully," said Ambassador Burgee. "And since it would be too risky for any one of you, I shall take it upon myself to get the word to the various broadsheet proprietors. At Lady Highleaf's insistence, each of them is in attendance here this very night. At any rate, I'll see to it that each is given, for starters, a tantalizing note. And they will be the recipients of a more detailed letter well before dawn. Do you think that will do?"

"I think it would be an admirable start," said Ashlord. "Hopefully, within but a few days, we can raise such a furor of concern that the King will be forced to convene a Congress."

"Now, what about that other attack you mentioned?" asked General Chadler.

"Yes. You have all heard and read the reports from Vanara concerning the attack on the Queen's Palace. So I will tell you now the true reason why Mr. Bosk and the rest of our company traveled west, why Commander Tallin and Robby Ribbon went to Vanara while the others of our party came here, and why Commander Tallin and Robby Ribbon were the targets of the attack that took place in Linlally. And, as you are certainly aware of the black eagles that have been a common sight over Duinnor these past many years, you may anticipate some of what I shall say. Billy, would you be so kind as to stand watch in the hall, for safety's sake."

"Certainly, Ashlord."

Billy closed the door behind him, and Ashlord turned back to his co-conspirators.

"What I have to tell you now has to do not with Tracia or the Dragonkind, but with demons, witches, monsters, the Bell of Tulith Attis, and, I hope, the next King of Duinnor."

● ● ●

"Oh, let us sit, I beg you!" panted Kecker, red-faced with exhaustion, his forehead beaded with perspiration. Four dances in a row with Lady Shevalia had quite done him in, and he put his hands on his knees momentarily to catch his breath. Sheila looked at him, smiling with amusement, appearing as fresh and lovely as when Kecker first saw her.

"Oh, but the music starts again!" she said.

"No, no! Please. Perhaps I might escort you aside for a less strenuous chat and a glass of refreshment?"

"Well, I suppose so."

They made their way to the servers, and General Kecker took two glasses of punch from a tray.

"Your archery skills must be..." He turned around, holding out a glass for Sheila, but she was gone. "...remarkable," he said, looking in vain for her.

In fact, Sheila had been unceremoniously pulled away by the very insistent Lady Highleaf.

"I must stay with Kecker," Sheila protested. "Ashlord counts on me to keep him occupied."

"That is well in hand, my dear, I do assure you," said Lady Highleaf.

Glancing back, Sheila saw General Kecker, craning his neck to find her, reluctantly handing a glass to the giggling Lady Bunsit, who immediately put it on the tray then dragged the hapless general back to the dance floor.

"My nephew has evidently flown the coop," Lady Highleaf said as she pulled Sheila through a private door. "But just so that the evening may not be a complete loss for you, I do have something else to share with you."

She led Sheila down a long hallway, through a door, then outside and down a flight of steps to a wide flat space under the stars.

"I have had my people working on this just for you. I think you'll need to sit on this bench just here."

"Why? What are you up to? What? Are these my skates?"

"Yes, they are," Lady Highleaf replied. Sheila looked more closely and saw stars reflected before her. Lady Highleaf then clapped her hands twice, and servants immediately began reaching with their long matches to light the many lamps atop posts that surrounded the area. Soon a wide circle of light illuminated a large frozen pool.

"I thought you might enjoy this," she said. "And I have not yet had a chance to see you on the ice. It is as wide around as Miller's Pond, and as solid as a rock."

"You made this? For me?" Sheila asked, quickly kicking off her slippers and putting on her skates.

"Of course, and why not? I know you are impervious to cold, now. But I am not. After I watch for a few moments, you shall have the place all to yourself, except for a few who will remain to look to your needs, should you have any."

"Oh, wonderful!" Sheila exclaimed, standing and kissing Lady Highleaf. "Thank you!"

"It is my way of thanking you, my dear. It isn't every day that someone like you comes along. You give me the pleasure of your friendship for its own sake, in spite of my overbearing ways."

"But you have done so much for me already."

"Then your enjoyment shall be my reward!"

• • •

"I don't know about you, Farby, but...Farby? Now where did he get off to?"

Farby was chatting with Billy in the hallway, having slipped out during a heated argument between his friends concerning the best way to defend Duinnor's interests.

"No, sir," replied Billy to Farby's query. "Just a private chat they're havin', I think. Between old friends, I gather."

"I see. And have you had a chance to enjoy the party?"

"Not so much. I've been keepin' close to Ashlord. Just in case thar's another attempt on the feller."

"Oh. But you are unarmed."

"I know. They took me weapons at the door. But I still got these!" Billy held up his fists.

"Watch it, there!"

"Oh, I'm very sorry 'bout that misunderstandin', I truly am," Billy said, referring to the jab to Farby's nose when he brought Sheila home on the day that her Scathing began.

"I was joking! You've apologized a thousand times, already. If you like, I can stand watch for you. Go have some refreshment, or a round on the dance floor, if you wish. If you are needed, I'll send someone for you."

"Hm. It's awful temptin'."

"Go ahead. I have my fists, too, you know."

"Well, maybe just for a sip. I'm awful parched. I won't be long. An' if they come out, just tell 'em ye threatened to sock me if I didn't go."

"I shall do so! Tell them, that is."

Farby watched Billy go, then put his ear to the door that Billy had been guarding. Hearing nothing more discernable than a word here and there, he shrugged and sat down across the hallway in a chair, leaning back so that the front legs were off the floor and the chair's back propped him up against the wall. He longed to go back out into the crowd, sure that he would see Shevalia instantly, but not at all certain that he would know what to say. Since the incident with the men in the alley, and after having gone to Mr. Sootking, whom he now knew as Ashlord, he had not ventured back to Crescent Avenue. He dearly wanted to visit, but had refrained from the temptation. He had obtained every assurance from Ashlord that Lady Shevalia was fully recovered from the Scathing. And, whereas before he knew that it was unlikely that she and he could ever come to have the relationship that he desired, now that she was Elifaen the gulf between them was impossibly immense. It would only be torture to see her, as wonderful as that torture might be.

Farby could not know how similar his feelings were to Robby's, a person whose existence he knew nothing of. And Robby, unaware of Sheila's affect upon Farby, had not been watching during any of the times when the two had been together, or else he might have seen the ardor in Farby's eyes or manner.

Still, they both felt the impossibility of having her love. Robby, at least, had much to occupy himself, which helped to keep him out of the emotional mire that Farby sank into. Some honorable men, when faced with unrequited love, threw themselves into terrible and risky adventures, as if life no longer mattered, marching off to war or sailing away upon the high seas, or contriving to insult others sure to call them out to a dueling place. Others, less honorable, drank heavily, or fitfully turned to other women that they could not love, growing resentful and sullen as time passed by. But Grantham Farby was neither of those kinds of men. He was honorable, but he suddenly had no desire for adventure. He could not drink his woes away, he knew, and it would be pointless to try. And, unless he was badly mistaken, he would never meet anyone that could make his heart spark brighter with such magic hope and excitement as Shevalia had done, and he could not see how he could even feign satisfaction with another woman. Farby was resolved in the hopelessness of his feelings. Yet it was in his nature, always somewhat contrary in attitude, to maintain just the very hope that was so impossible. If only he had the courage to stand before her and to declare himself fully to her. No. It was impossible. It was preposterous that she could have the least interest in him. Or was it? Such was his torment, back and forth, from determination to despair.

Suddenly the door opened and Ashlord emerged, surprised to see Farby and not Billy. Farby quickly righted his chair and stood, mumbled his explanation to Ashlord, then excused himself to hurry off. He found his way around to the kitchens, wandered the back halls and passageways of Starlight Hall, his mind still distracted by his previous thoughts, making his way aimlessly.

● ● ●

If only Farby knew what was in Sheila's heart since she had become Elifaen, it might have served as a severe tonic to him, ending forever any glimmer of hope he could ever have for her. For the moment, however, Sheila skated on the lamplit ice. The wind of her motion tugged at her gown, and the cold air invigorated her. She had thought she would never desire to skate again, so dark was the Scathing that she associated with her last outing. But she could not resist Lady Highleaf's gesture. And now that she turned and spun once more, she let the memories of her Scathing flood through her, unafraid of them, knowing that she could take the sorrow and could live through it to yet another endless moment. She knew that, somewhere, someone loved her. Not like Ashlord, who was like a father to her, and not like Lady Highleaf, or even Billy or Ibin, who were her good friends. Someone who knew her and who loved her before, who could still love her now. Someone who, if he was alive, would someday be like her, immortal, like the first children of the earth. Now she had time to find him, and for him to find her, even if it took a thousand years. What did it matter whether or not he ever became King? When, not if, they found each other again, things would be different. She was healed, and he was wiser, surely. They could have the family they longed for. Let the rest of the world be damned. He was all she needed. And she knew, as sure as she felt the burning on her back, he was all she had ever really wanted.

The slide of her skates, the air rushing past, and the reel now wafting from an opened window gave Sheila the sensation that she was dancing. It was as if she flew through the night sky, with the stars in the cold heavens above her head and those reflected on the icy surface below her feet all shining steadily, the Five Stars of Duinnor her companions, and the winter constellations her escorts. The music reached an end, and just as she turned and came to a stop, she saw a figure floating toward her from the other side of the ice, the shadowed shape of a man outlined by the lamplight behind him. She caught her breath with surprise, not daring to move. The man drew near without moving his feet, his arms down at his side, and as the orchestra struck up a waltz, the man halted close enough to touch her. He bowed.

"May I have the honor of this dance, my lady?" asked Farby.

"I suppose it would be alright," she said, relieved that it was Farby. He put her hand on his shoulder, his own on her waist as he took her other hand. "I'm not sure—"

"Sh-h!" he softly said.

Together they pushed off. His hand was firm, but yielding, and soon they were spinning together along a wide orbit on the frozen pool. She sensed his lead and turned as he indicated, and he quickly got the sense of her strength and sureness. Together they made their dance, and then he let go of her waist, giving her room to twirl around and around, coming out in a straight flight across the center, hand in hand, he going backwards with his arm outstretched and his hand in hers, pulling her smoothly along. She bent forward, letting her trailing leg lift, stretching the distance between them until only their fingertips touched. She spun around and reversed so that he held her close, his arms around her as they continued going backwards, her head tilted back onto his shoulder, her eyes closed. He spun her around, and she hooked a leg around his waist as he placed his hands firmly on hers. Bending backwards with her arms out, she let him pull her swiftly along with a power and grace that she would have not credited him to have before this moment.

Thus she let him speak to her, not with words, but with motion and strength and gentle urgency. It was a tale of longing, of loneliness, and of love. It was a flood of emotion too powerful to withstand, of hope, of futility, and of loss such as only mortals could face, when all moments may end and the memory of beauty and of pain pass away. And yet it was a flight of ecstasy, joining the two together with unashamed elation. For Sheila, it was heavenly joy, unfettered of the weight of history, and of sweetness unsoured by wistful regret. Thus, she discovered that she was wrong, so wrong, and was reminded of how she had felt, once upon a time, when she thought herself unfit for Robby's love. Here was Farby, not an Elifaen, but a man, only a man. And he, too, loved her. It was terrible, beautiful and terrible, and she suddenly wanted to love him, too. She needed to love him, and she desired his love of her. When the moment came to a close, when the music's final note faded away into the night sky, they came to a stop face to face under the stars. They kissed, long and fully. She felt her face redden and her heart beat as it had not done since she had become Elifaen. She looked into his eyes, sinking into the pool of his gaze. They put their arms around each other, and held each other close, her head on his shoulder.

"Oh, Grant!" she said, oblivious of the dull, clinking sounds that came into the place. "I did not know. But it cannot be. You and I, it cannot be."

She felt his back stiffen and his head move, and she knew that her words hurt him. Looking up, she saw such an expression of anguish on his face that she was taken aback. His eyes were wide, his jaw set as he pushed her around and behind him. Following his gaze, she saw, hovering at the edge of the frozen pool, the unmistakable shape of a red door, and Kingsmen fanning out to either side of it.

Chapter 12

A Gift for Lady Highleaf

Ashlord watched Billy dance with his lovely partner, his spidery movements and exaggerated steps miraculously replaced by an almost normal manner of dancing. In what must have been an extreme effort of restraint on Billy's part, he only occasionally dipped his partner too low or kicked his legs too high, all the while smiling, chin up, his demeanor gentlemanly and proper.

"Will wonders never cease?" Ashlord commented to Certina, now on his shoulder. Nearby, Ibin stood, his little finger protruding from his wineglass. Ashlord was about to take a dainty from a passing tray when he felt a hand on his elbow, pulling him away.

"Come quickly!" Lady Highleaf said, tugging his sleeve. "Shh! This way!"

Ashlord followed her through a side door, and she hurried him down a hallway, then turned into a parlor. Sheila came to him as soon as they entered.

"They have taken Grant!" she cried, tears running down her face. "The Red Door came, and Kingsmen! They led Grant away!"

"Ashlord, you must do something!" Lady Highleaf demanded. "You must go after him and stop Banis! I know Banis is behind it!"

"I don't see what I can do," Ashlord said. "When did they go?"

"Only moments ago!" Sheila said, taking Ashlord's hand. "It is all my fault! I insulted Banis in front of everyone!"

"No, my dear!" Lady Highleaf said. "I'm sure it wasn't on your account Grantham was taken. Ashlord, my nephew had words with Lord Banis earlier this evening. He has always been an impertinent boy! Oh, what am I to say to his parents?"

"Calm! Calm!" Ashlord commanded, and immediately the women stepped back in silence. "Allow me a moment to think."

Ashlord paced back and forth, his head down in thought. Whenever Sheila or Lady Highleaf made to speak, he held his finger up to stop them.

"Why would the King wish to summon Farby?" he muttered. "How could Banis know what Farby did?"

Ashlord stopped his pacing as he settled upon a plan. He looked from Lady Highleaf to Sheila, then nodded.

"There is only one way that I know of to intervene so quickly," he said. "Lady Highleaf, go fetch General Chadler. Bring him here immediately!"

● ● ●

As Ashlord drew together a scheme that he thought might free Grant Farby, Robby pored over the lists that Finn had delivered to him. Between Finn, Micerea, and Lafkin, over sixty candidates had already been identified for service in Griferis, more than he had hoped for at this early stage. None had homes or families, and none seemed obliged to the rulers of the Dragonlands or the Seven Realms. Most were impoverished craftsmen and service people who had lost their positions to one unfortunate circumstance or other, and some were renegades that Lafkin was certain would not survive the desert due to their unwillingness to sink into thievery and murder. Robby knew that it was a great chance they would be taking by bringing unfamiliar people to Griferis, and that it would only take one or two malcontents to upset things. But with Finn's growing dreamwalking skills, along with those other dreamwalkers that would, Robby hoped, soon be recruited and trained, they could perhaps be watched over for signs of impending misbehavior.

"That's a ways off, yet. Meanwhile, we'll just have to risk it." He got up to pull some maps down from a shelf. "Now all we have to do is get them here."

"My lord," Finn said as he approached from the doorway.

"Ah, Finn, how are you?"

"Well. And you, sire?"

"I am fine. Just going over the names on the lists. I think we are ready to begin."

"And have you found a way to bring these people here safely?"

"Yes. All is nearly arranged. You and Micerea must prepare the way by going to each of them with my invitation and my instructions, should they accept. But there are two people that I would like for you to visit, once you have seen Micerea."

● ● ●

Finn departed to begin the task. The first person he went to was the elderly Lord Threshmere. He found Threshmere dreaming of the past, of the days when his wife was still alive and they picnicked together with their newborn son on the hills above their estate. But before Finn found the heart to interrupt, Sir Wind jostled one of the shutters of the old hall and banged it harshly, waking Lord Threshmere. The old man threw his feet over the side of his bed, pulled on his robe, and shuffled with a candle through the dark and dusty house, and met Borwain coming from a side room.

"It was only the wind on a shutter, my lord," said Borwain. "I latched it and tied it with twine. I am sorry that it woke you."

"Do not be sorry," said the old man, putting his arm around Borwain's shoulders as he led the young man back. "I would have taken care of it. You should not be out of bed on such a cold night. Go back immediately. I think I'll take a walk about the place before I turn in again."

"Are you sure that you wouldn't like a cup of tea, sir?"

"Oh, no. Here we are, go in and rest easy, lad."

"I shall. You too, my lord."

Finn watched as Lord Threshmere leaned Borwain's crutch at the bedside and helped the young man pull the covers up around him.

"You should not serve me so," said Borwain, "for it is not your place, as I always say."

"Hush. You forget yourself. I am lord of this house, and shall do as I like."

"Yes, my lord."

Threshmere left the bedroom and pulled the door to, then shuffled a few steps away and halted. Finn saw the candle in Threshmere's hand shake, and then the old man wiped his eyes. Instead of walking about the house as he said he would do, Threshmere went back to his own bed, put out the candle, and lay awake for a long time with his eyes open, listening to the wind. But he eventually did go back to sleep only to have a frustrating dream wherein he could not find the proper papers on his desk, irritated by the ivy that kept inking its way across every page he picked up.

"Good sir," Finn said, stepping forward.

"Who are you?" Threshmere demanded. "Have you come from Duinnor to return the leases to me?"

"No, sir. I come from elsewhere with questions for you."

"More questions! It figures! What do you want to know now? How many crooked nails there are in this house? Or the size and weight of each chipmunk in the south wing? Or, perhaps you would like to inquire as to the style and manner of hats that rot in my closets?"

"No, sir. I care not for your hats, your chipmunks, nor even your nails. I am sent by a New King of a New Kingdom. Through me, he asks if you and Borwain would be willing to serve him. Would you?"

"What king? What kingdom? And what makes you think that we might serve another king? You are most impertinent, I think."

"My king says that you long for honor for yourself and Borwain. It is in Griferis, and under King Philawain that you may find new honor and purpose."

"Griferis?" Threshmere stopped shuffling through papers and stared at Finn. "I have heard of that place, sir. It is not a place for kings, but a place where, it is said, future kings are judged."

"That was once true. But it has been overthrown and transformed. King Philawain rules Griferis, and he needs good men who can be loyal servants. He instructs me that, since your own king does not respect you, in spite of your loyal service to him, perhaps you would not mind serving another for the period of one year. Philawain, King, instructs me to say to you that in return for one year of good service, he will have all of your leases restored to you, with a bounty for your grievances against Duinnor."

"He does, does he? I am a Kingsman, sir. I remain loyal to the one and only King of the Seven Realms, and will not be turned against him for some upstart warlord, no matter what grand title he claims to have, or what place he calls his kingdom!"

"King Philawain hoped that you would respond in such a manner. He says to tell you that he does not ask you to be disloyal to Duinnor or to its King. Indeed, it is his aim to save Duinnor from folly, and to preserve the throne of Duinnor under a New King, before that realm is lost forever."

Threshmere looked askance at Finn, then was distracted by the window. Outside it was fully dark, and stars shown brilliantly, even though the room was lit within by the light of day. He turned back to Finn and saw that behind the messenger were snow-capped mountains, and a marvelous castle resting on a cloud.

"Behold Griferis!" said Finn. "It is here that King Philawain bids you come, with Borwain, to serve for a year."

"This is a dream? It must be. For I do not recall mountains in my hallway."

"It is a dream, indeed. And Philawain is the King of Griferis and the Lord of Dreams. I am his servant, sent by him to you. As a sign that this is a true message, ask Borwain to tell you what manner of dream that he has had this night, and think on what I have said to you. I shall return to you in two nights for your answer."

• • •

Finn departed from Lord Threshmere and continued on to the next person on his list. While he did so, Micerea revisited a dreamer she had contacted already. He was a blacksmith's apprentice of Vanara, a youngish man, made old by his worries, who had spent twenty years under a master smithy. But he was let go without prospects or expectations when the smithy's son came home from service in the army and needed work. The destitute man had a young wife who was with child, and Micerea had discovered him, and first entered his dreams, while he was in the jail of Linlally, having been caught stealing oats from a stable so that his wife could make porridge. He was released after three days, on the word of an acquaintance, and given two silver coins, too, with which he had purchased as much grain as he could, along with a sack of coal for his hut. When Micerea finally located him once more, he sat with a blanket over his shoulders beside the straw mattress on which his wife slept. He nodded off to sleep, and slumped against the bed.

"I dream of you once more," he said to Micerea. "It is strange that I dream of a Dragonkind, for none of my own people can help me. But this dream is more pleasant than my others, full as they are of anxiety and terror. I prefer to remain in my dreams, rather than waking, for my waking thoughts are filled with despair."

"This is no mere dream, and tonight I shall give you proof of it. In the morning, ask your wife about her own dreams, and you will see. I repeat my King's offer to you. If you would serve him for a year, he will see to it that your child will not starve, nor your wife. You and she, when she is able, and if she wishes it, will have honorable work, too. Do you remember the offer made to you?"

"Yes, now I do. I was in jail when last you came to me. Did you also see to it that I was released? That my old acquaintance spoke for me and gave me his silver coins?"

"No, he did that out of the kindness of his own heart."

"Oh."

"Have you considered the King's offer?"

"I have. I would readily accept, but for my wife who, as you can see, is in no condition to travel."

"Then, if you are determined, a way will be made for you. On the night of the full moon, take your wife and go to the top of the hill that is behind the old river keep some mile or so from your hut. Tell no one! Carry only that which you can strap to your backs. You will not need food or coin. Dress very warmly for the cold night air, more warmly than you think you ought. When you reach the hill, you might meet others who, like you, wish for a better life. You and the others who wish to come to the Kingdom of Griferis must be fearless and patient! The King will send for you. Be not afraid of the King's messengers, who will come to convey you to him. Do these things and soon you will be warm and safe. Do you understand? I will not come to you again. Remember: the night when Lady Moon is at her boldest, so that you may also be bold!"

• • •

Robby watched from a hill a hundred leagues southwest of Edgewold upon the open plain. He waited for, and soon heard, a steady low rumble from the east. He saw the long line of trolls coming, their progress marked, even at night, by the cloud of dust rising in their wake. They had marched without tire, day and night since Thunderfoot led them away from Tallinvale, at a pace twice as fast and even faster than any man could walk. In single file, with Thunderfoot at the head of the line, they passed by the hill from where Robby watched, bearing west by southwest. Within two days, they would enter the lower territories of Vanara, then they would pass over and through the Tulivana Mountains and enter the Dragonlands, just as Robby had directed. In another three days, they would be near to the place where he needed them, and the next part of their task would be given to King Thunderfoot.

He was once again pleased with how things were shaping up, though he knew enough not to be overconfident. Too many things could go wrong. This part of his plan had little to do with those other things he had to accomplish. Yet he felt that he owed it to Micerea, at least—if not to the world—to try to use the trolls in this manner, even though it would be a long while yet before anyone would see the results of this work.

Turning away, he sped east, and saw that Lyrium was almost back to her refuge in Islindia, while Serith Ellyn and Thurdun were well on their way westward along the roads that followed upriver beside the Osterflo.

He then flew back the way he had come and went to Duinnor. Looking in at Crescent Avenue, he was surprised to see no one home but the landlady.

"I don't think that's a good thing!" he muttered as he spiraled in widening circles, searching the city for his friends. Passing over the Palace, he saw the Avatar entering the gates with a squad of Kingsmen escorting Grant Farby. Chiding himself for not paying attention to Duinnor for the past few days, Robby was about to follow them when he saw Ashlord and another squad of Kingsmen on horseback riding after the first group. Puzzled, and with growing concern, he watched.

"Kingsmen, halt!" cried General Chadler. The Red Door came to a stop as the Kingsmen surrounding Farby turned.

"None may delay the King's Avatar," called out the leader of Farby's escort.

"I do not mean to delay, only to join! I have here one summoned by the King!"

"We have the one summoned, sir."

"Then let there be two! My prisoner is wanted by the King for questioning, according to Royal Summons."

Chadler showed the summons to the Kingsman, and after the man looked at it and nodded, he offered it back.

"Keep it. I see no reason why you cannot escort both of them," Chadler said. "I only happened upon Ashlord at a party and took him into custody. You may take him from here."

"This is somewhat irregular, General Chadler," said the Kingsman. "But we'll do it. No doubt Lord Banis will be pleased, at least."

"No doubt. Carry on, then, the Avatar moves on as we speak."

Indeed, the Avatar was passing into the main foyer of the Palace as Ashlord dismounted and joined Farby.

"Hello, Mr. Ashlord."

"Hello, Mr. Farby."

"What brings you out?"

"Just thought I'd tag along."

"Oh? I hope Lady Shevalia did not put you up to it."

"In fact, she did."

"I had no idea you were a wanted man. How interesting you are!"

"It is the fashionable thing to be, these days, if you are the example."

"Indeed, I suppose it is, isn't it?"

As they came to the first long staircase, the Avatar stopped. The Kingsmen looked at each other, as did Ashlord and Farby. The Avatar resumed its ascent, and its entourage followed. Not halfway up, it stopped again.

"What is all this stopping and starting?" muttered a Kingsman.

"Most unusual," whispered another.

"Shh!" ordered their captain, eyeing the Red Door warily.

• • •

Far above them, in the King's High Chamber, Lord Banis was kneeling before his King. Banis's hands were over his ears, his eyes closed tightly, and he groaned in pain at the searing throb that ran through his head. The King, for his part, had for the first time perceived the shadowed place in the First Lord's heart, a place wherein he could not easily look.

"You hide something from me!" the King's silent voice boomed. "And I shall have it of you! It is something concerning Ashlord, whom you were to bring to me. Something more concerning Farby, who is being brought to us as we speak. And something about your daughter, going by the name of Shevalia. What is it?"

"My King!" cried out Banis, both in his mind and with his voice, straining to keep that hidden part of his heart away from the King, the hidden part that Secundur's witches had given to him. "Farby and my daughter conspire, somehow, to hide Ashlord."

"You lie! Your daughter is far away from Duinnor. Your black eagles have seen her in Tallinvale!"

"I do not know how she came so far so quickly, but I saw her myself this very night! At Starlight Hall at Wysteria Place."

The King saw that that, at least, was true. Banis did see Esildre this night. The King hesitated, unsure how to proceed. He saw that the darkened spot in Banis's mind was surrounded by thoughts of Farby, Ashlord, and Esildre. He saw glimpses of other things, too, going in and out of the shadow, certain men of the Duinnor Regulars, whom Banis used to his own ends, and a serving girl.

"You have overstepped your authority," the King said at last, easing his grip on Banis. "You came here with news that this Farby hides Ashlord, yet you have not discovered where. You would have me do with my Avatar that which I have charged you to do. Farby is of no interest to me, and I now have no wish to see him! And I do not wish to see you, either. Go away! Do not return to me unless you bring Ashlord with you!"

• • •

The Avatar turned around and descended the stairs, driving those that had been following back down to the foyer.

"What the blazes?" the captain of the guard exclaimed. "Now where?"

They followed the Avatar to the gate, and there it stopped, floating motionless.

"I think this means that Farby is to be released," ventured Ashlord. "And, as it turns out, the summons that General Chadler gave you is in error, and I am not to be taken up, either. Unless you wish another mistake to be made."

"What do you mean?"

"Let me show you," said Ashlord, gesturing at the paper the man carried. Suspiciously, the man held it out and Ashlord took it from him.

"Yes, see here? Come, let us all look together so that you may all see."

Ashlord held up the summons so that the writing could be seen by the Kingsmen.

"Look here, at this name," he said, pointing to his name on the summons. As he did so, it seemed that the letters of the name began to glow. "Look very carefully. It is a very interesting name, isn't it?"

The men, Farby included, nodded, unable to take their eyes from the name.

"I believe you have never seen the likes of it before, nor ever will again. All this commotion. You were sent to fetch one man, and only one. You have done so, and now he is to be released. Did the King ask you to bring anyone else? No-o, he did not. Look upon the name. See how it fades, as the paper fades, too. Look carefully. It is as if it never happened. Never happened. Now the paper is gone, and there is nothing but air."

Suddenly Ashlord snapped his fingers and the paper disappeared with a brilliant flash of hot white light that stunned and blinded all present. Ashlord quickly slipped away. A moment later, Farby and the Kingsmen were still blinking, as if waking from a dream, and looking at each other blankly. But it was a fleeting dream, carrying with it all memory of it save a vague and disconcerting feeling.

"Well," said the captain reluctantly, "tonight is your lucky night, son."

Farby, rubbing his eyes, looked around, every bit as disoriented as the rest.

"Get on, then! We can't have you loitering around the gates all night, can we?"

"No, sir," Farby said, hurrying off.

"And stay out of trouble, if you know what's good for you!"

"Yes, sir!"

Farby passed out of the Palace and through the many beggars who crowded around the walls at all hours. Once he was away, and was fairly certain that he was truly free to go, he slowed his pace, walking down the avenue back toward Starlight Hall. He was still trying to remember something that he was certain he ought to remember, something about what had just happened, when a hand reached out and grabbed his collar, pulling him into a side alley. Before Farby could react, he saw that it was Ashlord who now peered around the corner to make sure no one was following.

"I was not sure it would work," Ashlord muttered. "My skills improve, and I'm better than I thought I was."

"Mr. Ashlord! What are you doing here?"

"Oh, hello, Mr. Farby. Are you alright? Lady Shevalia told me you were taken, and imposed upon me to look for you. How was your visit with the King?"

"The King? I never saw the King. It's the most uncanny thing, Ashlord. The Avatar released me, just when I was being taken up to the High Tower. It just turned around and took me back to the gate. Then, then," Farby hesitated. "I don't know. Seems like we all stood around, the Kingsmen and the Avatar and I, just stood around for hours and hours. And they let me go."

"Oh? Is that all that you remember?"

"That's it. I mean, well, let's see, seems like there was something else. Something having to do with a bright light, I think. Hm. I can't for the life of me think of what it might be."

"Well, I'm sure Lady Highleaf and Lady Shevalia will be glad to see you safe and sound. I instructed them not to say anything to your parents until morning, if it could be avoided. Let's be on our way before the King changes his mind again."

"Yes! Let's do!"

They walked briskly back to Wysteria Place without sharing a word for a long while. Then, just when they were coming up the lane to Starlight Hall, Farby spoke.

"Has that ever happened before, I wonder?"

"Has what ever happened before?"

"Has the King ever changed his mind, once the Avatar was sent out to fetch someone?"

"Not in my recollection," answered Ashlord. "Let's take this walkway, here, and go in through a side door. No, I can't say that I have ever heard of it. But then, I have spent most of my years outside of Duinnor. So I am not an authority on the King's whims or the Avatar's inconsistencies."

Inside, and before Lady Highleaf could do so, Sheila threw her arms around Farby, hugging him tightly.

"Oh, Grant! You are safe! It was all my fault," she said. "I was too brash with Banis. I never meant to get you into trouble."

"You didn't," Farby said, releasing her so that his aunt could also hug him. "I can manage that all on my own."

"Oh, what a boy you are for causing worry and fret!" Lady Highleaf said. "We have not left this room since Ashlord went after you. And what did the King want of you?"

Sheila had already taken Ashlord's hand, and was hugging and thanking him as Farby told all that had happened, at least all that he could remember.

"But what of General Chadler?" asked Lady Highleaf.

"Who?"

"Chadler," repeated Sheila. "And the summons."

"It never came to that," said Ashlord. "Or else I would not be here, would I?"

"Came to what? What summons?" asked Farby.

"It does not matter," answered Ashlord.

"But won't Chadler wonder?"

"Yes, I am sure he will. For a moment or two. But he is too wise to dwell on it very long."

"What summons?" Farby insisted.

"I will tell you when it is good for you to know," said Ashlord. "Until then, by having no knowledge you will be innocent before the law."

"That's not very reassuring," Farby stated.

• • •

Robby had followed Ashlord, amused at the trick that had allowed him to escape, and stayed with him until he and Farby were back together. When Ashlord said that he came at the request of Sheila, a pang shot through Robby's heart. It was nearly more than he could stand not to go see her, but he was still resolved not to. He reminded himself every day that she was too young for a banged-up old man, and those reminders helped him resist the temptation to follow Ashlord and Farby back to her. Instead, he turned his attention to Lord Banis, who now flew from the Palace in a fury of anger. Banis harshly ordered his driver to take him home, and sat in his carriage holding his pounding head whilst he fumed and cursed Farby, Ashlord, Lady Highleaf, and the so-called Lady Shevalia, whom he still believed was Esildre.

"I'll have them. I'll have them all for defying me! For mocking me with their games!" he spat. "Damn the King and his Avatar! I do not need him! He needs me! To treat me so! Like some lackey!"

Robby did not know why Banis was so angry, but he saw plainly that the man was beside himself with seething rage. When Banis got to his home, he stormed upstairs to his rooms, and immediately sat at his desk, writing furiously. Robby watched as Banis wrote.

Sir,

At 3 Crescent Avenue, you will find four persons known by the following names: Sootking, Shevalia, Bosk, and Brinnin. Use whatever means you deem fit. Fill a basket with their heads and send it to Starlight Hall. You shall find the usual fee for each body in your accounts when news of Lady Highleaf's gift is made public.

Your patron,
Mr. D.G.R. Point

Banis folded the note, secured it with a nondescript wax seal, and wrote the name Sayboor Blodgruve on the opposite side. Satisfied, but still full of anger, he put the note on the morning tray, poured himself a glass of claret, and sat to drink it before his hearth.

Robby watched a moment longer, then departed back to Griferis where he instantly awoke and jumped up from his chair to pace back and forth. He knew what he had to do, but only wished it could wait a few more weeks until other things were in place. Ullin was still too far off, and Thunderfoot was not yet where he was needed.

"Griferis is not yet prepared, nowhere near ready," he said. "Yet, things are how they are. So be it. I'll do what must be done. If I act before the morning messengers come, the constables of Duinnor will find the note and will know the nature of their Lord Banis!"

He stared at the fire in the hearth, hesitating as a fleeting whisper of doubt crossed his mind, doubt as to whether he could carry out what was needed. Almost instantly he realized that, indeed, he would do what was needed because he had little choice, and he resolved to act before the sun was risen. It was lucky for him that he had learned to put himself to sleep after only a moment of effort. He threw himself back into the chair, went back to sleep, and rushed through the realm of dreams to do what he knew was his duty.

But Robby did not see Banis pull the bellrope, and he did not see the butler take away the note. The butler conscientiously took the note downstairs. There, the note was placed into the special pouch that was kept near to the servant's door. Three times each week, a man came in the dead of night to take from the pouch any notes left there for him to deliver. And tonight was one of those nights.

There was more that Robby did not see. Lord Banis did not settle down, after all. In fact, he became more agitated as a rising restlessness overtook him. This was something that had nothing to do with the note he had just dispatched. This restlessness came from a different source entirely. Banis tried to resist it, as he had all the day long, and each and every day. But it was the resistance of one resigned to his doom. Even as he undressed for bed, Banis tried in vain to resist. It was that hidden portion of his heart, he knew, that nagged at him, that made him restless, and that compelled him. It was that portion that was hidden from the King, the peculiar gift he had begged from Secundur, given to him with blood and incantations, and fire from Secundur's witches. Ever since, for hundreds of years, he had made good use of that gift, the gift of shadow, to hide his actions from the King. It was there, within that curtained chamber of his heart, that Banis conceived and pondered plots that remained unknown to the King, plots entwined with the intrigues and power of the throne but aimed instead to further the ambitions of Lord Banis.

He went to the washbasin and threw water into his face, but it was no use. Like a sudden squall, he felt the upswelling of darkness. The light of his eyes dimmed as his knees buckled, and he fell heavily against the washstand. He struggled to regain his balance as the peculiar condition of his heart made itself master of him, as a hand might pull the strings of a puppet. He staggered and swayed to his writing desk, and his perception of the world narrowed and tilted. Banis fell heavily, almost as limp as a ragdoll, into the chair before the desk. One of his hands snatched a stack of papers while the other grasped a quill and dipped it frantically. Then, with dripping pen, he wrote. As the record of his day flowed forth and stained the paper before him, his back stiffened, his arms outstretched to the desk. He threw his head back with his mouth open to a silent moan, his eyes rolling back into his head. He wrote and he wrote, no longer seeing the page or the quill or even the narrow mouth of the inkwell. In this posture, his body jerking as if jolted with pricks from a thousand unseen needles, his legs kicking with spasms, drool running from his mouth, and the shallow breath of his beating lungs, he scrawled. He shoved the line-filled sheet aside for another sheet, dipped without looking, and scratched without seeing what it was that he wrote.

Afterwards, drenched with perspiration but somewhat recovered, he saw what he had written, and he desperately grabbed the papers together, leaping from his chair to the fireplace to throw them all in. As he reached out to do so, he suddenly pulled away, clutching the papers to his chest defensively.

"No, I mustn't!" he cried, spinning around, turning his back upon the hearth. "I mustn't, I mustn't!"

He paced frantically about the room, glancing under the bed, pulling open his wardrobe and then slamming it shut.

"But where? Where, where?"

He remembered. Laughing quietly, fiendishly, he remembered and went back to his desk, throwing a quick glare over his shoulder as he hunched over the desk. With the papers secreted away, he was suddenly overcome with exhaustion and staggered to his bed. There he tossed and turned, thinking, "Tomorrow I will send them away. I will bundle them all off to Northgate where the others have gone. Yes, I will bind them in tight cord and wrap them in cloth and have them put into trunks to be carried to Northgate. That is what I have done before. That is what I shall do again."

Then he recalled that cell after dark cell in Northgate were already filled with trunks and trunks. It was due to this peculiar overcrowding that little room remained in Northgate for his many prisoners. He despaired briefly, then clutched his covers about him more tightly and turned over.

"No matter," he thought as sleep grudgingly overcame him. "I can simply dispose of a few prisoners and free another cell for my trunks."

Chapter 13

Red Doors

Day 196
49 Days Remaining

The small desert town of Almedian was one of those rare Dragonkind places where the Sun King's representatives seldom ventured. It was a pleasant enough community, located somewhat near the route that ran from Tyrsharat, the capital of the Dragon Empire, to the old city of Calamandor, sometimes called the Green Citadel. Yet Almedian was sufficiently far off the main route to be inconvenient for caravans as they went back and forth between the two larger cities. In ancient days, when the Dragonkind first began building towns, Almedian was settled around the several wells that were dug there, wells that never went dry even though they provided enough water not only to irrigate the meager fields around Almedian but also for the town's use in their households and workplaces. Almedian was a pretty place, too, with a bazaar shaded by colorful linen canopies, as were many of the rooftops of its stone and adobe houses. And though it was walled as most desert towns were, Almedian had never been assaulted, and probably never would. Nevertheless, its walls and watchtowers were manned day and night by the Al Sairs, the personal household guard of Gurasa, the once-famous general whose birthplace Almedian was, and where he had raised his own family. Under his watchful eye, the people of Almedian enjoyed a freedom that most other people of the desert did not know nor could imagine.

Through a mysterious arrangement, Gurasa saw to it that the people of Almedian had sympathetic priests with generous supplies of the darakal herb. He also encouraged those priests to administer darakal in greater frequency than would normally be done, and in a relaxed manner free of the rites and oaths imposed upon and exacted from people in other regions. So it was perhaps owing to this fact that Almedian's people lived longer than those in other parts, and they suffered far less from the crippling diseases that plagued the rest of the Dragon Lands. But they knew that their privileges might not last much longer than Gurasa's life, for his sons had all passed away, his wife, too. His surviving daughter, an indolent and spoiled child, had little to do with them. She rarely went out from her father's small but elegant palace. And when she did, it was usually only to pass through the town on her way to other far-off and more glamorous parts of the empire. It was said that she often went to the

Green Citadel to purchase the fine clothes that she always wore, and even to faraway Kajarahn, the Free City, where she participated in all manner of decadent activities. Still, as they had to admit, she was never cruel, as the children of powerful people often were. It was even rumored that it was she who arranged, through her many travels, for the supply of darakal herb that they all needed. They found such rumors difficult to believe, for they all knew Micerea to be too whimsical and flighty of mind to manage any such dangerous activity, for it was an offense punishable by death for anyone who obtained the herb from any but the Emperor's own agents.

As for Gurasa, he, too, rarely went forth from his palace. So it was a surprise when he did so, appearing in the marketplace alone, without any servants or guards, plainly dressed, a smallish man, unassuming and polite, shopping as anyone would, for a bit of dye, or a particular spice, or to commission a rug or carpet. Often he was not even recognized until his missing hand was noticed and a closer look was given him. And then a great fuss would be made over his presence, which was sure to make him quickly but politely conclude his business and retreat.

Gurasa's servants, who would never say a word against him, told others of the town how he spent his days writing verse, reading, or painting delicate scenes of the desert. They even said that within his palace were paintings that he himself had brushed, paintings that depicted places in the far north, of lands full of trees and green grass, mountains with gushing water running down their sides, and towns draped in the white of frozen snow. He seemed an enigma. They well knew that he was out of favor with the Royal Court, that he was wrongly blamed for the Northmen's sacking of the Green Citadel all those years ago, and was now living in a virtual exile. He was, as all knew, a broken man, frail and wizened, prone to chills and fever and bouts of deep depression, the hand that he lost in battle when he was a young warrior ceaselessly aching with phantom pain, and his heart aching, too, at the loss of his wife and sons, and for others whom he would not name. Such was their protector. They pitied him every bit as much as they revered him. And not a one would deny him anything, should he ever ask.

It was his daughter, all seemed to agree, who was most able to lift his spirits. The servants loved to tell how he and she would sit for hours playing cribbage, and how he entertained her all the while with fantastic tales of his youth. Those of the household staff told how Gurasa lovingly held Micerea close and kissed her head at every meeting of the day and before bedtime every night, as if she was still a little girl.

• • •

This night, after struggling to stay awake through her father's readings, Micerea could not keep from him the fact that she was distracted. He paused, gently closed his book, and looked out from the balcony where they sat. It was a cool and beautiful night, and though the lamps by which he read were bright, the stars were even brighter still. The town was long dark and asleep, except for a few lights at the weaver's house some distance off where, as Gurasa imagined, a loom still chattered and clicked and bumped away.

"Daughter," he said, "you seem to gain very little rest from all the sleeping that you do. I know that you dreamwalk, that you try to keep pace with Ullin Saheed and to watch over him, and I fear that it wears you down. But, tonight, I think something else troubles you. Tell me what it is."

Micerea looked down at her hands, then out across the desert.

"I wonder if Darish, your captain's son, might be brought into your trust, so that he and not I could go to the Free City next week?"

"Of course he can be trusted. And, though he is not as experienced as you, I am sure that he would make a fine messenger. But you know that within a fortnight he must go to Tyrsharat to enlist."

"Yes. I know. Could you not apply to have him enlisted into your guard, and have him absolved of any duties to the army?"

"I could. But, as you know, I have already had many of our town's sons exempted. I fear it would raise the hackles of the Emperor's generals for me to exempt another. And it might be seen by our people as playing favors with those attached to my house."

"Yes. I suppose it might."

"Why do you ask? Is there some reason that you do not wish to go to the Free City?"

"Yes, to be quite honest. Father, there are things that I mustn't tell you. The long and the short of it is that I need to leave, to go on my own journey, with my own purpose. I cannot tell you where. And I fear I will not return, at least not for a very long time."

Gurasa looked at his daughter with his gray eyes, his brow furrowed with concern. He relaxed somewhat, and nodded.

"You need not tell me where. I can guess easily enough. It is too far for you to go."

"No, Father. It may not be. Indeed, I think it will only take a week to go where I intend, or even less. If I am to go, I must leave at daybreak, or else it will be too late."

"At daybreak? And only a week? I don't understand. Perhaps I guess wrongly at where you aim to go."

"No, you very likely guess correctly. But you underestimate the power of the New King."

They sat for many moments, not speaking, looking out across the desert sky. The air turned cooler, and Gurasa pulled the blanket around his shoulders and stood.

"I knew this would come," he said. "I do not blame you. Indeed, it might be said that I have done nothing but encourage you in this decision, though I wish it could be otherwise. To keep you from it would be unkind. I am a grateful father, prouder of you than anyone I have ever known. Someday, I hope that our people will learn how you have served them and be grateful and proud of you, too. Go. Go with my blessing and with all of my love."

"Thank you, my Father!"

She hugged him dearly, and he took her in his arms, struggling to keep the smile on his face.

"Father, there is another favor that I wish to ask of you."

"Anything for you, my daughter."

"I need to take with me five of our best horses."

• • •

"Ashlord, I do not wish to stay here," Sheila said. "I want to come home to our apartment and be with you and Billy and Ibin."

"You are safer here than there," Ashlord said. "And tomorrow at dawn, we shall be finding a new place to live."

"Then one night won't matter, will it? And what if they come for you?"

"I hardly think they will. Banis is not so foolish. If he wanted me to see the King, I am sure he would not have tried to kill me. What baffles me is how Banis hides his actions from the King. However that is, something must have happened tonight. Perhaps something has at last come between Banis and the King. And, by the account you just gave me, Banis acted most peculiarly around you."

"It is likely that he acted so because I taunted him with my questions about Esildre. It was only because he said I reminded him of her."

"Ah! That must be it! He must have mistaken you for her."

"Oh, Ashlord. I doubt that very much! His own daughter? Besides, if that was so, why would he have Farby summoned and not me?"

"That I cannot answer. You are right. It makes little sense. No matter. If you insist, you shall sleep in your old bed tonight. However, tomorrow morning, I must send you back here while I look for another place for us."

Lady Highleaf entered the room and sat beside Sheila.

"What is this I hear? Sleep in your old bed?"

"Yes. Shevalia insists on returning with us back to our rooms for the night," Ashlord explained. "I know, I know! It is only for tonight. Tomorrow, she will return. By that time the last of your guests will have departed, I hope. And, after she returns to you, perhaps you could arrange for extra guards and watchmen? For the time being, while Shevalia is a guest."

"Of course. Well! It has been an eventful evening, hasn't it? Oh, Shevalia! I am very sorry things turned out the way they did. I so hoped that you and Grantham would hit it off. I am so dense. I had no idea you two already knew each other."

"I am very fond of Grant," Sheila said. "Much too fond, in fact. But I have been infatuated before, for no good reason, only to have my heart return to its true path."

"And what path is that, dear child? Is there someone whose affections cannot be replaced?"

"Yes, there is. It may be an impossible hope, but I do hope to see him again someday, and I hope to be faithful to him until then, and honorable in my conduct. I am afraid that I owe Grant an apology for my weakness. I have no wish to hurt his feelings. And, if things were otherwise in my heart, I am sure that he could win it."

"Oh, do not tell him that! Nothing could be more hurtful to a lovesick man, I am sure! If it comes about that you must say something, say only that you had a little too much to drink and that you regret that you cannot return his affection. Better yet, say nothing at all. Let him draw his conclusions from your actions henceforth."

"I shall try to do as you say."

"Good. Now, it is late, only a few hours before dawn. You had better go along so that your friends can have some sleep. And that includes me! I shall need a good rest before I read the morning stories about our little party. I'm sure that your name will be prominently and repeatedly mentioned!"

Lady Highleaf stood and gave Sheila's gown another look up and down. "Please put on a cloak before you leave."

• • •

They all rode together inside the carriage. Billy talked with Ashlord all the while about their meeting. Sheila and Ibin remained silent for the most part, listening as Ashlord explained to Billy that if a Congress was convened, he should prepare himself to address it.

"It may take several days at the very least to call a Congress, or weeks, or months," Ashlord said. "It all depends on so many things besides the King's willingness to do so. Banis will oppose it, for it would open his affairs to scrutiny and to questions about why he did not anticipate the Redvest threat, and why he did not warn Duinnor's armed forces."

"Oh," said Billy. "Then we are to wait even longer, I reckon. Ashlord, I'm about ready to go home, to be up front about things. Me ol' man'll be needin' me."

"I know, Billy. Please be patient. If the world goes to war, and if the Redvests and their Dragonkind allies gain the upper hand, Boskland will surely be overrun once more. I know you'd rather prevent that if you could."

"Why, certainly I would!"

"If Duinnor can be aroused quickly enough to send forces south, it may thwart that from happening. Would you not want to add your voice to those of others who call for action?"

"Yeah, I would. Them men were most respectful of me. An' I don't doubt they'll do what they can to move things right along."

"Yes, they will. I know you miss your home. I promise to have you on your way back as soon as I possibly can do so."

They bounced along the lonely streets as clouds blew in from the northwest, covering all stars but those Five that never moved from over Duinnor City. Whether due to the length of the evening, or because of the overcast skies, it was a somber and weary group that arrived back at Crescent Avenue, and they went upstairs to their rooms. Miss Tarrier was not about, it seemed, and anyway did not expect Sheila to return with the others after the party. But Mr. Yarman was kind enough to help them in, and he and Ibin brought in wood and coal, and soon they had all the fireplaces roaring and the stoves glowing. Ashlord made a pot of tea, but Billy and Ibin went off to bed before he had even poured, leaving only Sheila to sip with him in the upstairs parlor.

"Ashlord, what do you think has become of Robby and Ullin?" Sheila asked.

"I wish that I knew. I can only hope they have reached Griferis. But I hardly know what sort of sign to look for to indicate that they have done so."

"If they have, and if Robby has by now completed his work there, how might he become King? How might he overthrow the present one all by himself?"

"Again, I wish I knew. I hope that Robby will discover how it may be done. But do not think that he will be alone. He has his supporters, you know."

Ashlord's eyes twinkled over his cup at Sheila.

"Yes, he does."

"What is troubling you, my dear?"

"I don't know that I have words for it." Sheila shrugged, putting down her cup and pulling her shawl more tightly around her shoulders. She still wore the jeweled hairpins, and her eyes glittered in the firelight every bit as much as they did. "I was weak, during the time when we traveled here, and I am sorry for it. And, though I am stronger now than I have ever been, I still feel weak."

"Whatever can you mean?"

"I made a fool of myself in front of Ullin. On the day of the battle with the Wickermen. I think I was a bit out of my head. I said something to him that was not exactly true. At least, now I know it was not true. I was very mixed up. And now, just tonight, I realized what it must be like to be unable to love someone in return for their love."

"Ah. You must speak of Farby."

"Yes. Is it so obvious?"

"Hm. No, but I have eyes that watch, though I do not always see. He stayed here, as you know, all during the time of your Scathing. Even though he has his own home, one that is much more comfortable than this place. He did not have to stay. In fact, I urged him to go home. He would have none of that. I think he slept more in the hallway outside your door than he did in any bed during that time, unwilling to be even the short distance of the bedroom down the hall from you. More than his actions was the look on his face, in his eyes."

Sheila nodded.

"Have you told him about your feelings for Robby?"

"Yes, but without naming names. Oh, what a muddle!" Sheila stood and paced across the room. "Tonight we danced on the ice, and he held me, and we kissed, and I think I enjoyed it too much! What would I say to Robby?"

"Hm. Well, should it ever come up, which I doubt it ever shall, then simply be honest. Do not embellish. But hide nothing, if asked. However, and I do not mean to be unpleasant," Ashlord added gently, "I think you should not expect to see your Robby ever again."

"You have said that before. Or said as much. But that is my hope. And I will not give it up. Whether Robby becomes King or not, I will always love him."

Ashlord nodded.

"Then it is my wish that your hopes and your dreams shall come to pass," he said with a pained smile.

Sheila bent over and gave Ashlord a kiss on the cheek.

"Thank you, Ashlord. I think I'll lie down for a while and mull things over."

"Very well. Sweet dreams."

• • •

In those days, there was a small estate some thirty miles north of Duinnor known as Whitefall. It was an ancient village, located along the banks of the River Whitefall that poured into the Osterflo many miles to the north. Earlier that evening, while Lady Highleaf's party was well under way, and just about when Lady Shevalia made her grand appearance, a rider on a white horse bolted out from Whitefall Manor and galloped along the icy road leading southward. It was a hard ride, full of turns and fords across half-frozen streams, but the mount was one of those sired of two lines of fine breeds, and none in all of Duinnor was its equal in speed or as sure-footed. Snow Wind was his name, and this night he seemed to live up to it, for as soon as the lights of the old manor house were gone from sight, a cold north wind came at his back, spreading low clouds ahead, and, as horse and rider turned onto the main road to Duinnor City, the air filled with flakes. Heedless of the cold, horse and rider slowed only when necessary, to turn aside from a washed out portion of the road, or to halt so that the rider could take his bearings. Through a break in the trees between two hills, he saw the unwavering Stars of Duinnor far off ahead. They resumed their course, galloping across a frozen lake as a shortcut. Back on the road, they went as swiftly as the twists and turns would allow, vaulting over a fallen tree, and bearing on through the cold air with a determination that was nigh upon reckless.

At last, after many hours, they made the city at about the time when Sheila and Ashlord were having their tea and their chat. The horseman slowed Snow Wind to a canter, and they passed through the north gate of the city and then on along the avenues toward the Palace. Along the way, and not far from their destination, the rider guided his horse down a side street and along the front of an old factor's building. The grimy windows were lit from within, and he heard the strumming of a guitar. The front of the building was illuminated by streetlamps, and as they came before the door, he gently reined Snow Wind to a halt and stared at the door in amazement.

"It is just as was told to me, old boy," he said to Snow Wind. "And so must be the rest. It's to the Palace we go!"

• • •

Billy finally fell asleep after tossing and turning for the better part of an hour. He dreamt of home, of working in the woodshop to plane new timbers for the repair of Bosk Hall. He took great pleasure in working the block plane and the drawknife, and using the square to make sure of the corners. He was picking up the yardstick to take another measurement when a man appeared at the door. It was odd, because Billy felt as if he should know the fellow who came on into the shop and ran his hand down the beam that was taking shape. Then, with no comment on Billy's workmanship, the man said, "Come with me, if you please."

The man guided Billy out of the door and right into the night-time streets of Duinnor. There was something eerie about the fellow, for even though Billy strained and squinted and craned his neck to see the stranger's face, all he could make out was a beard. But what was even more uncanny was how, when the man took Billy's hand and before he could blink, they rose up into the air and then descended onto a rooftop not far from the gates of the King's Palace.

"Watch," the man instructed and pointed at the gate, "and listen to this man who comes yonder and approaches the beggars who sleep at the Palace gates."

Billy looked and saw a man on a fine white horse come into view, his travel cloak thrown back from his princely garments. He rode to the gate and dismounted. The guards, warming their hands at a brazier near the gate, saw the man and gave the challenge.

"Who goes? And what business at this hour of the night?"

"I have no business within. My business is here with the beggars and the homeless."

Those who huddled against the walls and around their meager fires stirred from their ragged blankets and approached the man.

"A coin for an old soldier?" asked one, offering his only palm.

"Have pity on a widow woman, my lord," pleaded another, old beyond her years.

"A mite for a slice of bread, good prince?"

Soon there was a large gathering of people around the young man, some who were truly pitiful in body and spirit among others recently cast out from their dwellings. Old women and grandchildren, young men ruined by drink or mangled by war, prostitutes desperate for trade, and old soldiers still wearing the tattered remnants of their age-old surcoats. The sentries shook their heads and turned away, impatiently pushing through the crowd to go back to their brazier.

"I am sent to tell you that a place has been made for you this night and for all of the rest of nights that you might need a place to stay. For all of you. Get you to the street called Traymont, in the factors district just yonder. Look for a warehouse with a red door. Any who go in will be fed and given warm clothes, and a warm place to rest and to sleep. Your wounds will be tended to and your needs provided for. Let those of us who are fit give aid to those who are infirm, and let us help them go to the place I speak of."

The crowd stared at him, and some backed away with looks of disappointment on their faces.

"Do you not understand?" he cried. "A place is made for you and is waiting."

"Sir," one of the old men spoke, "what is this place you bid us go to?"

"Is it a workhouse?" asked a woman. "Where they take away our children and demand labor that we cannot do?"

"No! Upon my word!" replied the gentleman. "It is not a workhouse. Though, if you desire work, it will be found for you. It is a gift made to you this night. Go, if you wish to be warm. If you wish to eat." Looking at one of the girls, he added, "Or if you wish for safety. No harm will come to you there."

"Well, I'll give it a try!" said one woman, pulling along her child as she started off.

"Me, too," said another beggar.

Billy watched as they filtered away from the gates of the Palace and moved into the streets and off along the well-lit boulevard. The princely man put several children onto his saddle and, leading his horse along by the reins, helped an elderly man who was blind.

"It was foretold to me that you would come," said the old man in a low voice.

"I do not see how it could have been known," replied the gentleman, "since I myself did not know until this very evening."

"I had a dream," said the blind elder. "And in my dream I was told by a kind voice to give up my place in the east market, where I have begged for nigh forty years, and to take up a place here, nearby to the gates of the Palace. In my dream, I was told that the King himself would send for me and would give me relief from my misery."

"I am not the King," said the gentleman.

"Then you are sent by him."

"I hardly think so, for I have never seen the King, nor have I had any word from him or any of his ministers. How I come to do this is by dream, too. I will not relate it to you, but it was terrible and beautiful. Now I do that which I must do, and that I ought to have done long ago."

"Then you heard the voice of the same King that I heard."

• • •

Billy and his guide watched all of the beggars depart except one who remained behind and returned to his place against the wall of the Palace. He sat down and wrapped a blanket about himself, pulling it over the top of his head for warmth.

"How come he stays," Billy asked, "when all the rest've gone on?"

"He stays as a sign to you. When you awake from this dream, come to him in haste and ask of him where the others went to and why it is that he alone has stayed behind. Do this to know that deliverance is nigh and that the New King is on his way."

Billy nodded and looked again at the beggar that remained.

"I will," Billy said. He turned to ask another question, but his guide was gone from the rooftop. He looked around and felt his heart jump a beat. Then he woke up.

"Gotta go!" he cried out, kicking off his quilts and springing from his cot to get dressed. "Gotta go!"

"Huh?" Ibin stirred in the bedroom next to Billy's, his cot creaking under his weight as he shifted and sat up. "Whatsamatter, Billy?" he called.

"What's afoot?" came Ashlord's voice from the next room.

"Gotta go!" Billy repeated. The door to his room was flung open, and Sheila rushed in, buttoning her bodice, her overcloak already across her shoulders. "Billy! Wake up!"

"I already am, ain't I?" he shot back, hopping on one foot as he tried to get his other boot on. "I gotta go out for a spell."

"Me, too."

"Did ye have a dream?"

"I did! Did you?"

"Aye! An' I gotta go see if it's true."

"Me, too!"

Behind Sheila, Ashlord appeared, alarm written on his face.

"What is happening here?"

"Are you to go to North Hill?" Sheila asked Billy.

"No." Billy hopped around, stomping his foot to get the boot firmly on. "To the Palace."

"To the Palace?"

"Why?" asked Ibin, stumbling into the hall as he pulled up his suspenders.

"Why do you have to go to North Hill?" asked Ashlord of Sheila.

In a babble of confusing explanations, Billy and Sheila told each other, and Ashlord and Ibin, about their mysterious dreams and how they each promised to go to certain places in the city to discover more.

"Wait! Wait!" Ashlord held up his hand. "The Palace is one way, and North Hill is a different direction entirely. Either we go together or else we split up. But the city is still dangerous for us. Need I remind you of last night's close call?"

"But this is surely the sign we have been waiting for," Sheila said. "Let's go."

"Right!" Billy agreed, putting on his coat.

"Dreams, eh?" Ashlord turned his head to look at Certina on his shoulder.

"Yes! An important one!" Sheila said.

"Mine, too, don't ye know?"

Ashlord nodded at Certina and looked back at Sheila and Billy. He was tempted to tell them about Robby's dreamwalking skill. And he knew that, if it was Robby who was behind all of this, he would not put his friends in needless danger. But that remained Robby's secret, to reveal in his own way. And perhaps this was the way he had chosen. Ashlord nodded again.

"You are right. It is time to act. Let us go to North Hill first, since it is somewhat closer."

Ashlord grabbed his cloak—he had already changed out of the red finery that he had worn to the party and into his less conspicuous attire—and for once it was he who was hurried along by the others as they went downstairs and out through the back door.

"Come on!" Sheila urged, pulling her hood over her head. "Which way?"

Ashlord pointed, and they hurried along the back lane. It was still dark, and snow drifted down steadily through the cold calm sky. A few people were already about, going to the markets or to their places of work, and none seemed to notice or care about the foursome that hurried along alleys and streets, turning this way and that as Ashlord directed.

"Which part of North Hill do we go to?" he asked Sheila.

"I don't know," she told him, "but I'll know it when I see it. There's a bridge. And, just across from it, a cobblestone street."

"There are four bridges that I know of. We turn left at the corner. Most all of the streets in North Hill are cobblestone."

"This one goes along a wall of sorts. There's a banister along one side of it. And it overlooks another street and some houses across the way."

"Oh," Ashlord glanced at Sheila with a look of concern. "I think I know it."

They kept on for nearly an hour, going more slowly as they went because of the steep hills in that part of the city that were glazed with slippery snow-coated ice. At last they came to a district where the shops and markets gave way to tree-lined parks and elegant mansions. As they crossed a bridge, Sheila shook her head.

"I know," Ashlord said before she could say anything. "But the one you described is farther along. Up this hill and around the curve there."

By now the sky was growing lighter, giving a grayish glow to the snow-dusted city. Lamplighters were performing their morning duties, going from lamp to lamp with practiced routine, and climbing their ladders to extinguish each one.

Indeed, as they moved out of the way of a carriage, and resumed their walk, Sheila saw a stone bridge, wide enough for two carriages to pass, and, beyond, the road continued atop a high embankment.

"I think that's the place," she said, pointing. "Just there, see?"

"Yes."

They crossed the bridge and went along the righthand side of the road where there was an iron-banistered sidewalk. Sheila stopped and, gripping the handrail, looked out at the tall houses that lined the other side of a street that ran below and parallel to where they stood. Ashlord and the others waited beside her patiently, as she seemed to be searching for something.

"These sure are some mighty nice houses," Billy commented.

"Apartments and houses of many high lords and ladies of Duinnor," Ashlord replied. "You see the guards that patrol below us, just there? They are Duinnor Regulars. Those streets are off limits to any who are uninvited. Sheila, what do you look for?"

"A window," she said, "with a blue curtain."

"There'sa, there'sablue, abluecurtain!" Ibin pointed to the third floor of a house directly in front of them, across the street, and to a window just a few feet above their line of sight.

"Yes! Yes, that's it!"

"Do not point, Ibin," said Ashlord.

"An' what're we lookin' for, 'sides a winder?" asked Billy.

"I don't know. I think we're just supposed to watch it."

• • •

Satisfied that all was ready, Robby prepared for the task at hand. He went to fetch Micerea, who had hastily prepared for her morning's departure and was dressed and ready to go. She had only just reclined for a few moments of sleep.

"Come with me. I want you to be a witness," he told her.

Surprised that Robby did not send Finn, she said nothing as they flew through the dreamscape to Duinnor City, and into the bedroom of a fine house.

"Wait here, and watch what I do," he instructed her.

Robby went to the person before them, asleep in a lavish bed draped with rich curtains, and as he approached, he conjured around him sights such as he had witnessed in Shatuum. He entered the man's dream, bringing his own visions with him. He knew that the nightmare he brought would be taken up and kindled by this man's own mind, and as

Micerea watched with horror, Robby backed out of the dream, leaving the man writhing in terror. Then, looking across the vague dreamscape, Robby made a beckoning gesture. Micerea turned and saw, as if coming over a hill, the awful dog-like creatures she feared the most, running toward the man's nightmare.

"You must watch this," Robby commanded as she shrank away.

The creatures tore into the man, and soon his dream was also stung by hundreds of swarming cindergnats, so much so that his dream seemed on fire.

"What do you do?" Micerea exclaimed, recoiling.

"I bring punishment," Robby said coldly. "This man is a murderer, and a traitor."

"This is terrible. I cannot watch!"

"It is only a dream," Robby replied coldly. There was cruel sarcasm in his tone that frightened Micerea even more. "But a mere bad dream is not enough for him. He is beyond the law, protected by his ill-gotten power and by the King, and he cannot be brought to justice by Duinnor. So I bring justice to him."

"I don't like this! This cannot be right! And, anyway, look. He rouses from his sleep."

"Not quite," Robby said, returning to the man as he struggled out of bed. Not understanding what Robby was doing, she saw him lay his hand on the fading nightmare. It rekindled anew, except now the man was on his real feet, stumbling around his bedchamber, flailing his arms at the goblins that came at him, knocking over chairs as he went, twisting around as if he was being pushed back and forth by a mob. Robby then conjured a red door, and stepped through it into the man's dream and held it open. The man, still swiping at the wraiths that swirled around him, saw Robby and was clearly terrified. Robby pointed at the open door, beyond which appeared a pleasant springtime meadow.

"Run!" cried Robby.

The man did, running madly away from the creatures that pursued him, past Robby and right through the open red door.

• • •

Sheila and her friends saw a figure crash through the blue curtains, arms flailing. The man's feet clipped the edge of the portico, and he flipped. They flinched at the dull crunch his body made when it struck the cobblestones. Shocked and flabbergasted, they stared in disbelief at the red star that blotched the snowy street around the dead man's head.

"Let's go!" Ashlord tugged on Sheila's arm. "We should not stay here!"

"Ohmygosh!" said Ibin, horrified.

"Did ye know that was about to happen?" Billy asked Sheila as they hurried away. Sheila was still looking over her shoulder, being pulled by Ashlord, a wry smile on her face.

"No," she replied. "But now that it has, I think we may all be safer."

"Why do you say that?" Ashlord asked, directing them west along the quickest way from the place.

"Because," she said, "in my dream, I was taken there, and I was told to go there when I woke up. I was told that I would see something happen that would make us safer within the city, and that would make Duinnor a safer place for everyone else, too. Something that would be the beginning of the end of this King."

"Well," Ashlord said to her, "we shall either be safer, or else the hornets' nest has just been kicked, for, unless I am mistaken, that was Lord Banis's house."

"No!" exclaimed Billy. "Do ye think that was Banis?"

"I do," Ashlord said, pushing them along toward a side street. "And one less enemy we now have."

"Then let's get to the Palace. We've a feller to meet thar!"

• • •

In the bedroom of Lord Banis, Robby spread a dream of sunshine and springtime, and the dream dogs of nightmare retreated, their meal having vanished. He turned to Micerea.

"I can prevent a person from fully waking up," Robby explained. "And I think I shall soon learn how to put people to sleep. I can summon and dismiss the dreamdogs that you saw. There is no need for you to be afraid of them. If ever you encounter ones that you don't want around, just conjure up a happy dream, something pleasant, and they'll go away."

Micerea looked at him aghast.

"You…you killed that man!"

"That man was responsible for many murders, including that of his own son. And he, through his daughter, was responsible for the madness that overcame Ullin. Not only that, but the attack against the White Palace of Vanara was of his making, and many innocent people were killed and hurt there. He was in league with those of your land who now strive to join with the Redvests of Tracia, those of your land who keep your people enslaved to the herb that they are made to think heals them. And he had an alliance with Secundur."

"What are you saying?"

"I am saying that it is up to us and others that we shall enlist to bring justice to those who are beyond the law. And to do other things that need doing. To reveal, when we can, to just courts those who do wrong, and how they do those things. And, when need be, it is up to us to punish those who cannot be brought to justice any other way. That man was preparing to murder others. If caught, he would have never been charged as he was too powerful for the present king's justice. But I could not permit him to harm my friends. It is time to act. If I am to be King, then my justice will go before me, and follow upon my hem. If there is to be peace, then those who make war must be stopped. Those who agitate and coerce others to violence and thievery must be stopped."

Micerea looked at Robby with a new appreciation and not without some fearful astonishment.

"What must I do?" she asked cautiously.

"Help Finn to raise my small army, since the three of us alone cannot be everywhere at once. I am teaching Finn how to find others who can dreamwalk, others like us. I shall teach you, too. And, when you locate them, how to judge if they be good people or not, and if they may be trustworthy to our cause. Right now, Men and Dragonkind have united against the Seven Realms. To oppose them, we must put forward a league of Men and Dragonkind, too, and of Elifaen as well. Fearless. Unafraid to work together. Those who long for peace and for healing. It is urgent. Are you ready to begin?"

Micerea looked at Robby, her expression full of confusion and, he thought, fear.

"Why do you hesitate?"

"I hesitate only because I must be away at first light, and I fear I'll not have much time for sleeping until my travels are over."

"Where do you go? Back to the Free City on your father's business?"

"No, sire. Please, do not make me tell you! I fear you would forbid what I do, and, if you did, I fear I would disobey you!"

"Then I will not forbid it, whatever it is, since you seemed determined to do it anyway," Robby said in an impatient tone. "Tell me. Where do you go?"

• • •

In the Great Tower, the King bent over the maps in his study. He leaned over his young companion so that the light from his Golden Mantle illuminated the chart that lay atop of all others. It was the latest one obtained from Vanara showing the mountains near Shatuum. There was a broad, blank space where Shatuum's details should have been, and the King unspun a filament of light and pointed with its tip at a place just on the southeastern edge of that space.

"This is where the eagles of Lord Banis say the outpost is," he said. "It is obviously an arduous journey from Vanara to there. The Gray Guard must number significantly more than the Queen has led us to believe, else they could not support such remote garrisons."

A loud noise suddenly came from the anteroom, a sharp, metallic groan. The King and his companion jumped at the sound, and raced through the door and then through the curtain into the waiting area. The doors to the outer hallway were closed, and nothing was seen but the Avatar. The Red Door, in the middle of the room, was swinging back and forth on its unoiled hinges, emitting the unnerving whine. They clearly saw how the plates of the hinges remained motionless, as if nailed to an invisible frame, whilst the door swung on the hinge pins. It opened and closed repeatedly as they stared at it.

"Sire, what makes it do that?"

The King made no answer, for he had none to give. He slowly approached the Avatar, still swinging back and forth on its protesting hinges, and he cautiously unwound a golden filament of his shroud to touch the door, to make it stop. As the tip of the filament touched the door, it came to a halt, and from the place where the King touched it, the door rapidly began to change from red to orange and then to bright shining gold.

"No, sire! Come away, I beg you!" cried his Melnari, taking a step toward the King. The door was now glowing so brightly that the light was unbearable, and the room was filled with a jarring buzz that vibrated the dust from the floor. It was as if the King could not pull away, but was held by the door's grip for a long terrifying moment. Then, with a loud pop, the King managed to pull away, and was sent stumbling backwards. The door quickly became red once more, and the King's Golden Mantle wavered and dimmed to silver, its threads dancing with dull yellow light. Slowly, the Mantle resumed its previous color, but it was not as bright as it was before.

The King's Melnari waited, shaking with fear as he stared at the King.

"The Avatar spoke to me," the King said. "But it made no sense. I saw Lord Banis, beset by terrible creatures, rushing for the door, one that was held open by a man. I felt a rush of cold air, and then, nothing."

"Oh, sire! What can it mean? Should we send for Banis?"

"Yes."

The King unspun another filament, to touch the Avatar again and to order it to fetch Banis. His young companion reached out his hand, as if to stop the King from touching the thing again. But it was too late, the King's Finger touched the door. Nothing happened. The King withdrew his touch. He touched it again, and a third time. The Red Door remained motionless. It did not change color, nor make any unusual sound. The King moved away and hovered without comment. The doors to the room opened, and two Kingsmen stepped in, immediately falling to their knees and shielding their eyes.

"Yes, sire?"

The King touched their minds briefly, and they rose and backed away, closing the doors behind them.

"I have sent Kingsmen for Banis," the King said, "since our Avatar seems unwilling to go."

"Unwilling, sire?"

• • •

Ashlord led his group quickly away, turning up and down streets until he came at last to a tea shop where he urged them inside.

"Let us have breakfast," he said.

"What? But we must get on to the Palace!" Billy insisted.

"Not just yet. Listen!" Ashlord pointed up. A horn was blaring over and over in the distance. "It summons the Kingsmen, likely sounded by those guards who found Banis's body in the street outside his house. Come in, come in. We stop to let things subside just a little."

They were shown to a table beside the front windows just as a squad of Kingsmen rushed by. After they passed, the waiter pulled a chair for Sheila, and they all sat.

"A pot of tea, please," Ashlord requested of the waiter. "And some bread. And, tell me, are today's broadsheets yet delivered?"

"Any time, now, I expect. Shall I bring you a copy when the bundle arrives?"

"Yes, please."

They were the only customers, and they watched the streets pensively as they waited for their breakfast. More Kingsmen came hurrying along, this time on horseback.

"It seems a busy morning," said the waiter as he brought their tray, along with a folded paper.

"Indeed, it does. Thank you."

"Anything else for you?"

"Not at the moment. Thank you."

"Well, then. Enjoy."

"Ibin, will you pour?" Ashlord asked, unfolding the paper. "Well! This may answer some of your concerns, Billy."

He turned the paper around and showed it to his companions. Across the top of the page was printed, in large bold letters:

WAR!!!
TRACIA ATTACKS THE EASTLANDS
The Dragonlands Are Her Ally
Tallinvale stands alone against the Redvest Invaders
Rumors from Altoria Abound

"My gosh!" said Billy. "Now, that's action!"

"Shall I read what it says?" Ashlord asked.

"Please do!"

"Very well. 'Reliable word has just reached this establishment that the Triumvirate of Tracia has amassed an army with the intention of invading Masurthia in the spring. Already, the Redvests have taken the Eastlands, emptying it of food and fodder, and taking slaves for its armies. In that Realm, only Tallinvale remains to stand against them. It has also been stated by an Unimpeachable Source that it is likely that the Dragonkind will soon invade Altoria, if they have not done so already. Tracia, our Source says, will unite its Redvest army with that of the Dragon King and march north against Duinnor, passing by Vanaran lands in order to come at all speed against us.' And so on, and so on, and so on."

Ashlord, smiling, gave the paper to Billy and picked up his cup of tea.

"I say! It's all here, Ashlord! Mebbe I made a difference, after all!" Billy said as he read. Ibin, sitting beside him, also appeared to read, leaning into Billy to do so.

Sheila seemed far away, gazing distractedly through the window. She shook her head, and turned her attention back to the table.

"Do you think it will be enough?" Sheila asked quietly. "Enough to arouse Duinnor?"

"No. Not by itself," Ashlord replied. "But with the other printers who surely are busy putting their own stories to ink, it is a start. And now that Banis is out of the way, others may have a chance to sway the King."

"Ye mean," said Billy, "if someone else don't come along, first."

"Quite so," nodded Ashlord. "But things will fall into place, one way or the other, I think. Which is as it should be."

• • •

By now, the day was fully come, not only in Duinnor, but also in the faraway deserts. There, the dawn broke clear and hot, and as the low beams of Sir Sun's gaze shot across the flat desert north of Almedian, it made five long shadows, fast moving and trailing a thin line of dust. Micerea, on the lead horse, leaned low in the saddle, pacing the gallop so that the others behind her, strung out on a long tether, could keep pace. She did not want to make this horse suffer too much, for it would need its strength when she turned it loose to fend for itself. She planned to move her saddle from one mount to the next, letting each horse free in turn, tossing away her waterskins as they were emptied. If all went well, she would reach the Nalamain Hills in time. There, she hoped to encounter others who, like her, wished for a new life.

She glanced over her shoulder to make sure her packs were still intact on the horse immediately behind her. He carried her clothes and food as well as her weapons and her fine light armor, which she had recently retrieved from where she had left it all those years ago, the day after she had first met Ullin. She hoped she would not need the armor, and that its weight would not slow them too much. But she wanted to have it, if for no other reason than it had been a gift from her father.

"Hie! Hie!" she cried, flicking the ends of her reins against her mount to make the gallop just a bit faster. "If you make me late, I shall find you and have you for dinner!"

It would be a promise she would make to each horse in turn that carried her toward her rendezvous.

Chapter 14

A Beggar, a Monk, and a Prince

"Did you carry out the execution, sire?" Finn asked, pulling up his collar against the cold breeze. Together he and Robby stood on the wall overlooking the north gardens, and they watched the new banner flying from atop the East Tower.

"Yes, Finn. It went just as I had planned."

"I'm sure that it was a most unpleasant test of your skill. But he was an evil man and a clear threat to the safety of your friends."

"Yes. All of that is true," Robby replied. "Very unpleasant. And I regret the need for my friends to witness it. But they, and especially Ashlord, needed to know immediately in order to take any appropriate action to further their safety. There is a risk that Banis had in his employ those who might carry out some form of retribution. I only hope that in his absence his web of corruption will quickly dissolve, allowing upright citizens the opportunity to do their duty."

"And thereby help to prepare the way, so to speak, sire."

"Yes, Finn. To prepare the way."

The flag straightened and snapped in the stiffening breeze,

"I have more to do, but I thought I could benefit from a stroll before I continue with things."

"I am sure that you have much to consider, my lord."

Finn followed Robby's gaze upward to the banner. It was of dark blue fabric, bordered in white, with seven white stars surrounding a winged key.

"Yes, I like it very much," Robby said. "Kinsiri and her girls did a fine job. Please ask them to make a quantity of them, as soon as they have time. And let's make the Winged Key our symbol, shall we?"

"Yes, sire. It does seem appropriate."

"How is Celia getting along with the other girls?"

"Most famously, I have to say. Already she has lost more than one hand of cards to each of them, and that actually pleases her. She does miss seeing you, sire. She told me to say so."

"Hm. And I miss her. Tell her that I'll visit her as soon as I am able. I hope Boxer is well?"

"Oh, yes, my lord. He scampers and binkies more than ever, perhaps due to the fact that he now receives affection from three more young girls."

"Good. Now, to more serious matters. Count Dialmor. I am afraid that we can ill afford such a scheming person free amongst us, especially while we strive to put all else in place. I mean to send him back to Vanara. Will you see to it that Seafar is prepared to receive him?"

"Certainly. I assume all else is ready?"

"Yes. Islindia supports us fully."

"And Queen Serith Ellyn? Have you managed to persuade her, sire?"

"I go slowly with her. She is on her way home, taking the River Osterflo westward. But I've decided against sending someone to take her Seven, at least for the time being. I need to find some way of coaxing the Queen to come around on her own."

Robby shook his head.

"She is quite moody, almost as sad as Islindia, and more easily provoked to anger than I thought she'd be," Robby explained. "I'll keep at it, though. Oh, I almost forgot. You could not but notice the tremor that went through Griferis early yesterday evening?"

"Not even the dead could have ignored it. It was a fearful quake, sire."

"That was my doing, and I apologize. I hope there was not too much damage."

"Your doing, sire?"

"Yes, I am still learning how things work. If I succeed without destroying the entire place, we'll not need Islindia's help for very long. I shall demonstrate when the time comes."

"Well, some dishes and some bottles were upset, and a few were broken. Sire, I hope you do not tax yourself too much."

"No, no. All in a day's work."

Robby felt wretched, and he knew Finn could see as much. Lack of true sleep was bad enough, for the night's dreamwalking required that he do much in a very short while, and he still had much else to do. Added to that, the death of Banis weighed upon him. He was, in fact, shaken by how easy it had been, and afterwards his stomach twisted in knots. It had been necessary, not only for the safety of his friends, but for Duinnor, too. Yet he feared that for every Banis he disposed of, a new one would arise somewhere or other. It was a gamble he had to take, and there was no helping it, now. Nonetheless, he did not enjoy killing Banis, to say the least, and he also felt somewhat guilty about forcing Micerea to watch. But she needed to know what to expect, should things require more such actions. That is, Robby needed her to know. How she reacted told him much of her character, for even though Banis was Elifaen, an enemy of her people, she was appalled.

The most painful aspect of the whole thing was seeing Sheila. He would have preferred relating his message to Ibin, but Ibin's dreams were too sweet to intrude upon, and he might not have been as assertive as was needed. And Certina, though reliable, was off flitting about town on her nocturnal hunt for mice. So he had turned to Sheila, pulling her from an anxiety-ridden nightmare. Robby sighed, looking back up at the new Standard of Griferis.

"Is that all, sire?" Finn asked.

"Yes, Finn. I think I'll take that stroll, and then turn in for a bit."

Finn bowed and departed, leaving Robby to ponder the change he had perceived in Sheila. It had been such a long while since he had seen her, and his self-imposed restraint—that is, his avoidance of her—had most certainly taken its toll on his heart. She was changed. It was not just the clothes or her appearance, although she was more beautiful than ever to his eyes. There was something new and different about her manner, her speech, and her mood. He had seen a similar change in her before, when he met with her at Ashlord's at Tulith Attis. She was much altered then, too, as a result of Ashlord's intense tutelage, and certainly by her terrible experience with Steggan and the awful loss of the unborn child.

"No, this is something else," he thought. He shoved his hands into his cloak pockets and made his way along the parapets. "I should not have lingered. I should have delivered the message, showed her where to go, and left it at that. I should have seen her back home in a flash, rather than strolling along with her that way."

But it was too sweet to resist. He bathed in her presence, no matter how melancholy she was. He wanted to make the dreamscape stretch out, to make the streets a hundred miles long, and the night into a century. Most of all, he wanted to take her into his arms and hold her very close.

"It was a mistake," he addressed himself aloud, "and now I'll pay for it with unbearable longing, as if it wasn't bad enough before. On top of that, she may have guessed who walked with her, which means that, if she still feels anything for me, I've teased her and nettled her. And if she doesn't miss me? Well, in that case, I'm sure she would wish for me to stay away from her."

• • •

"I am amazed," said Ashlord, "that it has been allowed."

He and his charges looked at the red door of the warehouse. They had already peered in through the grimy windows, and they had seen the many cots and partitions arranged around the old floor, nearly all of which were occupied by sleeping guests within. Walking along the front of the building, they came to the entrance and stopped, staring at the door.

"Why do ye say that?" Billy asked.

"Because the King ordered that no door is to be painted red," Ashlord explained. "Heavy fines are imposed on anyone found owning a door of that color, regardless whether it is the door to a bedchamber or water closet."

"Seems a silly rule," said Sheila.

"Yes, but the King fears red doors. It is rumored that each Avatar takes the shape of a thing that may play a part in the King's demise."

"Yeah,but, yeahbutAshlord, Ashlord, whataboutfryingpans, and, and-what, andwhataboutquills, and, and washboards, andlightningbugs, and—"

"Yes, yes, Ibin! You refer to past Avatars. No, it seems that this is the first year that the King has ever taken such steps. I think it is a foolish attempt to quell discontent, for, soon after the Avatar took on its current form, it became the thing to do as a protest, to paint one's door red, that is. Since the law banning red doors, those who do so willingly pay the fine, knowing their point was made. But some paint the doors of those they do not like, to cause them expense and trouble."

"Oh, good grief! What a place Duinnor is!" said Sheila. "Shall we go in?"

"No, no! Not yet," said Billy. He gestured down the street. "I've gotta go to the Palace, first. To see if the rest of me dream is true."

"Yes. That we must do," agreed Ashlord. "Let us go on, and, should it seem fitting, we'll come back here."

They hurried off, with Billy leading the way, and after a few turns along the busy midmorning streets, they approached the front gates of the Palace. Billy pointed at a lone man a few yards away. He sat with his back against the wall, his knees up in front of him, and he had an old blanket thrown over his head and shoulders.

"That's the man!"

Billy trotted over to the fellow, and he bent over him, saying, "Sir, sir! I don't mean to bother ye, but I was wonderin' if ye might tell me whar the others went off to?"

The man opened his eyes, looked up at Billy, and stretched his hand out.

"Help me up, laddie, if ye don't mind."

Billy gave the man a tug up, and the man stamped his feet and pulled the blanket back around his shoulders.

"They went to find the red door," he said. "An' that's where I'll be goin' now, too, since ye found me alright."

"Wait. What do ye mean, since I found ye?"

"Ye've been foretold to me, in a dream, don't ye know? A man came to me in me dreams an' told me to stay at me place until the red-haired lad comes along. An' he told me to say the followin', if some doubt crossed yer mind: The New King fears no door of any hue, nor any lock that may be put upon it, for no door may bar his comin' or goin', an' no lock may hinder his will."

Billy stared at the man, afraid to hope that the words spoke of Robby and his uncanny ability to unlock things. The man shrugged and sauntered off, apparently anxious to have a meal and some place warm to sleep. Then he stopped and came back, glancing at Ashlord with a suspicious eye.

"I nearly forgot. Somethin' else he told me. He said to tell ye that yer sis an' yer mum an' even yer dad are all safe. In case the bird hadn't told ye, he said."

The man jogged on off, and Ashlord patted Billy on the shoulder.

"I think we all know, by now, who sent that message," he said to Billy, "and who sent Sheila's message to her, too."

"I can't hardly believe it," said Billy as they began to retrace their way back to the warehouse. "I mean, ye already told me 'bout me family. But that man knew, too. From a dream, just like me an' Sheila. An' the man knew it was Certina what told us, after a manner."

"So it seems."

They arrived back at the warehouse, and just when they approached the door, they met with a Temple monk who was also approaching to enter. He was carrying a basket of potatoes, and Ashlord held the door for him.

"Thank you," said the monk, going in. "May I help you? Oh, it is you! How nice it is to see you once again."

It was the very same monk they had first encountered when they had arrived at the Temple, the one who had later made the arrangements for them to be smuggled into the city.

"Hello. It is good to see you again, too," Ashlord said. Meanwhile, Ibin took the large basket from the monk.

"The kitchen is over there, through that door. Thank you," the monk said, pointing at a far door.

"Is this a new establishment?" Ashlord asked.

"Yes, it is. Come in, come in. We opened just yesterday, in fact," the monk said. "It was brought to our attention that some who were reluctant to go across the city might need a place closer at hand to where they normally abide."

"I don't understand," said Sheila. "Why would they come here but not to your other places?"

"Most of the people you see here have come from the Palace walls," the monk said, "a place where the indigent and homeless often congregate in makeshift shelters. Many ask alms of the wealthy and powerful who come and go from the Palace. Others wait to be called by the Kingsmen so that their grievance may be heard by the King."

"Ye mean the King sees ordinary folk?" asked Billy. "An' helps 'em out?"

"It is the right of every citizen of Duinnor to apply to see the King," answered the monk. "But I have never heard of any applicants being called. Still, the hopeless often grasp at straws."

"How came you to open this place?" asked Ashlord.

"It was ordered by the Oracle. It came to him in a vision on the day before yesterday that the owner of this warehouse would rather it be occupied by us than to have it confiscated by the Crown."

"Confiscated?" asked Billy.

"It is a law that unless a place of business pays taxes to the King, it becomes the property of the King. Apparently, this place has been unoccupied for a year or more, and the owner grew tired of paying the tax on the empty building. He signed over a lease to the Temple yesterday, exempting him from paying the tax."

As they spoke, they moved a little farther into the place. There were hastily set up ropes crisscrossing the large room from which hung cloth partitions, somewhat like an infirmary. Indeed, from the coughing and sniffling and the crying babies and other sounds, it was apparent that food and warmth were not the only things these people needed.

"How many people do you have staying here?" Sheila asked.

"As of a few moments ago, over eighty. That includes children and infants."

"And the red door?" Ashlord asked. "Was it red when you moved in?"

"Yes, it was. Much to our dismay. We informed our Oracle immediately concerning it. He reminded us that in days of yore a red door was a sign of welcome. And he commanded that we were to make no change to the door unless ordered to do so by the Kingsmen. So far, they have not bothered us, yet they cannot have missed it, what with so many of them coming and going along these streets."

"I should say not. Hm. And does the Temple pay for the care and food here?"

"No, and that's an interesting bit. A sizeable sum of coin was given to us by a visitor. He came late last night, bringing with him most of the people you see here. His deed was also foretold to us by the Oracle. It was the Oracle's prophecy that a young prince would come to us and bring with him some who would need our care. And the prince would also give us the means, in gold and silver, to provide for the needy. I'm sorry to say that you just missed him."

"Did he say his name?"

"No. He helped us put things in order here, helping with the people late last night and through most of this morning. He made beds, worked in the kitchen, and helped with cleaning out the back rooms to make a pantry. He gave us a thousand-weight of silver and gold, and he departed. All he said was that he had a dream that compelled him to do what he did."

"Ashlord," Sheila said, pulling him aside, "you know as well as I do that all of this is a sign."

"Yes, and a most interesting one, too."

"And you know who sends this sign, don't you?"

"I think that I do."

"I think that I do, too," she nodded. "If it comes from," she glanced around, "from you-know-who, what is it that he means for us to do?"

"I can hardly guess," Ashlord said, then waggled his finger to indicate they should not speak just yet. Turning to the monk, he pulled out his purse.

"I would be honored if you would accept these coins to help with your new place," he said, putting a generous sum into the monk's hand. "And I thank you for being so patient with our questions."

"Not at all," the monk bowed. "Thank you for the gift."

"Tell me, how does the Oracle seem to you these days?"

The monk thought about the question for a moment as he held the door open for Ashlord.

"I would say that his time draws to an end," he said. "His countenance changed on the day that he instructed us concerning this new establishment. He washed himself. And he also ordered food brought to him. He actually ate, right there in the sanctuary, as he spoke to us. He seemed relieved, even happy."

"Hm. Thank you."

Outside, Ashlord led them the long way around, away from the Palace, and waved down a passing carriage for hire.

"Wysteria Place," he told the driver. "No, Ibin, not on the footboard. Let us all ride inside."

Once they had settled in and were on their way, Ashlord further explained.

"Snow begins to fall more heavily, and there are other reasons for taking this carriage," he told them. "We have taken an awful chance walking openly through the city this morning, and I do not wish to push our luck. And I can think of no safer place to hear the news than at Starlight Hall, so I plan for us to impose upon Lady Highleaf for a few days, at least. With the death of Banis, I fear there will be much confusion in the Palace. The King will no doubt be furious. Meanwhile, there are many who would love to take the late lord's place as First Lord of the High Chamber. Last night, when the Avatar suddenly released Farby, it was a sign of something else, of a different kind of confusion in the King's tower. Why should the King so suddenly turn Farby away when it was the King, through the Avatar, who had summoned Farby? Obviously Banis prompted the King do do so. But why didn't the King let it play out?"

"Mebbe somethin' Banis said made the King doubt him," offered Billy.

"The King does not talk to people, Billy, or rarely does, anyway. He reads their minds just as one might read a book, opening any memory like a page that he wishes to consult. No one may hide his heart from the King. But now that Banis is dead, we may never know what transpired. Meanwhile, this carriage is as good a place as any to talk about these things. We can hardly be overheard over the noise of the street. And with the windows closed and the shades down, no one outside can see us. I would very much like to hear about the dreams that you and Sheila had that brought us out this morning. Why don't you go first, Billy?"

"Well, it warn't like no other dream I ever had, I can tell ye that!" Billy declared. "In a way, it warn't even like a dream. It was too right, nuthin' out of place, 'cept that me an' this other feller flew over rooftops an' all. Other than that, it was like I was awake."

"And could you discern who your guide was?"

"No. An older feller, I think. Had a hood up an' it was dark. I could see a beard, but that's about all. He did glance at me a couple of times, sorta familiar-like."

"But you know who it was, don't you, Sheila?" said Ashlord.

"I'm not sure," she said. "The more I think about it, the more I wonder. The man in my dream was just as Billy described. Tall. Old, I think. A beard. And, like Billy said, when he took my hand we flew over the city. Then, after he showed me where I was to go, he flew back with me, holding my hand, and we landed, if that's what you call it, some few streets away from our apartments. He asked if he could walk along with me the rest of the way home. I didn't want to at first because, well, because for a moment I was afraid of him. But he seemed... Oh, you'll think I'm silly!"

"What? He, he, heseemedwhat,Sheila?" Ibin asked.

"He seemed kind," she said. "And, do you know how sometimes in dreams there's a mood?"

"I do not," Ashlord said.

"I do," said Billy.

"I do," said Ibin.

"Well, this mood, *his* mood, was sad. Or maybe lonely. I'm not sure, maybe both. Anyway, I said yes, that he could walk with me. Our footsteps didn't make any tracks in the snow, or any sound. We just walked. He didn't say another word all the way back home. Even though I had been somewhat afraid of him, earlier on, while we walked I felt very safe with him, and very warm. When we reached our apartments, he stopped, and he asked an odd question. 'What dream would you most enjoy having tonight?' And I told him, I don't know why, that I would love to go home. 'Home to Barley?' he asked. 'No,' I said. 'Home to Mira and to Mr. Ribbon. And to Robby.' That's when he looked at me, right at me, I mean, for the very first time. 'I wish I could give you that dream,' he said. And when he said that, I saw his eyes. They were black and watery. Then I recognized him! And when I did, I woke up! Oh, Ashlord! What has happened?"

Suddenly Sheila buried her face in Ashlord's shoulder and sobbed.

"It was Robby!" she cried. "It was Robby! What does it mean? Why did I dream that he was so old?"

"Come, come, dear," Ashlord put his arms around her, and Ibin reached over and put his hand on Sheila's knee. Billy was pale and nodded his head with the realization.

"What *does* it mean, Ashlord?" he asked.

"His age? I cannot say why or how he appeared that way to you," Ashlord said. "As for the rest, well, I think it means that Robby asserts his power. You see, I have known for some time that he is a dreamwalker."

Sheila pulled away from Ashlord and wiped her face, looking at him.

"A dreamwalker," he explained, "has the ability to visit your dreams, no matter how far away he might be. And a dreamwalker can also look upon the world as if he was awake, seeing those things that happen while he sleeps. I have come to surmise that Robby gained his ability very recently. While you and he made your way across the plains with Ullin. That is why he was so tired all the time, ever needing sleep and rest. It seems that while a person dreamwalks, he does not gain from sleep any replenishment of strength or spirit. And, as Robby explained to me, it has other peculiarities."

"But why ain't he come to us before now?" Billy asked.

"He may have tried," Ashlord shrugged. "Or he may have been prevented by other things that he has had to do. I can't say. But I feel certain that it was he who showed Certina that your family is safe, your father and sister and mother, and that's how she was able to relate news of them to me."

"I don't understand," Sheila said. "Maybe he has been busy. Maybe he's been in trouble. But why would he look so changed, so old? I mean, Billy saw him that way, too."

"I would not hazard a guess on that," Ashlord said.

"It all means that he's got the Name, don't it?" said Billy. "An' that he's gonna be King, right? That's what the man said, Robby said, that is. To go an' see the beggars at the Palace so that we'd know that the New King was on the way. An' remember what the beggarman said about the New King not bein' afraid of doors, an' locks an' such? That's gotta be Robby, right? Robby always had a knack with locks an' doors an' knots an' such. We all knew about that before he rung the Bell. An' remember them iron gates back at Nowhar? He opened them up lickety-split! So Robby's gonna be the New King, after all!"

"Your logic is, for once at least, quite impeccable, Master Bosk," Ashlord said. "I see no other conclusion to draw. I only hope he succeeds."

"An' why wouldn't he?" Billy said, grinning. "I mean, it oughta be a cinch for ol' Robby, right?"

"Perhaps. But let us not forget that the present King still rules. And his powers are considerable, uncanny, and inscrutable. He has reigned for over five centuries, so his own abilities must surely be formidable."

Ashlord's words were like icy water on Billy's enthusiasm. Billy sat back in his seat, frowning. They rode on in silence for a while before Sheila spoke.

"I would like to see him again," she said. "Before he becomes King, anyway. In person. I suppose that's not very likely, though, is it? I seem to go from one hour to the next all the way from hope and determination to feeling just plain nothing, no feelings at all. I don't know how much more I can bear. And, no offense, Billy, but it all seems so stupid and silly and temporary. I think I'd like nothing better than to plant an acorn and just watch it grow for a couple of hundred years, and then decide what to feel. I'm sorry. I don't know what I'm saying."

Her companions looked at her sympathetically. She impulsively pulled the blind away from the window next to her and stared out at the passing scenery.

"I would like to see him again, regardless," she stated. "If only there was a way to do so."

Chapter 15

Gladsten

A confident messenger resolutely strode along Halfton Way, that same street in northern Duinnor City where Sheila had naively ordered her driver to go when she was still new to town. It was a district of squalid pubs, brothels, and gambling dens, the domain of cutthroats and rakes, and the haunt of those with less than honorable intentions. The messenger was a big man, familiar with all the ways and byways of this part of Duinnor City, but his experience, his size, and the cudgel he waved served to prevent him from being molested. Most of the denizens of this place knew him well enough to know that the cudgel he carried had often been used to ward off muggers ignorant of his strength. His business was usually along the lines of taking or leaving messages, but he was also sent by some of his many employers to collect money that was owed to them. He was pleasant enough; that is, he said good morning when it was said to him, and he never took sides in the many brawls that broke out along the streets.

This morning, he made his earliest rounds, having already gone through the better neighborhoods. By night or in the early morning, he visited the back doors of mansions and estates, picking up his dispatches and coins, moving from one to the next before there were very many about who might wonder at his business. After his collections, and throughout the day, he delivered those messages, taking them to wherever they needed to go, and he guarded them along the way with the discreetness and cold ferocity upon which his reputation relied.

It was not long after he left the back door of Lord Banis, and just before the commotion broke out on the third floor of that house, that he turned down Halfton Way, stepping around the drunks who were passed out in the gutter. He walked down the middle of the street, as was his habit to better sense anyone who might make a move against him. When two men who had each other by the collar stumbled in front of him, he shoved them both away to continue their fight. They fell aside into a large puddle of dirty half-melted snow, rolling over each other as they swung their fists. Keeping on, the messenger passed a middle-aged woman in dripping eyeliner who, when she saw him coming, sauntered out from her doorway, smiling. When she recognized him, she gave up her act, dismissing him with a wave of her hand.

"G'mornin', Mixy," the man said as he passed.

She shrugged and went back to lean against the doorway as he turned the corner and disappeared down a narrow alley. Coming to a slit between two buildings, he gripped his cudgel firmly and squeezed his big frame through, trying not to get the grime of the brick on his cloak. The passage soon opened to a junk-strewn yard, and he walked up a flight of steps and tapped on the door, looking over his shoulder cautiously.

The door opened, and a woman took the parcel from him, nodding when she saw the seal.

"Are ye collectin' today?" asked the woman.

"Not today. Ye have 'til five more days, though, er else I'll be back with me helpers to fetch away yer things."

"Alright then."

The man nodded and went his way.

The woman watched him go, then closed the door. She bolted the door and turned within.

"A note for ye," she said as she tossed the parcel onto the table where her husband sat eating his breakfast. He was dressed and ready for work, as he always was at this hour, and he put down his bowl, wiping his mouth on a napkin as he looked at the seal.

"A job, I bet," said the woman, sitting across from the man and picking up her knitting.

"Yep. An' just in time, too," said the man. "We ain't done too bad since we got here, but things've kinda thinned out, ain't they, me dear?"

"Aye. But we got too many customers for it to go on too long. I'll bet ye'll be as busy as a bee afore long. A note from Mr. D is always a sign."

"That seems the way of it, lovie. Not much doin' for weeks on end, an' all comes at once. Let's see what the job is."

He opened the parcel and read the brief note. He blinked, then read it again. He looked at his wife and broke into a grin.

"A nice job, then?" she asked.

"Aye, a tidy job, indeed! A very tidy job, as is the usual way of things from Mr. D. A fortuitous job, apt to be mighty satisfyin'! Mighty satisfyin'!"

"Whatever do ye mean by that, sweetie?"

"Well, it's along the lines of disposal, an' a nice quantity, too."

"That's wonderful! A heavy purse it'll bring!"

"Aye. An' that ain't even the best of it!"

"Oh?"

"Listen at this."

He read the note aloud, lingering on the names, glancing up at his wife's reaction. She dropped her knitting into her lap and stared at her husband.

"Unbelievable!"

"This makes all worthwhile, don't it? Comin' all the way 'cross the plains, an' makin' our way here so profitably in such a short while. An' now we've got a bit of revenge handed right to us."

"Most unbelievable, indeed! That they're here in Duinnor!"

"If only thar bratty friend was on the list, too! That Bosk boy an' his idiot friend warn't never far off from the Ribbon lad!"

He stood and paced, clapped his hands and rubbed them in unrestrained delight.

"Oh, I'd just about do this job for free!" he declared.

"I wouldn't go so far as that," said his wife, "even though it's a fine way to get back at them horrible folk what kicked us out of Barley."

"I knew, I always knew, that makin' our alliance with Mr. D would pay off big! Let's see, I'll need the broadaxe sharpened up nicely. An' a big basket from Mr. Crawler. I'll use me usual boys to bring along our guests. Oh, an' ye'll need to fetch a lot of water for cleaning up the place. An' we'll get Ganner to make the delivery to Lady Highleaf once we've got all bundled up in a nice present. Why mebbe we should even put a bow on it!"

The woman got up from her seat and came around to her husband, giving him a hug.

"Me congratulations to ye, Mr. Gladsten."

"Why, I thank ye, Mrs. Gladsten."

"Now get on with yer breakfast, an' off to work ye go!"

"Yes, ma'am!"

• • •

Having become a man of a particular business shortly after arriving in Duinnor, even if it was an unsavory profession, and finding that he had a knack for the art of murder, Mr. Gladsten was proudly meticulous in his craft. This morning he wasted no time getting to his latest commission, immediately sending word for his accomplices to meet him at the usual place. Then, as he finished his morning tea, he put some final touches to his short-handled broadaxe by dressing the blade with a whetstone, and carefully packed it into his leather shoulder sack. He put on his long coat, slipping a couple of daggers into the pockets, and waited for his wife to get ready. Soon they walked down from their rooms, and through the alley to Halfton Way, where they kissed and parted company, she to fetch the needed basket, and he to meet with his colleagues.

All the way, Mr. Gladsten hummed, happy with the hand that fortune had dealt him, and looking forward to the day's work. Ever since the humiliation of being expelled from Barley, escorted all the way to the other side of Janhaven by Sheriff Fivelpont and his deputies, he had nursed the grudge within him. He longed to go back and burn the entire county to the ground. He passed a tavern, and saw pasted to the glass the morning's broadsheets. He stopped, reading with wonder the news of the Redvest invasion, relishing every detail of the reports.

"Well, the fates are aligned with me, it seems," he said with a note of satisfaction. "An' it seems I've got some Redvest friends I never knew I had! They can take care of them what's still in Barley, an' I'll take care of them what's come to Duinnor."

With a gleeful step and a jovial grin, hardly able to contain his mirth, Mr. Gladsten took a stroll over to Crescent Avenue. Striking an attitude of having some business there, he strode around the apartments, and he paid special attention to the doors and windows. Coming around a corner, he spotted Mr. Yarman who was checking the leads to his team.

"Pardon me, sir," Gladsten said, pulling a slip of paper from his pocket and glancing at it. He shoved the old bill back into his coat when he was sure that Yarman saw him do so.

"Yes?"

"I've got an order to be delivered, an' I'm just tryin' to figure if this here's the right place."

"Who is it for?"

"Sootking, Brinnin, an' Bosk. An' a lady, too."

"This is the place. But they ain't here at the moment."

"Ah, just as well, seein' as the delivery, which is quite large, ain't quite yet ready. I just happened by an' thought I'd make sure I knew whar to bring it. So they all live here? Tell me, since the thing I'm to deliver is quite unwieldy, is it many steps up to thar rooms?"

"They occupy the third floor, so yes."

"Oh, me! Well, that's good to know. I suppose they took them rooms 'cause the lower ones are all let out."

"Mebbe. But, taken or not, only the third floor is occupied by tenants."

"Oh, I see. Well, I thank ye, sir. I best get on an' see to things. Good day to ye."

"Good day."

Gladsten hurried off, retracing his steps back to Halfton Way and then to a gambling room in the vicinity. With the exception of the yawning proprietor, who nodded at Gladsten, the place was empty of customers. He passed through to the rear room where waited three sullen men. For the first time all morning, Mr. Gladsten frowned. It was not a group to be proud of, he mused, wishing that he had the silver to pay for a truly professional-looking crew, men who took some pride in their appearance. But they were what he had, and they were capable enough, each having proved himself on more than one previous commission.

"I surely hope getting up at this ungodly hour will be worth it," said one fellow as Gladsten approached.

"The usual kind of job," said Gladsten, "times four. Meanin', four times the pay for each of us, once the job's done to me satisfaction."

"Well! That's good!"

He briefly related their task, and they nodded casually.

"So I figure that we'll go in by the kitchen door, when the moment's opportune," Gladsten explained. "Now, thar may be somebody er other in the way, servants er whatnot, er meddlin' neighbors. But since our commission is only for the four, we'll not receive a penny more, regardless of how many we must take care of. Rest assured, our patron ain't the kind to be squeezed, so don't go gettin' idears. For ever' one of us, he's got two-score ready an' willin' to hunt us down if we cross him. Got it? An' it goes double if we don't do things just as ordered done. I'd be not at all surprised that his other agents don't watch our ever' move, with thar own commission to assure the work, ready to act on us without another word."

"So it's the mysterious Mr. D, again," said one of the men. "I think yer afraid of him."

"That's right. I am," said Gladsten. "An' I know for a firsthand fact, from havin' seen his handiwork at Northgate, that his folk love to take hours an' hours playin' with them what cross Mr. D. Do ye catch me drift?"

"Enough talkin'," said another man. "When's the time to do the thing?"

"Tonight. If all the other parts come along on time. I'll be wanderin' back over to make sure of things a bit later."

●　●　●

"Don't worry," said Ashlord to Ibin as they were being led upstairs to Lady Highleaf's sitting rooms. "I'll send for our things in a few days, including your mandolin."

The butler knocked and entered, then shortly reappeared.

"Lady Highleaf will see you."

Inside, Lady Highleaf was still in her dressing robe, sitting at her breakfast table which was strewn with the morning papers.

"Back so soon!" she said, putting down her teacup. "I was just reading the news of the day, and I am quite put out to find only two small reports concerning Starlight Hall. Really! And I thought my party was a great success!"

"I am sure it was, dear lady," said Ashlord. "But it appears as though someone has imposed upon the printers of the town to play up other events."

"Yes. And I suspect you are behind it."

"Come, now. Surely the printers delay their reports on your party only so that they may collect an adequate number of superlatives."

"Don't patronize me, Ashlord," Lady Highleaf said. "Shevalia, you'll be happy to learn that you are mentioned most prominently and almost exclusively in the few measly notes that serve as reports on our party. Oh, my dear!"

At last she noticed their grim faces. She stood and looked from Sheila to Billy, then to Ibin and Ashlord.

"What is amiss?"

"We have decided," said Ashlord, "that is, I have decided that we would be safer under your roof than ours. If we might impose upon you for a few days."

"Certainly. And it will not be an imposition, at all. I don't suppose this has to do with the news of war, does it? Do you think that you are suspected of being the source of the news?"

"No, that is not it at all. We think the days ahead may be full of turmoil due to events closer at hand."

"Closer at hand?"

"Yes," said Ashlord. "It seems that Lord Banis is now deceased. By all appearances, he threw himself from his bedroom window and fell to his death."

Lady Highleaf stared at Ashlord, then sat back down.

"By all appearances?" she asked.

"We saw it happen, Lady Highleaf," said Sheila. "We were nearby."

Lady Highleaf's eyes narrowed. "Did you…?"

"I assure you, we had nothing to do with it," said Ashlord. "But we all saw it happen. It was foretold to us, in a manner of speaking, and we went to his neighborhood to see what we might see. We were as surprised as could be at what transpired."

"And so we fear, knowing the recent narrow escape that Ashlord had," continued Sheila, "that we would all be safer here until things have settled down."

"I see," said Lady Highleaf. She absently looked at the papers before her for a moment, then stood once more and pulled on a bell rope. Her butler knocked and entered.

"Yes, my lady?"

"Denks, send the carriage for my nephew right away and have Harlson drive it over there in haste. He is to inform Grantham that it is a matter of the greatest urgency. Tell Harlson to do or say whatever he must to compel Grantham to come! On your way, please send in Alma."

"Yes, my lady."

"Grant had nothing to do with it," said Sheila once the door was closed.

"It doesn't matter if he did or if he didn't," said Lady Highleaf. "Grantham ridiculed Banis in front of everyone last night, and said other things about Banis that might have been overheard, so he will be suspect. And, if what happened later last night is any indication, it must have been on Grantham's account that Banis was further humiliated before the King. At least, that's how I put it together. Dead or not, the Banis people may still be loyal to him, and might try something."

Another knock came on the door and a woman entered.

"You sent for me, my lady?"

"Yes, Alma. It seems that I shan't be going out, after all. But I wish to dress quickly in case we have more visitors. What do you think of the dark green house dress?"

"I think it is right smart, my lady."

"Very well, then, have it brought to my dressing room. If you would excuse me, gentlemen, Lady Shevalia. I won't be but a moment. Please make yourselves comfortable."

Lady Highleaf departed, and Ashlord went to the papers, some of which he had seen at the teahouse. He shuffled through them as the others looked awkwardly at each other, then took seats around the room.

"Hm," said Ashlord, moving a saucer so that he could read more. "Hrumph! Indeed!"

"What?" asked Billy.

"Trifles about last night," Ashlord answered, tossing aside a paper and looking through another. "Lady Highleaf overstated the paucity of stories. It seems our Lady Shevalia did, indeed, cause something of a stir. I can only imagine what might have been printed if the other news had not required so much ink."

"What do you mean?" asked Sheila.

"I am loath to read it aloud."

"Please, do."

"Only a portion, if you insist. 'Perhaps if we had known before that Lady Shevalia is of Elifaen stock (which those of us who witnessed her skill upon the ice should have guessed), we might have been less shocked by her appearance last night. Still, the only attire that may have been more revealing of her prodigious natural beauty would have been a gown made of air, of the sort as it is supposed that her kind once wore, if legend is true, needing no other clothing for shame or protection's sake. But such was her grace and forthright lack of self-consciousness, that, to this observer's eye, anyway, she could not have been more innocent, womanly specimen though she is. Indeed, although some others in attendance used less fabric in their attire than was contained in half of Shevalia's, they had not the other attributes to be the least bit attractive whilst within the same room as she. And while Shevalia's manner provoked none, nor snubbed any, the ladies present were as unanimous in their jealousy as were the gentlemen in their admiration.' And so on, and so forth."

Ashlord looked up from the paper. Sheila shrugged. Billy screwed his mouth up to say something, but he suddenly and uncharacteristically thought better of it with a slight shake of his head. Sheila was about to ask Ashlord to read more when she saw that Ibin was frowning.

"What's wrong, Ibin?" she asked.

"Oh, ohnothing. Oh,nothingbutIwas, Iwas, butIwaswonderingwhen-wewe'regoingtogohome," he stated. He nodded, as if to say, "That's what's wrong."

"Oh," Sheila said.

"We'll be gettin' on our way, just as soon as we can, big man," Billy said.

"It has been a long trip, hasn't it, Ibin?" Ashlord asked sympathetically.

"Yes, yesit, yesithasbeen."

"Yes. It has been," Sheila agreed.

Ashlord put down the papers and gazed at the window.

"Much has changed since we left the east," he said after a few moments. "Not everything has gone the way we may have wished. I daresay we have all been changed in some manner or other along the way. But, Ibin, you have changed least of all, outwardly, that is. You keep your worries inside, and shore up the rest of us with your good heart. Yet, though you say little, I wonder if you are not the most deeply affected by all that you have seen and been through?"

Sheila detected, for the first time since she had known Ashlord, a deep tone of weariness, a note of doubt and darkness. It was odd to hear him, of all people, express such sentiments.

"No, no, I'm, noAshlord, Iamstillthesame," Ibin answered.

He began to hum, and after a few notes, he softly sang, his eyes to the floor.

I am just tired, my friends, but no more than you.
I feel so very out of place, but that is nothing new.
The things that you fret on are beyond my head,
My heart's on other things, from breakfast until bed.
I wonder why one fellow's bad, when another can be good,
I think on all the birdsongs, and of Islindia's wood.
I wonder 'bout the mountain witch, and Ullin's mandolin.
I recall the kindly Greenfar folk, and good ol' Robby's grin.
But I remember Buckie, too, and how happy he would be
To take an apple from my hand and give a ride to me.
I remember Barley stars up in the summer nights,
And Lady Moon's kind smile over Passdale lights.
I wish to see Sir Sun again on chilly Boskland morns,
And long to pick some blackberries, full amongst the thorns.
But they are not so far away, right here inside my chest,
And just as long as I'm with you, I'll wait for all the rest.

"Oh, Ibin!" Sheila exclaimed, getting up and kissing him on both cheeks. "You have been such a good, good friend. I am so very glad that you are with us."

"That goes double for me, big feller!" Billy agreed, patting Ibin on the knee. "Without all the kisses, of course."

Lady Highleaf re-entered, still buttoning her sleeves.

"It's all arranged," she announced. "Lady Shevalia, you shall have your same rooms as before, and the gents will be put up down the hall from you. Word has been sent to my nephew. And, Mr. Brinnin, lunch has been ordered, as I'm sure you are glad to hear. We'll dine as soon as we are called. Now, what does that leave for us to do?"

"I see you have quite a collection of this morning's broadsheets," Ashlord said. "I wonder if you would send a footman for those that might be printed this afternoon?"

"As a regular thing, I receive all and every edition of every broadsheet printed in this city," Lady Highleaf stated as if it could not possibly be otherwise.

"Ah. As I should have known."

"Not that there's all that much of interest," she said, looking at Sheila. "Last night's events are hardly mentioned at all, save for a few notes concerning attire."

"Oh?" Sheila said innocently.

"That is so. Now," she turned to Ashlord again, "I assume that you wish your presence here be kept quiet."

"Yes."

"In that case, you'll have to remain behind doors, so to speak, for a day or two. It will take that long for everything to be put away from last night's party. I brought in extra help for the party, and for the aftermath, so Starlight Hall is a busy place today."

"We will try to stay out of the way," Sheila said.

"And what should we do about your belongings?"

"Let us leave them where they are, for the time being," answered Ashlord.

"That might be best," agreed Highleaf. "I have already personally spoken with the footmen who brought you up, and the others of my house who have seen you this morning. They will say nothing of your presence, I can assure you. I take pride in my staff for their discretion, and they are accustomed to waiting on the occasional private guest or two."

"We thank you, Lady Highleaf," Ashlord said.

"Not at all. But would you perhaps inform me as to how it came about that you witnessed what you saw?"

"Well, it would be easy to explain, but not so easy for you to believe, I think."

"Oh? Try me."

"Very well, then. Lady Shevalia had a strong premonition, of sorts, and begged us all to go look for the place that her premonition told her she should go to and watch."

"A premonition?" Lady Highleaf looked askance at Sheila.

"Yes. Of a sort."

"An' that's not all," Billy put in. Ashlord waved a hand at him.

"Let us not tax Lady Highleaf with too many explanations and stories, Billy," he said.

"On the contrary, please tax me," Highleaf said. Then she turned to Sheila. "You had a premonition that Lord Banis would jump to his death, or be pushed?"

"No. I had no idea what we would see," Sheila explained. "Only that we should go to such and such a place along the street and wait to see what we might see. I was as surprised and shocked as anyone could be at what happened. And I don't know if he was pushed or if he jumped."

"Hm!" Lady Highleaf sat down beside Sheila. "It does stretch credulity a bit, doesn't it?"

"Yes," agreed Ashlord. "And so you understand better why we sought refuge here. We may have been seen in the vicinity, and questions will be asked. There is already a cloud over us concerning the servant girl, Reysa."

"Yes, of course."

Lady Highleaf leaned back in her seat, and she absently fiddled with the gold chain that dangled upon her bosom. She pursed her lips and squinted her eyes. She blew an exasperated sigh and abruptly stood.

"Ashlord," she said, "I should have known that trouble and danger would follow you to Duinnor. They always have, and always will, I suppose. But I shall stand by you, all of you. I wish you could trust me to tell me more, the whole story of why you are all here. I might be able to help you. You were a good friend to my father, and to his before him, and I have valued your kindness and friendship all my life, ever since I was a little girl. Now I am in this, too, you know. And, since we seem to have some time on our hands, why not just out with it all? Every last bit."

Billy raised his brows, looking at Ashlord and Sheila. Sheila shrugged.

Ashlord nodded and motioned for Lady Highleaf to resume her seat.

"Then I think we should all get comfortable," he said. "Let me think. Where to begin this tale? With Cupeldain? No, that's too far back, and I'm sure you know all those tales. Hm. Perhaps Esildre, the daughter of Lord Banis."

"Esildre? What does that whore have to do with you?"

"Lady Highleaf! She is not a whore," said Sheila. "At least, not any more, I don't think. If she ever truly was."

Lady Highleaf looked at Sheila as one might look at a child, shaking her head.

"No, that isn't necessary, either," Ashlord went on. "Lady Highleaf, do you remember the night when all the bells of Duinnor rang all by themselves?"

"Who doesn't remember that night? Or the wild days of panic that followed?"

"Well," Ashlord said, taking out his pipe, "I think that day is where we should begin our tale. And you will soon understand what very few in all of Duinnor might even suspect, about that night, and about what is yet to come."

• • •

"Ah," said Gladsten to Miss Tarrier. "So they ain't expected back, then?"

This was one of those inconveniences that annoyed Mr. Gladsten, but he was careful not to let it show, and kept smiling affably.

"I can't say," answered Miss Tarrier. "And I hope they don't come back, is all I have to add."

"An' where, might ye guess, would they all be off to?" persisted Gladsten. "I only ask 'cause I'm to make a special delivery of some goods, an' me note says to give 'em directly to Mr. Sootking."

"Like I said, I ain't got the foggiest, sir."

"Well, I'm a bit put out over what to do, ma'am."

"I guess you'll just have to go back to your shop, or wherever, and wait for Mr. Sootking, or Ashlord, or whatever his name might truly be, to let you know what to do with his things. And when he does, you might suggest that they fetch away all their belongings, too."

"I will do that, ma'am."

Mr. Gladsten moved toward the door, and Miss Tarrier held it for him.

"I knew no good would come of them!" Miss Tarrier said as he bowed and put on his hat. "And I only hope that Lady Highleaf don't get in the way, so to speak, of their troubles. All for taking a liking to Lady Shevalia."

"Lady Highleaf?" Gladsten paused in the doorway. "What does she have to do with them?"

By now, Miss Tarrier was on the verge of tears once more, shaking her head and wringing her hands.

"And all this, all at once, with my head swimming all morning, my eyes playing tricks on me, too!"

"What was that 'bout Lady Highleaf?"

"All morning, since just after breakfast, I kept seeing odd lights in the house. And, once, I could have sworn that I glimpsed a child standing at the top of the stairs. Then them odd lights flashed again, and when I rubbed my eyes clear of them, nothing!"

"I am sure ye've been through far too much, dear lady," Gladsten soothed her. "Perhaps a cup of tea an' a bit of a rest would do ye good."

"Perhaps so."

"An' what was it that ye mentioned 'bout the lady takin' to Lady Shevalia?"

Gladsten removed his hat and led Miss Tarrier back into the kitchen, pulling a chair for her to sit in. He did not mention that he, too, had the odd sensation of seeing a face in the parlor as they passed. A face that abruptly disappeared in a blur of soft blue light that seemed to linger for a moment. It was very uncanny, but Mr. Gladsten shrugged it off and put a kettle on.

"Why don't ye just begin at the start of things, Miss Tarrier, whilst the pot boils. I count meself a pretty good listener."

• • •

Robby saw that the King had weakened. He did not know why, but his visits to the High Chambers of the tower were frequent enough, by now, for him to notice the difference right away when he returned to the Tower on the day Banis died. The strange mantle that covered the King at all times was dull in places, grayish silver in color, while other areas of the mantle still glowed with brilliant golden light. It was baffling.

Robby's reason for coming so often was in the hope of finding a clue as to the King's ability to remain awake at all times. At first he thought the King might be a Melnari, like Ashlord, because he had no dreams that Robby could penetrate. But whereas Ashlord's aura was a mellow blue, just like Raynor's, the King seemed not to have one at all. The King's helper, the youngster who always occupied the tower with the King, was definitely Melnari, but the King? Robby concluded that it was the Golden Mantle that gave the King his powers, his long life, and his ability to do without food or sleep. But why did the mantle now seem so different than just the day before? Could it be that the death of Lord Banis had somehow weakened the King? Or had something else happened?

Emboldened by this new development, Robby for the first time approached the King and, with the hand of his dream's body, reached out and touched him. The mantle glowed brighter at his touch, and the King stiffened and turned as if to see who stood there, as flashes of the King's memory hit Robby's mind like hammers. He flinched, withdrawing his hand, and with it came a tiny thread of light from the King's mantle, snapping off after a couple of feet and falling to the floor. It glowed dully for a moment, then vanished.

The King groaned aloud, and Robby saw that he bent over to watch the thin thread disappear. Outside the tower, a cloud passed over the sun, momentarily darkening the room.

"I think I know what to do, now," said Robby. He had no joy in the realization. In fact, the knowledge that suddenly came to him arrived along with the shock that he would have to kill this King in order to take his place. To do so, he would pit the King and his young Melnari against each other. It made him feel very sad.

"This is turning out to be harder than I thought it would be," he said to himself as he returned to Griferis. He woke himself up, dressed, rang for breakfast, and stared out the window at the far mountains while he waited.

"Surely he also deserves to die," he muttered, "after all he has done."

Seeing the pale reflection of his own face in the glass, Robby shook his head. "Or does he? Maybe he had as much choice in becoming King as

I have. Maybe, after he became King, everything just went wrong. Or maybe Banis poisoned his mind. Oh, blast! Banis or no Banis, he has hurt an awful lot of people, if by no other means than his negligence!"

Turning around, he saw Halyari standing there with her sister Valcea, each holding a tray and staring at him.

"Come, come!" he gestured.

They put the trays on the table and began to prepare a plate for him.

"Thank you. But you may leave it. I think I can manage," Robby said.

"Very well, sire. Will there be anything else?"

"No. Thank you. I'll ring if I need something."

He sat and picked up his napkin. But suddenly he had no appetite. He thought again of Duinnor and the Sixth Unknown King.

If he acted against the King as soon as he wished, he might never learn all that he wanted to know. Why, for instance, did the King have a Melnari to serve him? Was he some kind of advisor? And how could that Melnari be blind to all the evil the Sixth Unknown King had done?

"Oh, I wish I had never come to this place!" he said, throwing his napkin onto the table and shoving his chair back. "It's all wrong, so completely wrong. I am no king, and don't want to be one. Not here, not in Duinnor, not anywhere!"

His shoulders sagged.

"I just want to go home and be with my father," he gulped. "To want such a thing! At my age! Oh, Daddy! Dear Mother! What has happened to me? What has become of me? How can I be doing the things that I do? How can Daddy ever forgive me? What's the point in even trying?"

He sat for a long moment, then shook his head again. "I'm in too deep, now, though. I had better get a grip. Too many people are counting on me. And, somehow, I've got to prepare everyone for what is to come."

A knock on the door interrupted his thoughts.

"Come! Ah, Finn. What is the news?"

"Sire, is something wrong?"

"Oh, no," Robby said, standing up. "Just off my appetite, is all. Do you bring news about our recruits?"

"Yes, sire. Both concerning those who will be joining us here, and those who might join us in the realm of dreams."

"The realm of dreams? I like the sound of that. Tell me about them first."

"Yes, sire. Even though Micerea sleeps little, and much of that in the saddle, she does as you have asked. Between the two of us, we have discovered well over a hundred dreamwalkers, spread out all over the world. And we are certain there are more to be discovered. None suspect they have the ability, though."

"That's hard to believe. Not a single one?"

"As far as we can tell, sire. Not a single one realizes it when they stumble into the dreams of others. Some are persistently hounded, pardon the expression, by the dreamdogs, since they are plagued by night terrors. Many are children, while some are very old. From every walk of life, too."

Robby went to the window and looked at the shadows of the east mountains receding from the western ones as Sir Sun continued his climb into the sky.

"I think we'll have to do things in a big way, Finn. So keep out of sight of them, if you can, until all is ready. On down the road, we may train others to dreamwalk, but that will take more time and effort than we can afford just now. And some who we would wish to have, like Ullin, just don't seem to have the ability at all. What about the others? The regular folk we have invited here."

"Micerea and I have instructed all of them as to what to do, where to go, and what to bring with them. I don't think any suspect what they are in for."

"I'm sure they can't imagine it. All that sounds very good, Finn. Excellent work!" Robby said.

"Thank you. Lafkin is preparing as best as he can, too. But he sorely needs the things that he requested."

"I know that he does."

"Sire, I know that I am no military man, but it seems to me that if Griferis is to be defended effectively, we shall need a much larger force than we can garrison here."

"That is so, Finn. Our position, floating over the great chasm, gives us our best defensive advantage, should it ever come to it. But, added to that, we shall eventually have new territories to put our people into, if all goes well. Until then, we'll just have to rely on our nearly unassailable location, and upon Lafkin's good planning."

"Yes, sire. Also, my lord, Dialmor grows restless, and I'm afraid he will soon try again to escape his quarters."

"That is to be expected. Ask Lafkin if he would consider posting a guard near to Dialmor's rooms. In a few days he will no longer pose a problem."

"Yes, I shall do so. Is there anything more that I might do for you at the moment?"

"No, Finn. Another busy day of dreamwalking is in store for me, I'm afraid. And you?"

"The same, my King. The same."

"Yes, of course. Finn, as far as you can tell, the Landing is still safe, is it not?"

Robby referred to the place on Algamori where the mysterious gate stood, and Finn nodded. "Yes, sire. Lafkin has set watches, between himself and our Elifaen, to keep an eye on it day and night. They use spyglasses that I gave them from the various libraries and workrooms. They watch from atop the Eastern Gate, and have reported nothing.

Lafkin has said to me that he wishes that he could go there himself and properly scout the Landing and the area nearby."

"Not yet. I don't want to risk it. Every time I put out the causeway, the storm that accompanies it serves as a sign to Shatuum of our activity. And I am sure that Secundur has his own watch upon us, too. Eventually, I hope to put out the causeway without making a storm in the process of doing so. I'll be seeing Lafkin later today, and we'll discuss the Landing. At least there has been no activity spotted. Otherwise, everything is ready, is that not so?"

"Yes, all is done that we can do, I think. If Islindia does her part, we shall most certainly be ready."

"I have no doubt that she will, Finn."

• • •

Later, Finn went from place to place, working with Kinsiri and her daughters to make ready the palace for more company, and meeting with her husband, Radasa, going over the list of things that were needed in Griferis and discussing where they might be obtained.

"But how are these things to be brought here?" Radasa asked.

"A little bit at a time, I'm afraid," Finn answered. "We should expect the first delivery in a matter of days. The larger items, such as the iron and the lumber, will be more difficult. Our King ponders through the method, and looks ahead to coming needs. Meanwhile, please inspect the larders and the cellars and make a better accounting of our food supply. Perhaps you could enlist your wife and girls to help, since they might know better than we menfolk how far it will go to feed so many mouths. That will soon be our most immediate concern."

"Yes, my lord. I shall begin at once."

It was a busy day, indeed, for Finn, yet he made time to spend with Celia, just as he did each day. Late in the afternoon, he walked with her and Boxer along the paths in the West Garden.

"I tire of snow," Celia said, picking up Boxer and tucking him beneath her cloak, holding the rabbit carefully so that only his head protruded from the folds, his ears back and his pink nose wiggling. "I suppose it must fall and fall until springtime comes."

"I suppose so," nodded Finn, pulling open a gate so that they could pass through to a courtyard where the bare limbs of overhanging willows drooped.

"I played a hand of cards with Robby today," Celia said. "And he nearly won."

"King Philawain, Celia. You should use his proper name, you know."

"I don't know why. He says I do not have to do so. He said so, right in front of the girls."

"Still, you should. It would be a way of showing him that you love and respect him."

"Oh. I did not know. Why? Why would it show him that?"

"Because, especially in front of others, it shows that you hold him in the highest regard and esteem. And it encourages others to do so, too. That is why he addresses you as Lady Celia."

"Oh. I thought he was just being funny. But I knew Robby before he was King Philawain. And I do love and respect him, and I am grateful to him for taking me and Boxer out of that glass jar that we were kept in all those years. I have told him so many times, Finn."

"He knows that you are grateful to him. And he would never in the world correct you in how you address him. Yet, along these lines, I have something for you to think about, something that occurred to me not long ago."

"Oh?"

"Yes, it is this. Even though you and I knew him as Robby all those years, he has always been King of Griferis, ever since he first came here, and maybe even long before that. Only we did not know it. And maybe he did not know it, either."

"Oh. I hadn't thought of that, Finn. Finn, you certainly are a thoughtful person, always considering this and that. Why, you must be the most thoughtful person ever there was."

"You go too far, my dear. I am just an old man who has much to think on."

•　•　•

Ullin had much to think on, too, and he was worried that he had not seen or heard from Micerea in four nights. He thought of little else as he made his way slowly and steadily eastward. From her, he now knew the extent of the conspiracy that brewed in the desert lands. All those years ago, when they had first met on the road to the Free City, he had unknowingly participated in that conspiracy. By delivering the dispatches that he carried, a long sequence of events was set in motion. And, by bringing back the letters that Micerea gave to him, a similar chain of events also took shape in Vanara and in Duinnor. Now, as she had related to him, her father's league was almost ready to act. But there was a hitch. Their intention was to establish a line of strong and independent city-states in the northern deserts, supported by allies in the Free City, the Green Citadel, and somewhat by Vanara, too. In exchange for a guarantee from Queen Serith Ellyn that they would not be attacked from the north, the Dragonkind under Gurasa's leadership would make a safe region to live in, free from the oppression of Tyrsharat.

However, the problem of the darakal herb vexed their plans. The black market in the herb was too inconsistent and unreliable and could never supply enough of it to Gurasa's cause. There were just too many people who needed it. If they broke away and managed to secure their independence from the Dragonkind King and his priests, Gurasa's followers would have to grow and refine the herb themselves. That could take years to achieve. Until then, it had been hoped that Vanara could provide all of the herb needed to alleviate the diseases of the desert, but with each year that hope grew dimmer. The few plants smuggled into Vanara did not thrive, as it was too cold, apparently, for too much of the year. This problem of the herb had to be resolved before Gurasa could move ahead with his other plans.

Now, on top of everything else, the Dragonkind armies massed in the far reaches of the south, drawing out men and resources from all other parts of the desert empire. But for the issue with the herb, it would be a perfect time for Gurasa to break away.

Vexingly, Micerea had not yet discovered how the Dragonkind armies intended to cross the Tulivana Mountains into Altoria. Those mountains were too precarious for any army to safely and quickly negotiate, made even more dangerous by a mountain of fire that was spewing ash and flowing lava down the eastern slopes. Even if a pass had been found, and roads built through it, there was still the Hinderlands, a vast area of marshlands on the east side of the Tulivanas through which no army could quickly move. It was filled with tidal estuaries, bogs, and broad stretches of fen. The only roadways there were built on pilings, constructed by the Altorians so that they could move squads of soldiers up to the foot of the mountains. But they were plank and board affairs that were too flimsy and narrow for much traffic, certainly not capable of carrying the weight of tens of thousands of heavily armed soldiers with all their needed supplies, even if the wooden roads could be captured. So the Dragon King must have found another way.

Meanwhile, Ullin's own path grew more precarious. Although the mountains were far lower than those behind him, their sides were steep and treacherous. More than once he had to backtrack many miles to pick his way around some sudden cliff that opened before him, or to locate a place to ford a broad, ice-choked stream. His supply of nuts and fish would soon run out, but he was unwilling, as yet, to make camp and take the time needed to catch and smoke more fish. He was resolved to do so only when he had no choice, and not a day sooner.

Four days he trekked, growing more worried over Micerea. She had always understated the danger that she faced as Gurasa's daughter and co-conspirator, but Ullin knew that her risk of discovery was considerable. So he worried constantly for her, and he relied on her nightly visits to reassure him that she was still safe.

The fifth morning came like the previous three, overcast with snow, but not as windy as before, and Ullin broke camp and began another day of his journey. He had gone no more than a league when he topped a ridge and stood before a steep slope that fell sharply to a narrow dale bordered by a thin stream on its far side. As he tried to figure the best way to proceed downward, Ullin pushed back his hood, took off his cap and balaclava, and rubbed away the ice from around his chin. Puffing out a long, weary sigh, he shook the rest of the ice from his balaclava and pulled it back on, jamming his cap down snugly.

"Another slope to stumble down," he said wryly, and was about to proceed when he detected movement and saw a lone buck bounding through the woods below, kicking up clumps of snow as it abruptly turned back and forth through the sparse trees, as if it could not decide whether to run to the left or to the right.

"What makes you run so desperately?" Ullin mused.

The deer leapt over a stream and was climbing up the steep far bank when Ullin spotted another movement in the wood behind it. He immediately dropped to his knees, and then to his belly in the snow, his flesh crawling at the sight of the predator. It was like a man, running through the snow on all fours, its shaggy coat frosted with snow. Even at this distance, Ullin heard the buck panting and rasping for air, and he heard the wolf-like snarl of the creature chasing it. He was not worried for the deer, since it was far too swift for the creature. But whatever it was that hunted the buck was surely a minion of Shatuum, and suddenly he felt exposed and foolish for brazenly tromping along in his own thoughts for days on end, thinking that he had outpaced Shatuum's reach.

Just as the pursuing creature came to the stream, the buck ahead of it screamed and stumbled, a smoking arrow jutting from its flank. The deer got its footing, and scrambled up the rocky slope, the dog-creature now upon it. Then, emerging from the woods below Ullin's ridge, there came yet another creature. This one rode a black buckmarl, and both mount and rider were enveloped in a cloud of steam. It was a thin, rail-like person, dressed in black and brown furs, with an iron helmet studded with horns. It drew a black arrow and then spat on the arrowhead, making it glow hot and bright red. The creature notched the arrow and pulled for the death shot, but the hunter suddenly eased up on the string, turning abruptly, its nose raised, sniffing the air. Ullin dug his chin down into the snow, with only his eyes and white cap exposed, and he watched the creature turn toward him. While the hesitant rider continued to gaze and sniff, its manlike dog engaged the wounded buck, tearing great rips into the beast with its claws. The buck kicked and butted its attacker viciously, sending the horrible beast rolling back down the slope only to spring up and attack again. The rider turned and loosed the second arrow, and the deer fell dead to be torn to bits by the snarling man-dog. Ullin watched as the rider put a horn to its mouth and blew a shrill discordant note, and the man-dog backed away from the dead buck a few feet and sat in the snow. The rider quickly approached its kill, dismounted and buried its head into the neck of the carcass, ripping out a morsel to toss to the waiting buckmarl and then another bit to the nervous dog-creature.

Disgusted, his heart racing, cold bumps coursing all over his body, Ullin began to slowly inch backwards and away when he heard a crash and looked again. This time it was a captain of Shatuum, just like the one he had fought on the ledge, riding headlong down the far slope on an armored horse. So noisy and intent on their meal were those at the dead buck that they did not see the new arrival until the last moment. Then buckmarl, dog-creature, and wraith all bolted, but not before the captain's whip cracked into the dog-creature, incinerating it instantly, then likewise the buckmarl which flew apart into braying cinders. Meanwhile, the wraith scrambled for its bow, but before it could notch an arrow, the weapon was snapped from its hands by the captain's whip.

"None may leave Shatuum but he whom Throgallus sends forth! All else must remain until their appointed time!" boomed the captain's voice across the dale. "None are to eat! None are to sleep! All are to watch! All are to work! All are to obey! And none may escape the wrath of Throgallus, the hand of Lord Secundur. Where are those others that stole out with thee from Shatuum?"

Ullin could not hear the response, only a metallic grating as the wraith fell on its knees in the snow and answered.

"Then I hope they tasted good to thee!" cried the captain as his hissing whip snaked through the air and cracked. In a flash of red fire and black smoke the wraith boiled and crackled away to nothing but a sooty stain on the blood-splattered snow. In the uncanny stillness that followed, the captain reined his beast around and rode to the southwest, disappearing over the far hill.

Ullin finally exhaled, catching a whiff of sulphur and pitch on the air, and panted to catch his breath, carefully examining every hill and branch, every rock and clump of brush for movement. Not satisfied that the captain was gone, he remained still for a very long while, letting the falling snow cover him over, listening for the slightest hint of any other creature. At last, not daring to proceed on his prior course, Ullin stalked away to the north, following the ridgeline as far as it went before turning again to the east. Soon it would be dark, and he needed to find a good place to stay, somewhere he could hide and build a fire that would not be seen. Sleep would be risky, too. He needed to do so, to rest and to be ready if Micerea came to him. But if he slept instead of keeping watch, and she did not come, he would be easy prey. And wild animals were now the least of his worries. As he made his way carefully and quickly through the drifts, his feet numb with cold and his mittened fingers clenched, he did not notice the black eagle that circled overhead and then turned away.

The eagle passed over the place where the dead buck lay, and it flapped up and over the trees and climbed higher into the gray snowing sky, following with its keen eyes the melted track that headed southwestward. A few miles away, it saw the captain nearing the top of the next high ridge. Tipping over, it banked sharply and descended rapidly until it was only a few feet from the ground, and it passed right in front of the captain just as he made the very top of the ridge. The captain halted as the bird circled him three times. The eagle then flew away, but the captain remained where he was, horse and rider as motionless as the still air.

• • •

Robby listened to Lafkin's report, feeling very pleased with him. He was turning out to be every bit the professional that the King of Griferis needed. It was not only Laftkin's appearance, although he did look much better than when he had first arrived, now wearing a new tunic and having recently cut his hair short and trimmed his beard. It was more in his bearing and his way of speaking that impressed Robby, respectful, but not reluctant to express his opinion, providing details, but not overly laboring his points. And Robby was sure that whatever task he gave his new general would be carried out with cool efficiency.

"No, sire," Lafkin said, "we have seen no sign of movement or activity of any kind at or near the Landing. However, our view of the place is limited. If you would authorize a sortie, I would dearly like to scout the place before the full moon."

"No, we'll have to chance it, General," Robby answered. "Each time I extend the causeway it is like a beacon to our activity. And I dare not leave it stretched across the void all the time for any and all to cross."

"Of course not, sire."

"Now. As for weapons. I take it you have found a way to arm your three Elifaen captains?"

"We all have taken heavy knives from the kitchen. And we are making staffs and strong clubs."

"Good. I suggest also that you try to make some crude bows and arrows, too. All this is just in case we are surprised by something or other."

"Unther is already doing that, sire. But he is loath to cut any of the few trees we have here. And, anyway, all would be green wood, and none are yew or any other very suitable for bows."

"I see. Hm. Well, let's hope they won't be needed until our supplies come. Now, as for the heavy iron and such, you'll have to do without until we can get a proper forge set up, so the emphasis at first will be on those things required by a smithy. Anvils, hammers, tongs, and the like. There is a small forge here already, but probably not suitable for serious weapons-making. Our blacksmiths, when they arrive, will be the judge. Until all that is in hand, we must depend on our deliveries."

"Yes, sire. I quite understand our limitations."

Chapter 16

Inquiries, Explanations, and Orders

It fell to Captain Thrubold to head the inquiry into the death of Lord Banis. He was getting nowhere in his investigation of the mysterious deaths of the men found near Crescent Avenue. He had learned only that they were somehow connected with the girl, Reysa, who was killed the very same day when she tried to murder a tenant living in one of the apartments nearby. He strongly suspected that Lord Banis was behind the girl's attack, but he was baffled as to the motive. Thrubold still had upon his person two orders, both issued by Banis on behalf of the King. One was the summons to have a man named Robby Ribbon and all of his party brought before the King, a party that was suspected to include the Melnari, Ashlord. The other order was a command to the City Gatesmen to be on the watch for a party of six that was suspected to be on its way to the city, a party comprised of the Melnari and five others, including a Kingsman. So why attempt to murder one of the members of the party that was wanted by the King? Obviously, Banis did not want the King to discover something that Ashlord must know.

Captain Thrubold also knew that the Kingsman that was supposed to be part of the wanted group was none other than Ullin Saheed Tallin. Commander Tallin had written Thrubold a few weeks earlier, requesting that he look into potentially illegal handling of leases for the Lord Threshmere's House of Hemlock. Thrubold knew the Kingsman. In fact, Tallin had saved Thrubold's life during an ambush in the Dragonlands that had left Thrubold seriously wounded. Tallin risked his own life to get Thrubold to safety. In gratitude, Thrubold's father had given Ullin Saheed a fine stallion, a horse that became Tallin's mount when he later became a Post Rider. Meanwhile, Thrubold had returned to Duinnor to recover from his injuries and was assigned to the King's Constabulary. Although Thrubold had not seen his fellow Kingsman in over a year, he knew that he rode as Special Courier. And the Post Rider who had delivered Tallin's letter had informed Thrubold about the group Ullin was with, so Thrubold knew that whatever Ashlord was involved in also involved Ullin Saheed. The investigation into the Threshmere affair had revealed many improprieties. And Thrubold suspected that certain fees collected from Threshmere had been diverted from the King's Treasure to a group of Duinnor Regulars, the same group that included the dead men.

All seemed to lead back to Lord Banis, somehow or another. But what could be so important about Robby Ribbon, a man from the faraway Eastlands, that would require Ullin Saheed's company? That would cause Banis to order the murder of Ashlord?

Thrubold was only too happy to turn his mind and his considerable skills to a new case, having been urgently summoned from his chambers to North Hill shortly after dawn. But even he, a veteran of countless investigations of the most scandalous kind, was surprised and confounded by what he saw upon his arrival.

Instantly grasping the ramifications for Duinnor that would be wrought by the death of Banis, Thrubold acted without hesitation to organize his investigation. He commanded that the entire block of houses be immediately isolated from any traffic, that all residents of the area be confined to their homes, with guards posted at every door, and that there be a complete curfew of the streets within the North Hill district until further notice. All of the Duinnor Regulars who had been on duty, whose responsibility it was to be watchmen of those exclusive streets, were gathered and sequestered for questioning while Captain Thrubold sent for more Kingsmen to take their place and to help him in his investigation. Knowing that the influential residents of the area would protest and challenge his authority, to say nothing of the commanders of the Duinnor Regulars that he held, Thrubold also sent an urgent message to his own commanding general who arrived within the half-hour. Since it was none other than General Chadler, a fair-minded man keen to duty, Captain Thrubold was given full authority to issue whatever writs or warrants that were needed, to blockade the neighborhood, and to search any home or building as he saw fit, even though the incident had every appearance of a suicide.

Knowing that word of Banis's death, once it got out, would sweep through the city like a fast wind, it was agreed that Chadler would go at once to personally inform the King of the event. Word would also be sent to High Judge Lord Arata. And it was at this juncture in their rushed discussion, standing over the body of Banis still laying where it fell, that a party of Palace Kingsmen came along to fetch Lord Banis. Chadler met them head on, preventing them from coming near or discovering what went on, and he wrote out a hasty note to Lord Arata to be sent by fast rider. General Chadler then departed with the Palace Kingsmen as his escort, telling them nothing but that Banis was unavailable and that he would explain the situation to the King in person.

Throughout the day, while Lady Highleaf received and entertained her guests, listening to Ashlord's accounting of their adventures, Captain Thrubold conducted his investigation, enlisting trusted men under his command to assist him. After quickly examining the body, he went up to the bedroom. The door was locked from within, so Thrubold had a soldier break it down. He glanced about the room and saw all the signs of a violent struggle, but no clue of anyone's presence other than Lord Banis. Going to the window, he made a quick examination and saw that it was still latched though completely shattered, the blue curtains fluttering out from it. Peering out, he saw no means for anyone to enter from the outside. To be sure, he sent a man to the roof to look for any ropes or signs that someone may have been lowered down from up there. That turned up nothing. Looking down once more at the street below, he surmised that Banis must have been running very fast when he exited the window, else he would have landed on the small portico below, and would have probably survived. Thrubold backed away from the window and jogged toward it to get a sense of the dive. He did it again. Yes, very fast, indeed.

"Sergeant," Thrubold said, "send men downstairs and have the body taken to the kitchen and laid out on the table there. I'll be down directly. And ask Waters if he has recorded all of the statements from the household staff. If so, have him meet me in the kitchen."

Thrubold stood for many moments, turning slowly to observe every detail that he could, eyeing the tumbled over chairs, the upset wine carafe, and the disheveled bedcovers. For the third time, his gaze fell on the writing desk, the only place in the entire room that seemed undisturbed. He moved toward it just as the sergeant returned and knocked on the door.

"They are ready for you downstairs, sir," said the sergeant.

"Very well. No one is to enter this room until I return. Understand? No one whatsoever."

"Yes, Captain."

An hour later, Captain Thrubold had completed his examination of the Elifaen's body, now stripped and laid out on the long kitchen table. One last time, he bent over and put his nose very close to the dead lord's lips, sniffing. Behind him, Waters held a tablet and copied down everything as Thrubold dictated.

"No," he said. "No odor of Sigh Mortabilis, or any other poison. Have it recorded that, in summary, I find no sign of any wounds anywhere on the body, save those sustained by his fall, which resulted in most of the contents of his head being upset and much now protruding from a large crack in his skull. This corresponds to the blood and brains found where he landed. Furthermore, I can detect no aroma of any poison, unction, or potion that would account for the erratic and violent behavior that apparently took place within the lord's bedchamber immediately before he apparently leapt from his window."

Thrubold dipped his hands into a basin of water and washed them, picking up a towel to dry them as Waters dipped his pen and wrote.

"Got it?"

"Yes, sir."

"Good. Now, get back to completing the copies of those statements for me, if you will. I'm going back upstairs to have another look."

"Yes, sir. Sir? What about the body?"

"Oh. Right. Have a couple of men get him back into his nightshirt for now. We'll decide what more to do a bit later. Bring those copies up to me as soon as they are ready."

Back upstairs, Thrubold reviewed the room once again, then began a very thorough search. He went through the wardrobe, the chest at the foot of the bed, and the bookshelf, then he settled himself into Banis's chair and pulled it up to the desk. He managed with little trouble to open all of the locked drawers, and he carefully examined the contents of each one. Then, since he had noticed the odd dimensions of the desk almost immediately, he began a closer examination of the desk itself, getting down on his hands and knees to look at its underside and even pulling it out from the wall to look behind it. He opened and closed the top drawer several times, noting how shallow it was, and passed his hands all over the underside of the desk until he found what he was looking for. With a firm click, the desktop shifted and, when he gave it a tug, it slid forward nearly halfway. Getting up, he saw at the rear of the desk a very large compartment filled with bound books, sheaves of paper, and tubes of scrolls. He looked through one of the small bound books, full of handwritten entries, and then glanced over several scrolls before looking at another book, this one a ledger of various accounts. Smiling, he put the book down and used Banis's ink and paper to write a note to Lord Arata.

"Kingsman," he said to one of the soldiers outside the door, "take a horse and ride quickly to Averboro Hall. You are to place this note into Lord Arata's hand and no other. Wait for a response and bring it back to me. If you cannot locate him, come back immediately."

"Yes, sir!"

"Sergeant, let Waters in when he comes up, but no one else."

"Yes, sir. Here he comes now, Captain."

"Ah. Waters. Good. Come inside. Sergeant, we are not to be disturbed."

"Yes, sir."

Inside, Thrubold carefully pushed the shattered door to.

"I hope you brought a lot of ink and paper with you today," Thrubold said to Waters.

"Yes, sir. I have a spare bottle in my bag, here. And a thick bundle of paper, and several quills."

"Good. We have much to copy. Look here. See these books and scrolls down inside this compartment? I have already quickly reviewed several of them. They contain records of the most secret and despicable activities. We must copy each and every one, every last entry, as quickly as we can. We'll send the copies we make to Lord Arata. And I shall want my own copies of certain portions. The originals, however, we shall put in a very secret place, for safekeeping. Let us get started."

• • •

Ashlord and his friends at Starlight Hall had an easy afternoon and evening. They were joined by Farby, who was somewhat flustered by his aunt's insistent summons. But once the situation was explained to him, he completely understood his danger. He was happy to be near Sheila, though he tried very hard to avoid showing it. He expressed confusion as to how Sheila and her friends came to witness Banis's death. Lady Highleaf then insisted that he be told all, so that he might fully know the circumstances of their arrival in Duinnor and thereby come to a deeper understanding of the many unsettling events of late. Ashlord agreed, and once everyone had settled down, he began to repeat what he had already told Lady Highleaf. For Farby's sake, he began the tale by describing how Sheila had first appeared at his cottage door near Tulith Attis. Ashlord avoided specifics, and he did not mention her rape or the particulars of her wounds. Rather, he spoke of Sheila's determination to learn and to change, "for the benefit of herself, and in hopes to make a better wife, I think, to a lucky man," as Ashlord tactfully put it. Who the lucky man was would be revealed to Farby, indirectly, as the tale unfolded. Sheila listened, her clasped hands in her lap, and her eyes, for the most part, upon them.

So they spent the afternoon and evening fairly isolated from others in the place, as the staff went about their labors cleaning and straightening up after the party. Farby listened patiently, asking very few questions, and Lady Highleaf listened again, watching Farby's reaction to Ashlord's tale. Ashlord elaborated, too, on other aspects of the story, about Robby's mother and father, the battle at Passdale, and many other things. Lady Highleaf realized that no matter how casually Ashlord told the tale, and however long it took, there would be much that he left out, for the scope of the story was truly vast, and deeply founded in myth and in history. Thus the afternoon passed, and evening came just as Ashlord reached the point when he had separated from the company so that he could find the witch's lair.

"I think Lady Shevalia would be the best one to pick up the story from here," he said, "since she was present and I was not. Do you mind, my dear?"

"No." She glanced at Billy, who always took more joy from telling stories than she did. His expression begged her to pass the duty to him, but, glancing back at Ashlord, she knew that if it were left up to Billy the telling would take all week. "Very well. Let's see. So Robby, Ullin, Billy, Ibin, and I left Ashlord behind and traveled on. As we moved through the final slopes toward the Missenflo, soldiers of the Damar warlord caught up with us. Ullin wanted us to flee across the river, but Robby insisted that we go first to Tulith Morgair, an old watchtower some ways off."

Sheila was interrupted by a gentle knock on the door, and Lady Highleaf waved away Ibin, going to answer it herself and to speak with someone briefly before closing it again.

"Dinner is ready," she announced. "We'll have it in the East Room. It is the most private. Perhaps you might take up your story while we dine?"

They repaired to the dining room, and once they were all inside, Lady Highleaf motioned at Denks, and he waved out the serving staff and closed the door behind them. He then uncovered the platters and poured the wine.

"There, my lady," Denks said. "I shall be just outside, should you require anything further."

"Thank you, Denks," Highleaf said. Then, to her company, she explained, "I thought it best that we eat from the sideboard, serving ourselves, for privacy's sake."

So they did. Sheila picked up where she had left off, and quickly related the rest of the tale, up to the point where they entered Duinnor City, with only the occasional added note on the part of Ashlord, and the occasional embellishment on the part of Billy. Farby ate as he listened, and Sheila managed to complete the story just as they finished their meal. Having kept an eye on Farby, Lady Highleaf could see that he appreciated the import of the tale. She also saw that, long before Sheila had completed the story, it had become apparent to Farby who it was that Sheila was in love with. He asked only a few questions, and by the time the tale was completed, he had become serious of expression, almost stern.

"I fully support the coming of a New King," Farby said. "It would be better to have no king, I think. But if we are to have one, it may as well be one that you, here, have some knowledge of and for whom, I can tell, you have true affection. I do not pretend to understand everything that you have told me. I cannot even form the proper questions to ask. However, there is one thing that I am certain of. It is simply that, if this man is someone you four think so highly of to endure what you have for him, and to count as your friend, then I shall do so, too. And I promise to you, since he is not here to make this promise to, that I shall defend you to the best of my skill, should it come to that, and do whatever is in my power for his success."

"I am so happy to hear you say that," Sheila said to him. "Robby means everything to me. And if he is to become King, he will be a great one. Of that I am certain."

Farby nodded and smiled.

"So!" he said, raising his glass. "To good friends, and good kings! May they ever be dear to our hearts, and may we always serve them well."

They drank to the toast, and Farby rose.

"My dear lady," he said to Lady Highleaf, "might I impose upon you to walk me to my room. I would like a word or two."

"Certainly, Grantham," she said, then to the others, "Please, do not rise. Enjoy the sherbert there, and more wine, if you wish. I'll return shortly."

They bowed and excused themselves, and together Lady Highleaf and her nephew went upstairs.

"You must be very disappointed in Lady Shevalia," said Lady Highleaf.

"How could I be disappointed in her?"

"I mean that you must be disappointed that she has her heart set on the impossible."

"In that, perhaps she and I are not so different," he smiled. "In my case, it was impossible from the start. I see that, now. In her case, who knows? I wish her every success and happiness."

"That is very good of you. But I know that it must sting."

"It is a sting that I might cherish, though. At least I have known her, and I have learned what it is like to, well, to feel the way that I do."

"Hm."

"I wanted to ask you about some of my things," Farby said, changing the subject. "I had a few bundles sent over years ago, for safekeeping. Do you remember?"

By now they were outside the bedroom that was to be Farby's, along the same hall that Ibin and Billy would occupy, and Sheila too, at the far end. Lady Highleaf smiled, pushing open the door.

"I think I know the things you mean," she said as they went in. "And I took the liberty of bringing them here earlier today."

Farby turned and saw resting on the bed a rapier and two daggers.

"I should have known you'd have them ready for me," he said, pulling the rapier partway from its scabbard to look at the bright and narrow blade.

"I took good care of them," she said, "hoping, of course, that you would never require them."

"Thank you. I knew my parents would toss them out if they ever found them at home."

"Yes, and who would blame them? Tell me, since you know Starlight Hall better than most," said Lady Highleaf, taking a seat while Farby strapped on the belts and frogs, "what would you suggest that we do to increase our vigilance?"

"I think I'd like to meet all of your watchmen, and for them to tell me their duties," he answered. "Perhaps you would have them come to me in the East Room as they report for duty. How many are there?"

"Just the four at night. Two during the daytime."

"Inside and out?"

"At night, two in, and two out."

"That isn't enough. Ibin and Billy can watch, and I can make rounds, too."

"Very well. What else?"

"You should inform your staff that a lamp is to be kept lit in each and every room throughout Starlight Hall, and all lamps fully supplied with oil. If anyone manages to get in, we don't want to give them shadows or dark rooms to hide in. Curtains are to be closed so that no one can spy in on us. The two of us should speak with Denks and your top staff."

"Yes, we shall do all of those things. Do you not find it strange that none of the afternoon papers mentioned Banis?" Lady Highleaf asked.

"Somewhat. But perhaps it is being kept under wraps until things are somewhat sorted out. My worry is that someone might have seen Lady Shevalia and the others, and they might now be looking for them. I don't fear the Kingsmen so much. Most of them are honest soldiers, just doing their duty. I fear Banis's people, and especially his Regulars, who would do anything to guard their secrets and their crimes."

"I quite agree. I have never felt the need for many guards or the like around here." Lady Highleaf frowned, rising from her seat and moving to the door that Farby was opening for her.

"Don't worry. We'll be vigilant. And, if needed, we'll come up with a plan to get Lady Shevalia safely out of the city."

"But where on earth would be a safe place for her? For that matter, for anyone, these days?"

"I don't know. One thing at a time, and first things first. Let's find Denks and have the staff and the watchmen gathered, shall we?"

• • •

General Chadler knew that if the King looked deeply into his mind, he would be discovered as a conspirator. Working secretly with Ashlord and others to bring about peace with the Dragonkind would, in all likelihood, be considered high treason. But Chadler had no choice but to face the King with the news concerning Banis. What he did not expect, however, was for the King to keep him waiting for so long. He had been here nearly all day, waiting and waiting, and he paced back and forth before the doors of the High Chamber with growing impatience to get back to Captain Thrubold.

"You must open the doors and let me in," he commanded the Kingsmen. "I must see the King!"

"Pardon me, sir, but you have no authority in this tower," answered a Kingsman guard, clearly uncomfortable with saying so to his superior. "And we are expressly forbidden from opening these doors unless the King orders them opened by, well, by ordering us to do so. I don't know what to say, General. This has never happened before, sir."

"You don't have to explain it to me, son. I didn't serve as commander of the guard for all those years for nothing. But something is clearly wrong. I grow afraid that the King is in danger. At least send for General Laless. As the new General of the Guard, he will surely be concerned."

"With respect, sir, I cannot send for him, unless the King says so."

"This is ridiculous! Open that door, or send for Laless, or stand aside!"

The door clicked and opened partway. Chadler and all of the guards were surprised to see a young man's head appear, cautiously looking out.

"What is the commotion out here?" the youth asked. "Why has Banis not been brought before the King? Who are you?"

"Who are you?" shot back Chadler.

"I am the King's servant. Who are you? Where is Banis?"

"Let me see the King!" Chadler pushed past the lad and through the door.

"No!" cried the boy. "You mustn't!"

Chadler halted and looked around. The Avatar floated nearby, but the King was nowhere in sight.

"Wait, wait! I shall fetch the King. Please wait, and remain where you are!" the boy implored, holding up his hands to indicate that Chadler was to stay where he was. But before the boy reached the curtain, a glow grew behind it, faint at first, then somewhat brighter as the King approached from the other side. Chadler immediately kneeled, bowing his head and averting his eyes as the King parted the curtain and came before the general. Chadler felt the King's touch, a sudden pain in his temples forming a searing headache that made him wince, and he heard within his mind a jumble of words, in no discernable order. The King's touch departed, leaving a throbbing sensation just above Chadler's eyes.

"I will speak to you with my own voice, today," the King said. "Where is Banis? And why do you come before me?"

"I come to tell you, my King, that Banis is dead."

"Dead?"

"By his own hand, King. He leapt from his bedroom window this morning and fell to his death."

"Leapt? Banis is dead?"

"Yes, Your Majesty. He is dead. My men continue to ask questions and to look into it. We strive to keep the news from the city until you are informed, sire."

"Leave me!"

"But, sire, what shall we—"

"I shall summon you when I desire your presence!"

"Yes, my King."

Chadler stood and backed away, keeping his head down, but he could not help but notice how the King's mysterious mantle did not shine as brightly as it once had. As he turned to pass through the door, Chadler threw a quick and careful glance at the King. Within the dull silver threads was the silhouette of a man.

• • •

Gladsten returned to his apartment, and as he hung up his hat and coat, he saw the large basket sitting nearby.

"We might not be needin' the basket after all, sweet thing," he called out. His wife came in from the kitchen, wiping her hands on her apron.

"An' why ever not? After all the trouble I went to!"

"Well, it seems our little chickens've gone to roost in the very place we were to send their heads to!"

"Ye don't say! Well that finishes it, now don't it?"

"Oh, not hardly, apple lumpkins! Not hardly, at all!"

"Oh, me husband's got a plan already, don't he?"

"Whenever do I not? But we'll be workin' tomorrow night, I'm afraid. I'll be needin' me crowbar, is all, a bit of bread an' cheese, an' me flask of foxdire, too. I've already talked to the boys, an' we'll head over this time tomorrow. This evenin' I'll need to get on over to Waresley for some large trunks an' crates an' such."

Mrs. Gladsten came over and gave her husband a hug.

"Well, come an' have a bite afore ye go," she said, giving him a tender kiss. "An' rest for a spell. Ain't I so lucky to have such a hardworkin' feller!"

Mr. Gladsten pecked her cheek, and then commenced to rubbing his eyes.

"I think that ol' Miss Tarrier's got some ailment, an' I might've picked it up," he said. "Little glarish glows off in the corner of me eyes what comes an' goes."

"Oh, me! I hope ye ain't got the pox again."

• • •

Long after Gladsten had his supper and darkness was settled over Duinnor, a black eagle returned to Shatuum. It flapped past the captains that guarded Secundur's tower gates and upward along the stairs until it reached the highest and darkest chamber. There it alighted on the cold stone floor before Secundur. What the eagle had to show Secundur angered him, for this feathered creature had also witnessed the duel between the missing captain and Ullin, and it had seen the bright painful light that came from the strange object that the Kingsman possessed. Secundur instantly knew what it was, and now he knew not only what had happened to his missing captain, but what the man was carrying.

"Tell my captain that his new prey makes for Duinnor. Tell him to wait for the darkness of night to kill him. He is to bring back the body and all of the man's belongings. All of his belongings! Go!"

As the bird squawked and departed, Secundur whispered the dark and secret words that only he knew, words that would float out from his tower, find their way to the armor of Throgallus, and strike him with an icy chill. Throgallus came, and Secundur immediately spoke to him.

"I have had news that the captain sent to track down the wraiths that escaped from you has succeeded in finding them. They are destroyed. He will now track the man who eluded us, the one who accompanied the boy to Griferis. It was this man who destroyed the missing captain. He now goes to Duinnor, doubtless to forge an accord between Griferis and the King. The man will be killed and his body will be brought to Shatuum.

The body and all of the man's things are to be immediately cast into the great chasm. You are not to examine the body or any of his belongings. He is to be cast straightaway into the chasm. Fail in this, and I shall remove you from your station and your rank and give you over to those who now serve you. Do I make myself understood to you?"

"Yes, my lord. But, Lord Secundur, how did a mere mortal defeat the captain? Will he not do the same to the one now tracking him? "

"The defeated captain succumbed to his own weakness. The one that goes forth will not make that mistake."

"Perhaps I should go and see to it, if this man is so dangerous to our cause."

"No! You shall remain and see that my will is carried out. Do as I have commanded, and remember that my eagles watch. Now leave me."

Throgallus had his doubts. He wondered at the strange command from Secundur, and it occurred to him right away that it was not the man that Secundur feared, but something the man possessed.

"He knows that I will learn of the captain's return as soon as he approaches Shatuum," Throgallus muttered as he made his way out of the tower. "If it were not for that fact, I am certain he would not have spoken anything of it to me."

As he returned to his own castle, Throgallus fumed at the insult, and he tugged at the armor, cursing the binding metal and himself for ever having put it on. Now, body and soul were bound up by Secundur's shadow, encased by the black iron of Secundur's will, encompassed all around by Secundur's enduring hatred. On one thing, at least, Throgallus and Secundur were fully agreed: The destruction of all life outside of Shatuum must take place. And Throgallus longed to be the bringer of that destruction. He resented being kept from it. After centuries of torment, it was vengeance upon existence itself that he craved. Redemption was not possible, Throgallus knew. But annihilation was.

Chapter 17

Relentless

Some twenty miles behind Ullin, and somewhat toward the southwest, the captain of Shatuum still sat on his horse and waited, just as he had done all day since the black eagle signaled him to do so. Underneath his horse the snow had melted, and every new flake that landed on his armor and his horse was so rapidly melted that a gray vapor enveloped them. The silence surrounding them was nearly complete, for no natural creature dared approach or even call within hearing of their presence, and only the occasional drip of warmed water from the flanks of the mount interrupted the stillness. Indeed, they were a stark blot of motionless black standing over a muddy brown splotch of ground surrounded by snow. And the scarlet hourglass on the rider's breastplate warned the forest denizens to stay clear of them if the other aspects of their appearance did not.

All day and all night, horse and rider waited, and they would wait for eternity for all it mattered to them, until orders were brought back from Secundur. Day came, sluggish and bleary under the thick clouds, and it slowly passed, and still they did not move. Eventually the leaden sky dimmed, and soon all hint of light was gone. Night, as black as pitch, descended, and still they waited. Then, in the heavy hours before the hope of dawn, the black eagle returned. The bird flew around and around them, its red eyes like cindergnats circling a nightmare, and it squawked the message from Secundur. Rusty light kindled and grew brighter behind the visor of the captain's helm. By the time the bird completed its message and had flapped away, the captain's eyes shown like red-hot coals through the iron slits. His horse's eyes, too, glowed through its head armor, and when the captain pulled on his reins, the horse snorted out a hot cloud of sooty air from its mouth and nostrils. They turned around and slowly came down from the ridge, going back to the place where the other creatures of Shatuum were executed. Each time the horse's hooves fell, the snow beneath hissed and steamed, and as they picked up the track they were to follow, gray vapors trailed them.

• • •

Thrubold and his assistant finished making their copies and sent them to Lord Arata as evidence of Banis's activities. Banis had kept a record of every person that was bribed by him or on his behalf, the amount of the bribe, when and why it was done, and, likewise, every murder and attempt at murder. There were statements in the journals of Banis about the many people he feared or those he considered threats or enemies. Thrubold found that there were two sets of journals that Banis had kept. One set of journals was more of a diary of his public activities, including his dealings with the King. The other set of journals pertained to his nefarious activities. Why Banis did this was baffling to Thrubold. Why would one create such detailed and incriminating records? The Kingsman could not know that these accounts were the result of a compulsion of the dead Elifaen, prompted by that peculiar gift of Secundur, the dark and hidden portion of his heart. But it had been that portion of his heart that was hidden from the King that drove Banis to report into his diaries and to make notes of those things that his King was not allowed to know. It had been a compulsion, a mania, a curse that Banis had never been able to control or resist. Every night, when all his day's work was done, sleep only ever came to Banis if he recorded his day's deeds.

As Thrubold immediately saw, the documents would resolve many baffling crimes, poisonings, murders, bribes, disappearances, blackmails, and unwarranted arrests. Thrubold also hoped that the documents would serve to bring about the downfall of all those who had been loyal to Banis and who would undoubtedly continue his malicious criminal enterprises. But he did not trust that his copies would be accepted by the courts, knowing that Banis's shadow would be powerful even in death, and that his servants were among the high and mighty of Duinnor.

So, late in the night, Captain Thrubold went alone to the Temple outside of the city with all of the original documents to give them to a monk that he knew for safekeeping. Such was the quantity of material that Thrubold and the monk had to make two arduous trips up and down the long stairs of the Temple, each carrying as much as their arms could hold. When Thrubold returned to the city, he went to his precinct headquarters, first for a brief nap and then to select four sturdy Kingsman to assist him on a special early morning task. Amongst those he chose happened to be Tom Blue, lately returned from serving with Teracue, and having been assigned just the day before to Thrubold.

"Sometimes we must blend in," Thrubold told his men after they threw long plain cloaks over their uniforms. "And we may have some unsavory business before us. I picked you four because you are all big stout fellows. Stay close, I'll tell you more along the way."

Thrubold picked up a heavy shoulder bag, and they stepped out together into the chilly predawn streets and pulled up their collars. They hurried along while Thrubold succinctly summarized what they were about to do. Passing quickly through the lonely streets, they made for a particularly dangerous part of town as the men listened carefully to their captain's explanations.

"So, there you have it," Thrubold concluded as he brought his group to a halt and peered around the corner of a dark street. "Word of Banis's death will surely leak out in but a couple of hours. If we can do our work beforehand, we have a chance of netting a few of his little fish, and perhaps make them give up some bigger ones. We turn here, a shortcut along that alley. Keep a sharp eye and a hand to your dirks; these streets are full of thieves and cutthroats."

• • •

The man who had delivered the note from Banis to Gladsten emerged from his lodgings to begin his rounds. He was a man of set routines, an orderly and meticulous person whose business depended on being prompt and reliable. Each day had its own duties, and his various employers valued the fact that he took orders, asked no questions, and invariably accomplished his tasks. Some of those who paid him did so because they knew their messages would be picked up and delivered, shielding the identity of the sender. Others gave him a good commission on the collections he made on their behalf, knowing that he was too big to intimidate, too dedicated to his work to be bribed, and too brutal for any but the most foolhardy to set upon. He was one of the nameless few who had free rein in the streets of Duinnor, whose name was known to none, but whose face was familiar to many. While the Avatar, in all its mystery, might strike fear into most when it appeared, this man was also met nearly everywhere he went with trepidation and caution. He was not to be trifled with, and on more than one occasion, he made examples of those who did so.

This was to be a light day of work for him, picking up a few payments here and there, dropping off a few notes, and delivering a few well-worded threats. He expected to complete all these tasks by noontime. The rest of the day would be his own. After receiving a shave and a trim from the only barber he trusted with a razor to his neck, he planned to spend the afternoon with a pot of tea and a fine old book lately acquired from a recalcitrant debtor.

As he turned down one of the darker alleys, he was thinking this might be the year he finally gave up on Duinnor and traveled back the long way home to Masurthia. Then two figures stepped out at the far end of the alley to block his way. Another figure suddenly came at him from his left. Immediately, he turned into the nearest assailant, raising his cudgel, but someone else knocked his feet out from under him before he could strike. A heavy foot stepped on his forearm, pinning it to the ground, while a knee fell on his throat and the tip of a dagger pressed against his cheek.

"Answer me truthfully and live," Thrubold said. "Yesterday morning you picked up a dispatch from Lord Banis. I know that you did, for his footman put it out for you, and his cook saw you take it away. I have had my eye on you, and by their description I knew right away who visited

Banis's back door three times each week for the past year. Who received the note you took from Banis?"

"I can hardly speak with your knee crushing my throat."

"You are doing just fine. You will tell me the name of the person you gave the note to."

"If I do, Banis will part my head from my neck."

"Banis is dead. Now tell me the name, or you'll join him."

"I don't believe it. And you don't know what you meddle in, you fool! If Banis doesn't kill you, I will!"

"Have it your way, then."

Suddenly a noxious rag was held to the man's nose. He quickly fell into a partial stupor and vaguely felt himself being rolled over and dragged. The distant sound of a hammer ringing against iron filled him with anxiety, and he struggled to shake off his grogginess. When he regained his senses only a few moments later, his legs were in iron cuff and chain, like his wrists behind his back, and he was being dragged to his feet.

"Get up! Up on your feet!"

He was urged and pulled. Then, as he managed to stand, he was pushed backwards to sit on a crate, and his five assailants faced him. They waited a moment for him to recover, and when he tried again to stand, they shoved him back down on the crate.

"What plays here?" the man cried out. "I'll gut you all, I swear!"

"You are in no position to do any gutting or swearing," Thrubold stated.

"What is your game, eh?" the man stammered, awkwardly trying to free his hands and making a useless attempt to kick at them with his feet. The length of chain between his cuffs was too short for success at either, and he realized that he was had.

"Tell me the name, and I may let you live."

"You may as well kill me, then."

"Oh, I don't mean to harm you one little bit. Not me. But I would like for you to consider how long you think you will last on these streets all trussed as you are."

"What?"

"I'm sure you have your fair share of enemies," Thrubold went on, "and you are likely carrying a nice purse, too. I imagine there'll be a bit of sport with you, too, before it's all over."

"You bastard! You wouldn't!" the man squirmed and tried to get up again, only to be shoved sideways to crash into a pile of rubbish.

"Let's go," Thrubold said, gesturing at his men. As they began to walk away, the man thrashed around and spat away a bit of rotted bread that had gotten smashed into his mouth when he fell.

"Gladsten! Gladsten's the name. Now get these irons off me!"

Thrubold turned back to him, pulling his cloak away to reveal his tunic.

"Gladsten? Well, that's a good start. Now, as soon as you tell me where to find Gladsten, I'll have you escorted to a cozy cell."

"Kingsmen! I should have known! But you'll not last long, none of you, when Banis hears about this!"

"I told you already. Banis is dead. Now, as for this Gladsten fellow. Where is he?"

• • •

Banis was truly dead, and the city was waking up to the news. It was soon on everyone's lips, and every printer scrambled to put rumor to ink. Mrs. Gladsten, who fancied herself a person of knowledge, purchased one of the earliest broadsheets along with two sweetrolls for her husband's breakfast. When she returned to their rooms, she put the rolls on his plate and the paper beside it.

"Ain't it a wonder?" she commented, tapping the broadsheet with her fingers. In fact, she could barely read the words at all and only knew they must be important ones due to the large size of the printing. And she had been assured of their importance by what the folks were exclaiming at the place where she had purchased it. She shook her head and clucked while her husband stared at the headline, his cup of tea halfway to his lips. He, too, shook his head, clucked, and sipped.

"Don't it just show," he said, taking a big bite of the roll and continuing to comment with his mouth full, "that ain't nobody, high nor low, above Master Death. Peculiar, too, as it says. Just took a runnin' dive through his winder, bashed out his brains all over the street. Much the pity when a man of the King such as that goes. I imagine the entire town'll be in mournin.' "

"But ain't that one an' the same as Mr. D?"

"Hush, woman!" Mr. Gladsten dropped his cup noisily onto the saucer. "Ain't I told ye a hunnerd times? Mr. D is Mr. D, an' nobody else!"

"But, dear," Mrs. Gladsten sat, lowering her voice to a whisper, "what about the job?"

"A job's a job, sweetie. What would things come to if it got about that I couldn't do a job that was rightly contracted? 'Sides, Mr. D always paid through his man. So I'm thinkin' all is still right in the world, so to say, an' when his man reads about Lady Highleaf's gift, we'll get our due."

"Well, if ye think so, then it must be so."

"Of course. Now, I've a long day an' a busy night at the end of it, so I must be gettin' on to me work."

"Yes, dearie. Please do be careful, an' take this other sweetroll along with ye."

• • •

Ullin puffed out great clouds of vapor from his hard trek, and he could go no farther for the moment, falling to his knees in the snow. He pulled away his pack and quickly undid his coat and pulled it off, too. He scooped up a handful of snow and shoved it underneath his blouse against his burning wound. Crying out in pain, he pulled up his blouse to have a look, not understanding why, all of a sudden, it began to burn and throb when for the past many days it seemed to be on the mend. It was a red welt that ran across his side, capped with a black festering scab.

"Oh, that can't be good," he muttered, scrambling to his pack and removing the tin of salve inside. The ointment was nearly as hard as rock, so cold it was, and he used his knife to cut out a lump, rubbing the greasy, pungent stuff in his bare hands to try to soften it, but it only rolled into a ball.

"A fire. I need a fire to thaw this," he panted as he pressed the lump back into the tin and put it away. "And to thaw me, too."

He looked around for a sheltered place, but the forest was so thick with trees that he could see no more than a few yards in any direction. Snow continued to fall, and he was not even sure that he was going the right way. His feet were numb with cold, his boots caked with ice, like the balaclava around his mouth, and his precious food was almost gone. Struggling to get his coat back on, and then his pack, he groaned back to his feet and shuffled on. He knew he had better find a good place and make shelter and a fire soon, before it was too dark to see anything.

"If only it would clear off," he thought, "and Lady Moon saw fit to lend me her light tonight. That might help."

Ever since seeing the awful captain of Shatuum the day before, Ullin had kept moving, trying to put miles between himself and that creature of Secundur. His painful wound was a constant reminder of the deadly weapons those knights wielded, and he was lucky to have survived his first encounter with one of them. And so, all throughout the day he trudged, and when nightfall came he did not stop, but stumbled along as best as he could through the snowy mountain forest, picking his way in the darkness. Morning came and he kept on. He stopped briefly beside an icy brook to have a drink and a nibble from a chunk of jawrock, then he set out again, the burning wound growing more painful with every yard. Fear drove him on, and he kept a sharp eye for anything amiss and often stopped to listen for anything out of place. He thought of Micerea, of Robby, of the things he carried, but his mind always went back to what he had seen the previous morning.

In fact, what he had witnessed baffled him as much as it drove him to keep moving. Ullin understood that the captain was evidently sent out to track down and kill the others, but why? Why would Secundur care if a few of his followers left Shatuum? And what of the captain's words that Ullin clearly heard from his hiding place?

"None are to eat. None are to sleep."

How were even Secundur's creatures to survive if they did not eat, if they did not sleep? The only conclusion that Ullin could reach was that a sinister reason was behind the incident, for what else could Shatuum hatch but dark plots and vile creatures? Perhaps Robby could make sense of it. If Micerea would only return to his dreams, he could tell her about it. If he could find a place to sleep and to dream, that is.

Though it was still difficult to hike because of the snow and his fatigue, at least now the way was not as rugged or as steep as it had been, and Ullin did not have so much climbing up and climbing down. He took this as a good sign, knowing that the closer he came to Duinnor, the milder the terrain would become, and the greater likelihood that he might come across a village or settlement. So when he topped an easy rise, his heart sank. As far as he could see was nothing but forest and snow, rolling up and down low mountains and high hills. He carefully studied the gray and white land for trails of smoke and for signs of a path or road. The falling snow limited what he could see to only a mile or two. He pulled out his spyglass and swept the scene to decide his way. He turned slowly around, examining the entire region within his view for anyone, or anything, that might be tracking him. In this, too, the misty snow hindered him, and he was unsatisfied even though he saw nothing more threatening than a fox scampering off through a thin copse nearby. Sighing, he put away the spyglass and marched down the hill and into the trees.

• • •

By noontime, Duinnor City was churning with the news of Banis's death. The Kingsmen contingents within the city were put on alert, and even the cadets of the Academy were called into service to assure order. Crowds gathered at the Palace, some to demand that the Congress of Realms be called, others who wished to petition the King to address their grievances against Banis. Many others went there merely to watch what might happen.

Meanwhile, on the other side of the city, the streets around Banis's neighborhood were opened, and they were soon filled with sightseers who came on foot or in carriages to gawk at the place where Banis had plummeted to his bloody death. Disappointed that his body was not still laying where it had fallen, and that his blood had been carefully washed away and the wreckage of glass had been removed, they had to satisfy themselves by gazing at the boarded-up window from which he had taken his fatal plunge.

In other parts of the city, generals met to organize against any disturbances that might arise, and ambassadors gathered with their counterparts to share information. Judges and magistrates assembled to discuss the ramifications of selecting a new First Lord, and, of course, the very highest of the land made their way to the topmost foyer of the High Tower to await the will of their King.

All of these things were witnessed by the agents of the various broadsheet printers, and by mid-afternoon they had produced so many versions of the events, and such was the demand for revised and updated news, that many began running low of ink and paper. At Starlight Hall, while workers continued the cleaning and reordering of things after the great party, there was one room within the place where all these editions were delivered. They were strewn over tables and chairs, covering teacups and platters, and they carpeted the floor around the chair in which Ashlord sat, as he had nearly all day, reading and tossing aside, reading and tossing. Some of the newspapers at Ashlord's feet were picked up by Denks the butler, who handed them to Lady Highleaf, who then handed what she had just finished reading to Lady Shevalia, and so forth, thence to Billy and then Farby until Ibin dutifully returned them to Ashlord only to be tossed away, beginning all over a confused and frustrating pattern of reading. Hardly did one broadsheet make a complete circuit of the room before another was delivered to begin its course from hand to hand.

"It says here that Captain Thrubold leads the investigation into Banis's death," read Farby.

"I know," said Ashlord.

"It says right here that the Congress of Realms might meet," said Billy.

"I know," said Ashlord, his eyes darting across the paper before him.

"Judge High Lord Arata has ordered a review of all prisoners arrested under Lord Banis's orders, perhaps to be freed," related Sheila. She looked over the corner of her paper. "Would that include your friend, Raynor?"

"I know," said Ashlord. "It might."

"Here's something odd: 'In Celebration,' it reads. And it is printed over a small advertisement for red paint," said Farby. "And it has a little drawing of a door. That's pretty daring."

"I know."

"Now, really! Not even a mention of our party?" declared Lady Highleaf, tossing aside her paper in disgust. "After all, it was the last event of consequence that Banis attended."

"I know," said Ashlord as he took the latest broadsheet from Denks.

"Well, what are we to do?" asked Sheila once Denks had left the room.

Everyone except Ashlord looked at her blankly.

"I mean, while the city sorts itself out. Are we to just sit around? Shouldn't we go see your friends, Ashlord? Arata and the general that you and Billy met with?"

"It would accomplish nothing," said Ashlord bluntly as he flipped his newspaper around and continued to read. "They have enough on their plates without our meddling, just yet. If the Congress of Realms is called, we'll endeavor to attend. Meanwhile, we must wait, watch, and be ready for Robby's next move. Could you pass that paper back over to me?"

Farby stood and walked the paper he was holding over to Ashlord, saying, "It is time that I made my rounds. Billy, would you care to join me?"

"Sure!" Billy jumped up from his chair. "Could use a little stroll."

"Grantham," Lady Highleaf called over to Farby, "I forgot to ask Denks about the cleaning work. Could you see how it goes? I think we'd all rest easier when it is done and all the workers have departed."

"Of course, Auntie. I intended to do so, anyway."

"It seems the aftermath of these things takes almost as long as the preparations!"

"Ashlord," Ibin spoke up, "Ashlord, whendo, whencanI, Ashlord, when, whenwillourthingscome?"

"It is a bit too soon, Ibin. I'm sure you miss your mandolin, don't you?"

"Yes, I, yesI, yesImissmymandolin."

"Oh, Mr. Brinnin! How very thoughtless of me!" Lady Highleaf exclaimed. "We have quite a collection of instruments in our music room. A piano forte, some violins and flutes, and, I believe, a mandolin. Shall I have it brought to you?"

"Oh,well, yesthat, Iwouldlikethatverymuch,LadyHighleaf!"

• • •

And so it went for the rest of the day, without much to show for it as far as Sheila was concerned. She did not like being cooped up, but she saw the sense of staying out of sight at least until the last of the workers departed. Lady Highleaf would never think it fitting for her to do so, but Sheila would have been more comfortable armed with her bow and sword, and keeping watch with Farby and Billy. As for that pair, they walked the long way around the premises, looking into every room and checking every ground floor window and door, until coming at last to the great interior hall and its adjoining rooms where the party had been recently held. They stood on the stairs watching a small army of men and women with buckets and mops and scrubbing brushes working away to return the floors to their previous luster. Before the line of cleaners, others worked to remove the last of the spare tables and chairs.

"It won't be long, now," commented Billy.

"No. I imagine they'll be finished in an hour or so," nodded Farby. "Perhaps we should take a turn around back, and look in on the watchmen at the garden wall?"

"Sounds good."

Billy and Farby sidestepped the workers and moved toward the rear of Starlight Hall while, out front, the last of many wagons were being loaded with all of the apparatus and equipment that the acrobats had used, and other workers carried out the spare tables that were no longer needed. It was a noisy affair, and would have easily descended into chaos but for Lady Highleaf's diligent overseers who directed every aspect of the cleaning. Supervising all this activity was Denks, who stood at the top of the front steps, arms crossed, frowning at the sorry way that a wagon was being piled with chairs. He was about to shout at the bungling workers when another wagon pulled up the drive and came to a halt directly before him. Recognizing the driver and seeing that there were several very large crates as well as a large wicker basket stacked within the wagon, and knowing that the glasswares had already been carted away to storage, he walked down the steps and met the driver who descended from the rig.

"Mr. Ganner, what's all this you have, eh?" Denks demanded.

"A delivery, Mr. Denks. A delivery. From Crescent Avenue," the driver answered.

"I do not know that address, and we have not sent for anything," replied Denks. "As you can see, we are taking things away today. And, anyway, it is rather late for deliveries."

"Aye, that's plain enough, sir. But these here things are for yer guests. They're the things belongin' to Mr. Ashlord an' company. Or, Mr. Sootking, dependin' on what he tells ye."

"Ashlord, eh?"

"Aye, sir."

"Well, I don't know. He has not notified me that he has sent for anything."

"Well, alls I know is that I was to bring 'em here. Then I'm supposed to drive over to Ingall Lane an' pick up some lumber afore dark. Oh, an' I was to say that the contents of these here crates're mighty delicate, glass an' pottery, in all likelihood, judgin' by the great weight of 'em. An' I was to say also that any place out of the way would be just fine. So long as they're inside out from the weather, an' they ain't stacked on one another, an' they're put somewhat close by to the rooms where yer guests are stayin'. But I doubt if they'll be needed anytime soon, seein' how they're all nailed up. So, what do ye say? Will ye take 'em?"

"Well, it is most irregular, at this late hour," Mr. Denks said, frowning and glancing at the other wagons now departing. "But I suppose we must, mustn't we, Mr. Ganner? I'll fetch some helpers."

"That is very good of ye, Mr. Denks."

It took a good while, but eventually men were found to remove the large crates from the wagon, some requiring six men to carry into the Hall. They managed to get all the way up to the third floor without dropping a single one, taking many rests along the way, and were directed to a large storage room just down the hall from the guests. There the crates were deposited until their contents would be needed or desired. Shaking his head at the distraction, Denks closed the door.

• • •

Ullin's fire crackled and popped. He gingerly picked up the tin that had been warming next to the flames, and he managed to spread a bit of the gooey unction onto his wound. Immediately he felt a little relief from the good stuff, and quickly worked to get his blouse and coat back on. He took his small pot of boiling stew, improvised from melted snow, dried fish, nuts, and chunks of jawrock, and began his supper. Hugging the pot in his cold hands and huddling under a low makeshift shelter made of pine boughs, he slurped and chewed carefully, not wanting to miss or spill a single drop or morsel. It was not much, it tasted horrible, and his stomach growled continuously while he supped, but he was grateful for it. After swallowing the last bit, he rummaged for dry socks, quickly changed into them and laid out the ones he removed from his feet onto the rocks beside the fire. He relaced his boots then set to work on his shelter. Once he had pulled additional boughs around him, he curled up within, his pack to serve as his pillow, and his tattered blankets for warmth. Then, being careful not to let anything fall into the fire, he pulled down his shelter atop of himself for the little additional warmth that it might provide.

"Oh, Micerea! If only I knew that you were safe," he thought, wondering again, as he nearly constantly did, where she was. He wished that he had her ability to dreamwalk so that he could try to find her. But dreamwalking was not within his kit of talents. In spite of being miserable with worry and cold exhaustion, he fell into an unsettled and restless sleep.

• • •

"I think all is well, so why don't you get some sleep," Farby said to Billy.

All of the work of cleaning up and putting things away had been done, and the house was long empty of the workers who had accomplished those tasks. After supper, Billy and Farby had made their rounds well into the night, checking all of the doors and ground windows, and making sure that the other watchmen were alert and vigilant. The two now stood at the top of the stairs that opened into the long hall where the guest rooms were.

"I reckon it's been a long day," he said. "But what about yerself? Don't ye think ye could use some shut-eye, too? It's nearly dawn, I reckon."

"I'll be staying up, I think. But if you would be so kind as to look for me when you rise, I'll sleep then, and let you keep the day's watch."

"Well, if yer certain."

Billy could not suppress a yawn, and Farby smiled.

"I'm certain. I'll see you later, Billy. Pleasant dreams!"

Billy nodded, yawning again, and turned to go to his room. Along the way, he passed by the room where the crates had been delivered. Seeing the door ajar, he put his head in. There was no lamp lit, against Farby's orders, so Billy picked up one from the hallway and took it in. Seeing the unlit lamp on a table nearby to the crates, he lit it with the one he held, noticing that all of the lids from the large crates were open and on the floor.

"Seems an odd place to keep empty crates," he thought as he peered into one. Seeing some crumbs of bread at the bottom, he shook his head. "Mighty large crates, too, for food an' the like. Why, I bet ol' Ibin could fit inside any one of these, with a bit of a squeeze. 'Course, thar was a prodigious lot of victuals served up at the party."

He shrugged and was about to leave when, passing another open crate, he saw at the bottom of it a pry bar.

"Folks 'round here just leave tools most anywhar."

He closed the door and put the lamp back on the table in the hall, then yawned practically the entire way to his room. As soon as he opened his door, a hand grabbed his arm and yanked him inside, spinning him around. A gag was shoved into his mouth and tied tight before he could cry out, and he was dragged across the room. At the foot of his bed sat Ibin and Ashlord, also bound and gagged, looking up at him with wide eyes. Standing over them was another man wielding a sword. Billy's hands were quickly tied behind him, and his legs kicked out from under him, making him fall on his rump beside Ashlord.

"Easy, easy!" said a voice from behind him. "Don't bruise the merchandise! I'll do all the damagin', if ye don't mind."

Billy twisted to see who spoke and saw the man come into view, holding a short-handled broadaxe.

"An' it'll be quite a pleasure, to be sure. Oh, good. I see that ye recognize yer ol' Barley neighbor, don't ye?"

"Mithtur Glathten!" Billy exclaimed through his gag.

"That's right! That's right! It's so nice to be remembered," Gladsten said with a grin. "Mighty nice. Mrs. Gladsten'll be so happy when I tells her. Warms the heart, it does."

Billy wrestled at his bindings.

"Now, now. Be still, an' don't make a fuss. It'll all be over soon, I promise ye. I only wish yer pal was here to enjoy our little party, too. Whatever happened to the Ribbon boy? Oh, but I imagine the Redvests got him when they came into Barley. Oh, well. A pity. I would've so enjoyed entertainin' him, as well. But as soon as yer little lady friend comes along, we'll do our chore an' be on our way."

"Why don't we go ahead and get started?" asked one of the men. "She's bound to be along soon, anyway."

"Naw, that wouldn't do at'all. Why half the fun is in the watchin'. Ye wouldn't deprive the lass of that, would ye? But let's give 'em a bit of foxdire, why don't we? Just to keep 'em settled an' quiet."

• • •

Sheila and Lady Highleaf sat up far longer than either had intended, chatting about Sheila's life in Barley. Lady Highleaf was understanding and sympathetic, and Sheila found herself relating more than she had ever done with anyone, except perhaps Robby and Ashlord. But at last, when Sheila noticed the frequency of Highleaf's suppressed yawns, she embraced Lady Highleaf and excused herself to go to bed. As she walked through the empty halls and made her way to the stairs, she wished she had the little book that Mr. Broadweed had given her so that she could read again some of the poems within it. Now that so much had changed, within her and elsewhere, she thought she might have a better appreciation of the sentiments expressed in those verses. Turning to climb the back staircase, she nearly collided with Farby who was coming down.

"Oh!"

"Oh! Pardon me, Lady Shevalia. Sorry to have startled you."

"That's quite alright, Grant. How goes the guard duty?"

"Fine, fine. All is quiet. Just as we wish it to be."

"That's good."

They looked at each other awkwardly for a moment, then Farby moved to go past her.

"I suppose I'd better look in on our watchmen once more," he said. "Good night."

"Good night."

Farby took a few steps down as Sheila moved up the stairs, then he stopped and turned back to her.

"Lady Shevalia."

"Yes?" Sheila turned and looked down at Farby.

"You must think me a complete ass."

"Why would you suppose that?"

"By the way I carried on, seeking your favors when they were obviously already given to another. One, by all accounts, worthier of your attentions."

"Don't be silly. How were you to know? I should have made things clear from the beginning," Sheila said. "And it is I who should apologize. For the other night. When we skated together. I should have kept to myself."

"If you had, you would have denied me the most enjoyable experience of my life."

"Please, Grant."

"You are right, though. I took advantage of you in a moment of loneliness."

"No, I think I had the advantage of you."

"Regardless, I assure you that you need have nothing to fear or dread from me concerning my feelings. Some things are just not meant to be."

"Yes, that is so."

"I would hate for my foolishness to come between us," Farby went on. "Perhaps we may still be friends, though?"

"I do hope so. You have already proven yourself a great friend to me. And I hope, for my part, that I can become a good friend to you."

"I am glad to hear you say so," Farby bowed. "Well, good night then."

"Good night, Grant."

Farby watched Sheila go up the stairs and turned just in time to meet Denks coming along the hall.

"You are up late, Denks."

"Yes, Mr. Farby," Denks said. "I was just putting away some things, but thought I saw some odd lights in the great hall."

"Oh? Aren't the lamps there lit?"

"Yes, they are. I thought it was my tired eyes playing tricks on me. But when I looked again, I thought I also saw some movement, and I thought that I should tell you."

"Yes, thank you, I'll go have a look."

• • •

Ashlord's door was ajar, and Sheila looked inside, thinking she might have a word with him. But he was not there.

"Oh, well. I imagine he's making himself at home in the library," she said, pulling the door closed. Passing by Billy's room, she heard a voice, and she knocked. Not waiting for an answer, she went on in.

• • •

Farby walked slowly around the perimeter of the great hall, but saw nothing amiss. Just as he completed the entire circuit of the room and was back at the base of the grand stairs, someone pounded on the front doors. He flew up the stairs, rapier in hand, and made the door just as Denks came hurrying from around the corner.

"Open up! We are the King's Constabulary! Let us in!" came a voice from the other side, accompanied by another round of knocks.

"What shall I do, sir?" Denks asked.

Farby nodded at the portal, "See who it is."

Denks opened the little portal and put his face to it to look out.

"Who goes?"

"Captain Thrubold, on urgent business."

"What business might that be at such an hour?"

"I have reason to believe that the guests of this house are in great danger. Let us in!"

Farby nudged Denks aside and put his own face to the portal.

"All here is quiet, Captain, I do assure you," Farby said, suspiciously. "I do not think you are required."

"I insist that you let us enter!" said Thrubold. "I believe you may have intruders within."

"We have kept good watch, sir. Thank you for your concern, though."

Farby closed the portal, only to elicit additional pounding from the Kingsman.

"Did you receive several large crates today?" Thrubold shouted. "If so, I fear you have taken delivery of the murderers and cutthroats of Lord Banis."

"Lord Banis is dead," answered Farby, turning away.

"I know that, you fool! Let us in for the sake of your safety. Or else we'll force the door!"

Denks pulled on Farby's cuff.

"Sir, we did take delivery of several very large items this afternoon," Denks said with a look of terrible distress.

"Why didn't you say so!" Farby jumped to lift the bar and open the door. Captain Thrubold and a dozen other Kingsmen charged in with swords drawn.

"Where were the crates taken?"

"Upstairs," Denks said. "To the guest wing."

Already Farby was running, with Thrubold and the Kingsmen right behind him.

• • •

"Right. Hold him still," Gladsten said. "That foxdire ain't as potent as it should be, an' he's liable to squirm."

Gladsten's assistant nodded and pulled Billy's hair, forcing his head down onto the chopping block. Owing to the vehement protests and kicks of his captives, Gladsten had ordered that each except the girl be dosed with foxdire, leaving only Sheila to watch. She was on her knees, her mouth gagged, her legs bound and her arms tied around the bedpost, and a burly man was holding her head to face Gladsten and Billy.

"That's right, just like that," Gladsten nodded.

He winked at Sheila as he raised his broadaxe and took aim at Billy's neck. The door flew open and, amid a bubbling of eerie light, Billy was pulled aside. Gladsten's axe was already sweeping downward, and it struck off his assistant's hand, still clinging to Billy's hair. In the next confusing moments, the man howled, holding his bleeding stump and falling away. Gladsten tried to free his axe from the block, while the man who held Sheila suddenly had his foot pinned securely to the floor with a dagger right through his boot. Gladsten wrenched the axe free just as a sword took off his right kneecap. When Farby and the Kingsmen finally barged through the door a moment later, they found three screaming men on the floor in a profusion of blood, Billy snoring off to one side, Ibin sawing logs, too, his head down on Ashlord's shoulder who was shaking his head and blinking. Certina shrieked and shrieked, going from one wounded assailant to the next, clawing and pecking at them each in turn. And they saw a little man standing beside Sheila, removing the gag from her mouth and untying her hands.

"Get away from her!" Farby shouted, going at Eldwin with his rapier. Eldwin reacted by lifting his own sword and putting his body between Sheila and Farby.

"Stop!" cried Sheila before either man could harm the other. "He saved us, Grant!"

While the would-be assassins continued to howl and cry, and as Thrubold's men crowded into the room, Farby eyed Eldwin suspiciously.

"This is our man!" Thrubold seized Gladsten by the collar, yanked him up, and shoved him at one of his Kingsmen. "Are you injured, my lady?"

"No, no. Eldwin, here, came just in time," Sheila declared. "Ashlord! Billy! Are you alright? Ibin!"

"Let me help ye," Eldwin said, untying her feet, while Farby undid Ashlord's gag.

"Those imbeciles used foxdire on us!" said Ashlord, more to Certina, now on his shoulder, than to anyone else. "They could have killed us!"

Billy, meanwhile, had slumped against the far wall and was snoring in spite of the commotion and yelling. Sheila, now free, scrambled to Ashlord and Ibin, and took Ashlord's hand.

"I will be just fine, my dear," he said to her. Ibin, his head still on Ashlord's shoulder, now competed with Billy's snores, as they always did when they slept nearby, and Ashlord gently pushed his drooling face away.

"Oh, Ashlord! Where did they come from? How did they get in?" Sheila asked.

"I am afraid I am at fault," said Farby, sheathing his sword. "And you have my deepest apologies. They apparently had themselves delivered to the house within large crates this afternoon."

"It is my fault, my lady!" called Denks from the doorway. "I should have suspected. And I should have informed Farby about the delivery. I am so sorry!"

"Help me up, child," Ashlord said to Sheila who pulled him to his feet. "There! Oh! My head spins!"

Suddenly Sheila flew to Eldwin and crouched before him, hugging him and kissing him on the head and cheeks.

"Eldwin! Eldwin! A miracle that you are here! Oh, thank you! But, how? How did you find us? Why did you come?"

"Many questions, indeed, good friend!" Ashlord offered Eldwin his hand. "We are truly in your debt, sir!"

"Well, sir, me lady, I, well, I...I have so much to tell! An' a lot of questions to ask, too," Eldwin stammered.

"I, too, would like to thank you," said Farby who also put out his hand, "and offer you my gratitude for saving our good friends. My name is Grantham Farby."

Eldwin shook Farby's hand firmly. "I am called Eldwin."

"Well, Mr. Eldwin," spoke up Thrubold, "you have saved the day! And I offer my hand as well, if I may. Captain Thrubold, at your service, sir."

By now the hall was crowded with servants of the house, and so intent they were on peering through the doorway that they hardly noticed Lady Highleaf pushing through them, only to be pushed back by Thrubold's men who were escorting their bleeding prisoners away. When she finally made it to the door, she took one long sweeping look at the room, the blood on the carpet, the severed hand, the weapons on the floor, the occupants, asleep and standing, and then, tugging her night robe tight, she took a deep breath.

"What in the blazes is going on here?" she shouted. "Do any of you have the least idea of the hour? And who," she glared at Eldwin, "are you?"

The men in the room stared at her, momentarily stricken speechless. But Sheila laughed and put her arms around the lady, saying, "I am so happy to see you again, too!"

"I can't imagine what you mean."

"I think I should explain my presence, at least," said Thrubold, bowing to Lady Highleaf. "But perhaps, if I may be so bold, we should first see to our two sleeping gentlemen here. If directed the way, my men can carry them to their beds."

Thrubold told the group about his work with Lord Banis's papers and how he had learned about the message sent by Banis to one of his accomplices.

"We managed to track the courier who told us where the message was taken. We forced the door into Gladsten's residence, but no one was there. I'm afraid at that point I was stymied. I feared I was at a dead end. Although we were disguised, that district is rather close-knit, and we did not want to put out a full-on search that would forewarn our fugitives. I could think of nothing else to do but wait. We paced around inside Gladsten's place all day, waiting for someone to show up. When Mrs. Gladsten arrived, very late in the evening and very drunk, we quickly extracted from her the whereabouts of her husband."

By now, Ibin was being put onto his bed by the servants and Thrubold paused as the door to his room was closed.

"And so we came immediately," he concluded, shaking his head. "I am so sorry we could not come sooner and prevent all this."

"And I almost didn't let them in," said Farby, "not trusting—no offense Captain—that it wasn't some ruse."

"No offense taken, sir. You do not know me, and caution is wise."

They made their way downstairs toward the parlor, and Thrubold begged his leave.

"I must see to the prisoners, and a few other matters," he explained. The group thanked him once more, and watched as he strode across the long great hall and up the far stairs.

"I'd dearly like to know how you got into the house, Mr. Eldwin," Farby said. "Or did you enter with the assailants?"

"Oh, no, I," Eldwin began to answer Farby, but before he could, Ashlord laid a hand on his shoulder.

"I think we should wait before we hear your tale, Eldwin," Ashlord said, glancing at the many servants who still lingered.

"Lady Highleaf, would you care to have a pot of tea or some other refreshment brought into the parlor?" asked Denks.

"A cup of tea would be just the thing, Denks," said Lady Highleaf. "And have the brandy cart brought in, please."

"Certainly, my lady. I'll see to it personally."

Soon they were back in the familiar parlor. When the door was closed, Ashlord turned to Eldwin.

"I fear your presence, though timely and fortuitous for us, is not a sign of good news from the east."

"I don't know where to begin, sir," Eldwin said. "Even though I've thought an' thought on what I'd say when I found ye. All is well back east, I suppose, if that's what ye mean. Tallinvale is safe, once more. The Redvest army that was there was defeated. I came as quick as I could, on a particular business of me own, ye see. There's somethin' that vexes me, sir. Somethin' most peculiar an' queer that I witnessed, that I thought I might put to ye. Somethin' that don't seem right. I'm not sayin' this very well."

Clearly nervous and upset, Eldwin struggled to speak.

"Lady Esildre," he started again. "She's dead! I was with her when she died. She just died. It was as if she gave up an' went to sleep! Just put her head down an' died. Why, Ashlord? Why would she do that?"

"Oh, my word! That is very distressing news, Eldwin." Ashlord offered him a chair, glancing at Sheila.

"Oh. Oh dear," she said with a confused expression as she took a seat next to Farby.

"No, thank ye, sir. I think I'd rather stand. An' I've got other bad news, too, I'm afraid. But where's Lord Robby an' Lord Ullin?"

"They are not in Duinnor. They went to Vanara to take care of their own business. Please. Begin at wherever you mark a good beginning, and tell us all the news, and let Esildre's death unfold in your telling, and anything else you might wish to tell us."

Eldwin did so. He told them how Esildre and her two great-nephews had remained in Nowhere to help train his people to fight, and how, eventually, the curse of Bailorg was lifted from them, thanks to Robby and Billy's idea of putting pigs up in tree lofts. He told them how he had gone to Janhaven with a small company of the Elders along with Esildre and her great-nephews. There, he said, they were told about the death of Robby's mother, Mirabella. So intent on speaking to Ashlord, whose gaze until this point was fixed and expressionless, Eldwin did not at first see the change in Ashlord's countenance. Eldwin hesitated and turned to see Sheila's face streaming with tears, her hands covering her mouth, her body shaking.

"Oh, pardon me," Eldwin, red-faced, declared.

"No, no," said Sheila, trying to stifle her emotions.

"Lady Mirabella was a friend to many," Ashlord gently said to Eldwin, his own eyes watery. "And to some a very good friend, indeed. Please. You must continue."

Eldwin hesitated, and he glanced back and forth from Lady Highleaf and Farby to Sheila. Ashlord stood and went to the window and pulled the curtain away. Dawn was nigh, and, with his back turned to the room, he gazed across the snowy gardens below. He heard Sheila release a soft moan. Certina fluttered to his shoulder and edged closer to his ear and put her beak into it. Ashlord nodded.

"Please, Eldwin," he said. "Tell us all."

• • •

Ullin awoke with a start and a spasm of shivers. But it was not the natural shiver of cold bumps that he felt running up his back and under his sleeves. Controlling his desire to jump up, he instead only opened his eyes to the dim early morning light that filtered through his cover of pine boughs. He listened but heard nothing. That was peculiar, for even the common titmice and nuthatches were seldom silent for very long, and morning was an especially busy time for them. Peering as best as he could through the branches and needles, he tried to discern any movement, anything out of place, but he could see very little one way or the other. Slowly, carefully, he moved out from under his shelter, stopping every other moment to listen. After a while, he was freed from his bed, and he knelt, looking through the tree trunks in the foggy light. As quietly as he could, he began putting his things together, and not until he had his pack on his back, his sword in one hand and Swyncraff in the other, did he rise to a crouch.

The uncanny sensation of danger remained, dancing up and down his arms as he moved off in what he hoped was an eastward direction, stopping every few yards to watch and listen. This he did for a long while, making slow progress for his caution, until he began to doubt himself and the warnings on the back of his neck. His heart fluttered as several wrens and quite a few sparrows shot around him, disappearing rapidly into the trees ahead. Suddenly he heard a sound, and he saw a white fox some many yards off, dashing in great strides through a drift in the same direction that he was going. Almost immediately, he heard another noise from his right and he saw three rabbits, bounding one after the other through the deep snow, darting around the gray trunks as they went.

"They all seem to be going in the same direction," he muttered, looking at the way he had come. "And I'll take my example from them."

He jogged clumsily away through the snow with little mind to the noise he made. Soon the rasping of his heavy panting was louder than the noise of his wading through the snow. He tripped over some buried brush and fell, immediately getting up to stumble on. Later, he lost his balance as he worked his way up a hill, and careened sideways into a tree trunk, banging against his wound painfully. It was a long slog upwards, and it seemed to take forever to gain the top of the hill, so long was its slope. When he reached the top, he fell to his knees to catch his breath. Looking ahead, he could discern a gap, some miles away, where it appeared that the forest parted, for he saw no treetops there. Perhaps it was a depression or dale that fell away from the hills, or maybe it was a field—his heart leapt at the hope—laying fallow during winter. The possibility that he might be nearby to a farm thrilled him and served to invigorate him.

Looking down the way he had come, he saw nothing alarming in the trees, no movement at all. Then, as he got to his feet, he looked at one of the hills he had passed over the night before, less than a mile away, one that was higher than most others. A strange heavy mist seemed to gather at the top of it, like a ball of lamb's wool. Perplexed, he watched the apparition until it dissipated somewhat, and saw within the vapor a motionless and black form that was shocking and stark against the surrounding snow. It was the captain of Shatuum on his horse, and the sight of it sent an electric terror through Ullin's body and pounded his temples with the hammers of his own heartbeat. Aghast, he realized that the creature watched him.

Ullin turned and fled.

Entr'acte

Entr'acte

The Oarsman

The long narrow channel of Grisland Strait was lined from south to north with burning and sinking hulks, and the choppy waters boiled with a thousand desperate men. To either side of the strait, the flotsam of ruin washed against sharp rocks and cliffs, and those in the water who were still alive thrashed wildly to keep from joining the many bodies tumbling violently against the crags. In some places amid channel, where the decks of stricken ships were awash and sinking fast, the current swept away long plumes of red, hardly distinguishable from the tunics and capes that adorned many of the bodies. Blue splotches, too, were everywhere in evidence, those of the Loyalists who, like their Redvest countrymen, were beyond the cares of any land.

With the unusual and providential southerly wind at his back, Captain Martin Makeig stood at the bow of the Golden Swallow and looked northward beyond the burning ships to either side of the littered channel. Through the black, smoky haze, licked here and there by oily flames, he saw the Sea Horse bearing the Prince's family just ahead of the Barge Royale that carried Prince Lantos and a large number of refugees trying to escape from the murderous Triumvirate. Both were about a mile ahead, nearing the northern mouth of the channel and open water. The Sea Horse was a Glareth-built ship, swift and weatherly, and once her oars were shipped and stowed, and the reefs taken from her broad triangular sails, she would easily outpace the lumbering Barge Royale. Gaining on them, however, was the Scarlet Lance, the pride of the Redvest fleet and the most powerful of their warships. She had already sunk two of the ships escorting the Prince and his family, and would no doubt soon add two more to her battle score.

• • •

Four days earlier, in what later became known as the Battle of the Marshlands, Prince Lantos and his small army of resistance were in retreat, virtually encircled by an overwhelming Redvest force. The Loyalists, including hundreds of women and children, were forced to fight a desperate rearguard action as they were pushed deeper into the inland mires and swamps. Annihilation seemed certain. However, the situation was at first unknown to the Triumvirate Navy, and they failed to reach the coastal waters in time to completely cut off the Loyalists. Thus, hundreds of tiny boats, manned by fisher-folk and tradesmen, made their way into marshes along the tidal estuaries and riverlets that flowed out of the swamplands. These small craft managed to ferry the defeated army and their people away to the sea where merchant ships, transports, and a few remaining Loyalist warships took them aboard.

While these weary Tracians embarked for the safety of faraway Glareth, the Prince and his family, along with a few resolute fighters, guarded their rear against the ever-encroaching Redvests. At the last moment, with enemy warships in sight, the Prince and his remaining people were taken aboard the Barge Royale and the Sea Horse. They immediately set course east by northeast, escorted by four warships, including the swift Golden Swallow. The aim was to round the eastern coast of Grisland Island and turn north on a long voyage to Glareth. But the Redvest fleet divided and cut them off, forcing the Loyalists into the treacherous Grisland Strait. Seven Redvest warships rounded the island and came down the channel from the north while six more came swiftly from the south. In between the two Redvest squadrons were the trapped six Loyalist vessels. There, constricted by the narrowness of the rock-strewn channel, battle was joined.

• • •

The two screening warships of the Loyalist fleet, the Trueblood and the Golden Swallow, cleverly engaged and sunk all seven Redvest vessels that sought to block the north channel, opening the path of escape. But the Trueblood was set afire and lost in the effort, and the crowded Barge Royale sustained damage. A mile to the south, two more Loyalist ships were set afire, rammed and sunk when they sought to shield the Barge Royale from the enemy ships still in chase.

Only the Golden Swallow remained to defend the escaping refugees. She immediately came hard about to south, swinging around and past the northbound Sea Horse and Barge Royale to bear swiftly down upon the six remaining pursuers. By sheer audacity and expert seamanship, the nimble and ferocious Swallow ran two of the enemy ships aground to be torn apart by rocks, and then set three more Redvest warships afire with her missiles and firepots.

But the Scarlet Lance escaped the little Swallow's wrath and slipped through the melee, daring to hoist full sails in the narrow confines. She expertly avoided the conflagrations that littered the way, skillfully twisting and weaving through the sinking and burning ships. The Scarlet Lance bore on, ignoring the struggling men in the water crying out for help, her two decks of oars sweeping at maximum cadence right through them. And the Golden Swallow, having put about once more, beat northward after the Scarlet Lance, her bow heaving against the current, every stitch of sail bent on, every spare sailor and marine at the oars.

• • •

Leaning over the rail, Captain Makeig looked down at his prow. There, rising and falling out of the water protruded the long iron ram. It was much beat up, and two men were lashed to it, hammering on a new steel tip, sharp-pointed and barbed. They timed their work, holding their breath as they went under only to gasp for air and work a few more hammer strokes at each rise before pitching under once again.

Squinting ahead, Makeig listened to the beat of his oaring drum from below decks, the rush of the bow wave, and the hammering of the ship's carpenter and his mate at the ram. But his eyes were fixed upon his prey's stern. The plan was set. There was no turning back, no turning away. Hearing a cry, he saw, only a few yards away, a dozen blue-tunics treading water just beyond the sweep of the oncoming oars.

"Go get 'em, Makeig!" cried out one of the men in the water.

"We'll be back for ye if ever we can!" shouted Makeig. But he knew it to be unlikely.

"Ne'er mind us, Capt'n," called another man clinging to a broken spar. "Only get the bas'ards afore they get the Prince!"

Makeig glanced down at the ram once more just as it and the men disappeared under the water. Even before the rise, they were swinging their hammers.

"If they don't drown," he said to himself, "if the men at the oars don't give out, if the wind holds steady, an' a thousand other ifs, we might just do it."

For a moment the smoke ahead cleared. It was now apparent that the Golden Swallow was gaining on the Scarlet Lance, only three hundred yards ahead. Makeig could clearly see the captain of the Scarlet Lance at the taffrail, looking back at him.

"Ha!" Makeig exclaimed grimly. "We've got ye, now. Bodwin!"

"Aye, sir!"

"Let's get set, shall we?"

"Aye, sir!"

The foredeck swarmed with activity as every man that could be spared from the oars assembled a framework of heavy timbers at the bow. The ship's carpenter and his mate were hauled up from the repaired ram, and they immediately lent a hand, putting layers of shields over the framework. Underneath, two ballistas with grappling hooks were winched, cocked, and elevated. The stern anchors were prepared. The winches and sheets controlling the sails were made ready. Meanwhile, the Golden Swallow closed on the enemy and would soon be within range of the Scarlet Lance's bowmen, already gathering at her stern.

Now the Swallow's marines were crowding under the frame of shields. Some were preparing to grasp the ropes from the grappling hooks while others were already sniping at the Redvest vessel with flaming arrows. In return, the Scarlet Lance let fly a flock of arrows, all landing harmlessly in the water or bouncing from the forward shields. All the while, Makeig shouted his orders and prepared the men by his speech.

"We'll not give in, an' we ain't lettin' up! We're stoppin' the enemy, an' we ain't gonna spare the Swallow to do it, else the Prince is a goner. So heave the grapplin' lines smartly to the stern anchors an' let 'em drop. Then at the signal make fast the lines an' cut away the anchors. We'll drop the foresail, an' fill the mizzen an' swing the main and spanker. The swing 'round'll be right harsh, so hang onto something firm. They'll pour it on, but we'll have 'em, an' our oarsmen'll heave their fire. When the work's done, ye'll know it. Lieutenant Bodwin will lead the way, and every manjack over the side after him. Make north for Glareth overland. Good luck! Long live our Prince!"

• • •

The captain of the Scarlet Lance watched, incredulous, as the Golden Swallow swiftly gained.

"It will avail him nothing," he said to his lieutenant. "He may close on us, but can only hope to tap us with his ram. Besides, if he grapples, he'll only be easy prey for our fire. So it is a symbolic gesture, no more, and he'll soon bear the folly of it."

As he spoke, the two small catapults nearby were readied, and a flaming pot was placed into each basket, ready to toss down onto the little ship that was now close astern.

"Let us make room for the archers," the Redvest captain said as he and his officer retreated to the helm. The rear deck swarmed with archers who began unleashing their arrows in thick flocks.

• • •

"Steady," Makeig said to the helmsman. "Steady."

Then things began to happen that the captain of the Scarlet Lance did not expect.

"Rammin' speed!" Makeig cried out.

The rowing master heard the order, and as the beat of oars quickened, the Golden Swallow rushed across the last fifty yards, then the last forty. Arrows from the enemy fell thick and useless on the sheltered men at the bow as the stern of the Scarlet Lance loomed at thirty yards.

"Let loose firepots!" Makeig cried.

Immediately, shielded platforms on the foremast were uncovered. Men stood, each swinging a smoking pot on a cord round and round and letting them fly high over the Swallow's bow, coming down upon the crowded taffrail of the Scarlet Lance. The pots burst into flames amid the archers as more pots flew and fell into the burning confusion.

"Grapplin' hooks away!"

The forward ballistas kicked, and two heavy iron claws shot over the flaming stern of the enemy ship. As soon as they landed, the men of the Swallow grabbed the lines and took out the slack, then, twenty men to a line, they ran astern, pulling the Swallow even faster toward her prey. The heavy lines were thrown around tackle affixed to the stern anchors, and the ends taken back to the mast and made fast.

"Let go anchors!" Makeig instantly bellowed.

The Swallow's heavy stern anchors were released. As they dropped, the tackle whizzed and the ropes whirred, and the Swallow lurched violently forward the last ten yards and crashed into the stern of the Lance with a tremendous shudder. The ram splintered through the Scarlet Lance's transom below the waterline, just to the port side of the rudder, and it passed through cracking timbers until up to the Swallow's beak.

Makeig immediately drew his heavy cutlass and shouted.

"Away, fors'ls! About the main! About the spanker! About mizzen! Hoist stern flyers! Cut away anchors! Ship oars! Hard a port!"

The anchors lines were cut, the booms of the middle and rearmost sails were hauled around as more stern sails were hoisted. The oars were drawn in and shipped, and men began pouring up from below decks, picking up their axes and swords along the way. For a moment everything became oddly quiet as the Scarlet Lance, her stern afire and hopelessly impaled by the ram, was slowed to almost a halt in spite of her sails and frantically beating oars. Then the Swallow's remaining sails, having been pulled around unnaturally, filled with wind, driving the small warship forward and sideways. The Swallow shifted at an angle, heeling to port, her stern coming slowly around, then more quickly, her ram now ripping out ribs and planking of the Scarlet Lance. The wind stiffened, pulling the Swallow nearly at right angles before her ram cracked as it pried away the stern post of the Lance, opening it up to the sea.

But the Swallow, too, was stricken. The ram splintered from her stem, snapped off, and she, too, was drinking water at the rupture. Freed of much of her bow, the Swallow now heeled all the more, swinging rapidly around by the stern, while the rudderless Scarlet Lance veered over at the bow, her sails heeling her against her leeway. While the crew of the Scarlet Lance fought to cut away her sails, the crew of the Swallow controlled their own, and she was now well past right angles to her opponent. The Swallow veered the rest of the way, crashing into the oars of the enemy ship. All the while, more firepots were slung onto the Redvest ship, arrows flew, and now, as the two ships came against each other, portside to portside, stern to bow, more grappling hooks were flung from the Swallow, these with chains that were drawn taut and spiked to the Swallow's decks.

Below decks, a few dozen oarsmen on the Swallow watched through their oar ports, waiting for the right moment. The enemy drew in his oars, which served to bring the Swallow's hull right against his own. Then the Swallow's oarsmen went to work tossing firepot after firepot through to the other side, and shoving long narrow troughs through and pouring casks of oil into the Lance, setting off an inferno below the Redvest decks. When this was done, oarsmen of the Swallow tipped over their remaining casks, and, as the last oarsman climbed up the ladder, he dropped a torch.

Now the battle was joined, and both ships were doomed, though only Makeig's men knew it. Redvest sailors and soldiers poured down onto the decks of the Swallow, and they met with a furious defense. But it was only a portion of the Swallow's crew who fought. Obeying their orders, most of Makeig's men dove into the water and swam for shore, taking their chances against currents and surf-battered rocks. Makeig and a few of his officers guarded the swimmers, fighting to keep the Redvests away from the landward side long enough to make a difference.

The Captain fought without care to danger, slashing and cutting viciously, slamming his huge frame recklessly into the Redvest throng. His men, as inspired as he to protect their comrades in the water, were reluctant to go over the side, and they kept up the fight with such vigor and determination that the Redvests were dismayed, though they outnumbered the small band nearly twenty to one. Soon all but the most foolhardy of the enemy were reluctant to face the Loyalist fighters, and many of the Redvests backed away, preferring to let their archers do the work from the safety of the Scarlet Lance. But there were very few Redvest archers left, and it was something of a shock when the boarding party turned to see that not only was their ship boiling with smoke and fire, but it was rapidly sinking by the stern, while flames shot up from the Swallow's own hatches.

Seeing their retreat, Makeig shouted at his men.

"Go Winterford! Get on with ye! Over the side, all of ye!"

There was one man in particular that seemed not at all inclined to leave Makeig's side. He was an oarsman, newly shipped aboard just before the battle, having specifically asked to serve aboard the Golden Swallow. Makeig did not even know his name. But now here he was, stripped to his waist, dripping with sweat and splattered with soot and blood, fighting next to his captain with a heavy fid in one hand and a dagger in the other. Makeig turned to him to order him off the ship, but was distracted by another rush of Redvests. Together the two fought them off as the deck slipped beneath their feet and tilted sharply down at the bow. The Redvests at last realized their fate and fell into confusion. Panting, Makeig glanced at his men in the water to judge if they were yet far enough off, then glanced warily at the hesitant Redvests. He did not see the flaming missile coming at him, but turned at the last moment, with not even time to flinch, as the oarsman shoved Makeig aside and tried to swat the ball of fire away. The oarsman slipped and struck the edge of the missile with his wrist, but it was enough to bat it clear of his captain. Makeig was momentarily stunned by the action and by the sight of the oarsman desperately trying to shake the sticky flaming pitch from his wrist.

But there was no time for expressions of gratitude, nor for nursing wounds, thanks to a deck now awash and rapidly slipping under. Makeig pushed the oarsman over the side, put the broad brim of his hat into his teeth, then jumped in himself. He came up, trying to get air, hampered by the hat that he refused to release from his bite, while at the same time trying to kick off his boots and squirm out of his heavy coat. He sank deep until, at last lightened of his coat and boots, he kicked to the surface. There he took the hat into one hand and began swimming for shore.

It seemed hours. But fortune favored Makeig and a fair number of his crew, the current taking them beyond the worst of the sharp rocks to a less dangerous stretch of shore. Makeig at last hauled himself onto land, and after lying on his back for a few moments, he stood. Out in the channel, some way north, the Golden Swallow and her victim slipped under the waves, leaving a few splotches of burning wreckage. He heaved a great sigh, and almost burst into tears. Blinking, he wrung the water from his hat, briefly mourned the ruined plume that hung limp from it, then jammed the hat on his head and began gathering his men together.

Knowing what was to come well before the last moments that doomed the Golden Swallow, many of Makeig's men had the presence of mind to go into the water with packs of provisions, kits of flint and steel, and a few weapons. His purser had even managed to bring some coin off the Swallow. Altogether, over a hundred men made it safely ashore. Subdued and weary, together they watched the fires in the channel subside, and caught a last glimpse of the faraway sails of the Sea Horse and the Barge Royale as they slipped into the hazy northeastern horizon. From time to time they called out to stragglers as a few more of their shipmates came out of the water or wandered from farther along the shore. But the new oarsman who had saved Makeig's life was not amongst them, one of the many comrades, known and unknown, who was lost that day.

Captain Makeig would have been very much surprised to know that he would meet that oarsman again one day in, of all places, an old troll cave. When that day came, the two former shipmates could hardly be expected to recognize each other, even though they would soon be fighting Redvests once again and side by side, just as before.

Part II

Chapter 18

Come Bright and Bold, Lady Moon

Day 199
46 Days Remaining

In Islindia's forest, the Faere Queen walked among the blasted ruins of her once beautiful wood. With her wings folded about her, she stepped lightly along the snow-covered path with hardly a track left behind her. She stopped and put her hand against the fallen remains of a mighty trunk, now reduced to a stony snow-covered log, hardly distinguishable from the icy ivy that overgrew it.

"Hello, old friend," she said. "Remember me? When I was a little girl, new to the new world, you were my favorite tree. I would alight in your branches, and you would hold me up to Sir Sun's gaze. At night, I often slept on your strong limbs, and you let Sir Wind play your full boughs, shushing me to sleep while Lady Moon covered the land with her silver light. Don't you remember me?"

Silence was the only reply. She removed her hand and backed away, her smile vanishing, and she sat down in the snow nearby, staring at the silent log.

"I am sorry," she said. "If I had gone with Secundur, if I had not been so proud and so terribly stubborn, you might have been spared. You and all your kin, and mine, too, who lived in these lands. Perhaps, if I had gone with him, I could have learned to forget things. Perhaps different stars would have turned in the sky above, and the world below would have been a different place. And, perhaps, Secundur's shadow would not have become so dark and so spiteful, and hearts not so filled with his hate."

She felt her father's spirit gather itself nearby, and felt, too, his anger and his desire to spite all in the world.

"No, Father. That is the Dark Lord's way, not ours," she said, not looking up. "Cupeldain's council should not have listened to you, and should have used their Keys to open the right way for us to depart. But what happened happened. Now the Keys are scattered and lost, Cupeldain is gone, with his beautiful wife, too, and his granddaughter sits on his throne. The power to open the way to Aperion's abode is gone from the world. Our lands are destroyed. Our people, our kin. And they will never be restored. And now your time, like mine, is quickly passing. Indeed, I hasten our end, do I not?"

It was true. Robby did not fully understand what he had asked of her. It was a hard thing, and yet so easy, for her to conjure into flesh and blood her memories of the wondrous forest where she first drew breath. It was hard because it made her all the sadder when her one day was done and all sank once more into mold and dust and mist, filling her days and her nights with restless melancholy, with terrible regret.

She was given by her curse one night and one day only each month, a day of her own choosing between the rising of one full moon and the next. And when Lady Moon came boldly once more to pass over her forest, signaling another chance to dream, to inhale the fine season of life for a night and a day, to laugh and sing and fly with her sisters and brethren, it was all Islindia could do to resist bringing forth the forest of her memory. And it was Islindia's way, to measure her own strength, not to dream immediately, but to wait as long as she could, her anxiety and anticipation growing and growing until she could stand it no more. It was only by chance, and by her strength of will, that she had put off doing so when Robby came to her with Micerea. And, willingly, at the next sunset, she dreamed her magic dream, and sent the trusted Ayreltide to Ullin's rescue.

But now Robby asked more of her. Soon, Lady Moon would be once again emboldened, and Islindia would have another night and day to bring it all back until, lost of her confidence, Lady Moon returned to the night sky with the edge of her fan across her face, putting an end once more to Islindia's sweet dream. Islindia knew the risk and the cost. If Ayreltide failed to return before Lady Moon crossed the threshold of the eastern sky, he would be lost, transformed forever into the creature that he was on all other days. Likewise all her subjects, for none could leave her forest without the greatest peril to themselves.

She did not tell Robby these things. If she had, he would have asked more about it, and discovered other things that she did not wish him to know. But the King of the Wood knew well the price his daughter paid for each conjuring of her memories. He knew how her own wings grew weaker with every passing month, so that she seldom used them at all as she once did, choosing instead to walk among the blighted spirits of the forest on her bare feet, saving her wings for those days when she could fly with her own kind, instead of alone. Soon, she would be able to fly no more at all, dream or no dream, and would be naked and in need of clothes and fire and food as mortals need.

Islindia nodded.

"Yes, Father. I know that the wings that fly beyond our forest are lifted by my strength. And I know that my strength fails. Soon I shall have none, I suppose. So I may as well use what is left to me in aid to those who might yet have some hope. For, in spite of Robby's words, we have very little, don't we?"

A snowflake fell. It was the last snowflake from the last cloud that trailed behind all others as the sky cleared from west toward the east. It drifted down, missing the stunted limbs of the struggling trees, blew across Islindia's face, and landed on her outstretched palm. She looked at it, studying its pattern as it slowly melted.

"Lyrium and her daughters have returned," she said, rising to her feet. "Perhaps her Sight is improved. I hope she brings back news that may be comforting. I hope it was not a mistake to give her refuge, or lend to her the old carriage."

Glancing up, she saw that morning was rapidly coming, and that it would be a clear day above.

"And tonight, Lady Moon will be at her boldest," she said as she turned and walked north to meet Lyrium, "and so it will be time."

• • •

All the day long, Ullin ran, if what he did could be called running. He continually slogged and waded through snow and drifts, stumbled headlong through frigid woodlands, and clambered and scratched his way over icy hilltops. He had no chance of escaping the hunter who patiently gained on him, and he only hoped for a place where he might make a stand, some open ground in which to rest for a few moments and prepare for combat. But he never found such a place, nor could his desperate mind find any means of making a defense within the winter wood. Several times he thought to stop and make a trap, some pit or snare. Each time when he examined what he thought might be a good place for one, he saw that the evidence of it would be too clearly marked in the snow. And each time when he thought to cut a sapling into a long spear, he struggled at it too long, having no woodaxe and ruining the edge of his sword in the trying, sensing on his arms and on the back of his neck that danger grew nearer. So he kept going, his pounding heart and aching lungs full of dread and clutching terror, and he watched as he fled for some little bit of open and level ground.

The hours of the day thus passed like the melting of ice, relentless but slow, quietly dripping away moment by insignificant moment. The snow ceased to fall, and the sky gradually cleared, giving Ullin some hope of using one of the Bloodcoins against this captain, just as he had inadvertently used it against the other one, and soon he found a small clearing at the foot of a hill where the low afternoon sun was bright and unobstructed. He slung away his pack, pulled out one of the Seven that he carried, and held it into the light with Swyncraff in his other hand, waiting for his attacker to close in, watching every approach. But it was as if the creature knew the sort of weapon that Ullin possessed, for the captain of Shatuum made no attempt to show himself or to come near to the clearing. As Ullin was keenly aware, Sir Sun did not wait and never would.

"Come on!" Ullin screamed, spinning around, ready at any direction as the shadows grew ever longer by the moment. Ullin watched the light turn yellow, and moved to stay in the slanting sunbeams until they faded along with his only hope of victory. As Ullin scrambled to put the

Bloodcoin away and to shoulder his pack once more, the captain of Shatuum spurred his mount and came in a cloud of steam over the hill above him.

Dusk saw the Kingsman racing up the far hill and down the other side. In the dale below, he stopped long enough only to push his pack under a rocky bank, pulling out his sword and shoving his ice axe through his belt. Thus lightened, he ran all the faster, gaining ground ahead of the captain. At the top of the next hill, Ullin did not look back and continued his headlong dash down through the trees and across a shallow stream and up the next hill as the last purple of day faded and night came. It was a steeper and higher climb than he realized it would be, and when he gained the top, he saw Lady Moon rising full and complete over the distant hills.

"At least I will see you when you come," he said hoarsely to his pursuer as he jogged along then began his descent. He tripped over a snow-hidden bramble and fell against his wounded side, and bit his lip to keep from cursing with pain. Still wincing, he got to his feet and staggered on.

Behind him, the captain trusted his mount to pick the best way through the woods, but he continually urged the beast with hot spurs into bloody flanks to keep a quick pace. This would be the night he would run the man down, and this would be the night he would turn back to Shatuum with the man's body. It would be a long while before he could do it, for his prey was stubborn. Though baffled by the man's determination, the captain of Shatuum was patient. Men are weak, he knew, and determination by itself is not enough.

• • •

Farby saw Sheila sitting on the south garden wall, her legs up and her arms around them, her head resting on her knees as she gazed away toward the Temple in the distance. Having spent nearly all day with Eldwin and Ashlord, listening to them go back and forth over Eldwin's tale, Sheila had slipped out for a breath of air. Some while later, Farby did likewise. Though he had looked all over for her, intending to speak with her, now that he saw her, he hesitated. Still unsure whether he should disturb her, he approached and took a seat on a bench below facing away from her.

"I am very sorry about your friend," he said after a few moments. Sheila did not respond, and so Farby remained silent, too.

"I was just remembering one of the chats that Mirabella and I had," Sheila said at last. "She thought that her husband would die before her. That she would live out her days remembering the love they had for each other. She was Elifaen, you see, and he was not. Is not."

"Ashlord said that you lived with her for a time. He is quite upset, too, though I daresay he thinks he hides it."

After a few moments, Farby stood and faced her.

"I just wanted to say I'm sorry," he said. "Ashlord and Eldwin are still talking. I think I'll rejoin them."

"Don't go."

Farby turned and watched Sheila climb down from the wall.

"Let's talk," she said taking a seat. "But I don't want to talk about Mirabella. Not yet, anyway, if you don't mind."

"Not at all."

"I didn't know Esildre well," she went on, "having only met her once. But Eldwin knew her from ages ago. From before she went to Shatuum."

"Yes, as he said. I never had the pleasure."

"I am amazed that Eldwin found us. That he came all this way in such a short time, and just to talk about Esildre with Ashlord."

"Yes, his ability to pop across great distances is truly remarkable."

"And he has been here for days and days looking for us. And going to our apartments probably right after we departed there, the morning Banis died."

"He seems to have gone to a lot of trouble," Farby nodded. "And it was lucky that he overheard Gladsten and Miss Tarrier talking about Starlight Hall. If he had not, he would not have followed Gladsten or found you in time."

"Yes. That Gladsten! In a way, it was on my account that he and his wife came to Duinnor. As I said earlier, they refused to help me when my uncle beat me. Robby's father had them kicked out of Barley for it. I suppose that set off the entire chain of events that nearly cost us our lives last night."

"Well, perhaps. But Eldwin handled him right neatly, didn't he?"

"Yes. He did. Poor Eldwin! All that he's been through. The awful battle he described, his friend Herbert, and then Esildre and Tyrin. Did you know that I met Tyrin?"

"Yes. Ashlord told me. At Edgewold. After the battle there."

"So unlike Mirabella! Esildre, that is. I suppose she simply could not live without Tyrin."

"Yes. Pretty awful. Very sad. Ashlord and Eldwin were talking about that when I left them. Ashlord was telling him about Esildre's curse, the one Secundur put on her. The one that made her, well, lascivious. Common knowledge around Duinnor, I'm afraid. As I said, I never met her, but her reputation was quite shocking. Apparently, your friend Ullin was not entirely immune to her curse."

"It's hard to believe," Sheila said. "I know what happened to Ullin, his madness. Ashlord told me, as I suppose he just told you and Eldwin. But she just didn't seem like that, not like everyone makes her out to be."

"Hm. I hope I don't cause offense, but Eldwin says that you and she look remarkably alike."

"So I've been told. I wonder if that's why Banis acted as he did at the party?"

"Who knows? But I think Eldwin was smitten by her."

"Smitten?"

"Oh, not in *that* way. Perhaps a poor choice of words. I mean to say that he must have felt a strong attachment, some powerful friendship, dare I say love? To come all this way. You know, I think he aims to spite Secundur himself! To get back at him for what he did to her."

"What do you mean?" Sheila shook her head. "Does he think it was because of Secundur that Esildre died? That she just gave up like that?"

"I think so. I don't know," Farby shrugged. "Eldwin seems to think that whatever happened to Esildre was just too much for her to bear. That when Tyrin died, it broke her. Ashlord seemed to agree, but I excused myself to look for you."

"That was kind of you. But I am fine. I may look like Esildre, but I am not her."

"And you have not given up on seeing Robby again, have you?"

"No. I know it seems silly, one way or the other. But, even if I never see him again, I'll do as Mirabella would have done, not as Esildre."

A sharp breeze cut across the gardens and whipped around the bench. Farby shivered, then tried to suppress a yawn.

"You haven't slept for nearly two days, I imagine," said Sheila. "You must be worn out."

Standing, she took his hand and pulled him up.

"I insist that you go at once and have a nap. It's getting dark, so you may as well sleep the night. Come, I'll walk with you back inside."

• • •

When General Mar Henith came to lay siege to Tallinvale, he brought with his army carpenters, experienced lumber cutters, and many blacksmiths. When they made their camps in the hills overlooking what would become their battlefield, the fields that would become their place of doom, they cleared the forest of virtually every useful tree within a mile radius of their encampments. The large trees with strong and straight trunks were used to make their engines, their towers and trebuchets, their bridges and their ladders. The leftovers from these fellings were used to stoke their furnaces, to heat the forges that prepared the rivets and bent the iron bands that bound the arms of their trebuchets. The smaller, sturdy-looking oaks and ashes, pines and poplars, hickories and walnuts were used to make their long pikes, cut into spears and tipped with sharp iron points. Countless lesser trees were also cut, to make space for the encampment. Some were used as poles to hold up the sea of tents, or as tripods and spits to support their stew pots and kettles, and, of course, as fuel for their cook fires and their watch fires. So cold was the winter that more and more of the younger trees were cut, and the older crooked ones, too, to keep the miserable Redvests warm. Scrub trees and bushes were gathered, too, and thrown onto their fires. In short, the invasion brought a devastating industry to Tallinvale, one that had been busy with the polluting art of war and weapons-making, the requirements of siege, and the travails of winter survival.

The lone young oak tree, no more than twenty-five feet high, that stood nearby to the graves of Esildre and Tyrin was spared only by luck. It happened that a soldier tied a rope to it, high up, and ran it to another tree some many yards away. This rope was pulled taut and used to support the broad tent of General Mar Henith, underneath which he had lived and from which he had directed his troops. But when the catastrophe of the north fields took place, and Mar Henith along with the bulk of his army was destroyed by fire and water, General Menslay, his replacement, ordered that all surviving men withdraw quickly to the southern fields of battle. While much in the way of tents and equipment was abandoned, the tent of Mar Henith was hastily struck and carried away, along with his tables and maps and chairs, his surveying equipment and his books, to be used by Menslay as his own headquarters in the south.

Now, after all the battles were done, the sapling stood nearly alone, amongst the stumps and leftovers, the trash and ruin of the hills. Not even a half-foot in thickness, with limbs bare of leaf, it stood as a thin, almost black silhouette against the gray sky. In the abrupt peace following the last battle, General Teracue and Lord Tallin ordered that the hills and woods be cleansed of the invaders' litter, and so workers nervously came from the town and made their way along the repaired road and crossed the sunken killing grounds, reeking with steaming pools full of corpses. Most kept their eyes ahead, looking at the less distressing sight of the north hills, and it was impossible for them not to glance at the sapling. The tree seemed an incongruous sight, so stark against the sky, standing over the wreck all around and the two fresh graves nearby. And as the people went about their work and labored to gather and clean away all materials left by the Redvests, it was as if the tree watched them, as it had watched all of the horrible proceedings of the recently passed days. Some of the more superstitious folk commented how, in future years when the oak was fully grown into a hulking tree, it would surely be filled with a mighty and terrible power. Others, less inclined to believe such things, simply shook their heads and went on with their work. But all alike came to view the tree with a kind of deference and respect, the kind that might be due to any uncanny survivor of a terrible fate which had swept away all others of its kind. So they kept a respectful distance from it. Alone and unmolested it remained, this silent witness, fated to keep its observations to itself.

During the days that followed the battle, winter reasserted itself upon the Old Eastlands Realm. On the day that Eldwin laid the bodies of Tyrin and Esildre to rest, snow began to fall once more. It continued to drift down lightly but steadily from the low gray sky for two weeks, with hardly a breath of air to disturb its descent. Soon the spindly limbs of the oak were coated, and all the lands surrounding were covered with a fresh white blanket that grew in thickness as the snow continued. The snowfall was enough to cover over much of what the workers of Tallinvale sought to gather and clear, so they gave up their work and retreated back to Tallin City to wait for spring's revelations. Their tracks were also soon covered, and silence descended peacefully over the place where the tree stood and where the two graves lay.

The days passed dimly and the nights darkly, for Lady Moon could not see through the clouds, and her husband, Sir Sun, had not the power to penetrate the thick gloom even with his brilliant gaze. Each day he tried harder and just a bit longer than the day before, but he went to his bed a failure. And each night, Lady Moon grew gradually bolder, determined to see the lands below her starry balcony. At each night's end, she, too, retired unsatisfied. To the inhabitants of Tallinvale, busy as they were rebuilding their town and preparing for what may come next, these days and nights were bleak and heartless. Many of the wounded died, and many friends remained missing and were presumed lost. Some, even those with hardly a scratch from battle, fell into deep morose distraction, their wounds having entered their eyes and scarred their hearts. But most of the Tallinvalers were sadly relieved to be safe, going about their days in mourning for the many dead, for the ruination of the land, and for the terrible waste that men bring upon one another.

Early one morning, very far away, a child of Sir Wind who had been circling up and down and around the western world took it into her heart to visit the sea. She passed out of Vanara, and easily strolled over Forest Islindia. Moving over the broad open plains, she came gently toward the Eastlands, crossed through the Thunder Mountains, and passed with the long, wide train of her clear robes through the region of Tallinvale. The clouds that had so stubbornly clung to those lands sullenly parted before Bonny Breeze. They reluctantly drifted away before her until, just before the end of day, Sir Sun looked over his shoulder back at the Eastlands, and the sky was filled with his red and purple robes. He smiled at his wife, rising beautiful and bold over the distant watery rim of the earth, and he longed to reverse his course to be with her. But his fate pulled him onward, and soon even the hem of his robe was gone from sight. Lady Moon, determined to look fully upon the Eastlands, folded her fan and put it completely away. She rose quickly into the clear starry sky, bathing the silent land with her blue-gray gaze.

When Eldwin made the two graves, he dug them on the west side of the lone oak and a few yards north of it, choosing the spot because of the nearness of the tree, and because it seemed the best place to dig. He had observed to himself as he dug that, should the little tree survive, someday its leaves might shade the spot from the hot glare of summer. So now, as Lady Moon made her way across the sky, the silhouette of the oak fell nearby to the graves, and the shadowline of its trunk inched closer and closer until it passed across them. It was at this moment that a black smoke-like tendril reached up from Esildre's grave, rising out from the snow-covered mound to gather itself in the thin shadow of the tree. The black smoke slowly churned and grew thick, rising from the grave into a low murky ball. Where the shadows of the oak's bare limbs did not touch the dense smoke, lines of light gave it some definition and form. Suddenly, pale arms shot up from the eerie mass, and an uncanny light illuminated it from within. A low painful moan came, then a cry of terrible anguish that shattered the winter silence, and the inky substance flew to pieces, evaporating in the moonlight, revealing a gray misty form. It stood, arms outstretched to the grave beside it, then it fell to its knees and covered its face, weeping terribly.

Far off, on the north wall of the city, Weylan stood watch and thought he heard a distant sound. Putting a spyglass to his eye, he scanned the moonlit hills, but could not make out any movement. Yet such was the silence of the night that the spirit's wail carried across the broad north fields and up to his ears. As a shiver spidered up his spine, he thought he heard words.

"No-o! No, no! Let me be with him!"

Weylan put down his spyglass, snugged his collar up, then pulled his hood over his head. He still heard the eerie sound as he continued his walk along the wall, but he said nothing of it to the others who also stood watch, their faces taut. They well knew that thousands of frozen dead lay before them, and it would come as no surprise to them if the restless spirit of at least one or two walked those fields, looking for a way home.

• • •

That night, while Weylan walked his watch on the walls of Tallinvale, and Ullin fled for his life, Robby paced back and forth in the East Tower of Griferis. His spyglass lay ready on the table near the window where he had put it a moment before. It was too early, he knew, but he worried all the same. So much could go wrong. Someone could fall and be killed. The distance could be simply too far for his couriers to travel. Or someone might be late at the rendezvous and left behind. But, he kept telling himself, if all went well this night, it would be the beginning of his plan, and the little Kingdom of Griferis would truly have its start.

He stopped and looked toward Algamori and the Landing where the gate stood at the edge of the chasm. The eastern sky was effused with the rising light of Lady Moon, but the mountain was still in shadow. Robby could just barely make out the gate, but he needed the spyglass to see what, if anything, went on there. Glancing below, he saw that his representatives were ready: Finn, Unther, Hathrain, and Lafkin. Each was armed with a sturdy cudgel that Lafkin managed to fashion, all gathered at the wall over the East Gate, with torches ready to light, if needed. In the courtyard behind and below them stood Dialmor, bound and tethered to a lamppost, with a sack over his head so that he could not see what went on around him. Watching over him was Radasa, who paced back and forth in thought, and Winnefras who also held a club in case Dialmor managed to free himself.

Satisfied again that all was in order, Robby turned away from the window and continued his pacing about the room. Glancing at the device that controlled the causeway, he steeled himself. It was a very unpleasant thing to do, downright painful, but he had practiced enough to know what to expect and to know that he would not be harmed by the jolt it would send through his body. Being Elifaen, he mused grimly, had its advantages, for he was certain that the process of making the causeway appear would have killed him if he were still mortal.

Passing back in front of the window, Robby glanced down once more at Dialmor.

"You haven't the foggiest notion of what is about to happen to you," he said, smiling wryly.

• • •

On the broad, trackless waste that was the northeastern Dragonlands, a tiny insignificant dot trailed a thin cloud of dust in the bright pale light of Lady Moon's full face. It was a lone rider, standing in the stirrups and leaning low over the horse's pumping neck, racing at a full gallop across the hard-packed flatlands. They made for the Nalamain Hills some two miles north. It was a gentle bump in the desert, barely a hundred feet at its highest, and it was the northernmost region of this portion of the Dragonlands that a person could go before reaching the dangerous renegade-infested badlands south of Vanara's Blue Mountains. Seeing the hills, and turning toward the middle part of it, the rider urged even more speed from the horse.

"Hie! Hie!"

Suddenly the creature plunged into a long-forgotten pit that was once part of a line of trenches in some forgotten battle, now covered over with an age of fine dust and sand. The horse sank and fell, throwing its rider over its head to land at the edge of the pit.

Micerea slowly regained her senses, half in and half out of the pit, and dragged herself out and away from it. Behind her, the horse was up to its bridle, struggling to swim out of the stuff, panting and snorting in panic.

"Easy, boy, easy!" Micerea coaxed, going back to the edge and getting down on her stomach to reach carefully for the reins. Taking them, she gently pulled. "Come along, come. Come on, boy."

Sensing that Micerea was only wishing to help, the horse calmed somewhat then made another effort. She continued coaxing, and the horse continued trying, and just when she was about to give up, the animal's front hooves gained some purchase and up it came out of the pit, shaking sand and dust from its coat and mane.

"Good, boy! Good! Uh, oh!"

The horse limped around her, and she could tell that he had given all that he had to her. She untied and pulled away her gear, then removed the saddle and picked up the last nearly empty waterskin. Holding it up, she took a few swallows then cupped her hand and let the horse have a drink.

"You've done better than I deserve," she said to him. "You have a good heart, and I am sorry for mistreating you so. But if you have it in you, go north and climb the mountains. Once across, you'll find water, I'm sure. Do not be afraid of the Elifaen. They appreciate fine horses such as yourself, and someone will take you in and tend to you and give you a good home."

She rolled out her bundle of gear, donned her light armor, cinched up her leggings and her plates securely, and slung her sword over her shoulder.

"Have the rest," she said, letting the waterskin run empty into her hand as the horse lapped it up. "I won't need any more of this, either way things go."

She licked her hands of the drippings, then she turned and began jogging toward the hills. Already Lady Moon was beginning her descent toward the west, and Micerea knew that it was quite likely that she had missed her appointment. If that was so, she would soon find out as she reached the base of the Nalamain and began climbing. Owing to its gentle slope and low height, she climbed quickly and easily, making the last few yards at a scramble. Suddenly she found herself at the top and in the midst of a small encampment. Blades rang from their scabbards all around her, and she drew hers just as quickly, facing the armed semicircle that cautiously approached. Behind them, she could see other people, but could not ascertain their numbers or nature.

"Who goes?" called out one of the swordsmen before her.

"I am Micerea," she answered, "who bade you come here, in the name of Philawain, King of Griferis."

The man put away his sword and approached with his hands outstretched.

"Then welcome. I am Mayhall, as I am sure you know."

Micerea smiled, put away her sword, and took his hand.

"It is good to see you," she said.

"And you, in the flesh, so to speak!" the renegade said. Turning to the others, he called out, "See! Truly our dreams are wondrous! And King Philawain is a great and powerful king!"

Soon Micerea was surrounded by other men and women, some of the north, but most of her own kind, greeting her with bows and outstretched hands, saying all manner of things about the wonder of all being at the same place this night.

"You see," Mayhall explained, handing her a flask of water, "things have been somewhat tense tonight, and full of mistrust. Men and

Dragonkind wandering up since yesterday, all telling something of the same tale. That their dreams bid them be here."

"Is there no sign yet?" she asked, looking at Lady Moon. "The hour grows late."

"No sign at all, I'm afraid."

"And how long have you been here?"

"Well, if you think we may have missed something," Mayhall said, guiding her to the middle of their gathering, "then I can assure you that we have not. I have been here since noon yesterday, not wanting to miss my chance. And not long afterwards, the first of the others began to arrive."

"I see," she said.

"I suppose we shall all share the same fate, now," said a nearby woman, "whether or not anything happens."

"Yes. I suppose we shall. How many made it?"

"We number seventy-four, my lady."

"Look, look!" someone shouted, pointing to the northeast. "There! Do you see it?"

All eyes strained at the northeastern sky and saw the stars winking as shapes passed before them. They continued to watch, some laying their hands on their hilts, others putting their arms around each other as the dark forms quickly drew near.

"Be not afraid!" Micerea shouted. "These are our allies."

She watched for a moment longer, amazed by the sight of the graceful flying horses.

"Put your warm cloaks on quickly! Where we go will be very cold!"

• • •

In Vanara, Lord Seafar climbed the ladder up to the newly repaired flight deck, and pulled his overcoat tightly about him against the cold wind.

"At your ease," Seafar said to the watch. "I only stretch my legs."

By the lamplight, added to that of the moon, he could see the newly laid planks and the orderly dots of their pegs, and the aroma of newly hewn lumber was a welcome replacement to the all-too-familiar smell of charred timber. A soldier on the far side of the deck was sweeping away snow, a continuous duty of late, keeping it safe for any landings that might occur. But the landing lamps were not lit, indicating no flight activity was expected this night. Looking up, he saw the dim red glow of the observation room at the cliffs, ever watchful over the Palace, and he could easily make out the gaping cave below where also no landing lamps were lit.

"All is quiet tonight," he commented to the guard.

"Just as we like it, sir."

"Indeed. But keep a sharp lookout tonight, would you?"

"As always, my lord. Is there anything in particular we should watch for?"

"No. No, I don't think so. But send for me should you observe anything unusual."

"Certainly, my lord."

Seafar climbed back down through the hatch and passed through the ready rooms, saluting the officer of the watch as he went. He jogged down a flight a stairs and made his way to the Scribblers Room, where he had just been not an hour ago.

"Strange," he said to himself, "how a simple dream can upset all one's routines."

Indeed, he should have still been in bed but for the odd nature of the dream that persisted in his mind. Normally, he would not have given it a second thought, but the message was so emphatic and clear, even if it was quite unbelievable.

"Griferis shall rely upon your judgment and the justice of Vanara," he repeated aloud as he re-entered the Scribblers Room. He had already used True Ink to verify the message, given to him by one claiming to be the Lord Chamberlain of Griferis, sent as an ambassador of goodwill.

"I am Finn, the Lord Chamberlain of the Kingdom of Griferis, come to you with tidings from my King," the man in Seafar's dream had stated. "He sends me in this manner because it is in his power to do so. The King says unto you: Watch the skies this night and through the morrow until you see his sign, for the King of Griferis sends unto you his gift of goodwill. Griferis shall rely upon your judgment and upon the justice of Vanara. So that you may trust this dream, go immediately and ask of your True Ink what is the name of he who rules Griferis. And you shall see it written: Philawain is King of Griferis."

Seafar pulled out a sheet, dipped his quill, and wrote the statement again. Again, it did not fade. Taking the sheet, he went to the duty desk, and asked the officer there to copy what he had just written.

"Just to be sure that my table's ink is not ruined," Seafar explained.

The True Ink did not fade, and the duty officer looked at Seafar questioningly.

"Yes, I know," said Seafar picking up the sheet. "It hardly seems credible. That, after all these centuries, Griferis has a king."

"And that you have guessed not only that, but also his name," said the officer.

"Yes. That, too."

Seafar retreated back to his desk, thinking that he would ask the ink to explain more to him. But he only stared at the nearby stove, hardly even aware when, some hours later, the watch changed, signaling the last hours before dawn.

"May I offer you a cup of tea, my lord?" one of the Scribblers asked.

Seafar looked at her blankly, then got to his feet.

"No. Thank you. I think I'll go back up to the Flight Deck."

• • •

Robby knew that those invited had far to come, and sometime after midnight, he was overjoyed to see the first arrivals swing around the mountain and begin their descent. These were from Duinnor and were fewer than a dozen. He put his glass to his eye and watched the winged horses swoop down and land lightly, their riders nearly all sliding off to their knees in relief. No sooner than the last horse from Islindia had taken off, than the next ones arrived. Excited and nervous, Robby watched and paced, repeatedly picking up and putting down his spyglass. The hours passed, and they kept arriving, sometimes in large flocks, sometimes singly or in pairs. The Landing on Mount Algamori was soon crowded with arrivals. Not only did the marvelous creatures bring newcomers to Griferis, but some of them also brought supplies and the needed equipment that Robby had requested. Down at the East Gate, where Finn stood, he saw his old friend grinning at Lafkin, just as pleased as any over the spectacle.

But, not to be overly confident in things, Robby began to worry that all might not be done in time. Islindia had hinted at some risk when he asked her this great favor. She wanted from Robby assurances that the flying horses would only be needed for the night, and would face no danger that would keep them from returning to her. She was not satisfied with his answers, for he could make no promises, but, without elaborating her concerns, she had agreed to his request. Robby was keen enough to suspect that her power to make real the creatures that populated her dreams had its limits and its perils. After all, it was the Queen of the Wood's dream that sustained the last goodness of her forest. He could only guess what would happen to her forest if something went wrong, if one of her magical horses failed to return. Her father's wrath would not be restrained, Robby feared, and the protection enjoyed by the good people of Greenfar might vanish.

Thrilled though he was at the success thus far, there was one horse in particular that he fretted over, that had farthest to go to deliver its rider, and farthest to go to return to Islindia. He had wanted to send it to Ullin, to ease his journey. But many of Islindia's horses would be bearing two riders, and others were devoted to bringing packs full of supplies. And the horse he had wanted to send to Ullin, as it turned out, would be needed by Micerea. Robby only hoped that Ullin would understand.

It was time to open the Gate and put out the causeway. He knew that it would terrify the new arrivals, and perhaps signal Shatuum that something was afoot, so he had dared not do it before now. Robby signaled with a lamp to forewarn Lafkin and the others. He turned the glass key, sucked in a deep breath, exhaled slowly, and placed his hands on the copper poles to either side of him.

· · ·

As he crawled up and over a steep ridge, Ullin only mildly noticed that a broad open space lay below and before him. Far off across the wide expanse, he saw a rim of what he took to be high hills, but at that moment he lost his footing and fell sliding and tumbling downward, crashing through brush as he went, unable to grab hold of anything that did not break away. He hit a drift of snow at the bottom, gained his feet and struck out, crunching through the drift into the bright moonlight. It was a large, perfectly flat open space, with no trees or cover of any kind. The captain on his horse topped the hill to see Ullin jogging away below, already some two hundred yards out.

The snow under Ullin's feet thinned, and as he began to slide he realized he was on a frozen lake. He should have known when he first saw it, and now, midway across, he clearly saw that the far side immediately ahead was rimmed by banks too steep to climb, and he altered his course toward what he thought was a milder shore. He heard noise behind him, and whirling around, he saw his pursuer charging down the hill and across the ice. Ullin stopped, panting, and bent over with his hands on his knees, watching the captain quickly approach, the uncanny eyes of the steed's, like glowing red coals, were matched by the ruddy light from the eyeslits of the captain's iron helm. Glancing at the shore, Ullin realized that he would never make it.

Drawing his sword and uncurling Swyncraff, he straightened up and walked toward his attacker. The iron-shod hooves thundered across the night, and in the silvery light Ullin could see shards of ice kicked up in a high spray. The captain made ready his whip, flinging it out like a red serpent, and spurred his mount on. Ullin crouched, set his feet, then, yelling, he charged the captain, hoping to dodge the steed and the whip, and perhaps strike a lucky blow as they passed. Before they met, a huge shadow passed over Ullin's head with the sound of rushing air. He ducked and slid to a halt at the new threat. The shape descended rapidly, and Ullin saw broad wings supporting a horse. On its back Ullin saw a rider and the flash of bright steel upheld in the moonlight as they swooped down onto the ice. The horse alighted on its rear legs, its wings flapping. The captain's steed roared in dismay, rearing up to fend off the interloper. Ayreltide struck the black steed's iron headgear with his hooves, and the beast stumbled at the blow and staggered. As his horse fell, the captain's whip struck Ayreltide's right wingtip, shearing it off in one fiery crack as the captain was flung skidding across the ice, his hot armor hissing as he went. Ayreltide careened away, screaming in pain, as his own hooves slid on the frozen surface. Ullin watched for but a moment, then resumed his own charge, closing the space as Ayreltide's rider scrambled off his back.

"Micerea!" Ullin shouted. "Get away!"

But Micerea ran for the captain who was struggling to his feet beside his stricken mount, and as she ran past him, she dealt him such a blow against his helm that it rang like a gong and sent a shower of red and yellow sparks flying into the air. Now Ullin was there, and saw that Micerea had thrown away her shattered sword, holding her arm. The captain staggered, but got to his feet while his horse squirmed on its side, panting and crying, its legs uselessly kicking as the ice under it hissed and steamed. Ullin threw Swyncraff as the captain faced Micerea and slung out his whip. As before, Swyncraff sliced through the weapon in an explosion of crackling embers. The captain roared in pain, reeling, and unsheathed his furnace-red sword. Ullin struck him on his side, shattering his own sword, and dove away after Swyncraff. Micerea threw a dagger that entered a chink in the captain's armor just under his chinguard. With a terrible groan, the captain pulled the dagger out, and Ullin watched the blade drip away in molten steel before it was dropped. With Swyncraff in his hand, Ullin scrambled to Micerea who was preparing to throw another dagger at the enraged knight.

"Run!" Ullin yelled, pushing her away as the captain loomed behind him, his wavering-hot sword held high.

"Ullin!" Micerea screamed, and Ullin turned to face the captain. As the captain swung down at Ullin, Ayreltide suddenly returned, spun around in the air and bucked, kicking the captain with both hind legs, first against his helm, then against his side, in two ringing blows. The captain staggered backwards, his sword striking nothing but ice, but he did not fall. Ayreltide crashed, his hind legs broken and useless, and he flapped his injured wings to lift himself up but only managed a pitiful tilted skitter, ascending only a yard or two before crashing again and sliding away helplessly.

Micerea cried out, and flung her other dagger at the captain who batted it away and now strode toward them. Ullin knelt, quickly pulled off his coat and then Robby's vest. Getting back to his feet, he shoved the vest into Micerea's arms, and he pushed her away. He turned around, backing into her to keep her moving as he pulled his ice axe from his belt, gripping it in one hand and Swyncraff in his other.

"Run," he said to her calmly, tears streaming down his face. "If you love me, then for pity's sake run!"

But whether she was too terrified to do so, or she loved him too much to abandon him, she did not go, and only backed away, unable to speak.

The captain came again. Slowly, in pain, his armor creaking oddly and glowing dull red where it was stove in by Ayreltide's blows, he came on. In those last moments, Ullin inhaled deeply, his senses acute, taking in every sound and color and smell. He could feel the heat of the captain as he approached. He saw the captain's mount become motionless, expiring with the uncanny sound of cracking sticks and falling into a heap of smoking and steaming coals. The scent of sulfur and ash was in the air, and some distance away, over the thudding crunch of the captain's steady steps, Ayreltide panted and whined. Ullin planted his feet, readied his ice axe, and took up his defensive posture, raising

Swyncraff. The captain was only ten yards away now, coming steadily. Ullin felt his footsteps through the ice and saw vapor rising from each hissing ironshod footfall.

Something snapped loudly, and a tremor ran up through Ullin's feet. Almost immediately, a loud, dense crack shot through the air, followed by several more in rapid succession. Where the captain's horse lay, the ice broke open and the remains of the beast sank into the frigid waters. Out of the hole erupted a geyser of steam and boiling water, spraying high and raining down warmly. Ullin almost lost his balance at the quake, and both he and the captain staggered sideways as screeching jagged lines shot across the ice with a sound like snapping limbs.

Ullin turned and pushed Micerea ahead of him.

"Run!"

They did, making for the far bank. Behind them, the churning water continued to spray up and outward, now bubbling furiously. The captain, confused and bewildered, only realized his peril when a large fissure cracked open between his feet and parted. He tumbled and sank as broad sheets of thick ice folded up and fell back down over him. A second geyser immediately shot up, blasting away layers of ice in a cloud of violently boiling and hissing water.

Ullin and Micerea stopped, staring at the cauldron in disbelief at their survival. Then Ullin stiffened and looked toward the distant Ayreltide.

"Come, we must try to help Ayreltide," he said. "But let's be careful!"

Skirting around the churning waters and broken ice, they made it to Ayreltide, who looked up at them as they knelt beside him.

"Oh, good fellow!" Ullin said, putting his hand on Ayreltide's head. "Once again you have saved me."

"Well," Ayreltide replied weakly as he panted, "that's something, anyway."

"Yes, it is, wondrous friend," said Micerea, putting her arms around his neck and kissing him behind the ear. "Thank you!"

"Let me look at your wing," Ullin said.

"It's only the tip that's gone," Ayreltide said. "Threw my balance off something terrible. But my hind legs took a awful shock from that foul creature's armor."

Ullin lifted the injured wing, seeing that it was missing the last foot near the wingtip. Then he went to examine Ayreltide's hind legs. Carefully running his hands across them, he could plainly see they were both shattered. He looked at Micerea and shook his head.

"Are you in much pain?"

"They burned and ached at first, but now I don't feel them at all. I'll be fine if I can get to the air."

Ullin and Micerea stood aside as Ayreltide raised himself up by his front legs. Then, with several powerful sweeps, he was in the air, floating up higher and higher.

"Oh, yes! I'll be fine!" he called down to them. "Farewell and good luck!"

"Farewell!"

"Farewell, with all our gratitude to you and to your lady!"

Ayreltide quickly receded toward the southeast and passed from sight over the distant hills. There, the sky was just beginning to show evidence of the coming day. Ullin slung Swyncraff around his waist, and put away his ice axe. He put his hands on Micerea's biceps, holding her at arm's length, grinning and shaking his head in disbelief. After a moment, she threw herself sobbing into his arms.

"My love, my love!" Ullin said.

"Oh, Ullin Saheed! Ullin!"

They wept with happiness, holding each other for a long while. They hardly knew what to say, but kissed and held each other tighter. At last, their eyes still misty with joy, they turned to look back at the spewing water.

"We must find a way off this ice," Ullin said, taking the vest from Micerea and putting it back on. "This way, I think."

They walked southward, toward the area that Ullin thought might offer an easier way onto shore. He remembered his coat, and darted off to fetch it, much to Micerea's worry, but was soon back, and, taking her hand, they continued on.

"I can't believe you are here!" he said, grinning.

"I can't believe I am with you at last. Truly with you!"

"But here you are!"

"I know!"

A dense fog was settling upon the frozen lake, rolling out from the obscured place where Secundur's creatures had been swallowed up. The eastern sky was quickly growing light as Lady Moon watched the far dawn from the end of her stroll over the western mountains. As Ullin and Micerea walked along, it seemed to them that there could not be a more beautiful place.

"I'm afraid I dumped my pack some ways back. Too far back to recover," Ullin told her. "In it are my rations."

"Hm. And I'm afraid I had to leave my supplies in the desert earlier tonight."

"You came all that way in one night?"

"Yes. Ayreltide is as fast as a falcon. Even faster. I thought the wind was going to tear my head off. As it was, I lost my helmet. And, as you can see, my cloak is in tatters. I think the wind of our passage was even more powerful than the terrible storm we endured the day we first met. And my hair!"

She passed a hand through her long, tangled mane as Ullin grinned.

"You are more beautiful in person than ever in dreams," he said, taking her into his arms once more. "There! That looks an easy spot to get ashore."

He pointed to the shore not many yards off just as another series of loud cracks and quakes knocked them to their knees. Turning over on their backsides, they watched as the thick ice before them broke apart and heaved up, grinding into the air before settling noisily back into the water. Unable to get to their feet, they scrambled backwards and away from the opening that fell away before them. Then, just as suddenly, the crashing quake ceased. The edge of the ice was now only a yard away. Before they could speak, or get to their feet, a fish leapt out of the water and slid across the ice between them.

"Oh!" Micerea cried out, laughing.

Then another fish popped out of the water, landing in Ullin's lap.

"Good grief!" he laughed.

Two more landed to their left, as more dove into the air and landed flapping to their right.

"Uh, oh," Ullin said, no longer laughing as one struck his face. He grabbed Micerea's hand and pulled her toward shore, and they slipped and stumbled as a rain of fish fell all around them. Just as they made the bank and scrambled up, the ice fell away while dozens of fish shot out to join them, the entire lake boiling and bubbling. They got to their feet and ran uphill, away from the frothy water as fast as they could climb. When they reached the top, they fell in a heap, panting and staring down at the steaming lake.

"Oh, my!" uttered Micerea. "The lake boils away! Feel the heat?"

"Yes," said Ullin, squirming as he fumbled with his hands in his large coat pockets. "But at least we'll have some breakfast."

He produced two fairly large fish, one in each hand.

"I have never eaten a fish."

"Well," Ullin shrugged, "it'll be a sight better than jawrock, I think."

• • •

"Another cold night nears an end," commented one of the Gray Guard on the Flight Deck, "and another cold day comes, my lord."

"Yes, invariably." Seafar nodded at the blue eastern horizon, growing brighter by the moment. "But at least we'll see the sun today."

Seafar had been pacing the deck for hours, shaking his head at his private thoughts. When the watch changed, he admonished all to "Keep a sharp eye aloft," but attempted to explain nothing.

"A signal from the mountain tower, sir!"

Seafar looked toward the northern top of the cliffs where a small outpost was, and saw the flashes of a signal lamp. Already, a guard rushed up with a slate, and copied as the officer on duty read.

"Flyer. Fast flyer. Not ours. Repeat. Not ours. Comes quickly."

"Sound action stations," Seafar ordered, loosening his cloak to free his hilt. A soldier ran to the hut and pulled a rope. Soon members of the Gray Guard were pouring out onto the deck. When they saw it, they gaped, for none had ever seen the likes of what swooped over the cliff and quickly descended toward them. It was a horse, a blue horse with the wings of a bird, bearing down upon them as naturally and as gracefully as any bird could do.

"Make room!" Seafar cried, backing away. The horse glided down and banked around the deck, revealing that it bore a rider, with arms bound around the horse's neck. It flapped twice and came to a landing on the deck, huffing as it folded its wings back. The creature turned its head back and forth, looking at the dumbstruck soldiers.

"Well," it said, "would one of you kindly remove this fellow? He kicks and squirms most stupidly. Come then. Which one of you is Seafar?"

"I am," Seafar said, stepping up.

"Do you, or do you not have the means to free me of this baggage?" the horse asked. "I don't have all day. And I can't tell you what a bother it is to go back and forth like this. My cousin Ayreltide gets all the best work, while I, mighty Shartide, must trundle inept riders. Come, come!"

Seafar shook himself, then pulled a dagger and cut the rope around the beast's neck. The rider, whose head was covered with a sack, slid off onto the deck with a thud.

"That's more like it! Goodbye!" Shartide said with an indignant snort, then galloped right off the deck.

All watched, wide-eyed, as the beautiful beast flapped up over the cliffs and out of sight.

"I demand that you untie me this instant!" the man said, struggling to his feet. "I will have you know that I am a special representative of Duinnor! Untie me, and get this bag off of my head!"

"I see you have a note pinned to your coat," Seafar said, pulling away a folded piece of parchment. "Hm. It says, 'Receive as a gift from Philawain and Griferis one Count Dialmor.' "

Seafar yanked the bag from Dialmor's head, and smiled as the Count blinked and looked around.

"No!" said Dialmor, recognizing Seafar.

"Oh, yes!" replied Seafar, walking away. "Put this man in irons, and throw him in the brig."

• • •

In Griferis, the new arrivals were guided across the floating causeway and through the gates and on to their temporary quarters. There they found steaming pots of tea and bowls filled with hot and hearty stew to help dispel the chill from their long cold ride. Lady Kinsiri and her daughters helped to serve the repast while Lafkin and Finn instructed the newcomers on where to sleep, explaining that certain rooms were set aside for the women and others for the men.

"We will return to see you all later today," Lafkin told them, "and begin to sort out how you will serve Griferis."

"Meanwhile, eat and rest," Finn added. "In a few days, you will all meet King Philawain. But, as General Lafkin says, we must spend some time with you to discuss your duties and who you will report to. For the time being, the doors leading out of this wing are locked, and captains of our guard are posted. Your curiosity about Griferis may be great, but do not let it get the better of you. Be patient and be calm. All is well, and let me say the King is very pleased by your presence. Eat, now, and rest. And by all means introduce yourselves to each other."

The new arrivals took full advantage of the opportunity to eat and to warm up, and did as Finn suggested by way of introducing themselves. Soon the north wing was full of talk and conversation, and they were all in good spirits and happy to be at the beginning of a fresh start in life, in spite of their fatigue.

Later, Finn returned with Lafkin and Radasa, and they began their interviews. This took the better part of the rest of the day and into the evening. At last, when night came once more to Griferis, and the evening meals were brought into the hall, Finn left Radasa and Lafkin to continue the interviews so that he could meet with Robby in his apartments. Finn found Robby pacing with eagerness to hear how things were going.

"So they all made it?" Robby asked immediately.

"Yes, sire, they have all come," Finn said, "all two hundred and seven."

"Wonderful! And are they situated for the time being?"

"Yes, in the north wing, sharing rooms. They are quite tired, but will soon be rested. They are excited to be here and are full of questions, naturally, but I think they are all anxious to begin their duties as soon as they may do so. Lafkin and Radasa are still with them. Our work ahead of time has made it all much easier. I doubt if there will be much need to change the assignment that we planned for each of them."

"Good. Very good," Robby nodded, and he yawned. Finn tried to suppress one of his own behind his hand. "I suppose we are both in need of sleep, aren't we, Finn?"

"Yes, sire, it has been a long couple of days and nights," answered Finn.

Chapter 19

The Hill Town Lass

To the east of Griferis were all the known lands of the world. But no one living knew what lay to the west, beyond the impassable chasm over which Griferis floated. Some called that canyon the Crack Between Worlds, and some legends named it the End of the Earth. It ran from north to south, as straight as an arrow, a league from side to side, and was made in the Time Before Time by certain Faerekind who, like Alonair, could speak with rock and stone and could raise them up from the ground as easily as a feather. This Crack they dug to cut off from the southwestern lands all water that fed the offspring of the ancient dragons whom those Faerekind feared and hated. Into this deep place flowed the clean, fresh water that once streamed across the southern lands, and to either side of this long ditch the ancient Faerekind piled up mountains to prick the sky and to make the heavy clouds release their rain and their snow so that little could reach the southern lands. And when their work was done, these Faerekind watched the deserts form where once forests and fields were, and where the Dragon People lived. Oddly, the Faerekind found that once they had made this great divide, they could not pass over it to the far western side. When they tried, it was as if some fierce wind held back the power of their wings. This angered many of the Faerekind who had nothing to do with the Dragonkind and cared not one way or the other for those lands that had become desert, for many loved the far west and now they were barred from going there.

Since Time was not yet arrived, it was to the Faerekind as an instant in which all these things happened, and like an eternity, too. They watched the Dragon People, who were once strong and handsome, grow sickly and infirm as dust spread across their lands and as dry sand replaced the once-green plains. They saw how the Dragonkind lived short lives full of suffering and disease, struggling to find food and shelter. And no one has ever been able to truly say why Beras allowed all this to happen, or why Aperion did not act to prevent it. Later, some of the Elifaen would come to think that it was the will of Beras, and the will of Aperion that it be so. And some of the Dragonkind began to believe that it was their challenge, and that Beras, through their Dragon Fathers, had made these things happen in order to try them, to test them, and to harden them.

Thus, as if to spite the efforts of those who made the deserts, the Dragon People survived and increased in numbers, adapting to the sands and making of that dry place a land they loved. And, as the legends tell, they would have their revenge upon the Faerekind, and upon the Elifaen.

Eons passed as the waters that once flowed across the Dragon Lands fell into the Crack Between Worlds. They fell and they fell, and joined into a great river that ran the length of the extraordinary canyon. In the untracked northern lands, far north of Duinnor, where the earth was always frozen and never knew the warmth of spring, enormous masses of ice creaked down from the heights that rimmed the chasm and fell like mountains into it, slowly melting as they floated away southward. As these icebergs tumbled and ground against each other, the thunder of their movement rose up from the great divide. And the mighty river that they made put out from its cold surface clouds of fog that rose up to obscure the river below.

But in the south, there was a place that Alonair had discovered, a place revealed by the digging of this chasm, where there was a peculiar and beautiful kind of stone, a kind that listened to him and spoke back to his heart. The stones complained to him of those Faerekind who cut through their home, and who piled up great heaps of rock to either side of the straight void. Alonair, in his eagerness to make of them his own creations, ignored their grievances and took from that place tremendous blocks for his own use. Of this stone he made the wondrous statues that graced Linlally and the lands of Vanara. He formed them into the likeness of animals that once prowled the long-gone forests of the Dragonlands, and the fair creatures that his kin once played and cavorted with. So lifelike were these works that they were the wonder of all who beheld them, and Alonair's reputation spread far and wide. Alonair's fame was heard of even in the Dragonlands, and stories of his works reached the ears of Kalzar, King of the Dragon People.

All know what happened, all know of the Great Stone that Alonair challenged Kalzar to cut and to move, and the impossibility of that task. But few could see into Alonair's heart to determine whether spite or ignorance or dark design was there.

And when came the Fall, and all Faerekind who remained in the earth were Scathed and parted from their wings, when Sir Time truly began his steady march, Alonair found that he could no longer do as he had done before; he could no longer harvest the marvelous stone as he once had. Like the rest of his kind, his wings were gone, the earth pulled him down, and things that once were joyously light became heavy and immovable. In those early days, the Elifaen still had some of their power, though it faded quickly, and from the scraps left to him, Alonair attempted to do that which only Beras can do, and from his efforts came forth the race of trolls. Yet, having lost what was most important in his art, Alonair was dismayed at his work, for the trolls were crude and without beauty, charm, or wit, and he banished them away to the east to live in the mountains there. Disappointed and heartsick, full of despair at his waning powers, and realizing his great mistakes and his great responsibilities, Alonair retreated from the world, and sought out places to hide and to meditate on his misdeeds and to await his chance to atone for them.

But in that place from where Alonair took his stone, the ancient river at the bottom of the Crack Between Worlds continued to flow, and it ran all the stronger and higher as the eons went by. Into the distant sea it crashed, cold and churning, crushing and grinding with its power the rocky coast, and there began a war between the cataract and the salty sea, a terrible, endless battle between the two. The sea, with its fury and power, sought to push back the roaring flow but could not do it. This was the place that came to be called the Craggy Sea, for it was full of sharp rocks and hidden reefs, treacherous currents for hundreds of leagues, roiling and crashing waves, wild tides and powerful maelstroms, ever dense with fog and mist. Along the coast, from the westernmost Dragonlands to the shores of Altoria, was the terrible domain of the Craggy Sea, where no one ventured but the desperate or foolhardy, and few who sailed or rowed into those waters were ever seen again.

And in that place from where Alonair took stone to make his statues and his other creations, far north of the frothy sea, far west of the badlands of the deserts, the mountains that rimmed the terrible chasm were not so high as all the rest. Indeed, Alonair's stone-delving made their valleys and their shoulders even lower than before, for he cut deep to take his stone. And it was here that the King of Griferis directed Thunderfoot, the King of the Trolls, to go and to take his people; here, back to the place from which they had come. And when they came nigh, having tromped across the foothills of the Blue Mountains and through the unknown lands beyond the Free City, they recognized the place, and remembered having been cut from it. Thunderfoot, their king, called them to a halt, and he stood on the very edge of the precipice, gazing across the void at the far mountains. For a day he stood, his people patiently waiting for his word, until at last he turned to them and cried, "Sleep!"

They obeyed, nodding off where they stood, to dream the slow dreams that only stone may have. King Thunderfoot sat and closed his eyes, and he had not long to wait before the mysterious figure appeared before him.

"It is not like it was before," Thunderfoot bellowed.

"Nothing ever is," came the tiny voice that answered.

"Our home is divided from us!" Thunderfoot declared. "This great ditch is in our way, and is cut through where we would return to."

"Then do as only your people can do," said the King of Griferis to the King of the Trolls. "Make the way open to you. Or is the task too great for King Thunderfoot and his people?"

"Ha!" cried Thunderfoot in his sleep. "You tease me!"

"Then make you a way across this void, if you can. And there, pull blankets of earth for your covers and let rocky boulders be your pillows."

"We shall! We shall!"

And so Thunderfoot awoke and called for his people to do so, too. They stirred and listened to his commands, and, for the first time in all their days, they worked gladly. They planted their square feet and spread their square hands, and they pushed. They pushed and pushed. Rock and stone tumbled, and earth heaved. Mountains rolled compliantly and fell over the side of the chasm as the trolls pushed and shoved. The ground shook and the lands resounded so that even in the far away Free City of Kajarahn their work was felt. And so it would continue to be felt for days and for weeks until it was all completed. The chasm slowly filled, and the waters slowly rose.

The King of Griferis came whenever he could to watch their work and survey their progress. And he was pleased.

"Two birds with one stone," he often chuckled, fond of his private joke. "In a manner of speaking."

Going back to Griferis, Robby woke and got up from the chair in his parlor and stretched. He picked up the book that had fallen out of his lap onto the floor, and put it on the mantel, and glanced out through the window at the noonday sky. He had not heard from Finn, but could only assume his hands were full with the new arrivals. It would not do to interfere so soon, though he dearly wanted to know how things were going.

"Tonight," he decided, "I shall sleep without dreamwalking. Real sleep. And, tomorrow, I'll have a good breakfast. I'm sure Finn will have a report for me by then."

He could not remember the last time he slept without dreamwalking. He was constantly on the move, going far and wide all over the world, watching Thunderfoot's progress, looking in on Ullin and Micerea, going about Duinnor or Vanara, or the Dragonlands. He studied Shatuum, too, though the place filled him with loathing. And, from time to time, he even dared to visit Passdale, so that he could look in on his father. But that only stirred Robby's remorse and sadness. Seeing how his father struggled at every moment to maintain, to find some way of carrying on, was nearly too much to witness, and sometimes Robby awoke to the sound of his own sobs.

Though it was without consolation, activity was Robby's distraction from the sad things he saw. His waking hours he filled with studies in the library and with learning more about how to manipulate Griferis itself. Night would come soon enough, and more dreamwalking duties. But it would do little good if he kept pushing himself. He needed regular, good, old-fashioned sleep if he was to hold up to the demands of the next few weeks. Spring was right around the corner, and the King of Duinnor would go out from his Palace to the Temple. All must be in place by then, or else everything else, all of his efforts, would be in vain. Though his mother's death and the suffering of his friends was his own fault, he was steeled by his regret, and he was determined that it would not be without purpose.

He stood thinking about all this for a long time, his hand resting on the mantel of the fireplace, staring blankly though the windows at the receding chasm that disappeared into the hazy southern horizon. He was Elifaen, now, and so the time he stood there did not pass as it may have done for a mortal. It was like a moment, like an eternity. But, long or short, he arrived at no new conclusions. And when he stirred himself once more, Sir Sun had passed from the highest step of his skyward stair to the lowest, and the long shadows of the western mountains reached the very tops of those on the east side of the chasm.

"Just to sleep!" Robby muttered, going to his bedroom and pulling the heavy drapes across the windows.

Crawling into bed, he tossed and turned in spite of his fatigue, obsessively turning over first one problem then the next. Suddenly he thought of Sheila. Before he realized it, he was flying across the dreamscape toward Duinnor. Just as he passed by the Temple, he halted, staring at the city as dusk descended over it, and at the Five Stars above.

"What am I doing?" he chided himself. "Have I forgotten how to sleep? I can't see her like this! I need to have my wits about me."

The city faded, Robby awoke and opened his eyes and sighed into the darkness.

"Oh, for pity's sake, let me sleep!" he whimpered.

As if this was the final expression of his exhaustion, his eyes became too heavy to hold open, and almost immediately upon their closing, he fell asleep. It was not a dreamless sleep, but it was deep, not given over to any particular sentiment or mood. When he had dreams, they were sweet ones of home and love, and he did not wander outside of their comforting cocoon, nor even did he know that he was dreaming. It was a delicious sleep, such that he needed and had not enjoyed for a very long time.

• • •

The next day, around noontime, Robby was the subject of Ashlord's thoughts, as he was very often. Things were coming to a head in Duinnor, and everyone knew it. In fact, there was a palpable sense of change in the air. It was five days, now, since the death of Lord Banis, and three days since his assassins had tried to murder Ashlord and his friends. Indeed, all events seemed to contribute to a looming crisis in the city, with Lord Arata issuing many warrants for arrests and summons for questioning while Lord Banis's supporters, especially those in the Duinnor Regular Army, were crying foul and woe to any who might inconvenience them. Kingsmen were out in force to maintain order, and so that the people associated with Banis would think twice before making trouble. The printers and papermakers, meanwhile, were kept busy relating wild stories about Banis and about who the King might select as the new First Lord of the High Chamber.

Amid all this commotion, Ashlord walked briskly along the streets, walking stick in hand, his long strides made even longer by his urgent pace, sometimes almost at a jog. He went the most direct route he knew toward the rear of the King's Palace, throwing up his stick to slow a speeding carriage as he passed in front of it, and waving his hand before him to part the throngs in his way. It was almost noon, and the crowd that was normal at this time was made all the greater by the latest news, the same news that sent Ashlord rushing from Starlight Hall.

Rounding a corner, he abruptly came to a halt, took a deep breath, and continued on at a more studied pace toward the back gate of the Palace. This was where prisoners who were released from their sentences normally emerged, often blinking and in a daze. Ashlord approached, the bells struck the noon chime, and the gate was opened. He watched as a few men unknown to him came out, some holding up their hands to block the glare, others pulling the tatters of their clothes around them against the cold winter air. Slowly drawing near, Ashlord saw a few more brought out on litters, greeted with relief by some who waited, as Ashlord did, for their friends or relatives. Raynor came last of all, grinning as he passed through the gate. Ashlord pushed through the onlookers as Raynor stopped, closed his eyes, his face up to the sky, and took a deep breath of pleasant free air.

"Ah, Collandoth! How nice it is to breathe clean, fresh air once more!" Raynor said before he had even opened his eyes.

"Raynor, old friend!"

The two Melnari embraced, and, smiling, they looked at each other.

"You haven't been worried about me, have you?" Raynor asked.

"Not at all," replied Ashlord.

"Because you needn't have, I assure you."

"I know. But I am still very happy to see you safe and sound." Ashlord broke into a grin. "Come! Let's go to Starlight Hall, where we'll find some decent clothes for you, a glass of wine, and a comfortable pair of chairs. I have much to tell you!"

"You do?"

"Yes!"

"About your odd complexion, perhaps?"

"Yes!"

"And perhaps about my little Beauchamp?"

"Why, yes. He is safe."

"And busy eating his way through the monks' precious herbs, I'm sure."

"Why, yes, he is at the Temple. But how did you know?"

"My jailor told me," Raynor laughed. "And he told me much else, besides. He had the most unusual dreams, for a jailor, that is, and he insisted on telling me each and every one of them."

"He did?"

"Yes, Collandoth. Does that surprise you?"

"No. And, yes, in a way."

"Starlight Hall, eh? Is that where you've been keeping yourself since coming to Duinnor?"

"I and my friends only took up residence there a few days ago. Until then, in fact, we had rooms upstairs of your place."

"Ah. Oh, my! Stop for a moment. Permit me to inhale this aroma!"

It was a baker's cart they stopped at, and Ashlord purchased a buttered roll for Raynor to nibble as they proceeded on their way.

"So Banis truly is dead!" Raynor mumbled, his mouth full.

"Yes, and you are released because of it. By edict of Lord Arata, all those arrests made by order of Lord Banis have been made null."

"They have, have they?"

"Yes. Tell me, what else did your jailor say to you? Or were his dreams confined only to furry creatures? And what, if I may ask, made him think to confide in you?"

"Fear, I think. He said that he feared a new King would not take so kindly to the servants of the present one, and that, according to his dreams, a new King was on the way. He hoped that by becoming lenient with his charges, he might win some pardon for his misdeeds."

"Oh?"

"Yes, and also he was afraid that the chains used to bind us might suddenly fall away as they did some weeks ago."

"What did you say? Fall away?"

"That is so. A most peculiar incident, I must say. And it terrified the jailor and all of his henchmen, too. After that, they didn't know how to treat us prisoners."

"Hm. Yet another confirmation that Robby already acts."

"The Ribbon boy? I was interrogated most severely concerning him. Before the incident with the chains falling off, that is. So he made it to Griferis!"

"Yes, apparently so."

"Splendid! Splendid! And the other members of your company? Are they all here with you?"

"No. Ullin Saheed Tallin, the Kingsman, went with Robby to find Griferis. To tell you the truth, I don't actually know what became of either of them. But I have reason to think that they made it and that Robby survived the ordeal of Griferis. Like you, those in my company have confided some of their dreams to me."

Raynor stopped and put his hand on Ashlord's arm.

"Do you mean to say he is a dreamwalker?"

"Yes. I know that he is."

"Dreams!" Raynor exclaimed more loudly than Ashlord would have wished in the crowded street. "I wish I could have one! I would dearly like to know what sleep is. Just for the experience of it, you see. And what it is like to dream."

"Come, let us keep on our way. Yes, I have found myself wishing something of the same," Ashlord nodded. "It seems odd that there is a power beyond our reckoning or experience that both the Elifaen and the Mortals share but that we are excluded from."

"Yes, it is odd that Beras did not bless us with that ability, or with that capacity. But we aren't the only ones."

"Who else do you mean?"

"Well, for one, the King. He does not sleep. And, if I understand what Esildre once told me, neither does Secundur."

Ashlord stopped and looked at Raynor with such a grim expression that the older Melnari's face reddened slightly.

"Oh!" he said. "I did not mean to exclaim his name so loudly."

"No, it isn't that at all, Raynor," Ashlord said. "It is something else altogether that you need to know. We have a newcomer to Starlight Hall, from the east, and his reason for coming to Duinnor is a sad one."

"Oh?" Raynor's smile vanished. "Collandoth, what is it?"

In the middle of a crowded street, as the pedestrians and carriages parted around them, the two Melnari were like an island in a river of motion and noise. But within the shores of that island, a profound silence followed Ashlord's next words. Certina, circling far overhead, watched over them, and she instinctively understood the need to leave them be, though she longed to perch on Ashlord's shoulder. She saw Raynor suddenly sit on the cobblestones and put his face into his hands. And she saw Ashlord lean heavily on his walking stick, then bend over to put a hand on his friend's shoulder.

• • •

At about the same time, Seafar went once more to see Count Dialmor in the prison of Linlally's lakebound palace. The past several interviews had been fruitful, and today Seafar hoped to make the breakthrough that was needed. He was confident that Dialmor required only a little more encouragement, and he carried in his hand the document that was sure to provide it. When he entered Dialmor's cell, he found the Count reading by the light that slanted down from the tiny window above.

"Good afternoon, Count," Seafar said as the door was closed behind him.

"Lord Chancellor." Dialmor rose and bowed, then put the book onto his cot. "What may I do for you, today?"

"I will get straight to the point, sir. You have been most forthcoming about the role of Lord Banis in your activities, and the information, should it be verified, will be invaluable to Vanara. However, there is the matter of the Dragonkind and the relationship between you, Banis, and the desert lands. You have already told me that you felt you would not be safe in Vanara and that you hoped to find refuge in the Free City of Kajarahn, and that is why you fled Vanara to the Dragonlands. But I have reason to think that there is more to it than that."

"I do not know what you mean, my lord," Dialmor answered. "I acted on my orders from Banis, but he could not guarantee my safety should his plot fail. Not here, certainly, and not in Duinnor, either. It seemed to me that the Free City was my only hope. That is all there is to it."

"Ah. As you have said before. But I find that Banis did not authorize Faradan. You did, since he reported to you. And I also know that the target of your plot was originally to be the Queen of Vanara and myself. Yet, it was well known that the Queen was not here at the time of the attack. Faradan and his men knew this to be so, as did virtually everyone in Vanara. And their attack was aimed at our guest wing, not the Royal Apartments. My only conclusion is that you acted without the authority of Lord Banis, or else did not need it. And, furthermore, I suspect that you aimed to go to the Free City because that is where your other conspirators are located."

Dialmor shook his head.

"No, my lord. It is as I have told you."

"I am not the only one who does not believe you. You know the fate of Faradan. He was tried and executed. I have here a writ of authority from the Courts of Vanara to present you for summary judgment tomorrow at noon."

Seafar handed Dialmor the document.

"As you can see, they have already made their decision concerning you, and leave it to me to cast the final verdict. I remind you, should you need reminding, that my verdict may overrule those of the other six judges who have recorded their decisions in the matter. As you can see upon that writ, they are all in favor of the same sentence as was passed upon Faradan."

"This is outrageous! I am a citizen of Duinnor, subject only to the King's Justice. The execution of Faradan was contrary to treaty and law."

"Your law. Your treaty. Not ours."

"But surely you would not risk the King's ire yet another time. You bluff."

"I do not bluff, sir. Tomorrow at noon, you will meet the same fate as did Faradan. That is, unless you give me good reason to keep you alive. Otherwise, your death will serve the cause of Vanara in its own way."

Dialmor was shrewd enough to understand that Seafar would learn his secrets with or without him, and he nodded.

"I see that I am beaten, then," he said. "If I give you what you desire of me, will you set me free?"

"I can only promise that I will not execute you."

"I have no desire to live out my days in a Vanaran prison. I may as well die."

"I could set you free, if you wish. But you should know that there are many who have sworn an oath of vengeance against you for the deaths of their kin. They have already petitioned the court to rule against our usual method of execution in favor of the stake, in keeping with how some of your victims met their end. I am confident that, if released, you would not get more than a league from Linlally before they found you. I haven't the means to protect you outside of the White Palace, nor do I have the least desire to do so."

"Then do you promise to spare my life?"

"I make no promise until I see what you have to offer me. Write down all that you know of Duinnor's liaisons with the Dragonkind, all that you know of Banis's involvement with them, too. I want names that can be verified and the methods by which that may be done. Every agent in Vanara, every plot and plan. You have from now until sunset. What you write will be brought before me at that time, and I shall decide your fate based on what I read and how convinced I am as to its truthfulness. At noon tomorrow, you will know my answer. You will not see me again until then."

Seafar tapped on the cell door. Several members of the Gray Guard strode in, and as two clutched Dialmor by the arms and shoulders another tied a gag in his mouth. Two more wheeled in and set down a large heavy block of stone. An iron collar at the end of a long chain was quickly pinned around Dialmor's neck as the other end of the chain was spiked into the top of the stone block. So efficient and quick was this work, and so firmly did the guards grip him, that Dialmor could neither struggle nor protest. As they completed their work, a small table was brought in, along with a stack of paper, a few bottles of ink, and several quills. They all departed but Seafar, who paused at the doorway as Dialmor pulled the gag from his mouth.

"Just so that all is ready for tomorrow," said Seafar, pointing at the table. "You have until sunset!"

• • •

In Griferis, Finn, Lafkin, and the others worked to sort out the new arrivals, as Robby impatiently awaited their report. He knew that he could leave things in their capable hands, and he spent hours studying in the great library, keeping himself out of sight until it was time to meet his new subjects. He pored over books on alchemy, history, and even took a few moments to read some poetry, recollecting a few of the verses from his lessons with Mr. Broadweed. But restlessness and worry overtook his attentions, and he made his way back to his own rooms. There, he plopped down in one of the comfortable chairs, closed his eyes, and set about dreamwalking with a mind to look in on events taking place in the east, particularly with the activities of Prince Carbane and his people.

• • •

Prince Carbane's plans were meticulous, and his fleet was prepared with every care to detail, but he knew that all depended on fair winds. He had ordered his trireme warships modified, with the lowest tier of oars removed and those oar-ports sealed to make the vessels more capable of withstanding the heavy winter seas and also to make room for additional cargo and bunks. His lumbering supply ships, with only their square sails for propulsion, were sent out first, beginning on the day Mr. Ribbon and Prince Danoss departed Glareth for Formouth. The supply ships were laden with stores of provisions, arms, and soldiers, and the faster warships, with their three great triangular sails and two decks of oars, would have no trouble catching up to them. As quickly as the modifications to his ships were completed, they were dispatched to sea in groups of five as more ships were readied. At last, all of Carbane's ships had left port, and he, too, aboard his flagship. Within three weeks of the first ships departing, all were united in one great armada of two hundred ships, plying their way south, with the fast warships circling the slower provision and troop ships so that all could stay together.

But only two days after the fleet was fully assembled, a powerful nor'easter battered the fleet with sleet and heavy seas, forcing Carbane to turn his fleet farther out to sea than he had planned. When the storm abated five days later, the fleet was scattered, and by the time they were reassembled, twenty of the two hundred ships were sunk or missing in the frigid waters. Another twelve ships were so damaged, including Carbane's own, that they had to be abandoned once their supplies, crews, and troops were transferred to other ships. It was another week before Sir Wind graced their sails with kind air, and the fleet headed southward again, making their first port at the town of Colleton on the shores of the old Eastlands Realm. They had been at sea for over a month and were much knocked about and in low spirits. It had been an abysmally poor transit time, even for the unfavorable season, and it was an inauspicious first leg of their long voyage.

At Colleton, while the ships were hastily repaired and refitted, Prince Carbane put ashore the first of his forces to secure the town ahead of his fast-approaching land army, and to make the port ready for the following ships that would provision the army from Glareth. There was little doubt in Carbane's mind that Redvest scouts would soon report the fleet's presence, and also spy the army. Indeed, the Prince counted on them to do so. But the army, led by the exiled Tracian Prince Lantos, was only a diversion in force. It took some doing to convince Lantos to be part of the diversion and not to accompany Carbane's ships. The plan depended on the Redvests being alarmed enough to send a sizable force to counter Prince Lantos, and hearing that the Tracian Prince in Exile was at the head of an army marching southward should do the trick. By then, Prince

Danoss and his forces should be in position to deal a counterstroke to the Redvests sent to intercept Lantos. United, the armies of Danoss and Lantos could then march on into Tracia together, spreading panic and alarm before them. Carbane hoped it would be enough to distract the Redvests from their coasts.

So, after only a week in Colleton, the fleet set sail again, and made a course northeast out to sea and out of sight of land, backtracking for two days so that coastal spies would think the ships were returning to Glareth. But on the third day, and out of sight from shore, the fleet turned again southward and made a course to take them east of the coastal islands of the region rather than risk the narrow straits and passages between them. They were nearly two weeks behind schedule, and still making slow pace, but fewer ships at least meant an easier time keeping the fleet together. Carbane was cautiously optimistic that they would arrive at their first landing on enemy territory in time.

Five days out of Colleton, Carbane stood behind the helmsman of his ship, looking aft at the following fleet, when he heard a call from the crow's nest atop the mainmast.

"Land, ho! Two points, starboard bow!"

Carbane turned around and lifted his spyglass and gazed until he saw the low hazy outline of land, the northernmost of the coastal islands. The ship's captain and several officers lifted their glasses, too.

"The island of Little Canis," said one of the officers.

"Yes. Hm. We're closer in than we thought," Carbane said. "Captain, let's give them a wide berth. No sense in letting our masts be seen by the enemy's lookouts. East by southeast until sunset, if you will. By then our running lamps should be beyond their vision."

"Aye, Prince," the ship's captain said, then turned to a nearby officer. "Signal the fleet. Change course, east by southeast. Resume south at sunset. Lieutenant Crowe, east by southeast, if you will."

"Aye, sir."

The flags went up, and the message went from ship to ship so that soon all were turning to go farther out to sea. The islands they sought to avoid marked the transition into enemy waters, and from here onward stealth was essential. Any ship or boat they encountered would be presumed hostile and would be run down and sunk before word could pass back to the Triumvirate. They could not risk making landfall, either, until well into Tracian waters, and then only to put ashore half of their remaining forces.

Carbane shook his head. It was a great pity, the loss of those ships in the storm. Over eight hundred souls. And much could still go wrong. The Redvests might not take the bait. Prince Danoss might not be able to rendezvous with Prince Lantos in time. Another storm could strike. A Tracian vessel might spot them and elude them.

"My gamble had better work," Carbane mused as he gazed through his glass at the nearby ships, one of which was wallowing dangerously low in the water, so burdened with supplies it was. "Or else many more good souls will be lost."

• • •

Robby did not understand Carbane's plan. He knew enough from his own experiences, the long sojourns imposed upon him during his trials, that a winter sea voyage such as this was fraught with hazards. And to risk so many ships crammed with men not accustomed to the privations of shipboard travel seemed foolhardy. He thought that Prince Carbane would have been wiser to put all of his efforts into the land army that was marching south along the coast. But when Carbane's fleet turned to go farther out to sea rather than risk being spotted, Robby realized that something more was afoot.

"I must know more about what he is up to," he said to himself. "If only I had time to linger."

However, other duties called. Finn and Micerea had located over a hundred other dreamwalkers, all over the world, and Robby desperately needed to make sure of them. But the experience with Galatus, the dreamwalking spy of General Vidican, had left him shaken and embittered; and since it resulted in his sending his mother to her death, he was in no mood to be too trusting of his own judgment, much less of other dreamwalkers. The thought of Mirabella jolted Robby with guilt, for he realized that it was the first time he had thought of her today. He left Carbane, his shame overriding the urge to look in on his father.

Waking himself up, he stood from his chair and looked around, shaking his head and trying to weigh what he should do. So suddenly distracted by the memories of his family and by his sorrow, he stood for several moments, unable to clear his mind. But at last he stirred.

"Yes," he thought. "We need more dreamwalkers as soon as possible."

There was simply too much to be done without recruiting others. Finn was hard-pressed by Robby's daily assignments, in addition to the running of Griferis, and Micerea needed her strength to travel with Ullin.

He went over to the bureau where there was a list, prepared by Finn, of one hundred and forty-two names. Until now, he had not even looked at it, being so filled with nervousness about it. It would be a great gamble, but no matter how many times he debated it, Robby knew it was a risk that must be taken. But there was the list, still where Finn had left it, waiting for him to look it over. Only now did Robby see the note written in Finn's neat hand at the top of the list:

"My King: This is the list that you requested. None of those named here know that they have the ability to dreamwalk, but all do it. Beside each name I have included notes on where they may be found, the nature of their dreamwalking, or other observations. Your servant, Finn."

Robby sighed, took the papers, and sat back down to look at the long list of names. On the second sheet, near the middle, he spotted a name he knew, and stared at it in disbelief.

"Sally Bodwin!" he exclaimed. And then he read Finn's notes pertaining to her:

"Hill Town, in the Thunder Mountains. She is of Tracian descent. She is vexed by night terrors, wandering into the dreams of her people who often dream of terrible events in their homeland. She shares a cottage with her godfather, a Martin Makeig, and her night cries frequently wake him. He often goes to her room and soothes her back to sleep with kind reassurances."

Robby glanced out the window. He was impatient to know how the new arrivals were doing, and how Finn and the others were managing them. But, again, he felt it best to await Finn's report. Meanwhile, Robby had much to do on his own, and since he observed that it would soon be dark, he decided to visit Sally Bodwin this very night, remembering her kindness to him when they first met and her lovely voice when she sang at the Green Sail in Hill Town.

"It seems like such a long time ago," he said. "I suppose it was for me. It will be nice to see her again."

Encouraged, he continued to study the list.

• • •

In Duinnor, Ashlord, Raynor, and Eldwin met privately in Lady Highleaf's library. They had much to discuss. Eldwin was determined to learn all there was to know about Esildre, and Raynor could fill in some of the gaps in what Ashlord had already told Eldwin. So while Raynor spoke, Ashlord calmly sat nearby, and Eldwin paced back and forth, growing more upset as Raynor's story unfolded. When Raynor concluded the tale of Esildre's life, such that he knew it, he fell silent and watched with Ashlord as Eldwin stared out the window.

"I don't understand why ye didn't stop her," he said at last, turning to face Raynor. "Didn't ye know something terrible would happen to her? I may be ignorant of the ways of the world, but not so that I don't know about Secundur! To send a fine an' valiant lady to *him* may as well been a death sentence!"

"Eldwin," Ashlord said gently, "it was not Raynor who sent her to Shatuum. It was her father, Banis, who sent her. And she went willingly. Raynor has understated his own efforts to stop her from going. But I know that he tried."

"He should have tried harder!" Eldwin shot back.

"I doubt if trying harder was possible," replied Ashlord, "unless some force was used."

"No, he's right, Collandoth," Raynor said. "I should have tried harder to stop her. Just as I should have tried harder to stop Navis from going after her. Eldwin, I don't know how to answer you, or what to say.

Except that sometimes things are out of our hands."

"And what's done is done," said Ashlord.

"No. It ain't done!" said Eldwin. "Somebody's got to take on Secundur, an' if ye big folk ain't up to it, then I guess it's up to us little ones, ignorant an' backwards though we may be."

"What do you mean?"

"I mean that one person may be a small matter to Secundur, after all the uncounted thousands that he's harmed. But one person is one too many, an' when he picked on Esildre an' put his curse onto her, he picked on me own friend. That makes him answerable to me! I'll find a way to get at him. I'll find a way, an' I'll get at him good!"

"Vengeance is futile, Eldwin, whatever the target is," Ashlord stated. "And Secundur will only turn it against you!"

"Ye may call it vengeance. But I shall call it justice! An' may both be served! This place makes me sick! Right on his doorstep an' not a finger lifted against him! By Men or Elifaen or Melnari! Fie on ye all for all yer talk!" He went to the door and flung it open. "I didn't come all this way just to turn me cheek, so since ye can't or won't tell me how to get at him, I'll find me own way!"

Eldwin raised his hand to snap his fingers.

"Wait!" Ashlord commanded. "Stay a little longer, and I will tell you who may be able to help you."

Eldwin hesitated, then lowered his hand.

"I am listenin'."

"Do you remember me telling you that Robby and Ullin Saheed had gone to Vanara, to find their own way and to take care of their own business?"

"Yes. I remember."

"Well. I think it is time for you to know what that business is. And where to find Robby."

Ashlord glanced at Raynor. Raynor nodded.

"You will need food and warmer clothes," Ashlord began. "With your ability you should be able to find Robby. He is at a place called Griferis, located somewhere beyond the land of Shatuum. And, by all accounts, he is no longer the Robby you knew in Nowhere, but has become someone else. And he is soon to be someone else, again. If you promise to stay the night, one night longer at least, then I shall tell you the full tale and strive to leave nothing out. That way, you may know as fully as any what stirs in the world and what you may encounter when you depart Duinnor."

Eldwin looked uncomfortable, as if the wind had been taken out of his sails. He stood in the doorway, shaking his head. At last he nodded and re-entered the room, closing the door behind him.

"Well, since it's late in the day, anyway, I will promise ye this night. But I doubt if anything ye say will change me mind about things."

"I don't expect to change your mind," said Ashlord, breathing a sigh of relief. "Please. Let us all sit. Let me just open the window so that Certina may enter, if she wishes."

So, as Ashlord had done many times over the past few days, he again recounted the story of the Bellringer, and all else that he knew of Robby's tale, his present whereabouts, and about Robby's ultimate destiny to become King of Duinnor. Day gave way to night as the hours of Ashlord's story passed, and, just as Ashlord promised, Eldwin's understanding of things was much enhanced.

• • •

Martin Makeig arrived back in Hill Town very late that night. He was just returned from Tallinvale to deliver Prince Danoss and to see for himself the defeat of the Redvests. Most of the Hill Town people already knew about the outcome, though, and with the additional news that their exiled Prince Lantos was marching with his army to free their homeland, many of Makeig's people were expressing desires to join with the Prince and wrest back their homes and lands. Others argued for caution, saying that it would be foolish to give up their Hill Town home just when security seemed assured. Makeig himself was torn between yearning for the sea and his duties to his adopted town and its people. As he rode slowly up to his cottage, he mulled over what he should do. He was glad that it was too late at night to meet with anyone, and he desired only some peace and quiet, and a bit of rest. In fact, he was heavy of heart, weary of strife, and sad. The fighting he had taken part in had been mean and ugly, full of hatred and anger. He had been merciless, and his fighters, too, and he was sick of it. He grieved for Mirabella, whose death continued to perplex and sadden him, and he grieved for her husband and all her friends who missed her. It was as if any joy that might be had from victory had died with her. And though he had known her only a short while, such was his respect for Mirabella and the intensity of their friendship that he felt as if he had lost a sister. While Mirabella was around, Makeig somehow knew that the people of Hill Town would have a true and powerful friend.

But she was gone.

Now, as he tethered his horse, Makeig longed more than ever for the wide open sea, to feel the surge of wind and sway of current, and to spread his worries across the endless expanse. Undoing the cinches and straps, he removed the saddle and led his horse into the small corral. He made sure there was ample feed and water, pulled off the bridle and gave him a good pet, thanking the animal as he always did for his patience and faithful service.

He watched his horse eat for a moment, then, as quietly as he could, Makeig went inside, put down his saddlebags, and tossed his travel cloak over the back of a chair. Pulling off his boots, he absently put them on the chair, then lit a candle and tiptoed down the hall. He carefully opened a bedroom door and looked in. In the bed, Sally Bodwin slept, the covers pulled up to her chin, and he smiled.

"Sleep peaceful, sweet lass," he said, gently pulling the door closed. Glancing into the room across the hall, he saw that his own bed had been made and prepared for him. He went back to the great room, put a few sticks onto the coals in the fireplace, and poured himself a spot of rum. He sat down wearily on a stool before the fire and he watched the sticks catch. They lit the room with their crackling yellow light, and as he sipped, he continued thinking over all that was on his mind, completely unaware that he was not alone in the room.

"So do you believe me?" Robby asked, standing with Sally Bodwin beside Makeig.

"I will if, when I wake up, I see Martin's things and hear him snoring in his room," she said. "For he's not due back for days, yet."

"Well, that will do, then." Robby smiled. "But if you do come to believe me, would you consider joining my cause?"

"Now, that I don't know about. Ye said that yer gonna be King of Duinnor, and that yer already the king of some other place."

"That's right. Griferis."

"And that ye mean to put an end to wars, if ye can, and do other great and mighty things."

"If I can. Yes."

"And that if I serve ye, ye'll teach me all about walking dreams."

"Dreamwalking. Yes. It is why I have chosen you. Because you already have the ability, among other reasons."

"Well, it's all very far-fetched. If I knew ye, that would be one thing. I might be tempted to believe all this. Or even tempted to do as ye say. But I'm not sure I like the idea of a stranger coming into me own dreams and, well, and so forth!"

Robby chuckled.

"Actually, I quite understand. I felt somewhat the same way as you do when I was first taught to dreamwalk. But as for knowing me, I told you my name. Philawain."

"*King* Philawain, ye said."

"Yes, I am Philawain, King of Griferis. But we have met before. I had a different name when we first met. And I looked very different than I do now. The fact that you don't recognize me tells me that either I truly am very much changed, or else you don't remember me at all."

"Ye are somewhat familiar-looking. As if I ought to know ye. But that just might be because this is a dream. Many things are so in dreams that aren't truly so."

"Perhaps. Perhaps not. Look at me again, very carefully, and tell me: Do you remember a boy called Robby Ribbon?"

"The Passdale lad? I do. I remember him well," she said. Her expression slowly changed as she recognized Robby's glimmering black eyes.

Suddenly, before Robby could react, she vanished, waking up in her bed and sitting up.

"Oh me!" she muttered. Then, without getting up, she called out, "Martin! Martin Makeig! Are ye there?"

Makeig jumped, knocking over his stool and spilling some of his grog as he stood.

"Aye, darlin'! I'm back," he called, going down the hall and knocking on Sally's door before peeking in.

"Aye, I'm home," he said. "An' just arrived, too. A wee bit ago, that is. I hope yer well. Didn't mean to wake ye."

"Ye didn't wake me, Martin. Only get yer boots off the chair, as I've told ye a thousand times."

She pulled up the covers and turned over to go back to sleep as Makeig stuck out his bottom lip and closed the door.

"It's mighty nice to see ye as well!" he mumbled as he went to do as she ordered.

"I'm glad yer home, Martin."

Smiling, Makeig took his boots off of the chair and put them on the hearth.

Sally opened her eyes and sat up again, remembering her dream.

"Martin?" she called out.

"Aye, little one?"

"Are ye truly home?"

"Aye, little one," Makeig replied. "I'm back."

"Good. That's nice. Good night, then."

"Sweet dreams, princess."

• • •

Robby left the two, satisfied that Sally would remember what she needed to remember, and would be ready to begin her training tomorrow night. So he went on to find Ullin and Micerea who were making the best time they could through the snowy forest mountains and were nearing the edge of the wilderness.

• • •

That day, Ullin and Micerea came across a tiny mountain village, and while Micerea waited out of sight, Ullin went to see if he could find food and blankets for the few silver coins left to him. Although the villagers were suspicious, they respected the Vanaran coat he wore, and when he pulled it open to show his Kingsman tunic underneath, they became even more obliging. Micerea watched from a hiding place overlooking the village as Ullin negotiated for the things they needed. She was relieved when she saw him returning with a large heavy pack.

"Well, there goes the last of my silver," he said when they had reunited. "But we have some blankets and some dried meat. Also a kit of flint and steel, and a good knife. I couldn't get a horse."

"Oh, we'll manage on foot," Micerea said, looking into the pack. "Blankets! This is wonderful! Perhaps we shan't shiver so much tonight."

"I hope not." Ullin nodded, hoisting the pack to his shoulders with a groan. "We'll skirt the village and bear back around to come onto the path some ways off. It should be easier going then. Oh, and here."

Ullin handed her a lady's brush.

"Oh! Thank you!"

Micerea took it and immediately began brushing her hair, pausing after a moment to deliver a kiss. Ullin smiled.

"Don't wear it out all at once."

"Be quiet."

Soon they were working their way around the village and down to the path beyond. It was much easier going once they were upon it, and they made more distance that afternoon than they had during any of the previous days. They found a good place to camp, made a fire, ate, and almost immediately fell asleep in each other's arms under their blankets. After hours of blissful sleep, Micerea was just beginning to dreamwalk when Robby arrived.

"I see you are a bit warmer tonight than before," he said to her.

"Yes, sire. Though I don't think I'll ever be warm again," she answered. "This cold has gotten into my bones, I think."

"It will be warm soon. Already the snow is melting out on the plains, and each day grows longer than the one before," Robby commented. "You and Ullin have done remarkably well, covering a great distance together. Quite remarkable, considering how little you have had to eat and how cold you have been. Just so you know, I think your coming to him was for the best, and not just because you saved him. It is a great and wonderful thing that you two are together. I can tell a difference in Ullin, in his dreams and in his spirit. He is much invigorated by you."

Micerea blushed.

"What I mean is, well, of course you two are lovers, but, besides that, you are friends. You lift his spirits, and by your company you give him renewed determination and hope."

"I, too, am much relieved and so glad to be with Ullin."

"Yes. You look tired, but happy."

Micerea did not miss Robby's wistful tone, but she did not presume to comment upon it.

"You come yourself, sire, instead of sending Finn," she said.

"Yes. Finn is busy. I have a new task for you. Tonight I have gone to see one of the dreamwalkers that you and Finn discovered. She happens to be someone that I know. She is a kind lass, a Tracian who is the adopted child of Martin Makeig."

"The Hill Town man?"

"Yes. I met her on the day I killed Bailorg."

"Yes, sire. I remember. I watched for you to sleep."

"Oh, of course. You drew me into your dream that night."

"Yes, sire."

"Well, she is a good girl. And with your instruction, I think she'll make a good dreamwalker. I must say that I find it strange that so few who have the ability know that they do. Their sleep-lives must be quite confusing."

"Yes, as my own sleep and dreams were to me before I knew about dreamwalking," Micerea said.

"Hm. Well, I would like to introduce you to her tomorrow night. If that goes well, then I would like for you to be her teacher, instructing her on how to purposefully dreamwalk until she can do without you. I'll be busy with the other dreamwalkers."

"I would be happy to do as you wish, sire."

"Good. Let me tell you about what I'd like for her to do for us."

Robby took Micerea to see Prince Carbane's fleet.

"Carbane plans to attack Tracia," he explained as they stood on the deck of Carbane's ship, completely invisible to the crew. "I need to know more about how he intends to carry it out. As soon as possible, I'd like for Sally to be my liaison to Carbane, coming and going from me to him, relaying messages. So, part of your training of Sally should be about how to convince Carbane to believe her, and how she can convince Carbane to trust her."

"I hope that I can do that," Micerea said. "It isn't always easy to convince others."

"I know. Sally can give Carbane signs in his dreams, ones that he can confirm upon his waking. Perhaps things aboard ship that she can observe while he sleeps, things that she can tell him to look for. I think it can be done. Sally will have to work some of that out. So. I'll leave you, now, and see you tomorrow night."

"Yes, my King."

•   •   •

Robby left Micerea to scout the way that lay ahead of her and Ullin. He flew as quick as a shooting star southward to the Dragonlands and to the place where Thunderfoot and his people labored. He saw that they had made prodigious progress. Great swaths of mountains on the east side of the chasm were gone, pushed over into the gaping void. With their massive hands, they were now digging into the place where those mountains had been, pushing rock and earth over the side and down into the great canyon. Already, after such a short time, the waters below had risen, and a churning torrent tore away the loose earth and soil of the dam that was being formed, as more rock tumbled down from above. Judging by the pace of their work, it would not be long, perhaps only a week or a little more, before the water rose up to the place where the trolls dug their trenches.

"I only hope that they keep at it," he said, turning away to go back north. He knew that he should check in on Ashlord and his friends in

Duinnor, but still he resisted the temptation. Until things were a bit farther along, there was little he could do for them, and little that he needed them to do for him. So he went back to Griferis, to take another look at the list of dreamwalkers.

• • •

Had Robby gone to Duinnor and looked in on his friends, he would have been surprised to see Eldwin there. He had not been back to Tallinvale or to Nowhere, and he knew nothing of Esildre's fate or Eldwin's travels. And he was unaware that he was the topic of continued discussion in Starlight Hall between Ashlord, Raynor, and Eldwin, though it was an hour after daybreak.

Eldwin had listened carefully to Ashlord's story all the previous afternoon, and all the night. He asked many questions concerning Robby, Griferis, and the prospects of a new ruler of the Seven Realms. But as the night wore on, he grew quiet. Around dawn, and especially after a meal was brought to them by Lady Highleaf's staff, Eldwin grew sleepy and finally dozed off in his chair, having not the sleepless constitution of Raynor or Ashlord.

"Well," said Raynor, grinning at Ashlord, "once again your speech has had its usual outcome upon the hapless listener."

"I was beginning to wonder," replied Ashlord. "But hopefully he'll sleep a very long while, and it will be too late for him to set out by the time he awakes. And who knows what delays might confront him after that?"

"He seems most determined."

"Yes. He does."

Ashlord picked up a shawl from the settee and put it over Eldwin.

"I think I'll wake Sheila and Ibin and see if I can impose upon them to come and take Eldwin off to his bed. I'm sure he won't be able to resist her coaxing, if he wakes, and Ibin can carry him if he doesn't wake."

• • •

Robby paced up and down in his room, the list of dreamwalkers in his hand. So encouraged by his encounter with Sally Bodwin, he had decided to look in on several more on the list, going quickly from one to another, but not letting himself be known to any as he had done with Sally. As he pondered the next names on the list, he heard a tap at the door.

"Come!"

Finn entered, bearing a tray with a decanter of coffee, and Leena, Radasa's youngest, came in after him with a covered breakfast tray. They put the things on the table, and Leena curtseyed as she departed, closing the door behind her. Finn poured a cup of coffee for Robby, and removed the cover of the tray, revealing a steaming plate of eggs and ham.

"Eggs? I thought we were out of eggs," Robby said.

"Yes, sire. One of our new arrivals brought with him five laying hens, and a basket of fresh eggs. It was all he had to offer you in exchange for taking him into your service."

"Oh, for goodness sakes! It is I who will be indebted to him, as I will be to all the others, too. Eggs!"

"Yes, sire. Please, I shall give you my report if you wish."

Robby sat down rather unceremoniously and began to eat.

"Mmm!" he intoned, savoring a first bite. "Please, won't you join me?"

"I have already had my breakfast, sire. But thank you. Shall I begin?"

"Let me begin with a report to you," Robby said. "I have looked in on thirty-something dreamwalkers, using your list. They all seem very good candidates, so far. And I hope to look in on the rest by this time tomorrow."

"I hope you do not tax yourself overly, my lord."

"No. I admit I was quite reluctant to begin the work, but now I find that I am much encouraged and very excited to keep at it. Once I have satisfied myself with each name on the list, I hope that you and Micerea will be able to work together on the next part of the plan."

"I am sure that I speak for both of us when I say that we would be very happy to do so."

"Wonderful. But we should limit how much we ask of Micerea. She must still scout the way for Ullin as they travel on to Duinnor. And I have also asked her to take on the training of one dreamwalker in particular."

"I shan't ask Micerea to help at all, until you feel that she is up to it. May I ask about the dreamwalker she is to instruct?"

"Yes. She is someone I know."

Robby told Finn about Sally Bodwin and about Prince Carbane's ships and the armies that were now sailing and marching south toward Tracia. They discussed how Sally might help with that, and then turned their conversation to events in Griferis. Finn reported that all was going better than hoped, and that already most of the new people were assigned to their tasks. Those assigned to the household staff were busy preparing rooms for everyone, while others were working with Lady Kinsiri to organize cooking and meals. Lafkin was spending a great deal of time with those who would be assigned to him, making sure that they understood what was expected of them. Radasa was meeting with the other arrivals.

"So tomorrow I'll get to see them at last," Robby said, putting his fork down and sitting back in his chair. "I look forward to it."

"I'm sure they also keenly anticipate seeing their king," said Finn. "If that will be all, sire, I think I'll leave you to get some rest."

"Yes. That's all for now, Finn. I'll send someone for you if I need you. Unther, or whoever is about. Thank you, Finn."

"Not at all. Good day, sire."

Chapter 20

The Apparition

Day 202
43 Days Remaining

Ullin and Micerea were on their way well before daybreak, walking off the chill of the night as the forest woke to the dawn. Birds seemed anxious for spring, squirrels chattered, and chipmunks chirped their protests as the travelers passed too close to the creatures' dwindling winter stores. The new-found path northward was easy and swift by comparison to the previous days of their journey. And though there was still much snow and ice in the shadowed forest, it was not so deep or thick as what they had encountered before, and what there was of it on the path was so little that it did not hinder them at all. In some places, as their way passed over hills sparse of trees, Sir Sun in his late winter stride had already melted much of it, and trickles of water ran away to join streams below. So this morning they were able to walk quickly, going up and down hills with relative ease, talking when they had the breath for it, making fifteen miles before stopping for a rest around midday.

"So you haven't any clue at all as to why we are to go to Nasakeeria?" asked Ullin for the third time in as many days.

"No, Ullin. Not yet," she answered patiently as she took a carrot from the sack that Ullin offered. She bit off the end of it, and said, "He'll tell us when he's ready to."

"I hope so."

Ullin took a carrot, too, and together they crunched away.

"What I wonder," Micerea said, "is why we are to give the Bloodcoins to Sheila. If the stories you have told me about them are so, it seems odd that Philawain gave them to you, risking their loss. Why didn't he keep them? For safekeeping, that is."

"Philawain. I can't seem to get used to the name," Ullin said, shaking his head as he handed Micerea the water flask. "Each time you say it, I must remind myself who it is that you refer to. I can only imagine that he has been in touch with Sheila, through dreams I mean, and they have some plan for them."

"He has not mentioned it. But perhaps so. He keeps much to himself. Maybe he did not know your way would be so filled with danger."

"Maybe. He must have a plan for them, something that Sheila is to do with them."

Ullin put away their food, took the flask back from Micerea, and helped her to her feet.

"Tell me again about Sally Bodwin and Prince Carbane," Ullin said as he slung the pack over his shoulder. "I must say that I wish I could dreamwalk."

"We'll try again tonight, if you wish," said Micerea as they started off. "I'm sure you can if you truly try."

"But I have been trying."

"We'll keep at it. As for Sally Bodwin, as I told you this morning, I am to help her dreamwalk on her own, so that she can keep an eye on Prince Carbane for us."

Micerea led the way, and they continued to chat as they hiked along, going over everything once more that they had already talked about earlier in the day. But after an hour or two, they fell silent again, and hurried northward at a steady pace. Looking at Micerea as she walked a few yards in front of him, Ullin recalled watching her shadow in the desert all those years ago, keeping his pace with her as she led him to the dead city. He smiled, remembering the rabbit that led him to the water, and how they lingered in the hidden oasis, surrounded by the colorful flowers. He wondered what had become of the little rabbit. He had taken it with them to the Free City, and then intended to carry it back to Vanara, to release it in the forest there. But, just as renegades closed in on him, the rabbit managed to squirm out of the sack within which Ullin had carried it, then it had scampered off amongst the rocks. He had his hands full trying to escape to look for the little thing. But, he consoled himself, if the remarkable rabbit had survived the deserts, surely it was able to make it home, wherever that was.

Micerea stopped suddenly, and Ullin nearly bumped into her.

"What is it?"

"I thought I saw someone," she pointed ahead, "at the bend just there."

Ullin looked but saw nothing.

"Going, coming, or just standing?"

"I only caught a glimpse," Micerea said. "I can't say for sure."

"Not just a shadow? Or a passing deer?"

"Perhaps. Now I'm not sure. What do your armhairs say, and the back of your neck?"

"Nothing," shrugged Ullin.

"It was probably just an animal." Micerea looked at him apologetically. "I'm sorry. I'm not accustomed to the forest, or to the creatures that live here."

"That's alright. Better to be cautious."

"It's so close, this forest," she shook her head. "I'm accustomed to the open desert. I'm sorry if I'm jumpy."

"I know. Don't be sorry."

They kept on, keeping a keen eye to their surroundings, but neither saw anything out of place, and Ullin never had any sense of danger. After a few more miles, the incident was forgotten, and once again they hurried along at a good pace. When the afternoon shadows grew long across the path, they began looking for a suitable place to make their camp. A bit later, Ullin spotted a likely place.

"Look here," said Ullin, pointing to the left. Micerea came back and saw a clearing just below them beside a stream.

"Looks like a good place to me," she said.

"Yes, somewhat sheltered, too. We can build a fire beside those large rocks and sleep there. It should be warmer than what we've been accustomed to."

Already he was making his way to the spot, and Micerea came after him. Ullin put down the pack, and looked the place over. It was about twenty yards around, bordered on one side by the path and along the other by a broad stream. A large outcrop of rock jutted out from one side, with a flat side toward the clearing, and other smaller, moss-covered rocks were on the far side.

"A natural place to make camp. Look, there's an old fire ring, so we're not the first to stop here. I think this will do nicely," he said. "So let's go ahead and gather firewood, first thing. And plenty of it. Snap off low, dead branches still on the trees, if you see any. They will be driest."

"Yes, yes. As you've told me before," she smiled.

They moved off into the nearby wood along the stream, picking up branches, or taking them from the pine trunks if they were dead and within reach.

"I think I see fish, Ullin," Micerea said, looking into the stream. Her arms were already full of wood, and Ullin snapped off a large branch, then broke it with his boot and came over with an even larger armload. Looking over her shoulder, he nodded.

"Trout," he said. "If there's light enough once we get the fire going, I may try to catch one."

"You could just open your pockets," Micerea laughed as they made their way back to the clearing. "Who knows? They might jump right in. Just like before."

"I suppose anything's possible," Ullin chuckled. As they came into the clearing, they both heard a chilling moan. Micerea stopped suddenly and gasped, dropping her sticks and backing into Ullin who bumped into her. He immediately saw what startled her, and his skin crawled. Only a few feet away, across the little clearing, was a person sitting on a low rock. It was a young lady, dressed in light robes of the sort that Temple pilgrims sometimes wore. She was crying and moaning, sobbing in a terrible way.

"Sheila?" Ullin muttered in disbelief, tossing down his firewood. He stepped forward, but Micerea clutched his arm.

"No. Don't, Ullin."

He patted her hand, unable to take his eyes from the crying girl.

"Stay here."

"No, Ullin!" Micerea pleaded in a whisper. "How can she be here?"

"Sheila?" Ullin asked, cautiously moving closer. He glanced around, half-expecting to see Billy or Ashlord. But no one else was there. "What are you doing here? What's amiss?"

She raised her head toward him, her sobs stifled for a moment. Ullin froze, shocked to see that she was blind, her face disfigured with scales that covered her eyes, and blistered skin around them.

"Oh, Sheila! What has happened?"

"Tyrin!" she cried out, reaching out toward Ullin. "Oh, Tyrin, is that you?"

"It is Ullin Saheed."

Hearing his name, her body shook as her arms dropped. A heartrending moan broke out of her and sobs of terrible grief. Ullin bounded the last few steps to her, but when he reached out to take her hand, she suddenly grew pale and drifted away as thin, dissipating smoke. Ullin's hairs tingled up his scalp and his heart raced as he stumbled backward in a daze. He heard a new cry, and turned to see Micerea backing away, her hands covering her mouth as she wailed in fear.

Rushing to her, he took her in his arms and held her.

"No, no. It was only a spirit. It won't harm us."

"Ullin! Ullin!"

"Everything is fine. We are safe."

"Oh, let us get away from here! Please, please! Oh, oh, oh!"

Micerea was shaking with such fright that Ullin held her all the more firmly, glancing back over his shoulder at the empty spot where the apparition had been.

"Yes, alright," Ullin said. "Let's go."

"Let's get as far from this place as we can!"

Tears were streaming down Micerea's face as they made the path and ran northward, and Ullin was barely able to keep up with her. After a mile, he shouted to her.

"Slow down!" he cried, shifting up his pack. Micerea turned, panic still in her eyes, then she came back to him as he stumbled and went down on one knee. "You are too swift for me!"

"Let's keep going, Ullin," she urged as she took his hand and tugged. "Come, let me have the pack."

"No, no. Let's just slow our pace a bit. And it will be dark, soon. We need to find another place to camp."

"No, let's keep going, Ullin. This forest is haunted, and I don't think it likes us being here."

"Nonsense! But did you see who it was?"

Micerea took Ullin's hand and pulled him along.

"It looked like your friend, Sheila."

"Yes. But her face, her eyes! Something terrible has happened to her. Oh, poor girl!"

"No, Ullin. Surely, Robby, I mean Philawain, or Finn would have told me if something has happened to her."

"Maybe they just don't want to give us bad news."

"No. I don't think so, Ullin. I don't know. It did look like her! But she just vanished. And what would she be doing out here?"

"Or dressed like that? But who can say what business spirits have anywhere?"

"And who was it that she called for?"

"Tyrin, I think she said. Yes," Ullin stopped again. "Tyrin. Not a common name. I've only known one Tyrin."

"Well, who or whatever it was didn't seem to recognize you."

"She was blind."

"Yes, I could tell." Micerea tugged his hand again. "Please. Let's keep going, Ullin."

Ullin glanced behind them, then nodded.

They kept on at a slower march than before. Eventually the last bit of daylight was long gone, forcing them to pick their way carefully along the turns of the path.

"We'll not have any moonlight for hours, yet," Ullin said. "If we keep going, we're sure to stumble and break our necks. I insist that we stop. Here. Let's press under this outcrop with our blankets and try to stay warm."

Micerea knew there was no use in arguing. They crawled under a rocky outcrop beside the path, huddled together, and pulled their blankets over.

"Will you go to Duinnor for me?" Ullin asked her. "And look for Sheila?"

"I'm not sure I can go to sleep," she said. "Oh, Ullin, I'm so frightened. I see the movement of shadows all around us."

"It's only the trees swaying in the wind. Close your eyes."

She did, putting her head on his shoulder. After awhile, she said, "First, I must go with Philawain to see Sally Bodwin. Then I'll go to Duinnor and look for Sheila."

"Thank you."

But when she dreamwalked, Robby was already standing with Sally Bodwin, and showing her the marvelous floating palace that was Griferis.

"Ah, and here is the one I was telling you about," Robby said. "This is Lady Micerea, of the Dragonlands."

Sally looked at Micerea, and curtseyed.

"I didn't know that ladies of the desert were so lovely," she said. Micerea, who was anxious to ask Robby about Sheila, was taken aback by the girl's comment and bowed to her.

"You are kind to say so," she answered. She turned to Robby, but before she could speak, he addressed her.

"I will leave you, now," he said. "Sally, please do as Micerea instructs. She is a good teacher, and quite experienced. Micerea, please take Sally to see Prince Carbane's fleet. Show Sally how to enter his dreams and give her some guidance on how to convince Carbane to trust her. Sally, I must know what Carbane plans to do so that I may decide how to help him, if that is needed. It may take some days for you to gain his confidence, or for you to learn your way around the dream world enough to do so. But Micerea, I hope, will come to you each night and help you until you can handle things on your own. Micerea, thank you for helping with this. I know that you'll both do just fine."

"Thank you, sire. We will do our best," Micerea said.

"I must go. I have much to do. Good luck!"

And, with that, Robby vanished, much to Micerea's frustration.

Turning to Sally, she shrugged.

"Well, I suppose we should be on our way, too. I think it will be easier if you give me your hand."

Together they flew eastward, and in an instant were approaching the coast.

"We'll only dreamwalk for a while," Micerea said to Sally. "I don't know how much the King has told you, but dreamwalking is not sleeping, and you get no rest from your sleep while you dreamwalk."

"No, he did not tell me," Sally replied. "But, if it is not sleep, and it ain't dreaming, neither, then it must be strange magic."

"It isn't magic. It's just the way things are. Like the sun and the moon and the stars. Very few reach those places, but all know they are there."

"That's a strange notion. Look! Are those Prince Carbane's ships?"

"Yes. Let us go closer."

"Do ye think ye might tell me about the Dragonkind? About yer lands? Lantin Rose, a man I know, was there when he was a lad. He said the deserts are very beautiful, but hot."

Micerea looked at Sally, pleased by her curiosity.

"Yes, there are beautiful places in the desert. And, yes, if you wish, I'll tell you about them. And, if we have time one night, we'll go there together to look at those places. But we have work to do."

As they settled onto the deck of Prince Carbane's ship, they saw cindergnats swarming around many of the sleeping men aboard, including Carbane himself. And, edging into view of the weird landscape, growling dreamdogs approached.

"Do not be afraid!" Micerea said as Sally saw them and began to panic. "I'll show you how to get rid of them."

"Oh, oh! What horrible creatures! What are they?"

• • •

Eldwin remained asleep all the morning and well into the late afternoon. His previous days without much sleep, the long night of discussion with Ashlord and Raynor, and the very comfortable bed that

Ibin placed him down upon and that Sheila tucked him into all contributed to his long slumber. It was the first time since leaving Nowhere that he slept deeply and soundly, and though he did so peacefully for many hours, his last few were filled with what he thought were anxious and uncanny dreams. He dreamed that he awoke, barely able to crack open his eyes as he lay on his side, baffled by the presence of a lady sitting on his bedside. He could not bring himself to speak, and his heart was gripped by a clutching sadness that pervaded the dream and choked his throat. He thought it oddly sweet that Sheila should sit with him, and strange, too, that he seemed to be able to see right through her, as if she was made of thin vapor rather than flesh and bone. But when she turned her head to face him, terror pounded into his chest as he saw that she had no eyes, only terrible black voids where eyes ought to be.

It was Esildre.

Eldwin sat up, gasping for air, his heart racing as he looked about the empty room. Then, after a moment, he flung himself under the covers, shivering.

Four times more he had the same dream, and the last time, when Esildre turned to him, he saw tears glistening down from her empty eye sockets.

He leapt out of bed and pulled open the drapes to let in the afternoon light, his lungs pumping so hard that his breath grated from his throat. The vapid figure, or the dream, faded from view. Quickly, he pulled off his nightshirt and tossed away his nightcap, dressing as quickly as he could, tugging his bootstraps as he hopped for the door. As he touched the knob, though, some wayward bird flittered onto a branch outside his window and tittered away, its singsong chirps in soothing contrast to his anxieties. He turned and saw the creature very near to the glass, its head up and its throat vibrating with its song, oblivious to the little man whose heart was becalmed by its emphatic joy.

Eldwin stood there for many moments, his hand still upon the doorknob, until the bird suddenly flew off. He sighed, and went over to the chair across the room and turned it to face the bed and sat staring at the disheveled covers.

"If ye need me," he said after a while, "I'll try not to be scared."

He immediately felt the room cool, and as a cloud dimmed the light through the window, he saw her again, now sitting on the floor in the far corner of the room, her knees up and her head down into her hands.

Her voice, small and distant, was not like an awful ghost or some tortured spirit, but like that of one of Eldwin's great-granddaughters after a skinned knee or other minor thing that seemed a great catastrophe. But what she said pertained to something that was a great thing, indeed.

"I haven't any friend but you, Eldwin," she said. "I'm sorry that I frighten you. I don't know why I am here. I don't know why I can't be with Tyrin, why they won't let me pass through to be with him. Oh, Eldwin, I don't know what I am. I don't know what to do!"

He instinctively got up and took a few steps toward her, just as he would have done for his own little ones, but she turned away, holding up a hand to stop him while keeping her other hand across her face.

"Don't look upon me! I beg you! I am hideous!"

"No, no, don't say such a thing!"

He came to her and knelt beside her.

"Can ye touch me? Can ye take me hand?" he asked.

She put her hand in his. It was like cold air on his palm, but when she touched him some color came to her form, some greater substance to her spirit, almost flesh. She burst into tears, trying hard to stifle them as she clutched his hand.

He did not know what to do. How does one give comfort to the dead who have no peace? What does one say to a creature no longer of this world, yet denied the next?

"We'll figure it all out," he said. "We'll figure out things together. Ye see, we're kinda in the same fix. I know what I must do, but I don't know how to do it. There's probably something yer supposed to do, too, but ye don't know what it is. So a pretty pair we make, don't we?"

She kept her other hand across her face, but nodded.

"Somehow, I'll help ye be with Tyrin," he said. "I know ye belong together. An' now, since I know a bit more about him, I know he wants to be with ye, too. I'm sure he's tryin' at this very moment, wherever he is, to find ye."

"Do you think so? Do you think he remembers me? It has been so long, Eldwin, since he departed. It seems so long! I have looked for him in the places where we once were together. But he is not there, not at any of them!"

"Well, I don't know much about how things are beyond death's gate. But I'm sure he's raisin' a ruckus wherever he is on account of yer not bein' there. From what I've heard about him, why, I imagine he'll soon wear out them that are the gatekeepers, an' he'll make a beeline straight for ye. Let's just be patient, shall we?"

"I don't deserve that he should come to me! Oh, the awful things I've done!"

"That don't have nothing to do with it, dear lady. Love's got its own rules, an' I doubt if whether one's deservin' or not is much in the accountin' of them. Besides, we're friends, ain't that so? So I can tell ye that it made me powerful mad when ye left me in Tallinvale. But I wasn't mad at ye, not so much. Just confused an' bewildered. The thing is, I came to understand it, in a way, an' realized something must've hurt ye so bad, so awful, that it couldn't be borne any more. An' losin' Tyrin was just the last straw for ye. So, since we're friends, I'll tell ye that I mean to go after the one that hurt ye so bad."

Esildre lowered her hand and lifted her head and looked at him in spite of herself. As the light played through her face, Eldwin could see the ghost of her amber eyes.

"That's what I must do, too!"

Then came a tap on the door, and Esildre cringed as her head jerked to see who was opening it.

Ashlord's head appeared, looking at the empty bed. He pushed the door on open and stood there, staring at the bed for a moment, then turned to see Eldwin crouching on his knees near the corner of the room.

"Oh, there you are!" he said. "My goodness, you gave me a fright. I thought you'd left us already without saying goodbye. Whatever are you doing?"

Eldwin got to his feet, but before he could answer, Ashlord shivered.

"Goodness gracious! It's freezing in here! And feels as damp as a rag, too!"

Eldwin shrugged as Ashlord's gaze seemed to penetrate him.

"Is there anything you wish to tell me, Eldwin?"

Eldwin shrugged again. "I don't think so."

"Hm. Very well, perhaps you'll think of it later. You must be famished, and we are sitting down to an early supper. Would you care to join us? All but Sheila and Farby, who are not yet back from some mysterious errand. What do you say?"

"Yes, Ashlord. I am quite hungry as it turns out. I would love to eat with ye."

"Good, good! Come along then, before Ibin has our portions."

Ashlord saw how Eldwin hesitated at the door, looking around his bedroom. Ashlord glanced around, too, but saw nothing more out of place than the bed covers.

"We must do something about your room," Ashlord said as they walked down the hall together. "It seems far too cold and damp."

"I like the room," Eldwin replied. "That is to say, it suits me just fine."

"This is a fine house," Ashlord went on, "but every house has its peculiarities. There's bound to be one or two rooms with seemingly inexplicable drafts, for instance. But there's always a reason for them. Seemingly inexplicable drafts, that is."

He glanced down at Eldwin, but the bait was not taken.

"Hm. In my experience, which is quite considerable, it all boils down to one or two reasons."

"Reasons?"

"For drafts."

"Oh."

"Yes. One has to do with doors or windows or fireplaces that allow air to move too freely about a room. So one reason is simply moving air."

"I see."

"Another reason has to do with other things that may also move freely about a room. Not air at all. Less substantial. But far more chilling."

"I see," Eldwin repeated.

"Yes. Hmm."

Ashlord gave up his line of talk, sensing that Eldwin was unwilling, or unable, to be forthcoming about things.

"Perhaps I might ask you to do something for me," Ashlord said, stopping a few doors away from the dining room. "Or, rather, I would like to ask you not to do something."

"I'm determined to go," Eldwin said.

"Yes, I understand. It is not that. It concerns Sheila."

• • •

When Billy came around the corner one or two moments later, he saw Eldwin nodding and shaking Ashlord's hand.

"Yer gonna have supper with us, ain't ye?" Billy asked as he approached the two, afraid that Eldwin was already making his goodbyes.

"Oh, certainly!" Eldwin said, smiling. "I've slept all day, an' have quite the appetite, I must say!"

The three joined Raynor, Ibin, and Lady Highleaf at the long dinner table. They were served a sumptuous meal, with Lady Highleaf presiding at one end of the table and Ashlord at the other end. Ibin, Raynor, and Billy sat between, along with Eldwin who was given a high stool to sit upon. Billy asked Eldwin about his people while Raynor and Ashlord chatted about the work of Lord Arata and Captain Thrubold. Ibin and Lady Highleaf had spent the afternoon making music together, she on her piano forte while Ibin strummed and picked the mandolin and sang, and that was what they now discussed.

"Starlight Hall has had a great many talented vocalists," Lady Highleaf said to Ibin, "from all over the Seven Realms. But I daresay none ever sang as beautifully as you do."

"You, youare, youareverynicetosaythat,LadyHighleaf," Ibin stammered, his cheeks red with pleasure at her statement.

"Oh, I do not say that merely to flatter you," she went on. "I only express my considered opinion. I have a fine ear for such things as music and song, and I can't abide false compliments. I do mean what I say. I can't tell you when I've had a more enjoyable afternoon. If you wish, we could try a few more tunes tomorrow. And, if you would care to do so, perhaps I could have some guests over in a few days, and we could put on a little concert for them. How does that strike you? I am quite certain that some of the songs from your homeland that you sang this afternoon would please and impress them. Especially the one about the apple orchard and the bluebird. Would you mind if we did that?"

"Thatwould, thatwouldbealright, thatwouldbealright. Aslongas, as, aslongasyoudidallthetalking," Ibin grinned nervously. "Idon't, Idon't, Idon'tliketotalktostrangers."

Lady Highleaf tilted her head, looking at Ibin as she dabbed her lips with her napkin.

"Is it because of your manner of speaking that you don't like to talk to strangers?"

"Yes, yesIstammerandrun, Istammerand, Istammerandrun, Iruneverythingtogether. People laugh."

"Not everyone laughs. Am I laughing? Those that do are not worthy of your notice. Tell me, have you always stammered?"

Ibin shrugged.

"Hm. And no one has ever told you how not to stammer?"

Ibin shook his head, looking at Lady Highleaf with an expression that told her he had never considered the possibility that he could speak any other way.

"My dear boy!" she said, putting her hand on his. "Ashlord! You ought to be ashamed!"

Ashlord stiffened with surprise, and bent sideways to look around the candelabra in the middle of the long table to see Lady Highleaf.

"What's that? Ashamed of what?"

"Never you mind," Highleaf said, patting Ibin's hand. "Really! Some men. Listen to me, Mr. Brinnin. It is quite simple. You must do two things whenever you wish to speak. First, you must think of what it is that you wish to say. That is always a good practice for everyone to adhere to, but it is sometimes very hard to do, especially for impetuous chatterers." She glanced down the table at Billy. "But there is a second, even more important thing that you in particular, Ibin, must do. And to you, this will be as easy as falling off a log, since you are so musical."

"Whatisit?"

Lady Highleaf explained.

• • •

Billy and Eldwin's conversation turned to the topic of Ullin. He told Eldwin about his own brief stay in Tallinvale, and about meeting stern Lord Tallin.

"Yes, I met Lord Tallin, too," Eldwin said. "It was only a brief meetin'. He thanked us Nowhere people for comin' to help at Tallinvale. It was the evenin' after the battle, an' he was badly wounded. He thanked us most graciously, an' he said that Tallinvale was in our debt. He didn't seem all that stern to me. That may have been because of his wounds an' because he had only just heard about the death of his daughter, Lady Mirabella. But he shook all our hands. It was awkward, because he had to use his left hand, bein' wounded in the other. Later that day, or so I heard, the physicians had to remove his entire right arm to stop poison from spreadin'."

"Oh, that's too bad," commented Billy. "I hope that he gets along well enough, now."

"I believe so. He must be a very strong man, for I heard that he was up an' in the saddle within only two days of losin' his arm."

"Billy," interrupted Ibin, "would you please pass the salt?"

"Sure. Thar ye go, Ibin. Only two days? Why, I remember once a field hand of ours got his foot stuck in a poacher's trap..."

"Ashlord," called Ibin, "did you like the meal?"

"It was a fine meal, Ibin. Thank you again, Lady Highleaf."

"Not at all, Ashlord," Lady Highleaf replied, smiling.

"If they call for witnesses," Ashlord said, turning back to Raynor, "then you would most certainly be required."

"Yes, yes. That I don't mind," Raynor replied. "But I would hate for Esildre's name to be brought up."

"I see no reason why it should."

"Raynor," said Ibin, who was now grinning, "would you like to play a hand of cards after dinner?"

"I might, Ibin. We'll see."

Ibin, beaming, turned back to Lady Highleaf, who nodded at him.

"See? They hardly notice. But they will soon enough," she said to him. "I think you will like the ice cream."

"I am sure that I will like it, Lady Highleaf. Thank you."

"You are welcome."

Sheila and Farby burst in, grinning and laughing. She carried a covered basket, and Farby had a large bundle.

"Back in time for supper, Ashlord," Farby said, putting his bundle beside the door. He then crossed his arms, smiling, and stood aside to let Sheila pass with her basket.

"Just as we promised," Sheila said.

She made her way around the table and glanced at Ashlord with a mischievous glint in her eyes. Ashlord nodded and leaned back in his chair, smiling with knowing anticipation.

"Here's a little something that I picked up this afternoon, just for you, Raynor," she said, putting the basket on the table beside Raynor's plate and removing the linen cloth that covered it.

"Oh? And what may this be?"

Two long ears suddenly protruded from the basket.

"Oh! Oh! Oh!" cried Raynor with delight.

• • •

"But she truly did look like Sheila," said Ullin for the fourth time that day. Micerea led on in front of him, and he did not see her roll her eyes. Micerea was sleepy and weak from a long night of dreamwalking. Her pace was slow, and even though they took many breaks to rest throughout the day, she yawned nearly constantly. The path they followed had broadened into a forest road, and it traced its way through the trees along the banks of a stream. They had passed several waterfalls, stopping each time so that Micerea could look in wonder at them, amazed at the continuous rush of clean water. Now, as they walked alongside a calmer and quieter stretch of the stream, their conversation touched upon the topic already much discussed earlier that day.

"I know, I know!" Ullin went on, shifting his pack as he walked behind her. "You saw her in Duinnor last night, sleeping like a baby, and she is just fine. But what a fright we had, eh?"

"Yes, and I'm still not very happy about this forest," Micerea replied. "It seems a bit close to me, so crowded with trees that it is impossible to see very far. Earlier today, when that fox ran across our path, I thought I was going to faint dead away!"

Ullin smiled, saying, "I'm sure your scream nearly made it faint, too!"

"I did not scream."

"You did!"

"I did not. I'm sure I only gasped."

"If you say so," Ullin chuckled. "Look. There's a clearing over there. Why don't we go ahead and stop. You need to sleep. After spending so much time with Sally Bodwin and Prince Carbane, then going to Duinnor to look in on my friends, only to get up at dawn and march all day, well, I know you must be worn out."

Micerea stopped and turned around, first looking at Ullin, then to the place where he pointed. He came up to her and put his arm around her.

"My love," he said. "The apparition we saw did us no harm. I don't think it meant us any harm, either. Whoever or whatever it was, and why ever it was there, we may never know. And I'm not worried about it if we do see another one. After bravely facing the warrior from Shatuum as you did, I know you would protect me from puny little spirits."

Micerea struck Ullin on the chest.

"Don't press your luck, Kingsman!" she laughed. "Very well. Let's make our camp."

There was still plenty of light left in the day, and once firewood was gathered and a campfire started, Ullin managed to catch a couple of fish using a makeshift hook and line from the sewing kit and a bit of carrot for bait. As the fish cooked, Ullin made for Micerea a bed of pine boughs to lie upon. He then stuffed more pine straw into the pack for a pillow. She watched his labors in silence, her fatigue truly catching up with her as she sat yawning by the fire, turning the fish as he had shown her to do so it would not burn too much. He finished his work and sat beside her, and they ate their supper. Afterwards, they sat gazing at the fire. He watched her head dip as she nodded off, and he lifted her up and took her to the bed he had made and eased her head down onto the pillow. As the first stars began to wink through the branches overhead, he stretched out beside her, pulling the blankets over them along with more pine straw. She was asleep, and as the light continued to dim, he looked at her, smiling. He kissed her cheek, put his head beside hers, and closed his eyes.

• • •

In Duinnor, a good while later, Raynor decided to take Ibin up on the hand of cards, along with Billy and Lady Highleaf, too. While they repaired to the nearby parlor, the others lingered, and Farby picked up the bundle on the floor and went over to sit near Eldwin.

"Eldwin, may I have a word?"

"Certainly, Mr. Farby."

"I took the liberty of going to my home this evening, on our way back from the Temple," Farby explained as he began untying the knots holding the bundle together. "Here are some things of mine that I can no longer use, but you may need," he said. "That is, if you are still determined, as I think you are, of going into the mountains to find Robby Ribbon."

"I am, sir. Determined to go, that is."

"Well, when I was a lad, I spent some time in Vanara," Farby said, pulling away the cord on the bundle. "It was wintertime, and I had to acquire suitable clothes for my little adventure, which was not sanctioned, you might say, by my parents."

"He ran away from home, is what he means," interrupted Sheila.

"Well, yes. But, as I was saying, when I was fetched back, I brought my winter things with me."

He tossed the cord aside, and unraveled a thick, down-filled coat, and took from inside of it a balaclava and cap. They were very much like those worn by Robby and his escorts during their trek to Griferis, except light tan in color.

"I think this coat might fit you," Farby went on, "and it is sure to be warmer than your present one. It is heavy canvas on the outside, oiled to be somewhat water repellant, but the coat and hood are lined with down-stuffed quilting. I don't know why I've kept it all these years. But now I'm glad I did."

"Oh, me! Thank ye," Eldwin said, standing to try the coat on. "But I think it might be too big for me."

"It is made big and puffy," Farby explained, "so as to withstand hard wind and snow, and so that you can wear sweaters and whatnot underneath. Oh, I think it fits perfectly. Even the sleeves are just right!"

Eldwin smiled, beaming as he turned this way and that for Ashlord and Sheila to see. He tried out the buckles and the pockets and even pulled up the hood for a moment.

"I think it's a wonderful coat, Mr. Farby," he said.

"Try this on." Farby handed him the matching cap. "I'm afraid the balaclava, here, may be too thin for where you're going, but it's yours, too, if you care to have it."

Eldwin took the balaclava, removed his cap, and offered his hand.

"I don't know how to thank ye, sir," Eldwin said. "This is very generous."

"Think nothing of it," Farby said taking Eldwin's hand to shake. "I only wish I had some mittens to give you. But I couldn't seem to find them."

"Do ye mean these?"

Eldwin pulled out a pair that was in the large side pocket of the coat.

"Yes, indeed! Do they fit?"

"Hm. A bit smallish," Eldwin said as he squeezed one on. "Me hands must be thicker than yers were when ye were…how old were ye?"

"Oh, about thirteen or fourteen. Take them anyway. Perhaps they'll do until you obtain better ones."

"I am very grateful," Eldwin said again, removing the coat and shaking Farby's hand once more.

"I am indebted to you, my dear sir," Farby replied, "for all that you have done for Lady Shevalia and her friends. Not the least of which was saving their lives. Now, if you'll excuse me, I think I'll look in on the card game."

Farby departed, leaving Sheila and Ashlord with Eldwin.

"So," said Ashlord, "it appears that you have little to keep you here in Duinnor."

"I suppose that's right," Eldwin nodded, taking his chair.

"And there's nothing that I can say to persuade you to stay on until spring?"

"I don't think I can wait that long."

Ashlord nodded.

"Eldwin," Sheila put in, "even if Secundur is to blame for Esildre's woes, and for her hurt, what might you do against him? I saw myself what he did to Islindia's forest, and I saw the witch that Ashlord slew, and the monster that one of his followers made out of vines, the one that nearly killed us. If they are any hint of his power, what hope might you have of harming him in the least?"

Eldwin shook his head and shrugged.

"I only know that I must try. I don't think I can live with meself if I don't. Ashlord says that I should go find Robby an' ask him."

Sheila looked at Ashlord. "He did?"

"It was only a suggestion," Ashlord said defensively. "If anyone has a chance of getting through to Griferis, then surely it is Eldwin with his ability to jump in an eyeblink a distance that would take us hours or days. And, if Robby's abilities are as we suspect, surely he must by now have some notions concerning Secundur."

Sheila was stunned to realize that it might be possible for Eldwin to do what she herself longed with all her heart to do. Ashlord's keen eye did not miss the subtle change in her expression. And when she nodded thoughtfully and leaned back in her chair, he was glad that Eldwin had given the promise asked of him earlier that evening.

"Well, I think I'll look in on our card players, too," Ashlord said, rising. "I hope you'll reconsider, Eldwin. Perhaps we might talk more about it tomorrow."

"Perhaps."

Sheila and Eldwin watched Ashlord leave, then, as he fingered his new cap, Eldwin yawned.

"Oh, excuse me, dear lady!" Eldwin exclaimed. "I guess I'm still quite tired, in spite of the long sleep I had today. I suppose I ought to go back to bed fairly soon an' get some more."

"Of course you are tired," Sheila said. "And I'm sure the staff would like to clear these things away. May I walk with you to your room?"

"That would be kind."

Eldwin picked up the coat and cap, stuffing the mittens and balaclava into its pockets as they walked from the room. They passed by the parlor where Billy was protesting Ibin's winning hand, and continued on through the otherwise quiet mansion and went upstairs, saying little until they came to the guest wing where Eldwin's room was.

"When do you think you'll go?" Sheila asked.

"Pretty soon."

"And do you mean to go straight on to find Robby?"

"No. I have in mind to look in on Lady Esildre's people, those she left behind at her castle. I think she'd want me to do that."

"Oh?"

"Yes. All her servants are blind. She told me that her castle had become something of a haven for them. Raynor told me the same yesterday, explainin' that they were immune to her curse. When last Lady Esildre an' I spoke about them, she expressed concern for bein' away, an' she hoped that they were gettin' along well enough."

"What do you think they'll do?" Sheila asked as they came to Eldwin's room.

"I don't know. I don't think she would have left them if she thought they weren't able to take care of themselves. But I ought to go see. Just in case there's something amiss, or something that I can do for them. An' someone needs to tell them what happened to her."

"Hm. Yes, I suppose so."

"Lady Sheila, or is it Lady Shevalia?"

"You can just call me Sheila, Eldwin."

"Sheila, I can't take ye with me. If that's what yer thinkin' of askin'."

"I was," Sheila said. "Please, Eldwin. I need to see him."

"I know ye want to, something terrible," Eldwin said.

"Do you? Do you know? It's as if I'm not right, not the same, since I said goodbye to Robby. I shouldn't have. I should have stayed with him, gone with him. I should be with him now."

Eldwin looked down at his feet, then back up at Sheila's glistening eyes. For a moment, as they spoke in the shadowed hallway, it was as if Esildre stood before him, pleading her case. He relived the moments watching Esildre sit beside Tyrin's bed, moments that stretched into days, not knowing at the time that she was wasting away all the while, just as Tyrin did, until the final moment of her final breath. But it was Sheila, not

Esildre, who begged, going to her knees and taking Eldwin's hand. And, as she did so, Eldwin saw Esildre's dim form appear behind Sheila. He looked at Esildre, who was slowly shaking her head, her empty eyes full of doom. In his mind, he said to Esildre, "How can I refuse her?" But with a weak voice, he said to Sheila, "I can't. Please don't be like her. Don't give up just because ye must wait. She couldn't take it. I think maybe ye'll find a way to see yer Robby again, but I can't help ye."

"Can't? Or won't?" Sheila took Eldwin's hand and clutched it to her breast. "My heart still beats. I won't be like her, I promise! I'll fight to keep Robby in my heart. I'll carry his love for me, and my love for him, forever, whether or not we ever see each other again. But, please, Eldwin! Take me with you, just so that, for a little while, anyway, I can have hope of seeing him once again."

"I can't. I've already promised to take someone else with me," he said.

Now the spectre of Esildre floated around to stand behind Eldwin, looming over him. When Sheila saw her, and saw her hollow eyes fix upon her, her flesh crawled, and she grasped Eldwin's hand all the harder as her breath quickened and her pulse raced. Just as Sheila was about to scream, Esildre tilted her head pitifully and put a finger to her lips. Sheila's terror instantly transformed into sympathy and dark understanding.

"Please don't tell anyone," Eldwin said. "I don't think they'd understand. I'm not even sure that I do."

Sheila bowed her head and let go of Eldwin's hand as her shoulders slumped.

"I won't tell," she said to Eldwin's feet. Then, not looking at either of the two, she stood and walked away, but stopped a few feet off. Turning her head slightly, but not daring to look back, she said, "I hope you find what you are looking for. Both of you."

Sheila heard a whisper, like an odd, ethereal echo.

"I hope you find what you are looking for."

Sheila nodded and hurried away to her room.

Chapter 21

The King's Artist

Eldwin watched Sheila disappear around a corner, then he entered his room. Esildre floated in after him. He saw no point in delaying his departure, and he dressed for the road, packed his few things into his shoulder bag, and put on the coat and cap from Farby. He popped quickly through the house, and once outside he traveled almost as fast to the southern gate of the sleeping city. He walked along the straight road toward the far-off Temple, the way lit well enough by the waning moon overhead. He had gone only a few hundred yards when he suddenly halted.

"Are ye with me, Esildre?"

A vague form hovered next to him, then became a wispy shape.

"I am here," she said. "You needn't worry, I seem to be able to keep up with you, no matter how quickly you pop along."

"That's good," Eldwin replied. "I suppose ye ought to show me the way, though, since I've no idea which turns I should take."

"Keep going straight until the crossroad at the base of the Temple mountain. Then take the right-hand road. It is well marked, I believe, for many miles."

"Is yer castle very far off?"

"Yes. Very far. But you will come first to a village called Averstone. Stop there and I will direct you to my castle."

"How will I know the village? Are there many other villages along the way?"

"It is the first one that the road passes directly through, though there are others nearby to the road, along side paths and trails."

"Very well," Eldwin said. "I'll do as ye direct. I'll pause between each little jump so that if I take a wrong turn ye may tell me."

"I'll be sure to do so, if that is the case."

"Then here we go."

Eldwin snapped his fingers, and in a fizz of bubbling blue light, he was off. He only popped as far as he could see, and repeated the process until he arrived at the crossroads at the base of the mountain. Pausing to look up at the mountain, he saw how the road straight ahead rose up a long incline as it approached the stairs of the Temple. He looked to the right, and snapped his fingers again.

After a few hours, and many hundreds of jumps along the twisting road, he was leagues and leagues from Duinnor, farther than one could walk in a fortnight, and well into the forested mountains. His jumps became shorter, sometimes going only a few yards at a time as the road turned, climbed, and dipped as the slanting moonlight became more diffused by the overhanging trees. When Lady Moon passed behind the western hills, and Eldwin could no longer trust his eyes to see the way, he stopped.

"I think I should walk until there is better light," he said.

"That seems prudent," came Esildre's soft voice, almost indiscernible over the shushing of air through the pine boughs overhead.

"How far do ye reckon we've come?"

"Many leagues. Many more to go."

Eldwin yawned as he nodded and began walking, then he stopped, sniffing.

"I smell smoke," he said, looking around. But he could see no fire-light.

"There are travelers camped nearby," Esildre said. "Their fire has all but gone out, and they sleep, as you should do."

"Hm. I'll walk until daylight," he replied, starting out, "as long as I can see the way by starlight. Then I'll find a place off the path to have a rest."

Eldwin would have been surprised to learn that one of the sleeping travelers at the campsite was none other than Ullin Saheed. If Esildre knew who it was, then she was too distracted by her own preoccupations and by her unsettled and pensive state of being to think that it was worth mentioning.

It is a peculiar thing to be Elifaen, caught between time and eternity, and doubly peculiar to be an Elifaen ghost, caught between the heavy world of matter and the equally urgent world beyond matter. It was confusing to her because there seemed little difference in being a ghost and being Elifaen. All Elifaen, she was coming to think, were like ghosts. Though she had never known any ghosts, she suspected that they were some other kind of Fallen Ones, stripped of something essential, pulled with contrary longings beyond their control, and filled with a sense of joyless inevitability. If she had not been Elifaen before she died, she might be more mournful than she presently was. But after a long life of mourning, this other creature that she had become was already accustomed to it, though that did not make her suffer any the less. And she was confused, too, that she had a sense of purpose without knowing what that purpose was.

All she knew was that she did not belong here, in this world, if she ever had. She needed to be elsewhere, with Tyrin, and she would do anything to bring that about. If it meant following her little friend back into Shatuum, then that is what she would do. If it meant—she shuddered at the thought and nearly let out a wail of terror, but stifled it—if it meant being taken once again by Secundur, if that was the price of her release, she would do it. But there was something at the edge of her mind, something she felt she ought to know or remember, something about Secundur that would help Eldwin.

The conflict of hope and hopelessness tore away at her, and she was terrified by every new moment. As she followed Eldwin, her mind thus ceaselessly circled around her heavy soul until, unable to withstand it any longer, she let out a long, low moan.

Eldwin trudged onward, hearing Esildre's grief and torment made into a hair-raising sound, a sound as cold as the night air, and as dark as the shadowed forest. He stopped for a moment, closing his eyes as he steeled himself against her pitiful whimper. Then, thinking of nothing he could say to her, he marched on. When dawn finally came, he resumed his popping along, covering a great distance once again until around midmorning, when he was done in.

"I must rest," he said, stopping to look around. He saw the little clearing off the path along the stream where Ullin and Micerea had encountered Esildre many days before. It was one of the places that Tyrin had made camp with Esildre when he brought her forth to Duinnor. "There's a good place."

"Keep going," Esildre said. "Do not stop here. Keep going."

"Is there something about this place that is not good?"

"No. Only memories," she gulped.

Eldwin shrugged and nodded, unable to see Esildre, but glad that she was still with him.

"Very well."

He kept on for another hour or so until he stopped once more.

"Would yonder rocks up around that fallen tree be alright?" he asked the air.

"Yes," was the nearly insubstantial reply.

Eldwin climbed up a steep hill to the base of a rocky overhang where a tree, heavy with snow, had fallen, and he crawled behind the trunk and kicked away leaves and brush to make a place to lie down.

"Will ye wake me up before the day is gone?" he asked as he unshouldered his pack.

"Yes."

Soon, wrapped in a blanket with his head on his pack, Eldwin closed his eyes. Esildre hovered, not knowing what to do with herself. She began weeping, trying her best to restrain herself so that Eldwin could sleep. But her soft weeping was only the trickle from a leaky dam, one that held behind it too much, one that might break at any moment and sweep her away.

After a while, Eldwin said without opening his eyes, "Don't cry. Things'll be alright. I didn't come all this way for them not to be. An' now that yer with me, I am bolstered in that determination. Only, I need hope, too. An' it makes me doubly sad to hear ye cry."

"I'll try not to," she answered.

"Do ye know how far we have come? Or how far it is yet to go before we reach yer castle?"

Esildre had to think about this because distance now seemed an odd thing.

"I think you have come more than half way," she said. "In life, it took Tyrin two weeks to bring me as far on horseback."

"Then, perhaps by tomorrow evenin' we'll see yer home an' look in on those who wait for ye to return."

"Yes."

"I must sleep, now."

"Yes."

• • •

The top of the wall of the south garden was Sheila's favorite place to sit. Starlight Hall and its grounds were on one of the highest hills within the city, and from her perch she could see across the spread of the city and beyond and across the valley to the other side. The Temple on the far mountaintop was still shrouded with the early morning mists that rose along its shoulders like long downy feathers. She remembered Alonair, and wondered how much longer he would remain living there. Ashlord, Farby, and Billy had all already departed to the Hall of Law, where a hearing was to be held pertaining to the activities of the late Lord Banis. Sheila and Ibin stayed behind with Raynor. Lady Highleaf had already come along, still in her housecoat, and begged Sheila to come down from her perch before she fell and broke her neck. But Sheila was in no mood to be compliant. Lady Highleaf shook her head in exasperation and hurried back inside. Sheila remained, having climbed to her place shortly after their early breakfast when it was discovered that Eldwin had departed without so much as a goodbye. She had not mentioned to anyone that she had begged Eldwin to take her along, nor did she say anything about the eerie apparition that accompanied Eldwin. Even though everyone took it hard that Eldwin was gone—even Lady Highleaf was put out over it, saying how rude it was of the little man—they could not help but notice that Sheila took the news with particular sullenness, but with no hint of surprise.

Now, after having studied for a long while the movement of a distant cloud, she looked back to a line of ants that came up one side of the wall, marched across the top right in front of her, and down the other side.

"You are too soon Elifaen to know patience."

She turned and saw Raynor standing a few yards off, bending over to put Beauchamp down to hop around the garden.

"But not too soon to know the pain and sadness of being Elifaen," Raynor went on, watching Beauchamp nibble a dried twig beside the path. Sheila wondered how Raynor could know.

"I have had many good Elifaen friends," Raynor said, turning to her. "Some started out like you did, as a mortal, and were Scathed as you were. And I have known others who were here from the time the earth was born. So I have some experience, vicariously, of the matter. Added to that, I am very old, older than Collandoth, and have had to learn patience, too."

"All we do is sit around and wait," Sheila said to him, "which would be fine with me if there was nothing else that needed doing."

"Ah. You worry about Robby. But what is it that you think you can do for him?"

Sheila shrugged.

"Be with him?" Raynor asked.

"Yes. That. And offer him my help. I don't understand why he doesn't come back to me in my dreams, as he did when he sent us to witness the death of Banis."

"Perhaps he does not love you any more."

Sheila shot him a look of astonishment that evaporated when she saw Raynor's smile. She smiled, too, and turned away to look at the Temple.

"You Melnari have a well-deserved reputation for upsetting people. Must you be so contrary?"

"I do so only to provoke the truth. Do you think that Robby still loves you?"

"Think? No. I don't know. I hope he does. You needn't remind me how silly that hope is."

"Hope? Silly? Never when it is for such an important thing as love."

"Well, Ashlord has as much as said that it is pointless. He has reminded me on more than one occasion that if Robby becomes King, the division between us will be beyond hope."

"I think you have mistaken what Ashlord has warned you against, which is not hope of love, but only the possibility that you two may never be together again. Ashlord cares deeply about you, my dear, and he would only say such things to help steel you against heartbreak. The notion that you may never see Robby again is, I am certain, a painful one to consider. I think that is why Eldwin's visit has stirred you up so much, his tale of Tyrin and Esildre."

"I know that if Robby becomes King there will not be a place in his life for me."

"No. You do not know that, else you would not hope for otherwise before it has come about. If your hopes are dashed, though, I wonder what will become of you? That, certainly, is behind any warnings Collandoth may give you."

Sheila looked at Raynor thoughtfully.

"Collandoth does not know all," Raynor went on. "And he does not always say what he thinks, deep down. I have often thought that, for a man of faith, he is far too rational. I think that he could do with a bit more, shall we say, imagination? Or at least he might allow for variations beyond his calculations. Perhaps he thinks that since he cannot foresee all possibilities that he must go on faith that things will turn out well. I, on the other hand, would rather apply hope, just as you do."

"Aren't they much the same thing, faith and hope?"

"Yes, like the sky, which at day shows us those things of the world, but at night shows us the heavens. You and I, perhaps, are creatures of the night sky. Though, at dusk and dawn, we see both day and night. Both faith and hope."

Sheila smiled again.

"You are kind. What do you think I should do?"

"I think you should be patient. Let Robby become King, if he can. Look forward to that day, if you can. Then, should Providence provide, perhaps you may seek an audience. It is said that the Kings of Duinnor may see into the hearts of those before them. I think it is true. So, if Robby becomes King, seek to go before him so that he can see the love within your heart. Once he sees that, be sensible to how he acts toward you, so that you may judge if he yet loves you."

Sheila nodded. "That is what I had resolved to do, more or less. Before Eldwin came, that is. You were right when you said that he stirred up much within me. I wanted to go with him and find Robby. Not wait. Not wonder. Just go. I begged him. He said no. So here I remain."

"But you can see how what I suggest may be much harder to do, though less audacious than running off in search of Robby."

"Yes. In a way. Much harder."

"Be patient. Be wise. Wait for him a little while longer."

"Do you think it will only be a little while? I am prepared to wait forever, but…."

"I do not think it will be much longer. He is putting all in place, and he has given us signs. He will come. You know, springtime is almost here, merely a few weeks away, and that is when all past Unknown Kings have come. I don't think the Seventh King will be any different."

"And if he doesn't come this spring?"

"Then he will come some other spring," Raynor shrugged. "Speaking of spring, it is already getting warmer each day. Before long, Lady Highleaf's frozen pool will be all melted away, and I would hate to have to wait until next year to see you skate."

"Oh, very well!" Sheila laughed, threw her legs over the side of the wall, and leapt down.

• • •

In Griferis, shortly after noontime, the great circular hall was crowded with the new arrivals, standing in orderly ranks and groups according to their assigned positions and duties. To one side stood Unther, Hathrain, and Winnefras with two dozen men and women chosen to serve in the new Palace Guard. At the other side of the room stood Radasa with a number of men and women who would be tradesmen and craftsmen. And in the center stood Kinsiri and Lord

Threshmere, who had been chosen to direct the estate of Griferis. Behind these two were all of those new arrivals who would be cooks and serving staff, gardeners, and others required for performing the day-to-day tasks and chores. Within this large group was Borwain leaning on his crutches.

Standing at a table at the side of the room was another newly arrived person, a young Dragonkind man from Kajarahn called Alzeeran. He had been a scribe's apprentice for fourteen years. He was a gifted writer and translator, as fluent in the writings and speech of the Dragonlands as he was of the Northlands, with knowledge and skills greater than his cruel master. Although Alzeeran was his master's most valuable servant, he was treated and kept as a slave. So while he earned for his master a great wealth of coin and trade, he received only endless toil and abusive treatment in return. At first, Alzeeran knew no better. He had only been five years old when he was first given over to his master's keeping, and he knew no other way of being treated. Over the years, from his reading and his writing tasks, he began to have a greater sense in his heart of the injustice and cruelty of his condition. At last, when he tried to defend another young servant from his master's whip, Alzeeran was publicly flogged and shackled for his defiant action. He was amongst the first persons Micerea had discovered who might desire a new life. One night, when all were asleep in the house above his cell, Alzeeran's chains burst asunder. Forewarned of this, he escaped and fled Kajarahn to the Blue Mountains, where he met others with similar stories as his. Some were Dragonkind, but others were not. And all told each other about their odd dreams, full of instructions and offers of escape. Today he was in Griferis, standing at his writing table, quill in hand, ink at the ready, and a large volume of paper opened before him. Alzeeran would be the Scribe of Griferis, charged by Finn to record all that would be said at this gathering. He had written a formal introduction of this day's record at the top of the first page of his book. Now, as he and the others waited, Alzeeran was afraid that his hand would shake too much once the King arrived, so excited and happy he was, and so anxious to perform his duty well. And though he had promised his faithfulness and his loyalty to Griferis and its King, he considered himself this very day to be a free man at last. It was a sentiment and a feeling shared by very many of those present.

Finn pounded his staff on the floor and cried out, "All attend! King Philawain, Lord and Master of Griferis!"

The door in front of them opened, and Robby strode in, attired in a resplendent dark blue suit made for him by Kinsiri, and behind him came Celia in a simple lavender dress and carrying Boxer in her arms. Having already been instructed by Finn and Lafkin on the etiquette of the occasion, all present, including Celia, bowed to their new sovereign, as Lafkin called out, "Hail, Philawain, King!"

"Hail, Philawain!" came the resounding chorus from those present.

Lafkin took his place to one side and behind Robby, standing next to Celia. Alzeeran dipped his pen.

"Sire, all are present and await your pleasure," Finn said, then bowed again and moved to stand on Robby's other side.

"Thank you, Lord Finn," Robby said. Then he addressed the gathering.

"I bid you welcome to Griferis! I should like to charge my various lords with their duties. I do this before you so that you know that they have my full authority. Lord Finn, if you will."

Finn stepped forward and bowed.

"This is Lord Finn, First Lord of Griferis. I charge Lord Finn as my overseer of all matters pertaining to Griferis. He speaks with my voice, and his decisions are final in all matters. He is a fair-minded person, and wise. Heed him as you would me. Lord Lafkin, if you will."

Finn bowed and stepped aside as Lafkin took his place.

"This is Lord General Lafkin who will lead the armies of Griferis. Although our ranks are few, they will grow in numbers and in might. General Lafkin will see to the defense of our realm. I authorize him to bid all of you to serve in that defense when required by him. You will obey without hesitation, for the defense of this, your new home, and of my throne. Lord Lafkin will order the ranks of my army as he deems best, using whatever means is required to fulfill his duty. Lord Radasa, if you will. This is Lord Radasa, who will oversee those aspects of trade and craft required to fashion or to obtain those things we shall be in need of. Under him I place all you who are woodworkers, smiths, tinkers, masons, seamstresses, tailors, and factors. Lady Kinsiri and Lord Threshmere: These two I charge with the ordering of our home and the management of our serving people. I bid and command that you obey your overseers as you would obey me and as you would wish to be obeyed if you were lord or king."

"Now. Though we are few, we who are gathered here come from every corner of the world. Elifaen, Dragonkind, and Men shall all serve me alike, here and elsewhere. You have been selected to serve here because you have already been found to be fair-minded and capable. It will be difficult, at times, to understand one another or even to get along with one another. There will be disagreements, and perhaps even heated debate. But if we do not get along well with each other, we shall fail, and Griferis shall fall. Let no person slight or insult any other with words or with deeds! Be slow to take offense from others, and quick to forgive. Treat every woman and girl as if she was your sister, and every man and boy as if he was your brother, each and every one with kindness, with respect, and with courtesy. I shall tolerate nothing less of you. When things go wrong, and they are bound to, do not cast blame upon one another. If there is a problem, strive to solve it together. But if you have problems, ideas, or concerns, take them to your overseers."

"Know this: in the same manner that you were informed of this place, through your dreams, you will be watched. Unseen by you, there is another realm of which I, Philawain, am master. In that place are my servants, who serve the throne of Griferis just as you do. Not only will they look upon us while we are awake, but they will watch over us in our sleep. I send them far and wide upon my business. They keep vigil by day and by night. I tell you this not to frighten you, but to give you fair notice.

"We all have much to do, so I shall be brief. I tell you that I intend to extend my reign over other kingdoms, over other realms. You will soon learn more. There are dark days ahead for the world, and we here shall do our duty to lessen the suffering that is to come, if we cannot prevent it. It is my wish that you will someday look back upon your days here as a time spent in honorable service not only to Griferis, but also to the world."

"I hope to see each of you privately. Some I shall require to wait upon me sooner than others, due to pressing matters, so do not be disheartened that I do not summon you before I summon others. There. I think I've said all that I need to say at the moment. I bid you all a good day, and good luck!"

Robby turned and departed, with Celia following, as again his people bowed and someone called out, "Long live Philawain, King!" which was spontaneously rejoined by the others.

• • •

"How did I do?" Robby asked Celia. "Do you think they were impressed?"

"Oh, I don't know, Robby Sire," Celia replied. "I'm sure they think you are a great person, but I'm not sure all the stuff about dreams was very convincing. I've never had a visitor to my dreams, after all. At least, not that I recall, since I don't recall dreaming."

"Oh? I'm sure that you do dream, though."

"Are you? What makes you sure?" she asked.

"Well, you have me there, Celia. I suppose I am not sure that you dream," Robby replied. "But, I tell you what: when next I get a chance, I'll send someone to look in on your dreams, if you have any, and report back to me. Then I'll tell you what you dreamed and see if you remember. How does that sound?"

"Oh, sire! That sounds like fun! Do you hear that Boxer? I shall have a dream visitor! Sire, do you think Boxer dreams, too?"

"I'm sure he must. All intelligent creatures dream. And he is most intelligent, is he not?"

"I think so. Sire, what am I to do?"

By now they had arrived at the stairs that wound up to Robby's apartments, and he stopped to look at her.

"Do? About what?"

"Not about. Just do. Everyone else has been given their duties and their chores. Shouldn't I have mine, too?"

"You need not have any chores or duties. You are my adopted daughter, and so you are different than the others."

"Sire, pardon me, but that doesn't seem fair. I *want* to do something."

"Well, Celia, everyone has their own talents, their own skills. Is there anything in particular that you want to do, or that you think that you can do?"

"No. I mean, I'm willing to do anything. The other girls cook and clean and tend to things. Perhaps I can cook, too. Or clean fireplaces. Or wash clothes."

"Oh, my dear girl!" Robby put his arm around her and drew her close. "You surprise me and do me a great honor by being so willing. Well, let me think on it. I have nothing against the idea at all, though. In fact, you are right. It seems fitting that you should also help out."

• • •

In the Hall, the gathering dispersed, leaving only Finn and Threshmere, who were discussing Threshmere's duties.

"Yes, Lord Finn," Threshmere said. "My estate is very large, and I have been forced to manage it without an overseer for years. The result of which was that I managed it right into the ground, so to speak."

"Lord Threshmere, the King assures me that you did no such thing, but that you did the best that you could under the circumstances that befell you. It was not your fault that you could not find workers, or that your fortune was taken by Duinnor. The King has every confidence that you will manage Griferis with skill and wisdom."

"If you say so, my lord. That is most kind, and I shall do my very best! But, if I may ask, what of Borwain? It seems that if he is to continue serving me, it would appear that I play favors with him. Yet, I am reluctant to do without him."

"Ah, Borwain," Finn glanced at the doors to make sure that the last of the gathering had departed. "The King knows that Borwain is your son, and that you have sought to protect him all these years by pretending to Borwain and to others that he is not. The King also knows that had you declared Borwain to be your son, he would have been forced to travel to Duinnor to have a fitness hearing before the Kingsmen. Philawain thinks that you feared Borwain would not survive the journey or the rejection by the Kingsmen."

Threshmere was astonished that Finn, and Philawain, could know these things. He blinked several times before he could form a reply.

"All that is so," he said. "I suppose I should not be amazed by the King's knowledge. But I am!"

"Do not worry." Finn patted him on the shoulder. "Your secret is safe. And don't worry about Borwain. I think Philawain has something in mind for him, to be revealed when the King deems fitting. Meanwhile, I'm sure the members of your staff are waiting for you. You have the lists and inventories?"

"Yes. And with Lady Kinsiri, we are already planning meals and rations."

"Good. Then I shall see you later this evening for a report."

• • •

Hathrain escorted Borwain to the small library in what they were calling the Royal Apartments, the southern wing of the palace where Robby had his rooms. Robby motioned for Borwain to sit.

"I know that you prefer to stand," said Robby, seeing Borwain's reluctance. "But I would prefer that we are seated."

"Yes, sire. Certainly."

"What do you think of Griferis so far?"

"Oh, it is a marvelous place, indeed, sire," replied Borwain. He leaned his crutches on the back of his chair. "I never imagined such a place. Floating like a cloud. It is like a dream-place!"

"Yes, it is, rather," Robby chuckled. "You do not remember me, but we have met before. I passed through your estate with some of my friends. One was a Kingsman, Ullin Saheed, who wrote a letter to Duinnor on Lord Threshmere's behalf. We accompanied a King's Post Rider who delivered to your father a summons. There were three other gentlemen with us, and a girl."

"Oh, yes! The red man. I mean to say, a man with red skin, sire. But, pardon me, sire, I do not remember you amongst them. And I rarely forget a face."

"I am not surprised that you do not remember me. To you, I would have appeared as a young man, roughly your own age, perhaps. But, to me, that was nearly thirty years ago, and I have much changed. Ah, I see that you now recognize me."

"Yes, sire. You are much changed. Taller, I think. And, yes, much older."

"Yes. Well, my companion, the Kingsmen Ullin Saheed, told me about the wonderful drawings that were inside your home. Ones that you created."

"Oh?"

"Yes, he did. And, though you may not believe it, I have seen them myself. They have a very peculiar quality to them. Lifelike. Uncanny."

"So Lord Threshmere has told me many times, sire. But I don't know how you may have seen my doodles."

"They are more than mere doodles. I saw them in my dreams, so to speak. But I mention your talent for a reason. You have seen a fair portion of my palace, I imagine, and you cannot have failed to notice that there are no drawings or paintings anywhere to be found."

"I did notice."

"Have you ever painted?"

"Yes, some. But I have confined myself to ink and quill for a long time, now."

"Because canvas, paint, and brushes are expensive, I take it?"

"Well, sire, yes. Lord Threshmere would have purchased them, would have sent all the way to Linlally or even Glareth by the Sea for them, had he known that I desired to have such things. He has always spoiled me most unlike a lord should do a servant."

"So you convinced him that pen and pencil was more to your liking."

"Well," Borwain looked down at his hands, stained by ink, then back up at Robby. "That is so."

"Would you be willing to make some drawings and some paintings for Griferis? I would provide a place for you to work, the things that you need, and so forth. There would be some conditions, though."

"Oh, I would be most happy to make whatever drawings or paintings that you desire!"

"Good, good! I have a list of subjects prepared. Don't get up! It is just here."

Robby handed the list to Borwain, who studied it for a moment as Robby sat back down.

"But," Borwain shook his head, "I do not know some of these people or these places. Lady Celia, of course, I have seen. And Lord Radasa, Finn, and Lady Kinsiri. And I have never seen the places that you list, though I have heard of some of them."

"Don't worry. I'll show them to you. And, though this may seem vain, I would like for you to first consider portraying some of my own experiences, as I may relate them to you."

"Your legacy and your life would surely be a fitting subject, sire. I only hope that I am adequate to the task."

"I am sure that you are. Tell me, do you work from memory? Or do you require your subjects to be before you as you work?"

"I work mostly from memory. From people and places I have seen. But I enjoy having what I draw before me. On fine days, that is, when my duties to Lord Threshmere permitted, I loved to go out and about. I like to see the trees and fields, the creatures of the world, and people as they labor and work. The changing light of day, from morning to dusk, and season by season. But because Lord Threshmere is overly concerned for my health, he forbade too many such forays. That is why I have learned to work from memory, my King."

"How extraordinary! Wonderful!" Robby grinned. "Very well, then. Hathrain, who brought you here, awaits outside. He will take you to your new rooms, in the southwest tower. There you will find windows and light, lamps and oil, and all the things you need to get started. If you need or desire anything else, just let Lord Finn know. Do not bother your fa—I mean, you needn't concern Lord Threshmere with your needs. All is arranged so that you will now be free of your duties to him in order to perform your duties to me."

"Yes, sire. I shall strive to please you."

"I am sure that you will. You know that I have some power within the world of dreams. So, do not be alarmed if you have strange and uncanny dreams. You will understand, after a while, that having them is part of your duty to me and the means of accomplishing your work."

"As you will it, King Philawain."

"Very good, then," Robby said, rising. He waited for Borwain to get to his feet and take up his crutches, then walked with him to the door. "And, Borwain, I would like for you to prepare a kit. It should contain materials and tools, ink, paper and whatnot, whatever you deem useful. I would like you to have the kit upon you wherever you go within Griferis. It would please me for you to make sketches of the people who are here as they go about their duties. Just try not to get in anyone's way. And try not to make anyone feel awkward."

"Yes, sire. Good day, sire."

Borwain bowed, not the least hampered by his crutches, and he departed. When the door was closed, Robby smiled and went back to sit in his chair. But as soon as he had done so, there came a knock, and Unther entered.

"Sire," he said, "Lord Finn wishes to see you."

"Please show him in, Unther. And, Unther, if Lord Finn wishes to see me in the future, you need not announce him. He is welcome to see me at any time."

"Forgive me, sire. I beg your pardon. It is General Lafkin's new orders, just given a few moments ago, that permission is to be asked before anyone is let in to see the King."

"Oh. I see. Then let it be as Lafkin so orders. I shall not contradict him. Is Borwain being seen after?"

"Yes, sire. I have relieved Hathrain, so when Winnefras arrives to take up her guard duty, I shall take Borwain to his quarters. It should not be long."

When Finn came in, Unther followed, closed the door, and remained beside it. Finn bowed, and Robby gestured to a chair as he eyed Unther quizzically. Finn waited for Robby to sit, then took his own seat, turning to Unther an amused smile before looking back at Robby.

"Sire," Finn explained, "Lord General Lafkin puts into place the first of his measures for the security of Griferis. He informed me this morning that he would be doing so."

"Ah," Robby said. "It is what I asked him to do, after all."

"Yes, sire. And you are not to be left alone with anyone unless you wish it so."

"Oh. Of course." Robby nodded. Then to Unther he said, "That will be all. Thank you, Captain."

Unther bowed smartly, tapping his heels lightly, and departed to stand outside.

"I suppose I'll have as much to get accustomed to as any, Finn." Robby shrugged. "I hope I won't disappoint you or the others too much by my ignorance, my lack of etiquette and so forth."

"I don't see how you could, sire," Finn answered kindly. "And Griferis is a new kingdom with, it is fair to say, new ways. Who is to know any better?"

"Good point, well said. So. How go things? Do you think some relief is in sight for you?"

"Yes, thank you. I think so. Already Lady Kinsiri and Lord Threshmere have relieved me of many household duties. So efficient are they that I only hope my usefulness to my king does not end."

"No, you aren't that fortunate," Robby laughed. "Your duties, your most important ones, are before you, I should say."

"And, along those lines, what do you wish for them to be?"

"First, I want you to be in charge of our dreamwalkers. Once enough of them are trained, and we are sure we may trust them, I would like for you to organize them. I have in mind that you should order them somewhat like we have done with those among us here in Griferis. A group for defense and security, a group for more mundane tasks and assignments, and another group as go-betweens. But, in addition to those, a fair number should be ambassadors and liaisons, such as Sally Bodwin is to Prince Carbane. And, as First Lord, I should like for you to be First Ambassador, too, in charge of all of them for a time."

"Hm. I'm not sure that I am adequate to the task. I have no training or experience with matters of state, or with dealing with royalty or foreign courts. And, sire, my own knowledge concerning the world is woefully limited by all my years of isolation here in Griferis."

"I knew you would bring up those concerns, Finn. Now you know how I feel. It's one reason I spend so much time reading. But there's no time to waste debating your qualifications. Frankly, there is no one else I might ask, and none that I would trust more than you. Put your mind to thinking on it immediately. In a few days, or, rather, in a few nights, I wish to have a meeting with all of our candidates. I will draw everyone together into one place at one time, to introduce myself, and to introduce them to you and to each other. I want you to be at my side, and I will ask Micerea to be at my side, too."

"So soon? And have you the ability to do that? To draw everyone's dreams into one?"

"Yes, I do. And I would rather it be sooner, but I need a few nights to arrange things."

Finn wrinkled his brow. "I'm afraid I don't understand how it is to work. A meeting place? In the realm of dreams? For all of us to be present at one place at one time? I worry that you may tax yourself. As for myself, although I am new to all this, it drains me terribly to dreamwalk. Is it not the same with you?"

"Yes, it is a drain on my strength. But only for a time. Since I am Elifaen, I think I may get along without true sleep somewhat better than others, and recover more quickly. As for the location of our gathering, it will be in several places at once, actually: Here at Griferis, at the Temple of Beras in Duinnor, and also in Nasakeeria."

"Nasakeeria? You have told me about that place, and about how those people are descended from the Dragonkind. Do you not send Ullin and Micerea there after they deliver the Seven to Duinnor?"

"Yes. I do send them there. But I have not told you all about the people of Nasakeeria. I have not told you about an old woman who lives there who has peculiar abilities. And, it so happens, she has one ability in particular that the Oracle at the Temple also has. And, if they are willing, I hope to enlist their help."

"Oh?"

"Yes. I'll tell you more once I have things settled with them. But, and I hope this is not pressing our luck too much, I want Borwain to tag along with us."

Finn's eyebrows shot up in surprise.

"He is not a dreamwalker, is he?"

"No, he is not. But I would like for him to be a witness and to put his impressions onto canvas, should he be able to do so."

"That would be quite a feat," said Finn. "I would hardly know how to begin describing the dreamworld, much less how to depict it."

"I plan to make it easy on him by creating a somewhat natural setting for us to meet. It will be strange-looking, no doubt, and our first order of business is with our dreamwalkers. We won't need Alzeeran, because others will be there to put things in writing. But it would be good, I think, to have Borwain make some artistic rendering of the meeting."

"For you to place such confidence in Borwain, his abilities must be remarkable, indeed."

"They are, Finn. Like nothing you can imagine. You'll see!"

"Then I am filled with anticipation."

Robby nodded, tilting his head in thought. He absently rubbed his wrist—the one that was burned by a fiery missile all those years ago during a battle at sea—a gesture that indicated to Finn that something was on his King's mind. It was only one of many injuries Robby had sustained during his trials, and Finn wondered, since Robby was now Elifaen, why it was still painful. While he waited for Robby to speak, Finn wondered if Griferis had done something to Robby, if it had made him into someone who was not Elifaen, nor Mortal. Just as the question occurred to him, Robby shifted in his chair.

"I do have a task for you, Finn," said Robby, "as my ambassador, if you will. Someone I'd like for you to visit on my behalf."

"Your wish is my command, sire."

Robby cocked a brow and looked askance at Finn. But then he saw that Finn's statement was made in all earnestness.

Chapter 22

A Messenger to the Queen

The following day, Griferis hummed with activity. In the large courtyard before the East Gate, Lafkin watched as Winnefras put some of the new members of the Griferis Guard through exercises meant to ascertain their fighting skills. Although it was windy and cold, she had stripped to her halter, and with a short staff instead of a sword, she pointed to each recruit in turn to come at her with their own staff. Lafkin was pleased to see how skilled she was. He was equally happy that, owing to their own skill, all of the recruits proved themselves to be nearly her match. While they exercised, a separate group of recruits went around and about Griferis with Unther as he familiarized them with the place. The remaining members of the Griferis Guard under Hathrain's command were on duty in and outside of the Royal Apartments, standing their watches and making their rounds within that wing.

Valcea, under her mother Kinsiri's guidance, busily sorted through fabric and materials for uniforms, while Halyari and Leena saw to the kitchens. Lord Threshmere worked with several of his people to set up all those more mundane places of work: laundry rooms, garden sheds, a woodworking shop, and a smithy. Threshmere suggested that Radasa, Finn, and Lafkin should each have personal waiting staff befitting their station, and that both Celia and Kinsiri have lady's maids assigned to them. Celia thought this quite silly, and Kinsiri was likewise skeptical, but Finn prevailed upon them both to graciously accept the help. However, Finn and the other gentlemen refused Threshmere's offer, for the time being at least. Meanwhile, Radasa spent a great deal of time with his King, who took a keen interest and seemed to have insight into trade matters, the business of obtaining goods, and the need for accurate records and inventories.

"Sire, it does seem unlikely that we will have anything of value to use as barter any time soon," said Radasa. He sat at a long table in the King's study, with Robby beside him. Before them, the table was strewn with papers and inventories.

"That is so," Robby nodded as he shuffled through several papers until he arrived at the one he sought. "We have no resources of the normal kind. No agriculture, mines, timber, or such. And we are not exactly situated on any trade routes, even if we did have such things."

Robby sat back in his chair and put an arm over the back of it, turning to Radasa.

"But there are valuable minerals, gemstones and so forth, very nearby. And as soon as we can safely send prospecting parties out, we will have treasure enough. All of which brings me to ask about my request concerning the storage and stacking of things. I spoke with Lord Threshmere this morning, and this afternoon he plans to see to his part of the palace. What about your people?"

"They work away at it as we speak, sire," Radasa said. "They are putting buttresses against the casks in the cellars, and are making sure that no tools or shelved things are situated so that they will easily fall down. But, sire, it seems unlikely that a severe earthquake could shake us very much, for we are not attached to the ground."

"When I said to prepare for an earthquake, it was in a manner to suggest the kind of shaking that Griferis should be able to endure. You remember the tremors that jolted us some days ago, do you not?"

"Yes, sire. Most mysterious, indeed."

"Not to me. I caused them. Since I have served aboard ships and am familiar with how things should be fastened down or secured against shifting, I will personally inspect all of Griferis and the work that you and Threshmere are doing along those lines. We may experience more tremors. I hope not. That is to say, I hope I can avoid causing too much excitement. I certainly don't want any injuries, and I want to avoid damage to our goods, too."

"I don't think I understand," Radasa said.

"You will soon enough. It is urgent, so let me know when you've got things secured," said Robby, smiling as he stood. "As soon as possible. Meanwhile, I'd like to look over these lists for a while."

Radasa stood and, with a quizzical look, bowed.

"I hope all will be done by this evening," he said. "I shall keep you informed, sire."

• • •

Finn was busy, too, although he remained within the great library nearly all day. With Robby's permission, which was gladly given, Finn read as much as he could find concerning the various Realms, their histories and rulers, and about the Elifaen. Robby told him about the Last Book of Nimwill and, even though it had not been copied from the archive in Linlally, there was a copy in Griferis. In fact, the library, a mind-boggling mystery in itself, seemed to contain a copy of everything that had ever been written from the beginning of the First Age to the time when Robby first entered Griferis. So Finn had no trouble finding more than enough to read, and so engrossed was he that the hours passed without his notice of them. Late that afternoon, he went up to a balcony to retrieve a certain volume of stories, and was surprised to see through the window how late in the day it was, with the shadows of the western mountains reaching out over the long chasm.

Finn had read enough to realize the profound change that Robby intended to bring about in the world. And he knew the risk. And Finn knew that tonight he himself would play an important role in Robby's great scheme. He looked forward to it only because it was something that his King asked him to do, and he admired his King not only as a subject should, but as a proud uncle might. But the King's ambition was greater than Finn had before imagined. Indeed, it had slowly dawned on Finn during his studies that King Philawain of Griferis intended to accomplish that which the greatest figures in history could not bring themselves to do. This realization served to make Finn even prouder of Robby and all the more determined to serve his King.

Finn sat down in a chair to think it all over. Night slowly fell as he continued to ponder, though the lamps kept the library bright. He remembered more of his life, now. As the glass before him darkened until he could see his own reflection, he remembered how he had once looked, when he was young and hale and happy in his work as an alchemist. Now his hair was white, his skin pale with lines of wrinkles. He could see the reflection's resemblance to the young man he had once been. How bright that young man had been! How full of zeal for knowledge and how energetic he was in his pursuit of alchemy and his desire to unlock the mysteries of potions and compounds. How sure he was of his own place in history, the discoverer of fire contained in mineral powders, with wealth enough to manufacture such great stores of the stuff in his workshops. He had discovered how to make powerful pastes, bright-burning sticks of it that flared with brilliant fire and sparkling colors. With his formulas and his secrets, he was sure to be the envy of all the world, sought after by every court of every land. How foolish! How ignorant!

Finn thought about Robby's mother, and his own family that was lost to his careless ambitions so many centuries ago. In a manner of speaking, Finn and Robby were alike. Both were determined men, but now they were made wary by their memories of those they had hurt. Although he was not tried in the same way that Robby had been, nor like any of the previous occupants of Griferis, Finn had been tried nonetheless. All those years of helping the others who had come here. Years and centuries spent as the butt of cruel and unkind words, the object of angry and contemptuous treatment. All that, yet Finn still waited upon them, served them, and tended their wounds and to their needs. And during all those years, Finn harbored a terrible sense that he deserved the treatment that he received.

Then came the boy who offered his hand in friendship on the very first day he arrived. It was a sign. During Robby's time here, he never spoke an unkind word to Finn, not even during the worst of his trials. And, inexplicably, Finn began to wonder whether he deserved such kind treatment. When it all began to flood back, when Finn began to remember what he had done, and all those who had suffered and died because of his foolishness, he knew that he did not deserve to live, much less to have and to receive kind affection and friendship. But whereas before Finn had sought to take his own life, now he intended to live it, what was left of it, for the boy who had grown up to become his King.

In memory, he stood again on the hill overlooking his village. He saw again the fire rolling into the sky, felt again the concussion of the conflagration, and saw once more the smoking remains of all his friends and family.

"I cannot redeem myself," he said to his reflection. "And I no longer own my life. I belong to those I killed and those I made to suffer. But since they are no longer here for me to answer, I shall answer to my King who stands in their stead. And I shall do so gladly."

To Finn, nothing could ever be as truthful, as inviolable, or as unambiguous as that sincere oath. As soon as the words were out of his mouth, the oddest sensation settled upon him. If one can feel a kind and forgiving smile when seen upon a sincere face, that is the sensation that he felt. The feeling came like a spirit out of the past, through the darkness, through Griferis itself, and it enveloped Finn within its earnest resolve.

Finn wondered about the men and women who had recently arrived. Though the Judges of Griferis were all gone away, the occupants of that castle, so it seemed, would continue to be tried in their hearts, forged and shaped and weighed for worthiness. Many would pass through this place of trials. Some to rule the world. Some to rule their passions. And a very few to neither rule nor be ruled, serving their faith and hope by giving their service to others. And if any could know the truth of Griferis, they would know it to be, as a place of trial, like all other places in the world. Like the Name of the Unknown King, the answer does not come from knowing the Name of the King, but from knowing your own name, whatever it may happen to be. Likewise, the first step to achieve worthiness is in knowing that you must achieve it, wherever you may happen to be. For some, it is in the trackless dusts of the Dragonlands, or on the long snowy path to Duinnor. And for some, it may be nearby to the Bentwide, in a lonely store, emptied of its little treasures and of its purpose. For others, Finn thought, it is in a place called Griferis.

Finn sighed as he pondered all this. For most, he thought, the true place of trial is within the airy castle of the heart, with its walls surrounding, with its lofty towers, its countless doors, and the abiding mystery of its existence. Back to that place—from the trials of their life, whether quiet and peaceful, or violent and injurious—all tried hearts are drawn. And it is within that place, the Griferis of the soul, that change might be wrought. Finn, at least, in this quiet moment, felt it to be so. And, he hoped, it was true also of the person he was to visit this very night.

• • •

Near the northern shoulders of the Carthane Mountains skirted the River Osterflo, winding around the base of the mountains that stretched their arms down as if to dip into its strong currents. The river lazed widely through snowy valleys only to constrict its course with churning furor through narrow defiles overlooked by precarious cliffs. In one long stretch of nearly fifty miles near the region of Karthia, it raced through a boulder-strewn channel, pouring over shoals and down dozens of waterfalls before settling to a more sedate pace as it flowed onward to Salfin Bay and past Glareth by the Sea. It was at the Karthian Rapids that the Fifth Unknown King ordered the construction of canals around those deadly waters. It was the greatest, most ambitious building project the world had ever known, spanning more than a hundred miles, with sixteen separate locks for raising and lowering boats coming and going between Glareth and Duinnor. But the Unknown King who had ordered it done would not see it completed, and it would be the Sixth Unknown King who reaped the glory of its completion some forty-two years after construction began.

As wondrous as the Locks of Karthia were, important to trade and travel, the Osterflo itself was a long and mighty river, stretching more than two thousand miles from the west to the eastern sea. Going west, against the mighty current, was arduous enough for the savvy boatmen who made their living on the river. Though the Locks of Karthia made it possible for a boat to make the passage the entire way between Glareth and Duinnor Realms, it was still a long and difficult trek. East of Karthia, the river was wide and calm enough to permit the use of sails to propel boats along, even against the current. However, traveling west from Karthia, teams of horses and oxen were required to lug boats upstream. In between, the west and east sections of river, the Karthian Locks made passage easy.

Just east of Karthia, along a calm stretch of river, many travelers made camps or stayed at one of the numerous inns along the banks of the Osterflo. In one of the nicer of these places, called the Floating Bottle, Queen Serith Ellyn and her party of Vanarans were the exclusive guests. Thurdun carefully set his watches and prepared to make the rounds himself all night long while his sister retired to bed. In the morning, their new boats would be ready, ones better suited for upstream travel, and they would begin the first leg of the canal passage. But Thurdun, who oversaw nearly every aspect of the Queen's safety, was not happy with their progress. He wished the boats were faster, the current against them less swift, and he hoped that they could avoid any Kingsmen along the way. He petted Celefar, his buckmarl, and gave him a handful of dried apple bits to chew.

"Only a week or so more through the canals," he said. "Then we'll find good horses for our people and hie down across the plains as fast as you like. With good weather, and fair fortune, we'll be home in just over a month."

Celefar snorted, licking and nudging Thurdun's hand for more apple.

"I know, but too much is not good for you," Thurdun replied, glancing at the upstairs window, which went dark as he looked.

Serith Ellyn, too, wished for more speed. She sorely regretted being away from Vanara for so long, and was deeply disappointed that she could not bring herself to broach the matter of her Seven with Prince Carbane. He probably guessed that she did not come all that way merely to see how her people were doing, those who had sought new homes in Glareth after losing their lands in Vanara to Duinnor cheats and swindles. While she made a great show of seeing as many displaced Vanarans as possible, promising to each one that she would do all that she could to have their lands restored to them, she was certain Prince Carbane suspected some other purpose to her visit. But it was not until after they arrived and she saw how miserably homesick her people were that she resolved not to give up her Seven to Glareth's safekeeping. Whether it was pride, anger, or just selfishness, she never even hinted at the matter.

She had remained too long in Glareth. And then there came the persistent dreams, Lyrium's visions, and her own nagging doubts that plagued her. Relieved to be on her way home, she was still restless and worried. War had come, and she was far from Vanara. New powers moved in the world, and she was not certain they would bring good changes. But the weariness of travel and her own constantly fretting heart wore her down. She did not want to sleep, did not want to dream, yet it was all she could do to stay awake once nightfall came.

So she slept. And she dreamed. Her dreams were not pleasant, for the most part, but not all were nightmares. And a few were quite peaceful. This night, after some anxious visions of Dragonkind overrunning Linlally, she suddenly dreamed of springtime, when the blue morning glories blossomed against the mountainsides, and of solitary moonlit walks along paths paved with Peller's Carpet, glowing steadily to show the way. She came around a bend in the path, where Lady Moon illuminated a small clearing beside a waterfall. She was somewhat surprised to see someone there, an older white-haired gentleman in a plain black suit leaning against a walking stick, looking up at the sky. When he saw her approach, he smiled.

"Queen Serith Ellyn," he said, bowing low.

"Hello, sir," the Queen replied. "You take the moonlight as I do?"

"Why, yes, I suppose I do, Your Majesty. It is a beautiful evening. And a beautiful wood, too."

"One of my favorite places in all Vanara. May I ask your name, sir?"

"Why, yes, ma'am. I am Finn. I am quite honored to meet you."

Finn bowed again.

"I am pleased to make your acquaintance, sir. Tell me, do you come here often?"

"This is the very first time ever, ma'am."

"And how did you come to be here tonight?"

"How? Well, that is not so easy to explain. But I came to have a word or a few with you, at the request of my lord and King, Philawain."

"King? Philawain? I have never heard of him."

"Few have, Queen. He is lord and master of a new kingdom called Griferis."

Serith Ellyn felt her heart jump a beat, and her breathing quickened.

"I know that place," she said.

"I know that you do," replied Finn calmly. "The old Judges of that place are gone, and a new judge sits in their place. Philawain, King. And he sends me to speak with you in this manner."

"Was Griferis overthrown?"

"Yes and no, Queen. It was overthrown, but it is better to say that it was inherited by he who suffered its trials for many years, by he who was judged and surpassed all others who went before him. By he who has learned the Name of the King. Philawain is that name, he who is King of Griferis, and who shall also in time become King of Duinnor."

Serith Ellyn felt dizzy. The dream had quickly become too perplexing, and it filled her with disquiet. She was surprised that she knew she was dreaming. She turned away from Finn, and watched the moonlight dance along the bouncing waterfall. It was still strangely peaceful, a paradoxical setting in spite of her darkening mood.

"What has your King Philawain instructed you to say to me?" she heard herself asking as she turned back to Finn.

"He has given me no instruction on what to say to you," Finn shrugged. "He merely wishes that I put his request to you again, in my own words and in my own way."

"His request? Again?"

"He told me that he has several times tried to persuade you to give over your Seven to him."

"That was he?"

"Yes. But he said that you were—pardon me for saying this—that you were quite resistant to the notion."

"Resistant? I would say that I absolutely refuse to believe that he, that anyone, would have the audacity to suggest such a thing! If he knows anything about the Forty-Nine, he should know their value. The Seven entrusted to me are symbols of my rule, to speak nothing of their other importance. Without them, I would be shamed before my people, just as Queen Therona was in the First Age when her Seven were lost. Like her, I would hardly be able to maintain my reign for very long without my Seven."

"Queen Serith Ellyn, my King knows their value. And he thinks that he may do with them what your people have not been able to do since they were given to the Seven High Houses of the Elifaen. And thus, he believes, he may release the Elifaen from their torment."

"He does, does he? How may he do that, I wonder? Does he know their secret, how they are to be used to open Heaven's Rainbow?"

"He does, madam," Finn responded calmly, still smiling, in spite of her tone.

"And with at the very most only forty-two of the Forty-Nine still in existence, how might he do that?"

"Queen, if you give yours over to him, he shall have all of the Forty-Nine."

Serith Ellyn stared at Finn in disbelief.

"That I cannot believe."

"He offers a way for you to know the truth for yourself. But he wishes for you to decide before the evidence is given to you."

"Why? I say prove it first, then I may change my mind. May."

"Queen, I remind you that he has not instructed me on what to say," Finn went on. "So I say to you now that which I believe, for I know my King better than any, perhaps. I know and have seen his power. I know his strength and his determination. I say this to you: He shall be the King of Kings, overlord of all the Seven Realms. And he shall add to his domain new realms and new lands and new peoples. All rulers will bow down to him and serve his throne. Those who refuse will bring suffering to their lands and to their people, not by his hand of might but by withholding his hand of mercy. Already the kings and queens, the princes and princesses of other lands prepare to swear their allegiance to him, and they do his bidding willingly. He gives each a test, and he shall reward their risk. This then is yours: Decide first if you will give over your Seven. But know this, Queen of Vanara: he asks only for that which he already has the power to take. You cannot hide the Seven from him. Give them to him willingly, I implore you, or have them taken from you, and much more besides. Those are my words, not his."

"Do you threaten me? How dare you speak to the Queen in that manner!"

"You threaten yourself, Queen, not I. And not Philawain. He holds you in high regard and esteem. But he also holds the key to your fate, and to the fate of your people."

Serith Ellyn was shaking her head and was about to speak, but Finn held his hand up.

"Queen, I beg you say no more. Philawain, King, gives you time to consider. He knows that you have many doubts, and that your heart is troubled. He prepares signs and omens to give to you. Watch for the first of his signs. It will appear in the form of a great sword hanging in the eastern heavens before dawn on the next moonless night. Each night thereafter, more signs will be given you. On the seventh night, the heavenly sword will pass out of sight and be seen no more. That night, Philawain himself will come to hear your decision. On the next moonless night, look to the east for the first sign. Remember my words. I bid you good night, Your Highness."

Finn bowed, then walked away. Serith Ellyn watched as a slit of light opened like a curtain briefly parted. Finn slipped through it and was gone.

Chapter 23

The Prisoner of Elmwood Castle

Day 205
40 Days Remaining

"Perhaps we should stop in the village to ask after any news about yer people," suggested Eldwin. He stood on a rise overlooking Averstone, not far from Esildre's castle.

"No. These people never cared for me," she whispered as she wavered nearby, a misty form in the bright noonday sun. "I doubt if they would have kind words."

"Kind words or harsh," Eldwin shrugged, "news would be news."

"No. Please, Eldwin, let us go on."

So he popped quickly through the village without being seen, stopping only long enough at a fork in the path for Esildre to point the way. The way soon descended, twisting and turning down through the mountains, and it became slick with ice and snow. Eldwin's jumps grew shorter and shorter, owing to his unsure footing and the steepness of the path. Sooner than he expected, he was looking across a mountain lake, crusted with sheets of ice, and in the midst of it rose up Elmwood Castle, dark-walled with grime and clinging ivy, gloomy and forbidding. No banner flew from its turrets, and the only sign of life was a thin trail of smoke rising from somewhere within it. Just ahead, though, he saw a little hut near the shore where a small barge was moored. A man sat on a stool in front of the hut with a staff across his knees.

"I see no way across, save for the boat," Eldwin said.

"It is the only way," replied Esildre. "Ask the ferryman to take you across. Beware that he may swing at you with his staff, to know if you can see or not. Those with sight have not been welcomed here for many years."

Eldwin walked down the path to the old man who stood when he heard the crunching footsteps.

"Who goes?"

"Eldwin, friend of Lady Esildre."

"If ye bring messages, ye may leave them with me."

"I come to look upon Esildre's servants, to know their condition, if they be well or not. So I ask that ye take me across, please sir."

Now the old man swung his staff, but Eldwin ducked as it swept over his head. Snapping his fingers, Eldwin then popped around to the other side of the man.

"I can see, if that's yer test," he said.

The man jerked around, bending his head to get a sense of Eldwin's new position and distance, and steadied his staff once more.

"Uncommon quick, ye are," said the ferryman, "an' rather short, I think."

"I am both, so save yer staff for someone worthier," Eldwin said. "Will ye take me across, or must I pull meself along?"

"The lady ain't home."

"I know."

"An' I ain't to take any across without fair reason to do so," said the ferryman. "If ye've a mind to pull, go ahead an' try. But ye'll spend a day untying me knots, I'll warrant."

"I mean to go an' see her people," said Eldwin, "an' I have a knife that'll cut through yer knots. So if ye don't wish for me to make a mess of yer boat, come an' take me along."

"*Take him*," breathed a cold voice into the ferryman's ear.

"Oh, oh!" he cried, shivering. "Me lady! I did not hear ye approach!"

"Let us go," said Eldwin, stepping aboard the barge.

The ferryman hesitated, his head tilted.

"Does me lady wish to step aboard, too?" he asked.

"She is already here," said Eldwin.

Skeptical, the ferryman came along, tapping his way with his staff. After untying his intricate knots, he began to pull the barge across. He worked slowly, but with steady strength, and the only noise of their passing was the bump of floating ice and the gurgle of water. The ferryman remained silent to his work until they were about halfway across.

"I well know me own craft," he said as he gripped the line for another pull. "I know its weight an' its speed by me pull, an' I can judge right well the size an' number of me passengers."

"I am small," said Eldwin.

"That I know," said the ferryman. "But yer also alone. Why did not Lady Esildre come aboard as ye said she had?"

"She is here," said Eldwin, "insomuch as she can be."

The ferryman shook his head and wagged his finger toward Eldwin.

"I think ye play with an old blind man," he said. "It is an unkind thing to do."

"I do not play with ye."

"*He does not play with you.*"

The ferryman gripped his line with both hands to steady himself, so shaken he was by Esildre's ghostly voice.

"I know that voice, but it cannot be," he said, "or else I no longer know me trade."

"I told ye we'd have to tell them," Eldwin said to Esildre. The ferryman heard this, and having stopped his pulling altogether, he listened as if his life depended upon it. But before he could speak, Eldwin came to him and put his own hands on the line.

"I shall help ye," he said. "Let us pull together."

The ferryman gulped, but permitted Eldwin to help, and together they pulled.

"How many live in the castle?" asked Eldwin.

"I reckon about five of us. No, six. I only come in when the weather's too cold to bear."

"All servants?"

"No. No, only five servants, an' meself. Thar's a guest of a rather permanent nature, though," said the ferryman. "Addled in the head, don't ye know, an' too pitiful to be let out."

"Oh?"

"Aye, me lord. Lady Esildre, fearin' to turn him loose, has him fed an' taken care of, when he's in the mood for washin', an' eatin', an' so forth. Been here for years an' years. Well afore I came along, an' I've been here a long time."

"Addled? How did that come about?"

As soon as the question was out of his mouth, Eldwin wished he could have taken it back. He remembered what Raynor told him about the single prisoner that Esildre kept, an Elifaen made insane by his desire for her.

"Well, um, that ain't for me to say. But for years, the gent would scream an' rant most fearfully, day an' night. We feared great violence if he was to be let out, er if he broke out. All that changed, fairly recently, though. Now, an' for the past three weeks er so, he just whimpers an' weeps an' sniffles most pitiful-like."

The barge bumped and cracked against the icy landing. There to meet them was Esildre's blind lady's maid.

"We've company," said the ferryman, somehow knowing she was there. "This gent says he's a friend of the lady an' wishes to look upon the place, an' see how things are."

Eldwin stepped up onto the landing, and bowed.

"I am Eldwin, a friend to Lady Esildre," he said. He knew, from his conversations with Esildre and Raynor, that all her servants were blind. Still, he felt awkward when she looked in his direction and curtseyed.

"How do you do? I am Hazel, Lady Esildre's maid. What may I do for you?"

"Well, ma'am, I've come to see what, if anything, I might do for ye."

"Whatever do you mean? I think we require nothing, and wish for nothing, other than our lady's safe return."

Eldwin hesitated, pulling his cap off and passing his hand through his thinning hair. He considered his next words carefully.

"Tell them."

"I am afraid that I have dire news," said Eldwin. "Perhaps all the servants can be gathered to hear it."

Hazel turned toward the open door behind her and then said, "I think we are all here."

Indeed, two elderly gentlemen and two ladies stepped out of the gloomy interior of the castle, apparently having waited just within earshot.

"We are all here," said one of the men.

Eldwin looked at the small group, remembering how fondly Esildre had talked of them, and how loyal to her they were.

"Lady Esildre is dead," he said. A whimpering moan came from Esildre, barely audible over the light breeze past Eldwin's ears. Hazel sat on the icy stones of the landing. The other women gasped and clutched each other's hands. The men's faces turned ashen.

"I am very sorry to bring ye this news," Eldwin went on. "I know her. That is, I knew her, from many, many years ago," he stopped, swallowing hard, seeing how distraught they were. "She died some weeks ago, in the east. At a place called Tallinvale."

Reaching down to Hazel, he gave her his hand.

"Come. The ground is far too cold for ye to sit upon it," he said. She gripped his hand but, silent until now, she began to weep, and for a few moments she had not the strength to stand. Only Eldwin's continued gentle urging got her up.

"This way, if you please, sir," said one of the men, motioning inside.

• • •

Except for the ferryman, who preferred to ponder the news while sitting on his barge, they all went inside and sat at the kitchen table near to the iron stove that kept the room warm. A hot cup of tea was put before Eldwin.

"Thank ye," said Eldwin.

"My name is Lyle," the man said.

"And I am his wife, Dora," said the woman sitting across from Eldwin.

"I am Garson, and this is my wife, Kate," said the other man who sat at the end of the table. He held his wife's hand firmly, as she daubed her eyes with the corner of her apron.

"Ye've all been with Lady Esildre a long time, then?"

"Yes," said Hazel who sat next to Eldwin. "A long, long time."

"There used to be more of us," said Kate. "But old age has taken many. My parents brought me here when I was a tiny thing."

"She's a relative newcomer," said Garson.

"My parents brought me here, too," said Lyle, "when they became too elderly to look after me any longer. But I was in my twenties. I suppose that was, oh, fifty years ago?"

"I came with Hazel," said Dora, "and we were the first of Lady Esildre's blind servants. You wonder, I'm sure. But I am Elifaen, having been scathed very late in life. My body does not age any longer, but my eyes could never see."

"Dora and I met in Vanara," said Hazel. "I am Elifaen, too. I was wounded at the Battle of Saerdulin, if you know of it. In fact, that is where I first met Esildre, though only in passing. I lost my sight there when struck by an arrow. It was after that wound that I was Scathed, so my eyes never healed."

She reached up and touched the top of each cheek with her fingers.

"The scars where it went through are almost gone," she said, "but my eyes have not healed. I was taken back to Vanara, and there I recovered. I met Dora at a home for blind people. A long time later, Esildre came there to ask for servants. We were afraid, at first."

"She had been in Shatuum, you see, which was bad enough," put in Dora. "Besides, who would want blind servants except those who might wish to take advantage of them?"

"But we wished to be useful," continued Hazel, "and not waste away in idleness due to our blindness. So Dora and I came here with Lady Esildre. It wasn't very pleasant for many, many years."

"Ye needn't tell me about it," said Eldwin. "I know about Esildre's curse, an' how she made this place a den of lechery."

Hazel nodded and fell silent as Eldwin sipped his tea.

"But things changed," said Lyle.

"Yes, I know. Raynor of Duinnor told me much."

"Raynor? You know Raynor?" asked Garson. "How is my old friend? Why I owe it to him that I found employment here."

"He seems quite well," said Eldwin. He put down his cup and looked around the room. Esildre had been present, earlier, floating about the kitchen in a rather anxious manner, but if she was now about, he could not see her.

"What will ye do?" he asked the group.

"I don't know what we can do but leave," said Dora. "I suppose Lady Esildre's father will take back the castle, now, and put us out. But I don't know where we can go."

"No, Lord Banis is dead," Eldwin said bluntly. "So there's no fear on that account."

"Dead?" asked Lyle.

"Yes. He leapt to his death, so I was told."

"Oh!" said Kate.

"Good!" said Hazel. "It was on his account that Esildre was made to suffer so! He made her go to Shatuum, and abandoned her without a care when she managed to get out from that place. I only wish I had been there to help him jump!"

"Hear, hear!" said Garson.

"But how do ye all manage without sight?" asked Eldwin. "I mean, there must be tasks that are beyond yer abilities."

"Yes. Plenty of them," said Kate. "Lady Esildre made special arrangements for regularly needed things, like fuel for the fireplaces and stoves, repairs to roofs, and the like. There's a man in Averstone that she'd hire, and he'd bring his own people to do the work. Occasionally, she'd send one of us up there with messages and such. We all know the way pretty well."

"And the same for food and the like," said Hazel. "All delivered to the ferryman."

"Lady Esildre's quite wealthy, though you might not think it," said Garson. "A Post Rider goes through Averstone every month or so, and so by messages she often sends away for things. That is, she used to. About twice a year, wagons come with new supplies, wine and beer, salt, cloth, and other things that were needed or desired."

"We are well set for several months yet," said Dora. "But when spring comes, I don't know."

"We never feared any from bandits or the like," said Lyle. "Lady Esildre was most capable of taking care of them, and of watching out for us. That's my worry, now."

"Well, I don't think very many nearby people know that she's away," said Hazel. "But do many know that she's dead?"

"Thousands may know, back in Tallinvale," shrugged Eldwin. "Her great-nephews know. An' a few people I told in Duinnor. Word is bound to spread, though."

"We must think hard on what we should do," said Kate.

Esildre floated back into the room, and Eldwin watched her as she moved around the table, a pale, bluish form. She now appeared to be wearing a gauzy gown, and though her eyes were hollow and dark, Eldwin was somewhat shocked at her beauty, and embarrassed for staring. Kate shivered, distracting Eldwin, and he looked over at Garson, who was rubbing down the hairs standing up on his arm.

"It is most peculiar," said Hazel, "that, since you have arrived, I keep thinking that I smell Lady Esildre's perfume."

"Do you smell it, too?" asked Lyle.

"I thought it was just my imagination," said Garson.

Dora just nodded, and Eldwin sniffed.

"I do think I smell a pleasant aroma," he said. "Oh! What about yer guest? The one kept here? What's to be done about him?"

"Vaspar? Now that is a question," said Lyle. "He has acted most peculiar lately, even for him. About three weeks, did you say? It was about then that his demeanor completely changed. I would tell you his story, but it is too shocking. Suffice it to say that he refused to leave this place, and was even thrown out. But he swam back, nearly dying of cold, only to pester and fawn after Lady Esildre. When she rebuked him, he became most agitated, throwing over tables, raving and foaming, even. She threw him out again, but again he came back. Finally, she locked him away, where he has been ever since. That was, let's see, was it two hundred years ago?"

"It's been a little longer than that, I think," said Hazel.

"Most days," Lyle went on, "Vaspar is incapable of dressing or feeding himself properly. While on some days, he seems perfectly calm between fits of hysterical laughter or crying without cause. Until three weeks ago, he would laugh and scream any time he thought Esildre might hear him, begging her to come to him. Then, about three weeks ago, his rants completely ended! He wept uncontrollably for an entire week. Since then, he has hardly uttered a word, and has not carried on at all."

"It is as if he somehow knew," said Dora. "Knew she was dead, I mean."

"He is Elifaen, then," said Eldwin.

"Oh, yes," nodded Garson. "He attended one of the last feasts that Esildre threw before, well, before she changed."

"What are we to do with him?" asked Kate.

"I don't know the man, of course," said Eldwin. "Nor do I mean to tell ye yer own business. But I think ye should let him go."

The servants became quiet, wearing somewhat startled expressions.

"It seems a cruel thing to keep him locked up if he can do no one harm," Eldwin added.

"He may do himself harm, though," said Garson. "He has, on many occasions, cut and wounded himself, perhaps thinking to get Esildre's attention that way. Or maybe just out of madness."

"He should at least be told that she is dead," said Hazel, nodding, "though he might not understand it. I sometimes think he does not understand a word we say. But, Eldwin is right. We should tell him."

"I am willin' to tell him," said Eldwin, "if ye fear to face him."

"Oh, he has never threatened to harm us. Unless throwing his soup at us counts as a threat," said Lyle.

"That was only once," said Dora. "And it wasn't very good soup."

• • •

They led Eldwin through the castle and up a flight of stairs to a bolted door. It appeared very much like what Eldwin imagined a prison door might look like. There was a slot at the bottom, for delivering food, and a little barred window for peering through, if only there was someone with eyes to look. Eldwin surmised that it was made before there were blind servants to wait upon the door.

"Are you sure?" Garson asked. "We can tell him through the door."

"No," said Eldwin. "I'm not sure, but such things are best done face to face, I think. I can take care of meself. Just open the door. I'll tell ye when I'm through it, an' ye can close it behind me an' listen."

Eldwin did not know what to expect. As Lyle pulled on the bar to open the door, he steeled himself, putting his hand on his dagger hilt and forming his other fingers, ready to snap.

The door groaned open, and Eldwin passed quickly through

"I am in," he said, and Lyle closed the door. Eldwin heard the bar put back into place as he looked around.

It was not like a cell at all, but a well-appointed room. There was a stove set into the wall, one that could be fed from the next room, a fair bed with good blankets and quilts, a table and chair, and a washroom off to one side, complete with an iron handpump for water. The only real clue that it was a prison were the heavy bars on the windows. The shutters were open, and there was more than enough light streaming in to see its occupant, sitting on the floor with his back against the far wall. He was unkempt, in tattered robes and leggings, though a nice set hung on a peg nearby. His hair was blond, long and tangled around his chin, and as Eldwin watched him, he slowly looked up with piercing blue eyes.

"You are different," Vaspar said. He then got to his feet and shuffled over to the window to glance out before turning back to Eldwin.

"It is still winter," he said. "Have you come to let me out?"

"If that is what ye wish," said Eldwin.

"What I wish? What I wish. What do I wish? I wish I knew why I behaved the way I did. I wish I had some recollection of peace. But all I can remember is shame and…and…desire. If you can call it that. I wish I had never come here. I wish I had never laid eyes on this place or its mistress."

Vaspar's words trailed off, and he looked aside as if trying to remember something.

"I have news concernin' Esildre," Eldwin said, sensing her presence beside him.

"She did not love me," Vaspar said. "And I did not love her, either."

"I know."

"Have I come to my senses?" Vaspar suddenly asked Eldwin. "What has happened?"

"She is dead."

Eldwin saw Esildre float toward Vaspar and reach out as if in pity. She let out a long terrible moan that sent Vaspar staggering sideways against the table, upsetting the unlit candlestick upon it. He looked around, but he could not see her.

"It was not entirely her fault," said Eldwin calmly, in spite of his own shivers at her outburst. "I believe her curse was made to be shared. But it was broken."

"Broken? By her dying, you mean."

"No. Not by dyin'. By something else. By someone else."

"So that was it," Vaspar said, his eyes lighting up as if a great thing dawned upon him. "This past fortnight, or more, I've tried to remember. I've tried to think what it was that kept me coming back after she cast me out. What the madness was that…"

He stopped abruptly, now looking at Eldwin with watery eyes.

"Although I desired her, with a desire that I could not control, it was folly. I remember, now. And, knowing it was folly, I was made a lunatic. I could not love her, and she could not love me, and that is what she most needed. It is what I needed, too. Just to be loved. I know it sounds silly and stupid. I haven't the right words."

"I do not think such a thing is silly," said Eldwin.

"What year is it?"

"It is the eight hundred an' seventy-first year of the Second Age," said Eldwin. "By Duinnor's way of reckonin', it is still the Year of the Red Door."

"That long? I've been here that long?"

"However long, I think it is time for ye to go," said Eldwin. "Since she is dead, her servants can hardly take care of ye, havin' themselves to look to."

Vaspar nodded.

"I see. I understand. I have been a terrible burden on them. They have done nothing but treat me with kindness, while I raved at them and perhaps said and did awful things."

"So, anyway, yer free to go, now."

"Free to go."

Eldwin turned and knocked on the door, and it was opened. Turning back to Vaspar, he said, "So ye ought to put on yer cloak yonder. It's cold out."

"Yes," Vaspar said, slowly pulling his cloak from the peg. He examined it and then pulled it over his shoulders as Eldwin stood aside.

"Are they still about? Hazel and the others?"

"Yes."

"I do not wish for them to look upon me," said Vaspar. "I cannot bear the shame of it after all that I have done. No. Wait. I must face them. If for no other reason so that they may watch me leave, and so know that I will burden them no more."

"Do ye not know, then, that they are incapable of lookin' at ye with disdain?" said Eldwin. "Or at all, since they are all blind, every one of them?"

Vaspar stared at Eldwin in disbelief.

"No! How can that be?"

"It is so. They are blind."

"Blind?"

"Yes."

"Oh, what a wretched fellow I am! Such was my madness. I never knew. All's the worse, my behavior."

Vaspar tentatively stepped through the door and into the corridor where the servants waited. He looked at them as if he had never seen them before, which, with sane eyes, perhaps he had not.

"I do not know the way out," he said meekly.

"This way," said Garson. Vaspar followed him, and the rest came along behind until they emerged outside at the landing. Vaspar looked at the sky for a long time, then at the lake and the mountains, smiling painfully.

Suddenly he turned back and knelt before Hazel, grasping at her hands. She recoiled, pulling away from him and backing into Lyle.

"I beg your forgiveness!" he cried, putting his hands down on the stones and lowering his head. "And I thank you all for your longsuffering care of me. Do I not now know my madness, my wickedness? Do I not recall every insult and every rant? What may I offer as token of my remorse? I know that you loved your lady, and that she is lost to you. I know that you looked after me as faithful servants to her, doing her honor. Never did you speak a single harsh word to me. Although my years of depravity are like a drunken, confused memory, I know that you treated me better than I would have if I had been you. Let me serve you, I beg, as you have served me! Allow me to wait upon you with meals. Give me wash to do, or hard work to accomplish! But do not send me away without first saying what I may do."

Vaspar's words of entreaty surprised Eldwin as much as the rest who heard them. Even the ferryman, patiently waiting on his boat, seemed confused by the outburst. Hazel slowly stepped forward. Reaching out her hand, she found and touched Vaspar's head. She crouched, and as he looked at her, she put her hands on his face, feeling with her fingertips his brow and the contours of his cheekbones, the curve of his nose and the outline of his lips. Then she cupped his face in her hands.

"You owe us nothing, sir," she said. "And we would have done better for you had we known how, or had we the strength to do so."

Vaspar gazed back at her, puzzled.

Lyle, with his keen hearing, bent to get a sense of Vaspar's posture, and that of Hazel, and he carefully approached.

"Rise up, sir," said Lyle, coming to him and finding his shoulder and taking his arm. "It is not seemly for a lord such as yourself to implore us so."

Shaking his head, Vaspar stood, his eyes watery, his shoulders slumped, glancing at Eldwin questioningly.

"I think, if ye are determined to be of service to these good people," said Eldwin, "that ye should offer them yer protection."

"It would be the least I could do, and not even a beginning to my debt," said Vaspar. "I was once a warrior of some ability, if that is the sort of protection I may provide. And, if you would have it, I shall purchase this estate from Lord Banis so that it can remain your home, should it seem suitable to do so."

"Banis is dead," said Eldwin.

"Then you who have served Esildre so faithfully shall occupy it as your own," said Vaspar, "until it may rightly be made yours by the laws of this Realm."

A slight movement caught the corner of Eldwin's eye, and he saw Esildre standing on the barge. Her hands were clasped in front of her, and though her insignificant outline was dim and her head was bowed, he saw that she was smiling.

Eldwin put on his cap and stepped onto the barge.

"I think I'll be on me way, then," he said. "I bid ye good fortune, good luck, an' farewell."

"Where do you go?" cried Hazel.

"I've business to attend," replied Eldwin. "Pull on, ferryman."

Chapter 24

The Oracle and the Witch

Day 207
38 Days Remaining

The same monk who had greeted Ashlord and his friends on the day when they arrived at the Temple of Beras now returned to that place, having turned over the care of the new shelter for the poor and needy to another of his Order. It was a long walk from the city, one that he was accustomed to, and he filled the time, as was his way, in contemplation. The year had been a busy one, full of strange happenings and signs. A fair number of visitors had come to the Temple, seeking refuge or shelter, or, in the case of a few, on other more mysterious business. Yet, as unsettling as the world outside was, peace and routine prevailed within the Temple, just as it had for over six hundred years. Six Kings of Duinnor had emerged during that time, and five times a new star settled into its place over the city as each new King replaced the one before. This monk, who was too young to remember the last time that had happened, knew from his studies and meditations all the history of the Temple. Because he was one of the few of his Order, doing the Oracle's bidding and understanding better than most the Oracle's nature, he knew that soon the Temple would once more, and for the final time, be called upon to anoint a New King. What would then become of the Oracle and the Temple was something this monk often meditated on, just as he did today, although he was not overly concerned.

"Beras will provide," was his mantra and his faith. As he trudged up the long flight of steps to the Temple, he was content with the work that he and his brothers had accomplished in the new shelter for the homeless and destitute. And he was happy that he would return to the Temple in time for his private meditation hour, a time he preferred to spend in his quiet cell.

He entered the Temple, bowing briefly toward the front of the sanctuary, and bowed again toward the chair near the brazier off to the side where the Oracle often sat. The Oracle was not there at the moment, but it was a gesture of respect to bow, and to say a prayer for the continued enlightenment of Beras. He turned and walked along the long corridors until he came to his own cell. There, he carefully removed and folded his outer cloak and put it onto the floor, then removed his sandals and placed them nearby. He bowed to each of the four directions, then settled onto his mat on the floor, his room not having even a cot, and crossed his legs to ponder, to meditate, and to clear his mind of all distractions. This he did quickly, from many years of practice and discipline, and he allowed the vibrations of the cosmos to move his spirit. All was peace. All was harmony. All was order.

Suddenly he stood. Not bothering to put on his sandals, he hurried out from his cell and along the cold floor of the hallway to the library just down the corridor. There he took up an inkwell, a quill, a writing board, and a handful of writing paper. He hurried back out into the hall, joining with several other monks who shuffled along with their hands folded in front of them as they went quickly to the sanctuary. While the other monks continued to enter and sit upon their prayer rugs, he went with his things to the front of the sanctuary where the Oracle was now pacing. Quickly sitting and arranging the inkwell on the floor, he dipped a quill and tapped it. As soon as he put the nib to paper, the Oracle cried out.

"Hear ye and give heed to the will of the King. Give now thy name before the King and hear his will!"

The Oracle paused, crouched, his head bent to the side.

"Shannon Weatherly, of Giyth in Glareth Realm!" the Oracle then cried out. "Shannon Weatherly, of Giyth in Glareth Realm, I appoint and commission thee to watch over the people of Greenfar. Do ye accept this office? I do, my lord."

In a quick but neat hand, the monk copied what the Oracle said.

"Harrald Delorick, of Whitefall in Duinnor Realm!" cried out the Oracle, pacing in front of the glass pyramid. "Harrald Delorick, of Whitefall in Duinnor Realm, I appoint and commission thee to watch over the people of Tallinvale. Do ye accept this office? I do, my lord. Tomas Oarsman, of Sorghwall. Tomas Oarsman, of Sorghwall, I appoint and commission thee to watch over the Dragonland town of Almedian. Do ye accept this office? I do, my lord. Ivana, of the Vanaran House of Starvine. Ivana, of the Vanaran House of Starvine, I appoint and commission thee to watch over the people of Nowhere. Do ye accept this office? I do, my lord."

The monk wrote, and the Oracle paced wildly, sometimes turning abruptly as if looking for something, sometimes twisting around, as if listening before proclaiming further. The other monks, chanting softly their mantras and prayers, may have wondered at the strange utterances, and at the many changes in the Oracle over the past fortnight. Though he was washed and clean, he now raved as madly as ever he did, almost desperately calling out names and places. They gave their prayers for him, for Beras to give him strength and to bless him with insight. They needed not understanding, nor did they desire knowledge concerning how the monk knew to take up quill and ink and to write down these things, though never had they seen him do so. It was important, they instinctively knew, for the monk to do this, and while they prayed silently for their Oracle, they prayed, too, for their brother so that he could keep apace with the Oracle's words.

For an hour, they prayed and watched and listened. One amongst them rose to his feet and hurried away, returning almost as fast as he could walk with more paper, giving it to the writing monk just as his last sheet was filled. Another monk came hurrying along and replaced the now empty inkwell with a fresh one as the Oracle continue to pronounce names and places. For his part, the writing monk was too busy recording what the Oracle said to wonder at the strange utterances, or at the repetitious nature of them. He dipped and wrote, dipped and wrote.

"Sally Bodwin, of Hill Town in the Old Eastlands Realm! Sally Bodwin, of Hill Town in the Old Eastlands Realm, I appoint and commission thee to watch over Prince Carbane of Glareth. Do ye accept this office? I do, me lord. Braddus Makesail, of Draymoor in Altoria! Braddus Makesail, of Draymoor in Altoria, I appoint and commission thee to be messenger, and to go whither I, thy King, may send thee, to say and to impart that which thou art told, and to repeat and to impart to thy King or his servants whatsoever is told thee, according to the wishes of thy King. Do ye accept this office? I do, my lord."

• • •

Several hundred miles away from the Temple of Beras, a similar scene was unfolding in Nasakeeria, at a place called Moon's Henge.

"Jarvin Tidewater, of Chiselpeck in Glareth Realm!" cried out Traveshia, her mouth foaming with spittle. "Jarvin Tidewater, of Chiselpeck in Glareth Realm, I appoint and commission thee to be messenger, and to go whither I, thy King, may send thee, to say and to impart that which thou art told, and to repeat and to impart to thy King or his servants whatsoever is told thee, according to the wishes of thy King. Do ye accept this office? I do, my lord."

Prince Nightar paced back and forth in front of the brazier, his arms crossed, his face etched with worry. For an hour without pause, the old woman raved, crying out names and places and other statements of an odd and perplexing nature. While she did so, Seleesa wrote furiously with brush and ink upon a long scroll of clean paper, her eyes closed, but her hand unerringly placing each stroke where it should be, dipping the brush quickly and efficiently as she went. Behind her stood the hunter, Aremon, fretting over Seleesa and as bewildered and worried as was Nightar and all of the others who had gathered within the circle of standing stones. Although Nightar paced nervously, he listened intently to every word uttered by Traveshia, every intonation and pause, and every gasp of breath that she made between phrases. It seemed to him, after some while of listening, that when she first spoke a name and a location it was different in tone and manner than when she repeated the name again and spoke the words of appointment and ordination. Realizing what this seemed to imply, he went to Seleesa and crouched to look at how she copied Traveshia's words. Indeed, as he saw, from the way Seleesa wrote the words and ordered the lines, it was as if one person said their name while another person repeated the name along with orders. Traveshia was dictating aloud what was being said at an important proceeding. It was more formal but similar to how Prince Nightar ordered his guards and gave them their assignments each month.

"But who does she hear?" Nightar whispered to himself as he stood once more and gazed at Traveshia. By now over a hundred names had been recorded by Seleesa, and the linen-paper that she brushed spread out in coils and folds before her. Nightar carefully took the end of the scroll and rolled it so that it would not flutter and tear in the breeze. Aremon knelt to remove a kink to allow Nightar to gather it, while Seleesa continued to brush ink, deftly dipping her brush and pulling the paper out from the roll on her lap to permit more space for writing.

"Talmadin, of the desert city of Calamandor, known also as the Green Citadel. Talmadin, of Calamandor, I appoint and commission thee to watch over the people of Forlandis in Tracia Realm. Do ye accept this office? I do, my lord."

"What does all this mean?" Aremon softly asked Nightar. "My lord, who are these people that Traveshia names? Why does she speak so? What king does she mean?"

"I cannot say, Aremon. I do not know the purpose of all this, much less the means by which Traveshia knows to say what she does."

"Lachlan Shurmarsh, of Glareth. Lachlan Shurmarsh, of Glareth, I appoint and commission thee to be messenger, and to go whither I, thy King, may send thee, to say and to impart that which thou art told, and to repeat and to impart to thy King or his servants whatsoever is told thee, according to the wishes of thy King. Do ye accept this office?"

Aremon was about to ask another question when Traveshia's routine abruptly changed. She stood upright, paused for a long moment, then said, "Do ye accept this office? No, my lord. I must refuse."

Nightar and Aremon looked at Traveshia who fell silent, as if in a swoon, rocking back and forth. Seleesa looked up, her brush poised. When Nightar approached Traveshia, she waved him away with her stick, and cupped a hand to her ear, listening, her eyes wild and bulging. During this long pause, in a realm that none present but Traveshia could see or sense, the mysterious proceedings also paused.

• • •

Robby severed the link of dream that bound his own to that of Traveshia and the Oracle. They fell silent, and waited, pacing back and forth with their heads tilted, as if listening carefully. Meanwhile, Robby turned to Lachlan Shurmarsh.

"Speak, then, and say why you refuse," said Robby.

"I do not know if you have the means to reach me or to punish me, my lord, though your power must be great. I accept your disdain, and I shall face your displeasure. But I must refuse. I am resolved that to look upon a person's deepest self, even in all its fantasy and confusion, is not proper. Yes, my lord, I have done it. But I have learned by what I have seen, and now I know better. I think perhaps that dreamwalking, for all that it might accomplish for good, may be a greater force for evil. To have the power to do something does not make it right, and I wonder if possessing this power of dreamwalking is not in and of itself an evil thing. Tell me, I beg you, how may temptation be resisted, on the whole, to toy and to play with others in such a manner? Sleep itself, our deepest repose in life, the schoolroom of our wisdom, is thus disturbed and is deprived of all, the dreamers and the dreamwalkers. Yet, knowing that our sweetest realm may be trespassed upon, even when it is not, must bring wary vigilance to every person. Who would not sink into miserable watchfulness, forever deprived of peace, suspicious of friend and neighbor and of every living person? Would you wish such a condition for your wife or children? Each one of us, my lord, is the king or queen of our own heart, and no other person may justly lay claim to the seat of that place. But by what arms may it be defended?"

For his part, Robby thought of the Ring of Hearing that he had refused from Lyrium, and the sword, too, that could have been his. Indeed, Lachlan's speech put Robby's own darkest reservations into words, concerns that he had pushed aside. Ashlord's admonishment, back when Robby had used his ability to coerce the ferryman to take them across the haunted lake, came sinking down upon his heart. Now, just as then, Robby felt rebuked by Lachlan, and, just as with Ashlord, Robby felt anger and embarrassment. For Robby knew that, like Ashlord, Lachlan was right.

He looked around at the many gathered in Griferis where he had brought them all together. Finn was there, and Micerea, and Sally Bodwin, too. They and all the others watched him, now, and waited for his response. He nodded.

"It is just as well that you all know that Lachlan Shurmarsh speaks truly. I commend him for speaking against what he views as improper. I may address him, but I speak to you all. It is as you say, Lachlan Shurmarsh. Dreamwalking is a dangerous power, permitting an invasion into the most private realm of a person's life. And it is not something that any of us should take lightly. Who may watch us to see that we do things rightly and respectfully? Who? Who but we here and others that we may enlist? I say that what we do is not a lark, and it is not an adventure. Dreamwalking is power, but it is the power of a tool. Language and writing and fire are such tools with great power. Swords and arrows, too. Who are we to possess such a tool, to wield such power? I will tell you: We are the first. Imagine the first person who harnessed and used fire. Imagine how this person may have made mistakes, may have been burned, or may even have injured others whilst trying to tame it. But imagine those people who received fire, their fear of the night lessened, and the killing cold of winter held at bay. They may have guarded it as a sacred thing, to protect and preserve its secrets. But who, now, does not have the use of fire? Who does not cook by its heat and read by its light? Like fire, we must guard this secret while knowing that others will discover this power, too."

Robby looked around at the gathering, and let them sense his determination.

"I tell you," he went on, "some will not be so inclined for peace as we are. Here, members of every realm, even the Dragonlands, stand together, Mortals and Elifaen, too. When may this ever happen again? Yes, Lachlan Shurmarsh, a great burden is upon us. But, seeing the flood coming, would you stand aside and let your neighbors drown? You know the flood comes. You have seen, through these sojourns, the armies arrayed in the field. You have seen your countrymen depart on ships that you yourself built and fitted for them. What would they say to you if they knew that you withheld your aid? How would you answer them? Yet they are ignorant of the greater threat, just as you are. Come, now, and look all of you upon the cauldron that is soon to spill forth!"

Robby guided them quickly, one by one, to Shatuum, into the very midst of that land. They saw the creatures there, busy at their smithies and furnaces. They witnessed together the torture and transformation of men into wraiths and beasts into monsters, and heard their tortured screams as man and beast alike painfully resisted. They saw an outbreak of violence, as hundreds of the bogles and wraiths and goblins of the place broke into a great slaughter of each other, and they saw the uprising quelled by the awful power of the captains of Shatuum with Throgallus at their head. Robby took them into the deep recesses of the caverns below Shatuum, and they saw witches and sorcerers binding spells upon weapons and conjuring fire from their spittle. Satisfied that the dreamwalkers had seen enough for now, Robby took them away and back to Griferis.

"With your own eyes, you have had a glimpse of what awaits the world. Secundur prepares for when our lands are at their weakest, torn apart by war. Think also of Vanara, long oppressed by Duinnor. Think of Tracia with her grievances against Glareth and Masurthia. Be mindful of the people of the Dragonlands, who have suffered ages of disease and war but are still strong and yearn for relief. The war that is upon us will rip apart the world and will set Realm against Realm. It is then that Secundur will unleash his legions. Who will face them? Will the Dragonkind render aid to Duinnor against them? Will Vanara stem Shatuum's tide from reaching Glareth?"

Robby walked about his dreaming guests until he came to Lachlan.

"What say you, Lachlan Shurmarsh? Will you help me?"

Lachlan looked at Robby, then at those gathered with him.

"I am not a man of faith, my lord," he said at last. "I do not easily trust new acquaintances. Indeed, what you have shown me is awful and wondrous, and I am deeply moved and disturbed by the horrors I have witnessed in Shatuum. But if, as you say, the world teeters, then how may we few prevent it? How may we put things right? How may dreams be properly used to such an end? How may so few, even with this power, turn the river of history? For the grievances you spoke of are as old as the world itself."

"Not so," answered Robby. "There was a time when all was right in the world, a time before time, when there was no suffering, no insult, and no need of vengeance or war."

"Do you speak of when the world was first made, my lord?"

"I do. And now it is come time for its remaking. Secundur senses it, and his will drives things along to make the new world his own. It is up to us, and to others who may help us, to drive things a different way."

"Then tell me how it is to be done, my lord," said Lachlan. "And then, truly I will call you King."

"I will do better than tell you," said Robby, smiling. "I will show you. But first, I insist that you give your name and receive your commission as the others have done, so that there is no discord among us."

And so Lachlan Shurmarsh repeated his name and the place of his home. Traveshia and the Oracle suddenly spoke again, repeating his words, whilst the monk and Seleesa copied. When Robby said to Lachlan his assignment and his commission, and asked if he accepted it, Lachlan said, and it was written, "I do, my lord!"

• • •

Thus ended the proceedings of the evening, and Traveshia sat down heavily as Nightar rushed to her. The Oracle walked over to his chair and sat, shaking his head.

"It is done!" he suddenly shouted. "Put the writing into a golden tube, and let it be sealed."

Meanwhile, one by one, Micerea and Finn escorted each new member of their army back to their homes, telling them more about their assignments. Robby himself took Lachlan back to his home in Glareth, and along the way he told Lachlan to expect to be summoned to deliver his first messages very soon.

"Rest today and tomorrow as much as you can," Robby said once they had reached Glareth and the house where Lachlan lived. "I'm afraid you will need your strength to be my messenger, and it is because I sensed that you are a determined and upright sort that I wanted you to be one."

"I will do as you say, my lord."

Robby returned to Griferis, to the last dreamer who still stood in the great circle room. He was not a dreamwalker, but a person that Robby hoped would provide a very different service to him.

"So, Borwain," Robby said. "Do you think you may make some rendering of what you have witnessed?"

"It will be difficult, my lord," Borwain said. "But I will try."

"Good. I'll let you rest and sleep, now. Thank you for attending, whether or not you are able to render a likeness of what you saw."

"It is my honor, King, to do whatever I may. And I look forward to our next outing. Where shall it be? Duinnor? Or will it be back to Barley?"

"I have in mind to show you some events that took place a number of years ago off the coast of Tracia, in a place called the Grisland Strait."

"Very well, my lord. Tomorrow evening?"

"Yes. If you are rested by then. I do not want to overly tax you, but things are becoming urgent."

"I understand. Perhaps you might come to my work room when it is convenient to see those canvases that I have painted thus far, and other little drawings that I have done. I would like to know if they meet with your approval, sire."

"I'm sure to like them," Robby said. "But I will come tomorrow, perhaps after noontime. That way, both of us can sleep a bit late into the morning."

Chapter 25

Signs for Serith Ellyn

Day 213
32 Days Remaining

In Duinnor, Billy and Sheila were required to give their testimony pertaining to Gladsten and Reysa before Lord Arata and other judges. Even on days when they were not required to speak, they had to attend while Captain Thrubold gave his evidence, and while other witnesses gave testimony, many of whom were new prisoners or newly released prisoners. They all related what they knew of the many illegal activities of the late Lord Banis, his henchmen, and others who were bribed or blackmailed to be in his service. When at last Billy was officially exonerated for killing Reysa, he was much relieved, though he did not feel any better about what he had done. Ashlord then hurried Billy off to meet with a hearing of Lords and Kingsmen. These men wished to petition the King to convene a Congress of Realms, but before doing so, they desired to question Billy.

So, for nearly the entire day, Billy stood nervously before the forty men telling and retelling his tale of the Redvest invasion and of the Dragonkind out on the Plains of Bletharn. Several of the Kingsmen were keen to hear military details from Billy that he could not possibly know. How many Redvests? Where did the Dragonkind come from? How were they equipped? What messages had gotten through to Glareth? And what was the role of the Damar and Galinot warlords?

The men spent as much time arguing and debating with each other as they spent questioning Billy, who stood in the witness box without respite. Just when Billy thought they might be finished with him, more questions were directed his way, and occasionally to Ashlord, too, who stood with him in the witness box.

At last, Billy's exhaustion and how he struggled to answer or speculate on the right answer was obvious, and General Chadler put an end to the questioning and thanked Billy for his patience. Relieved, nearly in tears and quite in shock over the ordeal, Billy finally stepped down from the witness box. Sheila met him and put her arms around him. She had stayed nearby the entire time, throughout all the days of Billy's questioning, and her presence might have served to temper the attitude of the men Billy faced.

"Oh, good grief!" Billy muttered as Sheila held him tight. "Is it over at last? I wonder if ye ever heard such a stammerin' fool as I!"

"You were just fine, Billy," Sheila said. "You spoke well, and you did far better than many others would have done. I'm so proud of you!"

"You Boskmen are certainly thick-skinned," Ashlord said, shaking Billy's hand and giving him a good squeeze on the shoulder. "I doubt if very many could have taken what you've been through these past days with as much patience and toughness as you've shown."

"I don't feel very tough," replied Billy as they made for the door. "An' I certainly ain't feelin' very patient. Do ye think they're done with me?"

"Well, I don't think you'll be needed again soon, if at all," said Ashlord. "And, instead of waiting around to find out, why don't we all go back to Starlight Hall for a good meal?"

"Ye reckon we could stop by a tavern on the way?" asked Billy, holding out his hands. "Look! I can't hardly keep from shakin'!"

"I think a good ale is the least we can do for you!" said Sheila.

"Do ye think they'll actually get the King to act?" Billy asked as they stepped outside.

"We'll have to wait and see," shrugged Ashlord.

A heavily guarded wagon filled with men in chains rolled past. Amongst them was General Kecker, the insignias of his Kingsman uniform stripped away and his face red with shame. The crowd lining the street jeered as the wagon lumbered by, and not a few lumps of rotted vegetables found their mark upon the prisoners.

"Those two men sitting next to Kecker are Norogus and Harmalway," said Ashlord. "They are the notorious proprietors of a trading firm that has handled many Vanaran leases. Associates of Bailorg, if you remember. I have good reason to think they are charged with a myriad of swindles and crimes."

"Are they? Well, it seems Duinnor begins to clean itself up," said Sheila.

"Yes. When Banis died, the rats began to scurry," Ashlord nodded. "And our good Captain Thrubold, thankfully, was quite ready to sweep them up, once he had proof of their misdeeds."

"Well," commented Billy, jutting a thumb toward the High Tower of the King's Palace that loomed over the city, "I only hope some sweepin' can be done up yonder, too."

• • •

At about the same time that Billy took his first sip of a refreshing beer, the boats carrying Queen Serith Ellyn bumped ashore at a small village called Montgate along the southern banks of the Osterflo. They were well out of the Locks of Karthia, much farther upstream, and in the western foothills of the snowy Carthane Mountains. The teams of mules that pulled the boats upstream were unhitched, gangplanks were laid, and when all was secured, the passengers began to disembark, the members of the Queen's Gray Guard going first to properly secure the area. Thurdun and Chanter, who had gone ashore two days before to ride ahead of them, were there to meet the boats and to supervise security. Once the guardsmen were situated and Thurdun was satisfied that all was safe, Serith Ellyn and Gaiyelneth came ashore.

"My brother," Serith Ellyn said, "what news?"

"Queen, we are favored with good fortune," said Thurdun. "We can leave the boats and move across land from here."

"Then you have found suitable mounts and wagons?"

"No carriage, but three wagons with teams as well as horses for all of our party."

"All?"

"Yes." Thurdun gestured for the ladies to come with him uphill to the village. "I was only hoping to obtain mounts for a dozen of us, but it seems that Chanter and I arrived just in time. A horse trader and his wranglers brought mounts and tack all the way from Duinnor to sell downstream, but the barges meant for them were wholly unsuitable. Or so he said, and he would not risk his herd upon them."

Thurdun paused and pointed upstream where six large barges were tied at the riverbank.

"When Chanter and I arrived, the trader and the bargemen were having a heated row, and were near to fisticuffs. It seems the bargemen were counting on the business, and had turned down other freight since they expected the trader. But the horse trader insisted the watercraft would not do."

"He must have a better eye than I do," said Gaiyelneth, still looking at the barges. "They look fine to me."

"To me, too, actually."

The three resumed their uphill climb.

"But," Thurdun continued, "the trader insisted that he had an omen, through a dream, that he would lose his investment if he were to put his horses upon their barges. The bargemen, in their turn, insisted they be paid for their loss if the trader did not adhere to their bargain."

"Through a dream?" Serith Ellyn asked.

"Yes, my Queen. I intervened, and negotiated with the two parties. I was able to pay the bargemen their fee, and purchase all of the horses at the same time, along with saddles and gear, and the three wagons, too. Everyone was satisfied, and we have the means for our entire party to hie forth homeward all together. I have also procured rations and water casks for our journey."

At the top of the hill, Thurdun and the Gray Guard escorted the ladies through the village streets, past warehouses and workshops, to an inn. The Queen stopped in front of the inn, looking at it.

"A humble establishment," said Thurdun, "but safe."

"That is not it," she replied. "I am sure it is perfectly suitable. Are the horses nearby?"

"Yes, they are corralled just yonder."

"How long would it take to prepare them, to load and team the wagons?"

"If we put our men to it, not very long. One wagon is already loaded with our firewood. Little more than an hour, I should think. Two at most."

"And are we very far from Middlemount?"

"This village lies at its northeastern flank," said Thurdun, "and the road, here, leads on for five leagues to its top."

"Then let us make ready and depart as soon as we may," said Serith Ellyn. "There are still several hours of daylight, and perhaps we could make the heights before we camp."

"Do you think it wise, Queen?" asked Gaiyelneth, speaking for Thurdun. "There will be no moon tonight, and it will be dark before we are halfway up it."

"Make it so, Thurdun," Serith Ellyn said. "Gaiyelneth and I shall help."

Thurdun and Chanter gave their orders, and all of their belongings were efficiently packed into the wagons, along with their tents and rations, and all of the mounts were saddled and ready. Soon enough the village was far behind them as they wound up and down through the eastern hills of Middlemount, and Serith Ellyn seemed glad, if not somewhat anxious, to be on their way. By sunset, their road had narrowed to a mere path, but it was not as steep or as winding as they ascended Middlemount. The company continued moving well into night, with lamps lit and carried on poles, crunching upward through the snowy hills, with Thurdun and his sister at their lead. Sooner than expected, the path leveled and they entered the treeless plateau of Middlemount, uncanny in its flatness. The stars were so bright in the cold air that they hardly needed their lamps at all as the snow-dusted vista fanned out before them.

"Are you still vexed by persistent dreams, Serith?" Thurdun ventured to ask.

"No," she answered, looking up to locate the North Star. "I have not had a single dream for just over a week. Indeed, my sleep has been unusually peaceful."

"Oh? Perhaps river travel agrees with you, after all."

She smiled. "Perhaps. But it is as if I wait for the other shoe to drop."

She twisted around in her saddle to look eastward.

"I should like for us to make camp, Thurdun," she said.

"Certainly, my lady. Captain Chanter!"

"Yes, my lord!"

"We make camp. Send out the rest of your scouts, if you please."

"Yes, my lord."

Chanter's men rode out in widening circles, to make certain of the land and to discover any other travelers who might be nearby. The rest of the company unloaded the tents from the wagons, built several small fires for supper, and saw to the horses. Guards were posted, some at obvious and expected stations around the camp, and others were sent farther out, with blankets and bows, to find hidden places away from the glare of the lamps and fires. Thurdun restlessly went about to see to these things, and as he did so, he kept thinking about the attack that had almost taken place the previous summer on their way eastward. If it had not been for the ringing of the Great Bell, things would certainly have gone badly. But the Bellringer, himself in peril, had saved them, alarming the camp so that every man had steel in hand. Unwilling to take on the elite fighters that surrounded the Queen, the enemy had withdrawn. Thurdun saw for himself, the next day, the tracks of the force that had surrounded their camp that night. He was determined not to slacken his vigilance like that again.

As Thurdun made his rounds, checking and double-checking everything, he kept thinking about that near miss. Much had happened since then, and many things had been revealed. And there was much to be hoped for, since the Bellringer was, as the Queen had speculated, the Hidden One, the one who would hold the reins of destiny. But now they were out in the open once more, and Thurdun knew that the Bellringer could not save them again as he had done before. The boy himself had said that it had been an accident. But Thurdun knew better. Such things do not happen by chance, or by accident. And all that had happened since—the events that drove Robby Ribbon westward, the emergence of Lyrium with her secrets, even Serith Ellyn's vexing dreams—were all but links of a chain, one thing to the next.

Thurdun paused and glanced at Serith Ellyn's tent across the campsite. He wondered if it had been a mistake for her to take the throne all those centuries ago. He remembered the first time their father showed them the Bloodcoins. He remembered the look on his sister's face, which he had taken as a look of astonishment at their beauty. Parthais even let her hold one, one with a sapphire as its jewel.

"This," Parthais said, "was once held by your grandfather, Cupeldain. And, before that, it was held by Aperion himself. No others, besides you and I, my daughter, have ever touched it."

When she became Queen, and again held that Bloodcoin and the others of her Seven, Thurdun saw the same look on her face. Her expression told him that she would never willingly give them up. Now, as he watched her tent, he sensed that she was, at that very moment, holding the sapphire-bejeweled Bloodcoin, and that the rest were spread upon her table before her.

"Is the expression on your face the same as it once was?" he mused.

"My Lord Thurdun."

Thurdun turned to see Chanter approach.

"Yes, Captain?"

"The men are posted, and the first of the scouts have returned, with nothing to report, my lord."

"Very well. Rotate your men as we discussed. Make sure everyone has blankets and hot food."

"Yes, my lord."

Thurdun walked to the fire at the center of the camp where many men were gathered for their supper, just as Gaiyelneth came out of the Queen's tent. She looked around and, seeing him, approached.

"How is my sister?"

"She retires for the night," Gaiyelneth said. "But she desires that you wake her if you see anything at all unusual."

"Unusual? Unusual in what way?"

"In any way, I suppose. She did not say. Only that you are to wake her should you see something unusual."

"Then I shall do so. Have you eaten?"

"Yes, I supped with the Queen earlier. Tell me, how long now, do you think, before we reach Vanara?"

"Oh, about a month, I'd say. If we hurry along, and if all goes well. But I think that the Queen has it in her mind to ride quickly ahead of the rest of our party in order to reach Vanara sooner."

"Oh."

"If she does so, I'm sure she would want you to come with her, Gaiyelneth," Thurdun smiled. "And I know that Seafar will be glad if you did."

"I hope so. That is, I hope that the Queen will have me ride with her if she hies forth."

"If she hesitates to have you along, I shall prevail upon her and insist that you come, too," Thurdun said. As he spoke, he noticed that several of the nearby men were looking out across the plain as they ate from their bowls, shaking their heads.

"Thank you, Prince. That would make me very happy. I think I'll do as your sister does, and go to my bed. Good night."

"Good night," Thurdun said. Curious, he approached the men who were now shrugging. "You all appear to have some quandary," he said to them.

"We were just wondering, my lord, what may cause such a light as that, resting yonder, on the eastern horizon. A bit to the southeast, just there."

Turning to look where the man pointed, Thurdun saw a bluish haze between the slopes of two distant mountains.

"Can it be the glow of some kind of fire?" asked one of the men.

"What manner of fire burns blue like that?" asked another.

"Wayregyle is that way, is it not?"

"I think Wayregyle is somewhat farther south," Thurdun said. "It is a peculiar light."

"And it seems brighter now than when I first saw it."

"Well, whatever it is, it is very far away from us, I should think," said Thurdun. "I go to my tent for a bit."

An hour later, Thurdun put away his ink, having recorded in his journal the day's events, and was preparing to pull of his boots and crawl under his blankets. Captain Chanter spoke from outside the tent flap.

"My Lord Thurdun. It is Captain Chanter."

"Come."

Chanter pulled aside the flap and stuck his head in.

"Pardon me, my lord, but there is something you might wish to see."

Thurdun hurriedly threw his heavy cloak back on and stepped outside.

"There!"

Thurdun saw that the blue-white light they had seen earlier was now clear of the eastern mountains, wheeling upward with the stars. Having risen above the low-lying haze, it was much brighter than before. It was long and slightly curved from one broad fuzzy end to a brighter point at its other tip, looking every bit like a ghostly sword. He turned and hurried to his sister's tent and unceremoniously rushed in. By the light of a low-burning lamp, he saw that she was asleep underneath thick layers of fine blankets and quilts, and he crouched to gently wake her.

"Serith. Serith."

She stirred, blinking at Thurdun. Her eyes widened, and she threw off her covers.

"Show me!" she cried, pushing Thurdun ahead of her through the flap and outside. He pointed, and when she saw it, she gripped her brother's hand.

"Gaiyelneth gave me your message," Thurdun said. "Is this what you meant by unusual?"

She nodded, unable to take her eyes from the uncanny object in the sky. Sensing some commotion, Gaiyelneth roused herself and came out of her tent to stand near Thurdun and Serith Ellyn. Soon enough, although everyone spoke in hushed tones, the entire camp was awake, staring at the sky. It was a stark sight, set against the black heavens with its twinkling constellations. The company watched for a long while, craning their necks little by little as it rose higher with the stars that surrounded it. Sometime after midnight, it was almost directly over their heads.

"An omen, surely," Thurdun whispered.

"But of what?" Gaiyelneth asked.

"Of beginnings," Serith Ellyn said as she turned away to go back to her tent. "And of endings, I think."

• • •

Once inside, she crawled back under her covers, and in spite of her dread, she quickly fell asleep and slipped into an odd dream. She opened her eyes and found that she was standing outside of her tent. The campfires and lamps were all extinguished, and the scene was lit only by the bright starlight and the brighter apparition above. There was no one in sight but a man, a few yards away, his back to her, looking up at the sky. He turned and approached.

"Your Highness," he bowed. "I am Lachlan Shurmarsh, messenger of King Philawain. You have seen the first of his signs." Shurmarsh gestured to the sky.

She nodded, swallowing hard.

"Tonight, and for each of the next five nights, if you are willing," Shurmarsh went on, "Philawain will send a sign to you. And, so that you will know that these are no ordinary dreams, each day following, you will receive another sign, for all in your company to see. My King does this so that you may know his power and somewhat more of the world. You must say whether you are willing to receive these signs. If you are not, he will not disturb you in this manner. But if you are willing, take my hand."

Shurmarsh put out his hand to Serith Ellyn and smiled. Hesitantly, she took it and felt his warm and firm grip.

"I bid you come with me," the man said, "to Forest Islindia, to see someone who lives there and who still remembers how things once were. Will you come?"

Serith Ellyn looked at the man and nodded.

As quick as a wink, they passed through the night and went to the great forest that was Islindia's domain. There, Serith Ellyn was taken to Islindia who stood among the blasted ruins of her forest. The man released Serith Ellyn's hand, and Islindia took it. Then he bowed and disappeared. Islindia smiled.

"Welcome, Queen of Vanara, to my domain," Islindia said. "Do you know me?"

"We have never met," Serith Ellyn said, "but I think you are Islindia, Queen of this wood."

"I am called queen by some. And, tonight, the King of Griferis gives us a gift, sending his dream, which is made of my own memories since I cannot dream it on my own before the next full moon. Come and see!"

The Queen of the Wood took the Queen of Vanara through the forest, just as she had taken Ullin some months before, happily pulling the mystified Serith Ellyn along by the hand. As they went, fireflies gathered around them and kept pace, lighting their way. Soon they came to the place in the ground from which a bright, golden light beamed upward. Islindia took Serith Ellyn down the stairs and to the mountaintop overlooking the ancient realm as it once had been, made for them by Philawain from her memories. At the precipice, they stood in shadowless sunlight, and they gazed over the magnificent valley with its vast forest of gigantic trees. As they looked, Serith Ellyn heard joyous singing, and Islindia's Faere denizens rose up from the forest below to greet them with song. Now with wings of their own, Serith Ellyn and Islindia flew hand in hand to meet Islindia's people and to rejoice in their company. Serith Ellyn was thrilled to fly, overjoyed to be free of all bonds, and delighted by the splendors of Islindia's forest and its beautiful inhabitants.

• • •

Long after Queen Serith Ellyn woke, and throughout the day of her westward travels, she remained quiet, answering Thurdun or Gaiyelneth pleasantly enough, but in a distracted manner. She sometimes forgot to urge her horse on, coming to a halt as she thought her thoughts until Thurdun came alongside of her on Celefar.

"My Queen?"

He saw that she was smiling broadly, but her face was wet with tears.

"Pardon me?" she said. "Yes, let's move along."

As the hours passed and they made their way southwestward across the broad flat Middlemount, Serith Ellyn would ofttimes just as suddenly burst into laughter as into tears, and often both at once. Everyone was alarmed and baffled, and Thurdun and Gaiyelneth begged her to say what was in her heart. But she did not try to explain it, nor could she put her feelings into words, and she only apologized for her outbursts.

Then, in the late afternoon, one of the scouts came riding back to them from ahead.

"My lord," he said as he pulled up on his reins, "I think you should come look upon something very strange."

"Is there some alarm?" asked Thurdun, glancing around to see the disposition of his men and the wagons.

"No, my lord, I don't think so. You should be the judge, I think. May it please the Queen, perhaps she should come as well."

Thurdun quickly assembled a squad as escort, leaving Captain Chanter with the van, and he and Serith Ellyn rode out with the scout, their guard riding close behind. They rode through a slight dip in the land and up the other side out of sight of the rest of their company. After less than a mile, the scout drew them to a halt and pointed to a low scattering of rocks that jutted from the snowy grass.

"There," the scout said. "Just there, see it?"

Indeed, the sunlight sparkled from some object on one of the rocks, and they slowly approached. Looking down upon the object, the group could hardly believe their eyes. Resting on a small pillow of folded cloth was the Crown of Vanara, the very one fashioned by Silmain's craftsmen, worn by him, and, later, by Cupeldain. It was the same crown, of untarnished silver and studded with rubies and diamonds, that Parthais wore when Serith Ellyn struck off his head; the same Crown of Vanara that was placed upon Serith Ellyn's own head when she became Queen.

She and Thurdun gaped at it, their hearts fluttering at the sight. Thurdun slowly dismounted and approached to examine it more closely, and, kneeling in the snow, he carefully lifted it up to do so. Serith Ellyn dismounted, too, and stood beside her brother.

"What the blazes goes on here?" Thurdun said with a look of complete astonishment. "There is no mistaking it. It is your crown."

"How?" she whispered. She felt lightheaded, as if she was about to faint. "How?"

Thurdun shook his head and stood, handing the crown to her. He fished under his shirt and tugged on a chain, pulling out a large key.

"I still have my half of the vault key," he said, shaking his head. "Seafar's half is useless without it."

Serith Ellyn stared at the crown in her hands, then looked at Thurdun, speechless.

"Even if Seafar had the means to take it," Thurdun went on, "how could he have transported it here? Piers!"

"Yes, my lord?" the scout dismounted and quickly approached.

"Any sign of horses or men?"

"No, my lord. A few tracks, just over here, beside the rock. See? But there are none leading and none going. I circled carefully around this place before reporting back to you. But these are the only tracks I found."

"It's impossible," Thurdun responded, walking quickly around as he examined the ground.

"I know, my lord. But I assure you there are no more tracks."

Serith Ellyn picked up the cloth and wrapped the crown with it.

"The day is late," she said. "Let us make our camp at the first suitable place."

• • •

At about the same time that the Crown of Vanara was found by Thurdun's scout, Lord Seafar, in the White Palace of Linlally, was shouting at one of the captains of the Gray Guard.

"What the devil do you mean it fell apart? Locks and chains do not just fall apart!"

"My lord, I beg your pardon, sir. Ask Telmon, here. He saw it happen, too! And so did Maywind."

Seafar struggled to get a grip on his anger, and through gritted teeth said, "Tell me again."

"We stood watch, as usual. Nothing at all happened until the outer door burst open. We went to investigate, amid strange lights, and then the inner door burst open, too. We saw no one come in, and no one come out, my lord. I swear it!"

Seafar had already examined the door and the inner vault. Both had two sets of iron bars, chained with heavy links, and both were shattered and twisted on the floor. Inside the main vault, where the Vanaran Royal objects were stored, the Crown was missing. In its place was found a note, which he now clutched. The men before him nervously waited as Seafar paced back and forth. He shook his head.

"Captain, you, Telmon, and Maywind are relieved," he said softly, at last gaining command of his temper. "Please confine yourself to your quarters. Commander Tide, double the guard here and in the corridor. Have new chains put on these doors immediately. And have spikes driven into the links as well. I shall inspect in one hour!"

Seafar pushed his way through the crowd of guardsmen who had come with him when the alarm had been raised. He strode down the corridor and away. He looked at the crumpled paper in his hand, stopped, and unraveled it to read again.

> Be not alarmed.
> I deliver to Queen Serith Ellyn that which is hers.
> Ask your ink.
> > Philawain.

Turning abruptly to climb a steep winding stairs, he made his way to the Scribblers Room.

"Great! Just great!"

• • •

Serith Ellyn went into her tent as soon as it was ready. The Queen had not told Gaiyelneth what had been found that day, or why she and the party who rode out were so upset when they returned. Thurdun ordered his men to keep it to themselves. He even begged Gaiyelneth not to ask about what had happened.

"And, Gaiyelneth, please do not engage my sister with conversation unless she speaks to you first," he said to her as she was taking a meal to the Queen. "I think she would prefer her own meditations."

"Certainly, my lord. But will you not tell me what is amiss?"

"I know that you love and care for her, but I can only say that I think she endures some inner trial, and grapples with great decisions. I cannot tell you more, but trust it will be revealed to you in its own time. Be patient with her, and with me for asking this of you."

"Yes, my lord. I shall do as you ask."

Gaiyelneth entered the Queen's tent with a tray of food. Serith Ellyn was sitting on her rugs, with a blank expression, staring at nothing. She barely noticed when Gaiyelneth knelt and placed the tray beside her, or when she uncovered a steaming plate and set out a cup of wine. Gaiyelneth waited, biting her lip, then, bowed and departed.

Gaiyelneth returned much later that evening and saw that the Queen's plate was untouched, her cup still full. Serith Ellyn clutched a cloth bundle in her lap. Gaiyelneth knelt to pick up the tray, but could no longer restrain her concern.

"This day we have seen a great change in your countenance, my lady," Gaiyelneth said. "Do you feel unwell? Perhaps the food we brought disagrees with you."

"There is nothing amiss with my constitution." Serith Ellyn almost whispered, she spoke so softly. "I have much to consider, and therefore little appetite. Tell me, does the great sword in the heavens shine again this night?"

"Yes, my lady, it does. Even brighter and longer across the sky than before. Won't you come out and gaze upon it with me?"

"I think not. I think that I'll retire now. You needn't help me. I shall manage."

"Shall I bring out the box of your Seven for you?"

"No. I am too tired to look upon them tonight."

• • •

This night, Serith Ellyn dreamed that she was back in Glareth, standing on a high windy bluff overlooking a stormy sea. Although the waves crashed, and the wind tugged at her robes, there was no sound at all. She sensed someone standing nearby. Turning, she saw a woman dressed in white winter garb, wearing boots and mittens and a heavy longcoat of white wool with a fur-lined hood. Her blue eyes glittered, and her pale face glowed as she smiled. She pushed back her hood, revealing close-cropped blond hair.

"My name is Ivana, of the House of Starvine, which I think you know. I am come to give you the next sign from my King, Philawain of Griferis."

"How is it that you call Philawain your king when you still have a Vanaran Queen?" Serith Ellyn shot back at her. "Did not the House of Starvine swear allegiance to Fairlinden?"

"We did, my lady, and bound the fate of our House to that of yours. And to the land of Vanara I am loyal, and to its Queen. But in this land of dreams, as elsewhere, Philawain is King and Master, and whilst here, he is my sovereign, as he shall someday be yours."

A statement such as that would have normally provoked a harsh and angry response from Serith Ellyn, but now she reacted with a nervous resignation.

"That remains to be seen," she said in reply.

"Yes, my lady, it does. Today, you found the object that Philawain sent to you. It is a sign that he moves not only within dreams but also outside of them. Now, he sends his next sign to you, if you are willing. If you are not, then ignore these instructions that he gives. But if you are willing and open to his signs, go to your True Ink and dip your silver-nibbed pen. Write what I say, and see whether the True Ink fades or not. Then ponder on what Philawain thus says to you. And look to tomorrow's sign as well."

"I am willing. What is it that I should write?"

• • •

Serith Ellyn awoke. She lit her lamps and went to her desk and took out her large amber vial. Within it was left only a small amount of True Ink, but it was enough.

Using one of the pens that Ashlord had given to her, she took out a bit of parchment and wrote two sentences.

Lord Banis is dead.
Pellen lives.

The ink did not fade. She changed the words, writing.

Lord Banis lives.
Pellen is dead.

The True Ink faded quickly.

She sat back in her chair. Banis was dead, and Pellen, Heneil's brother, was alive. A flood of realizations and possibilities swept through her mind. If Pellen was alive, then Lyrium held back much of her story. No wonder she refused to speak of the fate of her husband. All were led to believe that it was Pellen who was placed into the Bell Room of Tulith Attis to stand watch with his wife, Myrium, who was Lyrium's sister. That was what the legends said, anyway. Serith Ellyn then used the very last of her True Ink, and wrote:

Lyrium discovered Pellen's treachery.
Heneil is dead.
Pellen wanted Lyrium's Seven.
It was Pellen who betrayed Tulith Attis.

The ink did not fade. But much was still unexplained. No wonder Lyrium had her Bloodcoins smuggled away. No wonder she fled Tulith Attis instead of fighting and dying beside her husband. All the years since, spent in terror, in hiding, having lost her Bloodcoins, not knowing the fate of Pellen the Traitor, whether he died at Tulith Attis or whether he still searched for her. And for her Bloodcoins. No wonder Lyrium stayed aloof when in Glareth.

"She mistrusts me," Serith Ellyn said, standing and pacing back and forth. "Even me. It must have been an act of profound courage that she even came to see me at all."

She halted, staring at the bundle of cloth that held her crown, then at the small case that held her Bloodcoins.

"Have I become so like my father that the Firstborn fear to confide in me? That gentle souls fear to be my friend?"

She stood for a long while without moving. But her eyes stung with shame. Wiping her face, she hurried to her tent flap and flung it open.

"My Queen!" the guard bowed.

She glanced up at the apparition in the sky for a long moment.

"Bring Prince Thurdun, if you please."

When Thurdun came into her tent, and before he could speak, she shoved the paper with her True Ink writing into his hand.

"Pellen lives," she said. "Pellen! Remember how he was ever partial to Duinnor? Remember how we in Vanara heard that he frequented the court of the Fifth Unknown King of Duinnor?"

Thurdun nodded, holding the paper to the lamplight to read it.

"Pellen? Heneil's brother?"

"Is there any other by that name?" Serith Ellyn responded. She was pacing again, and as she passed by the stunned Thurdun, she tapped the paper in his hand. "And Banis is dead. Dead! One less enemy in Duinnor! And it is a great day for Vanara!"

Serith Ellyn came back to Thurdun and clutched his shoulders, grinning.

"Long has Banis been the bane of our good efforts, thwarting and twisting our entreaties to Duinnor with schemes and with obstacles while ever keen to rescue Vanaran lands from Vanarans with his leases and his Regulars!"

"And Pellen? He was not killed at Tulith Attis?"

"Apparently not."

"Where is he? Have you asked your True Ink?"

Serith Ellyn's smile evaporated.

"It is all gone. I have used the last of it."

"Oh."

"I wish to look upon the night sky!" she suddenly declared.

• • •

The two talked all night long, sitting in chairs brought out for them, and watching the ghostly sword move and turn with the stars overhead until the eastern rim of the world began to glow with the coming day.

"I wonder what we shall find today," she said to Thurdun as the camp began to stir and prepare for the day's travel.

"Pardon me?"

"Nothing."

That day, while serving as an outrider, Thurdun came upon Serith Ellyn's royal ceremonial robes, neatly folded upon a blanket.

• • •

When night came, and Serith Ellyn was once again sleeping, another messenger appeared to her and took her to the far away Dragonlands. She saw how, in the southeastern lands of that country a fiery mountain was rising up, spewing out molten rock as it rose higher and higher over the Tulivanas. It poured out lava that channeled eastward through the mountains like a fiery river, setting trees ablaze and hissing through streams. She saw how it was just beginning to pour into the Hinderlands of Altoria, sending up clouds of steam as it advanced through the marshes. Thus it was, she was told, that one of the ancient dragons had awakened, and whereas the people of the deserts once served the dragons, now the tables were turned, and this dragon served them. With its heavy molten bile, the dragon was making a road through the Hinderlands, a firm path that would rapidly cool and solidify in the marshwater. And along this road would pour out the armies of the Dragonlands that were already massed on the western slopes of the mountains.

Then Serith Ellyn was taken far away to the northwestern lands of the desert, to the distant mountains of the far west. There she was shown a new river that was gushing from the mountains and spreading out across the desert sands. She saw how the water poured from the great chasm at the edge of the world. Her guide then took her to see how the trolls labored to push mountains over into the chasm, causing the waters there to swell and spill over its colossal banks, creating the deluge that fanned eastward.

"King Thunderfoot and his people," said her guide, "serve Philawain's cause. And they do so at his bidding. Thus, already does Philawain become the King of Kings, exerting his might even over the Dragonlands."

• • •

The following morning, Serith Ellyn found her ceremonial armor. It could be none other than that of the Queen of Vanara, shaped for her own body, the polished gold breastplate adorned with a spreading linden tree of inlaid silver, its heart-shaped flowers of citrine against a sky of lapis lazuli. With it she found her backplate, likewise of gold, embossed with wings of silver. These items were inside her tent when she awoke, along with her chain skirt and leggings, her winged helmet, and her long narrow sword. Although they were made worthy for any battle, it was her custom to wear them only on great occasions of state. The last time was when she had ceremoniously displayed her Bloodcoins to the Ministers and Lords of the Realm, just before departing Vanara.

• • •

Her party did not cover much ground that day, owing to their Queen's distraction. She often let her horse wander aside or even stop altogether as she stared ahead. The entire company with her slowly followed, starting and stopping as she did.

"Perhaps she should ride in the wagon with me," suggested Gaiyelneth to Thurdun.

"No. Let us go at her pace. We all wish to be home as soon as we can, but let us be patient."

Chapter 26

An Uncanny Guest

"But what is it?" asked Sheila, looking across the garden at the night sky. Hanging among the stars to the southeast was the same long curved apparition that Serith Ellyn and her company watched, night after night. With Sheila stood Ashlord and Raynor, along with Ibin and Billy. Lady Highleaf was with them, too, and she pulled her cloak tightly as she stared at the sky.

"It is what some call a comet," said Raynor.

"It isn't the same as the one we saw last year, though," said Ashlord.

"No. This one is not known to me," Raynor shook his head. "Barian would know, perhaps. If he was still with us."

"Ain't comets a sign of bad luck?" asked Billy. "Me mum said one hung over our part of the country back when Tulith Attis fell."

"That is common lore," said Ashlord, "but there are no records to support it."

"The part about bad luck, or the part about Tulith Attis?" asked Lady Highleaf.

"If an object such as this had hung over Tulith Attis," Raynor said, "chroniclers would surely have made a record of it."

"But if such things are omens of misfortune," said Ashlord, "then there is some basis for believing so. It is said that such a sight hung in the heavens, briefly, during the time of Silmain, when he called together the Seven High Houses with their Bloodcoins."

"And it, or another thing like it, appeared again when Cupeldain tried to do the same," said Raynor. "Or so say the chronicles of that time."

"If I recall my lessons," said Lady Highleaf, "both of those kings met unfortunate ends."

"Yes, they did, eventually. But neither of their deaths coincided with any unusual celestial event," said Raynor. "At least not that I am aware of."

They all glanced over their shoulders at the High Tower of the present King of Duinnor.

"What, exactly, is it, though?" asked Billy. "Is it like ol' Will-o-the-Wisp, like is seen sometimes over in Boggy Wood? Or is it some other critter?"

"No one knows, Billy," said Raynor. "But I think it must be some heavenly object. That is to say, I don't think it lives on the earth."

They stood for a long while looking at the thing, as did people all over the world. Indeed, Thurdun, too, was watching it as he wondered about how his sister's ceremonial armor had appeared that day. Also watching the sky was Prince Carbane aboard his ship and Lord Seafar from the flight deck that reached out over the Falls of Tiandari. Lord Tallin, in Tallinvale, looked at it from the east wall of his city, in company with General Teracue and Prince Danoss. Robigor Ribbon saw it as well as he stood on the front porch of his shop, and so did Gurasa from his own porch in the far-off deserts. Ullin spotted it, and he woke Micerea to gaze upon it from their camp on a bluff overlooking the forest. Even Throgallus in Shatuum stared at it, and it filled him with trepidation and with impatience to begin his campaign.

Robby peered into the eyepiece of the great spyglass in Griferis, adjusting a focusing knob on the side of the device as he did so. Then he stood aside so that Lord Threshmere could look. Nearby were Lafkin and Radasa, and, outside on the catwalk that circled the glass enclosure, Borwain leaned on his crutch, holding a tablet while making a rendition upon it.

"It has no distinct form," said Threshmere as he squinted through the eyepiece. "Except for a very bright tip."

He stood aside for Lafkin to have a look.

"And, sire, you learned to look for it from the books in our library?" asked Radasa.

"Yes. It has come before, Radasa. It was recorded twice in the Chronicles of Vanara, during the First Age. Twice more, at different times, it appeared in records made by your people, and three times it was seen in Glareth. There was something peculiar about the span of years between each report. Some of the dates coincided with each other. Altogether, five different times it was recorded, once you accounted for various calendars. I did some tables, just as I once did to figure the value of certain things. Anyway, I worked out that it has actually come six times. For some reason it was not seen or reported by any accounts the fourth time that it appeared. It seemed time for it to come again, according to my sums."

Radasa eyed Robby with an incredulous look as he took Lafkin's place at the huge spyglass.

"It gives me a strange feeling," said Lafkin. "I mean, it is a most uncanny sight, sire."

"Yes, it is."

They heard someone climbing the ladder below them, then Unther's head appeared through the trapdoor.

"Sire, pardon the intrusion, but there is a movement of some kind on Algamori, near the gate," he said passing up his small spyglass to Lafkin. All eyes turned eastward toward the shadowy mountain as Lafkin searched with the spyglass.

"I don't see anything."

"It was a light, General Lafkin. Like a firefly, blinking just for a moment then fading quickly. Three members of our guard also saw it."

"Allow me," said Robby as he began cranking and turning wheels and knobs. The large spyglass moved on its gimbals and gears, slowly swinging around and downward until it pointed at Algamori. The eyepiece was now too high to stand at, so Robby dragged over a stepladder and climbed up. He looked through the apparatus as he continued making adjustments.

"It is too dark to see anything over there," he said. There was more noise at the ladder, and Unther came on up to give room to Finn, right behind him, who stuck his head through the trap door.

"Sire, we have company," said Finn, still in his nightshirt and out of breath from rushing from his bed. "One of our dreamwalkers reported a fast-moving person going through Shatuum. He reports that the person appeared as if out of nowhere, and shot through Shatuum at lightning speed, right up past Secundur's creatures and up the side of Algamori. He appeared to be making for the gate at the Landing there."

"Out of nowhere, did you say?"

"Yes, sire. I dreamwalked to the gate to see as soon as I received word. It is a little person, sire."

"Lafkin, prepare the Guard," ordered Robby. "I mean to put out the causeway."

"Sire?"

"I think I know who it is, who it must be. Let's be lively."

"Yes, sire! Unther, come!" Lafkin leapt for the trapdoor and disappeared down the ladder, with Unther right behind him.

"If you'll excuse me, gentlemen," Robby said to the others, "I must go to the East Tower."

• • •

An hour later, Robby paced back and forth in his parlor as Eldwin completed his tale. Finn and Lafkin were also there, standing at a respectful distance. As he paced, Robby frequently glanced around the room, then at Lafkin and Finn as if expecting one of them to say something. But he did not interrupt Eldwin, nor did Lafkin or Finn say anything. Eldwin was now explaining how terrified he was as he came through Shatuum, and how he did not know his way to Algamori.

"I only knew from Ashlord an' Raynor to get up onto the mountain, but I didn't know which mountain was the right one," he said. "I must've gone back an' forth across that cursed land six times, an' I'm certain I was seen. I'm afraid I stirred things up quite a bit, sir, er, sire. At last I popped right past the scariest tower, an' right through some awful terrible soldiers, in black armor, an' somehow found a path up the mountain. I found a hut, eventually, but pressed on. When I got to the strange gate over yonder, I thought I was done for. I could see yer kingdom, floatin' in the air, but I didn't rightly know a way to cross over. I'm mighty happy ye saw me, though I don't reckon I understand how."

Robby continued to pace, and he had rather absently listened to the last few minutes of Eldwin's story. Besides the disconcerting and sad news concerning Tyrin and Esildre, he was distracted by his feelings of embarrassment and shame that he had not watched over his friends more carefully. Finn could not help but notice Robby's agitation and his odd demeanor, but he said nothing, and shook his head a time or two whenever Robby glanced his way.

"I would like to say again how sorry I am to hear about Esildre," he said to Eldwin. "I must confess that I had ill feelings concerning her, and I feel bad about that."

"Because of Lord Ullin?" asked Eldwin.

"Yes, because of Ullin. So you know what happened between Esildre and Ullin. What happened to Ullin. Afterwards, that is."

"I do, sir. Ashlord told me all about that, an' he an' Raynor explained much about Esildre to me that I never knew. Though we spent a fair time together in Nowhere, she seldom talked very much. I knew something was amiss with her, something pretty awful. But until I went to Duinnor, I didn't understand. I'm still not sure that I do, exactly."

Robby nodded.

"Ashlord tried to set me straight concerning her," he said. "That it wasn't really her fault, what happened. Well. I am sorry. Especially since, having heard from you the manner in which she passed away, I feel that I know something more of her tormented life."

"That is kind of ye to say. As I said, that is why I came."

"And I can't say enough how thankful I am that you happened upon my dear friends at the moment of their need. I shall forever be in your debt for the quick and decisive action you took to save them."

"I only did what needed doin', sire."

"Nonetheless, Eldwin, you were there to do it," Robby said, wishing again that it had been he who saved Sheila and the others. He shook his head in an expression of relief as he wondered how many close calls there might be ahead, and how many people would be hurt because of his mistakes.

"I'd like to speak with Eldwin privately," Robby said to Finn and Lafkin. "But would one of you ask someone to bring up a meal for the two of us?"

"Certainly, sire."

• • •

"Won't you please have a seat?" Robby gestured to a seat as he took his favorite chair nearby. "I have news of my own to share with you, some of which concerns your friends and your kinfolk of Nowhere."

Eldwin looked uncomfortable as he sat, and put his hands in his lap.

"Ye've changed a great deal," Eldwin said. "More than I was led to believe."

"Yes, I have. I am much older, as you can see. And, in spite of my appearance, I am Elifaen."

"Oh."

"I would like to fill you in on things myself," Robby went on. "And I would like to ask you more about Lady Shevalia. I long to hear as much as you can tell me about her. Perhaps later, as we dine. I first need to tell you that I have wondered where you were. You see, I have been in touch with one or two of your people. Millithorpe, for example. I'll tell you how in a bit. The upshot is that they have agreed to do some errand-work for me. But, before I go into all that, I must ask you about your mission or your intent. You said earlier that you wanted to get back at Secundur. What did you have in mind?"

"I don't know, sir, I mean, sire," Eldwin shrugged.

"Sir, sire, or just plain Robby is fine," said Robby.

Eldwin nodded. "I think sire is fittin', if I can get used to it. I have no plan. I just got it into me head that I needed to do something about the feller who hurt Esildre so much. But I reckon I thought something would come to me along the way. Ashlord said I should come here an' see if I could find ye. He said ye'd know better than anyone what could be done. Only, well, I left out a few things. Things I didn't want to mention in front of the other gents."

"If you mean that Esildre's ghost came along with you, I know. She is standing behind you, and though Finn and Lafkin apparently never saw her, she has been in this room ever since you entered it."

Eldwin craned his neck and saw Esildre standing across the room, staring through the window at the apparition in the sky. Though she wore her armor and battle gear, Eldwin could see right through her form as she wavered in and out of distinctness.

"So I knew," Robby went on, "the instant she entered that something terrible had happened. And, I must admit, that is why I acted so coldly at first. Frankly, I was quite frightened. Especially when I realized that Finn and Lafkin could not see her. They could not fail to notice my agitation, I'm sure."

"I am sorry, sire. She is uncanny, an' strange. I've never known a ghost before."

"Neither have I. I've seen my share of weird things, many frightful things, too. Yes, she is both frightening and uncanny."

"An' she is moody, sire. The closer we got to Shatuum, the more afraid she became. I didn't want to come through that awful place, but saw no other way to get here. She wasn't very helpful, screamin' an' cryin', right up until we entered Shatuum. An' then she disappeared completely. I thought she'd gone away until I got onto the bridge that ye put out for me. Then she reappeared beside me, just as ye see her now. In her armor."

Esildre still stared away from them as Robby and Eldwin watched her.

"I think she knows something important about Secundur," Eldwin said.

"*I do*," came an emphatic voice. The sound set the glass in front of her buzzing and sent another stream of chills dancing up the back of Robby's neck.

"*I know how to kill him.*"

There was a change in her aspect as she turned around to face them. She became more substantial, the color of her armor darkened from light gray to dark blue, and her skin became almost life-like. But it was her eyes that were most alarming. At first, they were hollow shadows, but as she faced them, they burned with amber fire.

"*But I cannot do it alone.*"

"Ye know that I'll do me part," said Eldwin.

"And I'll have you know that I'll do mine, too," said Robby.

• • •

Meals were brought to Robby and Eldwin, and they ate. It was a strange conference that then took place between a king, a ghost, and a little person. It was difficult to work out what Esildre had to tell them, because she seemed so distracted. It was as if she heard sounds that neither Robby nor Eldwin could hear. Sometimes, while struggling to express a thought, she could barely speak, or her words were difficult to make out, as she passed from near-hysterical bouts of crying and moaning to angry silence, only to fall into pitiful whimpers, stuttering as if racked with shivers. As her mood changed and went back and forth, so, too, did her appearance, sometimes so thin that she could barely be seen, and other times as real as any person of flesh and blood. But eventually Robby understood what it was that she was trying to say, and he knew what must be done. And no one else but they three could accomplish it. So he told Eldwin about his plan, which first required that he tell Eldwin about dreamwalkers. Eldwin listened as Robby tried to explain. Afterwards, Eldwin remained silent, but Robby knew that he was skeptical.

"Well, you won't believe what I have told you until you see for yourself," Robby concluded. "But you will, this very night! And you'll see how my plan is to work, and how others of your people are already helping me. But you saw the nature of Shatuum. Are you brave enough to go back there?"

Eldwin looked over at Esildre. She no longer wore her armor, but was attired in the same way as when she traveled to Duinnor with Tyrin. And now she sat on the floor near the fireplace, her form so insignificant in substance that he could see right through her to the flames behind her. She sat with her knees up and her head in her hands, weeping softly.

"Yes," said Eldwin. "I had better be, hadn't I?"

Chapter 27

To Touch a Dream

As Robby and Eldwin discussed their plans, Serith Ellyn sat outside of her tent and watched the sky. Thurdun sat beside her, and Gaiyelneth nearby. Thurdun commented how the heavenly apparition appeared later each night, and Gaiyelneth observed that it moved slowly southward, from night to night, away from the constellation where it had first been seen. Engrossed by her own thoughts, Serith Ellyn was no more talkative now than she had been all day, and at last she rose from her chair and entered her tent without saying a word. A short while later, she was greeted by a Dragonkind woman who called herself Micerea. With her were two others, a Man and an Elifaen.

"We come together to show you that all races may serve Griferis and its king," Micerea said. "Indeed, our King respects not one race over another, nor any one realm over the next, but holds all to his own standard to be measured by his own judgment."

"Philawain, King, does not care whether his servants are amongst the high-born of the earth, or the meek," said the Man.

"He does not care whether they have been long upon the earth, or just born into it," said the Elifaen. "So that you may see this, come with us, and behold his kingdom, and see those who labor with Philawain to bring about a new world."

So Serith Ellyn was taken to Griferis to see it once again, for the first time since she herself was tried there. At first, she was terrified at the prospect of going back into the place, but she found her courage to go, and as soon as they entered, she saw how it was changed. Its once lonely corridors and rooms were now full of movement and sound. Some of the workers she saw labored with mundane tasks such as would be seen in any estate. Others toiled with books and scrolls, making tallies and entering figures beyond her comprehension. Standing on ladders, a few servants went about hanging works of art on walls that before had been completely unadorned, and they were the most amazing paintings and murals and drawings. Dragonkind men laughed with Elifaen as they worked together to move tables and chairs. Girls sang as they washed laundry, and old Men directed with their walking sticks how a tree was to be moved from one place to another in the garden. Small children sat in a vast room filled with books. Some of them read silently, and, in another part of the room, a woman stood, holding a newborn infant in her arms, bouncing it gently while still managing to hold a book, reading from it to several young children.

• • •

Late the next day, Serith Ellyn's tent was pitched, and when Gaiyelneth spread out a rug for the floor, out from within the folds rolled the Queen's scepter. Astonished, she picked it up and was staring at it when Serith Ellyn entered.

"Do you not know that only the sovereign of Vanara may touch that staff?" Serith Ellyn asked.

Wide-eyed and flustered, Gaiyelneth fell to her knees, bowing her head and holding the scepter out for her Queen to take. Strangely, Serith Ellyn laughed as she took it.

"It is a day to be remembered," she said, "when Gaiyelneth is at a loss for words!"

• • •

A man calling himself Harrald Delorick came to Serith Ellyn that night, and he took her again to the Dragonlands. They went to see the Great Stone.

"Do you know this object?" Delorick asked.

"I have only seen it in depictions," Serith Ellyn replied. "But who would not know it who knows of Alonair the Sculptor and how he challenged Kalzar to cut it from the mountains and to move it across the deserts?"

She walked around the massive block, resting unevenly in the windswept sand that piled around it. She was amazed by it, and was equally amazed that it had been moved as far as it had been before being abandoned.

"I wonder what Alonair intended to make of it?" she mused aloud.

"Who can say, my lady, but Alonair himself? Now that you have seen it, come with me to look upon another place."

He took her northward, to the ruins of an ancient city. It was the same place where Ullin and Micerea had stayed for a time when they first met, where they found water and a little rabbit, too.

"Do you know this place? Have you ever seen it before?"

"I do know it," she said. "I have twice seen it. Once, when I had wings, I looked down upon it from the high air as I flew over it. At that time, it was beautiful, and this broad circle of sand was a lake. From it came water to spread throughout the city, and into fields beyond where there were vineyards and wheat. It was then called Darini. I saw it again, a long time later, after I was Scathed. I came here with my brother on a dare, when Silmain was King. We heard it had been abandoned. The desert sands have covered over much more of it since then. But, though abandoned and forlorn, the desert cannot fully erase its beauty."

"Do you know how it came to be abandoned, or what happened to its people?" her guide asked.

"No."

"The people of this city revolted against Kalzar when he took their craftsmen as slaves to wrest the Great Stone. He took their wheat to feed his armies, just as he emptied all of the Dragonlands of its wealth to take the Great Stone out of the mountains. The people of this city could not resist his might, but nor would they suffer his abuse of them. To spite Kalzar, they stopped the waters that flowed here, and they abandoned their beautiful city. They traveled northward. With stealth and cunning, they traveled far away to be out of reach of Kalzar. Come, and I shall show you where they went to, and where the descendants of those people still abide."

Delorick offered his hand once more, and when she put her hand into his, the scene blurred as if the world spun. Suddenly, she found herself standing before a column of stone, topped by the likeness of a huge human skull.

"This is Nasakeeria!" she gasped.

"It is," Delorick said. "Have no fear. Only those of the waking world who pass beyond are slain by Aperion's Fire."

"Aperion's Fire?"

"Yes. When Cupeldain attacked the Dragonkind, those who had come from Darini and who had settled here were filled with fear. They were not a warlike people, and had no defense. And when they heard of the Scathing of those Faerekind who remained in the world, they pleaded with Beras for mercy. They knew that if they were discovered, they would be slain. Beras heard their prayers, and sent Aperion to make a border of fire around this place, so that no creature on two legs nor any carrying one might pass through its borders. But neither could the people of Nasakeeria leave this place, except for a few who might take the form of animals. Come. Let me show you this land and its people."

They passed over the border without incident or harm, being creatures of the dream world, and Delorick showed Serith Ellyn the villages and farms of Nasakeeria. She saw how the people there made their neat and clean homes, how they tenderly looked after their children, and how they worked diligently. She heard them tell stories of where they came from, filled with the hope and the promise that they might someday return to their ancient lands.

"But where are their fields of darakal?" Serith Ellyn asked Delorick. "They are a hale and beautiful people and must take the herb in copious amounts to remain so."

"No, Queen. There is no darakal here. When the Faerekind made the southern lands into deserts, they delved up rock and stone and raised a great dust. In that dust was poison, though they knew it not, a dust that salted and polluted all of the waters of the Dragonlands. It settled into the deepest wells and seeped into the fertile soils of the seaside lands. The darakal herb relieves the Dragonkind of the poison, but there is not enough of it for all. Did you think that Beras had cursed the Dragonkind with their chronic illnesses and their short lives?"

"That is what is commonly thought among the Elifaen."

"It is not true. Your own kind did that to them, and my King, Philawain, wishes you to know it. Long before the days of Kalzar, the Faerekind cursed them. It was the Faerekind, your own people, who wished to spite the Dragonkind by making the deserts. Your people poisoned them, not Beras. Your people thus sowed the seeds of tyranny in that land, the seeds that would grow and be nurtured by their desperation and watered by their blighted lives."

Serith Ellyn looked at Delorick with distress, not wishing to believe him.

"But here there is no such poison," the man went on. "The waters here are clean, and the food, too. And these people are how the Dragonkind once were. And how they may all be once again. Indeed, Philawain, King, works to make it so. For as long as the darakal herb is needed by them, they will be slaves to the powerful who control its cultivation and its allotment. And they will be herded to war, prodded by their rulers and goaded by the health and wealth of the Northlands. Did you never wonder how it was, during the Great Invasion, that the Dragonkind who swept across the earth became all the stronger the longer they remained in the north? When you fought them at the Battle of Saerdulin, were you not amazed by their strength and their endurance?"

Serith Ellyn felt dizzy. Although she had come into the world during the Time Before Time, it was after the deserts were already made. And now, though she had nothing to do with its making, she felt ashamed and embarrassed and insulted. If what Delorick said was true, and her own people were responsible for the squalor and disease of the Dragonkind, then how full of ignorance, how full of arrogance was the Elifaen's history of war, revenge, and hatred. And how chronically desperate must the Dragonkind's existence be!

As she considered this revelation, its sting quickened her pulse. Collandoth and his conspirators had been right all along. The right way was to first find peace, no matter how uncomfortable, then solutions. Collandoth's instinct, his intuition, and his work had all been directed to that end. She had tolerated his ideals, somewhat patronizingly, because there was no great harm he could do by consorting with the Dragonkind, and perhaps something could be learned.

The early risers amongst the Nasakeerians, handsome men and pretty women, were beginning their day, going out to their fields and into their kitchens and to their looms. As Serith Ellyn watched, she continued to consider Collandoth. She was full of beliefs, and Collandoth had virtually none. But his faith was the greater, and his accomplishments in the world would be greater, too, and subtle. She knew, now, that she had never wielded much power, because, in spite of her firm beliefs, she never had much faith. She felt like a child who, deserving of a scolding, was all the more humiliated by Collandoth's patient restraint. She turned to Delorick.

"I have seen enough," she said.

"Of course, my lady. On behalf of King Philawain, I bid you good night."

• • •

She woke up and opened her eyes. Her heart still fluttered, and she found it difficult to swallow. She sat up, blinking her stinging eyes in the dim light. She absently rubbed her hands together as if wiping away some stubborn substance. When she realized what she was doing, she stared at her clean hands, thinking the blood would never come off. And, now, it was no longer just the blood of her father that stained her heart.

• • •

"Brother, do you remember when, during the time of Silmain, that we stole away from Vanara and traveled back to see Darini? We told father we were going on an expedition into the mountains, but instead made our way south."

Serith Ellyn and Thurdun had decided to walk for a spell. She led her mount by the reins, while Celefar, Thurdun's faithful buckmarl, followed along beside his master. It was nearly noon, and by now they were over halfway across the broad top of Middlemount. They would have been much farther along, as all knew, but for the Queen's peculiar lack of interest in speedy travel. Some, like Chanter and his sister Gaiyelneth, were concerned not only for their Queen, but also for their company, because their supplies would not last forever, and they had not even made the Plains of Bletharn. Some many yards apart, brother and sister followed brother and sister, each pair quietly expressing their worries to each other.

"Like it was yesterday," Thurdun said. "We were very foolish, weren't we? For all we knew, an army of Dragonkind could sweep over the dunes at any moment."

"No, your scouting skills have always been far too keen for us to get caught."

"Father would have been furious. Not to mention Silmain. Why do you ask about the dead city?"

"Because I had cause to remember it last night," Serith Ellyn said. "It was a beautiful place, was it not?"

"Yes. And marvelous. Almost as beautiful as when we first beheld it, from high up in the sky, before the time of Kalzar. I dare say, our people could have learned a thing or two from the inhabitants of that city, had we possessed the will to learn. About tilework and building. About beauty. Not even the Green Citadel was its match in elegance. A sad place, though, its people gone, the waters gone, and avenues covered by sand."

She nodded, rubbing her eyes. Thurdun glanced at her, hiding his concern with a smile.

"Odd lights," she said, blinking.

"Pardon me?"

"Nothing. Let's ride."

They turned to their mounts and were surprised to see Serith Ellyn's feathered cape draped across her saddle. It was the one she wore when sitting upon her throne during occasions of state.

"It just appeared!" cried out Gaiyelneth, rushing up. "Out of thin air. And, just for a moment, I thought I saw someone toss it there. A little woman! Do my eyes play tricks? Is it truly your cape?"

Serith Ellyn pulled it from the saddle and held it up, examining the blue and green plumes and its golden clasp.

"It is mine," she said. "Put it with my other things."

She handed it to Gaiyelneth, and then took to her saddle, releasing a long, heavy sigh.

"Whatever may tonight bring?" she said to herself.

• • •

They traveled on across Middlemount, as did Sir Sun across the sky, and soon he and they ended their day's journey as night fell. Not long afterwards, the heavenly sword was low in the starry sky. It had barely risen high enough to clear the southern horizon before it began to descend once more. As it glowed softly, Serith Ellyn was met in the realm of dreams by Finn. They stood together upon the broad snow-covered plateau, far away from her camp, with no one else in sight. The starry sky spread from horizon to horizon, bright upon every side.

"I come once more to you," he said, bowing. "And, with your consent, I bring the last of Philawain's signs for your consideration. Do you consent?"

"Yes, my lord," she said to Finn, with a slight bow, "I do consent, though I am greatly troubled by the things I have been shown, and by the delivery of the symbols of my reign. No longer do I doubt Philawain's power, for as easily as he may deliver things to me, he may also take away my Seven. As you told me when we first met, I see that he may do so at any time, and I cannot prevent it. Yet he has not done so, and it is a mystery that weighs upon me that he has not taken them."

"Do not bow to me, Queen," said Finn, smiling. "For I am but a servant. And it is not for me to understand Philawain's restraint, nor do I comprehend his power. But his intent is clear to me, as I think it dawns upon you, too. Tell me not your decision, if you have made it, but wait until tomorrow evening when the King himself will come to hear it. Tonight, though, he bids you look upon these creatures who are gathered before you."

Finn waved his hand, and between him and her there appeared in a semicircle six creatures: an owl, a rabbit, a vulture, a praying mantis, a chipmunk, and a firefly.

"Know that these are but a few who were abandoned when the Firstborn were Scathed of their wings. These and their siblings remain, abiding in the world to await their own full Becoming, just as the Faerekind once were come into the world. Look upon them and hear what they have to say."

Finn bowed and withdrew into the darkness that surrounded the dream. Queen Serith Ellyn, perplexed, looked at the assembly, her gaze going from one to the next until settling upon the little owl that looked remarkably similar to that which often accompanied Collandoth.

"I am Certina," said the owl. Immediately she appeared to Serith Ellyn as a beautiful woman with brown skin and short wispy hair about her head. She had wings, too, such as those that a bird may have, wrapped around her form.

"I am Beauchamp," then said the rabbit. As he spoke, he stood handsome and strong, and he bowed as his brown and tan robes fluttered in the breeze.

"I am Fallendine," said the vulture, transformed into a handsome black Elifaen, his powerful wings outstretched to the air before they folded behind him.

"I am Telliniece," said the chipmunk. And now Serith Ellyn saw her as a little girl, with a brown, hooded robe.

"I am Hanion," said the praying mantis. And he, too, was transformed into a tall thin Elifaen wearing a magnificent velvet suit of green. He bowed, his hands held together as a monk might do, as his straight, shimmering wings folded across his back.

"And I am Wink," said the firefly, whose light now coursed all over her lovely body as she stood erect and proud, a beautiful Elifaen woman. "We are the Familiars of the Melnari," she went on, "and have served them faithfully. But only the Melnari of Certina and Beauchamp are still with their companions. We others are released to find our own way."

"We are the representatives of many others of our kind who have patiently waited since the Time Before Time to be fulfilled of our form and spirit," said Beauchamp.

"We would have become Faerekind, as you once were," said Fallendine, "but for the sins of Cupeldain and the disobedience of the Elifaen, acts which halted such things from happening."

"You see us now somewhat as we were intended to be," said Hanion. "None but you and King Philawain have thus seen us so."

"Not even our Melnari ever saw us as we now appear to you, though we have longed for them to do so," said Certina.

"With each Unknown King, there came into the world a Melnari," nodded Fallendine, "who was to be a companion to one of us. They were to help move the world so that our destiny could at last be fulfilled, and they were to do other things, too. But the earth is strong, and only two have survived it. And, of all our Melnari, only Collandoth, has been transformed."

"But now things have come to a pass," said Telliniece, "and even he cannot do that which the Melnari were put here to do."

"For to each of them was given the power to attain great knowledge and wisdom, and to make it so that the Elifaen would know their place," explained Beauchamp. "But Secundur, through his works, has killed all but Raynor and Collandoth."

"Tolimay was killed by a demon-child, sent by Secundur," said Fallendine.

"Secundur made a fiery rock fall upon Banion," said Telliniece.

"Micharam was flogged to his death by a moth of Shatuum," said Hanion.

"And my companion, Ishtorgus, was swallowed by the Great Sea, stirred against him by Secundur's whisperings," said Wink.

One after another, they spoke to the Queen of Vanara, revealing to her that which they were sent to reveal. Their words formed visions of the things they said, for they all spoke the First Tongue. She saw the Time Before Time. She watched as Ishtorgus the Mariner was swallowed by a maelstrom, and as Barian the Counter was smitten by a falling star. As they spoke, she saw the deaths of the other Melnari as well, each falling victim to Secundur's power.

"So only Collandoth and Raynor remain," said Certina.

"And they two, by themselves, cannot bring about the great change required," stated Beauchamp.

"Philawain, King, knows these things, and he knows, too, the peril that the world now faces. He, alone, may make use of the Nimbus Illuminas, and he, alone, may thus thwart Secundur's dark ambition."

"The Unknown Kings that went before Philawain did not know how they, in their ambition, only prepared the way so that Philawain could do his work."

"Those kings did not know, nor did they care to know, their true role within the world."

"And by their power, they did much evil, thinking that they did otherwise."

"Like the Elifaen, they refused to see why they were moved to do what they did."

"In spite of their evil, a force moved through those kings, an obsession to do that which the High Houses of the Elifaen would not do. But, like the Elifaen of the High Houses, the Kings of Duinnor were blinded by pride and power."

"Each King of Duinnor thought to gather the Forty-Nine Bloodcoins in order to enslave the Elifaen, to use the Bloodcoins as leverage over the Elifaen and to increase his might and the might of Men."

"But each Unknown King only advanced the purpose of he who now moves in the world."

"Even Secundur, in all his delvings, could not divine this outcome."

"And now, he comes, the Last King of all, who shall undo much, and remake the world as should have been done long ages ago."

She saw, through their words, how past Kings of Duinnor had obtained different sets of the Forty-Nine. How they sent expeditions to the far reaches of the frozen north and into the most distant corners of the world. How the Bloodcoins were found and obtained, through luck, through intimidation, and through thievery and murder. The Queen of Vanara felt their obsession, their lust for supremacy.

"Knowing now, as you do, all these things," said Wink, "you know that the Forty-Nine are being gathered. And you know, too, that ownership of them is above your station, for they were never to be owned."

"Aperion waits," said Fallendine, "as he has since the Forty-Nine were given, to welcome home his family."

• • •

With these words softly resonating in her heart, the dream faded, and Serith Ellyn slowly woke. She stared at the darkness of her tent, strangely peaceful of heart. She had not made up her mind, but was no longer worried. There was something about seeing the Familiars and hearing their words that deeply affected her, something that she thought she ought to know, like a distant memory, just out of reach. Whatever it was, she could feel it, although she could not delve its meaning nor comprehend its nature. But it was vast, as if there was a cosmos at her fingertips, full of peaceful mystery, full of joyous nervousness, full of being and becoming, full of hope. Insubstantial, immeasurable, yet critically essential.

She turned over onto her side and reached out from her covers, putting her hand into the darkness and upon the small wooden case that held her precious Seven.

It was like touching a dream.

Chapter 28

The Queen and the King

The following morning, Gaiyelneth went to Serith Ellyn's tent with her breakfast and found her sitting at her table. In her lap was the box containing her Bloodcoins, and she held the lid open, staring at them. Gaiyelneth placed the tray on the table, and stood aside. At last, Serith Ellyn noticed the food and put the box on the table, still open. She sipped the tea, holding the cup with both hands to feel its warmth and closing her eyes to enjoy its flavor.

"Would you ask Thurdun to come to me?"

"Yes, my lady."

A few moments later, Thurdun arrived.

"We are almost ready to break camp, sister."

"Sit, Thurdun, please. Stay, Gaiyelneth."

Thurdun took a seat across from his sister, eyeing the Bloodcoins, as Gaiyelneth stood nearby.

"Would you say that we are about half of the way across Middle-mount?" she asked.

"I think we are. Soon we should turn south and descend to the plains."

"I would like to linger," she said. "May we stay here for a day or so?"

"Of course, my sister. Has your sleep been troubled? Or do you feel indisposed in some other way?"

"I feel fine, Thurdun. I am weary, but it is not from travel, nor is it from bad dreams. I wish to stay in camp this day and decide on the morrow whether to continue on or linger for another day."

"Then it shall be as you desire."

"Thank you," she reached her hand across the table and took Thurdun's. "Gaiyelneth."

Gaiyelneth took her other hand.

"I wish I could say all that is in my heart, dear brother, dear friend. You two know it best, but much is hidden within it that I wish I could put into words. I am very sorry if I have disappointed either of you, as Queen, as a sister, or as a friend."

"Never in life, my lady!" said Gaiyelneth, kneeling beside Serith Ellyn's chair. "Pray tell me, why you think such a thing?"

"Dear sister," said Thurdun. "We all do the best we may, and you have done better than anyone else could have. Why do you worry?"

"If I have not disappointed either of you," Serith Ellyn said, "then I may yet do so, and our people, too. Gaiyelneth, you are young in the world and full of life. I would not have you spend your days in service to me, sacrificing your happiness for mine. I know that Lord Seafar loves you, dear girl, and I think that, for my sake, he and you play too cautiously with your hearts. Do not do so! Thurdun, you too, have given up too much. You are handsome and wise, and would make a fine husband and father. Yet you have not taken a wife, nor sought one to love. But I know there is love in your heart, like there is water in a deep well, clean and fresh. I wish to release both of you from my service."

"Dear Queen!" exclaimed Gaiyelneth, her eyes welling.

"Why do you say this?" Thurdun asked.

"When Vanara is once again under your feet, and we have this journey behind us," explained Serith Ellyn, "much in the world will have changed. I ask only your indulgence until that time."

"You shall have it, now and forever, dear lady," said Gaiyelneth.

"We are your faithful servants," said Thurdun, "and if you dismiss us, I daresay we shall serve you still."

Serith Ellyn smiled.

"Let us remain here for the day," she said, "and see what tomorrow brings."

• • •

And that is what they did. Serith Ellyn went out from her tent several times during the day to take the air. She spoke with every member of her company, walking out to sit with those who watched far afield, and to chat about nothing in particular. In the late afternoon, with Thurdun and Gaiyelneth at a respectful distance, she walked alone, looking at the deep, blue sky for a long time, watching birds fly overhead, and watching the rabbits and deer that crossed her path. She was still well outside their camp when the sunset came, and she watched until the last of Sir Sun's pink robes turn to purple and the first stars appeared.

That night, she sat at the fire in the middle of her camp, and taking a mandolin from one of the soldiers, she played and sang. Some of the songs were sad and lonesome, but some were ballads of love, or walking songs often sung by workers at their looms or in the fields of Vanara. She even sang a bawdy drinking song, laughing with the soldiers who sang with her, who were all amazed that she could even know such a song, much less sing it in such a flirtatious manner. At the end of it, as everyone laughed and applauded, she bade them all good night. Smiling, she then went to her tent.

• • •

She dreamed of a summer day. She was walking through a grove of apple trees, the branches drooping with fruit. It was a bright day, and warm, and beside her walked the King of Griferis. They did not talk about the Bloodcoins. They did not need to. Instead, they talked like old friends about happy things and things that excited them about life. Robby talked about the time when he was first getting to know Sheila, and how, without even realizing it, he fell in love with her.

"And, you know, in spite of her lessons, I never once caught a fish!"

Serith Ellyn laughed.

"The things we learn!" she said. "And the things we wish we had learned! But look at you!"

She turned and touched his arm, her eyes full of sympathy.

"I think you have suffered too much in too short a time," she said. "Yet, you have done, in Griferis and outside of it, what I could never have done. And, all the while, you were mortal and could have died at any moment."

"I did eventually die," he said, grinning. "At least I was a little bit dead, else I could not have learned what I know. But you have suffered, too, and for a very long time. Nearly since the beginning of the world."

"But it has been a slow suffering," she said, "easy to grow accustomed to. Too easy. And too easy to think very much of the suffering of others, I am sorry to say."

"Hm. Perhaps. I am Elifaen, too, now. And, being such, and having acquired the Name besides, I know something about the stretch of time and the stretch of memory. But I also know something about what might have been, had things gone a little differently, one way or the other. And I see what is to come."

"It is not all good, is it?"

"I'm afraid not. But it won't last forever."

• • •

The following morning, Gaiyelneth was aroused from sleep by the aroma of food, and, thinking that she had overslept and had missed taking the Queen her breakfast, she sat up abruptly. She rubbed her eyes, and blinked, seeing Serith Ellyn setting down a plate of breakfast on Gaiyelneth's little table and a cup of tea, too.

"Oh, my Queen! Have I overslept?" she cried, kicking off her blankets and scrambling to her feet. "Oh! Oh!"

"Calm yourself!" commanded Serith Ellyn. "You have not overslept. And if you had, it is not a concern. I only thought that I'd bring breakfast to your tent."

Gaiyelneth pulled on her morning cloak, as she stared at the Queen, who now sat crosslegged on the floor beside Gaiyelneth's chair.

"Please, sit. Do eat," Serith Ellyn said, smiling.

Cautiously, Gaiyelneth came over and sat, looking at Serith Ellyn with suspicion.

"I think it is not right, my lady," she said, "that you should serve me so."

"And why not? May I not do as I wish to do?"

"Of course, my Queen! But, I mean, of course you may!"

"Very well, then. Besides, I must practice."

"Pardon me, my lady? Practice?"

"Yes. That is to say, I must become accustomed to serving others."

"Whatever do you mean by that, my lady?"

"It is more the idea of it, than the skill of it, I mean."

Gaiyelneth, sitting, looked at her plate, then at her Queen.

"Once again you seem at a loss for words," Serith Ellyn laughed. "Twice within a week! Surely the world as we know it comes to an end!"

"My Queen!"

"Eat, so that we may depart as soon as you are ready."

"Yes, ma'am. I shall be quick about it, then."

"Take your time, there is no hurry."

"I long to get back to Vanara as much as any of us, my lady," said Gaiyelneth, stuffing too large of a piece of bread into her mouth and chewing rapidly as Serith Ellyn stood and went to the tent flap.

"I know that you do. But we must first make a detour."

Gaiyelneth, trying to swallow so that she could ask about it, stood as the Queen departed. She stared at the rustling tent flap and finally managed to swallow.

"Detour?"

Chapter 29

The Storm

Certina hovered momentarily over the high roof peak of the Temple where Robby sat, then she softly and silently descended to stand beside him. She looked at him, examining how he sat, and then, a bit awkwardly, she sat, too, letting her wings drape behind her. She pulled up her legs and put her arms around her knees, copying Robby's posture and glancing at him so as to get it right. She turned her eyes toward Duinnor City, a small sea of lights across the night-veiled valley before them, and watched as Robby did.

"I gave Collandoth your message," she eventually said.

"Thank you," Robby replied.

"I think he already knew, though."

"That would not surprise me."

On Robby's other side, Fallendine stretched out on the sloping tiles, leaning on one elbow that was hooked over the roof ridge upon which Certina and Robby sat, his long legs crossed in a relaxed manner and his even longer wings folded. Together, the two Familiars and Robby gazed out thoughtfully.

The night mists slowly gathered in the valley, and the lights of the city gradually went out, one by one, as its inhabitants went to their rest. The rooftop trio had nothing in particular to watch for, and nothing in particular to say to each other. They were content with their company, and the vista before them was conducive to their rambling thoughts.

"Someday," Certina said, "I would very much like to eat an apple."

Robby nodded. He liked apples and knew that Certina, should she ever get the opportunity to eat one, would like them, too.

"Someday," Fallendine said, "I would very much like to take a bath."

Both Robby and Certina nodded, perhaps wishing that Fallendine could take one right away. After a while, Robby turned to look first at Fallendine, then at Certina before turning his attention back toward the city.

"I know that there are many things you two have longed for. To do, to eat, to experience," he said. "Maybe it won't be too much longer before you get to do so. At least not compared to how long you've already waited."

"I hope that I will be a good person," Fallendine said.

"Me, too," nodded Certina.

"You are both already good persons," Robby said. "Trapped, perhaps. But good-hearted. If you keep your good hearts, and if you let them guide your actions, you will continue to be good persons, doing good things. It is hard, sometimes. Sometimes it seems impossible, too much. But one shouldn't falter on one's course because of a few wrong turns along the way."

"I will try to remember that," said Certina.

"Me, too," nodded Fallendine.

The mists thickened and obscured most of the few remaining lights so that only those within the loftiest spires and towers remained clear. The High Tower of the King was one of those, above all others, and the golden light that periodically glowed and then faded from its windows was evidence of the ever-restless and worried monarch.

Robby sighed.

"I suppose it is time I began," he said.

"Good luck," said Fallendine.

"Good luck," said Certina.

• • •

It was a clear day when travelers from the western territories first brought word to Duinnor City about a strange sight they had seen along the way. But none of the few who believed their tale understood its import. A few days later, riders came out of the southwest, galloping hard to the city, and they told the same story: a strange storm brewed over the snowy mountains, and it was moving. It rose up over the mountains, they said, a great black cloud, split with lightning and rumbling loudly, though the sky all around was clear and blue.

As night fell, the western sky flashed, and those in quieter places of the city could hear the low throb of far away thunder. Many climbed to their rooftops, or stood on the walls of the city to gaze at the uncanny light, speaking in subdued tones to one another. By noon the following day, the mysterious cloud could be seen in the distance, flashing purple and red, and none could ignore the powerful rumbles, each more dense and foreboding than the last.

Among those who watched the approach were Ashlord and Raynor, standing, as they had done all morning and the previous night, atop the west tower of Starlight Hall. In the late afternoon, they were joined by the other guests of the Hall, and Lady Highleaf, too, and they all peered out over the banister.

"Don't it seem like it's gettin' closer?" asked Billy, still trying to catch his breath after climbing the steep twisting stairs to the tower's highest platform. "I mean, since this mornin', anyways?"

"Yes, Master Bosk," said Raynor. "It comes this way."

"And if it keeps its pace and course, it will be here sometime tonight," added Ashlord.

"But it is so odd," said Farby. "Not a cloud elsewhere, and not a breeze to be felt."

"That will soon change, I think," answered Ashlord.

"And do you think it is what I think it is?" asked Sheila.

Ashlord nodded.

Farby and Billy looked at them, and at each other.

"It looks bad," stated Ibin in a song-like manner.

"You have no reason to be afraid of the cloud, Ibin," said Ashlord, putting a hand on Ibin's shoulder, "or what it brings."

"I wonder how the Palace is taking it," commented Farby. "Surely its occupants suspect."

"I imagine that the confusion of these past weeks continue all the more," shrugged Raynor. "They must be in a panic over what to do."

"But there's nothing he can do," said Ashlord, meaning, as they knew, the King.

"The city'll be in even more of an uproar," said Billy, watching a long series of bright flashes light up the distant cloud so violently that they could discern folds in the storm as a jagged fan of bolts etched across the billowing mass.

"The Kingsmen will keep order," Farby stated, glancing the other way over the city and toward the High Tower of the Palace. "I'm sure they've already doubled their usual patrols and such. And I imagine our Captain Thrubold will continue to have his hands full. No doubt he has already put men at the city gates to keep his suspects from fleeing."

A particularly long and powerful roll of thunder reached their tower, and it grew in density and strength, coming up from the floor as much as through the air, then faded slowly away.

"Oh my goodness gracious me!" uttered Lady Highleaf. "I shall not remain here a moment longer, and I advise all of you to come down with me at once. I'll have you know that this tower has been struck six times by lightning!"

"The copper roof and the long iron downspouts will protect us," said Raynor.

"I doubt that very much, sir," Lady Highleaf said as she made her way to the stairs. "Besides, I'm not sure how much shaking this tower can withstand. Oh! Oh!"

A powerful gust of wind blew from the east, upsetting Lady Highleaf's hat. She put a hand on her head and bolted down the stairs and away.

"Sir Wind races to the storm," commented Billy, "so it'll be a big one, indeed!"

"Yes, and I think it comes faster than before," said Sheila. "Listen!"

The bells of the city's watchtowers were ringing, a sign that the gates would soon be closed and barred. Sheila pointed to a chariot going along the street outside Wysteria Place. A Kingsman drove it along slowly, and another stood next to the driver with a megaphone to his mouth.

"What's he sayin'?" asked Billy, cupping an ear.

"…take shelter as soon as you may do so," came the voice. "We expect the storm will arrive shortly after sunset. It may prove to be a powerful one. Hear ye! Hear ye! Secure all outdoor items that may be damaged by wind or hail or rain. Shutter your windows and take shelter as soon as you may do so…"

"Well! This is the first time I have ever heard such a proclamation!" Raynor said. "And the city has seen many storms."

"I would guess that General Chadler is behind it," said Ashlord, "since he may well suspect what is taking place and wishes to assure order. Keeping people off the streets should help keep calm over the next days."

"Raynor, weren't you here the last time a New King came?" asked Sheila. "Was it like this?"

"Yes, and no. There was a storm, of sorts. But it formed only over the Palace, and it came suddenly, without warning."

"Then, if this is the New King coming, do you think he comes slowly for a reason? To make people nervous and full of fear?"

"It seems a terrible thing to do, if that is so."

"I think he means to say that he has business not only with Duinnor's king, but with Duinnor's people, too," suggested Ashlord.

"Like 'get ready, here I come?' " asked Billy.

"Something like that."

Another blast of wind swept through, stiffer than the previous gust, so that the group all cried out in surprise and gripped the rail for balance.

"I think Lady Highleaf's onto somethin'!" yelled Billy, hurrying to the stairs.

• • •

As the storm approached, panic slowly grew amongst the inhabitants of Duinnor City, in spite of the best efforts of the Kingsmen to instill calm. People hastened here and there, some to purchase bread, others to board up their storefronts or stable their animals. When afternoon waned toward dusk, the sun passed behind the eerie cloud, and its shadow darkened the streets and all of the surrounding lands. By the time sunset would normally have been expected, the lightning and thunder of the storm were almost constant, and the wind blew erratically, sending powerful gusts up and down the near-empty streets, banging shop signs off their hangers, making whirlwinds and dust demons at intersections, and upsetting the stands of a few street vendors who had not heeded the warnings. Those who had not yet gone indoors hurried to do so. As for the Kingsmen, they soon gave up their heralding cries and put away their megaphones to seek shelter themselves, for none but the dead could possibly ignore the fact that a mighty storm was nigh upon the city.

The first raindrops struck the western walls shortly before midnight, and soon they were falling cold and hard in heavy sheets mixed with hailstones the size of acorns so that, between the constant window-rattling thunder and the clatter of hail, the sound was nearly deafening. With that, the storm broke full across the entire city, blotting out the Five Stars above and flooding the streets with icy cold water. Parents clutched their children and held them tight within their houses, and those who had cellars fled into them. Horses kicked and cried in their stalls to be let free to escape, and birds in their nests and roosts put their heads under their wings and tried to hold onto their shifting perches. On the mountaintop where stood the Temple, the great gong rang every minute, but none beyond a furlong from that place could hear it over the noise of the storm. Inside the Temple, the monks gathered in the sanctuary to chant and to pray, while the Oracle paced up and down in front of the mysterious glass pyramid, crying out between fits of hysterical laughter, "The end of days draws nigh!"

All the night long the storm unleashed its fury upon the city, keeping everyone awake with its howling wind and cracking thunder. When dawn came at last, the storm relented, the rain eased, and a dense fog settled over Duinnor City. Somewhere above the King's Palace, lightning still flashed, followed by soft, grumbling thunder. As morning grew into day, the fog persisted so that no change in light could be discerned, as if Sir Sun was powerless to penetrate it or to part the mists. Pensive hours passed, and many brave souls ventured out to peer around tentatively. Eerie flashes of bright white lit the fog, and growling thunder resonated.

At the Temple, a monk approached the Oracle, and after a word the two went to the doors and pushed them open so that the monk and Oracle could step out onto the portico. A flat blanket of fog extended from their porch as far as could be seen, and through the mist above they could make out a hint of blue sky. But what the monk fetched the Oracle to see was an immense mass floating above the city, somewhat obscured by flashing clouds and billowing fog. They looked upward at it, and it seemed as if they peered at a mountain. As the mists and fog rolled and churned around the apparition, and as lightning blinked through, they had momentary glimpses of a marvelous castle, and atop five of its seven towers winked a star.

The Oracle's chair was brought to him so that he could sit and watch, and this he did for the rest of the day. Little changed until the late afternoon when the fog thickened, the lightning grew more frequent, and the thunder increased in volume. By nightfall, the storm had resumed and was pounding the city even harder than the night before. Once again, and all night long, it crashed and boomed, it blew and howled, and it hammered the city. And, when morning finally came, it was like the morning before, and the storm eased. So worn out were the residents that few bothered to venture forth, to open their shops or go to their places of work, choosing instead to remain indoors to sleep or perhaps to survey the damage to their homes. But in the late afternoon, a blinding light and jarring crack announced another night of frightful storms. Not only did it send the few intrepid wanderers scurrying back inside, but it fully awoke all who may have napped. Again, and worse than before, the storm beat the city. And each night and each day afterwards was the same and worse, with days dripping with fog and nights filled with terrifying wind and driving rain, with deafening thunder and blinding light.

On the sixth dawn, when all expected some relief, none was to be had. Indeed, as the hours passed, the storm only became more violent. Roofs leaked, and some were blown bare of shingles. Lightning struck many high buildings, scoring and buckling copper roofs and mangling iron balconies. Trees uprooted and toppled, and the streets ran like rivers, pouring through the gaps underneath the city gates to run away as gushing streams into the surrounding valley. No one could get a blink of sleep, and if it had not been for the violence of the storm, many would have pushed open the abandoned gates to attempt an escape from the beleaguered city. On and on it went throughout the day, and but for the lightning that flashed nearly constantly, it would have been as dark as night. There was no respite, no relief, and the wails of the people, children and adults alike, rejoined that of the wind.

• • •

"This is awful!" cried out Sheila, barely audible over the noise, her hands over her ears and her eyes shut tight as she flinched.

She and her friends were in the cellar of Starlight Hall, at the insistence of Lady Highleaf who was there also, along with all of her servants, sitting in chairs or on the floor among the wine casks and kegs and racks of bottles. Sheila was not the only one in terror of the storm, and many looked up at the ceiling, hearing the great hall above them creak and shudder in spite of its thick walls, strong timbers, and sturdy roof. In the candlelight, Ashlord puffed his pipe calmly, keeping an eye on those around him. Many of the maidservants held each other as they cried, while some of the men's eyes darted from shelf to ceiling as the wine bottles rattled and shook. He watched his friends, too, Sheila sitting on the floor between Ibin and Farby, and Billy next to Raynor. Lady Highleaf, sitting in an armchair brought down for her, had her eyes closed, and she clutched the arms of her chair so tightly that Ashlord feared she might crush the wood.

"It will pass, in time," Ashlord said.

"I hope Certina has found suitable shelter," said Raynor.

"If I know her, she is miles away, watching from a comfortable distance," Ashlord smiled. "But look at your friend!"

Ashlord gestured at Beauchamp who was close by, grooming his coat contentedly.

"Yes," Raynor shrugged. "For some reason, storms do not affect him in the least. I do look forward to going up to the Temple to thank the monks for taking such good care of him."

"Well, you should be able to do so soon. A couple of days at most."

"Ye mean this is apt to keep up for another few days?" Billy asked.

"The equinox is day after tomorrow, Billy. But I think the storm will abate before then."

• • •

Sheila, who seemed more affected by the storm than the rest, tentatively took her hands away from her ears and opened her eyes. Then, as another quaking boom resounded, she shrieked and put her hands back over her ears. Ibin put his arm around her, and she buried her face in his chest.

"Sorry! I'm sorry! I can't stand this!"

Ashlord got up and went over to Farby.

"Why don't we swap places for a bit," he said. "I'll see what I can do to relieve some of her anxiety."

When Ashlord sat beside Sheila, he leaned over and put his hand on her head.

"Come dear," he said, "tell me what it is that you are sensing."

Sheila, still clutching Ibin's hands, her eyes wide, turned to Ashlord. Though none could hear what he said, Ashlord spoke to her gently, in a low sing-song voice. As he did so, Sheila began to speak back to him, both of them speaking at the same time, one to the other. To Sheila's ears, Ashlord's words seemed to block most of the noise of the storm until it was a mere faraway hum, and it was as if the two were back at his old cottage at Tulith Attis, and he was coaxing Sheila to concentrate on a lesson, freeing her mind of her many worries in order to do so.

"My head is filled with awful visions," she said. "Like those I had when I was Scathed. But far worse, darker. I see a host of terrible creatures pouring across the lands of the world. Some are like wolves that walk upright as men do. Others are like the witch we saw in the Thunder Mountains, riding on the backs of loathsome-looking men that run like dogs, on all fours. I see horses with red eyes and black armor, carrying terrible riders also in black armor. These riders fling whips of cracking fire and hold up swords of red-hot iron. I see legions and legions marching behind these riders, with a red hourglass on their banners of black. And, at the head of them all, is a mighty warrior, more terrible than all the rest, riding a buckmarl that gnaws the bones of the conquered. This one I fear more than all of the rest put together."

Only Ashlord and Raynor could hear her words. And as she described her visions to Ashlord, he, in turn, continued his own speech to her, saying, among other things, "Let the fear of thy visions pass from thee. Let not the dread of what ye see blemish thy heart. Be not afraid. Speak all, and let it pass out of thee. Remember the visions, but let them be not frightful to thee. Be thou fearless before these things, confident in the will of Beras to bring peace and resolve to thee."

And so Ashlord, through Sheila, understood the time was nigh at hand for those things that all his years were but a preparation for. It did not make him afraid. He, Ashlord, who was brought back by Beras after being vanquished by Valkose the Demon, had yet to perform the greatest work of all his days. He smiled as he and Sheila ended their exchange and gazed into each other's eyes.

"I think you may begin to have Sight, my dear girl. And, I think that you will have much to do with how the world will soon be reshaped," he said to her. "And I shall help you in that work."

"I don't know what you mean, Ashlord," she said. "But I feel better now."

"Good. Then let me have a word with the others."

Ashlord stood and called out, "Hear me, friends!"

Immediately, all eyes opened and turned to him.

"This storm has no power over you," he continued, and though he spoke softly, all could clearly hear his words. "It is a warning only to those who have yielded to avarice, greed, and iniquity. Let the criminal be fearful. Let the evildoer tremble and the blameworthy be given notice. For, I say unto you: the New King cometh! Let us rejoice that we live in these days to see him come and may live to serve him, for the world has long awaited his arrival. I cannot tell you what to expect, what he may do, or what he may require of his subjects. Truly, terrible days are in store for the world, as its ancient evils are vanquished from it. But I tell you this: the New King of Duinnor shall be the last of all the kings of the earth, for after him, the fate of the world shall not be with the high nor with the mighty. He shall see the world remade. Blessed are we to witness his coming and to have our duty before us. Let us be glad, therefore, in our duty. Peace! Let peace be with you and within your hearts this night and for all the rest of your days."

As he spoke, it was as if a dark weight was lifted from those who heard him, for the power of his words was greater than his soft voice, and the fervent passion with which he spoke was shared with those before him. He bowed his head for a moment, and a loud peal of thunder cracked and shuddered the cellar, but none were frightened by it, nor were they afraid any longer. Indeed, as he took his seat on the floor beside Sheila, and she grasped his hand firmly, everyone began chattering away with questions and excited possibilities. This went on for several minutes until the door at the top of the steps burst open, making everyone jump with surprise. In the doorway above them stood a dripping figure, dressed in black with a hood drawn low. The figure turned away for a moment and called out, "They are down here!"

A moment later another figure appeared, in white clothing, just as wet as the first. He came down the stairs quickly, and then pulled back his hood to look around.

"Ullin!" yelled Ibin, jumping to his feet. "Ullin, Ullin!"

It was a raucous reunion, with Ullin's friends embracing him and all talking to him at once. After Ibin and Billy had a go at him, Sheila hugged

Ullin most tightly and unabashedly kissed him on both cheeks and the lips, then hugged him again.

"Have you seen Robby?" she asked at last.

"Just a moment, dear girl," interrupted Ashlord, grinning. "I'd like to give my greeting, too."

"Collandoth," Ullin said, taking both of Ashlord's hands in his.

"Ullin Saheed, my friend." Ashlord nodded, then they embraced and patted each other on the back. "Late, as usual."

"You know me," Ullin replied, smiling.

"And you brought a friend?"

"I would not be here otherwise."

Ullin held out his hand to Micerea. She stepped down from the stairs and took his hand. Her hood was pushed back somewhat, but her face was wrapped, all but her eyes, with caution for her reception. She glanced at Ullin's friends and the others who were there as Ullin pulled her close to him.

"If it had not been for this person, I would not be alive, and our New King would never come. My love, this is Collandoth, whom you have surely seen before, though not face to face. Collandoth, this is Micerea."

"I am honored, my lord," she said.

"The honor is truly mine. Indeed, this is a marvelous turn, I must say!" Ashlord bowed, taking her gloved hand and kissing it. "You do not know how happy this makes me! I congratulate you both on finding each other."

"Thank you," she replied with a dip of her head. "But it was Philawain, King of Griferis, who brought the two of us together, along with the help of Queen Islindia."

"Oh? Philawain? King of Griferis?"

"Yes, Collandoth." Ullin nodded, still grinning. "And soon to be King of Duinnor, too."

"Then you *have* seen him!" Sheila exclaimed.

"Yes. I have."

"And is he very much changed?"

"Ah. Yes, he is." Ullin's smile vanished as he glanced at Ashlord, then back at Sheila. "He is very much changed from when last you saw him."

"Oh, I don't think so!" Sheila smiled back at him.

"Oh?"

"Yes, yes!" Ashlord interrupted. "But we forget our manners. As you can see, we are gathered with other friends who have been kind enough to share their shelter and their hospitality with us. Let us acquaint you and Lady Micerea with them, shall we?"

"Certainly," Ullin agreed, "but, well, perhaps you would excuse Micerea for remaining somewhat modest?"

By now, Micerea had untied and removed her dripping cloak, revealing her light armor that none could mistake as from the Dragonlands.

"Let me take your cloak, my lady," Sheila said to her. "I'll just put it over here by the stove to dry. You must be freezing!"

"Thank you, Lady Shevalia. I admit I am cold, and drenched through and through."

"I suppose it should not surprise me that you call me that," Sheila said, looking askance at Micerea. "Though I suppose King Philawain has told you much about me."

"I know from my own skill."

"Oh. I see. And how do you come to know Ullin Saheed?"

"Nonsense!" Ashlord was saying to Ullin, then he turned to Micerea before she could answer Sheila. "My dear lady, allow us to make you as comfortable as we can. Surely your headdress is as wet as your cloak. I assure you that you are quite safe from persecution amongst us. Let us behold your face. Look upon us with confidence in our friendship, though some here may at first be surprised at who you are."

"Ullin told me it would be so with you and your friends," Micerea said, as all in the room listened, none more intently than Lady Highleaf, who was by now standing behind Ashlord.

"My dear girl," Lady Highleaf said, "if one could not tell by your clothes that you are from the Dragonlands, then one would certainly know by your beautiful accent. Come, dear. Worry not at how presentable you are, for you do not find any of us here looking our best, I dare say!"

Micerea removed her headband, and then her soaking shemagh, and let her shining black hair fall over her shoulders. She then looked up, first at Ullin, then at Lady Highleaf, who put her hand to her bosom.

"My word! We have amongst us two of the most beautiful women in all of Duinnor."

"You are too kind, my lady," Micerea said, bowing.

"She is," said Sheila, "though she does not exaggerate when it comes to you."

"May I present Lady Highleaf," Ullin said. "This is Micerea, daughter of Gurasa, of the House of Golden Sand."

"I am honored, my lady." Micerea bowed again.

"I am the honored one. The daughter of Gurasa himself!"

This began a flurry of introductions all around while Sheila helped Micerea off with her light armor and Billy and Ibin helped Ullin out of his wet things. Denks was imposed upon to brave the upstairs in order to fetch dry clothes for Ullin, and Sheila raced away to find some that were suitable for Micerea. Meanwhile, Micerea made the acquaintance of both Billy and Ibin, then, returning the grins of all of the others present, was introduced to each and every servant in turn, all of whom were fascinated by the exotic girl, none more so than Raynor, who was no stranger to the beauty of desert women. He immediately engaged her in conversation about desert wildflowers since he could not help but notice that her armor was engraved with floral embellishments. As all this went on, Ashlord spoke with Ullin.

"We have much to discuss, don't we?"

"Yes, but little time to do it." Ullin carefully removed the vest he was wearing. "Do you recognize this vest?"

"I most certainly do! It is Robby's, is it not? Does it still contain—"

"Yes. They are all here. All Seven."

"Marvelous! Then he has a plan."

"Yes, I'm sure he does, though I confess that I am in the dark about what it is. But, as you have no doubt surmised, he is here. Over the city."

"Yes. That much is apparent to me. But the means of his conveyance, beyond this persistent storm, is beyond me."

"He has brought his kingdom, and all of his subjects," Ullin stated. "Yes. Philawain is his name, and Griferis is his Kingdom. Micerea and I came by way of the Temple. We could see from those heights the vague form of his palace. One that we could not help but recognize as Griferis."

"A palace? In the sky? Griferis? Here? His subjects?"

"Yes, and the floating land on which the palace rests, in its entirety."

"But...?" Ashlord shook his head.

"I have no idea how he does it, Collandoth. Any more than I can guess how he does the other things that he does."

"Much to discuss, indeed! And what were you to do with your cargo?" Ashlord gestured to the vest.

"I am to deliver the Seven to Sheila," Ullin said, handing the vest to Ashlord. "But perhaps you will give them to her, and, if she does not know about them already, perhaps you could explain to her."

Ashlord stared at the vest that Ullin gave him, feeling in its folds the precious objects within.

"Why don't you give them to her yourself?"

"Because then she will ask me to explain everything, and that would delay us too long. Micerea and I are instructed by Robby, that is, by King Philawain to make for Nasakeeria without delay."

Ashlord blinked at Ullin.

"What? Nasakeeria? Why?"

"He has not told us why. And I don't think we should wait for the storm to pass. I have a feeling it is very urgent or else we would not have been asked to go."

"But you have only just arrived." Ashlord's eyes and voice was full of disappointment, though he quickly checked himself, seeing how it also pained Ullin to depart so quickly. "Of course, you must do what you must do. Do you have provisions? Horses?"

"Our packs are at the top of the stairs. The monks gave us food. I think we'll find what else we need along the way. No horses. We go on foot."

"On foot it would take you nearly two weeks to get there, at best."

"I know. So we must be on our way very soon, this very night."

Ashlord nodded, reaching into his pocket.

"Then take this purse," he said, handing it to Ullin. "There's not much there, but enough to keep you for a few days, if needed."

"Thank you."

Billy came up and interrupted. "Ullin ain't ye gonna tell us how Robby's gettin' along?"

"His name is Philawain, Billy," Ullin said, turning to face Billy. For the first time, Ashlord saw the bloodstained side of Ullin's blouse.

"You have been wounded!" Ashlord said, taking Ullin by the arm and turning him around to the light.

"Yes. I got into a bit of a scrape with a warrior of Shatuum," Ullin said. "Still hurts like the devil, too. He nipped me with his sword. Nearly got me with his whip, too."

"You encountered a warrior from Shatuum? A whip? Did he wear black armor, with a red hourglass?"

"Actually, I ran into two of them, on separate occasions. Yes, hot iron armor, black, with the red emblem, as you say. One of these," Ullin tapped the vest, "saved me from the first one. Micerea and Ayreltide saved me from the second one."

"Hm. Ayreltide? Islindia's winged horse? Pull off your blouse, and sit here in the light."

"Yes, the horse. I've been putting salve on it that seemed to help. It ran out five days ago. No. It's been longer than that."

"What did ye say Robby's name was?" persisted Billy, helping Ullin off with his blouse.

"Philawain. King Philawain."

Micerea jumped as thunder boomed and reverberated through the cellar. She was clearly nervous at the storm.

"Don't worry," said Lady Highleaf. "Ashlord has assured us that we are perfectly safe. Although I doubt if there'll be much left above us when we emerge from our little hole. Ashlord, won't you have a word with Lady Micerea concerning the storm? Perhaps you could ease her mind about it."

"Yes. One moment, please."

"Good grief! I hope there's a Duinnor left to reign over, and not just rubble and mud!" declared Ullin, wincing not from Ashlord's examination but at the jarring crash above them. "I'm sorry to cringe and flinch."

"I'd like for Sheila to have a look at this," Ashlord said to him. "Meanwhile, allow me to share few words with you and Micerea."

Ashlord gestured for Micerea to come close, and he began to speak to them, looking from one to the other with his penetrating gaze and his reassuring smile.

"He certainly has a way with words, doesn't he?" commented Lady Highleaf to Raynor as they watched from across the cellar.

"Yes, he does. If only they don't fall asleep."

"Oh, there are Denks and Lady Shevalia!"

Ashlord finished his short speech to Micerea and Ullin, who were now as calm as the others in the cellar, and Sheila took Micerea around and behind the wine racks to help her change.

"I don't know the manner of dress that you are accustomed to," Sheila said to Micerea. "But I have here a few things that I hope will do. I see that you dress as I prefer to do. Somewhat mannishly, that is. Is that usual for the women of your people?"

Micerea laughed, "I should say not!"

"Well, we are about the same size, I think, so I hope these will fit."

Sheila held out a dark green lady's tunic and matching breeches of a style popular among the Elifaen women of Linlally.

"Ah, so they have Vanaran fashions here?"

"Yes. Every fashion of clothes from every Realm, I imagine," Sheila nodded. "By the way, how did you and Ullin get into the city? I thought the gates were closed and barred."

"We came from the Temple, along the road that runs straight across the valley," Micerea explained. "The monks told us that the gates were closed, but we came anyway, fighting wind and pelting rain all the way across the valley. And when we approached, with lightning and thunder all around, the gate suddenly burst asunder, right off its pintles. We came right through."

"Oh! I suppose that was Robby's doings."

Micerea looked at Sheila and nodded. "So you know of his ability to open things."

"Yes. But you were going to tell me how you and Ullin met. Have you known each other very long?"

Everyone spoke nearly at the top of their lungs to be heard over the storm. Ullin changed into the breeches that Denks brought, and, with his blouse off, he re-emerged from a corner to wait for Sheila to have a look at his wound. Lady Highleaf introduced her nephew to Ullin, while she gazed all the while at Ullin's physique, embarrassing him with her approving expression. Ullin and Farby shook hands.

"You know, I think I have heard your name before," Ullin said to Farby as he pulled a blanket that Ibin handed him over his shoulders. "I think we have a mutual acquaintance, Reginald Bathwater."

Farby laughed. "Bothewater, you mean. Yes, it can be pardoned since we always teased him that if we got too rambunctious at a party, we be thrown out with the Bothewater! I know Reggie quite well. You?"

"I knew his father, and heard all about his son's antics when I was stationed with Lord Bothewater in Vanara. And, just so that you know, my mates and I made the same joke as you. But, Lady Highleaf, in point of fact, it was in this very place that I met Lord Bothewater's son, at an extravagant ball put on in honor of Kingsmen Cadets. Lord Bothewater was accompanied by his wife and son."

"Oh?"

"Yes, that must have been, oh, coming up on eighteen years ago, my lady. I was just beginning my studies at the Academy, the Year of the Lion."

"Oh. Then you must have kept to yourself," Lady Highleaf said, "for I'm sure I would have remembered you."

• • •

Like nearly all other residents of the city, those in the cellar of Starlight Hall (with the exception of Ashlord and Raynor) were exhausted after so long without sleep. Ullin and Micerea fared better, having slept regularly until their arrival at the Temple earlier that day. But they could not fail to notice the yawns and drawn faces of the others, heads nodding only to jerk back to full attention at the next clap of thunder. Sheila looked at Ullin's wound while he described how he had received it, jumping around in his tale somewhat as she and Billy peppered him with questions. Trying not to wince as she touched the area around the long burn-like welt on his side, he told them about the attack on Linlally, the long trek across the icy wastelands, and how they arrived at Mount Algamori where the marvelous gateway stood. Sheila asked Denks to fetch a few more things from up in the house. He hurried off to collect them, and Ullin described how Robby's appearance had changed so rapidly, instantaneously, it seemed, and how the stranger he had met, who turned out to be Robby, related tale after tale of Griferis.

"So he truly is much older," Ashlord commented.

"Just like in our dreams," added Billy. "An' ye really flew? Like birds?"

"Yes, like birds. And yes, he is older by two-dozen years or more," Ullin said. "Knowing now that it was Robby, that is, Philawain, who told me those tales, my heart aches at what he went through for so long. Terrible hardships on land and at sea, years of wandering, lost and destitute, until, in a time before us, he stumbled into Greenfar where those good people took care of him. Remember? It was just like the gentlemen in Greenfar told us had happened, years before we passed through. He was made to do and to suffer other awful things. In one night, he could not tell me all. But I see, now, that it was all in preparation. Oh!"

Suddenly Ullin closed his eyes in distress.

"I'm afraid that I have some very bad news. About Mirabella."

"We have already been informed, Ullin," Ashlord said.

"Oh."

"We were very saddened, to say the least."

"How did you find out?"

"Eldwin told us."

"Eldwin? The Eldwin of Nowhere? He is here in Duinnor?"

Ashlord told Ullin and Micerea about how Eldwin came just in time to save their lives, the news that he brought about Mirabella, the battle at Tallinvale, and about Esildre and the reason for Eldwin's journey to Duinnor.

"It was Esildre!" Micerea said to Ullin. "No wonder we made our mistake."

"What mistake?" Sheila asked.

"A few weeks ago, we had an encounter that frightened us terribly," Ullin explained. He and Micerea then told them about the apparition that they saw, and how Ullin had mistaken it for Sheila.

Sheila remained silent as they told the tale. Billy shuddered with goosebumps.

"But the spirit vanished," Ullin added, "and we hurried away from that place."

"It was terrible," Micerea said. "I was nervous and jumpy for days afterwards."

Raynor, who listened to it all in spite of being engaged with Lady Highleaf on some other matter, furrowed his brow, just as Ashlord did.

"I'm sorry that I mistook it for you, Sheila," Ullin said.

Sheila shook her head. "I have been mistaken for her," she said, "so I suppose it was only to be expected that she would be mistaken for me."

"So it must have been Esildre's spirit," Ullin said. "But why there? And why did she look the way that she did? Dressed as she was and with those scales and scars about her eyes?"

Raynor tactfully excused himself from Lady Highleaf and made his way to them.

"If the road you speak of threads through the mountains and comes up on the southwest side of the Temple, then I think I might answer you," he said as he sat on the floor beside Sheila.

"Yes, that is the road."

Sheila listened absently to Raynor's explanation of the apparition's scars and apparel. While he did so, she fingered a carefully folded scrap of paper in the pocket of her tunic. When Raynor told Ullin and Micerea that it was Tyrin that he sent to fetch Esildre nearly a year ago, Sheila drew out the paper, and carefully unfolded it on her knee to gaze at it.

"She told him that her name was Shevalia," she said, interrupting Raynor.

"Pardon me?"

"She told Tyrin that her name was Shevalia," Sheila repeated, staring at the writing on the scrap of paper. "I should have understood before. I should have put it all together when Eldwin was here. And I should have put it together even before then, when Lord Banis acted the way he did at the party."

She handed the note to Raynor, then looked at Ashlord who sensed, if the others did not, that Sheila was moved by something precious and tragic.

"He loved her," she said to him. "It wasn't just that she loved him. He loved her. And she knew it. When they met again in Tallinvale, somehow she knew, without a doubt, that she was loved. No wonder it was unbearable for her to lose him. No wonder, after her cursed life, that she, she... I should have given her the note."

Ashlord's brow shot up at the statement.

"I mean, I should have given it to Eldwin. And now he's off to do something terribly rash, I'm sure!"

Denks returned with a basket of salves and other things. Sheila took them and began mixing several unctions together.

"I found the note," she went on as she worked, "the first night we were here in the city. It was so strange to see it addressed like that, with what it said. I'm not sure why I kept it. Ullin, this might sting."

As she applied the salve, Raynor read the note. Somewhat smoothed by Sheila's hand, the wrinkles from when Tyrin had crumbled and tossed it away were still upon it.

"It is definitely Tyrin's hand," Raynor muttered.

He passed the note to Ashlord, and then it was passed to Ullin who read with Micerea, and he handed it to Billy and Ibin. It seemed, although there was no fear in the room, that some of Ashlord's spell wore thin as a weary sadness fell over his little group.

"When I sent Tyrin to fetch Esildre," Raynor said at last, "I almost immediately regretted doing so. A good man, honorable, and one of the best swordsmen around. But he was somewhat unpredictable. I feared that he might succumb to Esildre's curse, in spite of precautions. When he returned, and told me that Esildre was at the Temple, I noticed his subdued tone. But I thought that it was due to the fatigues of travel. And, during the week after the bells rang, and we were all forced to remain in the city, he drank more than I cared to see him do. He was anxious and downright moody. But then, so were we all. When I heard Eldwin's tale, I understood him better. I wish Tyrin had said something to me. I might have taken him into my confidence. I might have prevented him from running off. And he might have kept Esildre from doing so, too. They might both still be alive."

Raynor's words trailed off as he shook his head. He reached out and petted Beauchamp, now stretched out at his feet. Beauchamp looked up at him, and Raynor smiled back weakly. For his part, Ashlord felt that if Tyrin had remained in Duinnor, Robby might not have survived the Wickermen.

"Sometimes, it seems strange," Ashlord said to Raynor, "how things twist and turn, and how fates intertwine. But you should not blame yourself for that. It is how the world is made."

Raynor nodded.

"How is it that we may know what we were placed here to do?" Ashlord went on. "Sometimes we are certain it is this, and sometimes we are convinced it is that. But we are not so different from our friends, here. We do that which we may do, and face that which presents itself to us. You could not know that which you could not know. But if you had kept Tyrin here, and Esildre, too, a very different manner of storm might be breaking over our heads."

"Yes. All that is so," answered Raynor. "Yet, though I am filled with hope for what is to come, I am still saddened by what has passed."

• • •

In the sky above Starlight Hall, not a peal of thunder cracked and quaked away but that another took its place as the storm exploded and the wind shrieked across the city. In the cellar, the bottles and shelves vibrated and hummed ceaselessly. Longsuffering Denks was imposed upon once more, this time by Ashlord, and he went back upstairs, braving flying glass and the wildly lit mansion as lightning flashed to show him the way. He came back some while later, bringing with him sturdy rain capes and warm coats for Ullin and Micerea.

When Ullin's friends saw him stand up and help Micerea to her feet and on with her coat and then her cloak, they were at first baffled. Ashlord had said nothing to them about Nasakeeria. When Ullin donned his own outerwear, though, Billy and Sheila immediately protested.

"Where are you going?" Sheila stammered.

"We have an important errand to run," Micerea replied. "May I leave my heavy things here, Lady Highleaf?"

"Of course you may," said Lady Highleaf, equally distressed at their parting.

"Ashlord has something for you from Robby," Ullin said to Sheila. "It is on his business that we go. And we must hurry!"

"But ye only got here a little bit ago!" Billy yelled.

"Ullin, can't you and Micerea stay the night at least?" asked Ibin.

"There's something different about you, Ibin," Ullin said, gripping Ibin's outstretched hand. "You speak differently. And I think you have a confident bearing that you did not possess before. I wish we could stay, Ibin. And that I could learn more about your adventures."

"No!" cried Sheila. "Ullin, please don't go."

"We must," said Micerea, taking her hand.

Ashlord was the first to give Ullin a parting hug. Seeing this, the others followed his example, and hugged Micerea, too.

"I hope we will see each other again," Micerea said to Sheila.

"I do, too."

At the top of the stairs, Ullin stopped and looked down at his friends for a moment. Then he turned and disappeared as suddenly as he had arrived.

"Well, don't that beat all!" said Billy, staring at the door at the top of the steps. But no one heard him over the crash of the storm.

Ashlord took Sheila by the arm and gently pulled her away to the corner behind the shelves, carrying with him the vest left by Ullin.

"I have something very important to tell you, and to show you," he said.

Still confused over Ullin's departure, she saw what Ashlord held.

"That's Robby's vest," she said, taking it from Ashlord and looking at it in wonder. "Why is it so heavy?"

"Yes, it is Robby's. And it contains something that he wishes you to have," Ashlord said, producing a knife and cutting the threads that Mirabella had so carefully stitched, some of which had been repaired by Ullin.

Still holding the vest as Ashlord worked to free the threads, Sheila's eyes widened when he produced one of the Bloodcoins. He held it up so that the candlelight glimmered from the diamond at its center.

"Perhaps you remember this," Ashlord said. "I believe Mrs. Starhart left them with Robby's father."

"Yes," she answered, taking the coin to stare at. "I was there when she brought them to the store."

"Did Mirabella say anything to you about them?"

"No. Only I think she worried over them," Sheila said, unable to take her eyes from the coin as she turned it over in her hands. "I overheard her ask Mr. Ribbon about them one day. She wanted to look after them herself instead of them going into the store's strongbox."

Sheila looked at the vest draped over her arm, and felt it with her fingers.

"Blood money coins, Mrs. Starhart called them. They are all here? All seven of them? Robby had them all the while?"

"Yes, yes, and yes," Ashlord nodded. "You remember them, and that they each have a different jewel. Diamond, sapphire, ruby, amethyst, topaz, emerald, and amber. But they are called Bloodcoins."

"Yes. And it is strange, but I thought when Mrs. Starhart brought them that they looked strangely familiar, as if I had seen them before. Now, as I look at this one, I get the same eerie feeling."

"I think you *had* seen them before, long ago, when you were a very small child, before you ever met your Uncle Steggan."

Sheila shook her head. "Why do you think so?"

"Because I think it was Steggan who gave them to Mr. Starhart so that he could pay for the letters he was to post for Bailorg. Steggan probably squandered the coin given to him for that purpose on drink. He must have been desperate to barter the Bloodcoins in order to keep Bailorg's wrath at bay. It did not work. Robby later learned from Bailorg himself that he murdered Steggan. It was probably in the belief that Steggan cheated him and had not posted his letters. Bailorg probably thought Steggan had betrayed him."

Sheila was suddenly transported back to the awful night when Steggan had beaten and raped her.

"A blond-haired man was there," she muttered. "Dressed in fine clothes. He smiled while…while—"

"That was Bailorg," Ashlord said. "Somehow, Steggan had the coins all along, but dared not use them until his life was on the line. I can only guess, but I think Steggan somehow came to have possession of you and the Bloodcoins at the same time."

"A box," Sheila nodded. "There was a small wooden box. I remember it from when I was very young. It was always locked, and Steggan would often sit and drink and stare at it. And a man would sometimes come to look at the box, to look inside of it, I think."

"Oh?"

"I think so."

"Well, be that as it may, when Mrs. Starhart left the objects with Robby's father, Mirabella must have suspected that they were not merely rare and valuable coins. In fact, in Janhaven, when Robby's quest was decided upon, Mirabella must have thought they would be safer with Robby than remaining with her. Out on the plains, when I was reunited with you, Robby showed them to me. Mirabella must have believed that if Robby became King, he would know what to do with them."

Ashlord took the coin and the vest and carefully placed the object back into the hidden pocket, making sure it would stay there by pulling the threads tight again.

"Do with them?" Sheila asked. "What do you mean?"

"Put the vest on under your coat," he said, helping Sheila do so. "Ullin risked his life and Micerea's to bring these to you. Just as he did, you must guard them with your own life."

As Sheila buttoned the vest and put her coat back on over it, Ashlord dragged over a keg and motioned for Sheila to sit as he dragged another one over for himself.

"You must listen to me very carefully. I will tell you what they are, but this is a great secret that no one must know. Already many have died to protect them, and others have died trying to possess them."

• • •

The storm continued as Ashlord explained to Sheila about the Forty-Nine Keys to the Nimbus Illuminas. He told her about the pact that Aperion made with the Elifaen, that if they made use of the Forty-Nine, the Elifaen would be permitted to leave the earth and join with Aperion's host in heaven, becoming Faerekind once again. Ashlord told Sheila how Beauchamp had discovered that the present Unknown King already possessed thirty-five of the Forty-Nine, and how Queen Serith Ellyn possessed the Seven that were once held by Cupeldain, her grandfather. While he told her these things, their eyes locked together trance-like. The thunder and wind of the storm and the creaking of the house and rattle of the shelves seemed distant, the thunder like battle drums, the clink and rattle of the wine bottles became the noise of armor, and the wind moaned as the cry of legions embattled.

"But those Seven kept by Lyrium and Heneil were never found in the ruins of Tulith Attis," he concluded. "And they were not found among the Dragonkind who were slain afterwards."

Ashlord leaned back, nodding as he momentarily closed his eyes and broke the spell. A deafening crash violently shook the house, but Sheila did not jump or flinch at the thunder as she continued to stare at Ashlord. The thunder was once again only thunder to Sheila's ears, the bottles clinked mundanely, and the wind above carried no voices upon it.

"I think Lyrium's Seven were smuggled out of Tulith Attis and sent down river, to lands that are now part of Tracia Realm," Ashlord went on. "It was from Tracia that Steggan came, bringing his wife, and deeds to land in Barley, along with a small wooden box and a very young girl, barely even old enough to walk. A young girl, probably from a noble house, who would someday be Elifaen, just as her mother was."

Sheila's expression went from disbelief to wonder.

"Do you know what House?"

"I can only guess," Ashlord shrugged. "And I would rather not do so. But, in my opinion, you are a lady and the heiress of a very ancient house of Men, and, obviously, it was a Joined House."

"Oh," she said, her brow furrowed as she continued to absorb all she had just learned. "What am I supposed to do with these?" she asked, tapping her coat.

"I haven't the faintest idea. Meanwhile, shall we rejoin the others? Remember: tell no one."

• • •

Ullin and Micerea pressed their way back through the stormy city, holding each other's hand and finding their way by the almost constant lightning. The rain was too hard and the thunder too continuous and loud to speak, and several times they paused during particularly violent downpours, thankful for their new raincloaks. The streets and byways were all but abandoned, and quickly enough they made their way back out of the southern gate, which was shattered and torn asunder. As before, the gateway was not guarded, and the two would not have paused even if it had been. Soon they were making their way southeastward across the valley, and the farther they went away from the city, the less rain and wind they encountered until, some miles away, there was no rain at all. Indeed, here the sun was shining and the ground was completely dry. This made the two marvel even more at the tempest behind them as they moved quickly along the road.

Meanwhile, word had spread throughout the countryside concerning the storm that pounded Duinnor City, and the people throughout the land wanted to see it for themselves. There were a great number of campsites all around the valley, along the hills and open fields. The roads were busy with people still coming, entire families hurried along to find a suitable spot from which to watch, bearing bags and blankets and baskets of provisions. Wagons full of villagers rumbled toward the city, and sometimes a fine carriage flew along, bringing a lord or lady or some other powerful person. Against this thronging current Ullin and Micerea moved steadily, pushing their way south. They were well out of the storm, but kept their hoods low against the chilly air, sometimes looking back at the flashing clouds that obscured the Five Stars of Duinnor. They could sense the concern and wonder among the people they passed, and often heard them discussing what such a strange storm might forebode.

After only a few hours, the pair came to the crossroads where the south road toward Vanara bore on while the southeast road that would take them toward Nasakeeria cut off to the left. They continued on away from the city until nightfall, when they came to a small village. It seemed all but deserted with only a few lights showing in windows and no one about.

"This is the last village we'll encounter," Ullin told Micerea, "and there is a modest inn on the other side. Collandoth gave me some coin. Would you like to try for a room?"

"Do you think it safe?" Micerea asked, pulling her hood lower as a carriage passed by.

"I think so," Ullin said. "Just keep your hood down, and let me do all of the talking."

When they arrived at the small inn, they found it entirely empty of customers. The proprietor was sweeping the floor of the great room when they entered.

"Ah, sir and lady," he said, leaning his broom against the bar. "I'm afraid our kitchen is closed, and won't be providing meals until sometime tomorrow evenin' at the very earliest."

"We only need a room for the night," said Ullin.

"Well, you see, we all intend to go to Duinnor City first thing in the morning, so I ain't taking guests. I'll be closing up so that I can take me family to see the New King what comes. I'm sorry, but you and your wife'll have to find lodging somewhere else."

"We've been on the road all day, sir. We just need a little bit of rest," Ullin said, pulling out his purse. "Just a good warm room. We'll be on our way before sunrise, if you'll wake us. And we'll see to our own meals."

After a bit of haggling, the proprietor agreed to let them stay, and he accepted Ullin's payment. Micerea, still hooded, nervously gripped Ullin's hand as the owner saw to their room, lighting the fireplace, stacking wood nearby, and seeing to the lamps. Soon he was back and led them the way.

"Before sunrise," the proprietor said.

"Yes, sir," Ullin confirmed.

"Very well, then. Good night."

"Good night, sir."

Ullin closed the door, made sure it was bolted, and turned to Micerea who was standing by the fireplace, warming her hands.

"Well, I think this will do very nicely," Ullin said, dropping his pack and removing his cloak.

For the first time in eight years, since the two were in the Free City of Kajarahn, Ullin and Micerea enjoyed a bed together. It was not lavish, nor soft, but to the two weary travelers it was the highest of luxuries. Such was their enjoyment that, as soon as they were under the covers, they were both fast asleep.

● ● ●

"I shall need my heralds," said Serith Ellyn to Seafar.

She stood with him, in dreams, on the flight deck that overhung the Falls of Tiandari. Nearby stood the Dragonkind dreamwalker who had brought her and Seafar together. Seafar eyed the dreamwalker warily while Serith Ellyn looked eastward into the night. Below, Linlally stretched into darkness, but the blue light of Lady Moon made the River Iridelin a silver ribbon winding down shoals and falls to the place where it turned sharply south.

"Philawain has delivered to me the other things that I shall need," she went on. "But he has told me, should I do what I intend, that he would bring to me those people that I deem I would need. And he has assured me that those who come to me will be returned home as soon as possible."

Seafar was reluctant. He did not doubt the power of Philawain to do as Serith Ellyn said he would, and he had evidence enough, through the delivery of Dialmor and through other ways, of the might of Griferis.

"My Queen," he said at last. "If you do this thing, your reign will fail, and Vanara may pass away, for who else will there be to see to its safety and its security?"

"My reign is already failing, my lord. Slowly, inexorably, it fades. My reign may pass away, but Vanara will not. I will not become like my father, so obsessed with power that he sank into madness and despotism. When the people hear of what I do, they will undoubtedly be angry, at first. But they will see the light, in their own way, as I have done. They are weary, as am I. As is this land, and all the world. Should things go on as they have, all will sink into darkness. It will not be Secundur who brings this about, he only seeks to hasten that which is otherwise inevitable. But by doing this, I intend to strike a change and help put the river of history back into its ancient and proper course. Darkness may come, but I mean for it not to hold sway forever."

"Queen, I shall do as you command, of course," said Seafar. "I could hardly prevent it, could I? Nor would I wish to stand in the way of what you deem is hope. But the Dragonlands rise to war, and the Redvests join in conquest with them. Masurthia and Altoria cannot withstand them. By Duinnor's long interference, we are weaker than we should be. Now, of all times, to give over to Duinnor seems folly."

"So it would seem to you," Serith Ellyn answered. "But a new ruler comes to Duinnor, and great change is already being made. This very day, the Old King has been overthrown, and tomorrow a new ruler will take his place. You have helped this come about, and you have been witness to his power. I must submit to him, and I gladly do so, for Vanara's sake. You shall see! Take my heralds, ready to do their duty, to the place I have told you about, to the northeast banks at the bend in the river. Once there, they will not need their mounts, but they must trust the messengers who will await them. They are to do as they are told. Go yourself to assure them, so that they may have trust in their Queen, and to see yourself their departure from there. And so that you may know, once more, that it is I to whom you speak with, and that this is not a common dream, ask your True Ink where the Queen's heralds are to gather."

Seafar awoke, blinking, then threw off his covers and dressed. In less than an hour, he was in the Scribblers Room, and he had written much and learned more. He hurried out, put on his best uniform, and began giving orders.

By daybreak, Seafar was riding through the cold morning air out from Linlally, leading a dozen mounted heralds in all their finery across the River Iridelin to a lonely hill in the northeast. They rode to its top, and Seafar saw a small group of what he took to be youngsters standing there. But when he called his party to a halt before them, and dismounted, he saw that they were adults, none of them taller than his elbow. One of the little men approached, bowed to Seafar, and offered his hand in greeting.

"My name is Makewine," the man said. "And these are my companions."

"I am Seafar. And these are those whom my Queen has summoned."

"Very good, sir. We are sent by King Philawain to escort them to her, and we must depart right away."

Seafar looked around. Seeing no horses or buckmarls other than the ones of his own company, he shook his head.

"I am baffled," he said.

● ● ●

The proprietor's knock came at Ullin and Micerea's door all too soon. But, well rested, they quickly ate from the victuals they had been given by the monks. They were on their way by the time dawn was breaking. When they reached the outskirts of the village, Micerea pulled Ullin to a halt.

"Listen," she said, looking back the way they had come. Ullin looked, too, his head tilted to hear.

"No thunder," he said.

"And no flashes of lightning," she said, "but the sky toward the city glows brightly."

"Yes. The King has arrived, it seems."

Leaving the village behind, they continued south and east along the main road. There was hardly any traffic on the road at all, and just as they entered a stretch of road that ran between wide pastures, a dance of bubbling lights sprang up before them, quickly fading to reveal two little people, who faced them and bowed.

"Hello, Lord Ullin!"

"Millithorpe? Is that you?"

"It is! It is!" Millithorpe said, bowing again. "And this is Miladora, as I'm sure you recall."

The little lady next to Millithorpe bowed. "How do you do, my lord and lady?"

Micerea grinned as Ullin shook Millithorpe's hand and then took Miladora's.

"I am delighted to see you both!" he said. "And very surprised. But what brings you so far from home?"

"We have been sent to escort the two of you to Nasakeeria," said Miladora.

"We and some others of our people are serving King Philawain," explained Millithorpe, "running errands, fetching things from here to there, and so forth."

"So King Philawain has enlisted you, too."

"Yes, and many others, I'd say," said Miladora. "Some are presently looking after Queen Serith Ellyn's company. Others are back in Tallinvale, to assist your grandfather and Prince Danoss. And a few have even gone to the Dragonlands, to help your father, Lady Micerea."

"You know my name?"

"Yes, my lady. King Philawain has sent his dream messengers to us, to guide us and to bring his word to us. And, as you are one of his dreamwalkers, you very well know how that works."

Micerea looked at Ullin, shaking her head.

"I suppose the King is too busy to explain all to us," she said, "which shouldn't be a surprise. I have not spoken with him for a long while, and the last time I saw Finn was when he instructed me to go to Serith Ellyn last week."

"Yes," said Millithorpe. "Things happen quickly now, and it is very confusing. But our King has a plan and puts it into motion."

"Indeed," said Miladora, "it has been in motion for some time, I do believe."

"And we should also be in motion! If you'll take my hand, Lady Micerea."

Micerea took Millithorpe's offered hand, glancing at Ullin who took Miladora's. Before she could prepare, Millithorpe snapped his fingers and they shot across the countryside. When they stopped, Micerea felt extremely dizzy.

"Oh! Oh!" she cried, her head spinning. Ullin and Miladora appeared next to them in a blur of light.

"Oh, my!" she heard Ullin say.

"Don't be afraid," said Millithorpe to them. "We are quite good at popping around like this. But we cannot go all the way at once, so keep a good grip on our hands. We'll have you at your destination in a flash."

And so they crossed leagues and leagues in less than an hour, though Micerea lost count of how many times they paused. At last they came to Marker Number 1, at the westernmost boundary of Nasakeeria. Micerea was forced to sit, so overcome with dizziness she was. Ullin fared far better, and as soon as he appeared, she clutched his leg to steady herself, though she was sitting.

"My dear!" said Miladora. "Are you quite alright?"

"Yes, I think so. Just give me a moment. Oh, my!"

"I do apologize, Lady Micerea," said Millithorpe with distress. "I did not realize it would make you so very uncomfortable."

"Micerea?" Ullin crouched beside her. "Are you ill?"

"No, no. I will be fine. I should be accustomed to strange conveyances, shouldn't I? After having flown from the south, I mean."

"Oh, no. In my opinion, riding a flying horse is far, far worse than this!" said Ullin.

"Help me up," she said. Once she was standing, they all took a better look around. The warning pillar was their only company, and the place was marked with numerous cold fire-rings and old horse tracks. They knew where they were, she from her dreamwalks and he from his training days as a cadet and, later, from his travels which sometimes took him this way. The morning haze had lifted, and they could see well into Nasakeeria, and to their distant left and right, other warning markers dotted the border.

"Now what?" Ullin asked.

"I do not know," said Miladora. "We were instructed to bring you here, and that is all. Then we are to go on to perform other errands."

"We weren't told why," said Millithorpe.

"Oh."

Ullin pulled off his backpack and put it on the ground.

"It's been a long time since I was here," he said. He waved his arm. "See this campground? It is where Kingsmen cadets are brought for part of their training. I had training here, and, some years later, I led a group of cadets on their own training mission. Stone pillars such as that one surround Nasakeeria, every few hundred yards. Beyond is the border, across which no one may pass and live."

Micerea nodded, remaining watchful.

The region was silent but for the wind gusting across the tall dry grass, spotted with swaths of snow. Beyond the marker, the land rose gradually to a line of tree-covered hills some furlong away, and the top of a wooden tower could be seen rising over their bare branches. The four of them studied their surroundings, but there was nothing out of the ordinary to be seen, besides the odd watchtower and the stone marker with its foreboding skull. Outside of Nasakeeria, to the north and south and behind them toward the west, the land was bare of trees and stretched as far as the eye could see, the desolation of winter giving way here and there to patches of green. But the day was bright, and the sunlight was warmer, it seemed to Ullin, than he and Micerea had experienced in a very long time.

"Oh," said Ullin. "I just remembered. Today is Spring Day. It is the day when the King of Duinnor goes to the Temple."

"Except, today, a New King will be going there, won't he?" said Micerea.

"Yes," said Millithorpe. "Our people have learned much since you were with us, Lord Ullin. Esildre and her great-nephews taught us a lot about the world. And when we were in Tallinvale, and in Janhaven, we were told much, too."

"But Esildre spent a great deal of time with us, spending some time nearly every day to teach us about the world," Miladora said. "Until we went to Tallinvale, that is, where others told us their tales."

"And I wish to say that I am sorry about your aunt, Lord Ullin," said Millithorpe. "By all accounts, she was a brave and remarkable lady."

"Thank you, Millithorpe. Yes, she was."

"And we were saddened by the news of Esildre, which we only learned last night," said Micerea.

"She was a good friend to us," said Miladora. "She saved us from ourselves, you know. When Eldwin returned from Tallinvale and told us his news, we were all very shocked and saddened. Have you seen him, by the way? Eldwin?"

"No. He was in Duinnor recently, but he had already departed before we arrived."

"Do you know what he is doing, where he went to?" Millithorpe asked. "He would not say much about why he wanted to leave us. And he was most annoyed at our questions. His wife and children were beside themselves. He would not even take Tulleg and Kranneg with him, insisting that they stay with us until our lands could be deemed safe."

"We have known Eldwin for a very, very long time," said Miladora, "and have never seen him so determined. Angry, I think you could say."

"I'm sorry, but I don't know," Ullin said. "But I suspect, from what we learned last night from Ashlord, that he is on some business having to do with Esildre."

"That is what he let on," said Millithorpe. "But he would never say, exactly, what it might be. Although he did let it slip once that he aimed to look in on Esildre's people."

"Then your guess is as good as mine."

They fell silent once more, until Micerea spoke.

"Not long ago, I longed to be in the open," she said, "and out of the confining shadows of the forest. But now I feel very exposed. Do you think there is anyone in that tower? Who looks at us as we stand here?"

"Possibly. I wish I had my spyglass. Well. I suppose we must wait for a sign, or some such."

"Yes, I suppose you must," said Miladora. "But we cannot wait with you, as we are needed elsewhere."

"So good luck!" said Millithorpe. "And I hope to see you again!"

Suddenly Ullin and Micerea were alone, feeling somewhat disconcerted.

Chapter 30

Worthy of a Thousand Words

Day 228
17 Days Remaining

As dawn approached, the storm abated, and nearly all within the city immediately fell asleep, so exhausted they were. Even the city's Elifaen did so, though their stamina was greater than that of Mortals. Horses and cats, dogs and squirrels, every mouse, and every bird not long flown away, all slept at last. The city-shrouding fog rolled heavily along and billowed through alleys and avenues. It would have been a completely silent place if it had not been for the trickling of water that still ran down the soaked streets and dripped from soggy eaves. Surely Sir Sun had never seen such a strange thing as he did when he climbed the eastern stairs of morning and threw his warm gaze over the lands of Duinnor. All the countryside surrounding was as before, a patchwork of snowy fields and pastures, lined with roads and streams around the city. But Duinnor City itself was a gray blotch, its streets and buildings obscured by low mists. And, stranger still, hovering in the air over the center of the city was a magnificent palace surrounded by billowy purple and white clouds split with silent frozen lightning. Sir Sun intensified his gaze as he climbed his skyward path, and he urged the mists and fog to thin as they uplifted into the warming air. But he had no power at all to dissipate the strange storm around the floating palace. His fiery eyes could not loosen or push aside the clouds that stuck like plaster to the very air around the long thin bridge that stretched from the palace and attached itself to the High Tower of the Sixth Unknown King.

Shrugging, Sir Sun paid no attention to the lone figure who, dressed in fine garments and bearing a golden staff, walked along the narrow causeway, making his way from the castle in the air. This man stepped off through the strange arch at the end of the causeway and onto the south-facing balcony of the highest level of the High Tower. Passing inside, and into the High Chamber, he paused. Although he had been foretold what to expect, he was still shocked and saddened by what he saw. A dead man lay on the floor, as if in sleepy repose, his hands crossed over his chest. Beside him knelt a young lad, stroking the dead man's gray-blond hair. Nearby, the King hovered, filling the room with the awful golden light of his mantle. Next to the King floated the Red Door.

But for the occasional sniffling of the lad, the chamber was completely silent. The man stepped closer, heaving a sigh, and bowed to the King. A blunt force struck his mind like a hammer, and he clutched his staff in a brief spasm of shock as the King spoke into his heart.

"Go quickly."

Instantly the Red Door moved and the man turned and pushed open the doors of the chamber. The Red Door floated out, and the man followed, stepping around the dozens of sleeping Kingsmen and going down the stairs after the Avatar.

• • •

In the cellar of Starlight Hall, only Raynor and Ashlord were awake, sitting among their peacefully slumbering companions. They sat on the floor crosslegged across from each other, Raynor with Beauchamp in his lap. Though they were deep within their meditations, the two Melnari still heard the chorus of soft breathing around them as their companions slept. They heard Beauchamp's contented chomps, the creak of the great house above them, and the nearly imperceptible hiss of flame atop the candle that dripped its wax onto the old keg where it had been placed hours ago. They heard the door open two floors above them, the footsteps of the man who entered, and the tap of his staff as he came through the Hall and descended into the basement and neared the cellar door. When he came down the cellar steps, the two Melnari looked up at him, smiling. The man descended and stood nearby, looking around at the figures all over the cellar, lying on the floor, sitting in chairs, or propped against each other or against the shelves, all peacefully sleeping. He looked at Raynor and his rabbit, then at Ashlord.

"I am Finn," he said. "I am the King's servant, come to fetch Lady Shevalia to him."

Ashlord nodded and reached out to touch Sheila on the arm. She stirred, lifting her head from Farby's shoulder, and opened her eyes, blinking at Ashlord.

"I have just had the most marvelous dream," she said. Following Ashlord's gaze, she saw Finn, who was smiling down upon her, and she stood.

"Come," Finn said, holding out his hand. "The King awaits."

Sheila took his hand, and together she and Finn ascended the steps, her heart so full of wonder and amazement that she did not even see Ashlord's reassuring nod. She did not take her eyes from Finn at all as he led her up through the quiet house, looking upon her escort with an odd mixture of wonder, confusion, and trepidation. They passed through the great hall, crunching through broken glass and twigs, and up the stairs and onto the portico where the Red Door floated.

"Do not be afraid, my lady," Finn said to her when her hand gripped his more tightly. "The King's Avatar is his servant, too, and to show you that it means no harm, it will lend somewhat of its power to us."

As he spoke, the door tilted over until it was flat before them and floated down to rest on the top step like a gangplank. Finn stepped upon it, but Sheila, still holding his hand, held back. He smiled and nodded, and she stepped onto the door to stand beside him. She inhaled sharply and clutched Finn's arm with her other hand as the Avatar moved, carrying them with it as it descended over the steps to the lane. Hovering a foot or so above the ground, the Red Door transported them down the way and through the gate of Wysteria Place and thus into the foggy city.

"My King says that the streets of this city are unworthy of your tread," Finn told her, "and so he lends this conveyance to you, there being no better thing at hand for the purpose."

Sheila's heart thumped and beat so fiercely within her chest that tears threatened to blur her vision, and her breath was shallow and quick. Though she knew she had no reason to fear, it was fearsome indeed to encounter the very stranger who had visited her dream just a short while ago, telling her to prepare her heart. And it still seemed a dream as they moved along the empty streets of the quiet city. Looking down at her feet, she could hardly believe they flew along as they did. She wondered when she would truly awake.

As they came around a turn in the avenue, Finn lifted his staff and pointed upward across the city toward the High Tower.

"Behold, the Palace of the New King, wondrous and terrible, as is his might!"

Sheila looked up as a bank of fog rolled away revealing the strange storm, purple and red with harsh blue-white lightning that did not waver, like blinding cracks in the sky itself. Within those clouds, she saw the marvelous palace of Griferis, banners floating from its towers and ramparts, and the long floating causeway that stretched to the High Tower.

"Which king am I going to?" she asked, her voice small and tentative.

"His name is Philawain, King of Griferis, King of Duinnor, King of the Nine Realms, Lord of Dreams."

"Nine Realms? I know of only seven."

"Two more are now his sovereign domain, one of which is the Dragonlands of the south."

"Dragonlands? He has wrested that land from the Sun King?"

"No. He lays claim to it, and spreads his might across it, and it shall be given over to him."

Sheila's head spun. They continued along, came to the Palace gate, and floated within to the wide courtyard and then on through the tall doors of the Palace itself. As they went through the wide halls, they silently passed broad tapestries depicting the feats of the Kings of Duinnor. They passed by wondrous statues of great and mighty men of yore, and along stained glass windows that were like sparkling paintings of the Seven Realms. And they floated past groups of sleeping Kingsmen, stretched out on the floor or slumped against the walls.

"Do not be alarmed," Finn told her. "They merely sleep."

Sheila nodded as they came to the first broad staircase of pink marble, and they smoothly ascended.

"And the other realm? Where is it?" she asked.

Finn looked at her, smiling still, and said, "I think you know, for that is where we first met, but a few hours ago."

The Red Door, as solid as the ground itself, floated up the wide spiral stair, up and up and up, until Sheila became dizzy as they ascended. She felt her ears pop, and though the winding case was lined with windows, it grew darker as they went upward and as the tower entered the stormy clouds. Then they passed windows ablaze with blue-white light, outside of which a thunderbolt lingered in the air.

Reaching the uppermost floor, they floated down a hallway where more Kingsmen slept. When they approached a large double door, the Avatar descended to the floor, and Finn guided Sheila off of it. The Red Door righted itself, Finn pushed open the doors and entered, and he stood aside gesturing for Sheila to come in. She did so, the Avatar floated past her to take up its place, and Sheila saw what Finn had seen earlier when he first entered the High Chamber.

The lad still wept, the dead man was still in death's repose, and the King still hovered, his light almost unbearable. Finn bowed, and Sheila, her quaking knees unable to support her any longer, knelt and bowed her head, too, not daring to look upon the King. Now she knew what Ashlord had so often warned her about. He was right, and good-hearted Raynor had been mistaken to encourage her to have hope. She felt her heart crushing under the weight of the obvious: Robby was no more.

"My lord King," Finn said, his head still bowed, "allow me to present the Lady Shevalia."

Sheila felt the King's touch and she gulped, nearly bursting into tears.

"No, no. Be not afraid. It is I, Philawain, whom you knew before the trials that made me as I am. Long ago, I was known to you as Robby."

Sheila tried her best not to cry. She had cried too much this past year, and too often. Anger welled up in her heart, anger at herself for being weak, for losing the baby, for coming with Robby instead of staying with Mirabella, and then, after coming so far, for letting Robby go on to Griferis without her. But mostly, she was angry at her own present disappointment and at the gulf that was now all too apparent between her and her Robby. She felt the golden light bathe her, and it served only to illuminate the pathetic hopes she had clung to for so long. If she had felt unworthy of Robby when she had gone to Tulith Attis, she now felt herself wretched and lowly in the most extreme way. A mere speck, unworthy even of notice. All before, her hopes had been nothing but a dream. And now she felt she had awakened to things as they really were.

Ashlord knew all along, she thought, and had tried to warn her. Robby knew, too. He must have known. Raynor tried to be kind, encouraging her to keep her hopes. But it was a cruel thing to do. She gulped at her chagrin, at her humiliation, and hot tears rolled down her cheeks.

"I beg you," came the King's voice in her heart, "give me but a little of your time. Don't be angry. Do not judge things too harshly. And, so that you may not judge me too harshly, I, who am now King, beg your indulgence for a short while. Go with Finn so that he may show you my palace and some of the things therein. When you have seen them, come again to me, and decide if I am to be condemned in your heart, or if there is still a place for me within it. Will you go with him?"

Confused by the King's words, and with her head still bowed, Sheila nodded and obediently took Finn's offered hand.

"Rise, Lady Shevalia. And come."

She stood, dizzy and overwhelmed, confused, and filled with embarrassment, trembling with emotion. Too many things cluttered her heart and her mind, vying for space, pushing out from her soul. As Finn took her to the balcony, she paused and glanced over her shoulder. The boy was watching her, and she saw by his expression that he was confounded by his own confusion and sorrow. Like a bolt, his crisis of grief shot through her heart and transfixed her own grief. In that instant, Sheila ceased trembling. Suddenly she realized that there were too many things to wonder at, too many mysteries unfolding too soon to comprehend. Paradoxically, this calmed her enough for her to also realize that she had the strength to cope, if only for a little while longer. She was still overwhelmed, but it no longer mattered. She was Elifaen, now, and this moment expanded and encompassed her with a strange and accepting peace. She turned back to Finn and nodded.

She and Finn stepped out onto the balcony, and she saw the arched gate above her on the other side of the balcony, right against the banister. There was a chair on the balcony, and Finn stepped up onto it, then onto the banister. He helped her up, and together they stepped onto the landing of the causeway where stood the strange and eerie gate with its shining star-like disc. Finn guided her across the long causeway, walking in silence through the clouds, through fingers of frozen lightning bolts that fanned over them or struck downward into the clouds below. Finn did not urge her on, and she was not afraid. She felt drawn to the far side of the causeway. And soon they were there, at the looming gates of the strange palace.

The gates were open. Finn released her hand and gestured for her to enter. She did, and he followed her into a courtyard. Standing to either side of the broad walkway before her were men and women of every race, old and young alike, all in fine clothes, some in dark blue tunics and armed with swords over their shoulders. To her increasing wonder, they all bowed as she passed between them. Her heart was too much a-flutter with nervous wonder to be afraid, and she managed a tenuous smile as she acknowledged the people with a dip of her head. At the end of the two lines was General Lafkin, dressed in a fine blue tunic and greatcoat, with white trousers tucked into polished black boots. He smartly stepped out to face her, upright and stiff, clicked his heels together, then bowed low with his hand over his heart.

"Allow me to present His Excellency, General Lafkin of the King's Guard," Finn said to Sheila.

"Lady Shevalia," said Lafkin, "on behalf of the King and his subjects, I welcome you to Griferis."

Sheila curtseyed. "I am pleased to make your acquaintance, sir."

"The pleasure and honor are ours, Lady Shevalia."

Lafkin bowed again, and stepped back.

"This way if you please, my lady," Finn said.

Sheila glanced back at the now smiling crowd, noticing for the first time a little girl holding a rabbit and a young man standing beside her leaning on a crutch. It took her a moment, as she went with Finn, but then she remembered him, Borwain from the House of Hemlock. She glanced back quickly to be sure as she and Finn entered the palace doors.

They entered the palace, and Finn guided Sheila into the grand foyer.

"King Philawain wishes for you to look upon some of the paintings and drawings that hang throughout Griferis," Finn said, gesturing to a large painting on the far wall. Sheila nodded, then approached the work, a landscape depicting a pond on the edge of a wood. Green cornstalks waved in the breeze on the far side of the pond, and on the near side, sitting under a tree at the edge of the lapping water, were two figures looking out at the pond. One, a girl with long light brown hair, held a fishing pole, its line dangling into the water, while the black-haired boy beside her held a book. Sheila shot a look of confusion at Finn. When she turned back to the painting, she saw that the girl had put her head on the boy's shoulder, as his finger pointed to the indiscernible words on a page of the now-opened book. Sheila stepped back in surprise, with butterflies swarming in her belly.

"This is one of the King's favorite paintings," Finn commented, "because, he says, it was a very happy time for him. Come. There is much to see, and not much time to see it all."

Sheila reluctantly tore herself away from the painting, and followed Finn through a door and into an adjacent large circular room. Between the eight tall windows and over each of the doors were additional paintings. Finn stopped in the center of the room, and Sheila nearly bumped into him, so enthralled she was by the paintings there. One was of a violent and fiery sea battle. Oared ships rammed one another as their sails were ripped by the winds and waves that pounded the nearby rocky shore. Men flailed in the water, others clung to the side of wave-tossed wreckage, while those aboard the warring vessels shot arrows and flaming missiles at each other. Two of the ships had just collided, and both were sinking and on fire while men scrambled at each other violently. One prominent figure waved a broad feathered hat in one hand and a cutlass in the other, while men crowded around him, knives in their teeth, wielding axes, marlinspikes, and swords against the boarders that poured over the side of the larger ship onto their own. Above, a fireball arced through the smoky air, descending upon them.

"That's Makeig!" Sheila gasped, stepping closer. Her eyes suddenly became blurry, then immediately cleared. She blinked away an odd sensation, and saw that now the fireball was being deflected from Makeig by another man who struck it aside with the back of his wrist.

"Robby?"

"Yes. Our King endured many trials, among which were several battles," Finn said. "In this room are works which depict only some of those trials. There are many, though, that he will not speak of."

Sheila turned to another painting of the interior of a crowded hall. People pointed at each other and seemed to be shouting, and she imagined she could hear their angry voices. In their midst, standing alone, was a person who looked oddly like Robby, but with longer hair tied in a ponytail. She saw that many of the people pointed at a man who had his hands bound by rope and his head down, standing before Robby. A group behind the prisoner included an elderly man holding a crying woman, and a young lady with her hands clasped together, obviously pleading with Robby. As before, the scene seemed to momentarily shift and blur, and now Robby's own head was bowed, as he looked at the floor. The crowd that had been pointing earlier now had crossed their arms and looked on with expressions of satisfaction. The young lady's face was covered by her hands, and she had fallen to her knees.

"I don't understand," Sheila said.

"I'm not sure I do, either," answered Finn. "But I can tell you that the man was condemned and hanged, though, as it turned out, he was innocent, falsely accused by those who coveted his lands."

"Oh."

Turning to another painting, she saw a beggarly man with long unkempt hair and dressed only in thin rags in spite of the snow. Sheila could almost feel cold winter air coming off the canvas. The man in the painting had evidently just stumbled, and was trying to get back to his feet. Another man, dressed in good clothes and a long woolen coat, was hurrying to the beggar from the open door of a nearby cottage. Then, as if the paint on the canvas shifted from one place to the next, Sheila saw that the beggar now had the woolen coat thrown over his shoulders. The man who had before been wearing the coat was now helping the beggar to his feet, gesturing toward the open door of the cottage. She could make out the questioning look on the beggar's face, his hollow eyes glistening. In shock, she realized that the beggar was Robby, and she remembered the tale that Ullin had related, and the good people of Greenfar.

"We must continue," Finn said. "But perhaps you might look upon these other paintings another time."

Sheila nodded and followed Finn, glancing at a dark painting of a night-time scene. The moon faintly shone through clouds upon fields, and she could make out the dark shape of a mansion in the distance with one single small yellow light showing from a tiny window. In the foreground were brambles at the edge of the field and, just as she was passing through the doors behind Finn, she thought she saw an arm suddenly jut up from the briars, as if reaching for that insignificant light. The realization of what the scene depicted hit her like a hammer, and she groaned aloud.

"I can't!" she sobbed, putting her face into her hands. "I can't. Show me no more, I beg you. Why must I look upon these things?"

She felt Finn's arm around her.

"He tried to save you," Finn said. "He tried to save you and the baby. He turned back the banshee and even managed to get you as far as Bosk Manor, carrying you in his arms. But he was not permitted to stay with you, the Judges did not permit it. It was his first real trial, the first day he was here. I don't think he will ever get over it, and he still believes that he failed you."

Sheila wept, her body convulsing with grief as she buried her face against Finn's chest when he put his arms around her.

"Must I go on?" she cried. "Must I?"

"That is entirely your choice, my lady."

After a few moments, she stiffened and pulled away from Finn, nodding as she wiped her face of her streaming tears.

"Do you wish to continue?" Finn asked. "There is much more to show you, some of which I think you may find less disturbing."

"Yes. I am sorry. Yes, I am ready."

Finn took her through the passage that led out from the Circle Room. There were many pen and ink drawings of more mundane scenes, and a few small paintings, too. She saw winged horses, bearing her and her friends across Islindia's forest and over her lost city. Along the stairs that they climbed, she saw portraits of Billy and Ibin, and of Ullin conversing with Eldwin in Nowhere. There was a sketch of Ashlord speaking with Queen Serith Ellyn beside Lake Halgaeth. And, at the top of the stairs, there was a charcoal drawing of Micerea standing atop a desert dune, her black robes snapping in the wind.

As they rounded the landing and entered a broad hallway, Sheila saw a portrait of Robby's father. He was sitting at his desk at the store looking over his spectacles with a knowing smile on his face. And, a few yards farther along, was a portrait of Mirabella, tall and beautiful, standing on a wooded path strewn with autumn leaves, her long red hair tousled by a breeze. She was dressed as Sheila remembered her at Janhaven during the days just before she departed with Robby. Over one of Mirabella's shoulders jutted the hilt of her sword, there was a quiver of arrows over her other shoulder, and a bow was in her hand.

Sheila stopped to look, and Mirabella seemed to look back at her with her green eyes sparkling and an enigmatic smile on her face.

"There are many other depictions of the King's mother," Finn said. "Not all are so war-like. But it is evident that she was very beautiful and strong of heart."

"Yes. She was," Sheila said as her eyes watered once again. "I miss her."

"The King also blames himself for her death, though he might not wish for me to tell you so. I shall leave it at that. I have two more portraits to show you."

"Oh?"

"Yes, just this way. The first is of someone who has been in Philawain's thoughts ever since I have known him."

Finn gestured down the hall and Sheila followed, still looking at Mirabella, whose eyes seemed to follow her.

"Might I ask how long you have known him?"

"Since he first came to Griferis, twenty-eight years ago, by how we reckon things."

"Twenty-eight years?"

"Yes."

"Then he is much changed, just as Ullin Saheed told me."

"Yes, he is changed from when he arrived. But in many ways he is still the same as when I first met him. Older, yes. Wounded, and scarred, too, from his many ordeals. Some wounds, as I think you know, leave their scars within. Here we are."

Finn pushed open an ornate door and stood aside.

"These are the King's apartments," he said, following Sheila inside. Although curtains were pulled across the many windows, the hovering lightning outside shown through them and illuminated the room.

Sheila looked around at the fine tables and chairs, the beautiful desk and lamps, and the comfortable settee and divan, with books and scrolls and maps on or nearby to all of them and even stacked on the thick green carpet. She looked at Finn questioningly. He smiled and stood aside. Behind him on the wall was a full-size portrait of Lady Shevalia, depicting her at the top of the stairs of Starlight Hall just as she made her first appearance at Lady Highleaf's grand party. For a tiny moment, Sheila did not recognize herself, then her mouth dropped open.

"Is that me?" she whispered.

"It is," Finn said. "And it is the first thing he looks at each morning, and the last thing he sees before retiring each night. He often sits yonder, reading in that chair. But I think he just as often gazes at this portrait. At least since it was completed and hung there a week ago."

Finn looked up at the painting, then added, "And why not? You are quite beautiful, my lady."

"Was he there?" she asked, unable to take her eyes from it.

"No," said Finn. "But if you look carefully, you'll see someone who was, and who related this vision of you."

Sheila shook her head, then saw a little bird perched on the stair banister in the lower corner of the portrait.

"Certina!"

"Yes. Certina related this to the King, and to the artist, from her memory of you at Lady Highleaf's party."

"Would the artist be Borwain? Who used to live with Lord Threshmere?"

"Yes, that would be him. He has a prodigious talent, sometimes producing five or six works in a day, with hardly any effort. And, as you have no doubt noticed, all are of an uncanny nature and quality. As if the motion of his brush or pen does not cease after the paint or ink is dry."

"Yes, I have noticed," said Sheila.

"Well, I have one more portrait to show you," said Finn. "It is downstairs."

They made their way back down, and along the way, Sheila noticed a delicate painting of the girl she had seen earlier. She could have sworn that when they passed it before, the girl held a rabbit. But now she held a basket of flowers and the rabbit was at the girl's feet, nibbling on one she had dropped.

"That is the King's adopted daughter," Finn said. "Her name is Celia. As far as we know, she was orphaned and left here at Griferis. She has barely changed in appearance in all her years here, though I do not think she is Elifaen."

"Oh."

They went on, and they at last entered a large dining room where Finn, Lafkin, Radasa, Kinsiri, and Lord Threshmere were accustomed to having their meals, along with many others of Griferis. The room was now empty, save for the long table, set with many candlesticks. On the wall at the far end was a large portrait of the King of Griferis. He stood with a small book in his hands, regal in every way in his blue suit, his hair pulled back and tied with a small white ribbon, and his beard neatly combed. He looked down upon the room, and at Sheila, with sad but kind eyes, a slight smile across his lips, just as enigmatic as Mirabella's. In the background was a rampart over which flew a dark blue banner with seven stars in a circle, and beyond that were snow-covered peaks ranging to either side of a long chasm that stretched to the horizon. As Sheila studied Robby's aged appearance, she thought she saw the flag in the background flutter, and a loose strand of Robby's hair shift across his brow.

"Those who regularly dine here asked that the portrait be hung there," Finn said. "Philawain wanted you to see it, so that you would know how much changed he is in appearance. But, as you no doubt know by now, he is Elifaen. So this is how he will appear for the rest of his life, and he will age no more."

Sheila stared at the portrait, and saw Robby as a stranger, eerily like someone she once knew. She saw the gray along his temples and running through his beard, and the slight hint of lines that etched back from his eyes. Though he stood proudly, his chin up and his stance firm, Sheila thought his expression was somewhat weary.

"Why?" she asked. "Why did he want me to see all this? All these paintings?"

"It was the quickest way of telling some portion of his story," Finn said. "And he longs that you, above all others, should know it, and perhaps come to know him better than you do. He is now King of Kings, and must accomplish much in a very short while. Those things will require of him his entire attention. But he does not intend to always be King. Indeed, he already foresees the end of his reign. He will speak to you of those things when we return. But, now that you know something of his power," Finn waved his arm around, indicating Griferis, "and of his experiences that brought him to hold such power, he hopes that you will help him in those things that need doing. To that end, he hopes that you will abide with him this day."

"Well, of course I'll help in any way that I may," Sheila said, sensing something else in Finn's soft and gentle tone. "He has always known that, I think."

"Yes," Finn said, "his faith in that regard has never wavered. And, if I may be so bold, nor has his love for you. He will impose his will wherever it is necessary for him to do so. But he will not impose his will or his desire upon you, for he knows that doing so would avail nothing of value."

"What are you saying? I love him, too. And what I have seen today has only kindled my love for him all the stronger. I only want the best for him. I want his reign to be successful, and though I know little about what he must do, I will be his staunchest supporter, and would gladly lay down my life for him. Oh, Mr. Finn! What terrible thing do you prepare me for?"

"It should be the King who tells you this," Finn said, hesitating. "Although he is old in appearance, he is Elifaen and will remain as strong as he is now. He is resolute, and he will demand much of those who are to be his subjects. But of you he demands nothing. And though I may speak out of turn, I believe that I am correct in saying that he wishes for you to take all of the things that you have seen here and weigh them in your heart, in preparation for the request that I think he will put before you."

"His request?"

"Yes. I think he will ask you to become his wife."

Sheila stared at Finn for a moment as tears once again welled in her eyes. Then she took Finn's hand in hers.

"Oh, dear sir! Please show me the way back to him immediately!"

• • •

"Why do you think he summoned her?" Raynor asked Ashlord.

Ashlord stirred from his thoughts, and looked at Raynor incredulously.

"He obviously wishes to obtain her Seven."

Raynor shook his head and chuckled.

"Collandoth, my old friend, in some ways you are about as dense as they come," Raynor said, grinning.

"Why on earth would you say such a thing?" Ashlord asked, feigning offense, but with a twinkle in his eye.

"Because, dear fellow, you have known Shevalia all this time, and Robby Ribbon, too. You know what is in their hearts, and have no doubt even counseled one or the other or both pertaining to those matters. But you do not yet know the power of love, do you? I scold you! In the short while that I have known her, I have learned more about love's longings than I have in all my many years. Have you no eyes to see? Yes, the New King wishes to have the Seven. But they are his to have, more or less. He could have asked for them to be given over to Finn, his servant. But he did not. He could have had Ullin Saheed and Micerea take them to the Palace, when they were here. But he did not."

"I am not as thick as you think," Ashlord retorted, barely able to contain his mirth at provoking Raynor so. "I knew when she left with Finn that we would not see Lady Shevalia again. When we do see her, she will have a new title."

"You impertinent old Watcher! You knew all along, didn't you?"

"Pretty much. And who are you to call someone old?"

"And when did you first suspect this outcome?"

"I first saw the possibility, amongst ten thousand others, nearly nine months ago, shortly after the day the young lady appeared at my cottage door at Tulith Attis. Of course, I saw many other possibilities, too. But, one by one, those fell away until, on the day Banis died, very few conflicting possibilities remained to be resolved."

"Oh, is that so?"

"Well, yes," Ashlord shrugged. "But, of course, it wasn't up to me. And things easily could have gone an entirely different way, but for Eldwin's rescue of us. And so, in a very strange way, not only are we indebted to Esildre, but so is the world. For, should things now go the way that we think they will, everything will soon change."

"But in the short-term, at least, not all for the better."

"Perhaps not. But the world is not a short-term affair, is it?"

Chapter 31

The Last King

The city of Duinnor was slowly waking up. Although the fog and mist still swirled, oddly tinged with a bluish-white light, it was beginning to thin and lift. While most still slept, owing to their exhaustion, a few people cautiously emerged from their cellars and homes into the open air to look around, and they discerned faint hints of blue sky above them. They went about quietly, saying very little to each other. They were still trying to shake off the peculiar dreams that remained in the forefront of their thoughts, bewitching dreams that produced lingering sensations of mystery and peace. It was as if the world they walked in had somehow joined with that of their sleep and was reluctant to be separated. Then, at midmorning, all who were still asleep were jarred from their slumber by the great gong of the Temple. Although it was distant, such was the nature of the stark sound that none could mistake its import, nor ignore its summons.

The people of the countryside heard the gong, too. And those who kept vigil along the roads and hills surrounding and who had been watching the city from afar saw the floating palace long before the fog-enveloped city-dwellers did. They were filled with amazement and wonder, as well as a little fear at the sight of it and the long causeway that stretched out to the High Tower of the King. It was difficult to look upon for long, for the lightning that hung in the air lit the frozen clouds brilliantly. But those who had spyglasses saw movement along the unsupported bridge, a line of people going from the floating castle to the tower.

By the time noon approached, all understood the signal of the Temple gong, which was struck twice every minute. The people of the city lined the avenues leading from the palace to the south gate, and they joined with those of the countryside to gather in the valley along the road that ran to the Temple. Kingsmen filtered out of the city and formed two opposing lines along the length of the south road. At the noon hour, trumpets blared from the walls.

First, there came out of the gate two monks swinging censures of smoking incense, and behind them came four more monks carrying a litter upon which was the body of the Old King, his arms folded across his chest. Everyone, without knowing how, recognized him as someone they knew, or thought they knew, so familiar was his face to them, even though they had never laid eyes on him before. And they were surprised, too, by how young and hale he looked, even in death, his sandy hair and beard having but a few strands of gray. Two more monks came, one bearing a ceremonial sword wrapped in black cloth, and the other with a scepter of magnificent jewels. Behind them came a small boy, dressed in simple ill-fitting clothes as a beggar might wear, and he wept as he followed the dead monarch. Some many paces behind him moved the Avatar, the Red Door. But it floated not upright as a door should, but flat, and upon it stood the New King, glowing in his mantle. His aura was so powerful that one could only glance at him for the briefest of moments, as one might glance at the sun, but during that short moment, the eyes burned and watered, the mind was filled with a rush of spinning, confusing visions, and the heart throbbed with terrible dread. Instinctively, the people bowed to the passing procession, and most knelt on the ground. But the Kingsmen remained standing on either side of the road, facing the crowds, their swords drawn, and each of them mustered all of his will not to falter as the hum of their new ruler, silent except between their ears, shook their resolve. As the New King passed behind them, their sensation of his presence intensified, and the light of his mantle shot between the soldiers, throwing their shadows away from where they stood.

Following the New King, another group of monks carried an ornate sedan chair, one that was last used a year earlier, when the Sixth Unknown King went to the Temple, as each previous Unknown King did on every vernal equinox. Indeed, the chair was made to transport Duinnor's King, brought out only for that purpose, and it was the same ancient chair that had carried each of the previous Unknown Kings since the very first one had it constructed. Since then, it had emerged from the city six hundred and thirty-eight times before, and many people not privy to the workings of the Palace or the Temple may have thought that it was the King's Throne, but it was not. Each time before, the Avatar of the King would go before it, and the King would sit upon the chair, following along. But this day the New King went first, standing upon the Avatar. Upon the chair that followed sat a beautiful lady in regal gowns and robes who was known, until recently, as Lady Shevalia. If the onlookers were not already so amazed and bewildered by the procession, or if they had not been so distracted by their own fatigues of the past sleepless days and nights, or so disconcerted, still, by the dreams that seemed so real, they may have been more surprised by the sight of Shevalia. With her eyes firmly fixed ahead, her chin up, she was expressionless. Of those who had chanced to meet and speak with her before today, who knew of her kindness or had seen her joyous skating, she was as beautiful and as mysterious as ever. In her own way, she was as inscrutable as the King. But she was only one of the many mysteries that they were now to witness.

Behind Lady Shevalia strode a man wearing a dark blue military uniform with a white sash across his chest. He led two lines of similarly dressed men and women with scabbards on their backs and hilts protruding over their shoulders. Some of these stern and expressionless soldiers were obviously members of the fierce Dragonkind race, a fact that incited some considerable murmuring and pointing from the bystanders.

Next came a great and distinguished-looking lord, his chin held high and the whisper of a smile across his lips. This was none other than Finn in his fine green robes and jewel-studded hat, swinging his gold staff as he led a procession of people. To the crowd's further amazement came a Dragonkind man and woman, and three Dragonkind girls, Radasa and his family, attired in colorful and exotic robes and headgear. Indeed, nearly all of the servants of Griferis came out to accompany the New King, all finely dressed, and at the end of their line was a little man, Eldwin, walking beside the elegant Lady Highleaf. Behind her came Ibin and Billy, and, finally, Ashlord, Raynor, and Farby.

The procession slowly but steadily made its way along the straight road to the mountain and upward to the foot of the long stairs to the Temple. Still the gong rang out from the Temple, echoing across the country. The Avatar bearing the New King did not stop, but floated upward behind the still-weeping boy as he climbed the long stairway. Lady Shevalia's sedan was put down and she ascended the stairs on foot. Behind her, monks in ceremonial robes bearing ornate halberds barred the way while the other followers remained at the base of the stairs.

The Old King was taken inside the Temple, and his body carefully placed onto an altar of carved hickory wood near the glass pyramid that dominated the sanctuary. When the Avatar reached the portico outside, the New King stepped from it, and, when Lady Shevalia came to him, her head bowed in order to keep her eyes averted, the two entered the sanctuary behind the Red Door. Several armed monks stationed themselves outside the great doors of the Temple as they were pushed closed. On the portico, the monk who swung his mallet at the gong paused as an acolyte stepped up and stood at the top of the stairs.

"The King is dead!" he cried out, and the gong rang.

"Long live the King!" came a chorus from all those gathered around the Temple and the valley below.

A half minute passed, then the acolyte shouted again, "The King is dead!" And again the gong rang, and the refrain was shouted by the people as would be repeated for the following two hours.

Within, as soon as the great doors were closed, the bright mantle that surrounded Robby fell from him onto the floor at his feet, a brilliant robe of golden threads. A monk prostrated himself, then lifted up the robe in his arms and stood aside while another monk approached Robby.

"Behold the mystery of the Kings of Duinnor," the monk said to Robby, gesturing for him to approach to where the previous King was laid out. Robby nodded, and he offered Sheila his arm. He looked at her, and for the first time she saw him as he now was, the lines of worry etched from his eyes, the silver that shot through his hair and beard to make his once-black curls gray and straight. He smiled at her, and she smiled back, seeing the love and kindness in his eyes, and she took his arm with hers. Her own eyes blurred with emotion, with happiness, surely, but also with grief for what had befallen Robby. Together they walked between the rows of kneeling monks, who whispered their prayers and chants in unison as the gong outside was struck. Robby and Sheila were ushered aside and watched as the Oracle, dressed in only a loincloth, brought out a pail of water and placed it onto the floor while several monks undressed the corpse. The Oracle offered his hand to the boy who knelt nearby, and together the old man and the child ceremoniously washed the body of the dead King.

"Behold, the Old King," cried the monk, and then the gong was again struck.

In the jarring silence that followed, all eyes were upon the Old King. It was a heavy silence, somber and full of sadness. When the gong struck again, it seemed only to hammer down the melancholy proceedings, seemed only to focus all hearts upon the one person who lay upon the altar.

The gong struck again, and the Oracle spoke, his voice low but firm.

"Long has been his toil, and longer his trial. Let his works be known by their evidence. Let his sins fade from the earth, and be lifted from his soul. Let healing come of his deeds, and let new life come of his death. As his body is washed, so let his spirit be cleansed. As his troubles are dried away into the air, let him rest, for another has come to take his place."

As the Oracle and the boy turned to take up the washing of the body, the kneeling monks and the Oracle repeated his words in unison. The Oracle and the boy washed and dried the body carefully, with the Oracle giving gentle guidance to the youngster. When the washing was done, the Oracle gave a clean folded rag to the boy. Taking a cup from an attending monk, the Oracle poured drops of fragrant oil onto the brow of the dead man, and the Oracle put his hand upon the boy's that held the rag, and together they daubed and anointed the Old King.

Then three monks came, each carrying a tray, and they kneeled within reach of the Oracle. Upon one tray were strips of linen in long rolls, and upon another was a carefully folded robe of dark green silk. The third tray held a simple circlet of gold. Two more monks came, and as the Oracle and the boy assisted them, the man that had been King for so long was wrapped in strips of linen and placed into new robes. Then the circlet was carefully placed upon his head. The Old King was once more put upon the litter, and four monks lifted it to their shoulders. They bore him to the doors, and the monk outside at the gong put away his soft mallet and lifted two hammers of iron. As the doors of the Temple swung open and the body of the Old King emerged, the monk beat a rapid cadence, harsh and loud.

Those who saw the litter emerging fell to their knees. Many clutched their hands to their hearts, for the awful crash of the gong seemed to signal the end of the world and all things in it, a din of doom and grief. The sun descended behind the far mountains, and shadows crossed the land. The terrible noise of the gong continued, and the Old King who was dead was taken down the stairs of the Temple, unaccompanied by any but those that carried him. They turned along a path that wound around the mountain to its western face and disappeared from view as they made their way to the Tomb of Kings. There, the heavy stone door was already pulled open, and the dead king was carried within and placed into the sixth vault, the only empty one that remained. Thus the Sixth Unknown King of Duinnor joined the previous five. The vault was sealed with a heavy slab of marble. The monks then departed the tomb and pushed its great door closed. The instant it was shut, the hammering of the gong ceased.

An eerie silence followed the departing echoes of the gong. Noticing a bright light, the people turned and saw the Five Stars of Duinnor, hovering over the city and the strange castle in the air. The stars grew incredibly bright, then they faded and disappeared altogether. Hushed exclamations of wonder and dismay went up from the population. At that moment, night was come, and Lady Moon climbed her eastern stairs, putting her fan entirely away so that she could look fully upon the land.

Slowly, more and more campfires dotted the valley as the people kept vigil. They passed the night speaking in subdued voices to one another, speculating about the New King. What would he do? Would he bring an end to the turmoil that Duinnor City had been suffering for weeks on end? Who would he select as his ministers? What of the coming war with Tracia and the Dragonkind? And how would Vanara and the other realms react to the New King?

As they questioned one another, Ashlord, Billy, and Ibin, along with Lady Highleaf and her nephew, were introducing themselves to the citizens of Griferis who were in attendance, and who were all excited and happy to meet their King's old friends and friends of friends. Much was learned by all, albeit very little about what might be passing inside the Temple. They were further baffled when a great number of workmen came out from the city. They drove wagons of lumber and tools, and a host of them walked along until they came midway along the road between the city and the Temple. There, they chose a place and assembled a large platform, covering it with colorful awnings, and making it into a grand pavilion. Kingsmen worked, too, placing the staffs and standards of all their armies and battalions around it, and farther away, Duinnor Regulars also gathered under their own flags and pennants. At this sign, people hurried back and forth into the city, making sure that their own pennants were hung and flying. Soon the sound of rustling and snapping flags filled the air.

Within the Temple, a ceremony was taking place. The Oracle addressed those present as he held the hand of the small boy. He did not speak loudly, nor had any need to, for his old voice carried throughout the attentive room.

"This then," he said of the boy, "was ever the servant of Beras. He served long and faithfully, though burdened with a powerful ward, the Sixth Unknown King. As it was given to those who went before, his was at first the voice of wisdom and knowledge, provided to the Unknown King as counselor and advisor. His time stretched out as did the King's, and the years passed slowly. Not all his counsel was taken, not all his words were heeded, and as it has always happened before, both the King and this, his servant, were sorely tried by one another. As the years of the Sixth King waxed, the wisdom of his servant waned. He became, in body and in mind, in memory and in thought, more youthful, less confident, forced to give up his abilities. But know this: This child you see before you was the constant friend to he who could have no other friend, the companion to he who could have no other companion. As a friend, he loved his King. And as a faithful servant, he remained with his King when all others failed him. Until at last, provoked by the New King, the Old King did that which is forbidden, and in a fit of anger, he struck this child. Thus the Old King passed away as all those before him did, and fell victim to his own cruelty, thinking himself above the basest requirements of decency. And thus the Old King died by his own hand. But this child is not to blame."

The Oracle pointed at Robby.

"He, who stands yonder, brought this about. He provoked this death, not this child. And he, who took up the mantle of Kingship, has now the awful responsibility of his death."

At these words, Robby's visage hardened, though a tear dripped across his face.

Turning the boy to face him, the Oracle said, "You have been a kind and faithful servant. May Beras now release thee, and give to thee a new and happy purpose, full of peace."

The Oracle stood aside. The boy, who was now not much more than a toddler, looked at the Oracle. Then the youngster became fascinated by the strange pyramid nearby, which was now filling with a luminous cloud. He took a few quick steps toward it, then halted and looked at Robby. Robby was flabbergasted at the sudden realization that he recognized the boy's features, for his eyes and expression were just the same as Ashlord's. The boy broke his gaze from Robby and ran to the pyramid, passing right through the glass as if it was air, disappearing within the swirling clouds that now glowed even brighter than before.

The Oracle turned to Robby.

"It is ordained that he who takes the Golden Mantle is to become King," he said. "But your Kingship shall not last, for no secret guards it. You have spoken your name, so that others who seek your throne may easily know it is not yours but their own that they must learn. This naming and the discovery of the True Name was not something ordained by Beras, but a practice made by Men when they came to the shores of this world. The secret of it was guarded by the First Unknown King, and each Unknown King thereafter. But you have destroyed the secret, and cannot have its protection."

The Oracle paused, and Robby realized that he was waiting for a response.

"I do not wish for its protection."

"Then only three things may be given to assure your reign," said the Oracle. "The Golden Mantle, which has already revealed its power to you, and a servant who will be faithful during all the days of your reign. And, as a sign of your power, you may have the Avatar to command, and to be a symbol of warning to you, foreboding your downfall."

The monk bearing the bright-shining robe brought it to the Oracle and gave it to him. The Oracle then approached Robby, offering the robe to him.

"It has been cleansed of the ways of the Old King," he said, "and may now be yours."

"I do not wish to have it."

The Oracle smiled, but the other monks of the place looked aghast.

"I beg you to take it," the Oracle said. "For how else will you know the thoughts of those before you, and judge your servants?"

"I have no need to know their thoughts," Robby said, "if they are unwilling to share them. I would prefer to know their longings, and somewhat of their dreams. And I would prefer to have my own doubts about such things, rather than the conceit of certainty. Moreover, I would that those who choose to serve me and to advise me do so of their own desire rather than be compelled by the force of my will, or by the condemnation of this Temple. I wish to have no advisor from you, no mantle, and no Avatar, however wise or powerful or terrible they may be. I have my own means to bring terror, should I wish to. I have my own eyes to see with, should I wish to look. And I have my own friends to give me their advice and counsel, should they be willing to give me their friendship."

"Come the Destroyer!" cried the Oracle. He held up the mantle which suddenly lost its dazzling glow, fading until, for the first time since its creation, it appeared to be made of simple threads, golden and fine, but only ordinary threads that gave off no light of their own.

"It was foretold to me," the Oracle pronounced loudly, "that the Seventh King would resist such things. It was given to me in a vision that the Seventh King would destroy the Ring of Hearing. That he would reject the temptation of Ethliad the Sword. That he would refuse the boons of this Temple, and the golden raiments of power."

He then turned to Robby, and said to him, "And it was also foretold that the Seventh King of Duinnor would be its last, and his reign would be short and quick."

"Indeed, I mean for it to be so," said Robby. "And, to that end, I beg you to give final service to Duinnor, and then forever be set free from its dominion. For I have seen your visions, Oracle, and I have witnessed your ravings and your dreams. I know that as long as the Avatar goes forth this Temple cannot be fulfilled of its purpose. So I refuse your offerings, which you are sworn to Beras to make to me, and I ask you two boons in their stead."

Robby took Sheila's hand and drew her close.

"First, that you give that mantle, which is now merely a robe, to this lady to wear, as a sign of her authority."

"Only you may give it," said the Oracle offering it to Robby.

"Then I must know from you," Robby said, "do you recognize me as the rightful King of Duinnor?"

"Indeed, I must. And I do. And I declare you to be so."

"Then I have it in my power to act as King and to do all those things that a rightful King of Duinnor must do and may do? To make law, to reform the lands, and to reward and punish those who are deserving?"

"It is so. You are King."

Robby turned and placed the Golden Robe around Sheila's shoulders.

"With the offering of this robe," he said to her, "I declare you my wife and my Queen, if you would be so."

Sheila nodded, smiling.

"Do you," Robby turned back to the Oracle, "acknowledge this lady as my wife, to be Queen of Duinnor in her own right, whatsoever may happen to me?"

"I must. And I do," said the Oracle.

"And do you acknowledge in her all power and authority as monarch of this Realm, notwithstanding any condition or obstacle?"

"I do."

"Then, as King of Duinnor, I wish to abdicate, making her sole ruler in my stead. I relinquish any right or title to the throne of Duinnor, yielding to this Queen all authority and all rights of the King of this Realm."

Robby then knelt before Sheila.

"It is my desire that the Realm of Duinnor be united with that of Griferis, and that Duinnor and Griferis be as husband and wife, as are their sovereigns, in body and in soul. Will you agree to this, my Queen?"

"Be my husband," Sheila said, taking Robby's hand into her own trembling grasp. "And let me be your wife. Seal this pact with me as we have done before, with your lips upon mine."

The Oracle laughed, hopping and gesturing for all the monks to rise from their prayer rugs. A moment later, those monks who stood guard outside the doors heard a sound they had never before heard coming from within, the sound of joyous applause.

• • •

When Lady Moon approached the western rim of the world and looked back across the sky at her husband who now rose to his daily work, she smiled demurely at him, and he smiled back. At that very moment, the great pipes of the Temple blared forth a long deep blast, and all onlookers rose to their feet and turned to watch. The doors of the Temple were swung open, and the Oracle appeared.

"The Monarch of Duinnor cometh!" he cried. "Make ready!"

The pipes of the Temple blasted and blared, the armies of Duinnor marshalled, all of the Lords and Ministers and Judges of the land, and all of the people made ready. As Sir Sun stepped higher upon his stair and stretched his bright arms across the land, banners and pennants and streamers of every design and hue were fanned by a breeze, representing all of the Houses and Lords and Guilds of Duinnor, making the plain between the mountain and the city a tumult of color as the people thronged to the coming procession.

The blaring horns ceased, and the Oracle cried out, "Let the greatness of Duinnor be proclaimed throughout all of the lands of the earth, unto every corner, from the sea to the mountains. Duinnor the Mighty! Duinnor the Merciful! Duinnor the Bountiful! Duinnor the Just! Let it be thus as a sign to all people, that Duinnor thrives in the Heavens as upon the Earth! Receive your Queen!"

A brilliant flash of light came from overhead, briefly outshining the new sun, and then six stars appeared, all in an arc over the city, where before there had only been five. This brought cheers and clapping from the crowds that lasted many moments until the Temple pipes were blown once again and the mighty gong rang out, and the Oracle cried out, lifting up his staff to those Six Stars of Duinnor, "All hail Shevalia, Queen of Duinnor!"

From within the Temple emerged Sheila in her magnificent golden robe that glinted in the sunshine of day. A wave of wonder passed through the crowds who saw her, then a tumultuous cheer gathered and spread until the loud and happy noise filled the plains and the valleys and resounded from the mountains. During this, Robby came and stood beside and slightly behind Sheila until she took his hand and pulled him closer.

She raised her hand, and the noise of the crowd subsided.

"I am Shevalia, your Queen. And this is my husband, Philawain, King of Griferis, whose wondrous realm you see yonder in the clouds. We are joined, as our Realms are joined."

The Oracle stepped up and said, "Let this be a day of rejoicing! For the world shall soon be remade, and old strifes shall be put away."

Chapter 32

Homage to the Queen

In Duinnor, on the plain between the city and the Temple, the pavilion was completed long before the new ruler had emerged. And when, shortly after dawn, the First Queen of Duinnor walked, arm in arm, with the King of Griferis down the long stairs of the Temple, she did not ascend to her chair, but sent it ahead to be placed on the dais under the pavilion. When she and Robby came to the foot of the stairs at the base of the mountain, and to their friends and those gathered from Griferis, she paused as they all bowed low. She released Robby's arm, and he walked up to his old friends from Barley. Ibin was grinning, and so was Billy, although his face was wet with tears. Robby took him by the shoulders and then embraced him.

"I have missed you, old friend!" Robby said.

"Oh, I can't hardly speak," Billy answered. "I knew ye'd do it. I always knew it."

"I know. You knew better than I did, I swear. I'm sorry I put you through so much. And I intend to have you home just as fast as I can. You, too, Ibin. Come here!"

Ibin and Robby embraced, and then, over Ibin's shoulder, he saw Ashlord leaning on his walking stick, smiling.

"Ashlord, take my hand. You were right about so much," Robby said. "I made many mistakes, in spite of your warnings. But I would have made more had it not been for your advice. I hope you will not think too badly of me."

"How could I, dear King? How could I?" Ashlord embraced Robby, then stood back from him, each gripping the arm of the other. Ashlord looked over Robby's shoulder at Sheila. "I take it that things have worked out after all, between you and the Queen."

"Yes. I think they have. And you knew all along, didn't you?"

"No. Not quite all along. But things have a way of revealing themselves, do they not?"

"They do," Robby said, returning to Sheila's side.

"My lord," Sheila said to Robby, "I would have you meet two people that have found a place in my heart."

She beckoned for Farby and Lady Highleaf. They came forward, and Lady Highleaf curtseyed very low, while Farby knelt on one knee.

"Please rise," she said, "and make the King's acquaintance. My lord, this is Grantham Farby, to whom I and our friends owe our lives. And this is Lady Highleaf, who has been a very good friend to us all."

Farby bowed, then Robby took his hand to shake.

"I am ever in your debt, sir."

"I am at your service, sire."

"And I am happy to greet you, too, Lady Highleaf."

"The honor of greeting you fills me with happiness, sire," said Lady Highleaf as Robby took her hand. She would have said more but for the uncharacteristic lump in her throat.

"Come, then. Join us. We have business to attend, and I would have you with us as we do so."

"It would be our greatest pleasure."

• • •

Together, they slowly walked along the road to the pavilion, accompanied all the way by cheers and hurrahs. When they gained the pavilion steps and began to ascend, trumpets blasted a long fanfare, picked up by more trumpets on the walls of the city, and echoed by the pipes of the Temple. Sheila stood at the front of the platform, and Robby stood beside and behind her as the trumpets continued to blare and the bells of the city rang out.

"Hail, Shevalia!" resounded the crowd as loudly as the trumpets. "Hail to the Queen!"

Meanwhile, scribes set up their desks and dipped their pens, while Finn ordered those upon the dais behind Sheila into their positions. Thus behind her stood Billy, Ibin, Ashlord, and Raynor, along with Lady Highleaf, Farby, and General Lafkin. General Chadler was called, along with Lord Arata, and even Captain Thrubold, too. Only Celia was absent, but she watched with Boxer from the walls of Griferis high above them.

At last, Sheila turned and sat in her ornate chair, and Robby stood beside her as Finn held up his hand and waited for the noise of cheering to subside.

"The Kingdom of Duinnor and the Kingdom of Griferis are joined and shall henceforth be as one! Hail, King Philawain of Griferis, Lord of Dreams!"

Another great cheer went up, encouraged, no doubt, by the uncanny tidings that many of the people had received during their sleep, brought to them by various messengers of Griferis.

Robby stepped forward, and Finn bowed to him. Then Finn turned to the crowd once more.

"So that you may know the power of Griferis," he said, "remember your dreams and the messengers sent by Philawain unto you. Those of you who remember, tell others of what you were shown. All who dream are united under the banner of Griferis, whether man, woman, or child, whether Man, Dragonkind, or Elifaen, or any other race that may come upon the earth. Griferis is no respecter of Realm, nor of rank. Let no one treat another falsely unless he wishes for all to know. Let no one disobey the laws of the land, unless he wishes to be punished and disgraced. But if there be any law that is unjust or ill-considered, let it be known to your Queen and your King so that a just remedy may be found.

"And so that you may know the power of Duinnor, and the authority of your King and Queen, let those lords and princes of the world come forth to make their greetings and to give their allegiance! First, let the lords and princes of Duinnor come and be recognized!"

At this, a line of finely attired people were allowed to approach through the Kingsmen, lords and ladies all, generals of the armies, judges of the realm, and other powerful persons, including Blain Farby and his wife, Elyna, sister to Lady Highleaf. One by one, or in pairs, they were instructed to climb the dais as their names were called. They knelt before the Queen and kissed her hand, then knelt before Robby and repeated the gesture before exiting to stand separately from the crowd. This took a very long time, and once, during a pause while they waited for an elderly judge to be helped up onto the dais, Sheila glanced at Robby, who leaned over to her.

"Is all this necessary?" she asked, covering her mouth with her hand.

"I'm afraid so, my dear," he said in her ear. "I hope you are comfortable, for it only just begins. We must have Duinnor come first, so that they will know their place in service to you. Remember what I instructed you to say. Afterwards, I hope to reward your patience with a surprise."

It was a long procession. When Finn's voice grew hoarse from announcing the names of those who came, Lord Arata was imposed upon to continue, having been the first to give his own allegiance. But at last, Duinnor was done, and Sheila, taking her cue from Robby's nod, stood. Everyone on the dais bowed, and she stepped forward.

"I charge the forces of Duinnor, and its people likewise, in the protection of those who are our friends. It is our duty to show our goodwill to those who were formerly our enemies, so that they may show their goodwill to us. My husband, the King of Griferis, has already made known this duty to those who are in uniform, and they understand their duty. But I wish to offer my friendship and the friendship of Duinnor to any who wish for peace with this Realm. Let come any who wish for peace!"

Some distance off, a large group of people moved forward. They were dressed in brown robes such as pilgrims often wear, with hoods drawn up over their heads and their arms tucked within their sleeves. It was several hundred people who thus moved forward, and the Kingsmen around the dais had to shift their ranks to allow all of them to come before Queen Shevalia. When they had all gathered, shoulder to shoulder, rank upon rank, one of them stepped forward of their line.

"I bid you make yourselves known to us," Sheila said.

They stood and cast off their robes, revealing the glittering armor of Dragonkind. A great cry erupted within the crowds as they instinctively backed away, and the Kingsmen stiffened and put their hands to their hilts. In a clattering ring, out swept the Dragonkind's swords, but before any could react, they held them out and laid them on the ground and knelt before them.

"Hail, Queen Shevalia!" they cried out, bowing to touch their heads upon the bright blades of their swords.

"Hail, King Philawain!" they cried, touching their foreheads upon their swords once more.

While there was still a great tumult amongst the people, some of the Griferis guard smiled. Sheila addressed the Dragonkind who was at the front of the large group.

"Rise sir. Say your name, and tell us who these are that have come with you."

"I am Gurasa, of the House of Golden Sand, my Queen. These are the Al Sairs, guard of my household, loyal and cunning fighters all. We come to give our alliance, should ye wish it, and our friendship, should ye desire it."

"I do wish it, and desire it. What say you, my King?"

"Likewise, it is a great thing, such as never before seen or heard of," said Robby. "I wish and desire it with all my heart."

Finn then stepped forth, and lifted a scroll and read from it loudly.

"Let it be proclaimed, by order of the Queen of Duinnor and the King of Griferis, that from this day hence there is friendship and peace between the House of Golden Sand and our Realms. Let old enemies learn to be new friends. Let us together strive in solidarity for peace and for the prosperity of our people. Let no one interfere in this, nor let any matter come between us ever more! Let any act against you, be against our Realms, and let any act against us be an insult to your house and its people."

Finn motioned for Gurasa to come up as a small table was brought out. Gurasa came up the steps onto the platform, and he bowed to the King and Queen. Then he went to the table, took a quill, and put his name upon the document and then pressed his signet ring into it. Robby and Sheila then came to the table and did the same.

"Let this be but the first sign of many signs," Robby cried out, "of the new world, and of the new order. Let the night of Duinnor be turned to day, and let the old world thus begin its passing away."

Slowly, the murmuring of the crowds turned to approval until at last the people were crying out, "Gurasa! Gurasa!"

Sheila took her seat again, as Gurasa bowed to the crowds, then once more to Robby and Sheila before taking his place beside General Lafkin. Finn stepped up once more.

"Let there now come those who represent other lands of the earth!"

As Gurasa's men took up their swords and moved aside, there was strange popping at the rear of the throngs, and several glowing lights briefly appeared and disappeared with little notice. From that place behind the crowds came forth several men in regal clothes, including the Prince of Altoria, the Prince of Masurthia, Ruling Prince Carbane and his son, Prince Danoss, along with Prince Lantos of Tracia. As they made their way, they appeared somewhat bewildered, still shaken by the means of their transportation. They looked around, surprised and nervous before the great gathering. But they had all been told ahead of time what they should expect and what would be required of them, and all had agreed to come, though none could have imagined the manner of their travel.

Once gathered, the men knelt.

"Rise," said Finn, "and say whether you give allegiance to the King of Griferis and his Queen of Duinnor."

"We do, my lord," said Prince Lantos.

"Do you also swear to regard the King and Queen as your sovereigns, to support and to promote their will, and to defend and uphold their law?"

"We do," they said.

"Then come and put your names and your seals upon our pact."

They came up onto the dais, and like Gurasa before, they sealed their oaths with their signets. Each then knelt and kissed the rings of Robby and Sheila.

"Prince Lantos, Prince Carbane, Prince Danoss, please linger to hear me," said Robby, speaking so that all nearby could hear. "I have you know that Griferis and Duinnor shall endeavor to bring about an end to the revolt within Tracia, and bring to justice those who have committed violence in that land and elsewhere. However, as your armies presently march into Tracia and take up positions from which to launch their attacks, I warn you to treat the people of Tracia with gentleness and with patience. Long have they suffered tyranny, first under your brother's rule, Prince Lantos, and then at the hands of those from whom they sought relief and redress, the Triumvirate. Indeed, the Red Trio has encouraged violence in their ranks, corruption in their courts, and they have enslaved Tracia's people. They have brought ruin to their land. The long conflicts in Tracia have pitted neighbor against neighbor, and have created deep hatred and mistrust. You must be as bringers of freedom, not as conquerors. I advise you to see first to the well-being of the people, and to their recovery. The people must be fed and sheltered. You must minister to their wounds. They must be protected from reprisals and from unjust accusations. Hear the grievances of the people, and weigh carefully the evidence of their testimony. Let the guilty be disgraced and let them be punished with just labor and reasonable reparations, but not with their lives, nor may you allow suffering to be brought upon their families. Forgiveness must flow like water. I warn you: Griferis watches, and I put my own eyes upon the earth and its people. Rule your followers with a firm hand. Spare not your treasury for the relief of the needy, and permit no looting nor any uncivil act. Do these things justly, erring on the side of liberty, and Griferis will reward you. Do otherwise and be utterly destroyed."

"Yes, my King," said Prince Lantos, bowing and putting his hand over his heart. "I shall do my utmost."

"I, likewise, sire," said Prince Carbane.

Robby dismissed them with a wave of his hand, and Sheila gazed at him with wonder at the stern manner in which he had spoken.

A distant blast of trumpets interrupted her thoughts, and all eyes turned to the far eastern hills where coming over the rise were four columns of riders on buckmarls and horses. The outermost horsemen had trumpets and ram's horns to their lips, and from their upright lances flew the colors of Vanara. In between these, and at the forefront of the company rode a figure dressed in gleaming armor wrapped in feathery sky-blue robes. Upon her head was a jeweled helmet with feathered wings. Behind the Queen of Vanara rode Thurdun, likewise dressed in his ceremonial armor, and all the others of their company. In awe and somewhat in fear, the crowds parted as the riders streamed down into the valley and rode across the fields.

Sheila gripped Robby's hand. Grinning, Robby glanced at Finn who, smiling, gave a little bow of his head.

An opening through the Kingsmen was made for Serith Ellyn's company, and she rode up to the dais as her company fanned out behind her.

"Hail, Queen of Vanara!" cried out Finn as Sheila rose from her chair.

"Hail, Serith Ellyn," Sheila said. "I bid you welcome to Duinnor!"

"Hail, Shevalia! Hail, Philawain!" Serith Ellyn replied with a low dip of her head.

"Please come," said Robby, "and tell us why we have the honor of your company."

Serith Ellyn and Thurdun dismounted, as did all the rest of their company, and Chanter took their reins while Gaiyelneth stood beside him. Serith Ellyn, looking pale and nervous in spite of her fearsome attire, approached Robby and Sheila. Never before had any ruler of Vanara come into Duinnor Realm, and with all of the dire news of late concerning Duinnor's involvement in the attack on Linlally, the people present stiffened with nervous anticipation. Only the snap and rustle of the flags and pennants could be heard as a hush settled over the crowds, and everyone pushed forward to hear what would pass.

Serith Ellyn and Thurdun bowed to Robby and Sheila, who returned the gesture with bows of their own.

"I say again, welcome," said Sheila. "What gives us the honor of this unexpected visit? Unexpected, for I have been told that you were far away from these lands, and it has always been said that you would never come to Duinnor."

"Queen," said Serith Ellyn. "Until lately I have been far away. And, until lately, I would never have come. But," she glanced at Robby, then at Prince Carbane and the other dignitaries nearby, including Gurasa, "the heart may persuade one to do that which the mind is at first against. And the mind may come around to accept what the heart sees. Indeed, I have been shown many things, and though I do not understand them, I am compelled by my heart to be here. I come to offer my hand in friendship, and, as these others have done, to swear my loyalty and my allegiance to you."

She turned to Thurdun, who handed her a small box.

"As token of my sincerity, and to bind my realm and my reign to yours, I offer these gifts to you."

She opened the box, then held it up for all to see, revealing the Seven glittering Bloodcoins of her House. A murmur coursed through the crowd when they realized what they were. Then Serith Ellyn knelt, bowed her head, and held them out to Queen Shevalia. For a moment, Sheila stared at them, mesmerized by the power of their beauty, then she shook herself and glanced at Robby before speaking.

"Queen Serith Ellyn, these are symbols of your rule. Are you determined for me to have them? For if I take them, you will never have them back."

"I am certain, my Queen."

Sheila took them and gave them to Robby.

"It is a great trial you have endured," Robby said. "I bid you rise. Come and see this."

A large case covered in blue cloth was brought out by Hathrain and Unther and placed before them. When Robby pulled away the cloth, and everyone saw the other Bloodcoins within it, the murmurs of the people grew, with many expressions of astonishment. Robby placed each of Serith Ellyn's Seven into the case, filling the last remaining empty spaces, and turned back to face the others.

"Behold!" Robby said. "These are the Forty-Nine, gathered together for the first time since the days of your grandfather, Cupeldain. These will bring about the end of waiting for your people," he said to Serith Ellyn, "and will do much else, too."

As he spoke, cries of wonder swept across the throngs who were farthest off from the pavilion as seven flying horses swooped down low, going right over their heads. Upon them rode Lyrium and her two daughters, along with Tyrillick and three of his guard. There was quite nearly a panic as people ran left and right underneath the newcomers.

"Be not afraid!" cried Robby. "Let them come!"

The flying horses landed, and their riders dismounted, smiling broadly. Not waiting to be asked, Lyrium and her daughters stepped onto the crowded platform, and bowed very low to Robby, then to Sheila.

"We meet again, my lady," Lyrium said to Sheila. "And many mysteries are revealed."

Astonished by Lyrium's presence, Sheila remembered the night they spoke to one another in Tallinvale's moonlit gardens. She remembered sitting with Lyrium on the garden bench, chatting girlishly about Robby, and about the quest that was before them.

"Lady Lyrium, welcome to you and to your daughters," Sheila said. "I feel as if this is all a dream."

Nearly everyone smiled at this, but Lyrium shook her head.

"Someday, dreams shall be as real as this," she said. "And sweeter still."

"Do you come to celebrate with us? For there is much to celebrate today, not the least being the strange happenstance of me becoming a queen."

Lyrium and her daughters, their eyes glittering with delight, looked from her to Robby and back.

"Indeed, Queen Shevalia, there is much to celebrate. And that is enough reason for us to come, though we were invited for another reason entirely."

"Oh?"

"Yes, my Queen," said Robby. "I have a duty to fulfill."

He went to the case containing the Bloodcoins and removed all of the ones that had amber centers. Coming back to Lyrium, he held them out.

"These were given by Aperion's hand to your hand. You are the only one remaining of all those who received such tokens. You are the only one who may rightfully claim these Seven and decide their fate. I offer them to you, now, to decide for all those who are not here to do so."

"I know that Cupeldain is gone," said Lyrium, glancing at Serith Ellyn, "and likewise are Therona, Ormace, Pyros, and Lucinda. But what of Katrina? I see the Seven of Topaz, which were given to her. Am I to believe that, since you have them, she is no longer in the world?"

"It came to my knowledge some while back that she departed into the icy wastes of the far north, as you may have heard told," Robby said, "and she took her Seven with her. The Fifth Unknown King of Duinnor sent his agents to find her. She was dead and all her people, too, but they found and brought back her Bloodcoins."

Lyrium frowned, and she hesitantly accepted the Seven offered to her.

"I have not held all my Seven since Ormace forced us to divide them," she said absently. She stared at the objects in her hands, barely large enough to hold them all. Her voice softened to a whisper as she stared at them, and her words were barely audible. "And those that I carried to Tulith Attis, I thought they were lost forever."

She suddenly looked at Sheila with fire in her eyes, as if a burning hatred ignited within her.

"It is all upon you, now," said Robby, sensing the torment that Lyrium was enduring. Serith Ellyn looked aghast at Lyrium and backed away a step. Her daughters also sensed something terrible, and their cheeks reddened with growing shame.

"You must decide," Robby stated.

"Mother, please, say what passes here?"

"Give them back, their price is too dear!"

Lyrium shot an angry look at her daughters, as tears rolled down her face.

"Your father died for these," she stammered through clenched teeth, her body shaking. "As did our friends!"

She saw Gurasa, and then, as if in terror, she looked at his people standing some distance away. Lyrium screamed, clutching the Bloodcoins to her breast as visions of Tulith Attis passed through her and engulfed her. Gone were Robby and Sheila. Gone were her daughters and the crowds around her. She darted a few steps one way, then abruptly she turned and darted back. Then she fell to her knees, clutching the Seven to her breast, screaming as she saw her people slaughtered, crying out just as she had when she saw her sister's form turned to stone nearby to that of her own husband, Heneil. Belmira and Elmira quickly stepped forward to her, but Robby stepped more quickly.

"Leave her!" he commanded, gripping their arms. "It is her battle, not yours, and she must fight it alone."

"Robby," said Sheila, forgetting herself. "What is happening?"

Ashlord and Raynor, still standing with Billy and Ibin, watched. Raynor shot out a hand to clutch Ashlord's shoulder, but Ashlord barely noticed, his eyes closed, and he was muttering quick words that only he could know.

Now, in Lyrium's eyes, there was a darker force assaulting Tulith Attis. She saw again the one who called for the gate to be opened, and she saw how he strode in with the Dragonkind. His armor was black, with a red hourglass, and he wore a terrible war-helm with horns protruding from its cheeks of iron. Now, Lyrium swayed back and forth on her knees, and she saw him go into the Treasury and look upon the empty place where the Bloodcoins had been kept. The vision faded. Relieved, she fell on her side, her eyes still wide and filled with the uncalled-for Sight. But then came another vision of the dark warrior, standing atop the walls of Shatuum. Behind him, within that shadowed land, was rank upon rank of terrible creatures, silently awaiting his word. She did not hear what he said over the ringing in her ears, but the ranks poured out of Shatuum and flowed across the land, spreading like black oil on linen.

She screamed once more, then scrambled on her knees to Robby.

"Take them, I beg thee!" she sobbed and cried, spilling the Bloodcoins onto the floor and pushing them toward Robby's feet. "I give them up! Take them! Take them all!"

Robby crouched, picked up the Bloodcoins and handed them to Sheila. Then he lifted Lyrium to her feet, put his arms around her, and held her. Her arms hung limp at her side as she sobbed and wailed on his shoulder. Robby put a hand on her head, his own face contorted with grief. Serith Ellyn, by now, truly understood that her own Bloodcoins had never really been her own. She came to Robby and pulled Lyrium away and held her, each of them crying together, with Belmira and Elmira, too. Sheila watched them as she put the Bloodcoins back into their places.

After a few moments, Robby addressed the crowds.

"Surely you must wonder at what just took place," he said. "But those of us who are Elifaen know our curse. We know that our ancestors' defiance was made into our curse, one that has poisoned our existence, and has since filled the world with discord and violence. But these objects that you see here, these Forty-Nine, were given by Aperion as tokens of hope and symbols of promise that our curse could be broken. Of all those seven who received these objects, of those seven who were charged with uniting the Elifaen with hope, only Lyrium remains. You saw her anguish, for the stain of history is heavy upon her heart, and these Forty-Nine have been soaked with blood and strife and with tears. She came gladly to us, to confirm our possession of the Forty-Nine. But she, whose faith was ever truest, whose hope was ever the greatest of all the Seven High Houses, could not know how the hammer of history would fall upon her soul. Her faith was tested. Her resolve was tried. And her wisdom prevailed. Let this be a sign to all that the world shall soon be remade. Old powers pass away, and new powers gather and stir. Now come the days when all things shall change, Elifaen, Men, and Dragonkind, all. Let us thus celebrate the New World that soon comes. Good people, do me and my new wife, your Queen, the honor of your joy. Be happy in our union, and be hopeful for peace."

A group had gathered around the case that held the Forty-Nine, having been previously asked by Robby or by dreams that he had sent to them. They were Lafkin, Prince Thurdun, Tyrillick, Unther, Hathrain, Winnefras, and Alzeeran the Scribe, who gave over his ink and quill to Borwain for a time. Robby bowed to the people, then turned to those gathered at the Forty-Nine while the crowds, somewhat confused and baffled, clapped their hands.

"I do not need to introduce you to each other since you have already met in your dreams," Robby said quickly as he reached into the case. "You know what to do, and the risk you take in doing it. Go with my blessing, and all our hopes."

He took the Bloodcoins and passed them out, placing each set of Seven into a shoulder bag before giving it to one of them.

"Go!" he said. They hurried off to mount the winged horses, and were all quickly out of sight, flying away in separate directions.

Finn and Sheila stood beside Robby, watching the horses and their riders recede. When they were mere dots against the blue sky, Finn spoke.

"My lord, may I ask Lord Arata to announce the celebrations in my stead?"

"Certainly."

Finn nodded to Arata, who then turned to the crowds and began reading proclamations declaring that there was to be a period of feasts and festivities, celebrations and banquets in honor of the New Queen and her husband. Meanwhile, Finn once again turned to Robby, and gestured aside.

"And, my King, there are a few more men who deeply desire to greet you and your wife."

"Oh?"

"Yes, sire. Shall I bring them forward?"

"Certainly," Robby said, curious, but knowing Finn well enough to know they must be very important people. As Robby watched, Finn went to the side of the dais and gestured. A tall man climbed the steps. He was plainly dressed and had long white hair, and Robby saw that he had only one arm.

"Grandfather!" he exclaimed, hurrying to Lord Tallin. As soon as he took Lord Tallin's hand, he saw Billy's father come up the steps behind Tallin and fairly shouted with delight. Turning, he saw Billy chatting away with Gurasa.

"Billy! Billy Bosk! Look who's here!"

Billy nearly tripped over himself getting to his father, and Lord Tallin and Robby had to move aside at the Boskmen's exuberant hugs.

"Oops! I reckon we're forgettin' ourselves," said Mr. Bosk. He then turned back to Robby and bowed low, along with Lord Tallin.

"Yer Majesty!"

"Your Highness."

Robby laughed as Sheila came to stand beside him, grinning as Tallin and Bosk knelt and kissed her hand. Robby looked at her, shaking his head.

"That ol' Finn!" he said to her. "Who'll he bring along next?"

Sheila's expression changed, and her smile vanished as she looked past Robby.

"Oh, Robby," she said.

Turning, Robby saw that another man was coming up the steps with Finn. He looked somewhat lost and a bit feeble, holding his hat in his hands, and Finn held him by the elbow as they took the steps one by one. They took a few steps forward, then paused, and the man with Finn looked around, as if searching for someone. Robby slowly approached, and the man looked at him curiously.

"Son?"

"Daddy?"

Now it was Robby's turn to weep, and he clutched his father tightly, then fell to his knees.

"I'm sorry. I'm so sorry!" he sobbed. "I didn't know any better. I didn't mean for her to get hurt."

"Son? My son? Oh, me! What's become of ye?" Mr. Ribbon leaned over, sinking to his knees, too, as they put their arms around each other.

"Is it truly me Robby-boy?"

Chapter 33

The Seven Towers

Winnefras had far to go, and Shartide, not wishing to be late, spared not his wings to get her to her destination. Forewarned by those who had come to Griferis on the backs of Islindia's flying horses, Winnefras had cut her hair short to keep it from being a nuisance, and she leaned against the horse's neck to keep from being blown off its back. At her side hung the shoulder bag containing the set of Seven that was her cargo. Soon after taking the Bloodcoins that she was to deliver, the scars on her back began to throb painfully. Now, as she neared her destination, her scars tingled and burned more and more.

"…and I don't see how anything can be so important that needs doing that cannot be done in our own forest," Shartide complained.

He had not stopped complaining the entire time. If it was not the weight of his rider, it was her grip on his mane. If it was not that, it was the silly people who gawked from below. He took issue with birds that got in their way. He was offended by the tall peaks of the Carthanes that he had to fly over. And he grumbled about the breeze that blew from their left, though Winnefras could hardly notice anything but the powerful wind that tore at her from the speed of their flight. And Shartide seemed outraged when the air shifted before them, laden with the aroma of the sea.

"I must contend with all this while my cousin Ayreltide, who always craves the Queen's favor, remains in the forest doing nothing in particular. But he will nonetheless reap the greatest of honors, I'm sure, while I'll be lucky to receive a passing nod from my Queen," he went on. "Must you grip my mane so tightly? I'll have no mane left at all if you keep pulling so!"

Winnefras opened her eyes and squinted against the fierce wind. She had never told Philawain, nor anyone else that, like many Elifaen, she was completely terrified of heights. Had she done so, someone else would have been sent in her place. If Shartide had not complained so incessantly, she might have paid more attention to her fears. As it was, she was more than ready to be rid of him. By now they were well into Glareth Realm, and she looked for her destination.

"There it is!" she cried.

"I have eyes, don't I?" Shartide replied. "Or did you think I was blind? I promised that I would bring you, and so I have!"

Shartide stopped flapping and glided down toward the slender Tower Ulaman, rising up from its mountain perch. It looked a mere speck, but Winnefras had seen it before, from below of course, just as she had seen others like it, and she knew how tall and massive it actually was. At the foot of the tower, a dense bank of clouds covered the land and stretched out eastward as far as could be seen, with only a few other mountaintops showing through. Shartide banked into a spiral descent, coming closer and closer to the tower's point as he circled. Winnefras studied it carefully, wondering if anyone had ever before looked upon it from above as she now did. The top of the tower was a dome of pale orange, some fifteen yards around, and its faceted skin glinted in the sun. At the center of the dome was a silver cap with a tall narrow mast of silver rising another twenty or so yards high. The mast held aloft a broad band of silver, something like a large wagon wheel, held to the mast by several metal spokes. But her immediate concern was the dome itself and the platform upon which it was made; there did not seem to be anywhere to stand, much less for the flying horse to land.

"Well, I must let you off, now," said Shartide. "I wish I could say it was a pleasure."

"Wait, circle once more, I beg you!"

"Come, come. I'll hover so that you can slip right off onto the top, just as I was told to do."

"No, wait! I don't...!"

But Shartide not only hovered, but reared, too, so that Winnefras slid off his back and fell onto the rim of the metal ring.

"Farewell!" Shartide said.

Winnefras was too occupied with saving herself to reply. She landed with one leg through the ring and another outside of it, and immediately slipped over until she was upside down, her precious shoulder bag dangling. She scrambled to get a hand onto a crossmember that connected the ring to the pole, slipping several times. At last her grip held, and she pulled herself up until she was in no immediate danger of falling.

"Damn that insolent horse!" she cried out. "Oh, oh!"

Now her scars burned fiercely, and she exerted all her strength to hang on as fiery jolts ran up and down her back from her waist to her shoulders. She closed her eyes, grimacing. It was cold up here, colder than on Shartide's back, and the wind was a gale. She gripped so hard her hands throbbed, and she clung on even harder when a wave of dizziness set her senses spinning. It subsided just a little, and she opened her eyes and reached out to take hold of the nearby mast, then shifted her weight so that she hugged it, feeling something warm running along her legs as she did so. Looking down, she saw that her breeches were soaked with blood. It dripped out from the hems and over her boots, splattering the orange dome below in a windblown pattern. She knew that she did not have very long.

She summoned all her remaining strength to grip the silver mast with both hands. Her heart thudding with fear, she pushed off from her perch with her feet and before she fell very far, had her legs and arms wrapped around the mast. At first she was able to control her descent, but when she reached a section smeared with her own blood, she lost her grip and slipped forty feet down. The dome rang when she hit. The bones of both her legs snapped, and she was jarred from the mast. Screaming, she tumbled and slid down the side of the dome. At the last moment she saw a ledge, barely a foot wide, and she grabbed it as she went over the side, dangling by her fingers, her shattered and useless legs nothing but dead weight, her back and shoulders afire. Her fingers were smeared with blood, and she clawed like a cat to hang on, panting and grunting wildly. The ledge was too smooth, there was no lip or rim for purchase, and her hands were too bloody and slick. A hand clamped onto her wrist, and she felt herself being lifted straight up. After a moment of frantic struggle, she went limp, panting uncontrollably. A very tall, very thin man held her up by her wrist, looking blankly at her contorted face, her eyes bulging with terror. He wore an orange robe made of tiny shards of topaz, and had skin like snow. There was not a hair on his face or bare head, not even eyebrows or lashes, and his eyes were the color of his robe, glittering orange. When he spoke, she understood every word he said, though she had never before heard the language.

"*Do you bring something?*" he asked.

She managed a nod.

"*Seven?*"

Again she nodded.

Turning, he carried her, still dangling by the wrist, around the rim of the dome to a triangular opening, and then inside. The door closed behind them.

It was dark within, and Winnefras felt herself being lowered. Her legs were broken, and she cried out as she collapsed onto the cool smooth floor. She closed her eyes, seeing flares of pain against her eyelids. She felt herself fading, and fought to remain conscious.

"*Be healed.*"

• • •

At almost the same moment, Lafkin was crawling on his hands and knees around the green dome of Tower Zurlamont in a remote region of the far away Dragonlands. He had barely survived jumping from his mount onto the dome, and nearly slid off the narrow ledge, but he had managed to throw himself down on his side, pushing himself away from the precipice. That seemed like hours ago to him. By now, on all fours, he had crawled around and around the dome more times than he could count, panting with fear and growing desperation, but he had found no clue about what to do with his Seven. He inched along, stopping to examine the dome, then inched a few feet more, and stopped to look again. The dome was faceted, like thousands of emeralds fused together, but he could see no entrance, not even a crack or seam where one might be. More than once he had lost his balance, one knee slipping over the ledge, and now, tired and quite afraid, he moved more cautiously.

"There must be something!" he cried, feeling the edge of the stone where it came into contact with the lowest rim of the emerald dome. He tried to get his fingernails between the two materials, propping himself carefully to do so. Moving slowly, he traced the seam between stone and dome with his fingers, making his way around once again. After an hour of this, cramped and wishing that he was brave enough to stand so that he could stretch for just a moment, he had gone halfway around and was on the northeast side of the tower. He paused and looked out across the bright dry sands that stretched out into a wavering haze. Not a breeze stirred, and the sun hammered furiously. Sighing, he turned back to his work, putting his face close to his fingers to examine the seam more carefully. Shaking his head, he put his hand out to crawl another inch, and he touched a foot. Flinching with surprise and fear, he saw two bare feet standing on the narrow ledge before him. They were white feet, almost glowing in the blaze of the sun, and the hem of a shimmering green robe hung just above the ankles. Craning his neck, and awkwardly shielding his eyes against the bright sky, he followed the dazzling robe upward and saw a face, very far above him, looking down. The person had sparkling green eyes.

"Do you bring something?" he asked.

Lafkin swallowed, understanding a language he had never heard before. He nodded.

"I do."

"Seven?"

"Yes."

"Come."

The figure turned and walked away, and Lafkin followed, crawling quickly behind the trailing robe. There was an opening, where before there was none. The tall figure entered, and Lafkin crawled after him into the place. The emerald-robed figure stood at the center of the interior and then turned around to face Lafkin, who unsteadily got to his feet. Hearing a clinking sound, he turned and saw the opening that he had just come through was being filled with faceted emeralds, as if invisible hands placed each one into position as brick might be laid. The interior became darker and darker until, when the last gap was filled, it was pitch black within, and silent.

Slowly, his eyes adjusted. But it was not as he may have expected. Instead of standing within the interior of a dome, he stood on a glassy mirror of stars that stretched out as far as he could see. Above and around him shone every familiar constellation, those of every season of the year. Dizzy, he stumbled to one knee. Sensing the strange person still standing before him, he looked up, but saw only the barest outline as the stars shone right through him as if he was made of air.

"*You do not have the blood of the Faere.*"

"No. I am a Mortal."

"*You come on their behalf.*"

"I come on behalf of my King Philawain, who sent me."

"*I know of him. He is not of Ormace's House of Fairbirch to whom your Seven were given by Aperion, who is my King.*"

"No. He is not."

"*I hear my six brothers speak. They tell that they, too, have visitors.*"

"Then my comrades, who all serve my King, have reached their destinations, too."

"*We speak to all,*" the voice said, joined by six others.

● ● ●

Winnefras, her pain completely gone, cautiously stood and gazed at the stars around her.

"No," she said, "I am not of Katrina's House of Fairmaple. I bring these Seven by my King, called Philawain. Katrina is no more."

● ● ●

In the other five towers, a similar exchange was taking place. Tyrillick, who was within the yellow Tower Sirrian, found that the burning of his scars was now completely gone. He answered the strange figure who, nearly invisible, stood somewhere before him in a sea of stars.

"No, even Lyrium faltered, but she had the strength to willingly give up her Seven," he said. "I come on her behalf, and on behalf of King Philawain, who has sent me here."

● ● ●

In the blue Tower Medios, Thurdun answered the figure he met, saying, "Yes, I am Cupeldain's descendant, and on behalf of King Philawain, I now seek to accomplish that which my grandfather failed to do."

"*I hear my six brothers speak. They tell that they, too, have visitors.*"

"Then the time has come," Thurdun said, removing his shoulder bag.

"*We speak to all,*" the voice said, now joined by six other voices. "*Aperion foresaw that it would be as it is, if it was to come to pass at all. For no one may enter this tower, or any others of the Nimbus Illuminas, save those sent by he who has the power to turn the Key without touching it. For it is not gold or jewels that hands may grip or that the eyes may see that has power over this place. Only he who may behold the heart of things and who may touch that which has no substance may have power over this place. It was from such power that the Faerekind were born, and of such power that their wings were made. But so, too, was a portion of such power given unto the Dragonkind, and unto Men. It was for the Fallen Ones to discover this, and to know their brethren, and each other. But they never did. So it has come to pass. That which the Elifaen could not do, or would not do, a few Men and Dragonkind, together, have brought about. Some among the Elifaen serve them willingly, even those who were Firstborn, at last knowing their place. It is almost too late, but as a moment may contain an eternity, there is yet time. Reveal what you have brought.*"

As soon as each Bloodcoin was taken from the shoulder bags, it shot up and out into the stars, receding as a colored point of light. One after the other, the Bloodcoins flew into the heavens.

"*Return now to your King, and tell him that when Lady Moon and her husband Sir Sun are joined once more, Liberation is at hand. Your master will know what he must do.*"

• • •

"Why do you pace back and forth so?" asked Sheila.

They were in the High Tower of Duinnor, and the two had already made many appearances at their balcony so that the people could see them. Many of their guests had been ushered to Griferis, still floating outside, to see its sights and wonders. Among these were Serith Ellyn and Lyrium, guided by Finn across the causeway. While this was done, some of Eldwin's people took others, including Gurasa, Prince Carbane, and Prince Danoss, back to where they were fetched from. Eldwin, meanwhile, stood to one side of the High Chamber, while Esildre, as nervous as Robby, floated in and out of sight, variously dressed in armor and sometimes in a gown, but, at present, in robes such as what pilgrims to the Temple sometimes wore. Robby had given his father, Mr. Bosk, and Lord Tallin, along with Billy and Ibin into the care of Radasa and his wife, to show them about Griferis. But hardly had his guests stepped onto the causeway leading to Griferis than Robby's shoulder's slumped and he began to pace.

"I don't know where to begin," he answered Sheila. "But I may have just sent seven more brave souls to their death. Meanwhile, there are still two great armies on the march in the south, and, most urgently, a very important matter that Eldwin and I must attend to as soon as possible. I'm afraid we'll have to let things in Duinnor rest in the hands of Ashlord and Lord Arata, but I don't think they understand what may soon take place."

"I'm not sure I do, either," said Sheila. "Not that I understand anything that has taken place today, or last night, or, well, or ever!"

"I know, I know!" Robby said, coming to Sheila and putting his arms around her. "I'm sorry. There just doesn't seem to be enough time to do things properly. But making you Queen was the only way I could think of for us to be together, and to free me to do what I must."

"Oh, Robby. Is this one of your dreams? Nothing seems real. Yet, it is all too, too…. Robby, what right do I have to be Queen? I can barely even read or write, and I don't know how anything should be done."

"Welcome to my world," Robby said to her, stroking her hair away from her brow. "Only I've had years and years to think about things. And I've had help. Dreamwalking. Griferis. And good people. I want nothing more than to spend all my time with you, to tell you everything. I've missed you so much! I thought we'd never be together again. Oh!"

Seven people suddenly appeared out of thin air and a spray of multicolored light. They were Winnefras, Lafkin, Tyrillick, and all the others who had been sent out. They swayed and bumped into each other drunkenly and off balance for a moment. Then, seeing the astonished Robby and Sheila, they kneeled.

"My King," said Lafkin. "It has been done."

"Indeed, sire," said Tyrillick, glancing at the other six couriers. "The Forty-Nine have been delivered."

"Already?" Robby said, coming over to pull Lafkin to his feet. He went from one to the next, shaking their hands gratefully. "Tell me all! Did you find some way inside? Was there some device into which the Bloodcoins were to be placed?"

"No, King," Thurdun answered, shaking his head.

"My King," said Winnefras, "we were told that you would know what to do."

"Told? Someone was there?"

"Yes, sire. A strange being, unlike anyone I have ever seen," said Hathrain.

"Sire, did you not see, with your dreamwalking, that the towers were occupied?" Alzeeran asked.

"No. That is, when I penetrated them, all I saw were stars," Robby said, frowning. "I only surmised, from the make and color of the domes, which Seven went to which tower. I thought you would see what to do. Tell me what happened."

Lafkin then related what he had seen and heard, and the others were in agreement, taking turns to tell about the same strange beings they had encountered. They all described how the Bloodcoins that they had delivered were whisked into the stars.

"And then, I was returned here by some powerful magic," said Hathrain.

"As was I," said Winnefras.

"I was, too! As were all of us, it appears," said Alzeeran.

"Sire," said Unther, "they said the same to us all. That you would know what to do when Lady Moon and Sir Sun are joined."

"Are joined," Robby repeated. "Joined?"

He turned away in thought, shaking his head, clearly disappointed that it was not all over and done with. The others in the room, Sheila included, remained silent, watching him stare at the floor. Suddenly, he jerked his head up and spun around. "Two weeks! Eldwin! Esildre! Let's go!"

"Go where?" asked Sheila.

"We have business with Shatuum, and we should get right to it," Robby said. Eldwin looked from one to the other awkwardly.

"But Robby, we are expected to make our appearance at the feast, day after tomorrow," Sheila pleaded. "Can't you stay for just a few days?"

"Sire," put in Eldwin, "besides all else that's come to pass today, it's yer weddin' day. An' Queen Shevalia's. No one's keener than I am to strike at Secundur, but this day will not come again."

"We have much to plan, and to prepare," said Robby, none too eager, after all, to leave Sheila so soon.

"Stay. Please," Sheila said, coming close so that only Robby could hear her. "We have so much to talk about. And I need you with me. I do not know how I should act, or what I should say to people. And we have already given orders that the feasts and celebrations in our honor are to begin at noon on the day after tomorrow."

"I know, I know. Yes, of course. I'm sorry. I'm so accustomed to taking the bull by the horns, so to say, and acting whenever there's something I feel I must do. But, yes, I'll stay. Not that you need any help from me, mind you," he took Sheila's hand. "I must obey my Queen, mustn't I?"

"Yes." Sheila smiled. "You must."

• • •

For the rest of the day, Ashlord and Raynor acted as doorkeepers to the High Chamber. With Lord Arata and General Chadler nearby, Robby and Sheila greeted the many lords and ministers who came to wish them well and to determine what they might expect from the two monarchs. The generals of the Kingsmen came, and they were told to keep all of the Kingsmen in readiness. Robby and Sheila also met with several generals representing the Duinnor Regulars. These were given the same orders as the Kingsmen, but, at Lord Arata's suggestion, they were also told to expect changes to be made in their ranks. Ashlord and Raynor consulted with each other and Lord Arata before admitting each group of ministers and lords, some to go in before others did. Taking her cues from Robby, Sheila greeted them all courteously and formally, but most went away without much insight as to who would be asked to continue in their posts and who might be replaced.

"It is too soon for us to have decided such things," Robby said to each group. "Meanwhile, I hope that you will arrange to close your ministries on the day after tomorrow so that any and all of your servants and secretaries who wish to do so may join our celebrations."

When Raynor ushered in a group of high-ranking and powerful merchants and tradesmen, Sheila recognized Blain Farby, Grantham's father, as well as Mr. Sarb. Sarb was well-known to Ashlord, having served as his banker and money handler for many years. After a few moments of conferring with Lord Arata and Ashlord, Sheila and Robby greeted them and accepted their good wishes. Lord Arata addressed them.

"Mr. Sarb, the King and Queen have it on good authority that you are a wise and prudent man of finance, honest, well-versed with our laws, and familiar with our treasury."

"Thank you, my lord. That is most kind of you. Yes. I was employed by the Exchequer as a young man, and through my contacts, I have maintained an interest and knowledge in the Realm's finances."

"Then, as you know, Lord Banis exerted a great deal of undo influence, and there are many concerns with obtaining a true accounting of the Realm's affairs."

"I am certainly aware of that, my lord."

"Would you agree to put aside your personal and business concerns and act as our interim Lord of the Exchequer? Your first duty would be to present to the Queen a just and fair accounting of things."

"It would be my great honor, my lord."

"Then," Lord Arata went on, "the Queen would like to extend to you the full support of our courts in obtaining whatever assistance you may need, to summon those who have to this point been in the employ of Lord Banis, and to wrest from them our treasury, should that be necessary. We have yet to create a High Council to the Queen, but you will certainly be an important member. You shall have a proclamation elevating you to lordship tomorrow."

Each meeting was very brief, and no sooner than one group had departed than another was shown in. Before long, Robby and Sheila had spoken to and met with hundreds of Duinnor's most important citizens. Meanwhile, Lady Highleaf, at the behest of Ashlord, frantically and imperiously ordered her Starlight Hall to be made suitable for the Queen, as there was never a palace built to be the personal domicile of Duinnor's Ruler.

Several hours after dark, when the last group to meet with the new monarchs had gone, those who had toured the wonders of Griferis returned into the High Chamber. Serith Ellyn and Lyrium, along with Robby's father whom they had taken charge of, payed their respects to Robby and Sheila.

"Son," said Mr. Ribbon, "I think me old head spins too much! Not least at ye bein' a king, an' all that. But so much else on top."

"I know, Daddy," Robby said. "It seems too much to believe, even for me."

Mr. Ribbon looked around, glanced at Sheila and the other ladies who were chatting near the window.

"Well," he said, "I reckon thar's a lot ye must do, now. An' I don't mean to get in the way of it, but—"

"I've asked Lady Highleaf to look after you for a bit," said Robby. "Lady Lyrium and Queen Serith Ellyn have promised to escort you to Lady Highleaf's house. I'd like for you to remain in Duinnor, if you don't mind, for a couple of weeks. Just long enough for me to take care of a few things. Then I'd like to take you back to Passdale myself."

"Oh! Well, that seems alright with me."

Soon Mr. Ribbon departed, in the good company of Lyrium and Serith Ellyn. But Billy, Ibin, and Lord Tallin remained, along with Millithorpe, Miladora, and several of Eldwin's people.

"My King," said Lord Tallin, "Griferis is a wondrous place. I have been shown the most intriguing paintings there. Many, I'm told, are depictions of your experiences."

"Yes, Grandfather," said Robby. "Did you meet Borwain, the artist?"

"Yes, sire. His abilities are most uncanny. But, if I may ask, how came you to be in all those places, and for so long when so little time passed for the rest of us?"

"I can only say that it was one of the mysteries of Griferis," answered Robby. "I knew nothing of the world outside while I was there. So imagine my joy when I learned that virtually no time had passed at all for you and the rest of the world. I thought that surely all had been lost."

"Terrible!" said Tallin, shaking his head in amazement. "Wonderful, but terrible. You must have suffered an awful torment of mind. My grandson, did you never lose heart?"

"I almost did. I despaired of hope. But Finn was a good friend to me. Having someone like him nearby was at times all that kept me going. I should say to you, my lord, that I am deeply sorry that I was unable to help you during the siege of Tallinvale. I'm sorry that you were so badly wounded, and that you lost so many friends. And I am deeply sorry about your daughter."

"Hm. I don't know what you could have done, sire," Tallin said. "We managed through alright, with the help of Teracue's Kingsmen. And I will miss Mirabella more than I can say. But I know that you and your father will miss her the most. I wish I could offer some words to bring solace to you."

"Thank you," Robby shook Lord Tallin's hand. "I know that you wish to return to Tallinvale. So I bid you farewell."

"Farewell, sire. Farewell, my Queen."

Lord Tallin bowed and went to wait in the hall as Billy and Ibin approached Robby.

"Sire," said Billy. "We were wond'rin' if ye needed us to do anything in particularly."

"You'd like to go home, wouldn't you?"

"If that'd be alright, sire. I've got a sense that me folks could make use of me around the ol' place, if ye know what I mean."

"Of course."

"And, Robby, sire, er, Lady Shevalia, I'd like to stay, but, but," Ibin stumbled on his words.

"Oh, Ibin, of course you should go, too," Sheila said, giving him a hug. "I know that Frizella will be happy to see you, and Buckie will be, too. And what would become of Billy without his brave friend nearby?"

"Then I should like to go home, too," Ibin said.

Robby gave Billy a hug and a long handshake.

"I can't say how much it meant to me to have your company on the way out here," said Robby, holding Billy's hand firmly, "and to know that you were nearby to Sheila."

"Aw, it warn't nuthin', sire," Billy said.

"I'm sure that you'll tell your mother and father all about our adventures, won't you? And tell everyone that I send my greetings."

"Gladly, sire."

"Farewell, then."

"Farwell, me King."

"And, Ibin," Robby said as Sheila made her farewells to Billy, "I hope that you will look after everyone."

"I will, King."

"You can call me Robby, Ibin. But listen. I want you to look after yourself, too. There's many a fine lass in Barley who would be happy to fall in love with you, if you give any a chance to do so. So don't think that Billy or Frizella need you so much that you don't have time for your own happiness. I know that you would enjoy having your own cottage with your own family."

"I would, sire. I will think about that," said Ibin.

• • •

So Ibin, Billy, Mr. Bosk, and Lord Tallin all departed, swiftly taken by the people of Nowhere back to the Old Eastlands Realm. Eldwin went into Griferis where he intended to wait for Robby, with Esildre invisibly trailing along beside him. Saddened by their friends' departure, Robby and Sheila made their way down the long stairs of the High Tower to an awaiting carriage. They set off for Wysteria Place, smartly escorted by a squad of Robby's Blue Guard, and by a large contingent of Kingsmen. In spite of the late hour, the city avenues were bright with lamplight and by the light of the Six Stars overhead. The way to Wysteria Place was lined with throngs of cheering people. And though it was only the first of spring, flowers showered upon the King and Queen as they passed. Owing to the press of the crowds, and to the deliberate pace of the procession, it took a long time to reach Wysteria Place, where the gate was closed behind them. The servants and staff of Starlight Hall turned out in their finest, all beaming and smiling uncontrollably, since they all felt they knew the Queen more intimately than most anyone else in Duinnor. None smiled more, though, nor beamed as much as did Lady Highleaf, her face positively red with emotion and joy, and as full of nervous excitement as she had ever been in her life.

"Lady Highleaf," Sheila said to her, "I must thank you once more for all that you have done for me."

"My Queen," Lady Highleaf curtseyed once again, "it has ever been my utmost joy and honor, as it continues to be."

"I almost feel as if I am coming home," Sheila said.

"No greater compliment could I ever receive, Your Majesty. And I hope you will permit me to personally show you to your rooms."

"Thank you."

It took some while longer to reach the prepared suite, since along the way Lady Highleaf made every excuse there was for the paltry renovations that had been hastily made, talking nervously, almost giddy, about the rooms that had been quickly converted for the Queen's use.

"I would have been quite happy with my old room," Sheila said. "But I am astonished at what you have done. You must convey my gratitude to Denks and the others."

"Yes, ma'am. I shall, indeed. May I be so bold to ask if the King will also be staying the night?"

"Yes, Lady Highleaf," said Robby. "We'll stay here tonight and tomorrow night. The night after, though, I think I should like to entertain the Queen in Griferis."

"Very good, sire. I'll have Denks attend to your needs. My Queen, I would be honored to wait upon you myself, should that be suitable to you."

"Oh, Lady Highleaf!" Sheila said. "It isn't necessary. I doubt if we shall need much of anything tonight."

"In fact, if you pardon me for saying so," Robby added, "I think we would like to be left undisturbed."

"Oh, my, yes! I mean, pardon me, sire. Of course."

• • •

And so, at last, Robby and Sheila were finally alone. They would not sleep at all that night, nor had they any need to do so. They talked incessantly, laughing and crying at the stories they shared, and there were many, many stories to tell. They did not sleep, but that did not mean that they did not make use of the bed. Besides stories to tell and news to catch up on, they needed also to be reacquainted in other ways. Robby ran his fingers down the long scars of Sheila's beautiful back, and Sheila in return examined Robby's back, too, as well as the many other scars on his body. When she tapped a scar, he would halt his story only long enough to say, "sword," or "fire," or "My horse was shot from under me, and I fell onto some rocks," before continuing. There was no order to their stories, ranging back and forth, near and far, recent and long ago, covering a wide range of topics. They had very much to say, and could not possibly say it all in one night. In between tales, they enjoyed other intimacies, long desired, with new vigor and with greater ecstasy than they ever had known before, until, rested, they resumed their conversation.

Robby talked, and Sheila propped up her head on one elbow and gazed at his graying hair, running her fingers along his silver temples and caressing the beard on his chin. Sometimes Robby wondered if she even listened to the answers that he gave to her questions, so intent on gazing at him she was. And, truth be told, he could not resist gazing back at her, admiring her beauty, and he would have been content to do so forever.

When morning came, they did not stir from their room, but remained behind closed doors the entire day, while the capable servants of their two realms did their work. Robby showed Sheila, through dreamwalking, that preparations for the celebration were well under way. There were to be many feasts in various parts of the city, with the King and Queen making their appearance at each in turn. One would be at the King's Academy, in the great dining hall there. Another would be in the Court of Lords, where they would be feted by the Lords of the Realm and honored guests. And the last would be out on the open fields of the valley. There, hundreds of long tables were being arranged. Wagonloads of food and drink would be provided to all the people, with preference given to the poor and common folk, for Sheila had stipulated that lords must come and serve and ladies must wait and pour, if they wished to please their Queen.

So, during these preparations, Robby and Sheila kept to themselves. But they were not idle. Robby took Sheila to see where Ullin and Micerea had gone, and to see how Billy's people were getting along in the burned remains of Boskland. They went to visit Forest Islindia again, and they even looked in on Greenfar, to see how those people fared. Later, as the day waned toward night, Robby began to show Sheila things of great concern. He guardedly took her to see Shatuum, but made that visit brief, for he did not wish to terrify Sheila. He explained how he had recruited other dreamwalkers, even Sally Bodwin. Together they went to meet with Sally, to ask after Martin Makeig, who was at the moment taking Conner Faddus around to meet the Hill Town folk.

That night, they slept peacefully in each other's arms. And, in the morning, they began a busy but happy day of celebrations. It would prove to be a long day, but to Sheila's mind, it passed quickly. Everywhere they went, they were honored and celebrated not only as King and Queen, but as newlyweds. When at last they left the thousands who danced and dined under the open sky and went into Griferis, they were greeted by the people of that realm. Robby introduced Sheila to everyone, with Finn smiling proudly as he followed them through Griferis to the great circular hall where tables were set for a late dinner, with all of Griferis in attendance. Celia sat at the Queen's side, and, for the first time in what seemed ages, Sheila enjoyed a normal conversation (if Celia's manner could be called normal), with a girl who had no care that Sheila was the most powerful woman in all the world. Indeed, the entire hall was full of laughter and music, as Kinsiri's daughters sang and danced for the honored couple.

When the night was nearly spent, and the honored couple excused themselves, Robby took Sheila up into one of the towers of Griferis and showed her the marvelous spyglass. She watched him turn wheels and gears to point it at Lady Moon, who barely fluttered her fan before her face.

"Look," Robby said, standing away from the eyepiece. Sheila bent and squinted as she peered through the apparatus, then her eyes opened wide and she caught a breath.

"She is beautiful!" Sheila whispered. "She smiles most serenely. She looks at us, I think."

"Yes. I think she does."

"Does she see the whole world from there?"

"I think she must."

"Oh. I think she knows that we gaze at her. There is a blush to her cheeks."

Robby smiled, nodding.

"Within a fortnight, she'll be with her husband," he said. "That's when I'll try to open the Nimbus Illuminas."

"Why then?"

"I don't know. I'm only going by what Winnefras and the others said. There must be a reason, though."

"I think we should leave Lady Moon alone," Sheila said, turning to Robby. "Thank you for letting me see her."

"You are welcome. Perhaps we should go to my rooms for a while. We won't be seeing each other for a few days, at least."

"Except in dreams, right?"

"Yes. I will come to you that way."

"Good."

With Unther as their escort, they walked to Robby's suite. They took their time, stopping along the way to view some of Borwain's paintings.

"You said you didn't know how to work the Nimbus Illuminas," Sheila said as they entered Robby's rooms.

"I don't."

"How will you learn?"

"I don't know. I can find no books on the subject in the library. I asked Lyrium. But she said that when she gave them over to me, her memory of what was shown to her about how to use the Bloodcoins was removed from her. I'll just keep going to the towers, by dreamwalking, and I'll keep trying to figure it out."

"Hm. And you said that, even if you manage it, you still don't know what it will actually do, what will happen. Do you?"

"No. I don't."

"But we Elifaen will be forced to leave."

"I don't know. I'm not sure. I think so. But maybe only those who want to go. I don't know."

"Robby, we have just now found each other again," Sheila said, putting her arms around him. "What will happen to us?"

"We'll be fine, Sheila. Whatever happens, we'll be fine, I'm sure of it."

"How can you be sure?"

"I just am," he said, holding her close. "Let's worry about that when the time comes. Meanwhile, these are my rooms. What do you think of them?"

Sheila looked around, nodding.

"Very nice," she said. "But I'm not sure I like the way she's looking at me."

She jabbed a finger at the portrait of herself.

"And I'm not sure I approve of her attire," she added.

"Oh, I do!" Robby answered. "But if her gaze bothers you, come into the next room where we'll be out of her sight."

Chapter 34

Not Yet

On the day that Robby and Sheila went to the Temple to become King and Queen, Ullin and Micerea, having been delivered to the edge of Nasakeeria, waited and watched. The day was clear and indeed warmer than to be expected, even for the first day of spring, and they sat leaning against the warning pillar with blankets over their knees. With nothing more alarming or unusual than crickets chirping nearby, Micerea nodded off, her head on Ullin's shoulder, but she almost immediately awoke with a start and stood up.

"We must be off!" she said, tugging on Ullin's hand to help him up.

"What?"

"I've been told that we must go to the south side of Nasakeeria."

"How far?" asked Ullin as he bundled the blanket and strapped it to his pack.

"No, we are to have our blankets ready."

"Oh? Who told you all this? Robby?"

"No. One of his dreamwalkers. He was in a hurry, and said only that we are to go farther eastward and south around Nasakeeria. And to have our blankets ready."

"We can get at them quickly enough. Why couldn't Millithorpe and Miladora take us?" Ullin complained, following Micerea as she started off. "Instead of leaving us here?"

"I don't know, unless something has happened. Or perhaps they were needed elsewhere."

Somewhat frustrated, Ullin and Micerea kept on, putting mile after mile steadily behind them as the day wore on, keeping along a path that ran just outside of the stone warning pillars. They both felt an eerie sense of being watched, as all who ever traveled that path felt, and none too comfortable with the huge skulls atop the pillars that faced them. Behind the pillars some forty yards or so, an odd low mound traced its way along the border. From time to time, Micerea saw telltale flecks of white bone jutting up from the mound. She did not point them out or say anything about them to Ullin, for she knew that he was all too aware of them as well. When the path took them briefly behind the warning pillars and closer to the mound, Micerea felt oddly closed in and exposed all at the same time. She decided that the best thing to do was to keep her eyes ahead, looking to the path, resisting the urge to stare at the mound to their left and ignoring the stone pillars they passed on their right. But when they topped a mild rise, Micerea looked ahead and toward the southeast. Then she stopped. About a furlong away was a riderless horse coming toward them.

"Look," said Micerea.

"I see it."

The horse stopped and reared, tossing its head. Then it whinnied and broke into a gallop.

"I'm not sure I'm believing my eyes," said Ullin.

"I'm not sure I am, either," said Micerea as Anerath shot past them, then circled around to trot up to Ullin.

"Hello, old boy! Hello!" Ullin was grinning as he rubbed Anerath's neck. "How on earth did you get way out here from Janhaven, eh? How did you find us?"

Micerea, grinning almost as broadly as Ullin, patted Anerath's shoulder.

"It is good to meet you at last," she said. Then to Ullin, "I think we know how he found us."

"Are you willing to carry two?" Ullin asked. Anerath bobbed his head, and Ullin jumped up on the tall horse's back, and threw his leg over. Shifting his pack around in front of him, he reached out for Micerea, and soon they were trotting off eastward.

"I have waited a long time to be here, riding behind you," Micerea said, her arms around Ullin's waist. "Do you think he broke away just to look for us?"

"No, that's not something he'd do, I don't think. More likely, Mirabella released him."

"Oh."

They rode on in silence for a long while, covering many miles until Micerea spoke again.

"Ullin, do you think she knew? Knew that she would not need Anerath?"

Ullin shrugged.

"She may have known. I don't know. Listen. Whoa, boy. Hold. Listen."

It was the sound of drums, coming from within Nasakeeria. They looked but saw no activity. Another drum answered when the first paused. A third, even more distant, then took up the cadence.

"I wish I knew what they were saying," said Ullin.

"I suspect they are talking about us."

"Oh?"

"Yes. I doubt very seriously that our King would send us here without preparing the way."

"Walk on," said Ullin, nudging Anerath gently with his heels. The drums kept beating, and then ceased altogether, making the silence that followed even more powerful.

"Hold tight," Ullin said to Micerea. "Go, Anerath! Let's go!"

Anerath immediately sprang into a canter. After a mile, Ullin nudged him again.

"Let's pick it up!"

Anerath accelerated into a gallop over the rise and fall of the open plain, carrying the two riders with an ease that Ullin fondly appreciated. Micerea loosened one arm from Ullin's waist and pointed ahead and toward the left. There, several miles off, a trail of smoke was rising into the air from within the forbidden land.

"Perhaps that's our sign," said Ullin.

They hurried on, and in little more than an hour, they came close enough to see a fire on the top of a hill. Ullin coaxed Anerath to a halt, then slid his pack down to the ground. Once he and Micerea were on their feet, they approached a few steps closer and watched the distant hilltop. Many people were gathered there, several thousand at the very least. Some were stoking the flames while others were working on and around large squarish structures of logs and poles that were scattered all over the hill.

"What are those large things?" asked Micerea. "Those things made of wood."

"I have no idea," said Ullin.

They could see people moving onto those structures, many carrying large bundles. Some of the things already held horses or cattle. And many of the odd platforms seemed to have little tents erected upon them. They covered the hillsides like a jumble of huge box lids, some tilted on the slopes, others propped up in order to be level. Ullin had only begun to count them, and had reached fifty-eight, when a movement distracted him. A rider was coming down the hill toward them and, oddly, a fox loped alongside while a black bird followed. The rider stopped about a furlong away, just on the other side of the brown border beyond the mounds of bones. The rider lifted his hand in greeting, and Ullin returned the gesture. Meanwhile, the fox and the raven shot on toward them, the fox appearing and disappearing regularly over and under the top of the tall grass as it came, while the bird zigzagged in order to stay with it.

"Very odd," said Ullin, watching the approaching animals and keeping an eye on the horseman.

"I'm not sure I like this," said Micerea. "What sort of dog is that?"

"It is a fox. We saw some in the forest, remember?"

"Oh. But those were white."

"I know. This one's a different kind."

"Well, that's plain enough."

Now, as the two animals neared the border, the bird darted ahead, circling around and around Ullin and Micerea. It appeared to be carrying a small object in its beak. Anerath neighed and snorted at the bird, shifting sideways to keep an eye on it. As the fox came across and leapt up on the ring of bones not many yards away, the bird landed at the nearest warning pillar. Ullin and Micerea turned their heads back and forth from the fox to the bird, as the bird went behind the pillar and out of view for a moment. A man's head leaned out from behind the pillar.

"Oh!" Micerea exclaimed, backing up.

"What the…!" Ullin's hand went to his dagger hilt.

"Your blankets, please, to me give," the man said.

As the sun caught his face, they could see that he was Dragonkind. Ullin took the blankets from the pack and approached cautiously, seeing as he did that the man wore no clothes at all. The man took one blanket and quickly wrapped it around his waist, then took the other one, and, giving Micerea an odd look, he crouched as the fox ran up to him. With his back to them, the man put his blanket around the creature. A mist briefly appeared, then dissipated as the man stood, holding the blanket as a woman pulled it over her shoulders and wrapped it about herself. They turned around to face Ullin and Micerea, and they bowed.

"I am Seleesa," the young woman said in a strange accent, like Micerea's but more distinct. "And this is Aremon."

"I am Ullin Saheed Tallin," Ullin bowed, "of the House of Tallin and Fairoak. This is Lady Micerea, of the House of Golden Sand."

"How do you do?" Micerea bowed.

"We do very well," Seleesa said. "And shall soon do even better, I think."

"We are envoys of King Philawain," said Ullin.

"The King of Griferis is mighty," said Aremon.

"The King of Griferis is powerful," said Seleesa.

"And so, too, is the Queen of Duinnor," added Aremon.

"Queen of Duinnor?" Ullin shook his head and looked at Micerea who returned his confused expression. "We know of no queen in Duinnor."

"Nonetheless, this very day comes a queen to that land," said Aremon.

"She is made queen by her husband, King Philawain."

Ullin started to speak, then smiled. Micerea came up to him and put her hand in Ullin's.

"We are not the only lovers who are finally united," she said. Seleesa approached and looked at Micerea closely.

"You are Dragonkind," she said.

"Yes. As you are," replied Micerea.

"We were told that, as an omen of our deliverance from these lands, and as a sign that we would be restored to our ancient homeland, a prince of Men and a princess of the Dragonkind would come to us."

"I am not a prince," said Ullin.

"And I am not a princess," said Micerea.

Aremon laughed, stepped forward, and offered his hand to Ullin.

"We were told that you would say as much!" Aremon took Ullin's hand and shook it powerfully. "But the ring on your finger speaks of great honor bestowed upon you by an ancient house."

Ullin glanced at the ring he wore, given to him by Serith Ellyn.

"And, to be sure of these signs," Seleesa said, "we were instructed to ask the Princess what became of the ring that your father gave to this man's uncle."

"It found its way back to my father, who gave it to me. Later, I gave it to Philawain," Micerea said. At this, Seleesa smiled at Aremon and then bowed very low to Micerea.

"That is what we were told," Seleesa said, gesturing to Aremon. "And so now, Philawain returns it to you."

Aremon opened his other hand, and offered Micerea the ring just mentioned.

"Philawain, King, says that it is to be a token of his blessing upon you," Aremon said.

"And a symbol of your love for one another," said Seleesa.

Micerea took the ring, smiling.

"Let it be as they say, Ullin Saheed," she said, offering it to him.

Ullin grinned as he loosened Serith Ellyn's ring on his finger and offered it to Micerea.

"Yes," he said. "And take this in exchange for it."

They exchanged rings, as Aremon and Seleesa watched, then Ullin and Micerea kissed to seal their trade.

Afterwards, the four stood smiling at one another for a few moments. Ullin felt awkward, still mystified as to his purpose here. Anerath snorted. Aremon shook himself, then turned abruptly and waved to the man still waiting on his horse.

"Who is that you wave to?" asked Ullin.

"He is our Prince, called Nightar," said Aremon.

"Oh. What are those people doing around the hill near the bonfire?" asked Micerea.

"They make ready for our departure," Seleesa said. "All of our people gather. Many more are in the valley just on the other side of that hill. They have been told to bring all their important belongings, their tools and their clothes. They bring all the food that could be gathered, too."

"But," Ullin looked around. "How do they mean to cross over? Are they all like you, and can turn from people into animals and back? If so, how do they mean to carry their things, even if they safely cross the border?"

"No, no. We are the only two who may change into our totem animals," said Aremon. "And I am new at doing it."

"I do not know how it is to be done," said Seleesa. "But we were told, through dreams and through other signs, and through the visions of a wise old woman, that if we would but have trust in Philawain, and if we were prepared to forsake these lands, a way would be made for us to return to the desert land and to our ancient home. Philawain promised, through his messengers, that we would be safe. His messengers told us that we would not only be able to pass out of these lands without being consumed by fire, but that we would be guarded from danger during our long trek."

"I see. But I still don't understand. What are those large things?"

Seleesa looked over her shoulder at the many structures.

"That is the strangest thing of all," she said. "They are barges."

"Barges?"

"Yes. Though they are not for water," nodded Aremon.

"Instructions for their making was given to us. We know of boats, and use a few in our streams. But these are made without pitch or such. And they are very sturdy. We were told to make five hundred of them, enough for all our people and our things. You cannot see them all from here, as many are on the other side of the hill. Our people have been at it for nearly two weeks, felling trees and hewing timbers, making lashes and pegs, and moving everything here to be put together."

"It is work of trust," said Aremon. "We were hoping you would their purpose know."

"No," said Ullin, "I know of no use for barges that do not go in water. And the great fire?"

"We were told that we must burn anything that will not be brought out of these lands. And to make a signal fire."

"Oh."

Ullin looked up and around. The sun was setting, and the sky was now deepening toward night, with high pink wisps overhead, but otherwise clear as far as could be seen.

"I thought I heard thunder," he said. "No clouds anywhere, though. But perhaps it is the sound of the work that goes on over there."

Seleesa listened.

"I hear it, too," said Micerea. "It does sound like thunder. Very far off, though."

Aremon nodded, looking at the sky.

"But these are strange days."

Ullin was not satisfied, and with his keen eyesight, he scanned the southern horizon. There, obscured by the failing light, he saw the distinct discoloration of a dust cloud.

"Oh, oh!" he said, stiffening.

"What is it?"

"I think it is a stampede," Ullin pointed.

"A what?" Micerea asked.

"And I think it is coming this way!"

Aremon shook his head. "It is not the season for such. Very few herds move through this time of year. And none very large."

"Well, something is stirring up that cloud. Anerath!" Ullin hurriedly picked up the pack as Anerath came. "You must get back into your land and warn your people," he said to Seleesa. "Micerea and I will ride off. If it is a stampede, bees are sure to follow! Carrion bees!"

"No. Philawain said we would be safe," said Seleesa anxiously, unsure what to do.

"Will your Ring of Fire keep out herds?" Micerea asked.

"No," said Aremon, staring at the horizon. Now the low rumble was undeniable. "Four-legs that do not carry two-legs may pass unharmed."

Ullin looked up at the hills where the people still worked, thinking that, surely, they saw the approaching threat from those heights. The man on the horse had gone back and could be seen riding up the hillside.

"Ullin, what does your sense tell you?" asked Micerea, touching his arm.

He shook his head. "It has failed me before. It tells me nothing."

"It is a peculiar cloud," Aremon was saying. "It is narrow, as if riders approach."

"Riders do not thunder and quake the ground like this!" said Seleesa.

"No. They do not," said Micerea. "But I think we should trust a little longer, Ullin. Let it get closer."

Suddenly a ram's horn blasted from the hilltop, jolting the four as Anerath stamped impatiently, with Ullin's hands on his mane ready to leap onto his back.

"Easy, boy," he said softly. "Let's wait. Just wait a bit longer. Easy, easy."

Ullin trusted Anerath more than his own sense of danger. Although his arms did not tingle, and the hairs on the back of his neck did not rise, Ullin's heart pounded as he watched the odd cloud approach. He had to admit that it did not seem to move as panicked bison would, but seemed to come faster than galloping riders. And, strangely, the noise that grew had a rhythmic quality to it; they could feel it through their feet as much as hear it.

"It comes straight at us!" Ullin said in an urging tone, glancing at Micerea. She kept her hand on his arm, fighting to control her own fear.

Suddenly, Aremon sprang forward, and his blanket fluttered to the ground as a raven shot out of it, beating away toward the approaching thing.

"Aremon! Aremon!" Seleesa cried out, running a few paces after him.

"What are we to do?" cried Ullin at Micerea. "Flee or be overtaken?"

"Wait, wait!"

Anxious moments passed as the rumble grew and the dust neared, then the bird reappeared coming back at them as fast as an arrow. It landed and almost immediately turned into a mist out of which came the naked Aremon, running at them.

"Move away," he shouted, waving at them. "Move! Move!"

Seleesa was frozen with fear, seeing the strange shapes that were now coming into sight. Aremon reached her and clutched her arm, dragging her off. Ullin had already picked Micerea up and tossed her onto Anerath's back, then he grabbed Seleesa as Aremon pulled her past.

"Micerea! Take her!" he shouted over the rumbling din. He lifted Seleesa and tossed her behind Micerea, then he slapped Anerath's hind flank.

"Anerath, go!"

Ullin and Aremon ran after the galloping horse as the trolls tore over the place where they had just been standing. First came Thunderfoot, who stood aside as his people came in two long lines. As the first pair reached the warning markers, they threw themselves onto the ground. Two more piled atop of them, then more came and lay down before the first. More and more came, and the dust cloud they made covered the scene, obscuring what they did. Meanwhile, the thunder of their coming was matched by the thud of their stony bodies against the ground and the sharp crack of each rocky creature against another.

Still running, Ullin and Aremon lost sight of the women in the choking dust. Ullin felt a touch on his arm and saw Aremon, covering his mouth with one hand, gesturing behind them. Slowing to a stop, they turned and watched, but could see very little through the dust, made murky by the falling night. The noise of the trolls' labor was tremendous, cracking the air and shaking the ground. Ullin could discern enough from the sound to know that whatever the trolls were doing was slowly progressing toward the border. Still staring, the two men barely noticed Anerath and the women coming up behind them. Aremon coughed, as dust began to settle around them, and Ullin took off his travel cloak and handed it to him. Aremon nodded and put it on, never once taking his eyes from the source of all the noise. Without warning, brilliant blue-white fire shot up from the border into the sky, and, with a loud whoosh, flames ran east and west, roaring past the four onlookers. Everyone flinched and put their hands over their eyes, while Micerea clutched Anerath's mane with her free hand as he reared. Seleesa's arm shot vice-like around Micerea's waist, and the two barely managed to stay on Anerath's back. He settled onto all fours, and Micerea coaxed him as he continued to nervously stamp back and forth. Ullin, squinting to see, got to Anerath and put his arm over his neck.

"Easy, easy!" he cried as a blast of hot wind blew out from the strange flames. Oddly, he thought he heard a rumbling voice, laughing over the noise that the trolls made. He heard words, loud and full of defiance.

"We were here before ye were, Aperion!" the voice bellowed. "Ha! And we shall remain after yer gone, gone!"

Stranger still, another light had appeared in the eastern sky, a point that grew in intensity, a white star that made the sky blue and blotted out the stars as beams of light shone forth from it. The noise of the trolls ceased, and the flames nearby became silent. The dust settled, revealing a fantastic bridge made of stone blocks, passing over spans of arches and through the glowing flames that now dimmed into a shimmering blue, like the northern lights of winter. Ullin did not know which way to look—at the strange bridge, at the odd flames that rose up from the ground into the sky, or at the star that grew and grew in brilliance. But his eyes were drawn towards the star, and, blinking, he removed his hand from his eyes to stare fully at the celestial light. Then he perceived that it was not a star at all. Shimmering silver-white, as bright as a lightning bolt, was the shape of man standing in the sky. A man with wings.

Ullin's knees buckled, as did Aremon's, neither able to take their eyes from Aperion. The longer he looked, the more Ullin felt himself drawn upward, as if beckoned by the light, as if his soul was pushing out from his body, yearning to go up, go away, go. His heart cracked, but suddenly, as if he stood close enough to touch Aperion's face, he saw him smile and give a slight shake of the head.

"Not yet."

Ullin blinked at the sudden darkness, as did the others. He heard Aremon gulp. Slowly his eyes regained their seeing. The flames were still there, pale blue with wisps of white and yellow, like a strange glowing curtain that rustled in the breeze, lighting the countryside eerily. But there was no heat, and it was a beautiful starry night above. Ullin stood, glancing upward, but there was no trace of the vision he had seen before. He gave Aremon his hand to help him to his feet.

"Look, look!" said Seleesa almost in a whisper.

Ullin looked over his shoulder as he helped her down from Anerath, then helped Micerea down, keeping his hand in hers as they slowly walked toward the trolls. The way they had made passed clear over the border, like a paved roadway, blocking the flames where it went through and on into Nasakeeria. As the onlookers neared, they saw Thunderfoot, standing with his arms crossed at the end of the unnatural structure. He was grinning in a most disturbing way, which was his natural way of grinning, his square teeth crossing broadly across his square head. He saw the foursome approaching, and when they halted some many yards away, he laughed.

"Have no fear, little ones!" he bellowed, his voice easily heard throughout the land. "We are thy escorts, thy transports, and thy guardians from here all the way back the way we came."

Ullin, unable to restrain his fascination, stepped a bit closer.

"Might you be Thunderfoot, King of the Trolls?"

"Ha! I might be, I may be, I was, I will be, and I always am Thunderfoot! Ye know of me, then?"

"Your name is known throughout the world, great King."

"Call me not great, soft thing! Though, if I be great, then Philawain is greater, still, than I. Was it not he who freed me of the chains that I could not break? Was it not Philawain, King, who passed into my stony heart to speak into my dreams. Was it not he who showed me the way to take my people home? And is it not Philawain who rules the castle of the sky, making the crude rocks and stones of that place move and float as does the air? I am great, yes. But he is greater still!"

"Then strong sir, did Philawain command you to come here?"

"Command? Command me, Thunderfoot? Nay, fool! It pleases Philawain that I come hither. And it pleases me to please Philawain!" Thunderfoot roared. Then, in a relatively softer tone, he added, "Philawain asked if I might do this. And it is my pleasure to be here."

While they spoke, the people of Nasakeeria were busy. Although Ullin and his group could not see it happening from where they stood, Nightar was organizing his people onto their barges. These were then lifted up by the trolls and passed from one to the next over their heads to the bridge, where more trolls took them up to pass them along. When the first group of Seleesa's people came floating, as it were, over the bridge of trolls, Ullin was about to ask another question, one made unnecessary by what he saw. No sooner than the first barge emerged from Nasakeeria than the next one came, carried by four mighty trolls, and was taken out onto the plain. Each was inconceivably heavy, made of sturdy logs and filled not only with people, but with all their food and belongings, including their tools and horses, some livestock, as well as thousands of carefully gathered plants. Not once did a troll falter, not once was a barge tilted or jostled, so carefully and delicately were they handled. Needless to say, the people aboard each barge were fearful, but their fears had been allayed ahead of time by powerful dreams and messages that had visited each person's sleep and that now sustained their courage and their hope.

Ullin gaped somewhat stupidly at the procession. He still gripped Micerea's hand, perhaps a little too firmly, but she was too filled with wonder to notice. Likewise, Aremon and Seleesa stared, arm in arm.

"Can it be? Can all the tales be true, and all the eons of our people's exile are ended?"

"It was you, my love, and your predecessors who sustained us in our hope," Aremon said to her. "How else might it have ever been done?"

"I played but a little part."

"But a part, nonetheless."

"So you are truly Dragonkind," said Ullin. "And you have been living here, in this land, behind those fearsome fires."

"Yes, we are. And, yes, we have. Ever since the time of Kalzar."

"Oh, Ullin!" Micerea suddenly turned to face him. "Remember the city? The dead city? I think that is where they are going to!"

"Is the city still there? Darini? With its pools and springs, and its gardens? And, in the center of all, a lake as round as Lady Moon's bold face?" asked Seleesa excitedly.

Ullin and Micerea exchanged looks.

"It is still there," said Ullin, not wishing to spoil their hope. "But the water is nearly all gone."

"Nearly?" asked Aremon.

"Yes."

"It was supposed to be completely all gone."

"There was, when I was last there with Micerea, a trickle," Ullin said, shrugging.

"A trickle?" exclaimed Seleesa, turning to Aremon. "A trickle! All I need is a trickle!"

She threw her arms around Aremon, who was as baffled as Ullin and Micerea at her joy.

"Then I may indeed fulfill my purpose and do as I have been raised from childhood to do!" she exclaimed, kissing Aremon on both cheeks and on his lips. "And, when it is done, I will take your ring!"

"Oh, oh! Then, by all means, let us depart!"

Just then, the last barge came along, with Prince Nightar standing upon it, and as it passed over the bridge and out of Nasakeeria, the trolls behind it stood from their places and followed. In a short while, the land of Nasakeeria was emptied of its human inhabitants, and the trolls ordered themselves in ranks, some carrying barges while others made lines to the right and the left. Thunderfoot watched, appearing very pleased with all that he saw, and as Nightar's barge passed by, he signaled to those who carried it, and it was lowered gently to the ground. Then, with a movement that could only be interpreted as a bow, Thunderfoot motioned for Ullin and those with him to step aboard. They did so, along with the skeptical Anerath, and the barge was lifted up once more. But before Ullin and Micerea could be introduced to the Prince, Thunderfoot's booming voice addressed everyone present.

"Heeeeaaar meeeee! I am Thuuuunderfoot, King. We go now swiftly across the soft grassy plain, through the hard high mountains, and to the dry dusty place far, far away. We go swiftly, I say, running both day and night without tire. We drink not water, nor do we eat flesh or grain, nor do we need rest as soft creatures do, but take it when we wish to. We do this to take ye home so that we also may go to our home at last and in peace. Worry not, for no soft creature may assail us, and no storm may hinder us. No river may block us, nor may any mountain stand in our way. But be warned: Hold ye tight to the little stick-boats that float upon our hands. Do not fall out lest ye be left behind, if ye be not crushed by our heavy tread. Let it be known that it is my pleasure to do this thing, and the pleasure of my people, for the sake of my friend, Philawain, who is a great friend to my people. It is he who has bid me say these things unto ye, and so I do. Heed them well! Let us goooooo!"

As smoothly as a boat on calm water they went, but as swiftly as the wind the trolls ran, carrying the great weights as if they were mere sheets of paper. Their tramp and stomp rose to a noise so loud that many soon stuffed linen into their ears. Others, children especially, were so thrilled by the speed that they screamed with delight, barely able to hear their own voices, while their hair soon blew into tangles. Behind them, Nasakeeria's mysterious flames faded into the distance until they was merely a dim glow far to the north, then it, too, faded.

Nightar, shouting into Ullin's ear, made his acquaintance, and that of Micerea, and they found pillows upon which to sit, leaning close to ask their questions and tell their tales as the wind of their passing whipped by and the stars wheeled overhead. Lady Moon made her appearance, too, somewhat shyer than the night before when she was so bold. When dawn came, and Lady Moon shared the sky for a brief while with Sir Sun, the procession was already well out onto the Plains of Bletharn. Ullin's voice was hoarse, but he had barely begun to relate to Nightar the history of Men, much less answer Nightar's many questions or ask all of his own. They continued to converse on into the bright morning, long after Micerea and all the others on Nightar's barge had fallen asleep. At last Nightar, himself quite weary from many previous days and nights of labor, excused himself to stretch out beside his wife under a nearby canopy. And Ullin was quite happy, too, to nestle with Micerea. Taking a last look at the passing plains, he then gazed at those around him who slept, Aremon with his arm over Seleesa, Nightar and his wife, Rina, and several others nearby. Although they were asleep, all seemed to be smiling, and Ullin thought he had never been amongst a happier people outside of Greenfar.

"I suppose wonders never will cease, after all," he thought as he put his head against Micerea's shoulder and closed his eyes.

Chapter 35

To Catch a Shadow

Word of the events in Duinnor reached Shatuum, borne on the wings of black eagles. Six of these creatures arrived, one after the other, and, in his blackened chamber, the birds shared the visions that had been seared into their spying eyes. Secundur received their reports, and when he had the last one, he dismissed the eagles. An hour later, Secundur calmly summoned Throgallus and gave his order that the occupants of Shatuum were to be marshaled.

During the days when Robby and Sheila were celebrated by their subjects, the black eagles came and went from Secundur's tower, and his fearsome captains cracked their whips to drive ghouls and wraiths to their forges and their armouries. Thousands upon thousands marched through the vaporous valleys collecting their lances, their helmets, their swords and axes, and donning their armor of black iron emblazoned with the red hourglass. Crude bridles of biting wire and steel were put into the mouths of transmuted creatures that were once buckmarls, to be ridden by hags and warlocks. Other creatures, more like dogs than the men they once had been, were harnessed to long chains, and they snarled and bayed and strained to be set loose, but were held back by powerful wraiths who grasped their leashes. Witches of the place brushed swords with vile unctions, and they dipped the tips of arrows into their bubbling pots. The last of the prisoners were put to death, their bodies hoisted as ghastly standards to be carried before their legions. The black eagles squawked and flapped around these, clawing at each other with their talons to get at the gruesome drippings.

Clouds of stinging vapor blotted out the sky, belched from forges and boiling pots of poison. When day came, Sir Sun turned away his gaze from the place so that it remained as a sticky and offensive night in Shatuum, while the garish torches and braziers burned and glowed soullessly. When night came again, Lady Moon avoided looking upon Shatuum, turning her face away as she passed overhead. Day thus passed, and night, too, one into the next and the next as preparations continued and as the occupants of Shatuum grew more and more restless.

• • •

From his castle wall, Throgallus watched impatiently. It was taking too long, he thought, and all should have been done weeks earlier. It was now ten days since the first news from Duinnor had arrived, and the time to strike was now. If Duinnor was to be the objective, as Secundur had ordered, Throgallus yearned to go immediately, leading those who were ready while Duinnor was unprepared and in a state of confusion. But, if it had been left to him, he would strike eastward with his horde, ignoring Duinnor and Vanara. Throgallus wanted to march his army swiftly across the plains to take Glareth and Tracia, feeding his army as they went on the Men and Elifaen they encountered. Thus, his army's appetite truly whetted, Glareth and Tracia would be easy pickings. Then Throgallus, if he had his way, would turn back and march into the vast legions of the Dragonkind that were coming northward like sweet dainties. Vanara and Duinnor would be dessert, and Throgallus relished the notion of taking his time with the Elifaen of Vanara.

But Secundur's aim was otherwise. His plan was to take Duinnor first, which irked and irritated Throgallus. However, as long as the armor that Throgallus wore answered to Secundur's whispers, Throgallus would obey.

This anticipation was unbearable, and now that Secundur was almost prepared to release him into the world, Throgallus was more anxious than ever before. He turned to look up at the crooked tower looming on the nearby slopes. He waited to be summoned, to be given the final word. It would not be long, for soon the entire world would be torn by war and strife. Below him, the creatures of Shatuum worked in a growing frenzy. He knew that they, too, anticipated filling their teeth and their bellies with sweet meats.

• • •

The tortured mind of Throgallus feared many things, and his heart had long ago been eaten out by doubt and suspicion, fueled by Secundur's whispers. But he could not fear that of which he had no inkling. Even if he had known what was taking place along the eastern rim of Shatuum, he could not have fathomed its import. Indeed, it was so insignificant that none of those who occupied the watchtowers along the east walls even noticed the dim form that floated back and forth between the blasted trees and along the soot-stained path that led to the gate of Shatuum. While drums and horns continuously blared and beat from within the shadowed land, the tenuous form lingered for a long while, silent and hesitant. Then it came on, floating like a thin mist over the gate and snaking back and forth along the road that went westward through Secundur's realm. As it passed through ranks of marching goblins, the nearly invisible thread of mist touched one or two of them. Some fair memory sprang suddenly to their minds, and they screamed with horror at their surroundings, but when the strange mist passed by, they shook off the passing vision, resumed their dour attitude, and marched on.

The form drifted to Secundur's tower and passed between the two captains who stood watch at its entrance. Invisible in the darkness of the tower, it floated upward, back and forth along the climbing stairs, until it came to the uppermost chamber. Secundur, waiting for Tythos to come with his conveyance, immediately noticed the visitor, though it was completely dark within. Nonplussed, he spoke.

"You have changed since our last encounter, Esildre."

"And you, my Secundur, have also changed. You have given up the last vestige of flesh, and so have I."

"Yes. But you were forced to do so, whereas this is my true and willing form."

"It is a pity, for I thought it might please you to touch me again, as you once did. I have roamed the world, but I find that there are no others who please me, and so I came here, thinking that I might please you."

"Do you seek to seduce me as you once did?"

"It was you who had the power of seduction, not I. But it is too bad that there is no light in this place, for I think I may yet be pleasing to behold. And now I am no longer weak as before, nor as demure."

"You were never demure."

"Tell me, do you still enjoy the bed of your many mistresses? Are they as pleasing to you as I once was?"

"Such things are in the past. I have no need and no desire of such companionship now."

"Another pity. So you do not even have the power to feel my form?"

If one insignificant substance may touch another insignificant substance, then Esildre felt a slight sensation running along her bare side to the curve of her waist.

"Do you shiver, Esildre?"

"It has been too long, and none have been able to satiate me. I suspect you are to blame for that."

"It was a small, parting gift. Did you find it irksome, as I have heard?"

"I did, but I no longer do. I find that you have given me a peculiar power that cannot be matched. Who is that who looks upon me?"

"Do not be alarmed, my dear. He is a servant, and cannot see without light."

"He sees, Secundur, though he sleeps. I will leave you, now. For I would be seen only by you, or by none if you cannot see me."

"Do not go," Secundur said. "I shall awaken Herzees so that he cannot, in his dreams, see you. Wait."

There was a stirring in the chamber, and Herzees woke up.

"Yes, my lord?"

"Go. Take yourself outside of this chamber and await my will."

"Yes, my lord."

The poor fellow crawled across the room and found his way to the door, then crawled out and down the stairs to the nearest landing.

"There. He has gone."

"Good. But you are blind, I think, or else you could see me. Pity upon pity, for I think you would be pleased."

"Do not think that I cannot see. I have eyes, but they prefer the darkness."

"Oh, yes. You once said that bright light hurts your skin. But I can show myself without any source of light but my own. Come with me to the roof of this place and I shall show myself to you under the dark sky of your domain."

"There is no passage to the roof, nor any window here. Show yourself to me here, if you dare."

"Can you not follow me through the stones of this place? Are you not mere shadow?"

"I am pure shadow. But even shadow cannot pass through stone."

"I am beginning to suspect that you are a prisoner in this tower, Secundur. You cannot come and go as you please. Yet any may come in, even those bearing hurtful torches."

"It does not please me to come and go. When it does please me, I shall do so. And if any enter this tower bearing light, those chains there will loosen, and the door will swing to and lock long before they reach this chamber. This is my domain, and all here serve and protect me."

"Very well, look upon me, if you have eyes."

In the deepest darkness the dimmest light shines all the brighter, and when Esildre revealed herself, a black smoky substance somewhat resembling the shape of a man floated quickly away from her. Then, as she dimmed, Secundur floated back and swirled around her.

"Your form is as beautiful as ever it was," he said, running inky tendrils across the cold skin of her ghostly body.

"I thought you would say so," she replied. "Do your other senses still feel? Are you still as manly as you once were? Or have you given that up, too?"

Esildre screamed.

"What does that tell you?" Secundur breathed in a soft, pleased tone.

"It seems," she said, recovering, "that we may find some use for each other, after all. Tell me, why do you need so many servants, when none may please you as I can?"

"They have their uses, too."

"I have need of only one," Esildre said, trying not to bolt from the chamber. Secundur was now sliding around her shoulders and down the front of her neck.

"You have a servant? Why would you need one?"

"To carry my things, which I find too heavy."

"What need of things may you have?"

"I need nothing, but have a servant to bring something for you. A gift."

Secundur floated away.

"A gift? What may you have that I should desire, other than your company?"

"A small thing. Shall I have it brought to you?"

"I do not wish for you to leave me, even for a moment."

"I may summon my servant without need of leaving. And he always comes when I call."

"How may you do that? Have you hexed some amulet that he wears?"

"I have hexed his heart, Secundur. As you gave me the power to do when I left you."

"I am intrigued. Summon him, then, and let him bring the gift you spoke of."

"Very well. Come, Eldwin."

• • •

On the far side of Algamori, Eldwin paced around the gate of Griferis. Nearby, Robby slumbered on the ground beside an ornate chest that was recently constructed by the craftsmen of Griferis. It was some two feet long, and a foot wide and deep, made of heavy wood, its interior lined with polished silver. Outside, it was bedecked with jewels and finely carved wood. Robby suddenly woke up.

"It is time," he said to Eldwin.

Together they lifted the heavy chest until Eldwin had it on his back, hunched over and grasping one of its handles with one hand.

"Good luck," Robby said.

"I'll do me bit, sire."

"And I'll do mine."

Eldwin snapped his fingers. He made the many miles winding down and around the mountain in but a few minutes, stopping only long enough to get his bearings and to renew his grip on the chest before popping off once more. Down into Shatuum he went, becoming more careful, choosing shorter jumps to remain unnoticed. When he came around a bend and saw the two fierce captains standing at the entrance of the crooked tower, he hesitated. He knew it would be dark inside, and that he would not be able to see in order to do what he must. But he had practiced enough with Robby, and it was too late to back out. Hiding behind the outcrop of a wall, he peered at the two captains while the dense reek of Shatuum settled onto him. Hearing a noise, he turned and saw a squad of wraiths approaching with a pack of awful creatures on leashes. One of these dog-like beasts stood on its hind legs, appearing like a hideously malformed man. It pulled on its leash, sniffing as the wraith that controlled it cursed. Then, as the wraith realized the sign, the man-dog began to howl and snarl at the place where Eldwin crouched, jerking at the chains as the other leashed creatures joined in the howling. Eldwin snapped his fingers and shot between the two captains and through the yawning door of the tower. He hit the steps of the stairs and nearly stumbled under the weight of the chest. The wraith was pulled by his howling pack toward the two captains. Eldwin began to climb the stairs, feeling the way with his free hand as one of the captains outside unfurled his whip.

"Control your dogs," the captain said to the wraith. "No one may pass."

• • •

"He will be here very soon," said Esildre. "I think I hear him coming."

Eldwin was out of breath in the stifling confines of the tower stairs. He continued to feel his way along the grimy steps, his breath rasping when he made the landing where Herzees sat. Having heard someone coming, Herzees pressed himself all the closer to the wall, thinking it an odd sound, as if one of Secundur's servants struggled to come up. Knowing too much of Secundur, and knowing that Shatuum was filled with terrible creatures, Herzees prepared for some awful fate. When Eldwin stumbled onto the landing and bumped into Herzees, the both of them recoiled in fear.

"Are ye called Herzees?" Eldwin asked tentatively, in a whisper.

"That is my name."

"Then get ready."

• • •

"Here he is, now. Poor thing. Carrying my chest up all those stairs in the dark."

Eldwin stumbled into the pitch black room. When he discerned Esildre's glowing outline, he was too exhausted to react to her nudity, and too filled with terror to shrink away from the inky form that smeared its way over her skin. Eldwin put the chest down, and fell to his knees beside it, trying to get a breath of air.

"This is your servant? Such a slight thing, he is. I am surprised that with your charms you do not catch a more comely person."

"Eldwin serves me well, when no other can do so," said Esildre as she came over to Eldwin and put her hand on his head as one might caress a pet.

"His powers are uncanny," she went on. "How else do you think he managed to come through your domain unmolested?"

"Indeed. I wish to know more about him and how he managed that."

"First things first, dear Secundur. You are forgetting my gift."

"Is it within this chest?"

"In a manner of speaking. Eldwin, unlatch and open the chest."

Eldwin felt around to find the latch, and lifted back the heavy lid on its hinges. Immediately, Secundur floated over to it. Eldwin nearly retched as a finger of Secundur's shadow touched his brow.

"A peculiar fellow, indeed," Secundur said. "But what is this? I feel nothing within this chest."

"Ah, but it is not what is within, but what may not go within it. A very special chest, for when it is shut, no light may pass through it, not even a hair-width crack of light under the full sun. And, once that latch there is thrown, no one may open it except from within."

"An interesting gift," said Secundur. "But there are many such things."

"Yes, but I may freely pass into and out of it as I please," said Esildre, coming over to rub against Secundur. "It is so that we may be together within it, whenever we choose, in complete privacy. From within, you may learn from me whatever you wish to know concerning the outside. And, entirely secure within, with no fear of light or that anyone outside might open it, you may have your servants take us anywhere you wish to go."

"Ah. That is very kind of you, Esildre," Secundur said, "but I have my own conveyance which is being prepared for me as we speak."

"Oh? And is there room in it for two?"

While they conversed, Eldwin had been carefully feeling around inside his coat pockets, gripping the items there, and slowly moving away from the chest. Then, with a crash, the chains that held open the iron door of the chamber shattered, and the door slammed shut with a tremendous bang. Eldwin fumbled for a moment, then struck a brilliant white flare and held it up. An earsplitting scream filled the room, and Eldwin felt Secundur swirl around to be in his shadow. He flung the flare onto the floor, and dashed across the room, lighting another and another, tossing them about the room as Secundur's high-pitched whine reached such a crescendo that the stones vibrated and Eldwin felt as though his teeth would shatter. Still he lit flares, throwing them everywhere so that there was no place anywhere in the room with the least shadow. Then, as the first flare began to fade, Eldwin lit another one, hoping he would not run out before it was too late. As he held it high, Esildre's voice rang out.

"Traitor! Traitor!" she screamed at Eldwin, her aspect hideous and terrifying. She turned to Secundur, now no more than a wisp of smoke. "He has more of the lights!" she screamed. "Into the chest! Come with me quickly!"

Eldwin saw what was left of Secundur flow into the chest. He ran over to it and glimpsed the swirling, writhing smoke within, then slammed down the lid and threw the latch. Shaking, he took another flare, hurriedly twisted out a plug on the lid, lit the flare, and slipped it inside, banging the plug down with his fist. Eldwin then collapsed on the floor beside the chest with one arm over it, as if to hold the lid down. In the strange, sudden quiet, the flares hissed as they dimmed and burned out, and he heard a pathetic whine coming from inside the chest. Eldwin pulled out his last flare and looked at the door, praying that Robby could again do his part. Already he could hear iron shoes on the stairs far below.

"Please, please-please-please," Eldwin muttered.

Robby did his part again, and the massive door banged open. Eldwin scrambled to hoist the chest onto his back, and he struck the last flare. Putting it into the same hand that gripped the chest, he snapped his fingers and shot down to the landing. Herzees shielded his eyes, stunned by the light, unable to see Eldwin in the glare.

"Take the light!" Eldwin commanded. "Quickly, man! Now put yer hand onto mine, up here on this handle. Close yer eyes, an' when I say drop the light, drop it!"

Eldwin snapped his fingers, and they popped down to the next landing, then to the next and the next. When they came into view of the captains charging up the stairs, the captains momentarily froze, shielding their eyes. It was all Eldwin needed, and he popped right between them and on down the steps, leaving the captains literally in the dark. At the entrance of the tower, Eldwin stopped only long enough to survey his escape, seeing throngs of Shatuum's denizens crowding toward the tower gate, summoned, no doubt by Secundur's screams. Through the crowd pushed Throgallus, and several other captains cracked their whips before him to clear the way. Herzees, bewildered and by now truly terrified, gasped and clutched Eldwin's hand even harder.

"Drop the light!"

Herzees was incapable of reacting, and the captains loomed.

"Drop the light, I tell ye!"

Eldwin shifted around, and since he could not reach the arm of tall Herzees, he kicked him in the shin.

"Drop it!"

At that moment, a fiery whip snapped through Herzees. The flare fell to the ground as Herzees crackled to ash, and Eldwin snapped his fingers.

• • •

Without light no one could see the interior of Secundur's chamber. But Throgallus could smell the burned-out flares, and he felt his armor loosen upon him, as if that which had always pressed it from every side had eased somewhat. He and his captains stood motionless, somewhat baffled. No one spoke. Throgallus then took off his helmet, listening. The only sound was that which faintly echoed up through the staircase, nothing else was heard. Secundur was not there.

Throgallus smiled.

"Bring a torch," he said.

"My lord?"

"A torch! Bring a torch!"

When that was done, Throgallus looked at the room, littered with the remnants of the many flares.

"Whom do you serve?" asked Throgallus.

The two captains hesitated.

"Whom do you serve?" Throgallus demanded.

"Throgallus."

"Make it so that others serve me, too. Go! Do as I say!"

The iron-shod captains strode out, and Throgallus followed a little while later. As soon as he came out of the tower, he was greeted.

"Hail, Throgallus!" went up the cry as the throngs beat their shields and stamped their feet. He held up his hand and when silence crossed Shatuum, he eyed the masses before him, the wraiths and their dogs, the witches and hags on their buckmarls, ranks and ranks of ghouls and goblins uncounted.

"Let us eat!" he cried.

• • •

While Throgallus ordered his legions, Eldwin was back inside of Griferis. He stood beside Robby on the balcony of the Royal Apartments. With their backs to the railing, they gazed through the open door at the chest near the hearth. Eldwin was now wearing some of Robby's own clothes, for when he returned from Shatuum with the chest, he had outgrown his own, having burst the seams of his sleeves and pants so that he was almost naked. He was now only a little shorter than Robby, but still stocky and strongly built, though in appearance some two decades older than Robby.

Sensing a movement, Robby turned around to face the long chasm over which Griferis floated, the opposing lines of snowy mountains brilliant in the noonday sun. Eldwin turned also, and they saw Esildre floating in mid-air some six or seven feet away. She was dressed in a flowing green gown and a fine, golden circlet ran around her brow. She was smiling, her face bright with joy, and her eyes glistening like radiant honey. The means of her levitation unfolded from her back and spread wide and gossamer-like, undulating and iridescent as sunlight passed through them. She looked at Robby and then turned her eyes to Eldwin and nodded. She stretched out an arm above her head, her hand out as if gesturing, and looked up as she began to fade from view. They saw another hand take hers, and a slight blush came to her cheeks as she was lifted upward.

She was gone.

"Well," Eldwin sighed, "I reckon she's with Tyrin, now."

Robby nodded. They watched the sunlight sparkle from the icy slopes for a while longer.

"What will ye do with the box?" Eldwin asked.

"I think I'll eventually take it south. Just in case there's anything in it other than a burned-out flare. I'll take it to a place in the deserts, where, if it is ever opened, it might be under the bright sun. Unless you have a better idea."

"No, sire. That seems the thing to do."

"I suppose you are ready to go home."

"Yes. I am quite ready."

"I must find some way to thank you. And all your people, too."

"I don't think ye need to do any more than what's been done. Our curses have been lifted, an' that's plenty enough. But what of the things that we hold in trust from Tulith Attis? The Hoard."

"Just continue to look after it until Ullin returns. He'll know best what to do with it."

Eldwin nodded.

"Then, sire, if ye don't mind, I think I'll be on me way."

They left the apartments together. When Robby and Eldwin came out to the eastern courtyard, all of Griferis was gathered to see Eldwin off.

"One last thing, Eldwin," Robby said. Surprised at the turnout, Eldwin appeared somewhat embarrassed at the attention. Robby motioned to Finn, who unfurled a scroll and loudly read from it.

"By order of Philawain, King and Lord of Griferis, it is declared that Eldwin the Quick, for his service to Griferis, for his bravery and determination, and for his sense of duty and of right-doing, is hereby and forever to be known as Eldwin, First Lord of New Picathia, which has formerly been known as the land of Nowhere. Let it be known that Lord Eldwin shall enjoy every privilege and honor of this hereditary title and rank wherever he may go upon the earth, and that he and his heirs shall forever be Peers of Griferis."

Robby took Eldwin's hand and shook it, then turned Eldwin toward the ranks gathered.

"I give you Lord Eldwin!"

"Three cheers for Lord Eldwin!" cried Lafkin, unsheathing his sword. All of the Blue Guard, as the Griferis soldiers had come to be called, also lifted their swords in salute.

"Hip-hip, hurrah! Hip-hip, hurrah! Hip-hip, hurrah!"

"Now you may go, Eldwin," Robby said. "And carry with you my enduring gratitude and everlasting friendship."

Eldwin bowed deeply, then turned and passed through the saluting swords, and between the ranks of people who clapped and bowed as he went by. When he passed through the gate and stepped out onto the causeway, he paused. Robby saw his shoulders heave up and down as he sighed. Eldwin snapped his fingers, and in a burst of bubbling light, he disappeared.

• • •

Robby returned to his apartments, although he knew that Finn and Lafkin needed to see him, and that he should look in on his father, who was probably this very moment revising Radasa's inventories. He was somewhat surprised to see Celia sitting inside, and Boxer sniffing the chest.

"Hello, Celia," he said. Unther followed him inside, but a wave of Robby's hand dismissed the guard. He plopped down into a chair.

"So it is done? You have put the terrible spirit of Shatuum into that box?"

"Yes. It is done. But not all of his spirit went in."

"What do you mean, Robby?"

"I mean that he put much of his spirit into his followers, and elsewhere in the world. And, together, they may be stronger than he ever was."

"How could they be? Are they as bad?"

"Yes. And no. It depends. But now they are released into the world to do great harm."

"Oh. Will you do something about it?"

"I will try to. There is one thing more that I must do. Only one thing more. Then the world will have to take care of itself."

"Robby, why does that make you sad?"

"Because, dear Celia, I am tired. And, if I do what I must, I may never see you again."

"Oh. That is sad. That makes me sad, too. It means that you'll be leaving Griferis?"

Robby smiled.

"In a manner of speaking. Yes."

"What does Finn have to say about that, I wonder?"

"I have not told Finn. I have not told anyone but you, just now."

"Not even Queen Shevalia? She is your wife, isn't she? Will you go live with her?"

"No, I don't think so. I have not told her."

"Then she will be sad, too, I imagine."

"Perhaps. I think so."

"What will become of us, then? What about Finn?"

"I'm working that out, my dear. Everyone will be taken care of."

Celia looked at Boxer, then at her hands in her lap.

"I will miss my friends," she said.

"I know."

"But I will miss you and Finn the most."

"I will miss you, too."

Robby looked at Celia and smiled.

"You know who you are, don't you?"

Celia nodded.

"But you don't understand, do you?"

Celia shook her head.

"You will."

Chapter 36

The Red Hourglass Approaches

Day 240
5 Days Remaining

Robby remained seated in his chair long after Celia had departed. Weary though he was, the day's work, the destruction of Secundur, left him wondering about things. Things that he had doubts about.

Certainly, there was much that he knew. Not only did he have at his fingertips a vast library of knowledge and lore, but he also still retained many of the memories of his forebears, given to him with his name when he had crossed death's door. He was also now Elifaen, with a body that would no longer age, and he had their sense of guilt and loss, added to his own. The nature of that curse was, as all curses are, two-sided, and the dark side of it waged its battle within him. Like some lesser Secundur, his Elifaen aspect breathed doubt and hopelessness, it formed thoughts that spoke against his innate sense of duty, filling him with worry, and it goaded him concerning his mother's death, among other things. As Elifaen, he wished to do nothing, to let things rest, to be idle and watch the world pass by. But he was ever an energetic person, even from his earliest years, always eager to learn and to help, whether it was at his father's store or out running errands. There was little wonder that his parents had been so proud of him, little wonder that Billy admired him, and no mystery why Sheila, raised in ignorance and abuse, might have thought him to be somehow above her. None could deny that once he set his mind to a task, he was as tenacious and determined as any to see it through. And, as a young man, with his sunny outlook and his smiling face, he had been a joy to those he encountered, and a credit to his parents.

Perhaps those characteristics that were formed before he set out to Tulith Attis that fateful day, before he departed for the west or ever even saw Griferis, sustained him during his trials. Certainly he learned, though he did not enjoy the type of learning that Griferis had to teach. And he continued to learn, spending as much time as he could in the library and exploring the world through his dreams and the dreams of others. Although his knowledge was prodigious, and he might even be called wise, there was still very much that he did not know, nor could he even guess.

The creatures of Shatuum were still a mystery to him. If he could discover what it was that animated them without sustenance, what power enabled them to stay active without sleep or rest, perhaps he could have understood better the threat they posed to the world. As it was, all he knew was that they were horrible and despicable creatures, and, now that Secundur was removed from them, Throgallus would soon lead them forth. Like Secundur, Throgallus was Elifaen, too, and flawed. Without Secundur, who had been the shepherd of their flaws and the shaper of his creatures' power, Robby only trusted that they, and Throgallus, could be defeated by those with lesser flaws.

And soon, when the ferocity of the Elifaen would be needed most, it would be time for them to depart the world. Robby knew that if he failed, and the Elifaen remained in the world to fight, it would still be years and years before Throgallus could be defeated. If Robby succeeded, and the Elifaen departed, it could well be very much longer, perhaps an age before the defeat of Shatuum could be possible. That, at least, was Robby's worry, for it would be a dark time upon the earth. Nevertheless, he hoped the outcome, in the end, would be the same, that a new age would eventually dawn, one that was free of Secundur's shadow.

But Robby's mistakes haunted him. He had sent Mirabella to her death on a mission that was probably unnecessary. When given the chance, he had failed to save the baby that Sheila carried when she fled from Steggan that awful night. During his time in Griferis, when he was forced to be a judge, he had failed to properly question people who were brought before him, and he inadvertently set off deadly feuds. He had realized too late that he had the power to unlock things, to release chains and shackles and to open doors even in his dreams. He mentally ticked off his mistakes, those he had made inside of Griferis and elsewhere. All these thoughts left Robby with a nagging fear that Throgallus was unstoppable.

So, early the next morning, with these things weighing upon him, Robby took Griferis back to Duinnor, managing to arrive much faster than before, and with none of the terrible storms that had accompanied his previous arrival. He put out his causeway, walked across it with his escort, and went immediately to see Sheila, pleased that she was not at the High Tower. Indeed, since the tower was too austere for a great monarch such as Shevalia, she would remain at Starlight Hall until a suitable palace could be constructed for her. Lavishly decorated and furnished by Lady Highleaf, who spared no expense for the Queen's benefit, she had even turned the great hall into a kind of throne room.

There, guarded by the Kingsmen and by members of Robby's Blue Guard, and under the guidance of Ashlord and Raynor, Queen Shevalia held court. Although she was terrified at the prospect of Robby leaving her, they had been in touch through their dreams. During the several days of his preparations with Eldwin to capture and destroy Secundur, Robby had dreamwalked with Sheila in order to instruct and coach her on how he thought she should act.

"While in court," he had suggested, "or during any public audience, refrain from speaking directly to anyone present but Ashlord or Raynor. Put your questions to them, quietly so that no one else may hear, and have them speak for you. Insist that only Ashlord and Raynor are to be addressed by any who speak. That way, no one will be able to speak to you directly, and so no one will be able to put you on the spot. Also, that way, if ever you feel that you must speak, the people will pay attention to every word that you say."

Sheila took the advice, telling Ashlord and Raynor how it was to be. And, since she must sometimes be in the company of women, with no men about, Lady Highleaf was then to serve her as Ashlord might otherwise do. At first, it was awkward, but it worked, giving Sheila time to consider her questions and her words.

By now, during the week of Robby's absence, she had already heard many of the concerns put to her by the lords of Duinnor, and those expressed by representatives of other Realms, too. The great hall was nearly always occupied by one contingent or another, and the foyer outside was crowded with those seeking an audience. But when it was learned that Griferis had once again arrived, and that King Philawain approached Wysteria Place, the people immediately made ready. She knew that he was coming, and when Raynor bent to whisper the news in her ear, Sheila was already as filled with as much anticipation as any, and more so.

"...and so the prisons are full to capacity," Lord Arata was saying to Ashlord and, indirectly, to the Queen. "Captain Thrubold, here, may attest to the fact that the men and women that Banis had in his employ are from all walks of life. Some seven hundred within the ranks of the Regulars alone have been arrested on various charges, including unlawful possession of property taken from Vanara. And, I am sorry to say, several Kingsmen have also been arrested. I am afraid that the courts and the constabulary are already overwhelmed, and more arrests are expected. If some general pardon cannot be worked out, the situation will become dire, indeed."

"What are the conditions of the pardon that you propose, Lord Arata?" Ashlord asked.

"First, each person must confess the extent of their crimes, which will be printed in the broadsheets of our realm. Any who consider themselves victims must make known their claims. Then, if those found guilty have it in their means to do so, they must make restitution to their victims, as overseen by our courts. If they do not have it within their means, the courts will apply to the Crown for restitution. If any have committed murder, and they confess their acts, they will not be put to death, but made to serve in prison. If any have committed other violent crimes, such as assault, and they confess their acts, and if their victims are agreeable, they will be paroled after a period of not less than five years. My Lord

Ashlord, these measures are intended to alleviate the Crown of housing so many criminals, much less the years it would take to prepare and hear each case, and also to forestay reprisals."

"And what of the Vanaran leases?" Ashlord asked. "The Queen wishes that matter to be expedited."

"My lord," said one of the clerks assisting Arata, "if I may speak? All leases taken on Vanaran lands and property have been reviewed by our assistants. Since Her Majesty Queen Shevalia has already abolished the practice by proclamation, copies of the lists have been delivered to the Queen of Vanara to be taken with her when she returns to her realm."

Ashlord looked at Sheila, who nodded.

"Very good," Ashlord said to the clerk and to Lord Arata. "The Queen is pleased by your diligence."

It was at this point that the porter at the top of the opposite stairs loudly thumped his staff and proclaimed the entrance of King Philawain. All bowed as the King of Griferis, along with Finn and Lafkin, hurried down the stairs and crossed the hall. Sheila stood and smiled broadly as her husband approached, and when she offered her hand, Robby bowed and kissed it, then stood beside her as she sat back down. Robby gestured to Ashlord, who came onto the dais and bowed.

"My lord?"

"Ashlord, are the generals ready? And is Serith Ellyn still nearby?"

"Yes, sire. Serith Ellyn and Thurdun are here at Starlight Hall, and the generals you asked for are in the foyer."

"Then, if it pleases the Queen, conclude your business with Lord Arata, and have them come in."

Sheila nodded to Ashlord, who turned back to Arata.

"Lord Arata, the Queen must see to urgent business. But I think your proposals merit further discussion. The Queen will look at your proposals and decide. She thanks you for your service. Please convey her gratitude to the other judges, as well as to Captain Thrubold and his Kingsmen."

"Thank you, Your Highness."

Sheila took Robby's hand and he leaned down so that she could whisper to him.

"I love you."

"I love you, too, my Queen," Robby smiled.

"I was glad that you came to me last night and told me what happened. Do you think Eldwin is home by now?"

"I expect so."

"And Esildre?"

"She, too, I think."

"Did you bring him? I mean, the chest?"

"Yes. That is, it is in Griferis."

"So now war comes, indeed."

"Yes. Throgallus moves as we speak."

"Hm. I would like to address the generals first, if you do not mind," she said.

Robby nodded.

"King Philawain has just arrived," Ashlord said to the Kingsmen generals who were entering the hall, "and has important news."

They filed in, some six generals and their aides, and then came Serith Ellyn and Thurdun with Gaiyelneth and Captain Chanter.

When Sheila stood, they all bowed.

"Thank you for patiently waiting when I know that you are anxious to be at your duties," she said to them. "I would like for you to hear my husband, King Philawain. Also, should he instruct you, I bid you do as he says."

She turned to Robby and nodded. He bowed to her and waited for her to be seated.

"My Queen Shevalia, Queen Serith Ellyn, Prince Thurdun, Kingsmen. As you have been forewarned, Shatuum is on the march. You have all been shown, through my dreamwalkers, the power of Shatuum and its terrors. But Secundur does not lead them. He is destroyed."

There were brief expressions of relief on the part of those gathered before before Robby resumed.

"That only means that he cannot infect us with his shadow," he went on. "It does not mean that we will survive. Ashlord, here, was one of the Nine Banes. He can tell you how it took his company years, with all their power and cunning, to hunt down and destroy but a few fiends. And it cost them dear. Now come thousands upon thousands. They have at their vanguard witches who will cast awful spells. They march behind eleven mighty captains, each more than a match for a battalion of our best soldiers. And they are led by the traitor of Tulith Attis, who is as cruel as he ever was, and more so. He is called Throgallus by Shatuum, but was known as Pellen before."

"Heneil's brother?" Ashlord asked.

"Yes. The same. What he saw done at Tulith Attis, he now seeks to visit upon the entire world, and to do worse, if that can be imagined. And his power and strength have been magnified by his centuries within Shatuum, bolstered by the witches of that place, groomed by Secundur to be relentless. The Dragonkind who now pour out of the Tulivana Mountains into Altoria know nothing of Shatuum, but they will be fodder to Throgallus's purpose and food to his armies."

"Sire, if I may," asked General Chadler, "what is their aim? To where do they march?"

"Their aim, since Secundur is gone, is to eat. Sustained by dark enchantments, they have been kept from food, and now their appetite has grown so that it has no bounds. And they have been bred with a lust for human flesh. I am certain that, if unchecked, they will consume every living person upon the earth. I doubt if they need slaves, and they do not long for spoils or land. I do not know if they can have offspring, but let us assume that they may. So they will be as locusts. Their emblem is the red hourglass, upon a black field. An apt symbol, for Throgallus means to put an end to our time, and make the world dark. As of this morning, he began moving his armies out of Shatuum, pouring them through the mountains eastward, and the black eagles fly far afield of them. It is too early to tell if they intend to turn north or south."

"My lord," Serith Ellyn spoke, "what of the Bloodcoins? Why has the Nimbus Illuminas not been opened? Forgive the question, but do you intend to keep us here to fight Shatuum?"

"No, I do not. But the time has not yet come for the Nimbus Illuminas to open. In five days, we may see if it opens. If it does, I do not know what will happen. But if it does not open, the world will need your swords."

"My King," said Raynor, "if Queen Serith Ellyn and Prince Thurdun are to make it to Vanara, they must depart immediately, lest their route be cut off. Vanara needs her queen, sire."

"I agree," Robby said, looking at Serith Ellyn. "I doubt if Throgallus will split his army and send forces simultaneously against both Duinnor and Vanara. My guess is that he will turn north, since he knows that Vanara will soon have a Dragonkind army on its flanks and will thus be occupied with that threat. Before dawn, come into Griferis with all your people, and I shall take you to Linlally."

"Then, by your leave, sire, my Queen, we shall go, and make our preparations," Serith Ellyn bowed and departed.

Robby turned to the generals.

"Tell me what preparations are under way for Duinnor."

• • •

It was a brief session, and too soon for the generals to say how well their preparations for war were proceeding. Robby and Sheila knew they had only a few days notice, and that it would take every hour of every day to prepare against Shatuum. But there was little point in delaying things by ceaseless conversation and speculation, so the generals were soon excused to continue their work. Ashlord and Raynor also departed to assist, and Sheila walked with Robby to her apartments.

Finally alone, Robby and Sheila fell into each other's arms. Later, some long while after sunset, they lay together in bed, Sheila with her head on Robby's shoulder as they were once accustomed to sleeping. But they did not sleep.

"I want you to come back with me to Griferis," Robby said. "It is unassailable, and we can go anywhere we please, should it come to it."

Sheila shifted up onto her elbow to look at Robby.

"Do you mean for me to abandon Duinnor?"

"I mean for you to live."

"Robby, you made these people my people, and you made me their queen. I don't think I should leave them."

"Listen. If Throgallus comes, Duinnor will fight, I'm sure. And Duinnor may even hold out for a time. But those creatures will view the city as their larder. Did Ashlord ever tell you about the Free City? I have read the chronicles kept when it was attacked by witches. There were only four witches. And a few fiends with them. Less than a score of those creatures prevailed against an entire well-defended city. I do not think this city can have much hope against thousands of them."

"But we must try."

Robby sighed.

"I don't care what you say," Sheila went on. "I will not run away again."

"What do you mean?"

"I mean that I should have stayed in Janhaven with Mirabella. I should have helped her. I should not have come with you. Little good I did. But now that I am queen, I won't repeat that mistake. I won't have it upon my head."

"My mother died because I was stupid," Robby said, sitting up. "I was stupid, and she died stupidly because of me. It was my fault, not yours."

"Robby!"

"Look. I don't want to argue. It may be moot. We don't know what the next days will hold. But consider this: Would you want your loyal subjects to die trying to safeguard your life, as they would surely do? Or would you want them to fight for their own lives and for the lives of their families and friends?"

Sheila looked away for a moment in thought, then took his hand and turned it over and ran her finger over the scars on his wrist and forearm, examining them carefully.

"You have seen many battles, and have watched many die," she said. "And you have made a difference, preventing the death of many more. But now you are Elifaen, as I am, too. The Nimbus Illuminas is now the only honorable way of escape."

Robby nodded.

"So what have you not told me?"

"I do not think I can open it," he said bluntly. "I have looked, through dreamwalking, and I have looked and looked. I see nothing. I am no closer to understanding it than I ever was. So, if it does not open, you will have no choice but to remain. And, if you do not go into Griferis, when the ghouls come they will tear you apart and they will eat you."

"Then it will be over for me. And it will be over for Billy and Ibin, and Frizella and all our friends. Eldwin and Ullin and Micerea."

"I will take as many into Griferis as it will hold."

"And then what? Will we float in the clouds forever? What happens when the food runs out? Will we watch our friends starve? Or will we eat each other, and become like those who drove us there?"

"I don't know! I just don't know."

He stood and began dressing.

"Where are you going?"

"If you are determined to fight for Duinnor, then I will fight for you," Robby said, slipping on his shirt. "I need to see Lafkin and Finn and discuss a few ideas about slowing down Throgallus. I'll be back to say goodbye before leaving with Serith Ellyn."

Sheila got up, and began to dress, too.

"And where are you going?" Robby asked.

"Do you mind if I come with you to see Lafkin?"

"No. I'd be honored and happy for your company. And, as Queen of Duinnor, you might be able to help things along."

• • •

Lafkin and Finn were close by. In fact, they were dining with Lady Highleaf in the company of Grantham Farby. When the King and Queen entered, they all stood abruptly and bowed.

"Please be seated," said Sheila. "Lady Highleaf, pardon the intrusion. We would like to have a word with these gentlemen."

"Certainly, Your Highness." Lady Highleaf bowed and made to depart.

"You needn't leave," said Robby. "You may find our conversation interesting."

Robby got right to the point.

"I'll need to requisition as many bottles as possible, along with as much strong liquor and lamp oil. Also small casks, jars, and the like. All to be taken into Griferis as soon as can be."

"Lady Highleaf, please send for my scribe." Sheila asked. "Ask him to bring my seal and his writing things." Then, to Robby, she said, "I'll have an order made for you. We'll need men to gather and bring the things, so I'll address it to General Chadler."

"Very good," Robby said.

"Sire," Farby spoke up, "my father's warehouse has a great store of lamp oil, for use in our mines and mills. If I may be excused, I can arrange for deliveries to be made this very night."

"Why, yes. That would be most helpful. We depart at dawn."

"I am on my way, sire. Your Majesty."

Farby bowed to Sheila and Robby and hurried out.

"What do you have in mind, sire?" Lafkin asked.

"I mean to rain fire upon Throgallus and his armies," Robby said. "From Griferis, that is. We'll need flares, too. I believe Eldwin used most of those we had, didn't he?"

"Yes, sire. We have less than two dozen left," Lafkin replied.

"Then we'll have to impose upon Duinnor for those, too."

Chapter 37

The New River and the New Sea

The fleet of barges carried by Thunderfoot's trolls arrived at their destination about the same time that Robby left Sheila to go back to Griferis and make ready to take Serith Ellyn and her people back to Vanara. It had been a swift crossing of the plains, and there had been no mishaps along the way, even though the trolls forded many rivers and climbed up and down many slopes. When they arrived in the desert, the stony giants marched on, then they suddenly came to a halt. The trolls gently put down their loads and unceremoniously departed, having no time to receive the thanks of Prince Nightar's people.

It was dark, and the people of Nasakeeria did not know where they were, except that they were somewhere in the deserts. By the waning moon, they watched the trail of trolls disappear into the west, and once the sound of their tromping had passed beyond hearing, the silence of the desert was as deep and as broad as their surroundings. Ullin led Anerath off of the barge, as others did the same with their horses and animals. Nightar ordered that everyone remain close to their belongings, and they organized watches. But he forbade any fire or lamp until they were assured of their safety. Micerea joined Ullin as he walked Anerath around, taking his hand.

"Do you know where we are?" he asked.

"I think we are in the region of the old city."

It was as far as they got in their conversation, interrupted by a shout from one of the outlying scouts. Ullin quickly mounted Anerath and rode to catch up with Nightar, who was already galloping out to the perimeter of their encampment where Shazarra pointed south.

"Riders, Prince," he said. "There."

The moonlight was still bright enough that they could plainly see a large group about a mile away, a trail of dust rising behind them.

"They come slowly," said Nightar, taking out his spyglass.

"How many do you see?" asked Ullin.

"Hard to tell. At least fifty riders at the front, but it looks as though there are a great many followers. On foot. And I think I see wagons, too. Oh. Now four ride ahead swiftly, making straight for us."

Nightar handed the glass to Ullin.

"A standard bearer," he said as he peered at the approaching shapes, "and three others. Dragonkind soldiers."

By now Aremon and Micerea had caught up to them on foot, along with many others, and they heard what Ullin said.

"Shazarra, ride to warn the others. Have our men prepare."

Shazarra reined around and galloped off, as Ullin handed the glass back to Nightar.

"Let me ride out to meet them, Prince," Ullin said. "By how they react to me you may know if they are hostile."

"No, Ullin," Micerea said, putting her hand on his thigh and looking up at him. "If they are Dragonkind, how do you expect them to act toward a Northman?"

"Didn't our King say that we would be safe?" answered Ullin. "And would Thunderfoot have left us here if there was danger?"

"We'll ride out together," said Nightar.

"No! I mean, pardon me, Prince, but let Ullin stay."

"Micerea, what is wrong?" Ullin leaned down to better see her face. "My senses do not say there is danger."

"Then wait here."

Ullin glanced up toward the approaching riders, now only a furlong away. Nightar appeared uncertain.

"What is it?"

"I would not have the father of my child throw away his life needlessly," she finally said.

Ullin stared at her for a moment, then broke into a grin.

"Ha! I don't think that's very likely!" he said, leaning closer to kiss her. "Perhaps I know the Dragonkind standards better than you do. I think we are in no danger. The Prince and I should ride out to greet them. And perhaps you should come along. Come. Don't be afraid."

He reached down to give Micerea a hand and pulled her up to sit behind him, and they rode out. Micerea leaned around Ullin to keep an eye on those they rode to meet, and Anerath galloped smoothly, as if sensing that he should be as gentle as possible.

"I hope you are right," she said.

"I am. Prince! Prepare to meet one of the most famous men in all the world!"

"Oh, oh!" Micerea exclaimed as she suddenly saw the standard that flew from the lance of one of the Dragonkind. "I don't believe it!"

It was a green flag, and it had a white dragon rampant ornately embroidered on it. Micerea recognized it instantly, having known it all her life. A broad grin broke across her face as the two parties slowed and came to a halt before each other. Micerea immediately slipped off of Anerath's back and sprang forward.

"Father!" she cried.

Gurasa dismounted, and they reached for one another as Ullin and Nightar approached the embracing father and daughter.

"I was told you would be here," Gurasa said to Micerea. "King Philawain said so."

"Did he come to you in your dreams?" she asked, taking his hand and leading him toward Ullin and Nightar.

"No, daughter. He told me himself, in person, not even a fortnight ago. And his Queen sends her regards, too, as does Lady Highleaf. Have you not been watching Duinnor?"

"Yes. I mean, no. I mean, he must have wanted this to be a surprise. But why are you here?"

"First, I think introductions are in order, don't you?"

"Of course, Father."

"This can be none other than Ullin Saheed Tallin, of the House of Fairoak," Gurasa said, bowing to Ullin. Ullin nodded and bowed in return, putting his hand on his chest.

"Salam, dala Saltani Gurasa," Ullin said. "Salam, forala Saltani Philawain al Griferis."

Gurasa bowed again, returning Ullin's gesture.

"You do me great honor, Ullin Saheed," Gurasa said. "But I would enjoy speaking the language of the north, if you don't mind that I am somewhat rusty. I am no longer a saltani, but merely the leader of these people who come."

"Allow me to introduce Prince Nightar, my lord," Ullin said. "Recently of the far north, but whose ancestors are from these lands."

"Ah, Prince Nightar," Gurasa bowed. "I welcome you and your people to the deserts. Or, rather, back to the deserts."

"Thank you, Lord Gurasa," Nightar said as he bowed in return. "I have just recently heard of your exploits, and somewhat of your travels," he said, glancing at Ullin and Micerea. "I am honored that you have come to greet us."

"Oh, I come to do more than greet you," Gurasa said. "I come to join my people with yours, if you will have us."

Gurasa gestured toward the mass of people still approaching from some distance away.

"Allow me to explain," Gurasa went on. "We were forewarned that our town would be cut off from the northern deserts. Philawain, long before I met him in person, showed me that it would be so, and he said that we should abandon our ancient home and come to join with you. Together, he said, we should establish new homes for your people and for mine. Like you, we have brought all that we could bring. Horses, cattle, tools, looms, linen and other fabrics, all manner of things. Also we have brought seed and cuttings, food and salt. All our people have come from Almedian, our former town. Roughly ten thousand of us. It is a prodigious undertaking, and a mighty caravan we have made. But we have traveled with stealth in spite of our great number, and I do not think others of our kind have detected us. I see that you are truly surprised."

"Father, why? How has Almedian been cut off?"

"Then you do not know?" Gurasa looked at the trio. Then almost laughing, he glanced at his escort, who were all smiling.

"A great miracle is taking place," he said. "When I was told of it, by King Philawain's messengers, I immediately sent out my scouts to watch it, and we set to work preparing to leave our home. And tomorrow, or the next day, perhaps we shall ride to see it."

"What miracle?" Nightar asked.

"Watch what?"

"Ride to see what?"

"Three weeks ago, a thin stream of water coursed through the deserts coming from the west. At first, it merely soaked into the sands, filling depressions with mud. As our people worked in haste, the stream continued to grow, day by day, extending its reach farther east. During this time, our people began their trek northward. Two weeks ago, we crossed over it some fifteen leagues east of the Green Citadel. Our scouts reported that it was spreading out into a broad river, inundating the plain before the Green Citadel and sweeping away the sands. A week ago, it was reported to us that the river was beginning to flood the city, and the people there were in a panic. We turned west, and we followed along its northern shore for many leagues, watching it rise and spread day by day. And the mornings were unusually misty with fog which is rarely seen in our lands. When we left sight of it, it stretched out southward as far as the eye could see. The desert does not soak it up. Not very quickly, at least. But here our ground is higher, and will not flood."

Gurasa looked at his audience, who were so baffled that they did not know how to react.

"The desert is filling with water," said Gurasa. "I think, if it continues, there will be a great sea where there is now only sand and dust. Philawain said it would be so. And he said that the northern lands of the desert would be spared the flood, but the deserts would be cleansed of the poisons that afflict our people."

"But where does the water come from?" Ullin asked.

"Philawain told me, a few days ago, that it pours out from the western mountains. He said that Thunderfoot and his people made it happen."

"But where will the people go?" asked Micerea. "Those in the flooded lands."

"I asked our King about that," nodded Gurasa. "He said they must find their own will and way. But that the west would be opened to them as it has not been before."

"And, so," said Nightar, "we are protected by the waters from attack, at least from the south."

"That is so. It is now too broad and deep to be crossed by foot. And there are no boats."

By now the eastern horizon was showing light, and the rumble of wagons and horses could be clearly heard. Also, in spite of Nightar's orders, many of his men had gathered behind him, and were listening, though they had trouble following the dialect.

"And so," Gurasa went on, "we have only to occupy the old city, and to make our new start."

"Yes," said Nightar, looking around at the desert. "If we only knew where it was, or how far we have to go."

"You need only to cast your eyes yonder, and you will see."

Gurasa gestured to the west. There, a great distance away, was the vague outline of hills. They continued to gaze as the sky grew rapidly brighter and the stars were blotted by blue, and the hills they watched seemed strangely flat. As Sir Sun often loved to do in the desert, he suddenly walked up into the sky, sending a brief reddish glow across the land, then his bright yellow light. The people watched as their shadows shot away from them, long and thin, and what they took for hills they could now see were the ruins of the city.

Ullin smiled broadly, and Micerea, still gripping her father's hand, reached out and took Ullin's. Sir Sun swept away the morning chill and filled the air with his heat as they all marveled at the golden city.

"Darini," said Nightar. "That is its name. I think we should go there at once. And, after we have assessed things somewhat, we should begin bringing our things there."

Soon, in the company of Gurasa and many Dragon People, both of north and of south, Ullin and Micerea were retracing the steps they had walked many years before, when they had first met. And it was not long before they could see the two tall columns that marked the outer boundary of the ancient city. They kept straight on, stopping for a moment to gaze at the symbols carved into the columns. Nightar and his people could read them, but they did not share what the words told.

"You know, Ullin Saheed," Gurasa said as they passed between the columns, "we have met before."

"Three times, at least, I should say."

"Four. But at first I did not know who you were."

"I guessed who you were by the ring that you wore," Ullin said, lifting his hand to show it to Gurasa.

"Yes. When I learned who you were, and realized that you had not betrayed my identity, I knew you could be trusted. That you were an honorable man, like your uncle, and, by all accounts, like your father."

"That is kind of you to say, my lord."

"I was very sorry to hear about your aunt," Gurasa said. "Micerea told me. You may not know this, but there are accounts amongst my people concerning Lady Mirabella. She was known as a cunning and fierce warrior, expert with sword and bow. I was no longer in service, I am glad to say, when she fought at the second siege of the Green Citadel. But some of my townsmen participated in the defense of that city, and they saw her on more than one occasion. To this day, they say that if ever you see a Faere warrioress with long red hair, you must run away, for if you are ever close enough to see her green eyes, you will die. She and your father fought side by side, you know."

"Yes. I know. She told me. She also, years later, told me that she was disgusted by what she saw, and she described it to me in some detail. I think hearing her tale tempered my passion for war, which was, I'm sure, her intention."

"Hm. Yes. My heart was never in it, not even in the beginning, though I had some skill at it."

"Micerea told me how you came by the ring," Ullin said. "How you took it back from my uncle when you found him."

The group led their horses up the broad avenue that passed through the city toward its center. Nightar listened to Gurasa and Ullin, but he was as distracted as any by the magnificent buildings and structures. When they came to the broad round bowl that was once the central lake of the city, they stopped and stared in amazement.

"The sand is gone," said Ullin. "And what is that?"

Indeed, the entire bowl had been somehow swept clean of the dunes of sand that Ullin remembered. And, in the very center of the wide bowl, which was only some ten or twelve feet deep, was a massive cube of stone.

"It is the Great Stone!" Gurasa declared. "I swear it is! But how did it get there?"

"And look!" Micerea pointed toward its base. "Who is that?"

"And what is he doing?" Nightar added as he peered through his spyglass.

"It is my master."

They all jumped at the voice, coming from a nearby statue. The statue turned its head toward them.

"Oh! Who are you?" Seleesa asked, backing into Aremon.

"My master calls me Lythos."

"And who is your master?" asked Ullin.

"His name is Alonair."

Chapter 38

The Test

Day 241
4 Days Remaining

Griferis flew south, carrying Queen Serith Ellyn home. Besides the faithful company of a hundred or so who had traveled with her to Glareth, there were also nearly two thousand more Vanarans, traders, craftsmen, and soldiers along with their families. All were summoned hastily and told to come to Griferis should they wish to go home, and were given only the briefest account as to why they might wish to do so. They packed into Griferis, and Robby guided his domain swiftly southward with all its passengers. When they came over the village of Averstone, he halted so that they could see for themselves what was coming. As the clouds that surrounded Griferis cleared and parted, they gathered on the walls and at the higher windows, and saw the sooty torrent flowing thick and steady between the passes and over the hills below. Griferis was too high and far off for anyone without a spyglass to see the nature of those who marched, but the evidence of destruction was clear. They burned as they went, driving by their noise and fire herds of forest animals before them, leaving behind them nothing but ash and smoldering trees.

Robby took his hands from the copper rods that he used to guide Griferis, breathing hard against the pain that still bolted through him. At the window stood Unther and Hathrain, who watched what they called the East Wall of Griferis, where Lafkin and others of the Blue Guard prepared their weapons. Robby nodded to Unther, then turned to Finn, who was sitting in a chair. Finn was asleep, but roused himself, blinked for a moment, then looked at Robby.

"Throgallus rides about a mile away, some half-mile behind his vanguard," Finn said.

"I wish I could sleep while I do this, and see for myself," Robby said, rubbing his stinging hands together. "I wish we had brought the Oracle with us. He can dream while awake."

"Sire, there is a gap in the mountains just north of Averstone. It appears as if Throgallus will have to move through it."

"Right. Very well, then. Unther, go and tell General Lafkin what Lord Finn just said and that we'll be moving into position. Have him signal Hathrain when we appear to be over the best spot."

As Unther rushed off, Robby took the controls once more and Griferis slid across the sky, making for the place that Finn suggested. Finn went to stand next to Hathrain, grimacing himself at the obvious pain that moving Griferis inflicted on Robby. But it did not take very long at all before Hathrain spoke.

"Sire! We are there!"

The floating kingdom came to a halt, and Robby hurried down from the tower to be with Lafkin and the others, with Finn and Hathrain not far behind. Robby saw that Serith Ellyn and Thurdun were there, too, all looking out over the wall toward the approaching menace. Already the vanguard of Throgallus had passed below, and now came the thick horde, pressed shoulder to shoulder by the confines of the steep mountainsides, with those behind pressing into those that went ahead of them.

"Lo!" said Hathrain leaning out as far as he dared to see below. "What a stench!"

Robby looked around and saw that all was prepared. A small catapult was in the courtyard behind him, one that had already been tested many times. Its throwing arm was cranked back and ready, with a sizable keg as its payload. It was filled with highly flammable oil, and was wrapped in layers of oil-soaked cloth.

"Get ready!" Lafkin called out, peering over the wall with his hand raised.

Winnefras and Unther, beside the catapult, watched Lafkin. Winnefras held a torch, and Unther held the line that would trip the catapult.

"Fire the missile!"

Winnefras quickly touched the wrappings of the keg that flared into hot flames, then hurried away.

"Loose!"

Lafkin's hand swept down, Unther pulled the line, and the catapult kicked, sending the flaming keg up and over the wall. Everyone hurried to the edge and leaned over, watching it descend hundreds of feet, trailing smoke and bits of flaming cloth that tore away. It landed squarely in the middle of the vast black column below, exploding into a large ball of orange fire and boiling black smoke.

"Right on target!" cried Hathrain.

"Yes," Robby nodded, watching carefully, and leaning so far out that Finn gripped his belt to keep him from falling over the edge.

"Be careful, sire!"

"Look!" Serith Ellyn pointed.

The flames still burned, much diminished, but those who watched from above were horrified at what they saw. Not a single gap in the horde appeared. Indeed, although many of the creatures burned, or at least their clothing and fur did, none faltered, none fell, and they kept marching on.

"Again! Again!" Robby cried out.

Another keg was quickly prepared, and the catapult soon thumped once more, sending another missile over the wall and downward. It, too, struck its target, creating a brief inferno, but with little effect.

"I don't believe it," said Hathrain.

"They are impervious to fire," Lafkin said. He stepped back from the edge to face Robby, who was still watching. When Robby had seen enough, he turned to those around him who were looking at him with expressions of disappoint-ment and astonishment.

"Well," Robby said. "At least we know."

"I doubt if they can resist steel, though," said Serith Ellyn.

"Sire, permission to give them a volley?" Lafkin asked.

Robby nodded, and Lafkin waved at the small group of archers who were assembled a few yards away, some forty of Serith Ellyn's people along with a dozen of the Blue Guard of Griferis. Chanter gave his order, and a flight of arrows hissed over the walls. Some found their mark, and some of the creatures fell. But most of the arrows bounced off the crude armor, and now the creatures held their shields up over their heads.

"Stand down your men, General," said Robby. "I see no point in tarrying. Queen, I'll have you home in a few hours."

Robby walked away, going on down the wall toward the western side of Griferis, while Lafkin gave his orders. The others of the group somberly retreated from the walls, continually expressing their disappointment to each other and wondering what should be done.

"We could drop boulders on them," suggested Finn to Lafkin as they re-entered the palace.

"Yes. But we'd need to build up a tremendous stockpile of them. By the time we did so, Throgallus will be out of the mountains and his army not so pressed together as to make easy targets."

"And making them scatter too soon will only make hunting them down all the harder," said Thurdun.

"Hm. I suppose so," said Finn.

"What do you think Philawain will do?" asked Thurdun.

"I don't know."

• • •

Robby stood on the western wall. The dark river of Shatuum stretched and wound through the mountains as far as he could see. The scent of burning forests reached his nostrils, effused with another even more disturbing odor, that of rotting flesh.

"His army is an abomination."

Robby turned and saw Serith Ellyn standing not far away, looking down at Throgallus himself, passing beneath them far below. Robby looked, too, just in time for him to see Throgallus pass below on his buckmarl.

"I don't think he can be stopped," he said.

"If there is any way that he might be stopped, what might that way entail?"

"They don't sleep, so I can't attack them in their dreams, if that is what you wonder."

"I think that Secundur must have imbued his creatures with something of his own essence," she said, looking at Robby. "How else may such things exist?"

"That has occurred to me, too," Robby answered. "His capture was too easy. I think he must have weakened himself by spreading out his nature. Perhaps that is what sustains those things below. But Throgallus is Elifaen, and I think his captains are, too. Corrupted, made into monsters, but Elifaen nonetheless. But the others? Who can know what they are? Spawned by his witches and his demons."

"I want to thank you," Serith Ellyn said abruptly. "For taking the Bloodcoins. It is strange, but I have felt a sense of relief ever since. It is strange to feel so, since the end of things is nigh, but I feel for once in my life that, if things could be otherwise in the world, I could be happy."

Robby smiled.

"Better late than never?" he quipped. "I recently had a brief taste of that feeling."

"With Queen Shevalia?"

"Yes."

"Will you go back to her?"

Robby shot a look of surprise at Serith Ellyn.

"You are perceptive," he said with a wry smile. "I don't know. In four days, it will be time for me to do what I must try to do. Then, we'll see. But, yes, I'd like to go back. I long to go this very instant."

"And the world be damned."

"Yes, to be blunt."

"I have felt the same way." Serith Ellyn smiled. She turned her back to the wall and gazed for a moment at Robby's palace. "There is a gentleman in Vanara. He is but a commander who serves Lord Seafar, but he is handsome, and I think he has a liking for me."

"I'm sure that he does."

"I don't mean as Queen. I have seen how he has looked at me. I caught his gaze once, a year or so ago, and I think he actually blushed. It wasn't the way one looks at a queen. I must say, it sent a pleasing thrill through my heart to be looked at as a woman, even for a brief moment. Now, when I think about it, I find that I have very pleasant thoughts concerning him."

"Well! I must get you home right away!"

Chapter 39

One Last Night

Robby frantically turned the pages of the large tome spread out across the table in the east tower. This was the book that contained instructions about how Griferis could be manipulated through the sky, and how the long causeway could be put out. It revealed how only the ruler of Griferis could do those things, and how he must use his own body to capture and harness the power of lightning. It warned that doing so would kill any mortal. Robby suspected that the Judges, or whoever made Griferis, made this condition so that no mortal could use it. But the Judges did not count on Robby becoming Elifaen. Indeed, when he had first put out the causeway to rescue Lafkin, Radasa, and the others, Robby was not sure that it would work, in spite of what the book said. Had he tried but a few days earlier, when he was still mortal, the power of the lightning would have surely killed him. As it was, it was extremely painful, but by now Robby knew that the pain would pass quickly, once he let go of the controls. So, by practice and by studying the book, he had learned to manipulate the wondrous realm that was Griferis, to make it travel over the mountains to Duinnor, to make storms and to put out the causeway, and to make the causeway disappear.

But there was one thing that he desperately wanted to learn how to do, and the more he flipped through pages, the more he thought it was impossible. Simply put, he wanted Griferis to descend all the way to the ground. Yet each time he tried to guide it down, he could bring it no closer to the ground than a hundred yards or so. Granted, he had not yet read the book in its entirety, and he did not understand half of what he read. Now he was so agitated that he turned the pages back and forth so severely that if they had not been made of such sturdy vellum they would have surely torn right out. He heard someone clear his throat and looked up to see Finn.

"Sire, the Queen and her party have all disembarked. Lord Seafar begs to have a word with you before we go."

Robby glanced out the window and looked at the long stretch of causeway reaching out over the air and connecting itself to the flight deck that jutted out from over the falls.

"Very well. I'll see him."

"Shall I show him to your apartments? Or will you see him here? He is just downstairs."

"Show him up, please. Wait."

"Yes, sire?"

"Finn, I know you've looked at this before, but could you just take another quick glimpse?"

Finn nodded and came over to look at the book. He turned several pages back and forth, carefully examining each one. He turned pages quickly, shaking his head as he did so. He then leafed back to the first page of the book, where there was written, in the First Tongue,

For the Ruler of Griferis to See.

"Sire, except for this single page, all of the pages are blank. Just as they were when you first showed this to me."

Robby looked as perturbed as Finn had ever seen him, and he blew out a long sigh of frustration, then nodded.

"Thank you, Finn. Show Seafar up."

A few moments later, Seafar ascended the twisting staircase and entered the tower with Finn and Unther. Unther stood aside, as was his duty, as Finn and Seafar approached.

"King Philawain, may I present Lord Seafar?"

Robby smiled and crossed the room with his hand out. Seafar bowed, looking at Robby oddly, then took Robby's hand.

"My lord, King Philawain," Seafar said. "Thank you for seeing me."

"Not at all. It is I who should thank you for all that you have done for me," Robby said, shaking Seafar's hand firmly. "If it had not been for you and your men, I certainly would not be here. Commander Tallin and I would not have survived the attack, much less the trek to Griferis."

"It was the least I could do, sire."

"Have you had any word concerning Haskin and Gullwing?"

"No, sire. We have dispatched parties to look for them, according to the directions your dreamwalkers have given, but none have yet returned from their search."

"I see. I will look into it again. But I must express my regret for the loss of Strake, Buckwise, Tiller, and Sterns who flew over and fell into Shatuum. I did not realize their plan until it was done, or else I would have opposed it. But they were very brave men, and gave their lives so that Commander Tallin and I could reach Algamori. I am very sorry for what happened."

"It was Strake's plan, sire, and no fault of yours. At least Sergeant Hull and the others made it to Defiance. And, according to your dreamwalkers, they made it out before it was overrun by Throgallus. As of last night, they had evacuated Averstone and the nearby Castle Elmwood. They are well out of reach of Shatuum's army, for the time being, anyway, and are headed north toward Duinnor as fast as they can go."

"Yes. I know. Strake and the others were, and are, a credit to your leadership, Lord Seafar. Brave, dedicated, and capable men, every one."

"Yes, sire. It is good of you to say."

"Would you like to take a seat?"

"No, thank you. I will not take up much of your time. Just moments ago, Prince Thurdun told me that you dropped burning missiles on Shatuum's army, and that they failed to do them any harm."

"Yes. It was very disappointing. I hoped to use Griferis as a kind of warship against them. But there is not much hope of being effective. We thought of dropping stones and shooting arrows and such. That doesn't seem feasible. Unless we can deal them a crippling blow very soon, while they are still bunched up together in the mountains..." Robby shrugged. "I don't think we can take on enough boulders quickly enough to do much harm."

"I see. Sire, unless you have another plan, we are massing our armies to march against them, hoping to reach an encounter with Throgallus somewhere around Minion Gap, if not closer at hand. We will send another smaller force south to counter the Dragonkind, should they come up the Iridelin."

"They won't," Robby stated. "The Dragonkind are already pouring over the Tulivana Mountains and crossing the Hinderlands where a way for them was made by molten rock pouring into the swamps and marshes there, making a vast roadway for them. Altoria's people are presently fleeing eastward into Masurthia, hoping to join forces. A small Altorian army harasses the Dragonkind, seeking to delay their advance eastward, but to little effect. Tracia, meanwhile, has already driven into Masurthia, not knowing that Prince Carbane has attacked Forlandis and has captured the Triumvirate. A gutsy move, but it was successful. Prince Danoss and General Teracue, along with Prince Lantos and a large army are encountering very little resistance, and will be in Forlandis to relieve Carbane within the week. So, if nothing else, the Redvest army that invaded Masurthia will eventually collapse as its supplies dry up, and as news reaches them that Prince Lantos has retaken Tracia. But the Dragonkind will not wait for the Redvests. They will march northward across the plains. Indeed, small units already strike out toward Duinnor, to act as scouts and such."

Seafar nodded, quickly absorbing Robby's news.

"Sire," he said, "reports are coming out of the deserts of strange happenings. A new river is flowing across the land, dividing the northern deserts from the south."

"I know. You will receive an emissary soon, from a new nation that is forming in the northern deserts. One that will be friendly to Vanara. Much of the rest of the Dragonlands will soon be flooded. It will be a calamity, and those who do not heed our warnings will die. But it is the only way to cleanse the lands."

"Cleanse the lands?"

"Of the poison that the Faerekind caused to spread across it, poison that is in their water and their food and that gives them the desert sickness."

"Oh. I see," Seafar said, clearly not understanding the extent of Robby's knowledge, or his involvement in world events. "If the Dragonkind move north, sire, perhaps we should not march against Throgallus. Let the Dragonkind encounter them first."

"If Throgallus turns south, once out of the mountains, it is certain they will eventually meet the Dragonkind army. If they turn north, against Duinnor, the Dragonkind will be too late to help."

"And you are certain that the Dragonkind and Throgallus are not in league?"

"Quite certain. Shatuum is hungry, and the Dragonkind are merely flesh to Secundur's ghouls, just as we are."

"Hm. Then it is difficult to know what to do. It seems that we and the Dragonkind have a common enemy, but I doubt if we could reach any kind of alliance as long as they are intent on conquest."

"I have tried to reach out to them," Robby nodded. "I, myself, and my dreamwalkers, by showing their generals and even King Belsalza what is taking place. But Belsalza does not believe us, and his generals, who are far away from Belsalza, dare not refuse their orders. I'm afraid they'll have to learn the hard way that we are truthful. By then it will be too late. They will be obliterated. And, I'm afraid that until some armed encounter takes place, we will not know the capability of Throgallus. He has legions of witches and other conjurers with him, and my dreamwalkers have shown you his captains. I do not think steel will be an adequate answer to their offensive."

"I see. Thank you, sire, for being frank about things. Do you have any suggestions as to what we in Vanara should do?"

"I think you should remove as many people as you can to well-fortified and hidden places, and recall your soldiers to aid in that effort. To be honest, I don't think anyone will be able to hold out against Throgallus. His followers do not behave as men do, not even terrible men. You are well-educated, I'm sure. So you must be acquainted with the last time demons and witches came into the world."

"Yes. I have read many books on the subject."

"You have seen for yourself, and you showed me examples in your menagerie of the kinds of creatures that come."

"Yes, sire."

"Then you may draw your own conclusions as to our chances. But perhaps a few pockets of your people may survive."

Seafar gazed at Robby, slowly nodding his head.

"Yes. I see. Very well, then. We'll harvest as much witchbane as we can find, to make arrows and spears. And we'll do the best we can. Thank you for seeing me, sire."

"Not at all. I wish I had better news. I hoped I could take Griferis down to the ground and crush as many of them as possible, but I fear I lack the ability to make it so."

Robby walked Seafar to the stairwell.

"You must wonder at my appearance," Robby said.

"Yes. I do. I apologize for staring so."

"No matter. It was a long time ago, nearly thirty years, since I sat with you in the Scribblers Room. You perceived so much so quickly when I first arrived here, and you shared many important things with me. Added to what I learned here, I learned and discovered even more during my years of trial in Griferis. It seems like a long time ago, and like yesterday at the same time. I never forgot your kindness and your generosity. Good luck, my lord."

Robby offered his hand again, and they shook firmly. He watched Seafar go down the stairs, escorted by Unther, and turned to Finn who had listened to the exchange with polite silence.

"Well, Finn, what do you think we should do?" Robby asked, going back to the book.

"I hardly know, my lord."

"I wish I had not made the bargain that I made with Thunderfoot."

"Oh?"

"Yes. His people are not made of flesh, and Shatuum would surely not be able to withstand an attack by them."

"Sire, can you not appeal to him once more?"

"No. They have returned to their home, and have been taken back into the earth. It was my greatest mistake, thinking that other matters required them more. I underestimated Shatuum. I thought that removing Secundur would somehow weaken Shatuum irreparably. I was wrong. I think he put something of his spirit into his creatures. It was Secundur who was weakened, I now know. That is why it was so easy to trap him. Because of my blunders, the world comes to its end."

"I hardly think you should take the blame, my King. It was going to happen, regardless. But now, without Secundur leading them and casting his shadow across the hearts of men, perhaps the world has a chance. You have given the world that chance."

"That is good of you to say. But I don't like leaving things to chance. Let me study a bit longer, and then we'll depart Vanara."

"Yes, sire."

"I wish you would call me Robby."

"I shall endeavor to remember to do so, my lord."

• • •

As he pulled the chair over to the table, Robby glanced out of the window and saw Seafar just leaving Griferis and walking briskly toward the other side of the causeway. Forgetting to sit down, Robby bent over the book and turned pages, going back to the chapter that described how

Griferis could move. For the umpteenth time, he read over the instructions pertaining to controlling Griferis. Then he saw a passage that he had somehow missed before.

> Griferis may go east or south, but no farther than the sea. Griferis may go north or west, but may not pass over the Great Divide in the west, nor beyond the northern place where there is ice on the ground even in the summer. Griferis may go upward, but no higher than the highest cloud. Griferis may go downward, but no lower than the tallest tree.

"Well that explains things," Robby said. "What am I to do?"

He pounded the book closed and paced back and forth, then sat down, suddenly quite exhausted.

"Well, if the world is to end this way," he said to himself, "I must at least try to get as many out of it as I can. If only I knew how."

He was thinking of the Nimbus Illuminas, and how the mystery of it still eluded him. A dark thought entered his mind just then, and he wondered if it was all for nothing. The Bloodcoins, the Seven Towers, the haunting melancholia that plagued the Elifaen. Everything just seemed so cruel. At every turn, there was a new way of giving hope and of taking it away, ever punishing the Elifaen. He thought of Sheila and his mother, of Serith Ellyn and Thurdun, Coreth and Faslor, and Esildre's great-nephews. What did they do to deserve all this? Men and Dragonkind, too. Ullin and Micerea, Robby's father, Billy and Ibin, all caught up in such a violent tangle of history. Why did they deserve to be eaten alive like helpless prey? He envisioned Duinnor overrun by ghouls, and saw in his mind how bravely the Kingsmen fought, Ashlord and Sheila with them, until, surrounded and pushed back, they were overwhelmed. He tried to shake away images of Sheila dying under a pile of clawing and biting creatures, her beautiful flesh torn away in bloody tatters, her bones ripped out of her.

"No!" he cried out, jumping from his chair. "No, no, no! What has she done? What have any of them done to deserve such a horrible fate?"

He paced back and forth, sweat breaking across his brow. Then, in a fit of rage, he picked up the book and threw it across the room, kicked the chair the other way, and pounded the table with his fist.

"Not Sheila! Not her! I shall take her away!"

He thought of kidnapping her, of taking her by force into Griferis to keep her safe in spite of her desire to defend Duinnor. She would be furious, and she would probably never forgive him, but the two could have all of eternity to work that out.

"In time," Robby thought as he continued his pacing, "after a millennium, perhaps, she'd forget her anger. She'd remember that I love her. She'd come to love me again. What's a millennium, after all?"

He suddenly stopped pacing, looking down at his feet. It would not work. She would not forget.

"She is Elifaen, now," he said aloud. "Her memory is now perfect."

A day of her despising him would be an eternity, he realized. By taking her away, he would destroy her love for him. It would be a descent into a meaningless existence. They might as well be dead.

In the silence of the east tower, Robby's thoughts turned and turned, but for nothing. After a long while, standing like a statue in his circling thoughts, a slight sound penetrated his abstraction. It was soft and low and strange enough to erase all other thoughts for the moment. His entire attention was drawn to it, following it to the windows that looked over the southern side of the palace below. It was coming from outside the tower. Turning his head back and forth to hear better, it seemed to come from his own wing, from the place where his apartment was. Shivers coursed up and down his arms and neck, as he finally understood the sound, a soft persistent laughter, muffled, as if coming from inside a box.

Robby put his hands over his ears, turning away.

"Must I hear it even when awake?" he cried. He shook himself, taking his hands from his ears. He heard nothing.

"I'm going mad," he said. "I must get rid of that chest."

At that moment, it struck him that there was, indeed, something he could do. If he could not save Sheila, then at least he could make it so that she would not suffer. And he could do the same for others, too. Even if he could not open the Nimbus Illuminas, even if he could not save their lives, there was no reason why he could not prevent his friends from experiencing the agony of such a terrible end.

Robby jumped to the copper rods, and immediately the causeway disappeared with a flash of lightning and a clap of thunder. Griferis rose away from Linlally, shrouded in a stormy cloud, and Robby guided it north toward Duinnor as fast as he could make it go, desperate to have one last night with Sheila.

• • •

Only a few hours later, amid much noise and thunder, Griferis arrived back in Duinnor, and somewhat off from a high hill nearby to Wysteria Place. But before Robby put out the causeway, he commanded that all of Griferis be emptied.

"It is because I must go alone to where I need to go," he explained to the gathering of his subjects in the north garden, a space barely big enough to hold them all. He stood on a garden wall to address them, and they were clearly upset at his orders. Many of them knew as well as he did that they did not stand much of a chance below, in Duinnor or elsewhere, and he could see their reluctance, if not outright resistance to the idea.

"I do not wish it to be this way," he went on. "I did not foresee that things would come to pass this way. I will return for you if I can. Until then, I wish for you to serve and protect Queen Shevalia as you would serve and protect me. If I do not return within a week, consider yourself free of any obligation to Griferis."

"Sire," spoke Finn, "surely you will need assistance, whatever it is that you set out to do."

"No, Finn. No one can help with it. And, should things go wrong, Griferis may be destroyed. I am determined that you should all go." Then, to the crowd, he said, "Please make ready to depart immediately. You have until dawn to be out of Griferis. General, the Blue Guard will be the last to go, and I'd like to have an accounting from you of everyone so that I may know that none remain. I'll put out the causeway, now, and I should like to go to Queen Shevalia immediately while our people gather their things and make their departure."

• • •

When Robby and his escort of six Blue Guards under the direction of Winnefras and Hathrain arrived at Starlight Hall, he was pleased to see a sizeable contingent of Kingsmen guarding and patrolling the grounds, making it apparent that General Chadler wished to take no chances with the Queen's safety. At the gate, a group of Kingsmen was detailed to act as an additional escort for Robby, and they walked briskly down the drive toward the Hall. Along the way, they passed a large number of carriages and hansoms while fast-moving chariots came and went with Kingsmen messengers. Once inside, he saw that the foyer had been transformed into a large busy chamber, with numerous desks and bureaus, rows of chairs where waiting people sat, and even a bevy of young aides, some in cadet uniforms, scurrying here and there. Everyone stood when Robby entered, and bowed as he passed through. The doors were opened for him, and once at the landing at the top of the stairs, Robby paused to survey the large gathering inside the great hall. He put a finger to his lips to signal the porter not to announce his arrival. Instead, he watched and listened as Ashlord addressed the ministers of Duinnor.

"...and so it is with all these things in mind that Queen Shevalia wishes to make these changes. She hopes that the new ministers who join your ranks will be welcomed by you and given your every courtesy. She is mindful that many of the former ministers who have lately resigned from their posts will be viewed with suspicion. However, the Queen warns against any who may bear grudges against them to present their complaints to the courts and let it rest there. Duinnor will not abide any form of retaliation or prejudice against the former ministers or their families, nor shall their secretaries or aides be treated unjustly. Therefore, the Queen now charges each of you to uphold the oath you have just taken, and she has every confidence that you shall perform your duty to Duinnor with zeal and with diligence."

As Robby watched and listened, he was struck by the deep irony of mundane things moving along in spite of the looming catastrophe. It was as if the passengers of a coach calmly played cards as their conveyance careened over a cliff. It was play-acting, obviously, for Ashlord and Sheila knew full well what was coming. But it was a necessary act that Sheila performed, as it was in the continuity of mundane things that people placed much of their day-to-day hope. Ashlord continued to speak, while Sheila sat behind him on the ornate sedan chair that had become her throne. Hanging like a curtain behind her was a huge map of the world, and another map of Duinnor hung to one side of the hall. Beside her stood Raynor, and Lady Highleaf bent to put her ear near to Sheila, who whispered behind her hand. Then, sitting back in her chair, Sheila looked up and saw Robby standing at the top of the stairs. She smiled and acknowledged him with a slight nod. Ashlord turned around to face her as he concluded his speech, and he bowed as she rose.

"My lords," Sheila said. "I charge you with the well-being of the Realm, to maintain and increase its vigor. The Realm is in your hands, now, and Duinnor's success rests with you. I know you will do your utmost for our people. I have chosen certain members of your ranks to be my advisors and to act as my Privy Council. Lord Arata, Lord Ashlord, Lord Raynor, Lady Highleaf, Mr. Farby, General Chadler, Lord Crestwave, and Lord Sarb. It is well that you know the terrible threat that now faces Duinnor. You have no doubt heard or read that Shatuum is on the march. This threat is greater than that of any Dragonkind. There is little doubt that this condition will place great burdens upon you as you go about your duties. I beg your indulgence in these inconveniences, and I hope that once the threat to Duinnor is removed, we may truly enjoy the fruits of your labor. Thank you."

Robby was impressed with her speech, and wondered how much instruction she had received from Ashlord. As the ministers bowed and made their way up the stairs, Robby nodded to the porter.

"King Philawain of Griferis!"

Robby and his contingent strode down the stairs, the ministers parting and bowing as he passed between them. When he reached Sheila, he took her into his arms and kissed her unabashedly in front of everyone. Sheila did not mind this at all, though she was somewhat surprised.

"Lady Highleaf, Raynor. Hello, Ashlord. I hope you are all well," Robby said.

"We are quite well, thank you, sire," Lady Highleaf said with a curtsey. "And we hope that you are, too."

"Very well, thank you."

"Serith Ellyn and her party are in Vanara?" Sheila asked.

"Yes. Safe and sound."

"And, sire, what of the test of your fiery missiles?" Raynor asked.

"They proved quite useless against the creatures," Robby said. "They are not the least bit hurt by fire. But they do fall to arrows."

"Then Griferis cannot delay them?" asked Ashlord.

"No. I've tried everything that I know to try. The forces of Shatuum have reached Averstone and will soon be out of the mountains." Robby gestured to the map. "They have not yet made a turn north or south, but continue eastward along here, moving toward Minion Gap. Lord Seafar wants to move against them, to come at them from the south with a sizable force. But I have advised him not to do so. I'm sure he and Queen Serith Ellyn will soon decide."

Everyone looked at the map for a moment, trying to imagine how Vanaran forces could move northward in time to meet Throgallus at Minion Gap.

"Then we should send our army against them, too," said Sheila walking up to the map. "We can hit them from the north while Vanara strikes their southern flanks."

Robby was truly amazed at Sheila, and wondered how much was still changing in her since becoming Elifaen.

"I have warned Seafar against attacking them," Robby said. "And I warn you, too, that it would be a waste of men. May we speak in private about it?"

Sheila glanced at Ashlord, then nodded.

"Shall we go to my rooms?" she asked.

"Yes. I would like that. But first, I would like to ask if you would allow me to send my people down into the city, to stay here for a while."

"Yes. They are all welcome. But why?"

"Is there some threat to Griferis?" asked Ashlord.

"I am not certain," Robby said. "I hope not. I will explain it to Shevalia. I have ordered my people to leave Griferis by dawn tomorrow morning, if you will have them. I would also like to assign my Blue Guard as the Queen's private sentries while they are here. If all of that would be alright."

"I don't see why not," Sheila said, "if you think it should be done."

"Good."

Robby gestured to Winnefras, and she departed to carry confirmation of the plan to Lafkin.

"Now, may we have our chat?"

• • •

Once in Sheila's apartments, they waited until their escorts had been dismissed to stand in the hall. They kissed again, and Sheila sensed Robby's fatigue.

"You are tired and worn out," Sheila said. "We'll get things sorted, I'm sure."

"No, Sheila. I'm afraid we won't."

Robby pulled away from her and paced across the room and back. He saw a little book on the table beside a chair, and he picked it up. Sheila, waiting for Robby to explain, sat and watched him.

"This is your book of poetry," Robby said. "The one Mr. Broadweed gave you."

"Yes. It is."

Robby nodded, flipping through the pages for a moment, remembering the old schoolmaster fondly. A few verses caught his eye, lines from a song he once heard Serith Ellyn sing, but at the time he did not understand the language. Now, in the Common Tongue, he read:

Bright sun hides behind cloud.
Raindrop turns into snowflake.
Bare are the trees on the hillside.
Cold blows the wind on the lake.

He closed the book and put it down.

"There is nothing I can do to stop Throgallus," he said. "When his vanguard reached Averstone, they discovered a few dozen people still there who had refused to leave. Within moments, they were found and consumed in the most horrifying way. It was a frenzy. Do you remember the carrion bees? It was like that. As well they ate horses and anything and everything made of living flesh. Some deer were trapped between their lines, rabbits, and foxes, too. Whatever living thing they come upon, they eat. They don't bother killing them or cooking them. In fact, they seem to eat from the fingers and toes upward, until…"

Robby trailed off. Sheila stared at him. For the first time, she began to truly grasp what was coming.

"We must attack and destroy them," she said. "We must gather all of our forces and overwhelm them."

"Sheila. Throgallus must know the skill and power of Duinnor's armies, of Vanara's might, of the Dragonkind's lethal and determined fighters. He did not wait for all to be at war with each other, for our armies to clash, when the world would be at its weakest. He does not care. He knows that even if only one out of every hundred of his creatures survives, there will be more than enough of them to consume the world. He does not look to the next week, or month, or year to accomplish his aims. He has all of time, since he is Elifaen. His creatures do not die of starvation or old age. They will eat and eat until only his creatures are left. Secundur may be gone, but Throgallus was filled with his desire for the destruction of the world. And, for his own reasons, Throgallus will carry it out."

Robby sat down heavily beside Sheila and took her hand.

"Please come with me into Griferis," he said. "We can cultivate witchbane, and make arrows and weapons. Over time we can pick off those creatures. Even if we have to do it one by one, we can cleanse the world of them. In the meantime, in Griferis, we can find a way to raise our children. We'll be able to go where we need to go, to find food and the things our family may need."

Sheila shook her head.

"Robby, we can't. What kind of existence would that be? Knowing the fate that we left others to? Not lifting a finger to help?"

Robby nodded.

"So you are still determined," he said. "Well. I thought I would try again. But there are a few things I should do, should try to do, anyway. I'll be taking Griferis back to Algamori, but I don't know how long I'll be there. I didn't want my people to be stuck there; that's why I want them to come out of Griferis and come here."

"I know that you are going to try with the Nimbus Illuminas. Do you think that will harm Griferis? Or is there something else that you go to do?"

"Yes. But I can't explain it. It has to do with dreamwalking. I'm going to try to use it against Throgallus."

"Throgallus himself?"

"In a manner of speaking, yes. And his creatures."

"But I thought you told me that they don't sleep."

"I know. They don't. It's complicated. Anyway, I'll be leaving in the morning. I thought that we might have an evening together before I go."

"You said you didn't know how long it would take you. What you mean is that you may not be coming back at all, don't you?"

"No. I'll be back," Robby lied.

"But you don't know. Not for sure."

"Sheila. I don't want to go. I don't want to do any of this anymore. But there are a couple of things I must do before I can have any peace. If there's any to be had at all."

Robby stood up and gestured around the room.

"The whole world is made all wrong," he said, trying to keep anger out of his tone. "Things went wrong, and they continue to go wrong. It wasn't supposed to be like this at all. You know what I mean. You are Elifaen. You remember, as I do, what things were like before, when our ancestors still had their wings. It is a wonder that any Elifaen are left at all. A wonder that every Elifaen has not cut his own throat in shame and in sadness. You know what I mean. You feel it as much as I do. It's unbearable, yet we bear it."

"We bear up to it, Robby. We go on in spite of it."

"In spite. Perhaps that is the right way of putting it."

"No. That's not what I meant, and you know it. We aren't to blame for how things are. Not you. Not me. Not our friends. We had this whole thing dropped onto us by those who went before us."

"Yes, yes! I know. *We* are not to blame, so why should *we* be responsible for fixing things?" Robby said bitterly. "We only do the best we can. We muddle along, and muddle through. We manage, we cope. We pick out some little corner of the world to hide in."

"No," Sheila said, standing up and coming to Robby. She touched his arm and took his hand. "We look upon the world in wonder. We taste good food. We enjoy the company of our friends. We see beauty. We take pride in good work. We help others. We are grateful for what we have. We fall in love."

Robby smiled painfully, and kissed Sheila's hand.

"Those are good things," he said. "I am sorry. I must be reminded of them. You are right. I shouldn't despair. I should do what I must, as well as I can, and hope for the best."

"Yes. That is what all of us should do. Come. You are tired. Come to bed. Take off your clothes and lie down. I'll be with you shortly."

Sheila coaxed Robby to the bedroom, kissing him as she pushed him along. When he began to undress, she went back to the parlor and pulled the bellrope. A moment later, Denks appeared at the door.

"My Queen," he bowed.

"Denks, please have a covered meal brought up. There is no need for waiting people. The King and I will serve ourselves as we please. Once that is done, see to it that we are not disturbed."

"Certainly, my lady."

• • •

When Sheila slipped into bed beside Robby, he was already asleep. She pulled the covers up and snuggled beside him, wondering if he was dreamwalking or if he was enjoying real sleep. She had visited with him often enough, in dreams, to know much about that realm, but she had no ability, thus far, to go there on her own. Still, even when Robby was far away, she was able to enjoy his company. Since becoming Queen of Duinnor, she had seen and learned much as he took her all over the world. And, just a few nights ago, Robby had gathered Micerea and Ullin together and brought Sheila to see them in the marvelous city in the desert. Together, the foursome had chatted like old friends, and Robby insisted that they speak as though no one had any rank whatsoever. As they talked of the late happenings of the world, they watched Alonair work the massive Great Stone. Using only his hands, he coaxed chips away from it, speaking in low tones all the while, constantly moving, crunching on the flecks that piled at his feet. Some shape was already being formed by his hands, but it was incongruous and vague. At regular intervals, Alonair would climb to the top of the stone and work his way down, chips of stone falling away as he went. Sometimes he would make holes, reaching his arm deep into the stone to pull out bits. Sheila and Micerea chatted and watched while Ullin and Robby speculated on what Alonair might be making.

Sheila put her head on Robby's shoulder, reliving that night. It had been a good night. Ullin and Micerea were so in love. And when Micerea told her that she was pregnant, Sheila nearly cried with happiness. And she realized that the reason Micerea looked strangely aglow was because another life within her was also dreaming.

• • •

As Sheila pondered the realm of dreams, Robby was himself walking through it. He briefly looked in on Sheila, and felt her body against his. Soon he would awake and spend the rest of the night with her, but first he wanted to have another quick look at Throgallus and his army. Flying along, he saw a bundle of dream-bubbles not far from the vanguard of the army, and he realized that it was a large company of Kingsmen out on patrol, camping about a mile away. Almost as soon as he saw that, he saw a throng of creatures break away from the main body of the army and rush toward the camp.

"Awake, awake!" he cried, bringing visions of Shatuum around him as he invaded the dream of the commanding officer. The dreamdogs quickly came and began biting on the commander's dream, filling the Kingsman with anxiety. Robby stepped in.

"You are under attack! To arms! To arms!"

The commander immediately awoke, and sniffed as he sat up. The stench of Shatuum was carried on the air, and he leapt up, yelling orders. Quickly the company was roused and armed. They formed a tight circle with their lances before their shields just as the throng of creatures swarmed through the trees and surrounded their clearing. They held back, growling and drooling, as a witch rode up on her buckmarl. She leapt from her mount like a cat, and sprang at the Kingsmen, her jaw gaping in a terrifying grin of spikes that were her teeth. Seeing her, the Kingsmen stiffened and hunched for the attack. But she halted, and picked up a clump of dirt. When she spat on it, it burst into flames, and she hurled it at the soldiers. The surrounding creatures howled and wailed in delight as the fireball struck the shield of one of the soldiers and burst into a shower of smoking cinders. But the shield glowed so hot that the Kingsman had to throw it away. Meanwhile, specks of the fireball had also landed on helmets and swords, making them so unbearably hot that they, too, had to be discarded. Someone threw a spear at the witch, but it passed harmlessly through her as she pitched another fireball. As this one struck, disarming even more of the soldiers, the awaiting creatures charged into the gaps. It was all over only moments later.

Robby watched, horrified, as the last of the bones were cracked and eaten, and as even the ground where spatters of blood and flesh had fallen was licked up. Then, as if nothing had happened, the creatures turned away and silently went back to rejoin the army. But now, Robby saw, they were not as hunched, not as spindly-looking, and their eyes glowed red with their meal.

Quickly, Robby passed ahead of the returning wraiths and ghouls, and went through the army, trying to determine how many witches were amongst them. They were easy to find, given their form and that none of the other creatures would come within several yards of them. He stopped counting, only a little way into the horde, after three hundred and forty.

500

"There are too many!" he said to himself. "What can any army do against them?"

He rushed to Islindia and found the lady of that wood. She was not asleep, but Robby touched her, unlocking the bond that separates a person from their dreams. She yawned, then lay down on the path she was walking and was immediately asleep. Robby wasted no time.

"I have shown you the army that moves into the world from Shatuum," Robby said to her, creating around them a pleasant forest glade.

"Oh, Philawain! I wondered when you would come again. Yes, it was a terrifying vision you showed me."

"They come. Will your thorny vines, those that surround your forest, be able to stop them from entering as easily as they may stop those within from leaving?"

"If my father wills it, they may be turned outward. And he cultivated them of shadebane root, so that Secundur and his followers could not bear their touch."

"Can they be made to surround the fair land of Greenfar? So that those good people may be protected?"

"I do not know. The Ring of Thorns that surrounds this wood has never moved before."

"I beg you, speak with your father. Tell him what Secundur has done. Ask him if he would give satisfaction to those who serve Secundur by permitting them to destroy what your father seeks to protect, and those your uncle Solstice cherishes. I beg that he do this."

"Ye may speak to me directly," said the Green Man who walked into Robby's dream. It was the same figure that Ullin thought he saw when they first visited this forest, a man-like creature made entirely of holly and the leaves and berries of other plants.

"My daughter hast told me about ye, and she hast imparted to me the tidings ye brought concerning Secundur and his vile creations."

Robby bowed.

"King Ilex. They come. They are intent on the destruction of all living things made of flesh. Your forest, what Secundur has left of it, may survive. But those creatures within it will not, should they ever venture out from your realm. Your brother, Solstice, does not have it in his power to safeguard those who have enjoyed your protection. They have honored your forest, and your daughter, with their good thoughts and their good works. Never have they trammeled your forest, nor have they sought to cut its wood or take from it game or fish, but have remained in their own lands along your border. They have been a buffer to you all these past years, and you to them. I beg you, if you have it within your power, give them the protection of your thorny vines. Spite those creatures of Secundur who would destroy Greenfar just as Secundur, their creator, destroyed your own home and people."

• • •

Robby woke up. He was exhausted, in need of real sleep, and growing desperate. But he only had this night to spend with Sheila, and he did not want to waste it. Sheila stirred, and put her hand across his chest. He took her hand and pulled gently.

"Come here."

• • •

Finn put down his cards, showing the hand he held to Celia.

"Oh, my goodness, Finn! I can't believe it," she said. "You actually won."

"There is a first time for everything, I suppose," Finn said, bending over to scratch Boxer behind the ears.

"Yes. I suppose there is. Finn, may I ask you something?"

"Anything, my lady."

"Robby has not been himself lately," she said. "He is always worried and sad. And now he orders everyone away. Do you know why?"

"Well, he is worried because of the things that are happening in the world, to people he cares about. And I think he wants us to leave Griferis because he must think we would be safer elsewhere."

"Well, I don't want to leave."

"I don't want to leave, either, Celia. But we should do as he wishes."

"Hm. Finn, does Robby love Shevalia very much?"

"I think he does. Very much."

"Then if it is so dangerous down below, in the world, why does he not bring her here? Why doesn't he bring all of his friends here?"

Finn smiled and sighed.

"I don't think Queen Shevalia wishes to leave Duinnor. And the King has so many friends that I don't think they could all fit into Griferis. And, yes, I think he wants all of us to leave."

Celia reached down, picked Boxer up, and sat back in her chair, hugging the rabbit against her chin.

"Boxer and I will not leave, Finn. I don't care what Robby says. I know Griferis as well as anyone, perhaps better than anyone, and there are many places to hide. If I must hide, I shall do so. With Boxer, of course."

"I do not wish to leave, either," said Finn. "But I promised to obey him."

"Bad promises should not be kept, Finn," Celia said. "I should think you would know that, being so thoughtful as you are."

"Perhaps I am not as thoughtful as you believe, dear lady."

"I think you are, Finn."

• • •

As Robby and Sheila slept, and while Finn and Celia talked things over, a small army of workers labored to bring many large items up the winding stairs of the High Tower of Duinnor. Once there, they entered the High Chamber, and they began their work. They cleaned and washed the glass windows, cleared off the grime that coated the balconies outside, and they swept and mopped the floors. They tore away the curtain that divided the room, and they hung tapestries and lovely paintings on the walls. Rugs were rolled out, and lamps and elegant tables and chairs were brought in. They put drapes up over the windows, and at last, they erected a large high bed, with four finely carved posts and a little step so that one might easily climb into it. They arranged two thick mattresses on the bed, and covered them with fine sheets and thick fluffy comforters, and they lined the headboard with satin pillows. Around the bed they hung layers of sheer curtains, tucked with tiebacks to the posts. When all was done, they had transformed the High Chamber from an austere room to a luxurious bedchamber fit for a queen. The foreman of the workers inspected every corner, every fold of cloth, and the position of every piece of furniture until he was satisfied. For it was all to be fit for his own Queen, and he deemed at last that it was.

"Very good," he said. He pulled the door closed just as dawn was beginning to light the sky outside. Throwing a last look at the room, he said, "And may she have sweet dreams within."

• • •

Robby and Sheila were saying their farewells. They were both in apparent good spirits, having had an entire night to each other. They had made love, talked of old times, wondered together about the future, and they had eaten good food and drank sweet wine, and had gone back to bed to await the dawn. When it came, they dressed.

"Yes, I promise," Sheila said. "I will go there at sunset this evening. But I wish you would say what kind of surprise you have in store for me."

"You'll see," Robby said, smiling as he tightened his belt and picked up his jacket. "But my guess is that when you see it, you'll want to try it out."

"Try what out?"

Robby smiled even more broadly.

"What you'll see," he said. "I must go. I will be back just as soon as I can. Meanwhile, my Blue Guard will give me peace of mind by looking after you."

"The Kingsmen are more than adequate," Sheila said as they hugged. "But thank you."

"Oh, one last thing. Lyrium. Is she still in Duinnor?"

"Yes. But she has been keeping to herself. She is staying with Grantham Farby's parents, who have a large estate."

"I see. I have not visited her, in dreams, for quite a while, and I may not get a chance to do so. But will you send a note to her on my behalf? Tell her that I appreciate all that she has done for me, and that I will try my best to open the Nimbus Illuminas. It will be tomorrow, around noon. But mostly I want you to thank her for her bravery in giving up her Bloodcoins."

"I'll send a note right away, Robby. Is there anything else that you would like for me to do while you are away?"

"No. If I think of something, I'll let you know. But be sure to go to the High Tower at sunset, as you have promised to do."

"I will! I will!"

They kissed and held each other for a long moment.

"I love you."

"Know that I love you, too."

"I know it."

Robby released Sheila, giving her a last kiss, then stepped through the door, closing it behind him. His smile fell away as he stared at the door for a moment. Nearby, Kingsmen and Blue Guard stood at attention. Lafkin was there, too.

"My King," he bowed. "We are out of Griferis."

"Very good, General. Is my father here?"

"Yes, sire. He is in the downstairs library."

"Thank you. I'd like to see him before I depart."

Lafkin nodded, and he followed Robby along the corridors and halls and down the stairs.

"Where is Lord Finn?" Robby asked as they strode across the empty great hall toward a side door.

"I do not know, sire. He said that he wished to have a word with you."

"Hm. I won't be able to wait for him, so I hope he appears soon."

"Here we are, sire."

Lafkin opened the door to the library, and when Robby walked in, he saw his father asleep in a comfortable chair, his spectacles low on his nose and a book on his lap. Robby nodded at Lafkin, who quietly stepped out and closed the door. Robby sat in a chair across from his father and leaned forward, his elbows on his knees, his hands clasped, wondering whether to wake him.

"I know I should take you home," he said in a tone that would not disturb. "I know you'd rather be back in Barley, near Mother."

He leaned back, filled with indecision. After many moments looking at his father, he carefully stood and went to him and gently kissed him on the head. He quietly left, going in a fast stride with Lafkin and his escorts in tow. They passed out of Starlight Hall and marched away from Wysteria Place to the nearby hilltop upon which the causeway from Griferis descended. There, gathered all around the ringing arch at the end of the causeway, were the people of Griferis with their belongings. Robby went to them and shook their hands and bade them farewell. Radasa and his wife were most upset, and their girls were tearful, too. Unther, Winnefras, and Hathrain, along with all of the Blue Guard, were stiff and correct, but their stern faces clearly showed the stress of their unspoken concerns. Lord Threshmere and Borwain said little, bowing and shaking Robby's hand. Robby himself was moved by the clear sentiments of care and affection he was given. At last, he stepped up onto the landing under the shining gate of Griferis, and gestured to Lafkin as he took a note from his pocket.

"Where are Finn and Celia?" Robby asked.

"I cannot say, sire. Perhaps they are still in the town. Shall I give them a message from you when I see them?"

"No. No, I don't think so," Robby said. He handed the note to Lafkin. "These are your final orders, concerning the protection of Queen Shevalia. I know you will carry them out as faithfully as you have done all else. Lafkin, I want to say that I am sorry that I cannot offer you those things that I promised. The restoration of your honor and your name. But I thank you for the things you have done for me and for Griferis. I am grateful for your willingness and your help."

Robby offered Lafkin his hand.

"My King," Lafkin said. "You have restored more than my honor and my name. You have given me my life, and by permitting me to serve you, you have given me the greatest honor a man could have. I wish only that you would allow me to continue serving you, to come with you on whatever journey you intend to take, and to be at your side and help with your labors."

"Thank you, Lafkin," Robby said shaking the man's hand. "But no one can help with what I must do. You have been more than a faithful servant. I would be honored if I could call you my friend."

"The honor would be mine, sire."

Robby turned and walked up the long causeway as his people watched. Radasa put his arms around Kinsiri, and Lord Threshmere put his arm around the shoulders of his son, Borwain. By the time Robby reached midway along the floating bridge to Griferis, he could no longer blink away his tears. He was done with being angry, finished with feeling resentful over his lot in life, and he was through with trying to understand why it fell to him to do these things. He had given up wishing that he had never gone to Tulith Attis that fateful day, not even a year ago according to the world's calendars, and had even given up wishing that he had no feelings for anyone. As he came nearer to the walls of Griferis, he did not even bother to wipe his eyes. And with his vision so blurred he did not see the figure standing before him until he was nearly under the gate.

"Where do you think you are going, Robby Ribbon?" a firm voice asked. "And without even so much as a goodbye."

"Ashlord. I have had enough of goodbyes, I think."

"Then perhaps a fare-thee-well would suffice. But you still have not answered my question."

"I'm off to try to open the Nimbus Illuminas," Robby said, wiping his face, "amongst other things."

"I see," Ashlord said, leaning on his walking stick. When Robby's eyes cleared enough, he saw that Ashlord was smiling. His red features seemed to have browned to a dark tan, somewhat darker than his skin used to be, and his red hair was now streaked with gray.

"This is the end, Ashlord," Robby said.

"What makes you think so?"

"Oh, I don't know. Everything," Robby's voice cracked.

"Well, all things must come to an end, my friend. Some pass away easily, without much notice. Others go away surrounded by great turmoil. It is the same with beginnings of things. Some begin quietly, with hardly anyone noticing. Other things begin with a great deal of noise. But beginnings and endings are a false way of seeing. There is no beginning, no ending. Only a passing of one into another. You should know that by now."

"Words, Ashlord. Only words. Forgive me, but I have no hope that they are anything more than that. And, anyway, even if you are right, I simply do not wish for some things to go away."

Ashlord nodded.

"Nor do I," he said, reaching out to take Robby's shoulder. "And especially not good friends."

"I must do what I must do," Robby said, trying his best to keep a smile and not to break into sobs. He heard his voice cracking, and swallowed hard before arresting the need to mourn. "I will do what I can to prevent suffering," he went on, "but I am afraid I can't help you or Raynor."

"Whatever do you mean by that? Why should we need to be spared suffering?"

"I only mean that if there is a place where you can go and be safe, I wish you would go there. If I knew that you would be safe in Griferis, I would ask you to come with me. But I fear it, too, may not be a suitable place. I'm sorry. I'm not expressing myself very well. Look to your safety, Ashlord."

Ashlord gave Robby a look of sympathy, and pulled him close.

"Robby Ribbon. Bellringer. Hidden One. Lord of Dreams. King Philawain of Griferis. All these names you have had," said Ashlord. "But one name you have yet to acquire. So I bid you good luck and farewell."

Robby and Ashlord released each other, and Robby watched Ashlord walk briskly away.

"What name?" he called after Ashlord. "What name?"

Without halting or turning around, Ashlord called out the answer.

"Liberator!"

The word was like cold water in Robby's face, shocking him awake, washing away his sleepy preoccupations as he gaped at Ashlord's receding figure. It was what Robby needed. As much as he wished it could be otherwise, he was now suddenly confident that what was about to happen—what he would bring about—was what ought to happen and was that which was destined to happen all along. With a grim but renewed determination, Robby re-entered Griferis.

• • •

From the window overlooking Duinnor, high up in one of the towers of Starlight Hall, Sheila watched the causeway disappear. Clouds and lightning enveloped Griferis as it rose high into the blue sky and moved away toward the southwest. As it receded, she continued to stare after it.

"He goes to do something so awful, so terrible that he could not bring himself to tell me," she said to Raynor, who watched with her. Raynor nodded, but said nothing.

"I think he is just about used up," Sheila went on. "I wonder, if I had gone with him as he asked me to, would I have been able to help him? Or would I have kept him from doing what he thinks he must do?"

"I do not know, dear lady."

"If he opens the Nimbus Illuminas," she turned to face Raynor, "what will become of Men and Dragonkind? I mean, without the Elifaen to help against Throgallus. What about the rest of the world?"

"There has been much speculation, ever since the Bloodcoins were given to the High Houses, as to what the Nimbus Illuminas would do," Raynor answered. "I have read many theories, but none are convincing. Some have written that the Nimbus Illuminas will destroy the world, making it unfit to live upon, in order to force the Elifaen to find a way from the earth. Others say that it is no more than a portal, through which all of the Elifaen will be compelled to go, like upturning a bottle so that the contents may drain, and thus leaving the world to itself. But, dear Queen, no one knows. I doubt if even King Philawain knows."

Raynor glanced at the sky where Griferis was only a dot in the distance, and Sheila turned to look, too, as it disappeared behind the far mountains.

"We can only hope for the best, then. Isn't that so?" she said.

"That is always so."

• • •

When Griferis reached Algamori, Robby brought it to a halt, putting the floating palace where he had first found it. He took his hands from the controls, removed the glass key, and put it on the table. He went down the winding stairs and walked through the corridors of Griferis, the sound of his footsteps mildly echoing the emptiness of the place. Several times he paused to gaze at one of the paintings or sketches that Borwain had done of the recently departed inhabitants at their work. One was of Kinsiri and her daughters sewing away at the banners that they had made for Griferis, and it was particularly sweet, showing the industrious quality of the girls as well as their beauty and love for one another. Robby walked on, still quite amazed at Borwain's abilities, and at last came to his own wing, stopping again to look at the portrait of his mother.

"I hoped I would do much more than I have," he said as he watched the light across her face shift and change as it filtered through the autumn foliage. "But I failed to grasp the difficulties. Things are beyond my abilities, and there is no time left to hone them, or to learn others. I'm sorry, Mother. I wasted your life. I wasted so many other lives, too. I once hoped that I could redeem myself, to make Griferis a place from which good changes would come, to make up, somewhat, for all those who have suffered and died on my account. I wanted to give Ullin and Micerea hope in a new life together, I wanted to help Islindia, and, and I...I just wanted to help."

He turned away before Mirabella's smile could give any solace, and went on into his rooms, turning immediately to face the portrait of Sheila. There was something about the painting that was different, he thought. It was always shifting, as all of Borwain's works did, presenting slightly different aspects all the time. But today, there was a difference in Sheila's countenance, a slight change in her expression, perhaps, or the tilt of her head. She seemed to have a distant look, a new gleam in her amber eyes, as if she saw beyond Robby, as if she looked through him to something else. Perhaps it was only Robby's state of mind, though, that was so changed from when he had Borwain make the portrait. He was about to turn away when he noticed—and stepped closer to be sure—that Certina was no longer sitting on the banister of the stairs. He studied the painting carefully. In fact, Certina was nowhere to be seen at all.

"Yet another puzzle that I haven't time to delve," he said, going to a chair and sitting heavily to gaze out at the snow-capped mountains on the western side of the chasm. It was not even noon. But there was much to do.

Chapter 40

Sleep

Day 244
The Last Day

It began in the east, along the coasts of the world as Sir Sun passed out of the western sky, beginning a night during which demure Lady Moon would not show her face at all from behind her fan. Most of the people of Glareth went to their beds almost immediately at sunset, unusually tired from their day's labors. Others, growing so sleepy at their evening tasks, felt a dizzy fatigue overcome them so rapidly that they stretched out on the floors of their kitchens and workshops, or leaned over the tillers of their boats and quickly fell asleep. From north to south, and from east toward west, people slept. And, if one of them could have known the dreams of the others, he might have wondered at the fact that everyone had only pleasant dreams. In Tracia, where so many soldiers moved, and where stubborn Redvests still clashed with the forces of Prince Lantos, commanders could do little to keep their men awake, much less stave off their own irresistible desire to nap.

And so sleep came across the world. It was unnatural, so sudden and deep, and it spread so quickly that no one could take news of it westward. Travelers and innkeepers alike snoozed. Carriages came to a halt as drivers failed to shake their reins, and even the horses sagged their heads in tranquil repose. In the forests near Tulith Attis, rabbits stretched out and chipmunks curled up, deer fell asleep, and so, too, did wolves and wildcats, foxes, and owls. Geese tucked their heads under their wings, crickets wearily abandoned their chorusing, and frogs ceased their croaking as their eyes drooped and closed. The night grew quiet as no night ever had before. Even Sir Wind and all his children were not immune, as they all quit their nagging of the brush and dry leaves, and stopped rustling the pine boughs.

Lord Tallin, just coming home after a survey of the newly reconstructed bridges, barely made it into the yard of his estate before he slumped over in his saddle. Weylan, and all his men along the walls of Tallin City found that their legs were unable to support them, and after deep, uncharacteristic yawns, they all sat and dipped their chins in drowsy bliss.

This also happened in Nowhere, halting Lord Eldwin's exciting tale mid-sentence as he and all of his grandchildren who were gathered around his feet nodded off. Out on the Plains of Bletharn, down in Masurthia, and all along the north-south roads that ran to and from Vanara and Duinnor, the same thing was happening. Soon, too, the people of Altoria who had not yet fled from the invading Dragonkind, and the vast Dragonkind army itself, succumbed to the silent call of sleep. As swiftly as dusk deepens into night, from the southernmost reaches of the flooding Dragonlands, up through the ancient city of Darini where Ullin and Micerea were, into Vanara and on to Duinnor, came sleep.

But those who marched out of Shatuum did not succumb to the power of this event, for they had never known sleep, and they did not know what dreams were. They kept on marching, coming through Minion Gap unopposed, and spread east onto the plains.

In Duinnor, keeping to her promise, Sheila went to the High Tower at the time appointed by Robby for her to do so. Sir Sun had gone, but his pink and purple robes still streaked the sky, throwing soft light through the windows as she climbed the winding stairs. She had left her escort below, Kingsmen and Blue Guard of Griferis, and ascended alone, holding the skirt of her gown up as she went, her slippers softly tapping each marble stair step, and her golden robe flowing behind her. She did not notice the strange phenomenon that was taking place in the city below, nor did she notice how the usual evening sounds of traffic and carriages seemed to fade away.

At last she came to the High Chamber, she pushed open the doors and entered, and she was amazed by what she saw. Smiling and shaking her head at Robby's surprise, she closed the doors and leaned back upon them, gazing at the splendid room, half-believing that she would find Robby standing off in some corner to greet her. He was not there, of course, but she was comforted by this gesture, one that indicated to her that Robby truly wanted to come back to her. Grinning like a little girl, she threw off her golden robe and ran leaping onto the bed. She bounced a couple of times, then fell back upon the pillows and put her hands across her stomach, staring at the tapestry hanging over her head. It was finely embroidered with the details of a fantastic woodland where Faerekind floated over waterfalls and playfully splashed each other with their feet as they hovered over blue-green pools. As she looked at it, the light through the windows softened further and faded, and she yawned. Before she knew it, she was herself flying along with those Faerekind, laughing without care.

* * *

It was then that Robby turned to his most reluctant dreamwalker, Lachlan Shurmarsh.

"It is done," Robby said. "Now I leave it to you, sir. I put you in charge of all the dreamwalkers. I have unshackled their dreams from their bodies, and they cannot be awakened, nor can anyone else, while I live. So when Throgallus comes, at least they will not suffer. You know what you must do."

"Yes, sire," Shurmarsh said. "We will do our level best, I and the other dreamwalkers, to give the people of the world good dreams as long as we can. We have all gone into places that will be very difficult for Throgallus to find, so at least we may be the last to go. Until then, we'll keep the dreamdogs away, and all will dream sweetly."

"I'll watch over her for a little while," said Robby, looking at Sheila. "Come back when you see me depart. And, Lachlan, I thank you."

Shurmarsh withdrew a respectful distance out from Robby's dream to let him linger a while, to watch Sheila play and dance in the air of her dream. He smiled, longing to join her, but took solace that if anything went wrong, Sheila would know no suffering. He hoped there would be time to come back to her, and as he tried to rid his mind of her impending fate, he suddenly thought of Esildre and Tyrin. He wondered, if he could not be with Sheila here, would they be together in that Other Place? Pondering this question, he hesitated, looking at how easily Sheila floated through the rainbows at the base of a waterfall. He wanted to remain, but it was time to go.

• • •

He woke himself up and blinked. Standing before him were Celia and Boxer, along with Finn. Robby jumped up from his chair with a look of terror.

"What are you doing here?" he demanded. "Did I not order you to leave Griferis?"

"We disobeyed you, my lord," said Finn calmly.

"Well, I can see that, can't I? I'm taking you back immediately."

Robby pushed between them to the door, as Boxer binkied out of his way.

"You can't make us leave, Robby," Celia said. "You may say whatever you wish, but we won't go."

Robby was not sure whether to be angry or touched, and he was more than a little of both. He looked from Finn to Celia and back, having never seen such determination in their eyes.

"I beg you to leave," Robby said. "I don't know what will become of Griferis."

"Griferis was my home long before it was yours," said Celia petulantly. "And Boxer's, too. And Finn's. It is not right that you should make us leave. And it is hurtful that you should ask us to do so."

Robby, astounded by Celia's authoritative tone, felt his face redden at her words and his eyes sting with her rebuke.

"My lord," said Finn. "It is not only that we wish to stay in Griferis. But also that we wish to remain nearby to you during these next days."

Robby saw there was no use in arguing, so he shrugged.

"Then it is just the four of us, once more."

"I suppose so."

"Well, as you know, I have work to do. I have brought Griferis back to its original place, just where I found it. Tomorrow, I go to grapple with the Nimbus Illuminas. At least, if I'm lucky, some or all of the Elifaen will be able to depart. As for the rest...?" Robby shrugged again.

"I spied on you," said Finn. "I saw how you and the dreamwalkers induced sleep across the world. I know it is so that they will not suffer when the legions of Throgallus come upon them."

"You spied on me?"

"Yes. I apologize. And I am sorry that I conspired with Lachlan Shurmarsh to make you think that I, too, was put to sleep. But I was able to convince him that you needed someone to be with you. Lafkin would have been a better choice, I think, but he is not a dreamwalker. But he, too, agreed that Celia and I should stay behind, and he saw to it."

"So Lafkin was in on it, too?"

"Yes. I am sorry for the deceptions. But you left us little choice."

"Well. So that's how it is, then," Robby stated. He could not help but smile. Celia nodded and smiled back at him.

"Are you hungry, Robby? I can bring a dish for you from the kitchen."

"No. I'm not hungry, Celia. But thank you. I just need some real sleep before tomorrow. Would one of you be so kind as to wake me before dawn?"

"It would be my pleasure, Robby," said Finn.

* * *

So Robby slept. He did not dreamwalk, for there was only one place that he wished to go, and he dared not because he knew he would be unable to leave Sheila if he went to her now. And there was only one other place left that he had to go to, one more task, but it was not yet time. So he let himself sleep. He, alone, in all the world, slept ordinary sleep that night. He did dream, though. They were pleasant dreams, meaningless and ordinary and insignificant, yet filled with the profundity that such dreams often have. He worked at the account books in the store, under the watchful but kind eye of his father. He walked along the road to the Common House with Mirabella, holding her hand and chatting about the upcoming festival. He sat beside the River Bentwide, with a fishing pole in his hand, talking to his great-grandfather, watching their corks bob as they let fish steal bits of hard bread crust from their hooks. He even had a reading lesson with Sheila, but it was she who read to him, and he was enthralled by the tale she read, though none of it made any sense.

* * *

"It is time."

Robby felt a touch on his shoulder and opened his eyes to see Finn bending over him.

"Dawn comes," Finn said.

Robby threw his legs over the side of the bed and stood. He was still dressed, and now walked back and forth around the room to stretch his legs.

"Finn, do you have a first name?"

"Yes. It is Sheldin."

"Sheldin."

"Yes."

"Sheldin."

"But I prefer Finn."

"Very well, then. Finn, you must look after Celia from now on. I will tell you that when I next go to sleep, to dreamwalk, I may never awake. I do not want you to try to wake me, either. Do you understand? Do you promise?"

Finn gave Robby a painful look, then nodded.

"I promise. I'll take care of Celia, to the best of my ability, and I will not disturb your sleep."

Robby took Finn's hand, and gave him a hug.

"I remember when we first met," Finn said. "The first time you shook my hand. I thought then, and I still do, that you are a most remarkable person. Good luck, my good friend."

"None could have a better friend than you. Thank you for being mine. And good luck to you."

• • •

Finn departed, and Robby walked around for a bit longer, stopping at the windows to watch the day come. He opened the doors to the balcony, dragged a chair outside, and sat. In an instant, he was asleep once more, and flying through the dreamscape toward the Tower Medios in Vanara with its sapphire dome. He passed inside of it as easily as he passed through any door, as he had done so many times before. Nothing had changed from his last visit. It seemed as if he floated in a sea of stars. No matter which way he turned, there were only more stars, no sign of the Seven that were brought here, no sign of any floor or wall or ceiling, and no occupant.

"Today is the day," he said, "according to my books, that Sir Sun will hide behind Lady Moon's fan, and the two will kiss."

Oddly, his words seem to echo around him, as if repeated by a thousand soft voices, but at the end of the phrase was the word, "*Yes.*"

"Today is the day when the Nimbus Illuminas will open."

"*Yes,*" said the stars.

"What must I do?"

Robby was blinded by an incredible light that exploded from the stars, and heard a thousand voices say, in a tone that was kind and gentle and filled with power, "*Be willing.*"

The light passed, and as his eyes readjusted, he saw that some of the stars had become brighter than the others. They were distributed around the heavens in a circle, alternating in color from one to the next, blue, orange, green, white, purple, yellow, and red. He did not have to count them to know that they were the Forty-Nine, nor did he have to see the world outside of the dome to know that they shone so brightly that they could be seen through the blue morning sky. Then, he saw six more stars, blue-white, spin over his head and spiral down toward him. As they neared, they grew in brilliance and took on the form of six people, robed in silver clothes. They settled, and stood around him. He could not see their faces, so full of star-gleam were their robes, but it did not hurt Robby's eyes to look.

"It was we who failed, not you," said one of the figures.

"We came into the world before you, well-meaning, but flawed."

"We served the Kings of Duinnor, and filled them with a desire for the Forty-Nine."

"We sought to do that which the Elifaen would not do."

"We sought to free the world from its torment."

"But we only made things worse."

"For each of us thought that our King could do it."

"That our King could be just."

"That our King could accomplish that which the Elifaen would not."

"But we only realized, when it was too late, that each King of Duinnor had only one part to play."

"And that it could only be the Seventh King who could do it."

"The Last King."

"A king who would need no Melnari..."

"...no Avatar..."

"...no Golden Mantle."

Robby looked from one to the other as they spoke, realizing that they were the six Melnari who had each served one of the previous Kings of Duinnor, and who now were the Six Stars of Duinnor that shone above the city where Sheila slept and dreamed.

"Our twins also failed to do their part, those, our brothers, who were put into the world when each of us were put with our King."

"Barian, and Ishtorgus, Tolimay and Micharam, Raynor and Collandoth."

"They faltered because we faltered."

"They could not do their greatest works, because we did not make it so that they could do them."

Robby shook his head. "I don't understand."

The six figures merged, and then there stood a new, completely different figure, terrible and beautiful in aspect, with snowy wings and shining raiment.

"You do not need to understand," Aperion said. "The Seven High Houses failed, just as the Six Unknown Kings failed, because they would not give up that which they believed was their power. Even Lyrium struggled, she who alone still lives of those I gave the Forty-Nine. Since you are Elifaen, you know that when she grappled with the decision to give to you her Seven, those moments were to her as a thousand years. In what may have seemed an instant to others, she relived the terror of having her wings taken from her, the years and ages of struggle that followed, of betrayal, and of disappointment. She saw again all of the considerable suffering that her eyes have witnessed in this world. So she, too, was tempted to cling to her Seven, thinking them to be a tangible symbol of her people's struggle and their suffering, of her people's accomplishments and their shame. You saw how Serith Ellyn struggled and fought in her heart against giving up her Seven. It was nothing to Lyrium's ordeal."

"But she did give them," Robby said. "And the Forty-Nine have been delivered. What more is there to do?"

"One thing more. Someone must speak for those to whom the Forty-Nine were given. Since only you came, it must be you. If you wish for the way for all my people to depart the world, you must decide. For all my people."

"I would not be here otherwise," Robby countered. "I am here. I do not wish for anyone to suffer any longer."

"But you must decide. You. Yourself. What would you give? What would you give up?"

It was all immediately and irrevocably clear. The scars on Robby's back tingled and twitched. He felt heavy, as if every pound of his body weighed upon him like a stone.

He remembered. He remembered all of it.

Robby made the decision. And as he was transformed, his scars disappeared, and he smiled.

• • •

Darkness came to day.

As the forces of Shatuum spread out over the bright plains, they could not help but notice the odd light as the blue sky deepened and the sun dimmed. Then, although it was high noon, stars began to show. Throgallus pulled back on his reins, then fell from his buckmarl. When he struck the ground on his back, his helmet rolled away, and his armor shattered from his body. Likewise, the uncanny captains halted in their tracks, and pulled back on their whips, bending their backs to gaze upward at the mysterious multicolored stars that encircled the heavens. They raised their arms to block the light, as if the sky grew brighter instead of darker, as tiny blue-white lines of lightning danced across their hot armor.

The ghouls and wraiths and witches covered their ears at the silence that spread across the world, writhing in terror, unable to make any noise, their voices frozen in their heads. Throgallus, who was Pellen, cried out loudly, one single time, then lay still upon his back, staring, wide-eyed, at the heavens.

Inside Griferis, only a few yards from where Robby's sleeping body sat, the chest that held the remains of Secundur buzzed and hummed and vibrated across the floor. Then, when Sir Sun and Lady Moon had their moment together, the chest burst open. A black mass blasted out from the chest, and sprayed out through the shattered windows. The force knocked Robby out of his chair and onto the balcony as it passed and flew away, but it did not wake him. Like a long strip of shredded black cloth, it shot through the sky, accompanied by a terrible scream, coming in an instant to its army. There, as it swirled around the stricken creatures, every whisper Secundur had ever made, every word he ever spoke, came back through the air to that place. Out of the ancient reaches of time it came from Cupeldain's ears, it flew out from Parthais's heart, and it passed from Kalzar, too. Words of doubt and lies of shame shot from Ormace and away from Therona, too, and a thousand, million other words flew back to that moment and to that place on the Plains of Bletharn, where once, at the end of the Time Before Time, Aperion had gathered his host. Now, all of the words and all of the works of Secundur gathered, making a black pitch in the screaming air.

Sir Sun was completely hidden by his Lady's fan. The two of them looked away from the world, leaving it to the Forty-Nine that they had awaited for so long. Many times before, Lady Moon had rejoined her husband, and always they were disappointed when they parted company. But this time, they held hands earnestly and would not let go. For Secundur at last swallowed all his evil words into complete and awful silence.

• • •

It was the children of the world who decided first, having a greater sense of wonder and of adventure than their elders, and having more wisdom, too, in their own manner. They led the way, each with his or her own heart, and their bodies followed, lifted by the wings that children know they really do have.

Then came those who, in their pride or in their arrogance, had much to shed away, and much to be humbled by, for they were most like children, in life's way of making people so. As their dreams revealed to them the odd senselessness of time, and they understood at last where they had come from and what they were made of, they, too, joyously released themselves from the world, and found their true connection to the cosmos.

Lonely folk followed next. It did not matter if they were Men or Dragonkind or Elifaen. They saw, through the dreams that were not dreams, how to rejoin their lost friends, how to reunite with those they loved, and how, in doing so, they could at last know the world, both the heavens and the earth, through fellowship and companionship and love. Robigor Ribbon was one of these, and so was Danig Tallin, and even Lyrium. The love they had was undying, and in the twinkle of an eye, with new hands to hold their lovers, and new hearts that would never be broken, they found their way. Gurasa, too, was one of these, and when he took the hand of his awaiting wife, there was no greater joy to be had, unless it was that shared by Mirabella and her kind Barleyman.

Finally, those who were confused and bewildered by life's perplexities, by its sadness and its grief, and who never chanced to know companionship or love, who had always wished for meaning but never had the strength to find it. They saw a way for themselves, too. It was a Mortal Man's dream that took Serith Ellyn by the hand. Together they joined the dance of joy, leaving behind care and guilt, and they came into a new life with each other, one that was always new, but always as it should have ever been. Cuffdare, the anxious helper at Vanara's library, was another, and he discovered things that books could never say, peace that knowledge could never bring, and new things to learn that he could have never imagined, and he was welcomed into the fellowship of others with whom he was perfectly comfortable.

All over the world, a way was made for each person to choose. All were the children of Beras, as Aperion well knew, and it was only the right way of things for all to be offered this way, not only the Elifaen, but all people and every person. But not all accepted the gift. They would not be punished, for there was no disobedience in their choice. Those who remained in the world did so because the world was truly theirs, and they knew it was not separated from the rest of the cosmos. Ibin Brinnin was one of these, and he had every reason to think that everything would be just fine. And he was right to think so. The people of Greenfar also stayed, for they knew that their time upon the earth was a time of joy and friendship and love, and they understood the bounty of their existence and the beauty of their lives. A few others remained, too. Many of Nightar's people stayed, although Traveshia and Prince Nightar both departed. But Aremon and Seleesa stayed, and so, too, did Ullin and Micerea, for they saw, through their dreams and in their hearts, a joy that would come of healing and of abiding to witness the winding down of the old world, and the springing forth of the new one. Finn stayed, too, for he knew that Celia would not go, any more than she would ever leave Griferis, and she was his adopted niece. He was satisfied with his place, and his only concern, if he had any at all, was with his old friend, Robby Ribbon, to whom he was also devoted.

Nor did Sheila go. Not all could be foretold, not all could be predicted or foreseen, she knew. There were many things that might yet happen, and many possibilities that could come about. She slept peacefully. She was Elifaen, so it did not matter if she slept for a day or for an age. She was, as she had never been, contented to wait. When it was time for the Queen of Duinnor and the King of Griferis to leave, they would do so together. Until then, she would remain in unchanging beauty, slumbering in her High Tower.

• • •

But Robby, though he did not wish to remain, had to do so. It was his choice, and he freely made it. For he and only he could do that very last thing that needed doing. He awoke, and picked himself up from the floor of the balcony. Above, Sir Sun was just beginning to peek from behind his Lady's fan. Robby smiled, weakly picked up the chair that had been tossed over, and came inside. It was an effort, but he dragged the chair back to its place, and eased himself painfully down into it. Leaning back, he looked up at the beautiful Shevalia, and without closing his eyes or sleeping, he saw her dream.

"Why don't you sing?" he asked, sensing the presence behind him.

"Because all my songs are done," said Caparrashee.

Robby nodded, seeing Shevalia's portrait and her dream at the same time. In her dream, she laughed and played, dancing joyously across a breeze-rippled forest pool as easily as she had skated on Miller's Pond. But Robby saw that she kept looking around, as if hopeful that someone would join her. Caparrashee put her hand on Robby's shoulder as he smiled. Sheila would not have long to wait, after all.

• • •

Celia entered the room without knocking, with Boxer hopping along behind her. She looked at Robby and suddenly forgot what she had come to ask. After a moment, she stepped over to him and stood beside his chair. She gazed up at the portrait on the wall, her brow wrinkled in thought. Then she gently closed his eyes, her fingers shaking as she did so. Leaning over, she kissed Robby's brow, wetting his cheek with a tear, and went to find Finn.

• • •

Out on the plains, strange flowers began to bloom. They came up out of the scorched and tarred ground where but a little while earlier was a great and terrible army. Within hours, the blackened ground sank away beneath clambering stalks that opened into flowers of yellow and blue and red. All over the world, though few would ever know it, these flowers also sprang up from where Men once lay down their arms and slept, and from where Dragonkind once marched but had stretched out on the ground to rest, and from where Elifaen had suddenly dozed off. They sprang up from beds and chairs and from the decks of warships, from workshop floors and grassy fields where so many had fallen asleep the night before. Lady Breeze stirred to wakefulness, and seeing these marvelous blossoms, she took them in her gentle hands and lifted them upward and released them. The petals took to the air, spinning and winging higher and higher, passing into the sky and beyond the earth.

Ullin and Micerea saw them rise, having awakened moments before they took flight. Arm in arm, they watched them disappear into the endless blue. Aremon and Seleesa came to stand with them, and looked, too. They knew what they were. They remembered how every person's dream had been joined to their own. They said nothing, for no words were needed. They looked at the center of the round lake where stood a broad creamy-limbed tree of stone. Water dripped from the tips of its branches and covered its roots and slowly filled the lake with clean water, fresh and cool.

In Duinnor, the Temple was empty, its occupants gone away. Gone, too, was virtually every inhabitant of that realm, and every other one, as well. In the years that would follow, most of the old cities of the world, vanished of their citizens, would be slowly reclaimed by the earth. The towers and palaces would give back their bricks and blocks to the ground, and grass and trees would march determinedly along the cobblestones and roads so that every trace of the old byways would eventually be erased. As might have been said before, the stories of those things would be lost to forgotten languages and moth-eaten scrolls. Vine and root would grapple with the rune carved in stone, and, fleck by fleck, rust would carry away the great gates of iron.

But seven abiding stars would shine, by day and by night, in an arc over a place where a high tower once stood, where kings without names once ruled, and where a beautiful queen once slept and dreamed. And the highest and newest of these stars would shine the brightest of all, and forever after.

The End

Epilogue

Aperion's Daughter

Once, in an age long past, there was built a castle in the air. It was a fine place, with colorful pennants floating from its many towers, with gardens and groves, and with more rooms than one could explore in a week. It rested on a pillow of clouds and never knew a gloomy day, with Sir Sun and his wife Lady Moon holding hands and gazing down upon it with all of their starry children. The castle had a magnificent gate in its outer wall, and wonderful glass halls, and a fabulous magical library that was continually stocked with the latest scrolls and books from the time when the first ones were written. There were workshops and kitchens, parlors and dining rooms, and its great circular hall was airy and warm with light streaming through its tall windows. No moss encroached upon its stones, except where it was invited, and smokeless fires burned from its many fireplaces so that no soot or grime ever fell upon the castle. It was clean, spacious, and truly a wonder, and any who may have beheld it from the ground might have thought it was the abode of the Faerekind, for who else could gain its entrance or grace its halls?

But it was empty. No meals cooked in the kitchens, and no children played in its courtyards. No sound of occupants echoed from its walls, or disturbed the gurgle of the stream that ran from a cloudy waterfall and passed through its gardens. It was built and prepared by Aperion in the place where he and his host had gone to when they departed the earth. Then, in the same year that the great catastrophe struck the ancient lands of Men, when the seas swallowed up their home, and they set out upon the endless waves in their mighty city-ships, Aperion sent the castle to its place. And there it hovered, waiting, until came the time of Parthais. While generations of Men lived and died aboard their floating towns, slowly and gently pushed westward by wind and current, the castle remained in wait.

Then, not long after the first Men stepped ashore in the world where they would make their new home, Aperion sent his ram to tempt the hunter, Elrasil, to chase it into the high mountains. And thus Elrasil discovered the mystical castle and went to report it to Parthais. Later, when Serith Ellyn entered the place, the very first Judges came also, and the one called Finn and a girl named Celia were brought also to occupy the place. Finn was to be helpmate to those seeking to be tried. But Celia was brought there to serve a more subtle role. It would be she, not Finn, who would make the place a civil home to the one who would later claim it as his own kingdom. Celia would be the recipient of a father's love, from a man who was not her father, and an uncle's care, from a man who was not her uncle. She would have what many boys and girls would never know, the gift of love and kindness unbiased by blood, unconditioned by familial ties, and given without the asking.

Aperion made it so that Celia would not age until the time came that such gifts were hers. And he made her that which those of the forests and deserts and mountains could never be, free from all attachment except for that of her little rabbit. She would know heartache, in time, but not until after she knew that she was loved. She would grow old, too, in time. But not until the sweetness of youth was so firmly part of her that all the time in the cosmos could not erase it. She would also know pain, and, ultimately, she would die. But not until the pain could be endured without scarring her soul, and not until that other place was made ready for her, so that she could be a girl once again and forever.

For she was Aperion's youngest and dearest daughter, born without wings, but truly Faerekind. And she was what all Men, all Dragonkind, and all Elifaen longed to be. Restless, but at peace. Full of longing, but content. Curious, but without guile. Melancholy, but without sorrow. She was his witness. When all of the others had departed from the world, when the Elifaen were gone, when Men gave up these shores, and when the Dragonkind were returned to the earth, Celia would remain for yet another age. Though she would never roam, or take part in the happenings of the world, she would be its most enduring companion. It would be Celia who would witness the tiring of the seas, their waves no longer to beat upon the shore. She would watch Sir Wind go to sleep at last, never again to wander. And Celia would walk the parapets where once her adopted father strolled, deep in his thoughts and worries, and she would remember those tumultuous days in which she played hardly any role. She would look upon his tomb with fondness. And she would wait, still, until the last fleck of rust was swallowed by the forests and the last stone of the ancient cities was dust. She would wait until when the world was reborn, when Lady Moon walked again with her husband across the sky, and when time was meaningless. Until when, from the mists of the forests, there would come a new creature rising up to float effortlessly into the sky, and she would know her time was done. It would then be their world to witness, not hers. She would give her rabbit one last tender hug and kiss, peacefully give up her body, and rejoin all those who had ever loved her. Her rabbit, then, would also be free, and he would join those of his kind who soared like birds and butterflies, knowing happiness and joy, those with names like Wink and Fallendine, Hanion and Telliniece, Beauchamp and Certina. New air would stir across the earth, a new sea would arise, with new waves to beat upon the shores of new lands. And the creature that Boxer would become, when Celia was gone away, would live as Celia's spirit of love and of kindness, a legacy passed on to the newly born world from the old one which had passed away.

The Beginning

Afterword

Afterword

Thank you for reading *The Year of the Red Door*! I hope you have enjoyed this tale. And I cordially invite you to share your thoughts, questions, and comments at

www.TheYearOfTheRedDoor.com

There are many tales, legends, and people not mentioned within this story but nevertheless are important and interesting aspects of the world in which *The Year of the Red Door* takes place. It is my sincerest desire to assemble all of these into a compendium that, for lack of a better title, I will call *The Reader's Companion to the Year of the Red Door*. I hope you will look for it within the near future.

Meanwhile, the website mentioned above contains some of what will be within the compendium, and subscribers to my newsletter are already enjoying excerpts and backstories taken from my notes. And I heartily invite you to continue the journey, and the exploration, by visiting the website and by subscribing to my newsletter, should you so desire.

I also welcome any questions or comments that you would like to share. I try my utmost to answer each and every note, letter, and email.

Thank you once again for reading this tale, for sharing in this adventure, and for exploring *The Year of the Red Door*!

.

William Timothy Murray
Spring, 2017

The Door is Open!
www.TheYearOfTheRedDoor.com

Maps, Stories, Chronologies,
and much more.

Leave a comment or ask a question.

The Author would love to hear from you!

Sign up for the newsletter.
Get perks and exclusives
delivered right to your inbox!

The Year of the Red Door

Volume 1
The Bellringer

Volume 2
The Nature of a Curse

Volume 3
A Distant Light

Volume 4
The Dreamwalker

Volume 5
To Touch a Dream

www.TheYearOfTheRedDoor.com